The Dane Maddock Adventures

Adventures

Volume 1

David Wood

Gryphonwood

DOURADO

A sunken treasure. An ancient Biblical artifact. A mystery as old as humankind.

On January 25, 1829, the Portuguese *brig Dourado* sank off the coast of Indonesia, losing its cargo of priceless treasures from the Holy Land. One of these lost relics holds the key to an ancient mystery. But someone does not want this treasure to come to light. When her father is murdered while searching for the *Dourado*, Kaylin Maxwell hires treasure hunter and former Navy Seal Dane Maddock and his partner Uriah "Bones" Bonebrake, to locate the wreckage and recover a lost Biblical artifact, the truth behind which could shake the foundations of the church, and call into question the fundamentally held truths of human existence. Join Maddock and Bones on a perilous adventure that carries them from the depths of the Pacific to ancient cities of stone as they unravel the mystery of the *Dourado*.

CIBOLA

1539- In a remote Spanish outpost, one man holds the secret to the greatest treasure and deadliest secret in human history.

Utah, Present Day- Cave paintings in a newly-discovered Indian site provide evidence that Christ visited the New World. Or do they?

Dane Maddock returns in another unforgettable adventure! When Maddock rescues beautiful archaeologist Jade Ihara, he joins her on asearch for the legendary Seven Cities of Cibola. *Cibola* takes the reader on a journey across the American southwest, where the ruins of the mysterious Anasazi hide deadly secrets, and foes lurk around every corner. Maddock and his partner "Bones" Bonebrake must decipher clues from the fabled Copper Scroll, outwit their enemies, and be the first to unlock the secret of *Cibola*.

QUEST

149 B.C.- Escaping just ahead of the invading Roman legions, a Carthaginian soldier carries an ancient secret to places unknown.

1925- Percy Fawcett launches his final expedition into the Amazon, but what is his true objective?

Dane Maddock is back. Deep in the Amazon, a university group encounters a horror beyond their darkest nightmares and vanishes without a trace. Called upon to undertake a daring rescue mission, Maddock and Bones must trace the true path of Percy Fawcett's final expedition, but the secret that lies at the end of the search might be even deadlier than the enemies who seek it. From the streets of London to remote islands in the Atlantic, to the deadly jungles of the Amazon, Maddock and Bones must penetrate a secret lost to history, on their deadliest *Quest*.

AZTLAN

In a remote area of the American Southwest Dane and Bones stumble upon a place out of legend that changes their world.

CONTENTS

Dourado 7

Cibola 129

Quest 263

Aztlan 397

The Dane Maddock Adventures- Volume 1
Published by Gryphonwood Press
Copyright 2015 by David Wood. All rights reserved.

This book is a work of fiction. All events and characters depicted are products of the author's imagination or are used fictitiously.

ISBN 10: 1940095301
ISBN 13: 978-1-940095-30-1

From the Author

Thank you for reading the Dane Maddock Adventures- Vol 1. In each of these stories you might note that I have changed a few historical or geographic details. These are all minor changes that have been made for the sake of the story. I hope you enjoy them!

David

DOURADO

A Dane Maddock Adventure

And David said, "There is none like that; give it to me."
1 Samuel 21.9

Prologue
January 25, 1829-The Indian Ocean

The precious dream fled like the last mist of morning before the rising sun. Another wave broke against the side of the *Dourado*, the resounding crash booming like thunder in the tiny cabin. Monsieur le Chevalier Louis Domenic de Rienzi clutched the side of his bed to steady himself against the pitching and rolling. He had been dreaming of a triumphant return to France, where he would display the fruits of his years of hard work. He tugged the damp, musty blanket over his head, but it made a pitiful barrier against the shouts that penetrated from above. He squeezed his eyes closed and tried to force himself back to sleep, but to no avail. Muttering a curse, he pushed the sodden covers down to his chest and stared up at the aged wooden ceiling.

A man of his standing should have finer accommodations, he told himself. Of course, this was the best the captain had to offer. When he got back to France, when they saw what he had recovered, then he would be an important man. He would have only the finest lodgings. He smiled. For a moment, the aged wooden cabin was transformed into a luxurious berth on the finest ship.

Another wave sent the ship tilting like a drunkard, and his imagined stateroom dissolved in a dizzying roll. Rienzi held on until the ship righted before rising to don his boots and coat. The shouts on deck grew strident, tinged with an urgency that had not been there before. The storm must be more serious than he had believed.

He spared a moment to glance in the tiny mirror nailed to the wall opposite the bed. He was no longer a young man, but age was blessing him with a touch of the dignity he lacked in his youth. He had left home a young man but was returning as a seasoned adventurer with a fabulous story to tell.

His cabin door opened onto a narrow hallway. A petite woman in a dressing gown peered out of the door directly opposite his own. Her nightcap was askew, giving a comical bent to her pinched features. Their eyes met, and she gave a little shriek before slamming the door. Rienzi chuckled and made for the narrow stairwell leading up to the deck.

Tangy salt air filled his nostrils as he stepped out into the chill night. Fat raindrops struck his face, washing away the last vestiges of sleep. A crewman bustled past, jostling Rienzi in his haste. The sailor muttered something that might have been an apology, but Rienzi's Portuguese was very limited.

Angry black clouds proclaimed the ferocity of the storm that assailed the ship. The brig surged through waves that broke across the deck like hungry fingers clutching its prey. He drew his coat tighter around him to fight off the chill wind that sliced through him and thanked the Blessed Mother that it was summertime here on the bottom half of the world. What might this storm be like at home in the heart of a French winter?

With a fencer's grace, he stepped out onto the deck, keeping himself balanced on the tilting platform. Deckhands scurried about, obviously trying to put on a brave face in front of the knot of passengers who clung together near the mainmast. Strange that people felt safer on deck, where an errant wave might sweep them away than down below where it was warm and dry.

He soon found the captain, Francisco Covilha, who was fighting with the wheel and simultaneously barking orders.

"Captain," he shouted, "may I be of assistance?" Rienzi had some knowledge of sailing though certainly not as much as the veteran sailor. Yet, it seemed proper to at least make the offer.

The Portuguese sailor shook his head and called back in heavily accented French. "I am sorry, Monsieur. I must keep us from the rocks." Maintaining his grip on the wheel, he nodded forward and to port.

Rienzi spun and saw with alarm a jagged line of rocks protruding from the sea, the faint glow of dawn illuminating their jagged features. Despite the crew's best efforts, the *Dourado* hurtled toward certain peril, borne on the crest of deadly wind and waves.

There was no helping the captain and crew, nor did he hold out much hope that the ship would avert her impending doom. But there was, in fact, something Rienzi could do. Reeling with each ebb and swell, he made his way to where the frightened passengers huddled in fearful disarray. Taking him for someone in authority, they all began calling out questions.

Most of them spoke English, but a few were French. Rienzi could speak the uncultured tongue of the oafs from the north side of the channel, but he would not do so unless it was absolutely necessary. He did have his reputation to consider.

"Do not speak," he shouted over their confused questions. "There is little time." Though his words were in French, everyone seemed to grasp his meaning and fell quiet. He stole another glance at the looming rocks. They looked like the teeth of some primordial beast, ready to crush their fragile vessel. There was no time to get the others below, and should the crash be a serious one, belowdecks would not be the safest alternative.

He found a length of rope lashed to a nearby rail. It was one used by crewmen to secure themselves to the ship in just such a situation. He sat the passengers down and showed them how to double the rope around each of their arms so they all could tie on to the same rope. One of the Englishwomen complained about the cold and the rain, but he ignored her. When everyone was secure, he wound the end of the rope around his wrist and dropped to the deck, waiting like a condemned prisoner for the guillotine.

My treasures! The sudden thought pierced the veil of apprehension and embedded in his heart. A cold sliver of fear soured his stomach and sent a tremor of fear through him. Priceless, irreplaceable artifacts representing a lifetime's work were stored below. How many years had he spent collecting them? Above all others, one item, in particular, could not be lost.

With that thought in mind, he rose up from the deck to look out at the ocean. The rocks still loomed perilously close ahead, the waves crashing over them sending up gouts of foam that put him in mind of a rabid beast. They now seemed farther to port. Was the captain gaining some control of the craft? They flew faster toward the far end of the line of rocks, the cold rain now stinging his face. He held his breath. Were they going to make it?

Unwinding the safety rope from his forearm, he belly crawled to the side and clutched the rail, watching as the dangerous objects flashed by, the gap between the *Dourado* and these sentinels of doom ever narrowing. The last rock flew past with scarcely a foot to spare.

And then the world exploded.

A loud, ripping sound filled his ears, and everything somersaulted. He tumbled toward the bow, pain lancing through his cold, numb flesh as he half-rolled, half-bounced across the hard, slick deck. He crashed into the foremast with a breathless grunt and a sharp crack to the base of his skull. Dizzy, he struggled to stand. His feet and hands did not want to work, though, and his head seemed full of sand.

Surrendering with an agonized groan, he closed his eyes.

I have no choice, Monsieur Rienzi. I must give the order to abandon ship." A barrel of a man, Francisco Covilha stood a hand shorter than Rienzi yet managed to appear as if he were looking down his nose at the explorer. The moonlight accentuated his crooked nose and lined face.

"Captain, you cannot be serious," Rienzi pleaded. "You have kept us afloat since morning. Surely we can hold out until help arrives." He rubbed his head, which still throbbed from the blow that had rendered him unconscious. He had tried drowning the pain with wine, but had managed only to dull his senses to the point of being an annoying distraction.

"No help is coming." Covilha shook his head. "We lost the rudder when we hit those rocks just beneath the surface. Most likely, we have drifted out of the shipping lanes. We cannot expect anyone to come to our aid, and this craft will not be above water much longer. The pumps have not kept pace with the inflow of water. Perhaps you have noticed, no?"

Rienzi stared at the shorter man for a moment. He had, in fact, watched the rising waterline with an equally rising sense of despair. He could not afford to lose this cargo. It was too precious. The world could not afford for him to lose this cargo. How could he make the man understand?

"Captain, if you do not know where we are," he argued, "then how can you possibly hope to get the passengers and crew safely to port?" Perhaps it was selfish of him to try to keep the sinking ship in the water, but he had no choice. It was imperative that he convince Covilha not to abandon the ship and cargo. There remained the remote possibility that someone might come to their rescue. Any amount of time he purchased, no matter how small, increased that chance.

"I do not know precisely where we are," Covilha said, holding up a scarred finger, "but we have drifted south and southeast all day. I have a general idea of our location, and I know that I can get us to Singapore. That is if we get off this ship before we all drown." The Captain's face was a mask of determination, and in that moment Rienzi understood that he would never dissuade the man.

"Captain," called a voice from behind Rienzi. One of the crewmen, a short, swarthy man with a crooked scar running from his left ear to his upper lip, brushed past, a frightened look further marring his disfigured face. "The water is coming much faster than before. We may have only minutes!" He flashed a sympathetic glance at Rienzi. "I am sorry, Monsieur."

The moment of guilt he felt at having thought only of the sailor's ugliness dissolved with Covilha's subsequent words.

"Give the order to abandon ship," the captain instructed. Without further word, he turned away from Rienzi and began shouting hastened instructions.

Muttering a curse under his breath, Rienzi hurried to the foredeck and descended to the level where the crew bunked. He had made certain he knew exactly where his treasures were stored, the one in particular, and he quickly found the trapdoor that led down into the hold. The sounds of frightened passengers drifted down from above, as people who had believed the worst was over now found themselves abandoning ship. Fitting this should happen at midnight, he thought.

Yanking open the trapdoor, he mounted the ladder and began his descent. Only a few rungs down, he heard the sloshing of water inside. It must be filling rapidly. An icy sense of doom rising inside him, he strained his eyes to peer into the inky blackness, but it was too dark for him to see anything. He needed to find a lantern though it would likely do little good. Why had he not stored it in his berth? He knew the answer; it was too large for him to hide it in the tiny room, and it would have proved too great a temptation for either captain or crew. It had seemed safer to leave it crated with the other artifacts. It was certainly safe from prying hands now. Or soon would be. He gave a mirthless laugh at the irony.

He clambered up the ladder and back onto the deck. The *Dourado* was listing to port, and he was hard-pressed to maintain his balance as he hurried back to his quarters. Inside, he gathered his small lantern, along with his journal, which he kept safe in an oilcloth bag. Hastily lighting the wick, he returned to the deck.

The ship now listed mightily, and he was forced to place his free hand on the deck and scurry along like a wounded crab. As he made his way toward the foredeck, a noise caught his attention. He raised his lantern, and the light fell on two young women, their faces frozen in terror, clutching the mast.

"Get to the boats," he shouted. "Quickly!" The shorter woman, a blonde whose milky complexion was almost ghostly in the blended moon and lamp light, shook her head. The other did not respond at all. Fear held them rooted to the spot.

"Monsieur!" The Captain's voice boomed. "The second boat is leaving! You must come now!"

"Wait for us, Captain! There are yet passengers aboard!" Rienzi cried. If the man would not wait for Rienzi, perhaps he would wait for them.

"Hurry, I pray you!" Covilha's voice covered a remarkable distance. "The ship is sinking fast!"

"Mon Dieu," Rienzi muttered as he scrambled over to where the frightened women sat. "Come with me," he ordered. "I will get you to the boats." The one who had sat in mute silence a moment before, a thin brunette with brown eyes, nodded. She released her grip on the mast with obvious reluctance and crawled to his side.

"Come, Sophie," she called to the blonde. We must go quickly. There is no time." Still Sophie shook her head and refused to move.

This time not bothering to muffle his curse, Rienzi moved to the woman's side, his boots sliding on the damp decking. Gripping the oilcloth bag in his teeth, he used his free hand to pry Sophie's fingers loose from the mast. He grasped her around the waist and heaved her onto his shoulder. He felt the other woman's arms encircle him, steadying him as they stumbled together across the sloping deck.

The captain was waiting at the rail. Together, they helped the women into the smaller boat. A short distance away, the longboat awaited. Each craft overflowed with anxious sailors and travelers.

"That is everyone?" Covilha asked.

Rienzi nodded and tossed his oilcloth bag down into the boat. "Cast off. I will join you shortly." He turned and left the captain gaping open-mouthed at the top of the rope ladder. He stumbled and skidded his way back down through the crewdeck to the opening that led into the hold. He dangled his lantern through the open trapdoor and felt his heart fall into his stomach. Everything was under water. All would be lost. It would be lost. He should have taken it from the hold when the ship first struck the rocks. Burn it all, he had not believed that the ship would truly sink!

A pitiful whimper snapped him out of his dark thoughts, particularly when he realized that it did not come from his own throat. He looked down to see a small dog furiously paddling through the icy salt water that sloshed through the flooded hold. How had it gotten there? The water level was so high that he was easily able to reach out and catch the pitiful creature by the scruff of the neck, and lift it to safety.

The *Dourado* lurched, and now he could actually feel the craft sinking. If he did not get clear before it went down, the suction could pull him under. He tossed away the lantern, ignoring the tinkle of shattering glass. Clutching the frightened dog to his chest, he stumbled to the ladder and clambered up onto the deck. Not even looking for the lifeboats, he dashed to the rail and vaulted it. The *Dourado* was sitting so low that he scarcely had time to brace himself for the shock of the cold water.

When he felt his feet touch, he kicked furiously, trying not to go too far under. He raised the yelping, clawing dog above his head and managed to keep the tiny creature above water. He broke the surface with a gasp and shook his head to get the stinging salt water out of his eyes. He was relieved to see the smaller boat close by, and heading in his direction. Ignoring his body's instinct to curl into the fetal position, he fought to stay afloat as his rescuers rowed to him. His legs felt like lead, and his sodden clothes and heavy boots weighted him down. He kicked with desperate fury, but he was sinking. His shoulders sank beneath the surface of the water, then his chin, then his entire head. He was going to die.

Strong hands took hold of his shoulders and hauled him up. Covilha and the scarred sailor dragged him into the boat. He dropped to the bottom and slumped, exhausted, against someone's legs.

"All of that for a dog," a voice behind him whispered.

Rienzi was too tired and disconsolate to reply. Instead, he clutched the wet ball of fur to his chest, and watched with tear-filled eyes as the greatest discovery in the history of mankind sank into the depths of the sea.

Chapter 1

A dead ship makes better company than a live person. Dane Maddock propelled himself with two solid kicks through the gaping hole in the side of the sunken vessel. He drifted, careful not to upset the fine layer of silt that covered the boat's interior. It would be the underwater version of a whiteout if he did, and it would spoil his exploration. A school of bright blue sergeant majors, so called for their dark, vertical stripes that made them resemble a sergeant's insignia, swam past seemingly oblivious to this intruder into their watery domain. Maddock greeted them with a mock salute and they scattered out into the sea. Another small flip of his swim fins and he slid deeper into the bowels of the wreck.

It was a tuna seiner, and not a very old one. The outside was white with broad bands of green striping down the side. He did not expect to find anything of interest inside, but he desperately needed a diversion after a long and fruitless day of searching for the remains of the sunken Spanish galleon.

He switched on the dive light strapped to his forehead and looked around. More than likely, this had been a drug runner's boat. It was stripped down to bare bones on the inside, all of the trappings of the fishing trade absent. A fire extinguisher was still strapped to the wall, one of the few remaining accoutrements in this sunken tin can. He floated over to it and gently brushed away the silt over the inspection label to reveal the year 2002. He looked around a few moments more, his eyes taking in the crumbling upholstery on the seats and the bits of marine life that were beginning to homestead on the interior. There was nothing here to hold his interest. He took a quick glance at his dive watch and calculated that he had about ten minutes of air remaining. It was time to head back up.

He turned and swam out of the wreck. As he left the boat, a shadow passed over him, and something large and dark appeared at the edge of his vision. He looked up to see the thick, gray form of a bull shark circling above him. Maddock paused, watching the fierce creature swim back and forth. Aggressive and unpredictable, a bull shark was not to be trifled with. The best option was to wait until it went on its way.

The large creature swam a tight circle five meters above him. Maddock held tight, not wishing to draw its attention. Faint shafts of sunlight filtered down through the crystalline waters, shining on its tough hide. The beast's angry eye seemed to fix on Maddock though he knew it was only his imagination.

Minutes passed, with no sign of the shark leaving. He could have sworn the thing was standing guard over him. Its jagged white teeth seemed to grin back at him, daring him to chance it. Again, he checked his watch. Six minutes of air left. He couldn't wait much longer. He would have to chance it, but at least it was a shallow dive. The water was no more than thirty meters deep here if that, but it was safest to make a slow ascent, making a couple of stops to avoid decompression problems. His heart beating a bit faster, he suppressed the urge to strike out hard for the surface and began a slow, controlled rise.

He had read stories of men who had dived on bull sharks and had even met a few of the guys. Most of them were crazed adrenaline junkies. It was, however, at least theoretically possible to share space without provoking the beast. The problem was, it depended quite a bit on what kind of day the shark was having.

Holding his arms close to his sides, he stretched out, propelling himself with controlled kicks. He slowly drifted upward toward his waiting boat, remaining as still as possible and trying to resemble nothing more than a piece of floating debris. Don't rise faster than your bubbles, he reminded himself.

The shark continued to patrol the area, showing no signs of agitation, or so Maddock hoped. He now had a good view of the marine predator. It was at least ten feet long, probably a female. Viewed through aquarium glass or from within a dive cage, she would be a real beauty. Sharks were fascinating creatures; all muscle, teeth, and stomach, his Dad used to say. So far she gave no sign that she had noticed him. He flipped his fins, and he was now gliding upward at a steep angle. Just then, the shark veered to her left, heading directly at him.

Maddock tensed. The dive knife strapped to his thigh would do him little good against her tough hide. Struggling against his instincts, he forced himself to remain still, feigning death, floating free. The wide, ugly snout and rows of glistening razor teeth filled his field of vision as the shark barreled toward him.

His natural survival response battered at his will, screaming for him to take out his knife and start hacking. Just as he was about to give in, the shark angled past him, brushing his shoulder with her rough hide as she swam past. As quickly as she had come, she was gone again.

Maddock closed his eyes for a moment and said a brief prayer of thanks to the gods of the sea. Without looking around to locate the shark, he hastily pinched his nose closed and blew, forcing his ears to pop, before resuming his gradual ascent. He looked down at his wrist. Five minutes. Glancing up, he was surprised to see two boats floating above him. His attention had been so focused on the shark that he had not heard the second craft's arrival. He continued on with suspicious thoughts rising in his mind. The newly arrived craft floated directly above him. Warily, he surfaced just behind the stern.

The bright Caribbean sun danced on the cerulean water, and he squinted against the glare. The boat was an old Coast Guard cutter. Someone had repainted it an ugly shade of green with the Cuban flag emblazoned sloppily on the back. Four men stood with their backs to him, three of them holding rifles at the ready. One of them was talking to the crew of Maddock's boat, the *Sea Foam*. The newcomers were armed with old AK-47's and garbed in a motley mix of military uniform bits, as green and ugly as their vessel.

Aboard the *Sea Foam*, Maddock's partner, Uriah Bonebrake, known to friends simply as "Bones," stood facing the unwelcome intruders. A false smile painted his face, and his body was deceptively relaxed. The Carolina-born Cherokee, Maddock's friend since their days together as Navy SEALS, carried a nine-millimeter Glock on his right hip, out of sight beneath his loose-fitting Hawaiian print shirt. Willis Sanders, Matt Barnaby, and Corey Dean, the other members of Maddock's crew, stood behind Bones. Willis, the sun gleaming off his ebony skin and shaved head, stood with his muscular arms folded across his chest, staring coldly at the newcomers. Matt's lean, tan face was drawn in concern while Corey looked frightened. His crew was outgunned, but Maddock knew that all but Corey were looking for an opening, ready to fight back the moment the opportunity arose.

"You are in Cuban waters, Señor," the man without a rifle said. "We must inspect your boat for drugs." One of his comrades snickered, and he shut him up with a wave of his hand.

"These here ain't Cuban waters, Chief," Bones said, his deep voice relaxed, almost friendly. "Like I told you, we're marine archaeologists. This is a research vessel. If you're looking for drugs, there's this dude who hangs out on the corner near the Walmart by my house who can probably hook you up."

Bones knew as well as Maddock that these clowns might be Cubans, but there was no way they were government agents. They were self-styled pirates, thugs who preyed mostly on private pleasure craft. He needed to help his crew, but how?

"You, my tall friend, are not so amusing as you seem to think. I suggest you cooperate. Do not force us to harm you." The fellow's voice was as oily as his skin.

"No need for any of that now." Bones maintained his friendly tone. "We've got a cooler in the cabin. I don't share my Dos Equis, but maybe you dudes would like a Diet Mountain Dew or a can of Bud?"

Bones was stalling for time, waiting for Maddock to do something to help them out. Hoping he would not be heard over the sound of the cutter's idling engine, Maddock quickly submerged and dove back down to the tuna boat. He had an idea.

He re-entered the submerged vessel, scraping his shoulder on a jagged piece of metal. The salt water burned, but he had no time to think about it. He checked his watch again. Less than three minutes now. He had to hurry.

A quick swim through the dimly lit vessel, and he soon found what he was looking for. He hefted it and turned to find himself blind. In his haste, he had disturbed the silt on the bottom of the craft, and the interior of the submerged craft was now filled with a thick, opaque cloud of sediment.

More angry than concerned, he took a moment to orient himself. It was a small boat, and he should not have any problem getting out, but precious seconds were ticking away. He blew out a few bubbles just to make sure he knew which direction was up, and reached up to put a hand on the ceiling. He swam his way to the opposite side of the boat, the side in which the hole was rent, and hugged the wall as he worked his way back.

The way out appeared like a sliver of sky through gray clouds. Exiting the sunken craft, he made ready to return to the *Sea Foam* and his crew. Something moved in his peripheral vision. The shark again! This time he had no choice but to make a bolt for the surface and hope that the primordial creature would continue to ignore him. He set his jaw and swam to the surface as fast as he could. The shark ignored him, and he surfaced without drawing notice.

Tensions were at a peak. The leader of the intruders was waving his arms and shouting in Spanish. Maddock caught a few of the words, enough to know that they contained threats of bodily harm. Bones' eyes flitted in Maddock's direction for the briefest of instants. It was enough to let him know that Bones had seen him and was ready. Maddock kicked free of his flippers and slipped out of his dive tank just as the bull shark resurfaced on the other side of the boats and made straight toward him, its fin slicing through the calm gulf waters. The cut on his shoulder! It had scented him and now bore down on him. First things first, though.

This had better work, Maddock thought. He hefted the fire extinguisher he had retrieved from the drug runners' boat and opened it up full blast on the pirates.

Surprised shouts rang out from the men on the cutter, and gunshots erupted as Bones used the diversion to draw his Glock and open fire. The two intruders farthest from Maddock went down immediately. The man in the stern opened up wildly with his AK, spraying the *Sea Foam* with a deadly torrent of hot lead.

The shark was ten meters away and closing fast. Flinging the fire extinguisher in its direction, Maddock grasped the side of the boat and heaved himself out of the water. He tumbled over the stern and sprang to his feet, freeing his dive knife as he went. Only a few paces away, the confused attacker, still struggling to keep his burning eyes open, spotted Maddock and turned, bringing his weapon to bear.

Bullets buzzed past Maddock's ear as he closed the gap between himself and the Cuban. He lashed out with his left hand, smacking the barrel of the weapon to the side. Simultaneously, he thrust hard with his right. Still gripping his rifle, the Cuban could not protect himself. Maddock drove his knife into the man's chest. Giving it a quick jerk to the left, then back to the right, he yanked the weapon free, and shoved the dying, self-styled pirate away.

The last enemy was down on one knee, exchanging gunfire with Bones. He was armed with a .38-caliber revolver, of all things. Gritting his teeth, Maddock dashed toward him. The brigand must have espied him in the corner of his vision. He turned and leveled his pistol at Maddock, and pulled the trigger. The hollow sound of a hammer striking repeatedly an empty cylinder seemed deafening to Maddock as he charged in. Cursing in Spanish, the man threw the useless weapon at Maddock's head, and then jumped up to meet his attacker.

Maddock thrust low and hard at the man's midsection, but his opponent was a skilled fighter. The Cuban spun to the right, grasping Maddock's left wrist in both hands, and tried a shoulder throw. Maddock saw the move coming and managed to grab hold of the man by the loose fabric of his uniform pants behind his left thigh. He yanked up hard, throwing them both off balance. As they tumbled to the deck, the Cuban struck Maddock's wrist, sending his dive knife sliding across the deck. He rolled away, came nimbly to his feet, and lunged at Maddock again.

Years of combat training kicked in. Maddock dropped into a long stance, bending at the knees. He wrapped one arm around the man's waist and the other around his thigh. Allowing the attacker's momentum to carry him, he heaved the man onto his shoulder like a log. Ignoring the pain from his wound, he turned and dropped his opponent over the side of the boat and into the water.

The Cuban broke the surface, shouting angrily, but his cries quickly turned to frightened shrieks as the water around him began to churn and froth. The bull shark ripped into him in an eerie, silent assault. The man shrieked and beat at the shark with his fists, but to no avail. Maddock saw Bones, who had held his fire during the fight for fear of hitting the wrong man, raise his pistol and take aim at the shark. Just then, the Cuban ceased his struggles. Great gouts of blood erupted from his mouth as the ferocious predator carried him under, leaving a crimson pool spreading between the two boats. It was surely his imagination, but Maddock thought he could smell the coppery scent of carnage.

The strength left his legs, and he leaned heavily against the rail

"Thanks for coming to my rescue," he called across the intervening waters to his friends.

"Hey man, just because he didn't see the shark doesn't mean we all missed it," Bones yelled back. "The guy was a moron, anyway." The big, ponytailed native leaned his muscled, six-foot frame over the rail, cupped his hands, and shouted down at the water, "How many shots in a revolver, pal?"

"That's cold," Maddock said, feeling a touch guilty at his enjoyment of the dark humor Bones had adopted as a means of coping with the realities of combat they had experienced in the service.

"Yeah, but I'm right." Bones' mirthless grin reminded Maddock too strongly of the action they had seen in the SEALS. Bones was a good man, but a remorseless killer if he felt he had good reason to take a life.

Willis and Matt burst from the cabin, both carrying pistols.

"Man, y'all didn't save us any." Willis' shaved head and deep voice reminded Maddock of Dennis Haysbert's character, Cerrano, in the *Major League* movies. He turned to Matt. "After all we've been through together, these boys still don't know how to share." Like Bones, Willis was a former SEAL who loved a good fight.

"It's not our fault you left your weapons belowdecks. Some of us are prepared." Bones grinned.

"I thought Maddock was the Boy Scout in this group," Willis said.

"Where's Corey?" Maddock spoke a little more sharply than he'd intended. "The fight had him on edge and he was already fretting over the damage done to his boat.

"Downstairs. He put a call in to the Coast Guard when we first saw these guys coming, and now he's following up with them." Matt said, leaning against the rail of the *Sea Foam*. He ran his long, tan, fingers through his spiky brown hair, and scanned the horizon. The condition of his hair was always of paramount importance to him. "They should be here any minute." Matt was a former army grunt, but the skinny mate and engineer had proven himself an able seaman.

"They're almost here." Corey, the fair-skinned, redheaded computer specialist said as he strode from the cabin. He sat down on the deck beside Bones, propped his elbows on his knees and his chin cupped in his hands, and frowned. "You guys know what this means."

"I know," Maddock groaned, "back to the docks." They could not afford a delay. Business had been slow, and he had been counting on the Spanish galleon to change their fortunes. He had done his homework, researched it thoroughly, and was certain he had a line on it. But nothing remained secret for long in this business. His competitors would hear about the shootout and wonder what he was looking for out here.

"It should only be for a day," Bones said hopefully. "It's pretty obvious what these guys are. Or should I say were?" He twisted his mouth in a wry smile.

"It had better not be for long," Maddock said. "We've got to get back to work." He did not add, or we're going to go under. Everyone knew that fact already. "If somebody finds that wreck before us…" His words trailed away as a Coast Guard cutter appeared on the horizon.

Chapter 2

Maddock and Bones were surveying the damage to the *Sea Foam* when the hollow sound of approaching footsteps drew their attention. Though they had returned to port, they remained on edge after the attack. Even Corey, who was not the least bit prone to violence, had armed himself with Matt's spare .9 millimeter and was keeping an eye out for danger.

A young woman, perhaps in her mid-twenties, stood at the end of the dock. She was tall, with long, deeply tanned legs, which her khaki shorts displayed to good effect. A tight, white, sleeveless shirt clung to her trim, athletic body in all the right places. The intense Key West sun glistened on her long, white-blonde hair, which she wore pulled back, displaying a strong, yet attractive face that appeared untouched by the humidity. Her chin was a bit too small and her nose just a touch too big for her face, but that only added character to her appearance. She regarded Maddock with an intense, green-eyed stare that took his breath for an instant. She was a beauty.

"Holy crap," Bones muttered. "I wouldn't kick her out of bed for eating crackers."

"Good afternoon," the newcomer said, smiling broadly. If she had heard Bones' comment, she didn't let it show. "Permission to come aboard?" She asked the question as if it was a mere formality, which Maddock supposed it was. Beautiful women on the *Sea Foam* were few and far-between.

"Granted," Bones replied quickly, shouldering Maddock aside. He offered his hand to help the young woman onto the deck. She did not need his assistance, though, vaulting the rail and landing on the balls of her feet with catlike agility. Bones stepped back and grinned in approval. "Not bad. What are you, anyway, one of those Romanian gymnast women or something?"

"Hardly." She brushed some invisible dirt from her shorts. "Well then. I assume you would be Bonebrake and Maddock," she said, nodding to each of them in turn.

"As if we had a choice," Maddock replied, and immediately wondered if that sounded as dumb to her as it did to him. Bones was the clever one. "And you would be?"

"I am Kaylin Maxwell." She looked at him as if he ought to know her.

Maddock was certain that he'd remember that pair of legs, if not the name. "I'm sorry Miss Maxwell, have we met before?"

"Sure we have," Bones interrupted, his smile shining brighter than white against his deeply tanned features. "You know, at that thing, at the place…" His voice trailed off under Kaylin's bemused stare.

Kaylin folded her arms and looked down at the bullet holes riddling the side of the boat. "Termites?" she deadpanned.

"Cubans," Maddock said. "It's a long story."

"But it's a great story," Bones interrupted. "We were heroes. How about I buy you a drink and tell you all about it?"

"I'll take a beer if you have one handy," she said. "But I know enough of your reputation to not let you buy me anything."

Maddock waited for the woman to explain her presence here, but nothing was forthcoming. "You never told us where we know you from."

"You don't know me," the blonde replied, "but you both knew my father quite well."

Maddock paused for a moment and then took a step back. "Hold on! You're Maxie's daughter?" Commander Hartford Maxwell had led his and Bones' unit during their service in the SEALS. Maddock had held the rank of Lieutenant Commander under Maxie. "I haven't heard from him in years. How is he?"

Kaylin looked away, her bright eyes cloudy and her face crestfallen.

Maddock's heart sank. Somehow, he already knew what she was going to say.

"I'm sorry to have to tell you," she said, her voice husky with emotion, "that my father is dead." She paused, taking a deep breath. "He died a week ago. That's why I'm here."

"Oh," Maddock said, caught off guard by the surprise announcement. He did not know what to say, so he grimaced and looked down for a moment. He had seen his share of death, but he knew all too well that loved ones were different. The rest of the crew had joined them, and they offered their condolences to Kaylin, who nodded her thanks.

Willis, who had also served under Maxie, took the news like a gut punch. He sat down on the deck, bowed his head, and tuned the others out.

As usual, Bones tried to lighten the mood. "You're in the will, Maddock." He clapped Maddock on the shoulder. "Lord knows Maxie wouldn't have left me anything." The commander had appreciated Bones as a soldier. Unfortunately, Bones held his liquor about as well as any other Indian: not well at all. Maxie was constantly busting his subordinate for some shenanigan or another. Every time it had been when Bonebrake was drinking. It had taken years, but he'd finally learned his limits.

"I'm sorry, but I fear there's no inheritance," Kaylin said, smiling sadly.

"Yeah, I guess that wasn't very compassionate of me," Bones said, looking a bit abashed. "I gotta tell you, I'm not very good with the sympathy thing."

"No problem," Kaylin said. "As I said before, I've already heard a little bit about you, so I was prepared." She offered a sad smile to show there were no hard feelings, but then her face grew serious. She frowned and looked around uncomfortably. "Is there somewhere the three of us can talk?"

"Oh, sorry. Of course." Maddock said. The others suddenly busied themselves with odd tasks while he and Bones ushered her into the main cabin.

They sat down at a small table that was covered in charts and various books and papers. Maddock hurried to clean up the clutter while Bones rummaged through the small refrigerator and retrieved three bottles of Dos Equis.

"You two make an odd pair," Kaylin observed.

Maddock had heard that before. With his fair skin, blue eyes and blond hair, he didn't resemble Bones in any way.

"That's true," Bones said. "I'm tall and handsome. He's short and ugly." He added a squirt of juice from a cheap, plastic lime to each bottle of beer, and handed them around.

Maddock grinned. He stood a hair under six feet tall, but next to the six foot five Bones, he didn't exactly look strapping.

They made small talk, catching up on the years since Maddock had fallen out of touch with Maxie. Kaylin had graduated from college, traveled in Europe for a year, and finally settled in Charleston, South Carolina where she worked as an Art History professor and painted on the side.

They finally lapsed into a tense silence. Kaylin took a long, slow drink and sat in quiet contemplation for a moment before launching into her explanation.

"My father was murdered," she began. "The police say he interrupted a burglary in progress."

Maddock took a long pull from his beer. It was sharp and tangy, just the way he liked it and so cold that it stung his throat on the way down. Just what the doctor ordered on a hot day.

"But you think differently," Maddock prompted. He had listened to what Kaylin had not said, and that was what he responded to.

"I know it wasn't a burglary," she replied, meeting his gaze with a level stare. "Not long before he died, my father gave me a package and told me to keep it safe. He said it was something he was working on, and that people were after it. He planned to get it back from me when he felt that things had *cooled off*, whatever that meant."

"I don't get it," Bones interrupted, his beer forgotten as he concentrated on the issue at hand. "Maxie was good. If he knew somebody was after him, he should have been on his guard. How could someone have gotten to him?"

"That's another reason that I know it wasn't a burglary," Kaylin replied. "As you said, Dad was good. Whoever got him must have been better." She paused and cleared her throat, her eyes beginning to mist. She accepted the napkin Maddock offered with a nod of thanks and dabbed at her eyes.

"What was the condition of the house when the police got there?" He felt strange continuing the discussion when she was so upset, but he sensed that talking was preferable to sitting in gloomy silence.

"It looked like a burglary," she said, her voice thick with emotion. This was obviously difficult for her to talk about. "Drawers had been rummaged through or dumped on the floor. His DVD player was missing, and what little bit of jewelry he owned. Things like that."

"Let me play the devil's advocate here," said Bones, raising a long finger. "How can you be certain that it wasn't a burglary? You know, Occam's Razor."

"For one, it was too clean," Kaylin said. If she minded the question, she did not show it. "They left no fingerprints. Zero. No signs of forced entry, no alarm from the security system, and I know for a fact that Dad never went anywhere without locking up and arming the system."

"He never missed a detail," Maddock agreed. Maxie was the most professional officer he had ever known. "I can't imagine Maxie forgetting anything."

"Also, the hard drive on his computer was erased, save a few mundane files. All of his research was wiped clean. That isn't the sort of thing a burglar would do. The biggest reason, though, is what they didn't mess with." She paused. "Dad's study looked untouched: his desk, his filing cabinet, his books."

"Why would burglars mess with his books?" Bones asked. "Is there a big black market for old James Micheners?"

"People will sometimes hide money in their books," Maddock explained. "Or they'll get those fake books that are hollow on the inside and put their valuables in there."

Bones raised his eyebrows in surprise. "No wonder I made such a crappy burglar when I was a kid," he said. "Of course, I was mostly looking for beer and porn." He took a drink, gazing thoughtfully at the ceiling. "Rummaging through the desk, I get. A burglar would be looking for checks, credit card numbers, money, stuff like that."

"You said the study *looked* untouched." Maddock had caught the inflection in Kaylin's voice. "If that's the case, then what makes you so certain that someone had been in there?"

"The work Dad was doing," Kaylin looked up at the ceiling, seeming uncertain how to answer, "was sort of a research project. He told me that along with his real work, he kept a fake journal. Some of it was accurate, but with key information altered or missing. He kept it in the safe in his study. If someone got hold of it, they'd think it was real because he'd gone to the trouble of locking it up."

"The sneaky son of a..." Bones whispered. "Oh. Sorry. No disrespect or anything." He stared out the window with a faint smile and a distant look in his eyes. "I don't know if you remember him the way we do. It's all good, though."

"That's all right, he was sneaky." Kaylin laughed and reached out to pat Bones' shoulder. "He figured that if whoever was after him ever got hold of it, it would protect us, and also keep them from finding what he was looking for." She shook her head in admiration.

"I assume the false journal was missing," Maddock said, finding himself drawn into the puzzle despite his surprise at the news of Maxie's death.

Kaylin nodded. "The safe was locked. All his other papers appeared to be undisturbed, but the journal was gone."

Maddock folded his hands behind his head and looked up at the ceiling. He just could not believe Maxie was gone. The man had always seemed indestructible. Maddock's parents had died in an auto accident while he was in the service, and Maxie had stepped in to fill the void left by their loss, serving as a guide and role model. The two stayed in touch for a short while after Maddock left the military, but life had gotten in the way. Now, he regretted not having put more effort into the friendship.

"I truly am sorry to surprise the two of you with all this," Kaylin said. "Someone comes out of the blue and drops a bomb on you. It isn't the best way to deliver news. In any case, Mr. Maddock..."

"Please, call me Dane. Or just Maddock. That's what my friends call me."

"Like he has any friends," Bones jibed. "Except for me, and I only put up with him because he signs my paychecks."

Kaylin smiled. "All right, Maddock it is." The way she said it reminded him of how Melissa used to try a new flavor of lipstick: pursed lips and sort of a withholding judgment expression on her face. "I know this all comes as a surprise, and not a pleasant one at that, but I need your help." She reached across the table and laid her hand on his arm. Her touch was both soft and urgent.

"Wait, what?" Maddock was momentarily taken aback. What could he do to help with a murder investigation? He fixed the woman with a questioning gaze, but let her hand remain where it was. "I mean, you barely know me, yet you came all this way to ask for my help? I don't get it. Heck, how did you even track me down, for that matter?"

"Dad told me how to find the two of you." Her eyes darted to Bones and back to Maddock. "He said that if anything happened to him, I should come to you." She let that statement hang in the ensuing moment of stunned silence.

"Hold on a minute," Bones finally said. "Maxie wanted you to come to *me*?" His look of exaggerated shock would have been comical had Maddock not been so completely caught off-guard by Kaylin's revelation.

"He knew the two of you were working together. He told me that you," she gestured at Bones with her beer bottle, "were a character, but as trustworthy as they come. He's definitely right about the first part. As to the second part, that remains to be seen." She stood and looked down at the two of them. "The two of you have a very specific skill set that I'd like to take advantage of. Dad said you were the best."

"But we're treasure hunters, not private investigators," Maddock protested. What had Maxie been thinking? "We dive on wrecks and look for treasure. How can we help you?"

"Treasure hunters are precisely what I need," Kaylin said. She bit her lip and looked from Maddock to Bones and back to Maddock. It seemed as if she was uncertain whether to say any more. Finally, she continued. "I need you two to help me find a shipwreck."

Chapter 3

In my lifetime, I have had many joys and few regrets. The greatest of those things I regret, however, is the loss of my beloved treasures that January night. I was the first to rediscover the wonders and riches of those historic cities. I should have been the one to bring their secrets to light. But without that most precious of artifacts, no one would listen to me. I was scoffed at by my peers, ridiculed in scholarly circles, condemned from on high. I had no choice but to hold the truth close to my breast.

It is strange to think that I boarded the Dourado with the belief that I would return home a hero. The truths I had to share would have shaken the foundations of mankind. But alas, the fates have denied me the renown that I so richly deserve. Because I do not wish to hold myself up to the mockery of future generations, I will not record my findings in this journal. I will say only that truly, there is none like it.

Maddock closed the translated copy of Rienzi's journal. He ran his fingers across the smooth cover. Maxie had bound his translation in a simple, three-ring binder, and had printed "Journal" in his precise hand.

"So Maxie was looking for whatever this guy, Rienzi, lost. Do we have any idea what it was?"

Kaylin stood with her back to him, not answering, staring over the balcony and down at the Ashley River's slow moving waters where the river flowed into Charleston Harbor. Content to wait until she was ready to talk, Maddock left his seat at the bar that separated the kitchen from the living area of her small apartment, and joined her outside. Propping his forearms on the rail, he took in the peaceful view. A few sailing vessels plied the calm, gray harbor waters, their white sails glistening against the blue sky. He had always had an affinity for the water. If he could not be on the water, he wanted to at least be near it. He wondered if perhaps he had found a kindred spirit in

Kaylin.

He and Bones had arrived late the night before, three days after their initial meeting. Despite their reservations, it had not taken much coaxing from Kaylin to convince them to sign on for her project. Their latest expedition was a complete bust, and although the Coast Guard investigation had cleared them of all wrongdoing, it would be a while before the *Sea Foam* was ready to ply the waters again. The compensation Kaylin offered was more than enough to repair the damage to their craft. More, in fact, than he thought an art professor should be able to afford. When he had pressed her on the point, she explained that her father had provided well for her. That, Maddock did believe. Maxie was the kind of man who took care of his own. He and Bones admired the man greatly. But more than that, they wanted to see his last wish carried out.

"I'm sorry," Kaylin finally said. "It's difficult to talk about Dad's work." She turned to look at Maddock, her green eyes downcast. "Rienzi never names this treasure that was so precious to him. I've only had a few days to look over everything, but it seems that Dad was thorough in combing through everything the man ever wrote. He says all sorts of grandiose things about how important his discoveries were, but never reveals what, exactly he found."

"I picked up on the grandiose part," Maddock said. "He sounds like a character. Makes you wonder if it's all just bluster, or if he really did accomplish anything of note."

"He lived quite a life," Kaylin said. "He took part in the battle of Waterloo. He also fought for Simon Bolivar in Colombia, then came back to Europe where he was wounded at Marathon. He traveled most of the known world and became a self-styled discoverer. Not exactly a colonial era Indiana Jones, but something close." She grinned, and some of the strain melted away. She looked younger, more energetic. "He claimed to have been the first person to rediscover the ruins of Syre and Assab in Abyssinia. He also claimed that he was the first to excavate them, as well as Petra in Arabia."

"Wasn't Petra a crappy Christian band back in the eighties?" Bones called from the kitchen. He dropped a bag on the table and joined them on the balcony.

"It's also a famous city in the Middle East," Kaylin said. "It's literally carved into the sides of cliffs."

"You know, like in the third Indiana Jones movie." Maddock nudged his friend with an elbow to the ribs.

"Oh yeah!" Bones said as if this were all a startling revelation. "You guys are so smart."

The blonde rolled her eyes and continued. "Anyway, Rienzi was returning to France on the *Dourado* with all the treasures he had accumulated during his world travels. He lost everything when the ship sank."

"Bummer," Bones said. "Reminds me of the time I hooked up with this really cute sorority girl. We made it about halfway back to my dorm and then she hurled all over…" He took one look at Kaylin's disapproving stare and cut the story short. "Never mind. Rewind to where I said 'bummer' and just leave it there."

"Good idea." Kaylin folded her arms across her chest and frowned, but there was a twinkle in her eye that had been absent moments before. "Rienzi certainly thought it was a 'bummer' as you put it. He went back to France and made a bit of a name for himself writing. He never did get over losing his life's work, though."

"What happened to him?" Maddock asked.

Kaylin hesitated. "He killed himself eighteen years later."

"Ouch. Sounds like the guy had a flair for the dramatic," Bones observed, shaking his head. "So, what do we know about the last voyage of the *Dourado?*"

"It's a strange story," she said. "Besides Rienzi's belongings, the captain claimed to have been carrying more than half-a-million dollars on board when the ship went down. That was a great deal of money back then. When the survivors reached Singapore with word of the sinking, the British sent out a detachment of troops in three ships to guard the wreck against local pirates while divers tried to salvage the ship."

"I can't imagine trying to dive using nineteenth century technology," Maddock observed. He shuddered at the thought of braving the depths with only the aid of primitive dive equipment. Modern diving was hazardous enough.

"They didn't have to. The ships returned very quickly. They were unable to find the *Dourado*, and assumed that it had gone down in deep water. Less than a week later, though, the wreckage was found off the coast of the island of Bintan. Salvage efforts only turned up a few items: a silver statue, a box with some papers, and a couple of personal items. They found no sign of the money, nor of Rienzi's treasure. After three months, Rienzi gave up on ever recovering his property and returned to France."

The doorbell rang, bringing their conversation to an abrupt halt. Kaylin answered the door and returned a moment later with a tall, lean, ginger-haired man of middle years in a black suit and priest's collar. His thin-lipped smile was the only sign of emotion in an otherwise bland face. His eyes, narrowed in either curiosity or suspicion, flitted from Maddock to Bones, then back to Maddock.

"Father Wright," Kaylin said, "I would like to introduce two friends of my father. This is Dane Maddock." She gestured to Maddock with a wave of her hand. "And this is Uriah Bonebrake. They were in the Navy together with Dad."

The priest shook Maddock's hand first, then turned to Bones. "Uriah," he said, clasping Bones' hand. "A strong, biblical name."

"Let's hope I don't share his fate," Bones said with a mischievous smile. "Getting killed over a woman hits way too close to home." Maddock's surprise must have registered on his face because Bones frowned at him. "Think I don't know my Bible? I was raised on the reservation. Pentecostal preachers everywhere you look."

"I suppose we can forgive you for that," Father Wright said. He actually cracked a smile, but only a small one. "Kaylin," he continued, turning to their hostess, "I won't stay but a moment. I just came by to check in on you."

"Thank you, Father. I'm doing fine, all things considered."

"Glad to hear it." Father Wright paused, rubbing a pale, slender hand absently across his chest. He seemed nervous or uncertain. "I hope you'll forgive me, but I have a bit of an unusual question. Your father had in his collection a very old French Bible. I must not have hidden my admiration for it very well because he offered to donate it to the rectory library."

"Oh," Kaylin said, a frown creasing her brow. "I haven't gone through his things yet. I'll keep an eye out for it, though, and let you know if I come across it."

"Perhaps it is in his library?" the Priest asked. Maddock thought it a trifle rude for the man to persist, but he held his tongue. "I could drop by his house sometime when you are going to be there."

"Actually, that's the one place I have inventoried," Kaylin said. "After the burglary and the police investigation it seemed like it needed doing. As I said, I will look for it." Her voice had taken on a tone of impatience, and she stood with hands on hips.

"Thank you," Father Wright replied, touching her shoulder gently. "I just wanted to mention it. Please let me know if there is anything I can do for you."

"I will, Father. Thank you for dropping by." Kaylin showed the priest out and returned to the living room where Maddock and Bones had wandered in from the balcony. She had a puzzled look on her face.

"That was an odd conversation," Maddock said, dropping down onto Kaylin's black leather sofa.

"It was very odd," she said, taking a seat next to him. "Father Wright is a good man. It just feels so inappropriate for him to be asking for something of Dad's so soon after..." Her voice trailed away. "You know what I mean."

"You'd think a priest would have better bedside manner," Bones observed. He fished beer and a package of beef jerky out of the bag he had laid on the kitchen table. "Anybody else?" He held up his drink and snack.

"It's a little early for that much gas," Maddock said. "Thanks anyway, though."

"Breakfast of champions," Bones said. He joined them in the living room, dropping down into a Papa San chair beneath one of Kaylin's seascapes. The rattan chair creaked under his weight, and he overflowed it like a gorilla in an inner tube. Maddock chuckled at the mental image. Bones raised an eyebrow but did not ask what was funny.

"Cool artwork, Kaylin," Bones said, looking around at the paintings that adorned the living room walls. "You painted them all, huh? Anyway, I want to talk about this wreck we're supposed to find," he said. "If it was salvaged back when it first went down, and they didn't find much, it either means that Rienzi was full of it, or this alleged incredible discovery was lost somewhere between the point where the ship sank, and the point where the wreck was finally discovered. At best, we'll have to scour the ocean bed looking for some item which, by the way, we don't know what it is. I'd say it's impossible."

"It can't be impossible," Maddock argued. "Maxie wouldn't have wasted his time if it couldn't be done." Maddock had the utmost confidence in their former commander. He had no doubt that Maxie had been on to something. "There's something he knew that we don't. When we figure it out, we'll know how to proceed."

"Do you have anything other than the papers you showed us?" Bones asked Kaylin.

The girl shook her head. "We're missing something. I've been through Dad's journal and Rienzi's, and I can't find anything." She folded her arms and set her jaw. Her eyes were fixed on some invisible spot in the distance as she thought. "It has to be there. It just has to."

Maddock thought he knew someone who could help them. He excused himself for a minute and stepped outside to make the call. When he returned to the living room, Bones and Kaylin looked at him with curious expressions.

"I've got a friend on the case," he explained cryptically. He would leave them in suspense until he heard something back.

"So that's how you're going to play it?" Bones asked, grinning suspiciously.

"Yep," Maddock said. He did not want to get their hopes up until he found out what kind of results his contact could get. That and he enjoyed keeping them in suspense. At any rate, there was more that they could do in the meantime.

"Kaylin," he said, turning to the blonde, "What do you say we check out your dad's library?"

Father Michael Wright kept an eye on his rear-view mirror until he was well out of sight of Kaylin Maxwell's building before taking out his cell phone and punching in a number he'd committed to memory but dared not write down, much less save in his phone.

"*Yes?*" the voice on the other end of the line snapped.

Heart racing, breath short, Wright spoke a single word. "Dominion."

"*I'll transfer you immediately.*" The line rang again, and a familiar voice answered.

"*Robinson,*" the voice on the other end said.

"It's Wright." A police car passed him, going in the opposite direction, and he flinched. He knew it was a foolish reaction, but he'd never been completely comfortable in his dealings with this group, even if he did agree with their aims. He found himself on edge every time he spoke with one of them.

"*Report.*"

"I visited the subject's house. She claims to have no knowledge of the whereabouts of the article in question." Silence on the other end of the line. "I think she's telling the truth."

"*Then you'll have to keep looking. We need it.*"

Wright suppressed a shiver. The man was cold as ice. "I understand, but I'm at a loss as to how to proceed. He had no other living family, no close friends."

"*Find out where he banked. Perhaps there's a safe deposit box.*"

"Could be, but I wouldn't be able to get inside it."

"*You wouldn't but we would.*" Robinson paused. "*Anything else?*"

Wright took a deep breath. "Yes. She seems to have attached herself to some new friends. I'm no expert, but they look like they could be dangerous men to me. They served with her father."

"*Listen to me, Mister Wright.*" Robinson always omitted the priest's title. "*I don't care how dangerous the men you encounter are, I promise you we are more dangerous. And there are many more of us. Do I make myself clear?*"

"Crystal." Wright hated the sound of his own voice—tight and weak.

"*Excellent. Remember, you are doing the Lord's work. His dominion is at hand.*"

Wright swallowed hard. "His dominion is at hand." Ending the call, he realized he'd inadvertently driven past the rectory. Sighing deeply, he made a u-turn and headed home. He needed a stiff drink and time to plan his next move. Not for the first time, he wondered how he'd managed to fall in with such men.

Chapter 4

The books in Maxwell's library were arranged in meticulous fashion by subject, author and date of publication. The precise rows were totally in keeping with the commander's personality. Everything in the room, from the painting of the shipwreck on the wall above the computer to the single, framed family portrait, reminded Maddock of his mentor and friend. A pang of sadness welled up inside but was immediately overwhelmed by a wave of bitterness. He wanted to find whoever it was who had done Maxie in. He wanted them bad. He clenched his fist, imagining the murderer's throat.

"I wonder what Bible Father Wright was talking about." Kaylin stood next to him, looking over the books. "I know what Dad had in his library, and I never saw an old Bible."

"I didn't know Catholics even read the Bible," Bones said, "at least not in English."

"He didn't read it, genius. It was in French," Maddock shot back. "You don't see it anywhere? Maybe whoever broke in took it." He didn't know why someone would steal a Bible. He scanned the shelves but saw no obvious empty spaces where a book might be missing.

He set about the task of examining the library, pulling books off the shelves at random and thumbing through, looking for notations, papers, anything that might give a clue as to what they were looking for. Kaylin searched through the filing cabinets while Bones sat popping Maxie's thumb drives into his laptop one at a time, scanning their contents.

His cell phone vibrated against his chest. Maddock withdrew it from his jacket pocket and flipped it open. It was the call he had been waiting for.

"Hey Jimmy, what've you got for me?" Jimmy Letson was a writer for the Washington Post. He had access, legally, to a myriad of internet databases. He was also a hacker who had access, illegally, to resources Maddock didn't even want to know about. The two had been friends in the service, remaining in contact even after Jimmy had rung out of SEAL training and left the service when his tour ended.

"What's that? No, 'Wow, Jimmy, that was fast!' or 'Hey Jimmy, thanks for dropping everything to check on this for me,' or 'Gee Jimmy, thanks for risking your job…'"

"I get the point," Maddock said, laughing. "Fine, I declare you the Pope of Cyberspace. Now, what did you find out?"

"Funny you should mention the Pontiff. This guy, Rienzi, he came back from his world travels sounding off to anyone who would listen about all the great treasures he had lost."

"We knew that much already. Did he ever say what, exactly, he had lost?"

"He must have because, within several months, he had managed to tick off all of the scholars in his field, or at least the ones we have any writings from. Unfortunately for you, they all talk about his 'ridiculous' claims, but they never say what specifically those claims were. A year after his return, he pretty much shuts up and goes back to being a run-of-the-mill writer."

"Do you think the ridicule got to him?" Maddock asked.

"I think it was bigger than that." Jimmy paused. He had always tended toward the dramatic. *"NAILS turned up a letter from the bishop of Paris to a cardinal back at the Vatican, written nine months after Rienzi's return to France."*

NAILS was an acronym for "National Archive and Informational Linkage System," an interconnected system of informational resources used by the CIA. Jimmy had somehow found a way to clandestinely link up to the system. Maddock had told his friend on more than one occasion that he did not want to be around when Jimmy was finally busted. Jimmy just laughed and boasted that he was much too smart to be caught by those bozos. His cockiness made even Bones appear humble.

"I'm waiting for you to tell me why I should care," Maddock said, feigning disinterest.

"The cardinal wanted Rienzi excommunicated. Does that interest you, smart guy?"

Maddock reflected on this new bit of information. Could they be connected in some way? The timing was certainly right.

"I suppose it does. Thanks, Jim, that's great. Anything else?"

"Probably nothing you don't already know. I'll shoot a summary over to you. Anything else you

need?"

"Actually, would you see what you can find out about the ship Maxie was looking for? The *Dourado*."

"I suppose you're in a big hurry on this one too," Jimmy groaned.

"No, last night will be soon enough." Maddock ignored Jimmy's profane reply. "Thanks again. I'll stand you to a bottle of White Label next time I'm in DC." Maxie had taught him long ago how helpful it could be to know a man's weakness.

"You've got a deal," Jimmy replied and broke the connection.

Maddock hung up the phone and shared this new information with Bones and Kaylin.

"So Rienzi comes back from his trip and starts ruffling feathers," Bones said. He stood with his chin cupped in his hand. His brown eyes stared vacantly out the window. "Whatever claims he's making, they're enough to get somebody in the church all riled up. They threaten him with excommunication, and he clams up."

"With the kind of clout the church carried, it wouldn't be out of the question for the Vatican to find a way to get rid of any written record of Rienzi's claims, whatever they were," Kaylin added. "What could he have found that would upset the church that much?"

A flicker of movement at the corner of his eye caught Maddock's attention. "Did you see something out there?" he asked Bones, pointing toward the window.

His friend shook his head. "Sorry, man. Lost in space." He tapped his temple with a deeply tanned finger.

"Thought I saw something." Maddock drew his pistol, a German-made Walther P-99 and moved to the windowsill, carefully peering out over the narrow backyard that ran down to the shore of the Cooper River. It was a calm, sunny afternoon. Nothing seemed amiss in the quiet neighborhood. Bones appeared at his side, Glock drawn.

A knock at the front door broke the silence, causing the two of them to jump. Kaylin looked at him questioningly. Maddock nodded and walked with her to the door. She opened it to reveal an elderly black woman in a neatly pressed dress.

"Bernie!" Kaylin cried, crushing the woman in a tight embrace. The old woman smiled and hugged her back.

"Gently, child," she said in a tender voice, "I'm not as young as I used to be." She smiled a warm smile and patted Kaylin.

Kaylin pulled back and held the woman at arm's length. "It's so good to see you."

"It's good to see you, too. Can I come in?" The woman gave Kaylin a motherly pat on the shoulder and stepped through the doorway. After Kaylin had introduced Maddock and Bones, the four of them made their way to the kitchen, where they sat down around a stout oaken table in front of a wide bay window.

"Bernice took care of me when I was little; after Mom died," Kaylin explained. "I call her Bernie."

"I was so sorry to hear about your father," Bernie said. "I've been in Mississippi visiting family for a few weeks. It was such a shock when I got your call."

"I know it was. You're family to us, and you always will be," Kaylin said. Her smile underlined the sincerity in her words.

"I already miss your father a great deal. We kept in touch over the years and met for coffee from time to time." Tears welled in Bernice's eyes, and Kaylin took her hand and gave it a reassuring squeeze.

Kaylin turned to Maddock. "I was thinking about what Dad might have done with the Bible. I knew it wasn't among his possessions so he either hid it or gave it to someone he could trust. Someone whose connection to our family wouldn't be easily identified by outsiders. That's what made me think of Bernie."

"Well, I don't know if it's a Bible, but your father did give me something that he wanted me to pass along to you." The woman fished into her bag and produced a large, manila envelope with something thick and rectangular inside. Maddock could see that it was one of the padded packing envelopes used for mailing delicate items. "He gave me this several weeks ago. He was acting all nervous-like. Never seen him that way. He made me promise to keep it a secret. He said that I should give it to you if anything should ever happen to him." She shook her head. "I never thought it would be so soon if ever. Your father always seemed indestructible."

Maddock turned his head toward the window, giving the two a modicum of privacy to share this painful moment. Outside, a solitary boat drifted lazily down the Cooper River.

Kaylin nodded to Bernie, her eyes misty, and carefully undid the clasp on the envelope. Reaching in, she carefully withdrew a battered, old Bible, the leather cover worn with age.

Maddock leaned forward, his heart beating faster. This had to be it.

After a moment's pause, Kaylin opened the old book, and gingerly flipped through the pages. The writing was French! In various places, someone had written notes in the margins in a bold, ornate hand. The ink had faded with time and was, in parts, nearly invisible. Beside her, Bones whistled, and leaned closer. She turned back to the inside cover. There, on the front page, in the same flowing script, was the name: Louis Domenic de Rienzi.

"Rienzi's personal Bible," Bones marveled, his tone near reverential. "This is what the priest was after."

As Maddock sat staring at the ancient volume, something drew his attention. The boat had stopped drifting. A solitary man stood on the deck and appeared to be pointing in their direction. Immediately, Maddock realized what was happening, and he sprang to his feet.

"Down!" he shouted, grasping the edge of the table and upending it toward the bay window. The others fell to the floor as bullets shattered the glass and ripped into the heavy tabletop. An instant later, the sound of rifle fire drifted across the water, echoing hollowly through the house. Maddock drew his Walther with the futile knowledge that the boat was too far away for him to have any hope of hitting the shooter.

"Out the front," he ordered. He did not have a clue who was shooting at them, but he had an idea why. In any case, they had to get Kaylin and the Bible out of there right away. He reached up over the table and fired blindly, the report of the Walther loud in the small space.

"Come on, Granny!" Bones yelled to Bernie. His pistol in his right hand, he wrapped his left arm around the woman's waist and pulled her toward the door. Her eyes were wide with fright, but she did not argue.

Maddock followed behind, snapping off two more hasty shots at the boat in hopes of slowing the sniper's fire. He turned to see Kaylin rummaging through a drawer. "What are you doing?" he shouted. What could she possibly need from the kitchen that could not wait?

She turned back toward him, a .380 automatic and two reloads in her hand. "Dad kept guns everywhere. Let's go." She nodded toward the door.

He was impressed by her lack of panic, but there was no time to remark on it. He rushed to the front door where Bones and Bernie waited. He nudged the door open and looked up and down the deserted street. Behind them, the sniper continued to rain bullets on the house. From the sounds of shattering glass, Maddock determined that the shooter was methodically firing into each room, working his way across the back of the structure. They needed to get away immediately.

"Bones, you take Bernie in her car. Kaylin and I will go in mine."

They hurried to the vehicles, weapons at the ready. Maddock threw open the door of his rented green Tahoe and fired it up. He glanced at the rear-view mirror and saw a silver Taurus whip around the corner and come barreling down the street toward them. The passenger side window was down, and the man opposite the driver reached out the window and opened fire. Kaylin, Bible clutched in one hand, returned fire with her .380 before joining Maddock in the SUV. Maddock floored it, hoping to stay ahead of the attacker's vehicle.

He looked in the rearview mirror in time to see Bones make a u-turn in Bernie's cream-colored Lincoln and tear down the street, headed on a collision course with the Taurus. Bones thrust his pistol out the driver's window, blazing away left-handed with his nine as he charged their assailants.

"He's crazy," Kaylin whispered in awe. She climbed into the back seat, .380 still at the ready, and watched out the back window.

"You have no idea," Maddock said. In his rear-view, he saw the windshield of the Taurus shatter. The driver yanked the car hard to the right as Bones flashed by, still shooting. The silver car fishtailed as it drifted into Maxwell's front yard, but the driver recovered quickly and continued the pursuit. Maddock groaned. "Are you all right using that thing?" he asked, tilting his head toward Kaylin's pistol.

"Please," she said. "You knew my father." She turned back toward the rear of the vehicle, her .380 trained on the pursuing car.

He took a hard right, nearly bringing the Tahoe up on two wheels. He stepped on the accelerator and weaved through the sparse afternoon traffic heading into downtown Charleston. Behind them, the Taurus whipped around the corner, tires screeching. Maddock cursed as he watched the other drivers move out of the way of the speeding silver vehicle. How were they going to get away?

"Maybe they won't shoot at us with witnesses around," Kaylin said. Her hope proved in vain as shots rang out, and spider webbed cracks spread around a bullet hole in the bottom corner of the rear window. "Okay, forget I said that."

"Gotcha," Maddock said as he whipped the wheel back-and-forth, zigzagging as he sped along, but trying not to slip into a pattern that would make them easy targets. He heard the rear driver's side window roll down, then the report of Kaylin's pistol as she squeezed off rounds, maintaining a slow, steady fire at their attackers.

"Where are the cops when you need them?" he growled. The light ahead turned red. He pressed the pedal to the floor and veered into the oncoming lane to pass the traffic that had stopped for the light, narrowly avoiding a collision with a cab that was crossing the intersection. The cab screeched to a halt, and he heard the cabbie shout a physically impossible suggestion as they shot past. Once through the light, he yanked the steering wheel, bringing the Tahoe back onto the proper side of the road, and continued on.

"They're through," Kaylin called to him, snapping off another shot. Unfortunately, the light traffic worked in both drivers' favor.

A quick glance in the rear-view mirror showed the Taurus again narrowing the gap between the two vehicles.

"How can they possibly keep up with us when they're driving with a broken windshield?" Kaylin grumbled.

Maddock did not answer. It was further confirmation that whomever Maxie had run afoul of, they were good. He turned a hard right onto Market Street, the Taurus now in close pursuit. Kaylin exchanged a few more shots with the passenger in the pursuing car.

"Something has got to give, here," she said, popping a reload into her pistol. "They're way too close."

"That's an understatement," Maddock replied, glancing in his mirror. The traffic ahead of them was at a standstill. The oncoming lanes were almost gridlocked, and tourists packed the narrow sidewalks. The last thing they needed was an Old West-style shootout, but it might come down to that. He looked around for a side street, anything that would afford an escape. Ahead of him, the stalled traffic loomed ever closer. And then, to his left, he saw what he was looking for. It could work, but they would have to be fast.

He tapped the brake and then yanked the wheel hard to the left, nearly rolling the top-heavy vehicle. Horns blared as a he cut across the street directly in front of oncoming traffic. Hitting the brakes hard, he maneuvered the Tahoe into a controlled skid, then released the pedal and whipped the vehicle into an empty parking space.

"Out," he barked. He hopped out of the car and looked across the street, where the sheer volume of vehicles had managed to hold up the Taurus. The driver was trying to force his way across through the heavy oncoming traffic. Through the driver's window, Maddock was finally able to get a look at their pursuers.

The two could have been twins. Each had short, dark hair and wore wrap-around sunglasses and dark colored polo-style shirts. Dressed to blend in with the crowd, Maddock thought. That's what I intend to do. He took Kaylin's hand and led her away from the car. They hurried across the parking lot and into the Charleston Slave Market.

Chapter 5

The Charleston Slave Market was a long, narrow building that spanned the length of two city blocks. Contrary to common wisdom, the market was not a place where slaves had once been sold, but a place where slaves from the surrounding area had gathered to sell their wares. Now it had been converted into a sort of giant flea market, which drew thousands of visitors each day. Maddock hoped that the milling throngs would provide him and Kaylin with a way to disappear, at least long enough to evade their pursuers.

His cell phone vibrated. He opened it up and checked the display. It was Bones.

"Maddock, where are you?" Bones sounded calm despite the urgency of the situation.

"We're in the slave market. You know how to get here?" Maddock squeezed through the throng of shoppers milling about the displays. He turned to see the Taurus pulling into the parking lot.

"I'll find it. You got a SITREP for me?"

Maddock explained their situation and gave his friend a general description of their pursuers. Bones assured him that he would be there soon. Maddock flipped the phone shut and turned to Kaylin, who was turning off her own phone.

"I called the police, but I don't think the dispatcher believed me. She kept going on about the penalty for phony 911 calls. Useless."

"Two cars flying down the street, guns blazing have to have gotten someone's attention." Maddock hoped that was true. "Let's stay alive until they get here."

"Should we try and slip out of the market farther on down?" She stood on her tiptoes trying to see over the milling throng. The long, narrow market offered exits at the end of each section but was woefully lacking in side doors.

"I think we're safer in the crowd," he replied, as they moved deeper into the throng. He was walking sideways, pretending to look at the merchandise, all the while keeping an eye on the front entrance. So far, there was no sign of their pursuers.

A bit farther down, he saw what he had been hoping to find. He nodded toward the display of Hawaiian print shirts. Kaylin smiled, understanding his thoughts immediately. At the display, Maddock purchased two shirts, a straw hat for himself and sunglasses for Kaylin. They donned their new clothing quickly, throwing the shirts over what they were already wearing.

"You look totally lame," Kaylin said as she twisted her long, blonde hair up into a bun. "No one would believe you were once a badass Navy SEAL."

"That's the idea," he replied with a grin. "Tourist camo." He was fairly certain she was rolling her eyes behind her sunglasses. He offered her his elbow, which she took in a tight grip that conveyed her tension. Arm-in-arm the two continued to browse, looking, he hoped, like nothing more than a happy couple on vacation. All the while, they kept a lookout for the men who were after them.

Moments later, Maddock spotted one of their pursuers, the driver, he thought, enter the market. Trying to look inconspicuous, the man made a show of checking out the displays on either side of the aisle as he worked his way into the marketplace.

"Only one of them," Maddock whispered. "The other guy must be coming in from the back. That's what I would have done."

Kaylin examined a fat, silver bracelet inlaid with turquoise. "Buy this for me, honey?" she said in a syrupy voice.

"Not this close to our anniversary, sweetheart," he kidded.

"But you don't need a special occasion to show me that you love me, do you?" She screwed up her face in an exaggerated pout.

"Keep sticking that lip out there, and a bird's going to poop on it," he said, arching an eyebrow. He had to admit, she looked kind of cute when she made that face.

She frowned and smacked him on the shoulder. In response, he pulled her close and gave her a squeeze, giving himself a chance to look over her shoulder at the man who was coming toward them.

"He hasn't seen us yet, but he's getting closer," he whispered in her ear. Who were these guys?

"I still don't see anyone coming from the other direction," she whispered back.

They broke from the embrace and continued moving. Maddock guessed that they were about halfway through the first section of the market. He wanted to look back, but he could not afford to draw attention to them. A bit farther, then they paused at a book vendor's display. Maddock picked up a large picture book and held it up close to his face. He stole a glance back in the direction from which they had come. The man was no more than thirty yards away, moving slowly, but coming steadily closer. At least they had not yet been spotted.

"Maddock, here he comes," Kaylin whispered, her voice strident. "He's going to catch up with us soon."

Maddock turned his head and caught a glimpse of the second man, much farther away, but also headed toward them.

"What do we do?" Kaylin bit her lower lip.

"They're probably expecting us to bolt out the back door. Our best chance is to try and slip past the first guy."

"What if that doesn't work?" she asked.

"Then we might have to do it Old West style. Just make sure of your aim. Don't hit any bystanders. Got your gun ready?"

She nodded and patted the large handbag she carried slung over her shoulder.

"Good. Now we just need a way to get past him without him seeing us." He racked his brain. There was only the wide center aisle running the length of the market. Were their disguises good enough that they could just walk past the man? Not likely. He did not know what kind of look the men had gotten at him and Kaylin, but they would be searching for a man and woman fitting their general descriptions.

"What about this?" Kaylin took his face in her hands and forcefully pulled him toward her. Their lips met in a long, deep kiss. After an instant of surprise, he cupped her face in his hands as well.

He cracked his eyelid just enough to see the first man move past them on the far side of the aisle. He waited two seconds, then drew away from her. She looked at him with disappointment in her eyes. Whether it was disappointment over the quality or the duration of the kiss, he did not know.

"He's past us," Maddock whispered. They set off at a fast walk in the direction of the front entrance, with Kaylin walking just ahead of him. They wove in and out of the shoppers. After a few moments, Maddock stole a glance over his shoulder. He could not see their pursuers. Had they lost the two men?

Maddock and Kaylin continued at their hurried pace. The front entrance loomed ahead of them. Maddock cursed inwardly. No matter how fast they moved, the entrance seemed to get no closer. They dodged and sidestepped as they tried to make their way out of the market. Maddock looked back again, painfully aware that too much weaving through the crowd would draw attention.

As he turned around, someone grabbed him from behind by the shoulder. An arm clamped around his neck. He managed to shove Kaylin forward as he was dragged backward.

"Run," he grunted. One of the men shoved past him, going after Kaylin, who was pushing people out of her way as she ran toward the door. Maddock kicked out with his right foot, tripping him up. He could do no more for Kaylin until he got rid of the guy who held him in a chokehold.

Palms facing out, he grabbed his assailant by the wrist and inner forearm. He tilted his head forward and yanked it back up, catching his attacker across the bridge of the nose. As he bashed the man in the nose with the back of his head, he simultaneously pushed up and out with his hands, forcing that attacker's arm up off his throat. Maddock drove a solid left elbow into his opponent's stomach, stomped down hard on his right instep, then spun to his left with all of his strength, breaking the man's python grip.

Now facing his opponent, Maddock ducked under a right cross and punched the man in the throat, scarcely noticing the cartilage give beneath his knuckles. His attacker, already bleeding from a broken nose, stumbled backward, fighting to draw breath.

Maddock leaped forward, pistoning a right cross to the temple and following with a sweeping kick that took the man's feet out from under him. He fell hard to the ground, arms splayed. Maddock turned and sprinted after Kaylin.

The crowd had drawn away from the fight, giving him a clear path to the front door. Up ahead, the second attacker dove at Kaylin's feet, tripping her up. He scrambled up on all fours and grabbed at her handbag. She shouted and kicked him hard in the face. She continued to impress Maddock with her toughness.

Closing the gap, he flew through the air and delivered a flying kick to the man's chest, knocking him onto his back across a nearby table, sending the display crashing to the ground. From outside, sirens wailed over the din of the marketplace.

Kaylin's assailant climbed to his feet and drew his gun. Screams erupted from the crowd. For a moment, Maddock thought the man was going to open fire inside the crowded marketplace. Instead, he held the gun threateningly in front of him and dashed out the door. The man with whom Maddock had fought rushed by an instant later. Maddock drew his own weapon and gave chase, Kaylin following close behind.

Just as he ran outside, a sheriff's department patrol car screeched to a halt directly in front of him. Maddock raised his hands above his head, not wanting any misunderstandings. A deputy hopped out of the driver's side door, weapon drawn. Ignoring Maddock and Kaylin, he sprinted around the corner of the slave market in the direction the attackers had run. A moment later, Bones clambered out of the passenger side door and followed the deputy.

"Had trouble with the locks," he shouted as he ran by. "Glad you're all right."

Maddock could now hear sirens coming from both directions, and soon, three City of Charleston police cars pulled up to the front of the market. Bones and the deputy reappeared together a short while later.

"Lost 'em," Bones said. He holstered his pistol, cursing their still unidentified assailants.

"Where's Bernie?" Kaylin asked, a note of concern in her voice. The encounter in the slave market did not seem to have fazed her a great deal.

"She's fine," Bones said. "We flagged down the deputy here." He nodded to the man in the tan uniform. "She's in the back of the car." He turned and waved. Through the tinted glass, they saw Bernie waving back.

"The call came in over the radio about a running gun battle in the street just as your friend was telling his story," the deputy explained.

"Thanks for bailing us out," Maddock replied. He was confused and frustrated. Who were these guys, and what did Maxie have that they wanted so badly?

Chapter 6

"Hey, babe. Thought you'd be home by now."

"Sorry, I had to make a stop. I've got a surprise for you!"

"I hate surprises. What is it?"

"Maddock! You are no fun at all."

"I know. Now, what's my surprise?"

"I'm not…"

Maddock bolted upright, gasping. Sweat trickled down his cheek, or was it a tear? He didn't care. Wiping it away, he shook his head as if that could clear the memory from his mind. He hated the dream, and now he hated the sun that had made him drowsy enough to doze off. Rising, he snapped his notebook shut and went back into the condo. He hurried past Bones and Kaylin, who were working at the small kitchen table.

Inside the bathroom, he closed and locked the door, doused his face with cool water, and gazed at his reflection, calming his nerves. The empty look in his blue eyes matched the hollowness in his heart: both remnants of the dream that had nagged him ever since Kaylin had come into his life. What was the deal? Was it guilt because he felt attracted to her?

"Get a grip, Maddock," he said to the reflection. "You're not a lovesick teenager." He breathed deep and puffed out his cheeks as he exhaled. Pronouncing himself ready to face the world, he returned to the kitchen.

"Have a nice nap?" Kaylin asked. She looked up from Rienzi's Bible and smiled. "Nice digs you and Bones found, by the way. I forgot to tell you earlier."

Fearing for Kaylin's safety, and assuming that their assailants had the resources to discover Maddock's identity through the car rental agency, they had packed up and headed for North Carolina, where Bones' uncle, Crazy Charlie, who dealt in used Cadillacs and brand new casinos, owned this vacation condo. They had brought with them everything that might be pertinent to the *Dourado* investigation. At Kaylin's insistence, Bernie had returned to Mississippi to stay with relatives.

"How's the translation coming?" He sat down across from her, forcing his focus onto the case. He was getting good at walling away those memories.

"Challenging. Many of these notes he's written in the margins are so cryptic that I don't know if we'll be able to get any meaning from them out of context. A few of them are pretty interesting, though.

"Here in the book of Genesis, he's underlined a passage which describes a time when 'there were giants on the earth' who married the 'daughters of men.'

"Sounds like simple folklore to me," Maddock said. Religion and the Bible did not mean much to him anymore. God, if He existed, wasn't paying any attention to what was going on down here.

"That's what Bones said. But here," Kaylin pointed to a phrase jotted in the margin, "Rienzi has written 'could it be?' in big letters. He's at least considering the possibility that it's more than folklore."

The story of David and Goliath had strange markings on it as well. Maddock had not been much of a churchgoer since childhood, but, like most people, he supposed, he was familiar with the tale. A Philistine giant named Goliath had challenged any soldier of Israel to single combat. Only a teenage shepherd named David was up to the challenge. The story went that Goliath, nearly ten feet tall, was armed to the teeth, while David brought with him only a sling, some rocks, and his faith in God. David nailed Goliath in the head, knocking him out. While the giant was down, David cut off the Philistine's head with his own sword. It was actually a gruesome story if you stopped to think about it.

This, like most of the familiar children's Bible stories, was one Maddock assumed to be less history than fable. It was, in his mind, a story to teach a lesson about not giving up in the face of overwhelming odds, and, of course, to encourage faith in God. Maddock was not interested in any of that.

Rienzi had apparently seen something of great value in this story. Goliath's name was underlined in bold strokes. Oddest of all was a strange drawing in the upper right corner of the page. It was a stick figure of some sort. A series of dots of various sizes were linked by straight lines, creating an oddly familiar image.

Kaylin returned to translating Rienzi's notes while Maddock reviewed Maxie's work, and Bones looked over the research Jimmy had done on Rienzi.

"I don't get it," Bones said. "Whatever Rienzi found, he obviously lost it when the *Dourado* sank. That's not exactly a secret. Neither is the location of its sinking."

"What do you not get?" Maddock asked.

"Maxie was after the *Dourado*. Why don't the guys who are following us just try to beat us to the ship? What do we have that they need?" He tossed the stack of papers onto the table and sat back. Hands folded behind his head, he looked up at the ceiling and sighed loudly. "It's enough to make a guy crave a bottle of Jose."

"Not a chance, pal." Maddock didn't like Bones when he drank tequila. In fact, Bones didn't like Bones when he downed too much Jose Cuervo. The big man did not reply.

"It's a good question, though," Maddock mused. "Maybe they don't know what they're looking for."

"Why would that matter?" Bones asked.

"Think about what we know of the *Dourado*," Maddock said, turning the details over in his mind as he spoke. "The wreck turned up some distance from where it sank, with very little of the cargo remaining. Obviously, everything inside the ship spilled out over the course of several miles. There must have been something special about this one object that made Maxie believe he could find it."

Bones sat in silent contemplation for a minute.

Kaylin looked up from her work, a thoughtful expression on her face. She seemed about to say something, but then shook her head and returned her attention to her task.

"All right," Bones said. "We almost have to assume you're right. Nothing else has made sense so far. If that's the case, then what is it about this object that would make him, or us for that matter, believe that we could find it?" He folded his arms across his chest and fixed Maddock with a challenging stare.

Maddock had wrestled with this question since reading Rienzi's journal two days earlier. It was crazy to believe they could find a single object that had lain on the seabed for almost two hundred years. But he knew, without a doubt, that Hartford Maxwell was anything but crazy. If Maxie thought something could be done, it most likely was quite possible, if not probable.

"It could be a very large object," Maddock said. "Something he could have hoped to find with sonar."

"Like what? A statue?" Bones shook his head. "It could be buried in silt, maybe pitted and misshapen, grown over with all kinds of organisms. It's possible, but I don't like the odds."

"It's not totally out of the question that the cargo could be found, is it?" Kaylin asked, looking up again from her reading. "I remember reading about the discovery of some Roman artifacts. When the ship started taking on water, the crew threw things overboard in an effort to stay afloat. Underwater archaeologists were able to trace the ship's path by the trail of relics scattered across the seabed."

"That was in deep water," Bones protested. "The water between Singapore and Bintan is relatively shallow in most places. Storms and currents have more effect on shallow water wrecks than they do in deep water. There's a good chance there's nothing left of it." He paused for a moment, stroking his chin, his brown eyes narrowed. "Still, you're right. It's not out of the question."

"Okay," Maddock said. "Let's explore a completely different line of thinking. What if whoever is after us only knows that Maxie was on to something big, but they don't know what? The fake journal he planted probably wouldn't have mentioned anything about Rienzi or the *Dourado*. They might have discovered right away that the information was no good, and come after Kaylin to get the real story."

"That could be." Bones' frown indicated that he was not satisfied with Maddock's idea. "But they're coming at us awfully hard for something they know very little about."

"The information from Jimmy said that the church was ready to excommunicate Rienzi over the ramifications of whatever it was he claimed to have found. We also know from the journal that even the scholars of the day rejected his claims, whatever they were." Maddock chose his words carefully. "What if the implications of this discovery would be just as controversial today as they were back then?"

"Too many *what-ifs* for me," Bones groaned, rubbing his temples. "I just don't see…"

"Look at this!" Kaylin's soft voice trembled with excitement. She had returned to her examination of Rienzi's Bible. Maddock and Bones leaned toward her. Her slender finger was pointing to a single word, "vraiment," written in the margin next to an underlined passage.

"What does that mean?" Bones asked. "Sounds like some kind of stinky cheese."

"It means 'truly,' or 'truthfully,'" Maddock answered, drawing a raised eyebrow from Kaylin. "I took high school French. Good way to meet hot girls."

Kaylin narrowed her eyes and fixed him with a withering stare. When she was annoyed, she reminded Maddock a little bit of Melissa. Melissa… he was definitely not going to travel down that road right now. It was almost sad how easily he could push those thoughts away these days.

"Listen to the passage Rienzi underlined. Kaylin's knuckles whitened as she tightened her grip on the book. "And the priest said, 'The sword of Goliath the Philistine, whom you killed in the valley of Elah, behold, it is here wrapped in a cloth behind the ephod, if you will take that, take it, for there is none but that here.' And David said, 'There is none like it; give it to me.'" She slammed the Bible closed, dropped it hard on the table and smiled triumphantly.

"So he likes Goliath's sword," Bones said.

"Wait a minute!" Maddock snatched Rienzi's journal off the table and flipped to the last page. He read aloud, "I will say only that truly, there is none like it."

Bones whistled between his front teeth. "Son of a… Do you think he might have…"

"He found Goliath's sword," Kaylin said. She held the aged Bible in trembling hands. "That's what Dad was after. It would stand to reason. Rienzi was the first to rediscover those ancient cities in the Holy Land. Why wouldn't he find biblical artifacts?"

"The sword of Goliath." Bones said the words slowly as if trying them on for size. "I don't know anything about it."

"Jimmy can run it through NAILS," Maddock said. "Right now, we need to get ready for a dive."

Chapter 7

Kuala Lumpur, the capital of Malaysia, was an odd blend of modern and traditional. The city of more than a million people bustled with activity. Food carts intermingled with modern offices and clubs lined the banyan-shaded streets. Historic monuments and lush, green parks were sprinkled throughout the busy city. Even the skyline mixed the old and the new, boasting minarets and modern skyscrapers. Up ahead the Petronas Twin Towers loomed in the distance, and farther still, the Kuala Lumpur Tower, the world's seventh tallest free-standing tower. It was undeniably a beautiful and unique city.

Maddock and Kaylin made their way on foot along a traffic-choked street. Despite the oppressive heat, he felt energized by the surroundings. He always felt at home in a tropical climate.

"Something smells good," Kaylin said as they passed one of the food vendors.

"Maybe after our appointment." Maddock consulted his watch. They were scheduled to meet with a Dr. Tengku at the Muzium Negara, Malaysia's national museum.

"You're no fun," Kaylin said. "I want to come back here when we actually have time to be tourists."

Maddock noted her use of the word "we" but didn't have time to contemplate its meaning if any. It had been no mean feat to arrange transportation, as well as the needed ship and equipment, without drawing the attention of the people who were looking for Kaylin They had made the arrangements through a friend of a friend: one who asked few questions. An old Navy buddy had arranged transportation for the group on a cargo plane. No tickets were required, and thus no record of their flight. Maddock, Bones, and Kaylin had been careful not to use their credit cards, or do anything that might give away their whereabouts or their destination. Perhaps he was being paranoid, but his instincts told him to play it safe.

They skirted the edge of the Perdana Lake Gardens, Kuala Lumpur's version of Central Park. Up ahead, the museum came into view. The steep, double-roofed main structure was flanked on either side by twin wings.

"This is a beautiful example of Rumah Gadang architecture," Kaylin said.

"Good thing Bones isn't here. You'd be treated to a parody version of "Blue Moon.""

"What's that?" She cocked her head and frowned.

"You know: 'Ba ba bom ba ba Rumah Gadang...'" he sang in a deep voice.

"I'm beginning to think you and Bones are more alike than you'll admit."

"Maybe so, but it's only because he's rubbed off on me over the years. We hated each other during the first phase of SEAL training."

"Seriously?"

"Yep. Even got into a fight. Which I won, though Bones will tell you differently." He couldn't help but smile at the memory. It was hard to believe there had been a time when he and Bones weren't friends.

"How'd you work that out?" she asked.

"That was your dad's doing. He sent us on vacation. But that's a long story."

They reached the museum, paid their entry fee, and asked after Dr. Tengku, who came out right away to welcome them.

Dr. Tengku was a short, round-faced man with dark skin and hair. He wore a polyester blue suit so cheap that Maddock was surprised it didn't melt in the Malaysian heat. He greeted them with a moist handshake and ushered them into a tiny office decorated with model ships and Jimmy Buffett paraphernalia.

"Nice digs," Maddock said "I live in Key West, you know."

"Not many Parrotheads in Kuala Lumpur," Tengku said. "It gets lonesome sometimes but at least I'm unique."

"Thank you for seeing us," Maddock said. "We won't take much of your time. I understand you have an interest in ships and shipwrecks."

Tengku nodded. "It's merely a hobby but it's something I'm interested in. How can I help you?"

"We have similar interests. We are researching a ship that sank somewhere in this part of the world almost two hundred years ago."

"And which ship would that be?"

"The *Dourado*."

A flicker of recognition shone in Tengku's eyes and he smiled. "I have heard of that one. It's a mystery." He turned, removed a thick volume from a nearby shelf, and thumbed through it. Maddock didn't recognize the language, but it wasn't English.

"Here we are. Sank in 1829." He read the entry aloud to them. Unfortunately, it contained no information they didn't already have.

"Dr. Tengku," Kaylin began as he closed the book, "is there anything at all you can tell us about the wreck? Any artifacts at a been recovered? Any legends surrounding the sinking?"

Tengku shook his head. "I'm afraid the only legend surrounding that particular shipwreck is a far-fetched one."

"Far-fetched is okay with us." Maddock knew he was clutching at straws, but he didn't like the idea that this visit had been a complete waste of time.

Tengku shrugged "legend has it that the shipwreck is cursed and any who seek it are doomed to failure." He grinned and shrugged. "I told you. Far-fetched."

"Yeah, it sounds like the sort of thing you hear all around the world in relation to lost treasures." Maddock couldn't hide his disappointment.

"So, are you planning to search for the shipwreck?" Tengku's tone was conversational, but something in the man's demeanor made Maddock uncomfortable.

"No. We're here on vacation and thought it would be a good opportunity to poke around a bit. Shipwrecks interest me and this is one I've read about previously."

"I'm sorry I couldn't help you." Tengku offered his hand and Maddock reluctantly shook it.

"Thanks for your time. Look me up if you're ever in Key West. We've got some great bars that play Jimmy's music."

"Thanks. I'll do that."

Tengku saw his guests out and waited by the front door until they disappeared from sight. He hurried back to his office and rummage through his desk until he found the slip of paper on which the phone number had been written.

He felt decidedly uncomfortable making this call. Maddock and Maxwell seemed like perfectly nice people, but the people who had reached out to him had promised him a tidy sum of money in exchange for information about anyone who came looking for the Dourado. Exactly enough, in fact, to cover his gambling debts. The coincidence roused his suspicions, but he was in dire straits and couldn't afford to be too discerning about the people with whom he did business.

He swallowed hard and dialed the number. Someone on the other and picked up immediately but did not speak. Tengku waited and finally spoke.

"This is Dr. Tengku from the national Museum in Kuala Lumpur," he began.

"What do you have to report?" The speaker asked in clipped tones.

"Two people came to visit me. They were looking for information on the same ship you asked me about."

"What did you tell them?"

"Nothing. I mean, what is there to tell? The ship's been lost for two centuries. But I was told to call this number if anyone came looking, so…" Tengku broke off, uncertain how to continue.

"Did you get their names?"

"Yes. Dane Maddock and Kaylin Maxwell."

"Did they tell you what their plans are? Where do they intend to begin their search?" The man on the other end of the line actually sounded excited, or at least interested.

"He said he was here on vacation and was just asking around."

"He's lying." The man said flatly. *"Anything else you can tell me?"*

Tengku racked his brain. He sensed that the information he was providing had been measured and found unsatisfactory. "He's from Key West. He's interested in shipwrecks."

"Call me back if you learn anything useful."

"Wait a minute! When do I get my money?" Tengku's heart raced.

The pause on the other end of the line was so long that Tengku thought they had been disconnected, but finally the man spoke.

"You'll get your money when we get what we're looking for."

Chapter 8

Maddock sat in the cabin of the *Queen's Ransom*, the ship they had hired off a British expatriate living in Kuala Lumpur. They were now cruising the northern coast of the island of Bintan in search of the wreck of the *Dourado*.

He and Bones leaned over a chart, comparing it to the information Jimmy had put together for them. Jimmy had accessed an amazing computer program belonging to the Navy. The program factored in such details as currents, water levels, the terrain of the seabed, and historical weather data. Utilizing this information, along with the ship's last known location, the computer then made a projection, based on the size, shape, and composition of the *Dourado*, of where the wreck could now be found. The program had shown itself to be highly reliable in helping the Navy locate sunken ships, though to Jimmy's knowledge, the program had only been used to locate vessels of the World War I vintage, or newer. Nevertheless, he and Maddock held high hopes that they could locate the missing vessel. Whether or not they would find the sword, however, was another question.

"We're approaching ground zero," Corey Dean called from his seat in front of a computerized display behind them. Corey, a slightly overweight, balding thirty-something was a computer geek with a love of the sea and a nose for treasure. To Maddock's knowledge, Corey had never dived, but he was a vital part of the crew.

Maddock and Bones moved over to stand on either side of Corey. Staring at the GPS display, Maddock felt the same thrill that he always felt when he began a hunt. He never grew weary of it. It was not the treasure that kept him coming back; it was the challenge. He loved putting together clues to solve the mystery. He relished pitting himself and his crew against the sea, daring it to surrender its secrets. He even enjoyed the time-consuming sonar sweeps, waiting patiently for that anomaly on the sea floor that would tell him that he had nailed his target.

A few minutes later, they were circling the spot that Jimmy had pinpointed as the probable location of the *Dourado*.

"Slow it down, Matt," Corey called to the helm. "You want to take it a little to port."

"Thanks, Corey," Matt deadpanned, "I could never have read the coordinates myself." Matt and Corey enjoyed needling each other almost as much as they enjoyed working together.

"The game is afoot," Bones said, clasping Maddock's shoulder. Maddock smiled and nodded. Bones tended to enjoy the hunt for about forty-five minutes, after which time he was ready to dive.

"Get the sonar going, and let's start our grid," Maddock instructed.

"How big?" Matt asked.

"Let's go a quarter-mile square to start off." Matt nodded, and Maddock left the cabin. In the bow of the ship, Kaylin lay stretched out on a deck chair. Her red bikini left little to the imagination. She was chatting with Willis, who was doing an admirable job of looking Kaylin in the eye, but every time she turned away, he let his gaze drift.

"Are we there yet?" Willis asked.

"Yeah, get out," Maddock shot back.

"Sorry, Dad." Willis got up and stretched. Maddock noticed with a slight pang of jealousy that Kaylin was admiring his friend's thickly muscled back. "You need to make this quick, man," he said. "The ladies in the clubs like a medium skin tone, and if I don't get out of this sun I'm going to be invisible after dark."

"If you're in such a hurry, I think I'll pay you by the hour."

"Don't you dare pay that man by the hour," Bones called out as he exited the cabin behind Maddock. "He'll ride the clock for all he's worth."

"Go back to the reservation, Tonto," Willis taunted.

Maddock laughed at the surprised expression on Kaylin's face. Bones and Willis had always had an odd relationship. Their years spent together in the SEALS had helped them build a bond of trust that allowed them to say anything at all to one another without ever questioning the other's friendship. People who were unaccustomed to their banter sometimes found it disconcerting.

"Sorry, bro. Me got to make this dive first," Bones said in a gravelly voice. "Find gold, buy heap much fire water."

"I really don't understand you two." Kaylin peered over her sunglasses as she spoke.

"Don't worry, you're not alone," Maddock assured her.

Willis and Bones wandered off, heading for the ship's stern, still insulting one another.

"What happens now?" Kaylin asked.

"To put it simply, Matt draws a square on his map, with our target location in the center. He takes the boat out to one corner of the square and takes us back and forth, moving a little farther across the square with each pass until we've covered the entire thing. Corey keeps an eye on the sonar, looking for anything that looks like a ship. "

"What if we don't find anything?"

"We cover the same square, but we change directions. If we went east-west the first time, we go north-south the second. If that doesn't work, we expand our grid until we find what we're looking for."

"Sounds time-consuming," she observed, turning over onto her stomach. "Will you get my back?"

"Sure," Maddock replied, picking up the sunblock and kneeling beside her, "since we've got such a 'time-consuming' job ahead of us."

"You know what I mean." Kaylin gave him a half-hearted slap on the shoulder. "When you hear about hunting for sunken treasure, you imagine it being a lot more exciting than making grids and looking at sonar readouts."

"Fair enough." Maddock slathered the lotion across her back, and methodically worked it into her skin.

"Do you do everything that way?"

"Do what?" The question caught him off-guard.

"Systematically. Like the grids, or the way you put lotion on me." She turned over and sat up, looking him in the eye. "Don't you ever just, I don't know, wing it?"

"The Navy pretty much took that out of me," he answered truthfully. It was not the whole truth, but it was all he was willing to reveal.

"You sound like my Dad," Kaylin said, looking away. "He never lightened up."

"I know perfectly well what your father was like. He was a great man."

"Yes, he was." Kaylin turned and looked him directly in the eye. "And he was impossible to please. Everything had to be his way, and it had to be perfect."

"Is that why you're an artist? So you can be in control of what you create?"

"I'm an artist because I appreciate beauty. What do you find beautiful, Maddock?" She leaned close to him, her face inches from his, their gaze still locked.

She had hung him a big, fat curveball that he couldn't miss. Bones would have knocked that sucker out of the park. Somehow, he couldn't bring himself to take a swing. A part of him wondered why he didn't feel something for this girl more than physical attraction. He doubted he would ever feel that way for someone again. He sat up straight and looked out across the ocean.

"The sea is beautiful. The way the sunlight dances across the waves. The way the colors play over the surface. I love it."

Kaylin was silent for a moment, then reached out and put a hand on his shoulder. "Is there room in your life for any other love?"

Maddock was spared the uncomfortable necessity of answering that question when Corey called from the cabin.

"Hey Maddock, get in here!"

He hopped to his feet and hurried into the cabin. He was relieved that Kaylin did not follow him. He moved to Corey's side. Bones and Willis hurried in and stood behind him.

"What have you got?" Maddock asked.

"Sonar picked up something promising. Matt's taking us back for another look."

Maddock held his breath, staring at the sonar display, and waited for the ship to pass over the anomaly again.

"We're coming up on it again," Matt said. "Slowing down."

The image coalesced on the sonar.

"Print it," Maddock instructed. Corey had already captured the image and sent it to the printer. Maddock picked it up and examined it carefully. "It's a ship. Got dimensions for me?"

Corey clicked the mouse a few times.

"Too much of it's submerged, but it could be the *Dourado*."

"All right. We'll send Uma down." Uma was the nickname of their unmanned miniature submersible camera. Bones was a fan of the movie *Pulp Fiction* and felt that Uma was a "sexier" name than the acronym UMSC. That and UMSC was too close to the Marine Corps acronym.

Bones went back out onto the deck where the little submersible was prepped and ready to go. Just over a meter in length, Uma resembled, if anything, a half-flattened egg with three "eyes" set in the front edge. A camera lens was set in the center, with a headlight on either side. A propeller in a circular frame was attached to either side of the device. The entire frame could rotate forward and back, and each propeller could oscillate inside the frame, controlling the direction of the small craft. Another propeller set in the back provided thrust. Uma could also take on and discharge water for ballast and for diving. He carefully placed the instrument in the water and gave Corey the thumbs-up.

Controlling Uma from his console, Corey instructed the device to take on water in order to accelerate her dive. He flipped on the lights and the camera. The wreck was in relatively shallow water, and soon the sea floor came into view on the monitor. Fish scattered as Uma careened at them, piloted remotely by a maniacally cackling Corey.

"You're enjoying this way too much," Maddock told his colleague, placing a hand on his shoulder.

"Don't you want me to enjoy my work?" Corey said, still laughing.

"I want you to find the ship."

"Done," Corey replied. The faint outline of a sunken ship appeared in the distance. Corey picked up the pace, and the bulk of the ship gradually filled the screen.

"It's an old one," Bones whispered.

The wreck had gone down bow-first. The stern stuck out of the silt at a gentle angle, and the outline of much of the ship was discernible beneath the silt. A heavy mast lay half-buried. Everything was encrusted with sea life, but its old age was obvious.

"Take her around the stern," Maddock instructed.

Kaylin entered the cabin and stood next to Bones, as far as she could stand from Maddock and still be able to see the monitor. Maddock took little notice of her. His eyes were on the prize. As Uma rounded the far side of the wreck, his heart sagged.

"It's not her," he said flatly.

"How can you be sure?" Willis asked.

"See the rudder?"

Willis nodded. Beside him, Bones cursed loudly, and Kaylin hung her head.

"The *Dourado* lost her rudder when she hit the rocks. This ship has her rudder, and her stern appears intact."

Everyone was silent for a moment. Maddock took a deep breath and tried to lighten the mood.

"Hey, we didn't really think we were going to find her in five minutes, did we?"

"Hell yes that's what we thought," said Bones. "You know I don't like to wait." He turned and stalked out of the cabin. Willis followed behind, chuckling.

"Bring Uma back up," Maddock instructed.

"Gotcha," Corey replied. Under his control, Uma discharged the water she had taken on and began a steady climb to the surface, where Bones was waiting to fish her out. "Maybe the next one," he sighed.

Chapter 9

Maybe this one is it." Corey's voice was void of all conviction. They had struck out so far: three wrecks that had looked promising, three misses. Such results were not unusual, but it dampened their enthusiasm in any case.

Maddock stared at the screen, watching as the submerged ship came into view. This one lay on its side, a gaping hole where the center of the deck had been. The masts were long gone, but it was obviously a wooden sailing ship.

"Can you see the rudder?" Maddock asked as Uma approached the stern.

"Negative," Corey replied. He leaned closer to the screen, narrowing his eyes. "Let me get a little closer."

Uma banked sharply and dove down toward the ship's rear. Maddock leaned closer to the screen. It was difficult to tell beneath the crust of barnacles that coated the wreck, but the ship appeared to be absent its rudder. As the image clarified, Maddock's suspicions were confirmed. The rudder was missing.

"Looks good," Maddock said. "How close are we to where Jimmy predicted we'd find her?"

Corey consulted a chart, tracing his finger along the lines and moving his lips as he read. Satisfied, he looked back at Maddock with a broad grin on his face.

"Spitting distance."

That was all Maddock needed to hear. "Let's get wet!" he shouted.

Bones whooped and clapped his hands.

They hastily donned their dive gear. Willis leaned against the rail, a rifle held loosely in one hand, looking at them with undisguised envy.

"Man, I know y'all are gonna let me dive sometime, right?" He grinned. "No fair letting y'all two have all the fun."

"Let's see how it goes," Maddock said, strapping on his dive knife. "For now, we need your eyes up here." He hoped Willis would not, in fact, be needed on the surface, but he was playing it safe.

"I know," Willis replied. "At least I can chill with the lovely lady." He gave Kaylin a playful wink.

Kaylin smiled but did not answer. She took Maddock's hand and drew him closer to her. "I know this sounds cheesy, but I hope you can do it, you know, for Dad."

Maddock nodded. This one was for Maxie. He hoped they would not let him down. He turned to Bones.

"Ready?"

Bones raised his right hand, palm outward, in a sarcastic imitation of an Indian salute. Maddock returned the salute with an upraised middle finger. The two divers sat down on the rail, turned and nodded at one another, and flipped backward into the water.

The water was cool, but not unpleasant and the initial shock wore off quickly. Maddock got his bearings. A few strong kicks, and he was shooting down toward the wreck that lay beneath their boat. Bones swam alongside. The faint shafts of sunlight dissolved as they penetrated the depths of the ocean. As the darkness swelled around them, Maddock flipped on the dive light strapped to his forehead.

The sunken ship was just barely visible in the distance. Once again, he welcomed the shiver of excitement that ran through his body whenever he dived on a new wreck. They approached it cautiously, careful not to stir up any more silt than necessary. The closer they swam to the ship, the more certain he became that this was the *Dourado*. It was the right size, the right apparent age, and in the right location.

They swam to the stern and made a careful inspection. The rudder had definitely been broken off. Maddock ran his hand along the back of the ship, moving it down toward the ocean floor. There it was! He took out his dive knife and gently scraped at the barnacles that coated the ship's exterior. Where the ship disappeared in the silt, a jagged hole gaped like the mouth of an angry leviathan. It was just as Rienzi had described in his journal. He looked at Bones, who nodded his understanding.

Together, they swam toward the gaping hole in the deck. Bones, ever vigilant, peered into the hole, letting his light play around the hold in search of unwelcoming hosts. He gave Maddock the "all clear" signal and let his body drift down into the boat. Maddock followed behind.

This was the most dangerous part of a dive. The fine layer of silt that collected on the inside of a sunken vessel could easily be turned into a swirling maelstrom by an incautious flip of a swim fin. A diver could get lost inside an unfamiliar ship, blinded by the blizzard of dirt particles suspended in the water. Maddock was not worried, though. He and Bones knew how to take care of themselves.

He looked around at the interior of the ancient ship, but there was little to be seen. Random bumps and bulges beneath the surface of the silt indicated that a few items might remain inside the hold. If this was the *Dourado*, he did not expect to find much inside the ship, given that items had apparently been salvaged from it at the time of its sinking. Still, he wished he could find something, anything to confirm the ship's identity.

Bones waved to him. Maddock looked over and saw his friend gesturing for him to exit the wreck. He trusted his partner enough not to question his judgment. Maddock carefully turned and swam out through the hole in the deck. When he reached the outside, he turned about and peered back into the hold.

Bones was looking at something covered in silt. Occasionally he would look up toward Maddock, as if fixing his location, then look back down at the spot on the ocean floor. Finally, he began digging in the fine dirt. A massive cloud of silt erupted, spreading as if in slow motion to fill the hold. Maddock caught a glimpse of Bones scooping something up before the other diver vanished from sight. He held his position, keeping an eye out for his friend. Moments later, he made his appearance, bursting forth from the cloud that poured out of the ship, his fine mesh dive bag clutched in his hand. He held up the bag for Maddock to see. Coins! Maddock gave his friend the thumbs up, and they headed for the surface.

Breaking the surface, Maddock swam to the side of the *Queen's Ransom*, where Willis offered him a helping hand. The muscular, ebony-skinned man lifted him from the water with ease. Bones clambered aboard with help from Kaylin, who wore the expression of an expectant parent.

"Well?" she asked.

"Let's clean those up first," Maddock nodded toward Bones' bag of coins. "They ought to tell us a great deal." He tried to suppress his excitement. He had learned a long time ago not to get his hopes up, but right now he had a good feeling.

Retiring to the cabin, Maddock and Bones set to cleaning the coins. Patiently they scoured away two hundred years of tarnish and grime. Glints of gold began to peek out from the black circles. Soon, thereafter, details appeared: writing, numbers and images. Forty minutes later, a small pile of gold coins lay gleaming dully in a bowl of preservative solution. Maddock fished one out gingerly, held it up to the light and inspected it carefully, turning it around in his fingers.

"Portuguese," he announced. He could feel the grin spreading across his face.

"And the date?" Bones asked, leaning forward, his pearl-white teeth glowing in the sun.

"Hmm…" Maddock stalled, letting the tension build. "It's hard to say, but I'm pretty sure…"

"Oh, just tell us, Maddock!" Kaylin scolded.

"Fine," he said, chuckling. "The year of our Lord, 1824."

The room erupted in shouts of joy. Kaylin threw her arms around Maddock's neck and gave him a squeeze. Willis, still standing guard on the deck, pumped his fist and smiled.

Bones scooped another coin out of the bowl and examined it. His smile widened. "Portugal, 1821." He raised his clenched fist in triumph.

They repeated the ritual, taking turns examining the coins until they had inspected each one. The final tally was eleven coins: seven Portuguese, three Spanish and one French. All were dated four years or more prior to the sinking of the *Dourado*.

"Gentlemen," Maddock began, "and lady," he added, "I believe we have found our ship."

Chapter 10

The *Dourado* had definitely been salvaged though they went through the motions of excavating the wreck, carefully sifting through everything bit by bit. By the end of the day, they had found only a few more coins, a statuette, and a few pieces of china. The statuette, in Kaylin's opinion, was further proof that this was, in fact, the *Dourado*.

"It's definitely Middle-Eastern," she said. "It's very likely something that would have been found in Rienzi's collection."

The following morning, they mapped out their plan to search for the remaining artifacts. Utilizing the same program with which he had predicted the location of the *Dourado*, Jimmy had provided them with a chart that plotted the probable location of the remaining artifacts from the *Dourado*'s cargo. The search area was a crescent-shaped swath that swept down in an east-southeast arc from the initial wreck site to the spot where the ship had come to rest.

Maddock inspected the chart and shook his head. It was a large area to cover, with artifacts possibly spread thin across the sea floor. He was beginning to feel discouraged, but knew that a negative attitude would kill morale.

"We'll make our way to the wreck site keeping to the center of the target zone." His finger traced a path through the middle of the shaded area, up to Pedra Branca. "We'll run both the side scan sonar and the wave spectrometer, which ought to give us a unique signature for the different objects on the bottom. Once we get to Pedra Branca, we'll take stock of the readings we took along the way and start our grid in the most promising place."

"Let's do it," Corey said enthusiastically. He was still excited over their success the previous day in locating the wreck.

The others nodded their heads, but Maddock could read the skepticism in their faces: skepticism that he shared.

Maddock looked out at the rocks of Pedra Branca, so named because of the massive quantities of seagull guano that had colored them permanently white. These very same rocks had claimed the *Dourado*. Somewhere between this spot and the ship's watery grave, he hoped, lay the sword of Goliath.

The readouts they had taken along the way had not painted a hopeful picture. Admittedly, it was only a narrow strip in a wide swath of search area, but the lack of positive hits was worrisome. His cell phone buzzed against his thigh, and he answered it with an annoyed voice.

"Yeah?" he snapped.

"Maddock, how's the fishing?" Jimmy asked.

"Haven't caught a thing."

"Want to know why? Because I know." The hacker's voice had an odd lilt to it, almost as if Jimmy were taunting him.

Maddock closed his eyes, took a deep breath, exhaled and forced himself to relax. Jimmy could be annoying. A byproduct, Maddock supposed, of spending too much time at a computer terminal. "Jim, I'm tired and more than a bit hacked off right now."

"Fine, I'll start making sense. When you asked me to do some checking on the Dourado, I spread out the parameters of the search a bit. You remember how the captain claimed that there was half a million dollars on board?"

"Yes," Maddock said.

"Well, I checked on the colonial governor who reported the finding of the Dourado off the shore of Bintan. Seems that not long after the salvage efforts came up short, he found himself a quarter of a million dollars richer and living high on the hog back in England."

Maddock perked up. This was starting to get interesting.

Jimmy went on. *"Next, I followed up on the captain, a Francisco Covilha. He retired to America, a rich man. Settled in New York, and became a benefactor to several museums. Guess what he donated?"*

"Artifacts from the Holy Land," Maddock groaned. "The son of a gun was in on it with the governor. They hoodwinked Rienzi and made off with everything."

"That's the bad news. The good news is, I can't find any record of a Middle-Eastern sword turning up in the collections of any of the museums he supported."

"So either he held on to it," Maddock mused, "or it's still somewhere on the bottom of the ocean."

"Want to hear the weirdest part of all?"

"Not really." Maddock didn't think he could take any more of Jimmy's weird news.

"Just for a lark, I ran his name through Nexus, and I got a hit."

Maddock felt as if he had been plunged into an icy bath. He sat down clumsily on the deck. His legs were suddenly too weak to support him. "But, Nexus searches current periodicals. For Covilha's name to show up in Nexus means…" He paused, trying to get a handle on his thoughts. "Where did his name turn up?"

"In a small item buried in the New York Post. Someone robbed his grave."

After Jimmy had given him the details, Maddock gathered the group and relayed this new information.

"So, you think we're on the wrong track here?" Bones asked. "I can't say I disagree. The dive hasn't turned up much though we've got more ground to cover."

"I can't say with any certainty that the sword isn't here," Maddock said. "All we know is that it hasn't turned up, so there's a possibility it's still down there somewhere." He paused, weighing their options. "I think we need to explore all the angles and fast. We have to assume that whoever else is after the sword will find the same article Jimmy found, which means they'll be headed for New York. I want to get there first if I can."

"I'll go," Kaylin said. "I'm of no use here, but I can help you with any searching or research you do in New York."

"It's settled then," Maddock said. "Bones, you're in charge here. Keep up the search. Kaylin and I will get ourselves to New York as quickly as we can."

He only hoped they would get there in time.

Chapter 11

Maddock gritted his teeth as he weaved the rental car through the snarl of traffic coming out of LaGuardia. He felt he had made the correct decision the previous day to leave Bones and the crew behind to finish the search while the two of them pursued Jimmy's lead, but he hated splitting the group in the present circumstances.

"It says that the police apprehended the man who dug up the grave just as he was opening the coffin," Kaylin read from the article Jimmy had forwarded to them. "He was a local drug addict and trouble maker. He said that a guy he had never met before had paid him a hundred bucks, and promised him a thousand more if he would bring him whatever he found in the coffin." She turned and looked directly at Maddock. "Obviously, he didn't have a chance to take anything out of the coffin. That's good news, Maddock." Since their uncomfortable exchange on board the *Queen's Ransom*, she had taken to calling him only by his last name.

"I know," he muttered. "I just..."

"You're just a cynic," she completed the sentence for him. "How did you get that way, anyhow?"

Maddock was not about to tell her the truth. He shrugged and went on with his previous train of thought. "I just worry that this is a sign that whoever has been after you has gotten ahead of us. They knew about the captain before we did."

"Look at it this way. The grave was robbed last week. That means that, as of that time, the sword had not yet been located. Given that they were already working on the captain angle, we can safely eliminate the museum collections, or anything from his estate that might have been on record anywhere. That eliminates a lot of dead-end investigating on our part."

"And leaves us where? What new lead do we have to follow up on? If you're correct, the bad guys have already checked them all out."

"Have faith, my friend." She patted him on the shoulder, a gesture of condescension more than companionship. "My dad used to tell me there's always a stone unturned if you'll only look in the right place."

The problem they faced, Maddock thought, though he kept it to himself, was finding the right place. He glanced in the rear-view mirror and something immediately caught his attention.

"That's one serious expression you've got there. What is it?" Kaylin glanced in the passenger side mirror.

"It's probably nothing, but I swear the SUV back there is following us." He felt foolish saying it considering the number of vehicles on the highway, but this one had remained two cars behind him since they'd left the airport, matched his every lane change.

"Men in a dark SUV tailing us? Isn't that a bit cliché?"

"Someone was following us in Charleston. Is it really that big a stretch?"

Kaylin pursed her lips and gazed harder into the mirror. "I don't know. I guess you could make a few random turns and see if they follow."

"Already on it." He took the next exit. Sure enough, the SUV followed.

"Here they come." Kaylin's voice trembled.

"Stop staring at them. I don't want them to know we're onto them."

"Aren't you going to try and get away?"

"Definitely, but maybe not in the way you think." The heavy traffic made outdistancing their pursuers impossible. He took a couple of turns at random just to confirm his suspicions. Sure enough, the men followed. He quickly considered his options. It had been a while since his last visit to New York, but he quickly formed a plan.

As they cruised across the Brooklyn Bridge, he outlined his plan to Kaylin.

"You're sure it will work?"

"Nope. Not sure at all, but I think it's worth a try."

They parked in a public lot on Liberty Street. As instructed, Kaylin retrieved her camera and a notebook from her luggage and they made the short walk to Battery Park.

"Did they take the bait?" Kaylin whispered.

"We'll see. Give me the camera and strike a pose for me."

Kaylin did as instructed. Pretending to line up a shot, Maddock scanned the crowd behind her. Two athletically built men loitered about forty feet back, looking at nothing in particular.

"I think so. Let's go." They passed through the park, enjoying the breeze blowing in off the Hudson River and sparing a few minutes to admire the Statue of Liberty. Maddock snapped another picture of Kaylin and spotted the same two men a short distance away.

"Still on our tail. Let's keep going." His heart raced as they moved away from the heavy crowd and into a less-crowded part of the park. Clearly, the men who followed them were after information. If they planned on kidnapping him and Kaylin in order to learn what they knew, they would likely make their move as soon as there were no witnesses around. Maddock hoped he had found a way around that.

They paused at the water's edge and Maddock pointed to a statue at the end of a pier. Depicting four sailors aboard a sinking ship, the American Merchant Mariners' Memorial stood on a stone breakwater just off the shore and memorialized the thousands of merchant mariners who had died at sea over the course of American history. Based on a photograph from an actual sinking, it was a disturbingly realistic representation of an American ship sinking after a U-boat attack. One mariner lay on the deck, clutching the hand of a comrade who had fallen into the water.

"It's kind of disturbing," Kaylin said, "but the artistry is exquisite."

"When the tide comes in, the man in the water is submerged," Maddock said. "It's powerful." The image brought back memories of his time in the Navy and comrades he had lost over the years. He shook his head and returned his thoughts to the present. "Okay, time for the show."

He raised the camera and began snapping photographs of the monument from various angles. Meanwhile, Kaylin opened her notebook and began scribbling notes. She too moved from side-to-side, scrutinizing the sculpture from different viewpoints. Out of the corner of his eye, Maddock watched as the men who had been following them moved ever closer, finally stopping on the other side of a tree no more than ten paces away. To his relief, they too produced a camera and feigned interest in the surroundings. Time for act two.

"Any ideas?" he asked Kaylin in a voice intended to travel.

"I'm not sure," she said. "I think we'll have to go out there and examine it closely. My guess is the head comes off of one of the men. That would make the most sense. You could make it so it twists off. The seam would be easy to conceal. And if one of those guys is hollow, there will be plenty of room to hide something inside."

"And you're sure it's hidden in there?" Maddock said, continuing their planned charade.

"Dad spent years researching it, and that's the conclusion he came to." A shadow seemed to pass over Kaylin as she spoke of her father. That wound was still raw.

"I suppose it makes sense." Maddock scratched his chin and stared out at the memorial. "The sinking of the *Dourado* was perhaps the singular moment in his life. A memorial to drowning sailors would be fitting."

"So what's the plan?" Kaylin asked.

"We can't go out there in broad daylight. I say we come back at midnight when no one's around."

Kaylin nodded. "I hate to wait that long when we're so close, but I guess we have no choice. Let's find something to eat."

They headed back to their car, walking at a leisurely pace. It was not until they were once again on the road that Maddock breathed a sigh of relief.

"I think it worked. As soon as we left, one of them made a call."

"And they aren't following us." Kaylin laughed. "Those guys must be idiots. That sculpture was installed in the early 1990s. How could it possibly be connected?"

"As someone who has been Bones' best friend for more years than I care to count, believe me when I say a conspiracy nut will believe almost anything. Or at least give it serious consideration."

"Thank God for that." She reached over and squeezed his hand. "Now, how about you step on it so we can get to our real destination before the bad guys figure out they've been duped?"

Chapter 12

The basement of the Stoney Falls Public Library was damp and musty, a terrible place to keep books, particularly old ones. The walls were ancient brick, discolored by years of leaks and a light dusting of mold. The shelves looked as if they had been donated by a local warehouse or automotive repair shop. The dull gray metal was pitted by rust and most of the shelves sagged in the middle. Maddock scanned the spines of the aged volumes, withdrawing them one by one, flipping them open to the inside cover to look for Francisco Covilha's name.

Jimmy had learned that one of the captain's descendants, a great, great granddaughter, had died without heirs and had left her estate to her church. The estate included a number of very old books, which the church had in turn donated to the local library.

Given that the woman was the granddaughter of Covilha's granddaughter, his surname was in no way associated with her in any public records. This, Maddock and Kaylin hoped, would provide a new angle to the investigation.

The librarian, Mrs. Meyers, was of little help, expressing first surprise, then suspicion at their interest in the aged volumes. She was reluctant to let the two of them see the books, citing the need to "protect them from damage." Kaylin concocted a story about searching for her ancestors. It was a plot replete with lost loves and parents she had never known. Maddock thought it sounded like a pile of crap, but it won over the aging woman who looked to him like she spent her free time with her nose buried in a gothic romance. She took them down into the dark basement and guided them to the area in which the books "should" be kept.

"Found them," Kaylin called. She held open an old book. Written on the inside cover was the name "Francisco Covilha."

Maddock knelt down next to her. A number of very old books were grouped together on the bottom shelf. He pulled out a thick tome that was obviously written in a foreign language. He was not familiar with Portuguese. He opened it at random and held it out for Kaylin to inspect.

"Portuguese," she said and returned to paging through her book.

Maddock leafed through his own volume, crinkling his nose at the musty smell. Page after page passed across his vision with nothing catching his attention. "What do you hope to find?"

"I don't know," she said. "Truthfully, I had hoped to discover his personal journal. Short of that, maybe we could find some personal correspondence that belonged to him. If the sword was passed down to his descendants, maybe we could find some hints from one of them. I know I'm clutching at straws here, but there has to be a clue somewhere. The sword is too important to have just disappeared."

"Do you think he knew it was important?" Maddock asked. "I mean, what if, to him, it was just a sword?

"I can't believe that. Rienzi considered it his greatest discovery. Given how much he liked to boast, I wouldn't be surprised if he bragged to someone on the ship if not several someones. There would be few secrets from the captain on such a small ship."

Maddock could tell by the tone of her voice and the expression on her face that she was picking up steam now.

"Also, Rienzi lost nearly all of his personal papers in the wreck. Allegedly, `some' of them were recovered. I'll bet a lot if not all of them, were found. Just not by Rienzi."

"So you think the captain knew something about the sword's significance," Maddock said.

"I believe he hid it away somewhere. I think the clues are there if we can just find them."

Maddock waited for a moment. "Kay, how much of this is about your dad?"

Kaylin's eyes widened. "Who are you to ask me that?

"It's just a question." Maddock was already wondering why he had gone down this road.

"Have you ever let me in? Have you told me what makes you tick? Shared your pain with me?" Kaylin stood up, hands on hips. She looked down at him like a vulture circling over dead meat.

He looked her in the eye, staring for several heartbeats. Perhaps he should tell her. "You're right, I..."

"I'm not finished." Tears welled in her eyes. "Yes, it's about my dad, but the why of it is none of your business. Furthermore, that does not mean I don't believe in what we're doing. I know we can find the sword!"

"Fine, I'm sorry." He did not truly feel like baring his soul, and she seemed to be in no mood to make nice. He returned to the book he had been looking at, letting an uneasy silence fall over them. Something caught his attention, and he chuckled. Kaylin flashed him a resentful look, so he explained quickly. "Somebody was a doodler."

On one page, on the bottom inside corner, was a rough sketch of a large tree, perhaps an oak. He held up the book for her to inspect. She nodded and returned to her work. Maddock shrugged and flipped through the remaining pages. He saw nothing else of interest, so he set the book aside, and selected another. This one was in English, but the date, if he remembered his Roman numerals correctly, marked it as old enough to possibly have been part of Francisco Covilha's collection. Again, nothing but a small drawing on a random page in the book's center. This one was drawn on the same spot on the page, the bottom left corner next to the spine. Instead of a tree, this one was a rough illustration of what appeared to be a wrought-iron fence. He inspected it for a moment and then scanned the remainder of the pages before placing this book atop the other.

"Here's another," Kaylin said. "It looks like some sort of weird hat, or something."

"It's a sinking ship," Maddock corrected. He pointed to the wavy line that she had apparently taken to be the brim of the hat. "This is the water."

"Now I see it," she said, gazing at it a bit longer. "I wonder if the *Dourado* weighed on his mind." She suddenly cocked her head to the side, like a dog hearing a strange noise. "Wait a minute. Isn't the captain supposed to go down with his ship?"

"Not this captain," Maddock said. "It's kind of strange. Usually, the captain would make certain that everyone else is safe before he abandoned ship. Sometimes, if it went down too fast, he really **did** go down with the ship."

"If you believe Rienzi's story, he was the last one off the ship, and Covilha would have left more people aboard if Rienzi hadn't saved them." Kaylin looked thoughtfully up at the ceiling.

Maddock caught himself admiring the slender blonde's profile and had to shake his head to clear the haze.

"Covilha didn't exactly act ethically in stealing Rienzi's loot, either. If he had any sort of conscience, I wouldn't be surprised if the memory of the *Dourado* shadowed him all the way to the grave." Maddock understood how one day could darken the rest of one's life. "Guilt is a terrible thing."

Kaylin nodded but, lost in her own thoughts did not reply. Obviously, she was haunted by her own demons, apparently relating to her father.

Maddock pulled three more books off the shelf and sat cross-legged on the floor. He was not optimistic about finding anything meaningful in these volumes though some of them had obviously belonged to the captain. The first book on the stack he flipped over and went through it backward, just for a change of pace. His optimism, which had not been high to begin with, continued to wane as he looked at every page, and again found only a doodle.

"This is getting weird," Kaylin said. She held a slim book in her hands. The front cover, old and worn, simply read *Poems*.

Maddock looked up at her, waiting for her to elaborate.

"Do all of your books have a drawing in them?" she asked, frowning and pursing her lips.

"So far," he replied, uncertain of her train of thought.

"Do all of them only have a single drawing on the bottom left hand of the page?" She held up her book to illustrate.

He nodded, thinking. It was a little odd. If the man were a doodler, one would think he would draw in various places in each book. Another thought occurred to him.

"Come to think of it, books were usually treated with respect back then, weren't they?" He did not wait for her to reply. "It's strange that a grown man, even one who absent-mindedly draws pictures, would sketch childish cartoons in his books."

Kaylin stared at him, an odd expression on her face.

"Now what?"

"Isn't it even stranger," she said slowly, as if thinking her way through the problem as she spoke, "that he always drew on page one hundred twenty-five?"

Maddock picked up the stack of books he had already gone through, and added them to the pile in his lap. He checked them. Each of them had a small sketch drawn in the bottom left corner of page one hundred twenty-five. Obviously there was some significance, but it escaped him at the moment.

"I think we should copy these down," Kaylin said. She checked her watch. "I'll do it. You go through the rest of these books and see what you can find."

"I love it when you boss me around," Maddock teased, hoping to melt the icy wall that had risen between them. She responded with a smile that, though tired, seemed sincere enough.

Maddock searched through the remainder of the books on the shelf while Kaylin set herself to the task of copying the sketches onto a notepad she had brought along. As he flipped through the last book, this one with no drawing in it, a piece of paper, folded in half and yellowed with age, fell onto the floor. He picked it up and opened it, being careful not to tear it.

The ink was badly faded. The words, barely discernable, were written in a tight, choppy script. The letter was in Portuguese; he had now looked at enough books written in that language to recognize it easily. He could not translate the writing, but one word instantly jumped out at him: *Dourado*.

He was about to share his discovery with Kaylin when the sound of footsteps rang hollow from the nearby stairwell. The librarian appeared in the doorway, a look of apprehension on her pallid face. Maddock hastily turned his back to the woman and slipped the paper into his jacket pocket as he re-shelved the book.

"I'm sorry to interrupt you," the librarian said, sounding anything but sorry, "but the library will be closing soon."

"We were just finishing," Kaylin said, her voice syrupy. "Thank you so much for your help today, Mrs. Meyers."

She was really laying it on thick, Maddock mused. He would have to ask her why she was never that sweet to him. Then again, he had upset her enough for one day.

"I also thought you might like to know that a man is upstairs looking for you," Mrs. Meyers added. Her voice carried a tone of suspicion, bordering on judgment.

Maddock and Kaylin exchanged glances. This was an unexpected and unpleasant surprise.

"What does he look like?" Maddock asked, trying to keep his tone conversational.

"Short brown hair, average height, expensive sunglasses that he is too rude to take off." As the woman rattled off the details, Maddock could see why she made a good librarian. "Blue oxford cloth shirt, navy pants, fair skin, thin."

He sounded to Maddock like one of the guys that had pursued them in Charleston.

"Thank you," Kaylin said. "So, you didn't tell him we were down here?"

"No," the woman replied, blushing a bit. "To tell you the truth, I didn't care for his manner. He was rather abrupt. I told him that I was certain you had left. He asked where I had seen you last. I told him you had been checking the census records up on the second floor. He went up there looking for you. Did not even thank me." She folded her hands across her chest and frowned at Maddock as if the man's behavior were somehow Maddock's fault.

"I'm sorry about that, Ma'am," Maddock said. He racked his brain for a good story, but he couldn't think of anything.

"It's my ex-boyfriend." Kaylin entered the conversation smoothly. "It's embarrassing, but he's been stalking me. I can't seem to go anywhere without him finding me. I have a restraining order against him."

That was all the librarian needed to hear. Her eyes flared and she scowled.

"That is just terrible. One of our regular patrons was stalking me just last summer," she shook her head and tapped her foot on the concrete floor. "I thought I was going to have to turn him over to the proper authorities."

Maddock struggled not to smile at the thought of anyone stalking this dowdy old woman.

"Is that so?" he asked, keeping his facial muscles in firm check.

"I shall go back to my desk and call the police," the woman said firmly. "There is a utility entrance in the back. I will let the two of you out there."

"Maybe I should deal with him myself," Maddock said. A clean getaway would be preferable, but he was tired of running.

"Absolutely not. I'll have no unnecessary confrontations in my library. You should go before there's trouble."

They thanked her for her help and began picking up the books they had been looking through.

"Don't you mind those. I will reshelve them later." The librarian shooed them out of the room, down a narrow hallway, and up a small flight of stairs to a metal door. She unlocked it and ushered them out.

"Are you going to be all right?" Kaylin asked the woman. They certainly did not want the woman's kind aid to cause trouble for her later. She was a bystander in all this.

"I'll be right as rain," the woman replied firmly. From the look on her face and the tone of her voice, Maddock did not doubt her for one moment.

As they hurried to their car, Maddock wondered how their pursuers had caught up to them so quickly. Was it possible they had planted a tracking device on the rental car when he and Kaylin had stopped at battery park? He'd have to check it out. His thought were interrupted when his cell phone beeped once, indicating he'd received a voice mail message. As he entered the car and turned the ignition, he retrieved his message. Apparently, he had not been able to get reception in the basement. There was static on the other end, then shouting, and a sound like a gunshot. *"Maddock! We..."* a strained voice shouted, then a loud thump. The message ended.

"You look like you're going to be sick," Kaylin said. "What's the matter?"

Maddock swallowed hard. For a moment, he thought he might actually prove her right, and lose his lunch right there. "That was a voice mail from Corey. Something's wrong."

Chapter 13

Bones looked up at the man who was holding him hostage in the cabin of the *Queen's Ransom*. Thin nylon rope held his wrists together tight behind his back, cutting into his skin, and was knotted around his ankles. Next to him, Matt was similarly bound. Corey lay on the floor, blood trickling from a wound he had suffered when one of the attackers had hit him in the head with the butt of a rifle.

"You have found the *Dourado*, no?" his captor asked in heavily accented English.

Bones did not reply. He looked up at the man with what he hoped was a defiant glare.

His captor merely smiled and shook his head.

"My friend, we can play games all day. But I promise you, sooner or later, you will answer my questions." He knelt down in front of Bones and smiled. "Oh yes, you will tell me everything I want to know."

"And then what? You'll kill me." Bones had no illusions about the situation and would not believe any false promises the man or any of his cohorts might make.

"Yes," the man said, taking a long drag off his cigarette.

Bones was taken aback by the man's candor.

"The question is, do you want your last hours to be painful, or pleasant? If you cooperate, I promise you will die of a bullet to the back of the skull. Quick. Painless."

Bones stared at him. The man seemed to be waiting for him to ask what would happen if he did not cooperate. He wasn't about to give the jerk the pleasure.

"What if we don't cooperate?" Corey groaned. He was trying to sound tough, but Bones could hear the strain in his voice.

"You will be made to suffer. And then you will die in the most painful way imaginable." The man stubbed out his cigarette on the bottom of his shoe and flicked the butt out of the cabin door and onto the deck.

Bones eyed him. The man was tanned, with black hair and a slightly oily complexion. His face was wide, with eyes set a bit too far apart. He paced back and forth in front of his captives, his hands folded behind his back.

"I believe what I shall do is to begin with you," he nodded toward Corey. "Your friend shall watch what we do to you. Perhaps that will convince him to talk to us."

"Take me first," Bones said. "Neither of them knows anything. Leave them out of it."

"Oh no, my friend." The man leaned down close to Bones' face. "I know the reputation of the American Indian. You can remove your spirit from your body, and watch your own torture, even death, dispassionately. I am wagering that your weakness is that you cannot watch the suffering of your friends with the same lack of concern."

He smiled, confident in his theory.

"You don't really believe that fairy tale crap, do you? That's just something we made up to scare white people," Bones said. "Besides, what can we tell you, anyway? We're a research…" A loud pop burst in his ear as the man kicked him in the side of the head.

"We will not make satisfactory progress if you insist on playing games." He looked at Bones with empty, dispassionate eyes. After a moment, he casually removed the pack of cigarettes from his breast pocket and shook out another of the cancer sticks into his palm. The pack was white with a black sailing ship set in front of a blue wheel. They were Esportaziones, an Italian brand. The armed peon rushed from the cabin door he had been guarding and lit the man's cigarette with a hastily produced Zippo. The oily man took a deep draw, held the smoke in for a moment, and slowly exhaled.

"I will give you one last chance," the man said, walking over to where Corey sat. He held the cigarette near Corey's cheek. The computer whiz winced and turned his head away from the glowing ash.

"First," the man said in a calm, conversational tone, "did you find the wreck of the *Dourado?*"

"Yes," Bones replied. He saw no point in denying it since the man obviously already knew. Now, he needed to buy time until Willis could do something to help them. The two of them had been underwater when the attack came. Bones had surfaced only to find guns drawn on him. They hauled him aboard, relieved him of his dive knife, and tied him up. He cursed his own laxness. Things had proceeded so uneventfully up to this point that he had not insisted that Willis stand guard, convinced there was no danger.

"We found it two days ago. You can see the spot on the chart over there," he nodded toward Corey's instrument panel, above which a chart of the area between Bintan and Singapore was mapped. Straight pins were pressed into the map, marking the location of the *Dourado*, the probable site of the sinking, and places in between where they had successfully recovered artifacts from the ship. These had been few and far between.

The man glanced at the chart, then back at Bones. He seemed satisfied with the answer.

"What did you find?"

"Gold coins, a few statues, stuff that you'd expect to find on a ship." Where was Willis? "The *Dourado* was salvaged years ago. There's almost nothing left."

The man thought about this for a minute as he took another long drag off his cigarette. He turned and blew the smoke in Corey's face, then held the ash close to Corey's neck. "You are certain?"

Bones nodded, his heart racing. If these people knew about the *Dourado*, then they had to know that the ship had been salvaged. That was part of the historical record. It was the other information, about the sword and the captain that he needed to protect.

"Can I at least know your name?" Bones asked. He had to stall as much as possible.

"I do not see the harm in revealing my name to a dead man. My name is Angelo."

"Thanks, Angelo," he said, feigning friendliness. "Good to know you. My name is…"

"Your name is Uriah Bonebrake. You work with Dane Maddock on the *Sea Foam*, along with Matthew Barnaby and Corey Dean. At present, you are working for Kaylin

Maxwell."

"Nice job," Bones said. "I was never much for homework, myself. I just copied off of the cute girls."

"Enough of this." Angelo made a slashing motion with his hand. "After you finished your excavation of the wreck of the *Dourado*, what did you do next?"

Bones took a deep breath and exhaled slowly, trying to appear as if he were debating whether or not to answer the question. Anything to stall.

"We went to the spot you see marked on that chart. It's the pin farthest to the northwest. That's where we think the *Dourado* went down."

"And then?" Angelo fixed him with an impatient glare, the cigarette dangling from his fingers burning down slowly.

"We started scanning and making short dives at places in between the site of the sinking and her present location." Behind his back, he worked at the ropes. He had tensed his arms as much as he could while they were tying his hands together, but the bonds were on tight. He didn't have much wiggle room.

"What have you found on these dives?" Angelo leaned toward him, an intense look in his eyes.

"Again, almost nothing. We figure the cargo gradually spilled out onto the seabed between the place the ship went down and the place it turned up off of Bintan several days later. Over time, the currents will have scattered it pretty wide."

Angelo, without changing expression, buried the cigarette into the exposed flesh of Corey's upper arm. Corey screamed, as much in surprise, Bones supposed, as from pain.

"What the hell did you do that for?" Bones snarled, jerking in his bonds.

"I did not ask you what you think happened to the cargo. I asked what you found. You will answer me specifically and explicitly." Angelo's eyes now held a slightly demented look.

"Fine." Bones pretended to rack his brain though their take had been so small that he could probably rattle off the list without a second thought. "Two statues, both in poor condition. Each of Middle Eastern origin."

"What country?" Angelo snapped.

"Not my specialty." Bones shrugged, using the motion to mask his struggling with his bonds. "We'll have them checked out when we get back."

"No. We will have them checked out when we return. You will not be returning."

"Whatever," Bones pretended to dismiss Angelo's words with a shrug, using the motion to twist against the ropes around his wrist. He felt them give just a bit. "We also found a small, ornate wooden box that had probably contained someone's personal papers once upon a time."

"There were no papers?" Angelo leaned toward him again, frowning as he spoke. Suspicion dripped from his words. "You are absolutely certain of this? I caution you. No attempt to deceive me will work. You will succeed only in making your friend suffer."

"It was a wooden box, genius," Bones said. "It filled with water. Whatever was in there has pretty much dissolved into some mush in one of the corners. You're welcome to scrape it off and try to read it if you like."

For a moment, Bones thought that Angelo was going to punch him, or burn Corey again, but the dark-haired man relaxed visibly and nodded for him to continue.

"Seven coins... no, eight...no, it was seven." He was running out of stalling tactics.

"Seven or eight. I do not care! Get on with it."

"Sorry, you said to be explicit." Bones had worked his wrists looser. He had to be careful to keep Angelo from noticing any movement. "Beyond that, we've found some dishes, a pistol, and a small cannon that might have been kept aboard the *Dourado* for defense, but we aren't sure about that. We couldn't have raised it, anyway. That's everything." Having finished his list, he stared at Angelo defiantly. "What else do you want to know?"

"What else?" The man seemed agitated now. He stamped his foot and crossed his arms in front of his chest.

"I told you, that's everything," Bones said. "Of course, we're not finished with our search. Who knows what else we'll find if you let us keep working?"

Angelo did not seem satisfied with the answer. He began pacing again. After a moment, he stopped and scrutinized the map on the wall. He dropped what was left of his cigarette on the floor, and put his finger on the site of the wreck. Silently he traced the path they had marked out on the map.

"Where is the rest of your crew?" He asked, almost nonchalantly. Bones did not know how to respond. Angelo didn't wait long before he continued. "Come now. I know that you are missing both Mr. Maddock and Ms. Maxwell."

Bones relaxed a bit. So they didn't know about Willis. That was a point for their side.

"They went back to the states." He wouldn't be surprised if the guy had the resources to know where they had gone.

"Why did they go back?" His voice took on an impatient tone.

"There was a death. Someone in Kaylin's family. I think it was maybe her cousin or somebody. Maddock went with her since she's been attacked before." He stared intensely at Angelo. "But I guess I don't have to tell you that."

"You are not being completely truthful with me, Mr. Bonebrake," Angelo said. "Mr. Maddock and Ms. Maxwell left because you found what you were looking for, didn't they?"

"What?" Bones didn't know what else to say.

"You were left behind as a ruse, continuing the search so it would seem to outsiders that you had not found that for which you were searching."

"We're not looking for any one thing." Bones' searched for a way to stall Angelo further. "We're just excavating the wreck. Kaylin's father had researched it all of his life. It was his pet project, and she wanted to finish what he started."

Angelo produced his own lighter, lit another cigarette and moved back to Corey's side. He knelt down and held the burning end next to Corey's left eye. He gripped Corey's hair in the other hand.

"My patience is at an end. I will know what you found, or I will blind this man."

"We didn't find anything," Corey grunted, trying to jerk his head away. "He's telling you the truth. Everything we've found is on board the ship."

Angelo thought this over. He did not, however, move the cigarette away from Corey's head or loosen his grip. "For argument's sake, let us say that I believe you. Answer this, Mr. Bonebrake; what is it you expected to find on this wreck? And no more lies about not looking for one specific thing. There was something special aboard the *Dourado*. Tell me what it was."

Bones could tell that the time for stalling was at an end. As he watched Angelo push the hot ash of the cigarette ever closer to his friend's eye, he hoped Willis had come up with a plan.

Chapter 14

"I can't get in touch with any of them." Maddock snapped his phone closed and slammed it down on the table. "I don't know what's going on!"

"We've notified the authorities in Singapore. There's nothing else we can do," Kaylin said. "Besides, if you smash your cell phone, they definitely won't be calling you anytime soon."

"I shouldn't have left them," he muttered, the feeling of helplessness was driving him crazy. Her assurances didn't make him feel any better. He stood up and walked across the room they had rented under a false name in a rundown roadside inn. Reaching the far wall, he turned and stalked back to the window. "I need to do something. I can't stand waiting around like this."

"You've already done something. You found that tracking device under our bumper. It was a nice touch planting it on a police car. That'll make a nice surprise for our new friend."

Maddock tried to smile but managed only a grimace. "That doesn't help Bones and the guys. I should be with them."

"Well, you aren't, and you're not accomplishing anything by walking around the room. Sit down and help me with this letter." She sat at a small table, rickety and badly stained, comparing the letter Maddock had found against a Portuguese-English dictionary they had picked up at a local bookstore.

"I don't know any of that stuff," he grumbled. He slumped down in the cheap, fake leather chair across from her, feeling every bump against his back. He folded his arms across his chest and stared. He knew he was acting childish, but the frustration he felt at being unable to help his friends, or even know what was wrong with them, was almost more than he could bear. But he also realized it was pointless to sit and complain about something over which he had no control.

"What do you want me to do?"

"Here. See what you can make of these." Kaylin slid her notebook across the table to him.

He flipped it open to her copies of the sketches they had found in Covilha's books. His eyes took them in with only moderate interest. He exhaled long and loud, sighing impatiently.

"I don't know what we're going to learn from these," he complained. They were just doodles, after all.

"And you never will if you don't shut up and get to work," Kaylin snapped, not looking up at him.

"Fine." She was right, but he did not like to be reminded of it. He looked them over again, this time more slowly. The sinking ship was probably the *Dourado*. But what to make of the others? A wrought iron fence, an old house, a river, an oak tree, a tombstone... He turned the page. There were more on this sheet, but nothing caught his eye as being of particular significance. What could they mean, if anything? And why were they all written on page one hundred twenty-five? After mulling it over for a few long, boring minutes, he flipped the notebook closed and pushed it back toward

Kaylin.

"How's your translation coming?" he asked, more to fill the silence than because he expected her to have discovered anything of significance so soon.

"Slowly," she replied. "If I've got this right, it's an unfinished letter to his mistress. He mentions someone named Domenic and talks about his regrets."

"Maybe they had a son together?" Maddock asked.

"Could be. The mention of the *Dourado* isn't of much significance. He just talks about how his life changed when the *Dourado* went down 'on that January night.'" She bit her lip and looked up another word.

Something in her statement seemed to trip a switch in Maddock's subconscious. "Say that again."

"What?" She looked at him with a blank expression.

"That last part about the *Dourado*," he said, closing his eyes and pressing his hands to his temples. "Read it back to me."

"All right. 'I tell you, darling, my life was forever changed when the *Dourado* went down that dark January night.'"

"What date, exactly, did the *Dourado* sink?" His heart beat faster as a wave of adrenalin surged through him.

Kaylin picked up another notebook and turned to one of the first pages. "January twenty-fifth. Why do you ask?"

"That's it!" He pounded his fist on the table. "January twenty-fifth! One-twenty-five."

"Page one twenty-five!" she cried with delight. "You're right. That's got to be it!" She pushed the letter away, grabbed the notebook, and scooted her chair around the table so that she could look at the sketches along with him.

"Now that we're fairly certain these symbols are tied in with the *Dourado*, we need to figure out what he was trying to tell us," Maddock said, feeling confident for the first time since getting Corey's cry for help.

"Could it be a cipher of some sort?" Kaylin asked.

"I don't think so. There aren't enough icons to cover much of the alphabet, and nothing repeats."

"Perhaps it's more complicated than that. Maybe we take the words for these different things, combine all the letters, and rearrange them to spell out a message?"

Maddock turned and stared at her, his eyes wrinkled in a frown. "How in the world do you think of these things?"

She shrugged. "Ciphers were common back then, and some of them were pretty complicated."

"I hope that isn't the deal," Maddock said. "It would be hard enough to unscramble in English, but if he did the cipher in Portuguese…" He left the rest unsaid, as understanding dawned on her face.

"Does your friend have access to a computer program that could decrypt a message like this?"

"First of all, we aren't sure that there is a message to decode." He was growing frustrated again, and with the feeling came renewed concerns about Bones and the crew. He pushed away from the table. "I want to get out of here. Let's get a drink."

"I'm really not in the mood for a drink," she said.

"Fine, you can watch me." He grabbed his jacket and keys and left the room without waiting to see if she was following.

"Maddock, wait a minute!" she called.

Something in her voice, some underlying tone of revelation, made him turn around.

"What if we're making this too complicated? What if it's just a simple map?"

Maps he understood. Curious, he returned to the table and stood looking down over her shoulder.

"The sinking ship is probably the *Dourado*, so that's most likely the first symbol in the sequence. Maybe these other images represent real places. Put the clues in the right order, they lead us to the sword!" Her eyes were bright, her face positively aglow. Maddock stared at her for a moment, admiring her fresh, youthful beauty.

"Are you still with me?" she said, waving her hand in front of his face.

"Oh, sorry, just thinking." Maddock shook his head, trying to get his thoughts back to the subject at hand. Guilt soured in his stomach as he thought of Melissa. "If they're real places, what is this thing?" He pointed to a drawing of four arrows emerging at right angles to each other from a central point, pointing up, down, left, and right. Another smaller arrow pointed down and to the right at an odd angle.

"What's the matter, sailor boy? Never seen a compass before?" She smiled up at him, and he grinned in spite of himself.

"Fine, you got me on that one." He settled back into the chair he had vacated moments before. "The problem I see is that so many of these drawings are too generic. How many streams are around here? Or wrought iron fences? Where do we even start?"

"How about the house? It's a little more detailed than the other images."

Maddock looked at the sketch. It was certainly distinctive, with a large porch running across the front and wrapping around the right side. An odd, tower-like architectural feature graced the front left corner. Chimneys peeked up from either side of the steeply pitched roof. Two second-floor windows extruded Cape Cod-style from the front of the roof. Ornamentation had been sketched on the porch rails and posts. It might be possible to locate the house. It was as good a way as any to pass the time until he could find out what happened to Bones and the crew.

Chapter 15

Antonio stepped away from the door of the cabin. Angelo had everything under control inside while Louis and Vincent patrolled the deck. He pulled a brand new pack of cigarettes out of his pocket and slapped the bottom of the box a few times before removing the wrapper. It was a personal tradition of his; bring a new pack on the job and do not open it until the work is done.

This one had been too easy. The people on board had not been expecting anything out of the ordinary, and the diver who had been down at the time had not heard them coming. He was supposed to have been a SEAL, but their reputations must have been exaggerated; they had subdued him quickly. According to Angelo, two of the crew members were missing.

It would not have mattered if the entire crew had been there, Antonio thought, smiling. They had taken their victims completely by surprise.

"And to think they wanted to send Stefan," he said to no one in particular. Stefan was good, there was no doubt, but Angelo's team, of which Antonio was a member, was good as well. If only their superiors would let go of their foolish attachment to Stefan. Antonio hated being underestimated.

He leaned against the rail and admired their speedboat. It was a sleek model with a low profile and a powerful but nearly silent engine. The hull was painted a swirl of blues and greens, allowing it to blend in with the sea. A bulletproof, green-tinted windshield swept back in a tight curve. It was a beautiful piece of workmanship.

A loud splash from the stern drew his attention. He looked back but saw nothing. A porpoise, perhaps? He scanned the horizon. The blue-green waters were choppy today, and devoid of any crafts other than their own and the one they now controlled. There had not been any since they had taken control of the boat. He shrugged and dug out his lighter.

Antonio thumbed the lighter and raised it only to freeze. It suddenly occurred to him that when he had looked to the stern it had been empty. Had not Vincent been sitting there just a minute ago? Surely, he would not fall in. It seemed a bit strange. Perhaps his comrade was in the bow with Louie.

Antonio lit his cigarette, inhaled deeply and blew a cloud of smoke into the air. He made the short walk to the ship's bow, skirting the exterior of the cabin and stopped short. The bow was empty as well. His jaw fell and the burning cigarette dropped to the deck.

He looked around. Where had they gone? He needed to tell Angelo. He hurried to the cabin door but the sound of Angelo's voice, raised in anger, gave him pause. He needed to at least check the situation out before reporting to his boss that half of their team was missing. He did not want to think about delivering such a message. Angelo's was a prodigious temper.

Perhaps they were in the cabin. He wanted to check, but that would risk incurring his leader's wrath. He thought for a minute. No, they could not be in the cabin. He would have seen or heard at least one of them pass by. Something was very strange here. He turned a complete circle, reassuring himself that there was nothing on the horizon. There had to be an explanation. Rifle firmly in his grip, he walked quickly to the stern where he had last seen Vincent. He peered over the rail and saw nothing. He turned back toward the bow of the ship and scanned the entire deck. Where were they?

A cold, wet hand clamped down hard across his mouth, and he felt himself yanked backward. Frantically, he dropped his weapon and grabbed for the railing, trying to prevent himself from tumbling into the sea. A hot, searing pain shot through his throat, and consciousness fled as he fell into the cold, dead arms of the sea.

Bones worked furiously to free his wrists. On the other side of the cabin, Angelo had duct taped Corey into a chair and had begun his questioning. Corey was holding out, denying that they were after anything other than whatever could be salvaged from the *Dourado*. Angelo stood, cursing loudly and shouting.

"You are lying to me!" he cried, shaking his fist in the crewman's face. "You know it, I know it, and your soon-to-be-dead Indian friend knows it as well." He drew an automatic pistol from an ankle holster and aimed it at one of Corey's fleshy white thighs. "I warned you. Perhaps I can impress upon you just how serious I am."

"No!" Bones shouted, thrashing around and struggling to work free of his bonds. "Leave him alone!"

Angelo turned toward him, smirked, then returned his attention to Corey. As he turned, something caught his eye, and he looked to the deck with an expression of disbelief on his face. He grunted in surprise, then seemed to regain his composure, and leveled his pistol toward some unseen target.

Willis! Bones had almost reached Angelo's side. Rolling onto his back, he raised his feet, still bound together, and struck with both heels, driving them into the side of Angelo's knee.

There was a loud pop, and Angelo cried out in pain as his knee buckled under the force of Bones' kick. His arm flew up, and his shot went through the ceiling as a blue and black blur hurtled through the cabin door, bowling him over.

Willis, clad in his wetsuit, rode Angelo to the floor. He held the man's right wrist with his left hand. He clutched a dive knife in his right. A faint smear of blood, apparently not his own, stained the chest of his blue neoprene suit.

Angelo frantically fired off a shot that flew harmlessly through the cabin roof. He held Willis' thick ebony wrist, struggling to keep the stronger man from bringing the knife down on him. He shifted under the man's weight and brought his left knee up hard between Willis' legs.

The former SEAL grunted. Bones saw his friend's face contort in pain. His grip slipped ever so slightly on Angelo's gun hand, and his knife ceased its steady downward descent. Bones twisted and contorted, and finally succeeded in freeing one wrist. There was no time to loosen the bonds that held his ankles. He pushed himself up to his feet and jumped.

Javelin had been his sport in high school, but his standing long jump hadn't been too bad. He came down feet-first with his full weight on Angelo's face, hearing the satisfying crunch of cheekbones snapping, and the squeal of pain that leaked from the man's ruined face. The squeal turned to a shriek as Willis buried his knife in Angelo's chest.

Their former captor's struggles ceased as the life drained from his body along with his blood, bright red on the stark white cabin floor. Willis lurched to his feet and cut the ropes from Bones' legs, then set about freeing Corey while Bones worked on reviving Matt.

"What kept you?" Bones called over his shoulder as he tended his crewman's wounded head. "I got so tired of waiting for you I was going to take care of them myself, but then you dragged your tail in at the last minute and played hero."

"Grateful as always." Willis rolled his eyes. "I had to wait until they split up and weren't paying attention. The guy in the bow made it easy for me. I guess he heard me and thought it was a fish because he leaned way over the rail. I grabbed him by the collar, put my knife in his throat, and eased him on into the water."

"How did you 'ease' a two-hundred pound man down from the bow while you were still in the water?"

"I'm good," Willis replied firmly. He stared at Bones for a moment, and then rolled his eyes. "Maybe there was a splash, but it wasn't a big one. Got the others the same way."

Bones was impressed. "Divide and conquer. Not bad for a hired hand."

"You didn't warn me this hired hand was going to be a hired gun. My salary demands just skyrocketed."

"Talk to Maddock," Bones said. "He's the boss."

After tending to their colleagues, Bones and Willis searched Angelo's body for identification. They were not surprised to find that he was clean. His black jumpsuit was also devoid of identifying marks. The only personal object he carried was a silver necklace that was tucked into his left pocket. Bones held it aloft.

A silver pendant dangled from the chain. It was a crucifix unlike any he had ever seen. In the place of the cross, the Christ figure, his face staring angrily forward, hung from crossed swords.

"Jesus," Willis whispered.

Bones felt the blood drain from his face. He stared at the object for a moment, then said the one thing that came to his mind.

"Literally."

Chapter 16

Maddock rapped smartly on the door of the small white cottage. He turned and looked up and down the street. It was a typical pre-World War II neighborhood. The long, narrow thoroughfare was lined with ancient oaks, the roots of some of which were breaking through the sidewalk in places. All of the houses appeared to be in good repair, with neatly trimmed lawns, each bordered by a manicured row of hedge. He should have felt at peace in such surroundings, but he was not. Though he was relieved to have learned that his crew was safe, his senses were on heightened alert. The people who were after them were every bit as dangerous as he had feared. They were well armed, and seemingly had the resources to track their every move.

An elderly woman answered the door. Maddock immediately took notice of her sharp, blue eyes. The intensity of her stare was hawk-like and contrasted with her gently lined face, soft white hair and grandmotherly frock. She regarded them through the screen with an undisguised look of suspicion.

"Mrs. Russell? My name is Maddock. This is my friend, Kaylin. Ms. Meyers from the library called you about our visit?"

The woman's face brightened. "Oh, yes. Come in." She pushed the screen door open wide, and motioned them inside. They settled onto an overstuffed love seat. Their host pulled up a rocking chair in front of them. "I understand you're doing some genealogical research?"

"Yes," Kaylin lied. "We've found some drawings in an old family book, and were wondering if you might recognize this house." She held her notebook open for the woman's inspection.

The old woman leaned forward, her nose nearly touching the page. After a moment, she leaned far back and peered down her nose at the picture. She shook her head.

"No, I fear I have never seen that house. I have been the unofficial town historian for fifty-three years. I know most every old house in town. That does not mean, however" she added, noticing Kaylin lower her head in disappointment, "that it was never here. Quite a few old homes were torn down in the forties and fifties." She suddenly cocked her head and stared at the page again. "May I see that notebook?"

Kaylin handed it over, and the historian inspected it carefully.

"These other drawings remind me of the Riverbend Cemetery north of town. There is a stream that runs alongside it, an old wrought iron fence in the front, and there used to be a giant oak tree on a hill in the center of it. There is a print of it from the nineteenth century that hangs in the funeral home in town."

"Is there a covered bridge?" Kaylin asked, her voice raising an octave. She leaned forward and turned to the next page of the notebook, where she had copied a picture of such a bridge.

"Why, yes there is," Mrs. Russell replied. "I see the gravestone here," she pointed to the sketch. "Is one of your ancestors buried in this cemetery?"

"That's what we're wondering," Maddock replied hesitantly. "We heard someone dug up a grave there recently."

"Yes, it was a terrible thing." She pursed her lips and frowned. "An old drunkard from town said some people hired him to do it. What foolishness."

"Was the grave anywhere near the spot where the old oak tree used to stand?" Kaylin asked.

The historian cocked an eyebrow as if this were a very odd question. "I do not know for certain. I have a layout of the cemetery in my records. It shows the locations of the plots, and who is buried in each. Perhaps I can help you find your ancestor."

She led them through a clean but cluttered old house jammed with antique furniture and walls lined with paintings in faux-gilded frames to a room in the back of the house. A stout wooden table stood in the center of the room. The walls were nigh-invisible behind bookcases overflowing with books, file folders, and loose papers of various shapes and sizes. The room was the very antithesis of Maxie's meticulously organized library.

Despite the chaos, Mrs. Russell had no difficulty finding what she was looking for. She walked over to one of the shelves and withdrew a cardboard tube, from the inside of which she produced a long, rolled paper. She smoothed it out on the table, pinning the corners down with stray books.

The boundaries of the graveyard were marked in bold blue lines. Plots were denoted by faint dotted lines. Each had a name and number written in tiny, precise print. Pathways crisscrossed the entire cemetery.

"Here is where the grave was desecrated." She pointed a knobby, liver-spotted finger at a spot not far from the cemetery entrance on the south end of the graveyard. "A man named Covilha, I believe. A Spaniard, or some such." She moved her hand across the page. "Here is where the oak tree stood." She indicated a point near the center of the graveyard. "And here is the covered bridge." Her finger drew a line to the northwest.

"Do you have a string, or a ruler?" Maddock asked, struck by a sudden inspiration.

"Certainly." The old woman exited the room, returning momentarily with an old yardstick which she handed to him.

Maddock grinned and smacked it into the palm of his hand. "Just like Mom used to beat me with."

"I whipped my son with that very same ruler," Mrs. Russell replied, a wistful smile on her face. "He still frowns when he sees it."

Maddock laid the ruler across the map, angled downward from the top left. He then lined it up so that the edge lay across the center of the drawbridge, as well as the spot where the oak tree had grown.

"Would this line cross the wrought iron fence?" he asked.

"It encircles the graveyard, so yes."

"What would have been up here, outside the cemetery," he indicated the place where the ruler left the page, "back in, say, the mid-eighteen hundreds?"

"I do not know. I suppose I could check." She moved quickly to one of the shelves and began browsing through some oversized books.

"What are you thinking?" Kaylin whispered.

"Just a hunch." He didn't want to tell her until he was fairly sure he was right.

The historian laid an oversized book on the table, opened it, and flipped to an index in the back. After a moment, she turned to the page she was looking for.

"Here we are. This is from 1860." She looked at the cemetery map, then back to her book, did a double-take, then checked each again. "This is a strange coincidence. There was a house here that belonged to Francisco Covilha. I believe that is the same person who…" her voice trailed off.

Maddock and Kaylin exchanged excited looks. They were on the right trail. They had to be. Kaylin's eyes narrowed. Maddock believed he could read her thoughts. If Maddock was correct, and the clues ran in a straight line, they would not lead to Covilha's grave, but possibly to that of another person.

"Let me check something," the historian said. She pulled from the shelf a small clothbound book with a tattered cover and paged through the yellowed pages. "This book was written just before the turn of the century. It has pictures of some of the older buildings that were in the town at that time. I didn't think of it before." She found the page she sought. "May I see your sketch, please?"

Kaylin showed her the drawing of the house.

"This is it." She turned the book around to show them what she was looking at. It was a print of the house in the sketch. At the bottom of the page was a single word: "Covilha."

"Well, that certainly is interesting," Mrs. Russell continued.

"Now, about the ancestor you're looking for; I assume his name was Domenic?" She pointed to the name Kaylin had found in one of Covhila's books.

"Um, that's right," Kaylin said.

"Well, let me see. There is a plot with the name Domenic LaRoche right here." The location she indicated was on the opposite side of the oak tree, in perfect line with the house and covered bridge. "Is that the person you were looking for?" The elderly woman looked at them with a smile that said she was quite pleased with herself.

"That's him," Kaylin said, grinning. She clasped the woman's hand in both of hers. "Mrs. Russell, thank you for your help."

"You are most welcome." The woman smiled kindly.

"There's one other thing," Kaylin began. "If someone were to come asking about me…"

"Ms. Meyers told me about your situation with that terrible man. I'll be happy to keep your confidence."

Maddock added his thanks, and they left the house. As they climbed into the car, Maddock quietly contemplated what they had learned.

"Do you think that's the answer?" Kaylin asked. "The sword is buried with this Domenic person?"

He turned to face her, his heart racing. "I think we should go to the cemetery, and follow the clues."

Chapter 17

They parked on the shoulder of a narrow road that ran between the Burnatches River and a gently sloping hill. Covilha's home had once sat atop that hill overlooking the

Riverbend Cemetery. They crossed the old covered bridge, now open only to pedestrian traffic, passing over the river, and arrived at a wrought iron fence.

"It looks just like the drawing in the book," Kaylin said, inspecting the fence.

Maddock looked out across the graveyard. It was an old place that carried the evidence of its years in the weather-stained tombstones and eroded statuary. The paint on the fence was chipped. Patches of rust stood out everywhere on its pitted, black surface. Thick patches of clover stood out on the green carpet of grass. There being no gate nearby, he vaulted the fence, and then gave Kaylin a hand up.

They stood in the midst of several old gravestones. Maddock knelt down to inspect the nearest one. It was dated 1841. He looked around.

"Where do you want to start?" he asked Kaylin.

She opened her notebook and looked over the images she had recopied onto one page. She had drawn a rough outline of the cemetery and placed the house, river, bridge, fence, tree, and the name "Domenic" in their proper places. At Maddock's suggestion, she had sketched in the compass alongside the house. He pointed out that the objects they had located all were directly southeast of the house; the same direction the compass was pointing.

"Let's orient ourselves with our backs to the house, facing the hill where the oak tree was," Kaylin said. "We'll walk straight ahead, and see if we come across anything that might be represented in these other sketches."

They began their walk, taking care to appear to the casual observer to be a couple on a leisurely stroll to visit the resting place of a family member. Not, Maddock noted, that there seemed to be anyone around. He looked carefully at each headstone they passed. The oldest ones were so eroded that he could not make out anything carved into them. One of the stones, however, drew his attention.

"Kay, look at this." He knelt and rubbed a bit of moss from the discolored face of the old marker. As the gray-green moss was scraped away, it revealed the faint outline of a dove carved into the stone. It was weathered, but still easily recognizable.

"Check one more off the list," Kaylin said. She crossed out the picture of the dove at the bottom of the page and sketched it into its location on her rough map. The ground sloped gently upward as they approached the place where the oak tree had stood many years before. As they rounded a large, above ground vault, she laughed.

"The torch!" She pointed to a statue of a woman that topped the crypt. Dressed in a flowing robe, the figure held a torch aloft in her right hand. We're tied," she said, adding this new find to the map.

They each located one more item. Maddock found a headstone with the outline of a cross carved in the top while Kaylin found a fleur-de-lis. Kaylin added these to the map, leaving only the sketch of a bird unaccounted for. As they topped the rise, they stopped and looked out over the old burial ground. This was the view that Covilha would have had from beneath the oak tree. Might he have stood on this very spot and created his code?

"Maddock, look there." Kaylin indicated a small, worn headstone just down the hill from where they stood. It read, Domenic LaRoche. "That's it."

"I don't know," he said. "We're still missing the bird." He scanned the nearby headstones, but nothing immediately caught his eye. Where was it?

"The bird," Kaylin said to herself. "What if it was carved onto one of those stones. The ones that were so badly eroded that we couldn't make out what was written on it? Or," she held up a finger like a schoolteacher giving a lecture, "the drawing might have represented birds that nested in the oak tree."

"Maybe," Maddock agreed, "but let's keep going just to make sure." It was his nature to be thorough. He did not want to miss an important detail because he had made an assumption based on incomplete information or a bad presupposition.

They continued their trek down the hill and across the graveyard. By the time they reached the far boundary, they had seen no bird symbol. Hoping that Kaylin's earlier assessment would prove to be correct, they returned to the grave.

Kaylin knelt in front of the small tombstone. There was a faint inscription beneath the name. She ran her fingers across it gently.

"What does it say?" Maddock asked.

"I can't make it out. Hold on." She tore a sheet of paper from her notebook and held it flat against the stone above the inscription. Fishing a pencil from her purse, she made a rubbing of the headstone. When she had finished, she held it up and read aloud. "Domenic LaRoche, Son of Marie-Louise, 1834-1836." She stared at the paper for a moment, then looked back at the small marker. "He was just a baby. That's so sad."

Maddock nodded. It was sad but not unusual for that period in history. Something else was bothering him.

"Don't you think it's strange that only the mother's name is listed?" he asked.

Kaylin pursed her lips thoughtfully. "Maybe he was illegitimate."

"If that's so, I'm surprised he had a proper burial and a headstone. Most mistresses couldn't afford it, and the fathers wouldn't usually spring for it."

"Must have been an unusual circumstance," she mused. A frown creased her brow. She opened her notebook, found the page she was looking for, and grinned broadly.

"Tell me," Maddock said.

"The letter you found in the book. You remember, I said it sounded like a letter from Covilha to his mistress? Look at her name." She held the translation up for him to inspect.

"Marie Louise," Maddock marveled. "He buried the sword with his son."

"That's why they didn't find anything when they dug up Francisco's grave." Her hands trembled. "It's right here, Maddock! Right here beneath us!" She jumped to her feet and wrapped her arms around his neck.

He hugged her awkwardly and gave her a pat on the back before pulling away gently. Something was not right. He thought about it for a moment, before realizing what was bothering him.

"I'll be right back." He hurried down the hill and over to the fence that encircled the graveyard. A brief inspection of the wrought iron revealed a loose bar: a vertical post topped by a spike. A few twists and the old solder broke, freeing the rod.

Kaylin greeted him raised eyebrows. "What's that for?"

"You'll see." Choosing a spot in line with the center of the headstone and about three feet out, he pushed the spiked end of the bar into the earth. The ground was fairly soft, and he encountered no large rocks. With only a bit of persuasion, the bar sank slowly into the earth.

"Maddock, don't tell me…" Kaylin covered her face. "You're not going to dig up that little boy's casket, are you?"

"Think about it," Maddock said as he continued digging. "Would a regular sword fit into the coffin of a two-year-old? We're talking about a sword that was wielded by a nine-foot tall warrior." He stopped as the bar struck something solid. He wiggled it gently and felt it slip over the side of the object. Ignoring Kaylin's questioning look, he gently drew the bar back up and continued to probe.

He quickly found the other edge. He guessed the object, the sword, he hoped, was about six or seven inches wide at this point. It was certainly too narrow to be a casket, and it was at a depth of just over two feet. He turned to Kaylin and smiled.

"I think we've got it." They definitely had something. He just hoped it was the right something. What if it wasn't the sword? What if they had come to New York for nothing? He pushed the worries from his mind. Such defeatist thoughts wouldn't get them anywhere, and he'd find out soon enough what lay buried in this child's grave.

Kaylin beamed back at him, confidence gleaming in her eyes.

"Turn around and screen me from the road," he instructed. "Pretend you're writing in your notebook, but keep an eye out."

"No way," she said. "Don't you think we should wait until after dark to do this?"

"And have somebody beat us to it? Those guys have been one step behind if not a step ahead of us, the whole time. Besides, with Covilha's grave being dug up, they're likely to keep a closer eye on the place at night."

"Right," she said, "because no one in his right mind would rob a grave in broad daylight."

He rolled his eyes and started digging.

Kaylin gave him a mock frown, then turned and pretended to be writing something in her notebook.

Maddock chopped at the ground with increasing vigor. He tore up thick clumps of sod before breaking through to the soft dirt beneath. He wished for a better digging implement, but, as his grandpa used to say, you make do with what you got. He had made substantial progress before Kaylin called out a warning.

"Here comes a car!" Her voice was calm, but he could sense the tension in her tone.

He tossed the bar behind the little headstone and knelt down over the trench he was digging, pretending to be reading the inscription. The car passed without the driver taking any apparent notice of them. They were interrupted two more times by passing motorists. Maddock had exposed a foot-long by ten-inch wide section of what was obviously an old metal box. The surface was pitted with rust, but still solid.

"Cops!" Kaylin called, this time with a touch of alarm in her voice. "And he's looking this way."

Maddock hastily repeated his ruse, tossing away his digging apparatus and kneeling over the hole, which was now starting to resemble a latrine. He hoped the cops didn't take too close a look, as he could not think of any plausible explanation for digging up a grave.

A brown and tan sheriff's department vehicle cruised by, slowing as the deputy in the passenger seat peered at them with undisguised distrust. Kaylin mimicked writing furiously in her notebook while Maddock joined in the charade by pretending to read the inscription aloud to her. The car slowed further, and the deputy rolled down his window. Maddock's heart pounded. He was not afraid of going to jail. He feared that if the deputies discovered what they were doing, the authorities would take possession of the sword, or worse, whoever was following them might somehow get hold of it. They had to get the sword now, or face the real possibility of losing it.

Kaylin pretended to have just noticed the patrol car. She smiled and waved. Maddock waved as well. They held their breath as the car slowed to a near stop before the deputies nodded to them and accelerated around the bend and out of sight.

Maddock let out a breath he didn't realize he'd been holding before returning to his digging. Kaylin looked like she was going to crumple to the ground. Instead, she knelt, found a flat rock that Maddock's digging had turned up, and joined in. While she worked, scraping away at the soft loam, she kept an eye on the road.

They attacked the ground with a fury. After a few minutes, the piles of dirt around the forming trench had grown too large to hide. Maddock felt his adrenaline surge at the realization that this was it. They had to get the sword out before another vehicle passed by. Droplets of sweat beaded on his forehead and rolled off into the moist dirt in the trench. His shoulders ached from the awkward digging motion necessitated by the wrought iron bar. His hands stung, and blisters were forming on his palms. Beside him, Kaylin panted as she hacked at the soil. He did not know if it was out of fatigue or fear of discovery.

Inch by inch, they exposed the box. It looked to be more than five feet long. When the entire top surface was exposed, he used the point of the bar to scrape the dirt from around the sides. He then placed the tip underneath the bottom end of the box, and gently pried it up. Slowly, the box broke free of the soil that had ensnared it for more than a century and a half. He soon raised the end of the box high enough to get his fingers underneath. Straining, he lifted it until he could get two hands under it. It was remarkably heavy. Kaylin lent a hand, and the two of them dragged the box free from its grave.

It reminded Maddock of a large gift box. The top was slightly wider and longer than the bottom so that it fit neatly over the bottom half. The lid had been welded all the way around at the bottom edge.

"We can't open it," Kaylin complained, her face taut with tension and frustration.

"Not yet," Maddock said, "but in any case, we need to fill this hole in before we do anything else."

They hastily kicked dirt and rocks back into the trench they had dug. With the box missing, there was not enough dirt to fill the hole back to ground level. Maddock gathered a few stray rocks and sticks, tossing them into the hole, then patched the top with chunks of sod. It would not hide what they had done, but someone would have to be right on top of it before they noticed.

Maddock took off his jacket and laid it across the box. Kaylin did the same. Together, they hefted the large metal container. Holding it at waist level, they stumbled down the hill to their car.

When they reached the wrought iron fence, Maddock propped his end on the rail and vaulted over. He cautiously dragged it toward him, letting the fence support its weight, and held it while Kaylin clambered over.

As she topped the fence, she looked up the road, her eyes widening and her face pale.

"Maddock, it's the cops again!"

Maddock grabbed the box around the middle and lifted it with a grunt of pain. He stumbled to the car and heaved the box down on the ground next to the rear tire. He stood up in time to see the car rounding the bend in the road.

Kaylin calmly walked to the driver's side door, trying to put herself in a position to prevent the deputies from seeing what lay underneath the car. She fished in her pocket for the keys, not realizing they were in Maddock's jacket, which lay draped over the box.

The cruiser rolled to a stop. The deputy rolled down the window and leaned as far forward as his wide-brimmed hat would allow.

"Afternoon," he said. His words were friendlier than his expression. His hazel eyes gleamed with suspicion and his narrow face and thin lips were set in a firm manner that said he would brook no foolishness.

"Good afternoon," Kaylin replied, smiling sweetly, leaning forward ever so slightly.

"You folks visiting a loved one?" He smiled as if that were some big joke, eyeing Kaylin with more interest now than suspicion.

Given that the cemetery had met its quota of residents more than a century ago, Maddock supposed it qualified as a joke. He smiled and let Kaylin do the talking, as she seemed to have captured the deputy's attention. Maddock supposed that sometimes there were definite advantages to being female and attractive.

"We're doing some genealogical work," she said. "We were trying to find the grave of one of my ancestors."

"Any luck?"

"No. We thought we had found it, but we were wrong." She frowned and bit her lower lip as if she were about to cry. "We're so close, too."

"Sorry to hear that," the deputy replied though the words held little empathy. He looked down and frowned. "What's in the box?"

Maddock could have smacked the guy. He told the first lie he could think of.

"Art supplies: an easel, paint, brushes and such." He nodded to Kaylin. "My girlfriend was thinking of painting the cemetery."

"It's quite lovely," Kaylin agreed.

"So I guess you were drawing in that notebook when we drove by a while back?" The deputy acted as if Maddock were not there.

Maddock didn't care if he was noticed or not. He only prayed that the man would not ask to see Kaylin's sketches.

"Yes, just a few sketches," Kaylin said, beginning to look nervous. "Would you like to see them?"

What was she doing?

"No, thanks. I'll warn you folks, though," the deputy said, removing his hat and running his fingers through his short, brown hair. "There've been some strange goings-on around here. If you see anything out of the ordinary, call 911."

"We certainly will," Kaylin agreed, smiling again. "Thank you for letting us know."

The deputy looked them over again, then nodded and told his partner to drive.

They watched until the patrol car disappeared from sight before they loaded the box into the back seat.

"Now what?" Kaylin asked.

"We check out of the hotel," Maddock said, "load up the car, and get as far from here as we can. Then," he turned and smiled at her, "we see what's inside this box."

Chapter 18

The knife struck the post dead center, its razor tip piercing the soft wood and burying itself a full three inches into its target. Stefan smiled a wicked grin. He never missed. He retrieved the blade with a deft yank and held it up in the afternoon sun, admiring the way the sunlight played along the razor edge. It was a KA-BAR knife, the style used by United States Marines. The weight and feel of it in his hand was perfect.

He flexed his bicep and drew the knife point across the muscle, drawing a faint trickle of blood. He no longer felt pain, and the cutting reminded him of killing. He loved killing with a knife; it was so… personal.

Sheathing his knife, he returned to his training. Placing his palms on the ground, he flipped into a handstand, put his heels against the post from which he had taken his knife, and began his regimen of inverted pushups. One-hundred repetitions and then time for his run.

He was on ninety-seven when his phone vibrated. There was no need to check who was calling. He already knew it would be Robinson, and the news would not be good. He ignored the phone while he finished his exercises. When he finished, he went inside, poured himself a drink, and waited for the next call, which he expected would come in short order. He was not disappointed. The phone buzzed again almost immediately, and he answered on the first ring.

"I have been waiting for your call," he said.

"Stefan, you are needed." Robinson sought to give his voice the weight of command, but Stefan could read vocal inflections, and the man was agitated. It pleased him.

"Angelo has failed, as I told you he would. The Italians are less than useless." They had been foolish to entrust an important mission to that buffoon. Angelo was good for bullying wayward priests and holding the door for his betters. Nothing more.

There was a long pause on the other end of the line. Robinson had already lost whatever advantage he thought he had. They needed Stefan, but Stefan did not need them.

"The operation was not a success," he admitted.

"Obviously, or you would not be calling me." Stefan wished the man could see his smile.

"We… should have entrusted this to you at the outset. We need you now. God needs you."

That admission was all Stefan would get. It was enough.

"Very well. Give me the details of the operation."

He listened to what Robinson told him, asking an occasional direct question. He wrote nothing down. He would remember everything. He was about to hang up the phone when the man actually managed to surprise him.

"They claim to have found what?" Stefan asked, his head abuzz with surprise. He set his jaw and let the information sink in. "This cannot be. It is heresy."

"That sort of outdated thinking will serve neither of us," Robinson said, clearly pleased to have scored a point in their heretofore one-sided verbal joust. *"We must deal with the situation on the ground. If what they say is true, it must be suppressed."*

"Of course it does. You absolutely should have called me first."

"I'm calling you now. Remember, His dominion is close at hand."

Stefan snapped the phone closed and laid it in its place atop the antique roll top desk. Dropping to the oak floor, he sat cross-legged with his hands in his lap. He gradually slowed his breathing and willed his heart to slow. He instructed his mind to slow as well, the whirling cacophony of disconnected thoughts and images coalescing into a single ball, which he crushed and discarded. He had one focus: the mission.

He visualized his enemy. He envisioned stalking him, looking him in the eye before killing him. He could not allow this artifact to come to light. The man who sought the artifact, this treasure hunter, would die for his folly. Stefan would not fail in this quest.

The orphan rescued from the streets of Venice had risen to a unique standing. Important men begged for his services. He named the price and set the terms. His was an uncanny knack for anonymous killing. Many had died by his hand, but suspicion had never fallen upon him. In fact, he did not officially exist. He was a phantom, a product of the organization that had raised and trained him. He owed his life to the order, and his service to it was always free.

He fingered his crucifix, the symbol of his order, feeling the sharp blades that formed the cross on which his savior claimed the victory. Anticipation welled up inside of him as he envisioned the hunt. He forced himself to remain calm. This assignment was not for sport; it was a grave responsibility, a holy quest the like of which he had never undertaken. This would be his finest hour. He would recover the relic, kill the heretics, and claim the head of Dane Maddock as a trophy.

Chapter 19

Maddock smiled as he and Kaylin walked the grounds of the United States Naval Academy. It had been years since he was last here, but he remembered it like it was yesterday. The campus, or "yard" as it was called, covered over three hundred acres and held a trove of fond memories. Up ahead, the domed roof of the chapel peeked out above the trees, a comforting sight.

They made their way to Maury Hall, which housed the departments of Weapons and Systems Engineering and Electrical Engineering. They made their way down to the building's lowest level—a floor he had not known existed. There, a welcome sight greeted them—his crew.

"About time you two showed up. You been making out in a dark corner somewhere?" Bones asked.

Maddock greeted Bones with a rough hug and a slap on the back. He then turned and shook hands with Corey, Matt, and Willis. It was a relief to see them safe.

"Thanks for waiting for us," Bones said. "I know you're dying to open that box, but we didn't want to miss this." The others added their thanks as well.

"Kaylin didn't want to wait," Maddock said. "Truth told, I didn't want to wait either. But you guys deserve to be here. Everything worked out all right?"

"No problem," Bones said. "We recovered the bodies, searched them, stripped them down, took them out to deeper water, and fed 'em to the sharks." He said this as if recounting a trip to the grocery store or a day of chores around the house. "Done deal."

"Did you find anything that will tell us who these guys are?" Maddock asked. Why they were being followed was obvious, but the question of exactly who it was that was after them had confounded Maddock and his friends.

"Just those weird crucifixes with swords for crosses. Corey took some pictures and emailed them to Jimmy. We'll see what turns up." Bones looked around before continuing. "Sorry, I just feel like someone's going to walk up on us any minute. This is not the kind of stuff anyone else needs to hear. We were defending ourselves, but..."

"I understand," Maddock said. "This is the most desolate floor of any Naval Academy building I've ever been in. I think it's safe to talk here. Go ahead."

"We burned the clothing, put the ashes, crucifixes, and weapons into their speedboat, and blew the whole mess to kingdom come."

"Man, I hated blowing up that boat," Willis said. "That thing was sweet."

"No kidding," Matt said. "Bones wouldn't even let us take a spin in it first."

"Which is why we were able to clean up the mess, get the boat back to its owner, and get the hell out of Dodge before the authorities caught up with us," Bones said.

"Get out of Dodge?" Corey echoed, grinning. "Indians aren't allowed to make cowboy jokes. It's in the rulebook."

"How about we get on with it, gentlemen?" Maddock asked, opening the door to the room where Kaylin was waiting, along with Dr. James Sowell, and engineer with a strong interest in archaeology. Jimmy had found Sowell's research online, and Maddock had used his Naval connections to persuade the man to help him, which hadn't been difficult. Sowell had arranged for the use of the laboratory and gained entrance to the campus for Maddock and his friends.

The room was utilitarian: plain white walls and lots of stainless steel. The metal box, the box holding the sword, Maddock hoped, lay on a table in the center of the room beneath a bright fluorescent light. They all circled around, eager to find out what was inside.

"All right, everyone put on your safety glasses," Sowell said. He donned a pair of dark-tinted laboratory goggles and picked up his saw. The tool consisted of a small handle with a diamond-tipped circular blade. "Watch for sparks and tiny shards of metal," he instructed, then began to cut away the welds that held the lid securely to the box.

The thin, high-pitched whine of the saw rose to a shrill squeal as the blade cut through the ancient bonds.

Maddock was so excited that he could scarcely hear it. A tingling sensation ran up his back and down his arms as the moment drew near. He watched as Sowell worked his way down one side, then around the end, and back up the other side. When only one end of the box remained, he felt Kaylin grasp his forearm in both hands and squeeze.

The professor completed the last cut, put down his saw, and knelt to inspect his work. He used a brush and a small vacuum tube to clean away the loose bits of metal from around the cut. Then he probed the cut with a thin bladed knife.

"Should we just come back tomorrow?" Bones asked a touch of annoyance in his voice. "I mean if you're gonna be a while..."

"I was asked to do a job," Sowell replied, not looking up from his work. "It's going to be done properly."

"Sorry," Bones said. "We've been through a lot to get this thing."

Sowell finished his inspection and nodded as if satisfied. He stood up and addressed the group.

"Everyone put on masks and rubber gloves, please." He pointed to a table against the far wall.

"Why?" Willis asked.

"We don't know what's in there. There could be some sort of mold spore that might be harmful if inhaled. And frankly, even if whatever is in there isn't potentially harmful, I don't want you sneezing on it." He turned to Bones. "Since you're so eager, how about you give me a hand with this lid?"

Bones donned a mask and a pair of gloves and positioned himself at one end of the table. He and Dr. Sowell each took hold of one end of the lid.

"Okay, lift," Sowell instructed. Each lifted his end of the lid. It did not budge. Bones tried to jiggle the lid, to no avail.

"Don't try to force it," Sowell ordered. He took a small hammer and chisel and began working at the corners of the box, carefully tapping the tool's fine point between the two halves. When he was satisfied, he nodded to Bones, and the two of them pulled up on the lid. With a little persuasion, it came free.

Maddock's mouth dropped open in slack-jawed disbelief. The box was filled with moldy burlap. He wanted to curse. Just as quickly as the thought had entered his mind, it fled. The burlap was obviously packing material to protect whatever was inside. He chuckled at his own foolishness. Kaylin glanced at him, a look of curiosity in her eyes. He shook his head.

Sowell carefully lifted the bundle out of the box and laid it on the table. Slowly, delicately, he unrolled the burlap from around the object. Maddock held his breath. Around him, the others gasped as the last layer of cloth fell away.

It was a huge broadsword. The pommel was broad, the handle wrapped in dry, aged leather. The scabbard was simple, without ornamentation. When Sowell drew the blade, however, even Maddock sucked in his breath with surprise.

The sword was unlike any he had ever seen, and not only in terms of its size. One side of the blade was perfectly straight, and obviously razor sharp. The other side, apparently equally sharp, was oddly shaped, with irregular waves and indentations along the length of the blade, some of them nearly an inch deep.

"It looks like a big key," Bones observed.

Maddock was too mesmerized by the magnificence of the sword to comment.

"It's so shiny," Kaylin marveled. "It looks brand new."

"Is it steel?" Maddock asked. The sword should not have been in such pristine condition, especially not a three thousand-year-old sword.

"No, it isn't," Sowell answered slowly. "It's surprisingly light." He hefted the sword with one hand and cut a figure eight in the air. "It feels almost like titanium." His puzzled voice was a match for his frown.

"May I hold it?" Kaylin asked.

Sowell nodded and held it out across his upturned palms as if making a formal presentation. It glistened in the artificial light.

Considering that this was the fulfillment of her father's dream, Maddock agreed that a bit of ceremony was not out of order. He laid a hand on her shoulder.

"Congratulations," he said softly.

Bones began clapping. The others quickly joined in, whistling and applauding with enthusiasm. Kaylin turned toward them and held the sword aloft. The tears streamed down her cheeks, framing her brilliant smile.

"Thank you all," she said, lowering the sword, and gazing at it with a mixture of wonderment and adoration. "You all worked so hard, and put yourself in such danger to help me finish Dad's work. I can't tell you how much..." She broke into sobs.

Everyone surged forward to hug her or pat her on the back. Maddock held back. He did not know why, but he felt as if he should not be a part of this moment.

Kaylin quickly regained her composure. She scrubbed her tears away with the back of a sleeve and smiled anew.

"Who wants to hold it?" she asked, looking around at the others.

"Let Maddock hold it first," Bones said. "You guys found it. I mean, all we did was get beat up."

"No, you go ahead," Maddock declined, laughing. "This was a team effort, and you guys certainly paid your dues."

Bones took the sword from Kaylin and held it aloft, letting the light play off the keen edges of the blade. Despite what Sowell had said, his face registered surprise.

"Man, this thing is light. And there's not a scratch on it. The edge of the blade is perfect." He gazed at it for a moment before passing it around the circle.

First Corey, then Matt, then Willis took a turn holding the sword. To a man, their faces registered bewilderment at the weight and condition of the ancient blade.

"No way this could be the real thing," Willis said as he passed it to Maddock. "I'm sorry to be the stick in the mud, man, but they didn't have metals like this back then."

Maddock grasped the hilt of the sword. Light though it might be, it was perfectly balanced.

"You're right, Willis," he said. "They didn't have this kind of metal back then. But there's another problem." He waited to see if anyone was following his train of thought. When no one spoke up, he continued. "We know that, at the very least, this sword is nearly two hundred years old. It's been in the ground almost that long."

"I hear you," Willis said, a sly smile spread across his face.

"I get it," Bones said, pounding his fist into his palm. "Whatever kind of alloy or whatever this is would have been almost as much out of the question in 1825 as it was way back when. It's an anachronism regardless."

"Ms. Maxwell, will you allow me to analyze the blade?" Sowell asked. "I have some tests I can run that will not damage the blade. Perhaps I can shed some light on this puzzle."

"Please," Kaylin said, obviously confused by this revelation. "I thought that finding the sword would be the end of the mystery, but it seems that it's just the beginning."

"Let's assume that Rienzi is correct, and this is truly the sword that belonged to Goliath," Corey said, scratching his head. "How was this thing made?"

"Maybe it was a miracle," Kaylin said. She blushed a little as everyone looked at her. "Why not?" she asked with a touch of defiance in her voice. "David was God's chosen warrior. Maybe when he used the sword to cut Goliath's head off, God did something to it."

"Back to reality," Maddock muttered. Religion of any sort was not his favorite topic.

"What's the matter Maddock, don't you believe in God?" Kaylin rounded on him, hands on hips and a look of challenge in her eyes. "Don't you?"

Maddock did not reply. He focused his attention on the sword, and tried to ignore the heat that was rising up the back of his neck.

"I don't want to talk about it," he said. His voice sounded like winter in his own ears. He knew from experience that if there was a God, He did not intervene in events to help good people. In any case, he was not going to talk about it. Something else had captured his attention.

He held the sword up to the light and looked closely. Sure enough, there it was. Strange, alien characters were etched into the metal. They seemed to flow together in a regular, but ornate script. Something about them made goosebumps rise on his flesh. The words seemed powerful…and sinister. The others needed to see this.

"What is it?" Kaylin asked, her voice sharp.

He turned the flat of the sword blade outward for everyone to see. "Maybe the answer is in the writing etched into the blade."

Chapter 20

So, what have we learned about Goliath?" Bones tossed a folder on the table, pulled up a chair, and produced a can of Diet Coke with lime from the pocket of his leather jacket. He popped it open and took a swig.

"You might know what we've learned if you helped us," Kaylin grumbled, looking askance at him.

"I'm hurt," Bones answered, clutching his chest and twisting his face in mock anguish.

"Sorry," she said. "I'm just stressed out." She took a sip of coffee and grimaced. "Ugh, who made this?"

"I like it strong," Maddock said. He turned to Bones. "What's up with you?"

"I'm celebrating," Bones said. "Ask me why." His eyes twinkled as he spoke.

Maddock was still in a bad mood after the religious discussion of the previous day. He knew that he shouldn't be angry at the others. The problem was his own. Nonetheless, he wasn't in the mood to bandy words with his friend.

"Why?" Kaylin asked, her voice tinged with annoyance.

"Because I found a connection between the notes in Rienzi's Bible and the tall man." The brightness of his smile made Maddock's headache worse.

Maddock waited for Bones to continue, but to no avail. "Bones, if you're going to make us ask you a question after every sentence you utter, this is going to take forever." He tossed the printed e-mails he had been reading onto the table and squeezed his head between his hands. The pressure relieved some of the throbbing.

"Fine, ruin my fun, why don't you?" Bones pulled his feet off of the table, sat up straight, and took another drink before continuing. "I was doing a little research this morning, and came across a website that claims that the story of David and Goliath is a fable inspired by the stars. Specifically, David is the constellation Bootes, the sling is Corona Borealis, and Goliath, drum roll please…" He began drumming on the table with his palms. "…is Orion." He sat back, folded his hands behind his head, and waited for their reply.

"But we know that Goliath is real," Kaylin protested. "So how does that help us?"

"Think about Rienzi's Bible," Bones said. "Remember the stick figure drawn in the margin next to the David and Goliath story? Did it remind you of anything?"

"Orion," Maddock said. How had he not recognized so familiar a constellation? "You're right. That's what the drawing is. I should have recognized it."

"So Rienzi knew about this idea that the constellations inspired the story," Kaylin said, her voice bland. "I'm sorry, but I still don't see how this is helpful." She paused, waiting for an explanation.

"Think about it this way," Bones said. "Rienzi, at least in his mind, knew that Goliath was a historical figure. After all, he had the sword to prove it. So he must have seen some other connection between Goliath and Orion."

"Like what?" Maddock feared this was one of Bones' fancies. "Wait a minute. Maybe I don't want to know." He held up his hands as if warding off an attack.

"Like little green men." Bones rolled his eyes and waggled his fingers as he spoke.

Kaylin buried her head in her arms and groaned.

"Bones, if you had any idea how hard I've worked at doing real research, you would never come to me with this ridiculous idea."

"Why is it ridiculous?" Bones propped his elbows on the table and fixed her with a blank stare.

Maddock knew his friend well enough to know that Bones was being serious. At least, as serious as he ever got.

"Come on," Kaylin said, looking up at him. "You expect me to believe that Goliath was a space man?"

"Not a spaceman," Bones said. "But he was a descendant of an alien race."

Kaylin chuckled and shook her head. She was not accepting the idea at all.

"Let's hear him out," Maddock said. He wasn't quite sure why he wanted to hear what Bones had to say. It was, after all, pretty far-fetched. Perhaps it was because he knew it would get under Kaylin's skin. Sort of a petty payback for last night.

"First of all," Bones said. "Remember how Rienzi had marked the passage about the giants being on the earth, and mating with human women?"

"Yes," Kaylin said in a voice that was part tired, part bored. "I remember."

"I did some cross-referencing between my research and Rienzi's notes," Bones continued. "Did you realize he marked every scripture that referred to races of the Nephilim or the 'giants?' He noted the Emim, who the Hebrews called 'the terrible ones,' the Rephaim, and the 'stranglers,' the Anakim."

"All right. So the Hebrews came to a new land where some of the native tribes were bigger than they were, so they called them 'giants', and gave them scary names," Kaylin said.

"The Bible says that the Anakim were so big that the Hebrews were 'as grasshoppers in our own sight,' Bones argued. "That's more than just bigger. And remember, these are the descendants of the Nephilim. They've been interbreeding with regular humans for generations."

"Still, Goliath was a big guy," Kaylin said, refusing to give ground, "so it would make sense that Rienzi marked all of the passages that referred to these 'giants.'"

"Goliath is generally accepted as being one of the Anakim. By the time the book of Joshua is written, which is well before David, we are told that there are only three places where the Anakim still live. One of those three places is Gath, Goliath's home. Rienzi would have had no reason to note any of the other races unless he was trying to make a connection."

"But why aliens? Why couldn't they just be big people?" Kaylin protested.

"Actually there are several reasons." Bones took a final swig of his soft drink, draining the can. He belched loudly, crushed the can against his forehead, and dropped it on the table. "The most important of which is that it is the only way to explain that sword." He paused for a moment and stared at Kaylin as if challenging her to argue with him.

"That sword is the ultimate anachronism. It's made of some combination of metals we've never seen. It hasn't aged in thousands of years. It has been used in battle, but never nicked or scratched. I don't know that it could be duplicated even today."

Maddock could see that Kaylin was thinking this over. Suddenly, he had an idea.

"It also explains why Rienzi was threatened with excommunication," he said.

Kaylin looked at him, frowning while Bones smiled and nodded.

"Now you're getting the idea, Maddock," Bones said.

"Something that's been bothering me is the fact that the church effectively shut

Rienzi up about his discovery. You would think that discovering an ancient artifact that proves the truth of a story in the Bible would be a good thing, but in this case, the church didn't want the word to get out." Maddock's mind was operating at a fast clip now. "Obviously, Rienzi was making claims about the sword and what it signified that went above and beyond simply claiming that it had belonged to Goliath. Claims that the sword was the creation of a superior alien intelligence, and that Goliath was part alien would have been objectionable to the church."

"And it would explain why his peers scoffed at his claims," Kaylin said thoughtfully. "I'm still not convinced, but I'm willing to keep listening."

"Fair enough," Bones said. "A million or so years ago, according to anthropologists, Homo Erectus migrated out of Africa. By thirty thousand years ago, the only hominids around were Homo Sapiens. Oddly, despite the fact that Homo Sapiens is a much more highly developed being, there is no fossil record of a progression from Homo Erectus to Homo Sapiens. It's as if we just burst onto the scene with our big brains and frail bodies.

"There's also the issue of structures like the pyramids. How did our ancestors build them? There are megalithic structures all over the world made up of giant stones that people did not have the technology to move. Take the walls of Sacsayhuaman in Peru. One of the stones was measured at eight and a half meters high and weighs over three hundred sixty tons."

"We can move objects bigger than that," Kaylin argued. "I read about a lighthouse that was moved a while back. It weighed in the thousands of tons."

"You're talking about today, not thousands of years ago," Bones replied. "And then there are the accounts of aliens in the historical record. There are carvings of images that look remarkably like astronauts, rocket ships, even light bulbs. There are also written records. Take the Tulli Papyrus, for example. He opened his folder and selected a single page printout. He held up the page and began to read.

"In the year 22, in the third month of winter, in the sixth hour of the day, the scribes of the House of Life noticed a circle of fire that was coming from the sky... From the mouth, it emitted a foul breath. It had no head. Its body was one rod long and one rod wide. It had no voice. And from that the hearts of the scribes became confused and they threw themselves down on their bellies ... then they reported the thing to the Pharaoh ... His Majesty ordered ... has been examined ... and he was meditating on what had happened, that it was recorded in the scrolls of the House of the Life. Now after some days had passed, these things became more and more numerous in the skies. Their splendor exceeded that of the sun and extended to the limits of the four angles of the sky ... High and wide in the sky was the position from which these fire circles came and went. The army of the Pharaoh looked on with him in their midst. It was after supper. Then these fire circles ascended higher into the sky and they headed toward the south. Fish and birds then fell from the sky. A marvel never before known since the foundation of their land ... And Pharaoh caused incense to be brought to make peace with Earth ... and what happened was ordered to be written in the Annals of the House of Life so that it be remembered for all time forward."

Maddock tried to digest what Bones had read to them. It just seemed so far-fetched. He was impressed, though, that Bones had obviously done his research.

"There's also the fact that our ancestors had a great knowledge of astronomy. They knew that the sun, moon, and planets rotate. They also knew the circumference of the earth and included it in their architecture. Ancient maps have been discovered that showed things that ancient humans shouldn't have known, like the coastline of

Antarctica beneath the ice."

"Let me see if I've got this," Kaylin said. "You're arguing that aliens not only intervened in human pre-history, but interbred with humans, thus making the aliens the 'missing link.' And that Goliath was closely descended from one of these alien races."

"I'm saying that some people believe that," Bones corrected.

"So we're all aliens?" Kaylin asked, with a sick look on her face. "That's hard to digest."

"I guess so. At least, we're all part alien. The Anakim and the others might have been a remnant of aliens who continued to breed mostly among themselves until so few remained that they had no choice but to mate with humans."

"Did you do all this research, or did you have your friend Jimmy help you?" Kaylin asked.

Bones stuck out his tongue.

"Okay, I think I've heard enough," Maddock said. "Without agreeing with you that Goliath was an alien, let's operate on the assumption that Rienzi believed that he had discovered proof of that very idea. The sword, amazing as it is, would not have been sufficient proof, especially two hundred years ago. They would have dismissed it as an undiscovered metal, or perhaps a miracle."

"You're right," Bones said. "There's more that we haven't discovered. Something Rienzi found that supported his claims. We have to find it."

Chapter 21

They arrived in Professor Sowell's office to find him seated at his desk, an expression of amused bewilderment on his face. He motioned for them to take seats opposite him.

"We've run tests on the composition of the sword. Frankly, it does not belong."

"It doesn't belong in that time period, you mean?" Maddock asked, dropping down into an uncomfortable, straight-back wooden chair.

"I mean it doesn't belong on this planet." The professor paused while this bit of information sank in.

Next to him, Maddock heard Bones chuckle.

"What'd I tell you?" He stood behind Maddock and clapped a hand on Maddock's shoulder.

Sowell ignored Bones' comment and continued.

"The component elements are terrestrial. The metal, however, is an unknown alloy. Whatever that alloy is, it gives the sword its strength, durability, and lightness. The blade is harder than titanium, lighter, and has an extremely high melting point though I have only managed a rough estimate. There are other tests I could do, but I do not want to risk damaging it. Not that I have any confidence that I could damage it with anything short of a nuclear explosion."

"You think it's an alien artifact," Bones stated, squeezing Maddock's shoulder.

"I can't tell you what it is," Sowell said, "I can only tell you what it is not. And it is not of this earth, at least not of any known alloy."

"Did you learn anything from the inscription on the blade?" Maddock asked, eager to change the subject.

"Yes," Sowell said. "I was able to scan the images and send the information to your friend Jimmy. He just updated me on his findings. The writing resembles hieroglyphics and will take some time to decipher. That is if we can decipher it all. He has managed to translate a small portion, and is confident that he is correct."

"Forgive my ignorance, but why are hieroglyphics so hard to translate?" Kaylin asked.

"No frame of reference," Sowell explained. "Decrypting an alphabetic cipher, for example, involves finding patterns such as frequency of occurrence of certain letters or finding double letters and using them to identify words. Once the code is broken, its child's play. With hieroglyphics, each symbol can represent a word, a sound, a concept, or even a story. That is why Egyptian hieroglyphics were a mystery for so long. Until the Rosetta Stone was discovered, there was no reference from which to translate them."

"How did Jimmy manage to break any of the code, considering the sword may not be of earthly origin?" Maddock asked. "It almost sounds too easy."

"Apparently the computer found matches from a variety of sources: Egyptian hieroglyphics, Viking runes, even some Central and South American Indian pictographs. Much of what he has at present are bits and pieces that are meaningless out of context."

"You said he was able to translate a portion of the writing. What does it say?" Maddock's curiosity was piqued. Having been the one to first notice the writing on the sword, he was eager to learn what it said.

"Not what, but where," Sowell said, pushing a computer printout of a map across the desk. He turned it around so that the three of them could see it. "The writing pinpoints a location in southwest Jordan." He circled a spot on the map with a ballpoint pen. "A few of the other words he has translated include "rock" and "red." Coupled with these coordinates, we are confident that the writing on the sword is pointing to this location."

"Petra," Kaylin breathed the word more than spoke it. She turned to Maddock, her eyes wide with excitement. "Rienzi claimed to have been the first to rediscover Petra. Many of the artifacts he lost on the *Dourado* were discovered at Petra. That must be where he found the sword."

"I take it this is good news?" Sowell asked, his smile unreadable.

"Absolutely," Maddock said. Standing, he clasped the professor's hand. "I can't tell you how much I appreciate your help."

"I should thank you," Sowell said, also rising to his feet. "It is the most amazing artifact I've ever seen."

"It certainly seems to be so. Well, I guess we'll be taking it with us now," said Maddock. "Where is it?"

A sudden change came over Sowell. His face seemed to harden. His ears reddened, and his fists clenched.

"The sword?" he asked in a clipped voice.

"What else would I mean?" Maddock asked. Warning bells were going off inside his head. He stepped closer to the desk. Out of the corner of his eye, he saw Bones position himself between Sowell and the door.

"Mr. Maddock, the sword requires further study. If we could reproduce this metal, do you have any idea what the implications for industry and defense would be?"

"Give me my sword," Kaylin said in a cold voice that caught Maddock by surprise.

"Why do you need it?" Sowell asked. "You completed your father's quest. We will pass all our findings along to you. You have had the satisfaction of finding it. Now let us, your countrymen, get something out of it as well."

"My father bought that sword with his blood. It belongs to me, and it's not for you to ask why I need it." Her voice remained calm, but her eyes were shining with barely contained rage.

Kaylin's expression suggested she was on the verge of climbing over the desk to get at Sowell. If that were to happen, Maddock did not know if he would try to stop her.

"Give us the sword, Sowell," Maddock said firmly. "You have your test results to study. Don't make this hard on us and depending on how things unfold, Ms. Maxwell might permit you to study it again at some point in the future."

Sowell's eyes flitted rapidly between Maddock, Kaylin, and the door where Bones stood.

"Commander Wrexham deems it in the interest of national security that the Navy takes possession of the sword." He swallowed hard. "He took it this morning."

"You're lying," Maddock said flatly. Sowell reached for the bottom drawer of his desk, but before he could get it open, Maddock grabbed him by the wrist and yanked, dragging him face down across the desk.

"I'm telling the truth," Sowell sputtered.

"Shut up," Maddock ordered. Sowell lay on his desk, head hanging off one side, legs off the other. Maddock grasped the hair on the back of his head with one hand. The other held Sowell's arm pinned behind his back. Maddock knew just how far the arm would bend before popping out of its socket, and he held it at the threshold.

"You forget that my friend, Bones, is a Cherokee. Indians have ways of making people talk, don't they Bones?" He looked at Bones, who nodded, smiling wickedly, his white teeth gleaming like fangs.

"You don't think I believe that voodoo hocus-pocus, do you?" Sowell wheezed. The pressure Maddock was putting on the back of his head was forcing his throat down against the edge of the desk. His face was turning purple from lack of oxygen.

Bones knelt down in front of the man. "We Indians do have our ways," he crooned. He reached into his jacket pocket and pulled out his Swiss Army knife. "But they aren't mysterious, spiritual ways. They're just plain nasty." He opened the corkscrew and held it up to Sowell's eye.

The professor squirmed and kicked, but Maddock held him firmly in place. The man had to be running out of air by now. After a moment, the struggling ceased, and Maddock felt the man relax.

"It's in the safe," he said, his voice a faint whisper.

Maddock decreased the pressure on Sowell's neck enough for the man to draw a breath and tell them the combination to the safe, which was, predictably, hidden behind a framed Ansel Adams print. While Maddock continued to hold the professor, Bones opened the safe and retrieved the sword which, along with its scabbard, was now protected by a layer of bubble wrap, which seemed odd considering what they knew about the sword's durability. He supposed it was a good idea to protect the aging scabbard.

"The commander was going to pick it up tomorrow," Sowell said, as Maddock let him stand. A miniscule flick of his eyes toward the clock on the wall was enough to give lie to his statement.

"Tell him we knocked you out and stole the sword," Maddock said and drove the heel of his palm into Sowell's temple. As the professor crumpled to the floor, Maddock doubled up his fists and struck the man a two-handed blow to the base of the skull. He turned to the others.

"Sowell was lying about Wrexham picking it up tomorrow. We've got to get off this campus now. He's probably going to be here any second."

The three of them scrambled out of the basement office and hurried to the elevator. Maddock looked at the numeric display. The elevator had stopped on the first floor and was now descending to the basement.

"Come on!" he shouted, dragging Kaylin down the hall. Behind him, the bell rang, and he heard the elevator doors begin to open. They were not going to make it to the end of the hall in time. Their options exhausted, he darted through an open door, with Kaylin and Bones right behind him.

It was another office, much like Sowell's. Fortunately, the occupant was out as was the light. There was no way to shut the door without drawing attention to whoever might get out of the elevator. They stood just inside the office door. Maddock strained to listen but did not hear anything. For a moment, he thought he had overreacted that the elevator had been empty, but then he heard footsteps. Someone knocked on a door.

"Sowell?" a voice boomed down the tiled hallway. "Open up!" The person knocked again. A pause, then the sound of a doorknob turning. Maddock heard the sound of the commander entering Sowell's office. "Sowell, what in the…" He heard thumps as if someone were shoving furniture aside. Wrexham had found the professor. Perhaps there was a chance.

"Go," Maddock mouthed to Kaylin and bobbed his head toward the door. To his surprise, she neither questioned him nor protested.

Hastily removing her shoes, Kaylin hurried to the door, glanced toward Sowell's office, then sprinted in the opposite direction. Maddock watched her disappear around the corner, and then moved to the door himself, with Bones behind him. Just then, he heard the sound of the commander coming back out of the office.

After a moment, footsteps again echoed down the hall, followed by an insistent tapping sound, which Maddock took to be Wrexham pressing the elevator button. The metallic ring of the elevator bell a moment later confirmed his instinct. He heard the doors open, and then close seconds later.

Maddock placed his hand on Bones' chest. They needed to make certain that the commander was really gone. He silently counted to twenty, all the while listening for the sound of footsteps that would indicate that they were not alone in the basement of the building.

Twenty seconds. Nothing.

He nodded to Bones, then peered around the door. Still nothing.

He moved silently on the balls of his feet out into the empty hallway. He had taken no more than five steps down the hallway when a firm voice rang out from behind him.

"Stop right there."

Chapter 22

A short, stocky, balding man with pale skin and a neatly-trimmed gray mustache stepped out of the next office. He held a Beretta pointed at Bones, who clutched the sword against his chest. Maddock was tempted to leap at the commander, but the distance between them was too great. Besides, if Wrexham were any kind of soldier, his reflexes would be too quick.

"Commander Wrexham, what a pleasant surprise," Maddock said, filling the words with as much sarcasm as he could generate.

"Spare me the small talk," Wrexham said. "I want the sword. Give it to me."

"No can do," Bones said, keeping his eyes trained on Wrexham's pistol.

"You can and you will," Wrexham snapped. "When the M.P.s find out how you attacked Dr. Sowell and stole Navy property, I think you'll be all too happy to surrender the sword."

"The sword is not Navy property. It belongs to Kaylin Maxwell, the daughter of…"

"I know all about Maxwell," the officer said. "He was acting on behalf of the United States Navy. It is a matter of national security. The Navy is grateful for your assistance in recovering the sword. Hand it over, and I'll let you leave unharmed."

"Don't think for one minute I believe you're going to let us out of here," Maddock said. Over Wrexham's shoulder, at the far end of the hall, something caught his attention. Kaylin had circled around and was coming up from behind. She held her father's .380 trained on Wrexham's back. Maddock could not believe she had smuggled that thing onto the campus of the academy. She was too far away at the moment to be of any help. Maddock needed to keep Wrexham talking. Careful not to let his eyes betray their only hope, he continued talking.

"We're the only ones who know about this," Maddock said. "You are acting on your own. If this were a Navy operation, Sowell would have immediately turned the sword over to his superiors, but you had him hold on to it for you."

Wrexham turned his pistol toward Maddock. "Maybe I should shoot you both right now. You talk too much."

"What about me?" Bones asked, apparently trying to help Maddock's stalling tactic. "I haven't been talking. That's not fair!"

"I don't like your face." Wrexham smirked.

Kaylin, still in her stockinged feet, was about halfway down the hall, about even with Sowell's office door. Close, but not close enough.

"Wait a minute," Maddock said thoughtfully. "You aren't going to shoot us."

"You are sadly mistaken my friend," Wrexham said, adjusting his grip on his pistol.

"You can't shoot us. If you try and use this story of us stealing Navy property, you're going to have to turn the sword over to them. You want it for yourself. I don't know who you're working for, or what your angle is, but I'm willing to bet that you've already negotiated a fat bonus for yourself."

Kaylin was creeping closer, narrowing the gap between herself and the commander.

"Who is it?" Maddock asked, watching for the officer to make a mistake. "A private corporation, or another country?"

Wrexham's eyes twitched at the mention of a private corporation, but otherwise did not react.

"I'll bet it's the French!" Bones shouted.

"Excuse me?" Wrexham said, raising an eyebrow.

Maddock was grateful that Wrexham had not recognized their stalling tactics, and had allowed himself to be distracted by the absurdity of Bones' exclamation.

"The French, they're always pissing Americans off." Bones looked at Maddock, feigning earnestness. "Wouldn't it piss you off if they had the sword?"

Maddock shot Bones a withering glance and shook his head.

"Well, wouldn't it?" Bones acted as if all was normal. "I mean, everybody hates the French."

"The only person who is pissing me off right now is you," Wrexham said. "Drop the sword or die."

"Drop the gun!" Kaylin had finally crept up behind Wrexham and now held her pistol pressed against his temple.

Wrexham slowly turned his gun hand sideways, the back of his hand facing upward, and began to spread his fingers. He knelt with equal care, Kaylin's gun remaining pressed to his temple.

It happened suddenly. Wrexham dropped to the ground, spinning to his left. He drove his left elbow into Kaylin's side. He simultaneously fired off a wild shot. Bones fell back with a grunt. Kaylin, apparently not expecting resistance, stumbled awkwardly, nearly losing her grip on her pistol.

Maddock, having expected Wrexham to try something, sprang forward the moment the naval officer moved. He grasped Wrexham's right wrist in his left hand and banged the man's gun hand hard against the ground twice. The gun clattered to the floor. With his right hand, he pressed down on the commander's windpipe. The man struggled in Maddock's grasp but could not get loose.

Kaylin appeared at Maddock's side. She had recovered her pistol and held it trained on Wrexham's forehead. At the same time, Bones stepped up and delivered a vicious kick to the officer's temple. The man ceased his struggles.

"I thought he shot you," Maddock said to his friend as the two of them stripped off Wrexham's jacket and bound his arms behind his back.

"I think it bounced off the sword," Bones replied, his eyes wide in amazement. "I heard the ping."

There was no time to discuss it further. They dragged Wrexham into Sowell's office and dumped him behind the desk alongside the still-unconscious professor.

"Let's move," Maddock ordered. "Someone is bound to have heard those shots. I don't want to be here when they come around to investigate."

They dashed down the hall and around the corner. Maddock heard the elevator bell ring again. He was growing to hate that sound. At the far end of the hall, where it made another right turn, was a door marked Stairs. Maddock threw it open, and they sprinted up, taking the stairs two at a time. When they reached the first floor, Bones grabbed for the stairwell door.

"No!" Maddock shouted, and continued running up the stairs. Bones and Kaylin followed. "If anyone did hear the shots, they're probably watching the stairwells as well as the elevators."

"We have to leave sometime," Kaylin huffed. "What do you want us to do?"

"I've got an idea," Maddock said. Below them, he heard the first floor stairwell door open. He halted and motioned for the others to stop as well. They stood silently, listening as the clatter of footsteps echoed from below. The noise diminished, then, with the sound of a closing door, faded away.

Maddock led them to the fifth floor. He pressed his ear against the metal door but heard nothing. Cautiously, he opened the door and led the others into the corridor. He led them quickly down the hall and breathed a sigh of relief when they came to a glass door labeled, Admiral Franklin J. Meriwether, Professor Emeritus. Suddenly wondering if this was such a good idea, after all, he took a deep breath, turned the handle, and stepped inside.

An attractive woman, probably in her late thirties, sat behind a small desk. She had short, blonde hair, green eyes, and fair skin. The nameplate on her desk read, Jill Trenard. A civilian, Maddock noted.

"May I help you?" Her smile was polite but perfunctory. She took in Maddock's sweaty brow and disheveled appearance, and her brow creased. Her eyes widened when she caught sight of Bones.

"Yes," Maddock said. "Dane Maddock to see Admiral Meriwether, please."

The woman consulted her computer screen. "Do you have an appointment?" She knew perfectly well he did not, but she was a military secretary, and she had to go through the motions of asking.

"He's expecting us sometime today," Maddock said. "We weren't certain what time we would be getting here."

Ms. Trenard was apparently too professional to point out that the Admiral had said nothing to her of their expected arrival. She gave him a long, sour look.

"Just a moment," she finally said. She tapped a button on her telephone console and spoke softly into intercom.

Maddock stepped away from the desk, so as not to appear as if he were eavesdropping on her conversation. He pretended to take an interest in the photographs of World War II-era naval vessels. All the while, he kept watch on the hallway outside. After a moment, Ms. Trenard spoke to him.

"Admiral Meriwether will see you now, Mr. Maddock." Her surprise was evident in her voice and her expression.

Maddock smiled and thanked her, then followed her into a small office, Bones and Kaylin following behind.

Admiral Franklin Meriwether, a broad, white-haired man, sat behind a massive mahogany desk. A laptop computer, telephone, and a ship in a bottle were the only items on the dark, wooden surface. Covering the wall behind him were framed degrees, certificates of achievement, and photographs of Meriwether with various comrades which told the story of his naval career. One of the photographs, a framed color print, showed Meriwether with his arm around the shoulders of his former underling, Dane Maddock.

"Maddock," the Admiral greeted him in a surly tone. "When will I ever get to stop pulling your chestnuts out of the fire?" He stood and reached across the desk, clasping Maddock's hand in a firm shake.

"Come on, now. Why would you say that, Admiral?" Maddock feigned innocence, knowing that he was not fooling his old commanding officer for one moment.

"I'm not sure. Either it's because you show up in my office unannounced after my not having heard from you in two years or because you had the audacity to lie about my expecting you." Meriwether sat down, an angry look in his eyes.

"I'm sorry I haven't kept in touch," Maddock said, truthfully. "After Melissa…" He halted. If he said no more, he could still retain his composure. Even after two years, it still hurt more than he could stand.

"I know, son," Meriwether said, his voice softening. "It was a shock to us all."

From the corner of his eye, Maddock saw Kaylin cock her head and fix him with a questioning glance. Bones tapped her on the shoulder and shook his head.

"Besides," Meriwether said, "the phone lines work both ways. I have not been in touch, either. Sit down, all of you." He gestured to a large leather sofa that sat against the wall opposite him beneath a framed oil painting of a three-mast sailing ship battling a vicious storm.

The three of them seated themselves; then Maddock introduced his companions.

"Admiral, this is my friend, Uriah Bonebrake." Bones stood and shook hands with the retired admiral, who fixed him with an appraising look.

"A SEAL," he said, nodding at Bones, "if I don't miss my mark. And I rarely do."

"Yes, I was," Bones said, looking surprised. "Do we know one another?"

"No, I can just tell sometimes," Meriwether said. "I've had a few years of experience with your lot." He turned his attention from Bones to Kaylin.

"And may I present," Maddock said, "Miss Kaylin Maxwell. Her father was…"

"I remember your father," Meriwether interrupted. "A fine officer, Maxwell was. Damn fine."

"Thank you," Kaylin said, her head bowed a little. Maddock suddenly remembered he was not the only one grieving a loved one. "That's kind of you to say."

"How is he doing?" Meriwether asked. "Haven't heard from him in more years than I've heard from Maddock here. Hope he's enjoying his retirement."

Kaylin's face turned red, and her eyes glistened. She looked away, unable to reply.

"I'm sorry to tell you," Maddock answered quickly, "Maxie died last month."

"Oh, I didn't hear," the Admiral said. An odd look crossed his face. "You have my sympathy. I wish I could have been there to pay my respects."

"We kept the memorial service very small," Kaylin said quietly. Apparently being around Navy men was bringing back painful memories.

"Now, tell me why you're here," Meriwether said. "I assume it's important, so you'd better fill me in."

Maddock quickly recounted their tale, beginning with Maxie's search for the *Dourado*, and finishing with the details of Sowell and Wrexham's treachery.

When Maddock had finished his story, Meriwether sat quietly, rubbing his chin. He turned around and stared at the pictures on the wall behind his desk for some time. Finally, he spoke.

"How did you come to choose Professor Sowell to examine the sword?"

"I know him mostly by reputation," Maddock admitted. "Bones and I have used him as a resource for a few projects. We've mostly exchanged e-mails." He folded his arms across his chest and stared at the ship-in-the-bottle, thinking how foolish he had been to trust a relative stranger. "I figured whoever was following us couldn't infiltrate the academy. I didn't count on an entirely new adversary."

"Sit there for a minute. Let me check something out," Meriwether said in his abrupt manner. He picked up the phone and dialed an extension. He asked the person on the other end a few pointed questions about Sowell and Wrexham, punctuated by disapproving grunts. Finally, seeming satisfied with the answers he received, he hung up the phone and returned his attention to Maddock and his friends.

"Neither Sowell nor Wrexham has reported anything about this sword to their superiors," Meriwether said, clearly annoyed. "They are definitely acting on their own. That alone is probably enough to keep the three of you out of hot water."

"Thank you," Bones and Kaylin said in unison.

"Not so fast." The Admiral held up a beefy hand to silence them. "Maddock beat up a Naval Academy professor. Then you," he turned to Bones, "knocked out an officer, tied him up, and left him in the basement.

"I believe I could let those things slide, considering that the two of them were dishonest at best, traitors at worst. What concerns me is that this sword might actually be of some benefit to our armed forces. If this metal has the qualities that you say it does, I think the military needs to know about it." He turned and fixed Maddock with an intense gaze. "It's quite a conundrum, isn't it?"

"Admiral Meriwether," Kaylin spoke up, "my father lost his life in pursuit of this sword. We have to finish what we started. There's a mystery that must be solved."

"Why do you need to solve the mystery?" Meriwether boomed, slapping his palms on his desk. "You've found the sword. You've done what Maxwell set out to do."

"My father was killed because of this sword. We have almost been killed as well. We have no idea who is after us, or who killed him. Perhaps if we can solve the mystery, we can find out who these people are."

Meriwether stared at Kaylin. His face betrayed nothing.

"It's also possible," Bones said, "that even if we were to turn the sword over to you, those people could still be after us for what we know, either to get the information or to suppress it. The only way to end this is to solve the puzzle."

The Admiral nodded thoughtfully, cupping his chin in his hand and staring at the portrait behind them.

Maddock saw an opening and took it.

"Admiral, the Navy has all of Sowell's findings to work with until this is over. Let us finish what we started, and I promise you that when this is over, we will do our best to see to it that you have the opportunity to study it." He looked at Kaylin, hoping she would not contradict him. She looked back at him angrily but nodded in agreement.

Meriwether exhaled long and loud. With a shake of his head, he returned his gaze to Maddock and the others.

"Well then," Meriwether said, clapping his hands, "I'll make a deal with you."

Chapter 23

Maddock rubbed his eyes and fought to stay awake as the tour guide droned on. The guide was an American and appeared to be in his early retirement years. A fringe of white hair showed at the back of his head beneath his tan pith helmet. The sun was apparently not agreeing with the man, as his burned, red face attested, but he did seem knowledgeable if a bit dry.

"Petra was the stronghold and treasure city of an ancient Arabic people who were called the Nabataeans. It was situated near the points of intersection of great caravan routes from Gaza on the Mediterranean Sea, Damascus, Elath on the Red Sea, and the Persian Gulf. From the fourth century B.C. until the second century A.D., Petra was the capital of the Nabataean Kingdom. The Romans conquered it at the beginning of the second century A.D. and made it part of the Roman province of Arabia Petraea. The city continued to thrive in the second and third centuries, but later, when the rival city of Palmyra took away most of Petra's trade, its importance declined. It was conquered by the Muslims in the seventh century and captured by the Crusaders in the twelfth century. Afterward, it gradually fell into ruin."

Maddock looked at Kaylin, who was seated next to him. She was studiously making notes in a small journal book, despite the fact that they both already knew these things.

"The site of the ancient city was rediscovered in 1812 by the Swiss explorer Johann Burckhardt," the guide continued.

Maddock was tempted to ask him who was the first to excavate the city, but knew that he should not risk drawing that sort of attention to himself. He shifted in his seat and exhaled loudly. Kaylin frowned at him and kept writing.

"Petra is known both for its natural beauty and for its magnificent monuments. You will see, when you approach the city, that it may be entered only through a chasm which is, in some places, no more than twelve feet wide. Along the ravine are the ancient structures carved out of the walls of solid rock, the most famous of which include the Khaznet Firaoun, a temple also known as the Treasury of the Pharaohs, and a semicircular theater capable of seating about three thousand persons. All along the rock face are rows of tombs hewn out of the solid stone. The remains of Petra bear witness to its former power, wealth, and prestige."

Maddock looked around. About twenty yards away, Bones sat in the midst of a different tour group, probably getting the same boring spiel. He wore a ridiculous looking wide-brimmed straw hat, wraparound shades, and an orange and yellow Hawaiian print shirt. He appeared to be amusing himself by constantly raising his hand and asking questions. Maddock could not hear what his friend was asking, but judging by the look on the tour guide's face and the snickers of the group's other members, Bones was up to his usual foolishness. Next to Bones, looking annoyed, sat Admiral Meriwether.

Meriwether's "deal" had been to make all of the arrangements for this trip to Petra, including false identities for the four of them and inspection-free transportation on a Navy plane, in exchange for Maddock and the others allowing him to take part in the "adventure," as he called it. Maddock wondered if his old commanding officer were regretting his decision right about now.

The four of them were registered in separate tour groups for today. Beginning the next morning, they would be volunteering for one of the archaeological digs that were taking place within the ancient city. Maddock hoped that they could slip away in time to find whatever lay at the coordinates the writing on the sword had pinpointed.

"If there are no questions, we'll head down to Petra," the guide said. He removed his hat and ran his fingers through the fringe of short, white hair. The look on his face indicated that he was not eager to field questions. Hearing none, he motioned for the group to follow him.

The track wound down the hill from the small village of Wady Musa, with its neatly terraced gardens and vineyards looking more like a model than reality. Upon entering the valley, Maddock had his first impression of the strangeness of the place. Rocks weathered by time into rounded masses like domed towers stood above them. As they continued on, the facade of an occasional tomb showed in a side valley or recess. Everything was so different from what they had just left behind that Maddock had the sensation of having wandered into another world. It felt nightmarishly surreal like he was walking through the abode of the dead.

The valley narrowed. A sheer cliff in front seemed to offer little promise of further progress. Rounding a corner, a great dam built of carefully dressed blocks of stone filled the valley from side to side and confirmed the impression, but the guide led them through a narrow cleft in the cliff face just by the wall.

"So this is the road to Petra," Maddock said to himself. "A handful of men could hold it against an army."

Kaylin nodded in agreement.

The path ran along a dry torrent bed, the sheer cliffs on either side rising higher and higher as they penetrated deeper into the heart of the mountains. Here it seemed to be perpetual twilight, with an occasional glint of sun on the cliff face high above. The pathway widened and narrowed intermittently. Maddock looked above him and saw that, in places, the cliff tops nearly touched. There was little sound beyond the shuffling of feet and the occasional rustle of shrubbery in the faint breeze.

"This road is called the Siq," the guide announced. "As you can see, on this side is a channel cut in the rock, which originally carried water to the inhabitants of Petra from the springs at Wady Musa."

The road twisted and turned. At this point, Maddock could only see a few yards ahead. The way became interminably slow, one featureless stretch giving way to another, then another. He was beginning to feel antsy when suddenly, startlingly, the end of the chasm appeared.

Framed in the cleft before them was the facade of a great tomb, dazzlingly bright in the sunlight. The change from the gloom of the Siq was so sudden that, for a moment, Maddock felt dazed and bewildered. He glanced at Kaylin, who was squinting and shading her eyes.

Gradually their consciousness began to absorb the glowing beauty and perfect proportions of the sculpture, the subtle coloring of the rock, and the soft green foreground of oleanders.

"This tomb is called the Khazneh or Treasury, and the urn at the top carries the marks of many bullets which have been fired at it in the hope of shattering it and releasing the treasure which local tradition says is hidden there. The rock face in which it is carved is sheltered from winds and rain, and the Khazneh is in consequence the best preserved of all the monuments. Most others are badly weathered, for the soft sandstone quickly submits to the battering of wind-driven sand and rain, and the sharp lines of the sculpture are reduced to a vague outline. Even here the bases of the columns, where it is a softer strata of stone, have weathered somewhat." The guide quickly led them through the open area.

Maddock looked at his wrist, checking the GPS monitor that was made to look like an oversized watch. Meriwether had made certain that all four of them had one. They were not far from their target location.

Beyond this clearing, the gorge narrowed again, with great tombs on either side. A little farther on was a theater cut out of the living rock. Apparently, in the course of cutting this theater, many tombs were sliced in half, and their inner chambers now stood open to the sunlight.

Soon they came to a place where the hills fell back on either side, leaving an open space about a mile long and three-quarters of a mile wide.

"Here, on the slopes," the guide said, "was the actual city, its temples, palaces, baths and private houses, with a fine paved street following the line of the stream, and bridges reaching across at intervals. This was the great capital of the Nabataeans, from which, at the height of their power, they ruled the country as far north as Damascus. There was an earlier Edomite town on the site, but of that, practically no traces now remain. The city was extensively occupied from about the fifth century B.C. to the fifth century A.D. and was at its heyday during that time.

"All the monuments and buildings now visible belong, however, to the Nabataean and Roman periods. The extreme softness of the sandstone prevented any finely detailed work being done, and the sculptors had to devise a style to suit their material. This they did very effectively, and it is a tribute to their skill in design that none of the tombs, however small, seems dwarfed by the great cliffs which tower above them. They all fit perfectly into the general picture and do not in any way detract from the natural beauties of the site.

Maddock looked around. From the open space of the town site, valleys went off in all directions. Thank goodness for the GPS units. Otherwise, they could spend hours wandering up and down these narrow ravines. The ravines appeared to be lined on both sides with houses and tombs, of infinite variety and size. Occasional flights of steps wound their way up the sides of the mountains. They were not straight channels, but winding courses, their depths hidden by twists and turns.

"Many of the tombs are occupied by Arabs. During the day, you will hear them herding their flocks of goats. After sunset, you will likely see their campfires, and perhaps hear occasional snatches of song."

Maddock was surprised at this bit of information. He had always been under the impression that the entirety of Petra was abandoned, like the cliff dwellings of Mesa Verde. At least the throngs of tourists and the many natives would make their searching around less noticeable.

The guide paused and motioned for everyone to circle around. He began describing some of the larger tombs, which were found in the northeast area of the city. Maddock gradually worked his way to the back of the crowd. When he was out of sight of the tour guide, he consulted his GPS again and then looked around to get his bearings. If his estimation was accurate, the location indicated in the writing on the sword lay to the northeast of where they stood. Looking in that direction, he saw that two narrow defiles snaked out of the canyon. Either could be the right one. Kaylin squeezed through the crush of the crowd and sidled up next to him.

"Well, boyfriend," she said the word with intentional irony, "what do you want to do first?" She had a pretty smile. More than pretty. Why hadn't he noticed it before?

Maddock ignored the boyfriend comment. Meriwether had suggested that the two of them pose as husband and wife. Maddock had refused, but Kaylin took it in stride though she seemed disappointed.

"The tour ends in an hour," he said, pushing away thoughts of her smile. "We don't have to report for the dig until after lunch. Let's see if we can 'accidentally' wander away from the group."

She nodded her agreement and reached out to take his hand. They walked slowly around the ring of tourists, pretending to take in the scenery. When they were certain that their guide's attention was diverted, they strolled quickly but casually away from their group.

About fifty yards away, they blended into the fringes of another tour group. Bones and the Admiral were in this group, but the two pairs made a point to pretend that they did not know one another. Maddock and Kaylin casually skirted these people in the same fashion that they had moved around their old group. When opportunity arose, they wandered away.

They were now very close to the two ravines that Maddock had identified as likely candidates. Still pretending to gawk at the scenery, though in truth the gawking came easily in this magnificent setting, Maddock pulled out his cell phone and called up Bones' number. He felt a bit foolish calling someone who stood less than a hundred yards away, but it was the only way he could communicate with his friends without anyone seeing them talk to one another.

It took what seemed an interminably long time for the connection to be made, which was fine with Maddock. Not that he believed anyone would realize that the two of them were talking to one another, but the delay did not hurt their ruse.

"Yep," Bones answered.

"We're headed northeast," Maddock said.

"East northeast," Bones corrected, "I saw you pass by."

"I can't tell for certain where exactly the GPS is going to place us. We'll take the ravine on the right. Let us get out of sight, and then you and Meriwether take the defile on the left. I'm assuming the cliffs will block cell phone reception, so let's get back into the open in one hour and call each other."

"Do you really want us coming out of the clefts at the same time?" Bones asked.

"Negative. We'll head out in fifty."

"If I don't hear from you, I'm coming after you," his friend said.

"Same here," Maddock replied.

"Yes, Kemosabe," Bones joked and ended the connection.

Maddock and Kaylin entered the narrow cut in the rock façade. Maddock half expected to hear someone calling for them to rejoin the tour group, but apparently no one had noticed their departure. They came to a sharp bend in the rock, and behind them, the tour groups disappeared from sight.

The shade was even deeper in this constricted space. Faint sunlight bounded down the walls, casting a dull pink glow on the hard, sandy loam at their feet. Maddock consulted his GPS. Fortunately, the unit was still receiving a strong signal. They were coming closer to their destination. He picked up the pace.

They made two more turns, eventually ending up at a blank rock face. Maddock scanned the rocky ledges above, letting his sight gradually trail down the walls to the ground below. He saw nothing. He felt Kaylin tugging at his arm.

"I see something up there." She pointed up and to the left, high up in the rocks.

Maddock looked in the direction she indicated. Behind a small outcropping of scrub lay what appeared to be a small cave. In the half-light of the gorge, his eyes had passed right over it.

"How do we get there?" she asked. "Did they have hand trails like the Anasazi?"

The ancient settlers of the American southwest had built their cities in rock overhangs high in cliffs not entirely unlike these. The dwellings were accessible by hand and foot trails, which were little more than depressions chiseled in the wall.

"I don't know," Maddock said. "But I believe the hand trails usually ran from the top of the cliff down to the overhang. Looks like we'll have to free climb."

Kaylin consulted her wrist unit.

"It's in the right direction," she said. "Ready for a climb, monkey man?"

"Sure," Maddock said, laughing, "send the scuba diver clambering up the precarious rock face."

"Forgive me," she said, grinning, "but doesn't SEAL stand for 'sea, air, land?'"

"No," Maddock replied with a straight face. "It stands for 'seduce every attractive lady.'"

"I guess I should be offended, then," Kaylin said. "You certainly haven't tried to seduce me. "What's the matter? Am I not pretty enough for you?"

Her tone was playful, but there was a questioning look in her eyes. Why did women always have to twist everything you say into some weird criticism of their physical appearance?

"I'm retired, remember?" Maddock said, trying to lighten her mood a bit.

"Sorry, but you're not using that line on me. Once a SEAL, always a SEAL. Now let's check out that cave."

Maddock scanned the rock face from the ground up to the opening of the cave. He studied it carefully, selecting the cracks and outcroppings that would provide the best handholds. When he had planned his route, he set to climbing.

He made his way up the face of the rock at a steady pace. He looked neither up nor down but kept his eyes just ahead of his hands, picking out the next hold. He trusted the route he had selected and allowed himself no second-guessing. Foot by foot, he scaled the wall. It was a strenuous climb, but not a particularly challenging one. The route he had chosen avoided sections in which the rock wall leaned out over the chasm. Without the proper equipment, he would not have attempted to scale any of the most dangerous outcroppings.

After what felt like an hour, but was probably more like six or seven minutes, he hauled himself up onto the narrow ledge in front of the small cave. He turned and offered his hand to Kaylin, who shook her head and pulled herself up.

Maddock felt a pang of disappointment when he looked at the cave. It was small: no more than five feet high, and about the same width. It ended in a blank wall about twelve feet back.

"Sorry," Kaylin said, clearly disappointed. "All of that climbing for nothing."

Maddock checked his GPS and found that they were very close to the targeted spot. In fact, their targeted location was to the west of where they stood: either atop the plateau between the two ravines or inside the mass of rock. He took a few steps into the cave, hunching so as not to hit his head on the ceiling. He could have sworn that he felt a gentle breeze on his face. He dug deep into his pocket and found the mini Mag-Lite he always carried, flicked it on, and played the beam across the back wall.

"Kay, look at this!"

The cave did not end in a blank wall but took a sharp turn to the left. Kaylin, her enthusiasm apparently renewed by this bit of good fortune, hurried to his side.

They turned the corner and found themselves in an even tighter passage. They could still walk side by side, but barely so. The ceiling gently rose to a height of over six feet, allowing Maddock to stand up straight though he still instinctively felt that he ought to duck down. About twenty paces in, he noticed goose bumps rising on his arms. The air had grown markedly cooler, and he could still feel the faint breeze on his face.

The tunnel snaked back to the right. The path began to slope gently downward and was slightly moist. Maddock put his hand out against the wall and was surprised to feel that it was smooth to the touch. He halted and shone his light along the wall.

"Pictographs," Kaylin whispered in awe.

There was no one around to hear their voices, but it somehow seemed appropriate to speak softly.

"Do you have your notebook with you?" Dan asked in an equally quiet tone.

"I've got my digital camera," Kaylin replied. She produced a small camera from her fanny pack and began snapping pictures of the carvings.

The pictographs ran horizontally from left-to-right, just above Maddock's eye level, along the left wall in a single row for a distance of about eight feet. Below them was a row of characters that resembled writing. Maddock could not decide if they looked more like runes or alphabetic figures. There was something vaguely familiar about them, but he was no scholar. He checked the opposite wall and confirmed that it was bereft of any carving.

"Got them," Kaylin said. She checked the display on the back of her camera, using the zoom feature to ensure that she had gotten a clear picture of every part of the carving. Apparently satisfied with her work, she led them deeper down the tunnel.

Maddock estimated that they had traveled about seventy yards, including the jog to the left. Measuring from the outside wall, he guessed they were about fifty yards deep into the massive stone plateau. Though he knew it was a futile attempt, he checked his wrist unit. Sure enough, the rock walls precluded any signal from reaching them.

As they progressed down the tunnel, Maddock caught a faint whisper of sound, like wind rustling through tree branches. As the sound grew louder, he realized that he was hearing the sound of running water. Somewhere far beneath them was an underground stream. Was there a passage leading down?

The tunnel veered to the right, and they came to an abrupt halt. A narrow crevice, no more than six inches wide, cut across the tunnel. A few feet beyond the crack, a massive rock fall blocked the tunnel. Most likely, some sort of seismic activity had caused both the fissure and the tunnel collapse. Maddock stepped across the gap and carefully inspected the pile of rocks and debris. There was no sign of any opening. He shone his light all over the pile, looking for a sign of empty space behind the wall, but he could see nothing. Even if he had believed that it might be possible to clear away some of the debris, he dared not risk another collapse. Based on his inspection, though, he was satisfied that the tunnel in front of them was impassable.

"There's no way through?" Kaylin asked, her voice tinged with disappointment.

Maddock shook his head as he turned. He knelt and shone his light down into the crevice. Kaylin added her brighter beam, and they peered into the depths of the ancient stone. The cut was incredibly deep. Dan thought he could make out a slight twinkle of light reflected on water, but he could not be certain. The sound of the underground stream was audible, and the cool breeze, though faint, was decidedly refreshing. They sat there for a moment, silently peering into the thin defile. Maddock finally broke the silence.

"I guess we'd better head back. Bones will be looking for us if he can't reach us by phone."

Kaylin nodded, her face twisted into a disappointed frown. She said nothing, but Maddock believed he could read her thoughts.

"We're close," he said, laying a hand on her shoulder. "I can feel it."

Chapter 24

Bones muttered a curse under his breath and adjusted Goliath's sword, which hung strapped across his back inside a long, leather, camera tripod case. Neither he nor the others of his crew had come up with a good idea of how to safely store the sword while they were out and about. They all had also agreed, perhaps irrationally, that the sword should remain with them at all times. Consequently, the camera equipment bag had been the best idea they had devised. Bones had concealed the sword inside a black cover made of the same material as the camera bag and kept it inside along with a camera and an actual tripod. He had maintained the ruse by setting up the apparatus and taking several very bad pictures. He had not actually developed the film, but he knew what his talents were, and photography was not one of them.

The dig had quickly grown boring. At Maddock's instruction, he and Meriwether, or 'Franklin' as the Admiral insisted on being called, had explored this same ravine the previous day, and found nothing but an occasional tomb or shallow cave. Nothing like the passageway that Maddock and Kaylin had discovered. According to the GPS readouts, their target area lay somewhere in the center of the giant mass of rock directly between the gorges.

"This blows," he said aloud to no one in particular. "Some vacation."

"Come now Uri," Meriwether said, hefting a bucket of parched earth, "archaeology is fun."

"Tell you what, Frankie, you call me Uri one more time and I'll scalp you with my tripod."

The broad-shouldered man chuckled and returned to his task of putting buckets of dirt through a mesh sifter.

So far, they had uncovered some fascinating rocks, and something that Bones believed was a fossilized goat turd. Muttering a curse, Bones took off his straw hat and fanned his face. Archaeology required a meticulous nature. That was why it was a perfect pastime to an officer, and a total drag to an impulsive, eccentric treasure hunter like himself.

"Mister Uriah, would you come here, please?" The dig foreman called.

Bones, unaccustomed to being called by his Christian name, did not respond at first. The man called his name again. Bones had quickly earned the reputation of being a bit surly. The foreman, a wisp of a man who looked to Bones more like a missionary than an archaeologist, seemed more than a bit intimidated by the tall, muscular Cherokee with the long ponytail and perpetual scowl. Bones had not helped matters by constantly playing with his hunting knife.

"Mister Uriah, a word, please?" the man said. He stood with his arm folded across his chest, his chapped lips pursed in a petulant frown.

Bones stood and slowly turned and faced the man. He bared his straight, white teeth in a predatory grin, and narrowed his eyes wickedly.

"You want something, Mr. Jonas?" he asked. Behind him, Meriwether whispered something disapproving. Bones ignored him. He was hot, bored, and anxious to do some exploring.

"Uh, yes," Jonas said, drastically altering his tone of voice. "I was wondering since you don't seem to be, shall we say, enjoying yourself if you might like to take some photographs of the dig?"

Bones inwardly cringed. The last thing he wanted to do was to take more pictures of these pasty skinned, middle aged, Indiana Jones wannabes in their fresh off the rack safari clothes, and their John Lennon-style shades that he supposed were supposed to make them look professorial. Framed by sunburned faces and perched atop zinc oxide coated noses, they looked silly at best. He took a deep breath, looked up at the sky, and tried to think of a good lie.

As he stared up at the crest of the ridge, inspiration struck. His cold smile melted into one of warmth and sincerity.

"I'd love to," he said. He was amused at the look of surprise on Jonas' face at this sudden bout of agreeability. "Tell you what. I'd like to get some overhead shots. I'm going to climb this ridge over here," he pointed behind them, "and take a few pictures from up above. Shouldn't take too long."

Before the dig supervisor could protest, Bones turned and strode down the defile, leaving the thin man standing open-mouthed behind him.

A few quick twists of the gorge and he had reached the spot where, yesterday, he had observed the remains of an ancient staircase running down from the top of the cliff. Time and weather had worn away the bottom portion of the stairs, and they ended about halfway down the stone face. There had been neither time nor opportunity to explore the cliff top on the previous day. He wanted to get up top and take a GPS reading, to see if there was anything suspicious-looking up above. He positioned the sword comfortably on his back, tightened the straps of the camera case, and began his climb.

The rocky face was irregular, with lots of protrusions upon which to find footholds. An experienced climber, he quickly made his way up the face until the rock wall smoothed out about ten feet below the foot of the ancient staircase.

Bones inspected the stone above him and noticed a thin crack running upward from left to right at about a thirty-five degree angle. The crack appeared to be just wide enough to fit his fingers inside. Taking a deep breath, he let go of the rock with his left hand and reached over and upward for the crevice. He could not quite reach. He drew his hand back, carefully centered his right foot on the outcropping on which he stood, and slightly loosened his grip on the wall with his right hand, allowing his fingertips to slip back until they had only a small purchase on the rock. Sometimes, it's a matter of inches, he thought. He refrained from mentally turning the thought into a crude innuendo and instead focused on the task at hand.

Biting his lower lip, he raised his left foot and stretched out to his left, reaching again for the crack in the wall. His stomach fluttered, and for a brief instant, he felt certain that he was going to fall. Then, he felt his fingers grasp the lip of the crevice. Pressing his body against the rock, he worked his fingers deeper into the fissure until they were in up to the second knuckle. Certain now of his grip, he scrabbled with his left foot until he found what amounted to little more than a rough edge against which to brace the bottom of his foot. He exhaled slowly, took another breath, and pushed up hard off his right foot, at the same time pulling up with his left hand.

His right hand caught the edge of the crevice, and he hung suspended on the cliff face.

"Why the hell am I doing this?" he asked aloud. No one answered, so he decided to keep climbing.

He pulled up as much as he could with his left hand, allowing his weight to swing to that side. He then scooted his right hand farther up the crevice, gripped tight, and shifted his weight to the right. Repeating this process, he worked his way up the wall. It was slow going. Twice he had to stop to catch his breath. The muscles of his shoulders and neck were knotted, and his fingers screamed in agony. He felt around with the bottom of his foot and found a tiny indentation in which he could fit the tip of his boot. It was a small relief, but it took some of the burden of his body weight from his fingers.

A strange tickling sensation ran across the back of his right hand and slowly down his arm. He looked up.

"You have got to be kidding me!" he shouted.

He had read about the black scorpion but had never seen one in person. It was monstrous, nearly four inches long. Rather than black, its color was a dark reddish-brown. Its stinger, thick and menacing, curled up above its body like a snake poised to strike.

Bones froze, irrationally hoping that the deadly arachnid would turn around and creep away. No such luck. The scorpion paused, then proceeded further along his arm. Bones tried blowing at the creature but to no avail. It held fast to his arm and continued to make its way ever closer to his head. Up close, its pincers looked like crab claws. Bones flexed and relaxed the muscles of his arm, blew another hard puff of air, and then another, but could not dislodge the scorpion.

He groaned. As he saw it, there were two choices. Climb to the top and hope that the scorpion did not sting him before he could get it off him, or let go with his left hand and try to dislodge the scorpion without falling or being stung. Figuring his odds were better if he reached the top before dealing with the nasty creature, he made up his mind to continue his climb. His plans changed when the scorpion, for no apparent reason, put on a burst of speed and shot over his shoulder and onto his neck.

Instinctively, he grabbed for it with his right hand. His stomach lurched as he swung to his left, holding on with one hand. Without thinking, he grabbed the scorpion and flung it away in one quick motion. He exhaled slowly, unable to believe what he had done, and even more surprised that he had not been stung. His adrenaline pumping full-force now, he hauled himself the last few feet up to the ancient stairway.

He reached the top of the steps and took a moment to catch his breath and gather himself. After a moment, he stood and surveyed the wide plateau. It was a featureless landscape, save a few stray boulders and some sparse patches of dry grass. At least it would be an easy walk. Bones consulted his GPS and found that his target location lay to the southeast. He quickly made his way to the site, keeping an eye out for more scorpions. When the GPS display told him that he had hit his spot, he stopped, looked down, and swore.

He saw nothing. The ground beneath his feet was flat, clear of any debris. Whatever the sword was pointing to must be underground somewhere. After a visual inspection revealed nothing out of the ordinary, he set about inspecting the area around the target location.

Keeping his eyes on the ground, he began by walking the spot in a pattern: four paces, turn left, four paces, turn left, and so on. With each complete circuit, he stepped out two paces, and enlarged his square. Eventually, he had covered most of the plateau and found nothing.

He supposed he had better snap a few pictures before the folks at the dig started wondering what had happened to him. He unslung the long case that held his camera equipment and the sword and removed his camera and tripod. Making his way to the ledge directly above the dig, he wondered if perhaps the blocked tunnel Maddock had found might be the passageway they sought. From what his friend had said, that would be a hard row to hoe.

The faint sound of shouting caught his attention. It seemed to be coming from beneath him. He laid the camera down, knelt and looked down over the edge. The dig was deserted, but at the base of the cliff, he could see several people milling around and talking loudly. They appeared to be looking at something in the face of the rock. He called down to them, but they seemed to be unable to hear him above the sound of their own conversation.

His cell phone rang. Maddock was calling him.

"Yeah?"

"Bones, you've got to get down here right away," Maddock's voice, though tense, sounded excited.

"Sure. Where are you?"

"Look down."

Bones peered back over the edge and saw Maddock standing on the outer fringes of the crowd. Neither of them ventured to gesture to one another, maintaining the fiction that they were complete strangers.

"What are you doing with my dig group?" Bones asked. "Mr. Jonas will smack you with his pocketbook if he catches you."

"Just get back down here. You'll see when you get here."

The connection went dead. Bones cursed and debated dropping a rock down on Maddock's head. Just a very small pebble, something that would sting a bit. He thought the better of it, though. He was eager to find out what exactly was going on down below.

The climb down was much easier than the climb up had been. A few minutes later, he trotted up beside Maddock, who was standing at the edge of the crowd. He fixed his friend with a questioning look. The blond man merely nodded toward the wall. Bones turned toward the wall and gasped.

Someone had apparently uncovered a false wall in one of the broad recesses in the rock. The wall had been knocked down, and the rubble hastily cleared away. Real archaeologists will have a fit at the impulsiveness, Bones thought, but they won't scream too much once they see what these amateurs have uncovered.

Beyond where the wall had been, was a deep alcove. In the foreground was what appeared to be a well, but it was the back wall that drew everyone's attention.

Carved into the back of the alcove was an incredibly well-preserved relief sculpture depicting five giant men engaged in battle with a throng of much smaller warriors. The two giants on either side were displayed in profile, laying about with heavy broadswords. Dead soldiers lay strewn about their feet, graphically depicted in various states of dismemberment.

In contrast, the warrior in the center was rendered from the front, facing directly toward them. Bones was fascinated by the detail. The towering warrior was outfitted in typical Bronze Age armor and a small helm, from which flowed a wild mane of hair. His face was framed by a thick beard, and his eyes seemed to bore into Bones with evil intent. He held his giant sword upraised, and his small, round, shield in the center of his body.

Maddock turned to Bones, smiled broadly, and whispered one word. "Goliath."

Chapter 25

Maddock, Bones, Kaylin, and Meriwether crept along the pathway that led down into Petra. The full moon cast odd shadows among the tombs and dark recesses in the walls. In the places where the pathway narrowed significantly, the darkness was almost complete.

"What do you think we're going to find?" Bones whispered, looking around.

"Hopefully, a doorway of some sort," Maddock answered in a hushed voice. He was not certain what they would discover, but he had a strong suspicion. "The carving in the center," he began.

"The one you believe represents Goliath?" Kaylin asked.

"Right. You notice he's facing forward, but the others are all facing sideways. Well, there's another difference." He paused, waiting to see if anyone was thinking along the same lines. "His shield is different, as well. It's much smaller, perfectly round, and held at the very center of his body."

"You're right," Bones said after a moment. "I didn't really think about it at the time, but it does look...wrong."

Maddock held up a hand to silence everyone as they approached the dig site. Though the discovery had initially caused a bit of a stir, it had quickly become business as usual in an area rife with history. Only one person, an archaeology student from Tel Aviv, minded the site. The term "minded" was used loosely, Maddock thought, as the young man was apparently asleep in his tent, a good fifty yards away.

They crept closer to the site, moving cautiously so as not to disturb the sleeping scientist. They cautiously made their way around the ceremonial well, gaping black in the darkness, and walked to the center of the wall.

Maddock knelt in front of the center figure of the carving, produced a small flashlight, and shone its tight beam on the carved shield. After a brief inspection, he put the flashlight between his teeth, stood, and grasped the shield with both hands. Meriwether and Kaylin added their flashlight beams to his. His heart pounded. He hoped this would work.

He gave the shield a great twist to the right, grunting with the effort. Nothing happened. He took a breath and tried again, with the same result.

"What do you think?" Bones whispered.

Maddock did not answer. He was thankful that the darkness kept the others from seeing the redness in his face. He had been so certain. What if...

He grasped the shield again, and this time twisted counterclockwise. The stone held fast. He threw every ounce of his strength into the effort until he could feel the veins in his head bulging. He was about to give up when he felt the stone give. Slowly, inch by inch, the shield rotated. It spun a full quarter turn to the left before grinding to a firm halt. Maddock let out the breath he had held, and then pulled. The shield came free in his hands. His eyes widened with excitement when he saw what lay in the center of the carving.

Where the shield had hung in the middle of the warrior's chest was what could only be described as a giant keyhole. It was a large, iron circle, with a vertical slot slicing through the center. It appeared to Maddock to be rust-free, and in good condition, protected by the dry climate. The others pushed forward to examine it more closely.

"How do we open it?" Kaylin whispered, running a long, slender finger around the edge.

Maddock paused, taking a moment to gently lay the stone shield on the ground. Perhaps he should be nervous, but having been correct about the shield, he was even more confident in his hypothesis. He removed the scabbard and slid the sword free.

"Ahh," Bones intoned, understanding now evident in his voice. Maddock shone his light along the length of the blade, examining it carefully. He then turned the light onto the keyhole and inspected it. Satisfied, he took the sword's hilt in both hands and leveled it at the keyhole. He rotated it so that the serrated edge faced up, and before doubts could arise, he thrust it forward.

The sword slid home with a scarcely audible hiss. Kaylin gasped as the blade disappeared into the slot. Maddock pushed it in until it stopped about ten inches short of the hilt. He let go of the hilt and grasped either side of the crossguard. He first tried turning it counterclockwise, as he had done the shield, but the sword held fast. He then twisted it clockwise. Nothing. He gave it another twist and felt something give. Slowly, the sword turned in the keyhole, rotating a half turn. It halted with a metallic clank, followed by the sound of something behind the wall snapping into place. In the silence of the night, the noise sounded like a thunderclap. All four of them jerked their heads toward the darkened tent but saw no evidence of anyone stirring. Suddenly, Maddock felt the sword being pulled from his grip.

He turned to see the carving of Goliath recede into the wall, revealing inky blackness on either side. Instinctively, he had tightened his grip on the sword when he first felt the tug, and he was pulled off-balance, stumbling toward the dark opening. He loosed his grip on the crossguard, and felt someone grab his belt, steadying him.

"That was graceful," Maddock said, looking back at Bones, who had caught him. "Are we ready to go in?" he asked the group. They all nodded in affirmation. In the dim flashlight glow, he could see that each of them wore the same look: a mix of wonder and excitement.

"You do the honors," Bones said, motioning for Maddock to lead them into the inky blackness behind the wall.

He stepped through the narrow space between the receded carving and the wall. He played his light around in front of him, involuntarily sucking in his breath at what he saw.

"What is it?" Bones whispered, concern in his voice. "Are you all right?"

"Get in here," Maddock said. The others were quickly at his side, shining their lights in front of them.

The cavern was enormous. From the wall behind them, the ceiling swept upward at a sharp angle, reaching a peak about fifty feet above their head. Maddock played his light down the wall, revealing a stone well, the twin of the one outside, and five huge, lidless stone coffins fanned out along the wall behind the well. He took a step forward and then remembered the sword. He turned to see that Bones had already removed it from the keyhole. Accepting the blade from his friend, he returned it to the scabbard.

Meriwether scrutinized the back of the door.

"It's actually a very simple mechanism," he said with surprise. "It's counterweighted and set in a track. Whoever forged the sword didn't make this." He sounded disappointed and more than a bit puzzled.

Kaylin moved ahead of the others to inspect the well. She shone her flashlight down into the blackness. Maddock joined her and peered down into the depths of the hole. Far below, he could see the glint of their beams on water. He heard a faint gurgle.

"An underground river," Kaylin whispered, "and look!" She focused her light at water level. Maddock could barely make out an archway on either side of the well shaft. "It's more than just a ceremonial well. There's something down there. A tunnel?" she mused.

"I don't know," Maddock said. "But this must be how Rienzi got into the tomb without having the sword to unlock it."

"How did he climb up?" Kaylin asked, frowning.

Bones stepped up to the opposite side of the well and squinted down.

"Ha! I thought so. Turn off your flashlights." Maddock, Kaylin, and Meriwether extinguished their lights, leaving the depths of the well illuminated only by the light of Bones' flashlight, which he held above his shoulder, pointing down at an odd angle.

"If you look at it in just the right way," he explained, "you can see handholds carved up one side. I'll bet the well outside is the same."

Maddock tilted his head and moved to his right until, as if by magic, a series of small, oval shadows appeared on the wall. "So whoever made this place sealed it up and climbed out through the wells."

"But what's beyond here?" Kaylin asked.

"Why do you think there's anything else to see?" Meriwether asked, placing his meaty hands on the rim of the well and leaning forward. "Perhaps this is all there is."

"The tunnel goes both directions," Kaylin explained. "I think if we were to climb down and follow the river, we'd find more."

"Why don't we take a look at what's in here, first?" Maddock suggested, turning to face the coffins. He walked to the coffin on the right and shone his light down inside.

The coffin contained a large, humanlike skeleton. The man must have been nine feet tall, with a broad chest and shoulders. The bones were intact but appeared to Maddock to be brittle. Behind Maddock, Bones whistled softly. The man had been buried in full Bronze Age armor. His arms were crossed over his chest, and his sword lay behind him. Though all that remained of him was a hollow shell, he seemed to exude power.

"This one in the center has no head," Meriwether said.

Maddock and the others hurried to the Admiral's side. The skeleton was the twin of the one they had just inspected, or at least from the shoulders down, he thought.

"I guess we've found our friend Goliath," Maddock said. He gripped the edge of the open stone coffin and silently gazed upon the remains of the legendary warrior. He realized, after a few moments, that he was holding his breath. Goliath! Even when they had recovered the sword, he had not truly believed that it was Goliath's weapon. It was a remarkable and mysterious artifact, to be sure, but to be proof that a biblical tale was factual? The idea had been hard for him to swallow.

He had never been a religious man. After Melissa died, he gave up on any notion of a loving god looking down on creation. But now, looking down upon the remains of the unfortunate half of the children's Bible story, he wondered what it all meant.

Beside him, Kaylin fell to her knees and crossed herself, like a good Catholic. Bones and Meriwether knelt down on either side of her, the full impact of what they saw evident in their faces.

"It's true," Kaylin whispered, tears running freely down her cheeks. "We did it. I wish Dad could be here."

"He's here," Meriwether whispered, putting his arm around Kaylin's shoulder, and giving her a grandfatherly hug. She laid her head on his shoulder and continued to gaze in disbelief at Goliath.

Maddock did not say anything. They had proved that Goliath was a historical figure, but that was all. It did not prove anything about God, or life after death, or anything else. He was not selfish enough to say so, not when Kaylin needed to believe it. He stood in silence and tried not to imagine that Melissa was looking over his shoulder.

"It's not enough," Bones suddenly said, raising his head to look at the others.

"What?" Meriwether asked, fixing him with a quizzical glance.

"This doesn't answer everything. There's got to be more somewhere."

Maddock nodded. He understood exactly what Bones was saying. He was feeling the same lack of…completeness was the only word he could think of to describe it.

"We know that this is Goliath's sword," Maddock said. "We know how Rienzi got it. But it doesn't explain the sword itself: how it was made, what the writing signifies."

"Not to mention," Bones added, "why the writing on it pointed to this location."

"Because Goliath and his brothers are buried here," Kaylin said, a look of bewilderment painted upon her face.

"No," Maddock said. He turned the conundrum over in his mind as he spoke. "According to the Bible, David took Goliath's sword after he slew him. The priests kept it for a while, and then David took it for himself when he needed a sword. Obviously, the Philistines recovered it some time later. Which means…"

"Which means that either the writing was etched into the sword long after Goliath was dead," Meriwether interrupted, his face aglow with understanding, "which is unlikely, considering none of our tools could do a thing to it, or it was etched into the blade when the sword was forged."

"Meaning that the coordinates for this location point to something else," Maddock said. By the time he had finished saying it, he was certain. There was more to be discovered.

"You're right," Kaylin said. "Why would you put directions to a gravesite on the sword, and then bury the sword in that same grave?" She stood and put her hands on her hips, looking around. "So what now?"

"I don't know about you three, but right now, I'd like to find a way out of here," Bones said. "We've got company," he whispered.

Chapter 26

Maddock turned and peered through the opening in the rock face, back in the direction from which they had come. Shadows moved stealthily across the moonlit sand. He caught a glimpse of pale light glinting off the barrel of a gun. He could not tell what type, but the length of the barrel told him all that he needed to know.

"How many?" he whispered to Bones.

"At least eight," Bones said. "Probably more. Either way, they've got much more firepower than we do. "

"Should we turn out our flashlights?" Kaylin asked.

"No, then they'll know we've spotted them," Maddock said. "Let them believe they're taking us by surprise, and maybe they'll be less cautious." Maddock hoped his voice carried more optimism than he felt.

"Who do you think they are?" Meriwether whispered, drawing his pistol, an old, Swiss-made SIG P-210, from his fanny pack.

Maddock shrugged. "Probably the same guys who've been after us all along. Either that or Wrexham's got friends."

"How would they find us?" Meriwether protested. "We've been so careful in every detail." His words sounded like a statement, not a question.

"Right now, I don't think that's as important as how we're going to get out of here," Bones said, "because there's no way we'll be able to get back out the way we came."

Maddock knew that his friend was right. He scanned the room one last time, seeing no sign of a secondary egress. He knew what they had to do.

"Down the well," he said, "and make it quick. Bones first, Kay next, then Meriwether."

Bones clamped his small flashlight between his teeth, tucked his Beretta into his belt, and swung over the side into the well. The others complied without protest, although Kaylin appeared quite displeased. Cautiously, they climbed over the edge. Finding their footholds, they slowly disappeared from sight.

Maddock knelt behind the well, positioned so that he could see outside. His Walther he held trained on the opening. In his left hand, he played the flashlight back and forth across the far wall of the cavern, trying to create the illusion that they were still inside looking around.

He stole a quick glance down into the well. The others had not yet reached the bottom, their flashlights bobbing far below where he stood. His heart pounded. How much longer could he wait? He wanted to cover their descent, but if one of their stalkers appeared in the doorway, Maddock would have no choice but to shoot him. After that, the odds of him making it safely down to the bottom would be slim indeed.

He strained to listen for the sound of approaching footsteps. He heard nothing. Whoever these people were, they were good. They had to be close by now. He looked down the well again and thought he saw the reflection of light on the water. The others were close to the bottom. He could start his climb down.

He laid his flashlight on the ground with its beam pointed at the coffin farthest to the right. Perhaps the intruder's attention would be temporarily diverted from the well when they first entered the room. Tucking the Walther into his waistband at the center of his back, he climbed onto the edge of the well, all the while certain that, at any moment, an armed man was going to appear in the doorway while Maddock was at his most vulnerable.

He hung his left foot over the edge and felt for a toehold, but there was none to be found. He moved his foot in a circle against the smooth stone, seeking to gain purchase in the darkness. I should have spotted out my path before I put the flashlight down, he thought. Frustration welled up inside of him. Finally, he found a niche in the wall. Gripping the edge with both hands, he swung the other foot over and quickly found another hold. Cursing the darkness, he began a slow descent. The sword made movement awkward, and he was grateful for its incredible lightness.

He had descended no more than twenty feet when he heard a shuffling above him. Someone had entered the burial chamber. The sword bounced off the back of his thigh as he went. He paused, hastily adjusted it, and then quickened his pace, wondering absently how deep the water down below was, in case he should miss a step.

The hand and footholds were set at regular intervals, and he soon fell into a rhythm. He stole a glance upward and saw that he had covered a good fifty feet. He guessed that he was about halfway down.

He heard a clattering sound, and the faint glow above him seemed to waver. He guessed someone had kicked the flashlight. The followers had obviously proceeded with caution, thoroughly searching the cavern before declaring it empty. He wondered how long it would be before they looked into the well.

He had his answer sooner than he would have liked. A shadowed form appeared in the faint circle of light up above. Now grateful for the darkness, Maddock scrambled down the wall at a pace that bordered on incaution. The figure up above moved away. Maddock kept his eye on the circle that seemed to grow no smaller no matter how quickly he moved down the wall. They couldn't be giving up, could they?

As soon as the thought entered his mind, two faces appeared above him. A gleam of dark metal, and then the sound of automatic weapons fire shattered the cloak of silence. Maddock froze as the bullets ricocheted off the wall behind him and down the shaft below. Holding on tight with his left hand, he freed his Walther as a second burst of gunfire ripped along the wall, this time farther below him.

Taking aim, Maddock squeezed off two shots. He heard a scream, and one of the shadows disappeared from sight. The second man, however, ripped off a long, steady stream of bullets that tore into the wall only a few feet above him. Sharp, stinging pain danced across the top of his skull as fragments of ancient stone cut into his scalp. Idiot! You gave them a target! Hoping that the others were clear of the shaft, he let go and plunged toward the river below.

As he fell, he pulled his knees to his chest, tucked his chin, and drew his hands up to his face. He had only a moment for the fear of being hit by ricocheting bullets to do battle with that of too-shallow water, before the tickling sensation of falling was replaced by the icy impact of his body striking the surface of the underground river.

He kicked downward, and fanned his arms out, trying to keep himself from plunging too deeply. The dark, cold water enveloped him, and then his feet struck bottom. The impact sent waves of pain coursing up his legs, through his groin, and up his spine. He felt his body crumple. A coppery taste filled his mouth. For a brief, panicked moment he thought, *I'm paralyzed.* Then his legs seemed to find a life of their own. Reflexively, they kicked out, and he felt himself rising toward the surface, even as a hard current swept him down the tunnel and away from the deadly gunfire.

He broke the surface in total darkness. He blew a mixture of water and blood from his sinuses, and took a wet gulp of air. Coughing and spitting, he struggled to keep his head above water. He was surprised to find that his arms worked as well as his legs. The cold water dulled the pain in his back, knees, and ankles, but the sensation was there, and that was a good sign. He was also surprised to find he'd maintained his hold on his Walther. He hastily shoved it into his waistband as he swam.

He'd only managed a few feet when his head struck something hard. A loud sound burst through his ears. He felt a brief flash of pain, and then fading…

"Hey, babe. Thought you'd be home by now."
"Sorry, I had to make a stop. I've got a surprise for you!"
"I hate surprises. What is it?"
"Maddock! You are no fun at all."
"I know. Now, what's my surprise?"
"I'm not telling."
"Come on. You know I'm going to get it out of you."
"Fine, just be that way…Daddy."
"What did you say?"
"You're going to be a…AAAAAH!"
Scream. Tires screech. Crash. Glass shatters.
Silence.
"Melissa! Melissa, speak to me! Melissa!"
Silence.

"Melissa?"
Call ended... 0:59

A scream of primordial rage filled his throat, and he rent the veil of unconsciousness. His head was still above water. He must have only been out for a few seconds. Suppressing an angry sob, he focused on staying afloat and pushed the memories back into the recesses of his mind.

The channel was narrow, and he quickly paddled to one side. He tried to find something to grab onto, but the arched walls were smooth and slick. He kept treading water, concerned that hypothermia would set in if he did not get out of the frigid stream sometime soon. He wished that he still had his flashlight. What if he passed by a side passage and could not see it in the darkness?

He banged into the side of the tunnel as the current swept him around a bend, and then silver light exploded around him. Blinded after so long in the semi-darkness of the burial chamber, and the underground waterway, he squeezed his eyes shut. He felt something tighten around his throat. Then several hands were on him, pulling him free of the water. He opened his eyes to see Bones, Kaylin, and Meriwether leaning over him.

"Good thing you had the sword on," Bones said, grinning. "I missed you, but I caught hold of the scabbard."

"Are you all right?" Kaylin asked, looking frightened. "You aren't hurt, are you?"

"Oh yeah," he groaned. "I feel great."

Accepting a hand up from Bones, he climbed to his feet. His ankles screamed in hot pain, but he did not think they were broken. Likewise, his knees and back hurt, but he was still in one piece, which was all that mattered.

"We heard shots," Meriwether said.

"They almost got me," Maddock said hoarsely. He paused and hacked up the last of the water in his lungs. "I don't know if they'll try to follow us, or not. We'd..." He stopped and took a good look at his companions. "Why aren't you wet?"

They all laughed.

"Three tunnels branch off of the shaft of the well just above water level," Bones explained. "They were pretty well concealed, so we couldn't see them from above. Lucky for you, we picked the one that came out downstream."

Maddock looked around. The room was wide, about one hundred feet square. The walls were incredibly smooth, seemingly cut with laser precision into the native rock. Ornate, ivy-wrapped columns climbed the corners. The underground river flowed through a channel, twenty feet wide, that divided the room. Where the water flowed in and out of the room were archways adorned with sculptures of angels dueling with swords.

On either side of the room, wide steps led up to high, arching doorways, each opening into a dark tunnel beyond. Above the arch on either side was the carved figure of an angel in flight. Its wings, rendered in painstaking detail, swept downward around either side of the doorway. Each angel, its face an implacable mask of fury, held aloft a fiery sword in its right hand.

High above, small window-like openings, one in each wall, looked down on them. Maddock craned his neck to look at them. He could not make out anything in the darkened recesses behind the windows, but he could tell that there was open space beyond them.

A random thought broadsided him without warning, and he looked at the other three in confusion.

"Wait a minute," he said. "Where do you think all of this light is coming from?"

"From these." Kaylin pointed to a diamond-shaped stone protruding from the wall nearby. It was about the size of Maddock's hand and glowed an opalescent white. A row of them ran at regular intervals around the room about a third of the way up from the floor. Another row circled the room about two-thirds of the way up, and more were set in a grid-like pattern in the ceiling. How had he failed to notice them?

"Watch what happens," Meriwether said, his voice an excited whisper. He shone his flashlight on one of the stones. When the beam hit the diamond-shaped object, the surface seemed to swirl and flash in an array of colors like mother-of-pearl. The glow that emanated from the stone grew in intensity, and as the light that it generated touched the lights on either side of it, they too shone more brightly. "It absorbs the light and amplifies it." Meriwether sounded entranced.

"What is this place?" Maddock marveled. Before anyone could answer, footsteps sounded from the other side of the room.

Maddock whirled and drew his pistol, hoping that the water had not treated it too roughly. He had allowed himself to be mesmerized by the magnificence of what he was seeing, and now their pursuers had caught up to them. Four men in dark clothing, armed with automatic rifles burst through the doorway on the far side of the room. They looked around in confusion for a moment, and then caught sight of Maddock's party.

"Get up the stairs!" Maddock yelled. Bones shouted back, but his words were lost in a raging torrent of gunfire.

Chapter 27

Maddock dropped to one knee, bringing the Walther to bear on the four armed men, all the while expecting to feel hot lead ripping through his flesh. However the roar that filled the room was not the staccato rattle of automatic weaponry, but the sharp report of large caliber rifles. Across the room, two men crumpled to the ground. The remaining pair fired wildly into the air as they backed up, seeking shelter in the passageway from which they had come. The rifle fire continued unabated.

Maddock, now retreating toward the safety of the doorway on his side of the room, looked up to see men leaning out of the upper windows, sending a steady stream of bullets toward their pursuers. What is going on? Not waiting to find out, he turned and ran as fast as his injured legs would allow. Bones waited at the top of the stairs, covering his retreat. The big Indian grabbed Maddock's upper arm and helped him into the dark hallway where Kaylin and Meriwether waited.

"Who are those guys?" Meriwether asked.

"Which ones?" Bones replied, still watching the room behind them.

Maddock looked back. The two fallen black clad men still lay at the foot of the stairs on the far side of the room. The others had disappeared, and the gunfire had ceased.

"I don't know who any of them are," he said. "Let's stick together and try to find a way out of here. Do you remember which direction you came from?" Meriwether nodded and led the way.

All four had their weapons drawn, and they moved together down the hallway. Bones kept an eye out behind them. About fifty feet down, the passageway ended in a cross-hall. Meriwether paused and peered around the corner, checking in both directions. He turned back to Maddock and the others, and tilted his head to their left. "That way?" he asked softly.

Bones and Kaylin nodded in agreement. Meriwether nodded, turned, and stepped around the corner.

A blistering peal of gunfire shattered the quiet of the hall. The old Navy man was spun half around as bullets ripped into him. Instinctively, Maddock dove forward, hitting the ground and rolling, his gun held out in front of him. Another of their dark-clothed pursuers, rifle in hand, sprinted toward him. The man had obviously been watching at head-level for someone to round the corner. His brown eyes widened in surprise as he looked down at Maddock, and he swung his rifle forward, but too late. Maddock opened fire, catching him full in the chest and knocking him flat on his back. Maddock regained his feet and looked up and down the hall for more attackers. Seeing no one, he turned to check on Meriwether.

Kaylin and Bones knelt over the Admiral, who held both hands clamped over his stomach. Blood soaked his shirt, and his face was ghastly pale. Maddock moved behind Kaylin and placed a hand on her shoulder. He looked down at his old friend, a mixture of fear and anger roiling inside.

"We've got to get you out of here Meri," he said hoarsely though his words rang false in his ears. They all knew that Meriwether was not going to make it out of here.

"Leave me here," Meriwether whispered, grimacing with the pain of speaking. Kaylin started to protest, but he shook his head vigorously. "Sit me up," he gasped. Maddock and Bones grasped him under each arm, gingerly brought him up to a sitting position, and propped him against the wall. Meriwether's face twisted as they moved him, but otherwise he made no sound. He was still as tough as old leather, Maddock thought. He could not believe the old sailor might die.

"I am going to be fine," Meriwether said softly, his face placid. "Don't you worry about me."

"You're not going to be fine unless we get you out of here and to a doctor," Kaylin said. Her fair skin was flushed, and unshed tears glistened in her emerald eyes. "We'll find a way. We will."

"That's not what I mean," Meriwether grunted. "You see, I have cancer." He paused to take a raspy breath. "They give me six months, a year if I'm lucky."

The words hit Maddock like a sledgehammer. His blood seemed to turn to ice.

"I don't know what to say," Maddock said after a long pause. Bones and Kaylin were silent.

"It's all right," Meriwether said. "When I first found out about it, I was scared. I realized I was afraid to die. I had too many unanswered questions. But after what I've seen tonight, I don't have any more questions." He closed his eyes. For a moment, Maddock thought the man might have expired, but then Meriwether opened his eyes again. "So, like I said, I'll be all right."

"I wish there was something I could do for you," Maddock said. A feeling of helplessness swelled up inside of him, all thoughts of their pursuers were forgotten in his pain and frustration. First his parents, then Melissa, and now Meriwether. What good was he? He had not been able to do anything for any of them.

"You've already given me a gift that I couldn't repay if I lived forever. You've given me hope." He coughed, a loud, rasping song that was painful to hear. He winced, and then extended his hand, first to Bones, who shook it regretfully. He next took Kaylin's hand. She took his in both of hers and kissed him gently on the forehead.

Finally, Meriwether reached out and clasped Maddock's hand.

"Good luck, Swabbie," he said hoarsely.

"You too," Maddock replied. After a moment, he let go of the older man's hand, but Meriwether held on.

"You need to have hope, son," he whispered. His eyes had gained a sudden clarity. "It's nobody's fault." The intensity of his expression took Maddock aback.

"What isn't?" Maddock asked.

Meriwether did not reply. He closed his eyes and let his head rock back against the wall. He sighed deeply. Maddock leaned closer and could hear the man's shallow breathing. He gave his old friend's shoulder a squeeze, and then stood.

"We need to go," Bones said. "I hate to leave him as much as you do. We're too vulnerable here."

Maddock knew that his friend was right. Someone could come upon them from any of three directions. He stood and addressed the other two.

"All right, let's get out of here." Maddock turned and led the way down the passage he hoped would lead them back to the well. Over his left shoulder, he could hear the faint rushing of the river through the main hall. Approaching the end of the hall, he paused to relieve their attacker of his rifle. It was an older model NATO CETME. At .51mm, it carried serious stopping power. He tucked the Walther into his belt and stood, rifle at the ready.

Bones knelt down over the attacker. Reaching under the man's collar, he grasped something. With a curse, he gave the object a forceful yank. He held up his hand, displaying a silver chain with a familiar pendant.

"The sword crucifix." Kaylin's voice was scarcely a whisper.

"The same guys who came after us before," Bones said bitterly. He stood and gave Meriwether's assailant a vicious kick in the ribs. "Too bad he's dead. I'd like to hurt him a little bit before I kill him for good."

"I'm sure there are more of them." Maddock gritted his teeth. He would find out who these people were, and he would make them pay. He stalked angrily to the end of the hallway. He peered around the corner to the right and saw another short hallway, twin to the one in which he stood. To his left, a spiral stone staircase wound upward. He heard a faint sound coming from the stairwell and held up a warning hand to Bones and Kaylin.

Moving to the inside wall, he knelt down, and waited. Bones squatted behind him, gripping his Beretta. The faint sound came again. Someone was coming down the stairs. A brief glimpse of black clothing was all the motivation Maddock needed to open fire, cutting his target down. Bones hastily appropriated the man's rifle and pointed back down the hallway.

Maddock led them along the featureless passage. The corridor was dimly lit by the same diamond-shaped rocks that illuminated the main hall. They made a sharp right at the end of the hall. Far ahead of them, he could see the pathway leading to the tunnel. He made a mental note that they were now moving parallel to the inside hall where Meriwether lay, and to the river.

He paused where the passageway intersected a hall on the right. A careful look revealed no pursuers, but in the faint light he could just make out a spiral staircase at the far end. Kaylin came up beside him, her gaze following his. "Do you think…"

"It's a big old circle," Bones said, pausing between them. "Or a square, I mean. I guarantee you, you go down there and hang a right, you'll be in the hall where we left Meriwether."

Bitterness and frustration welled up inside of Maddock as he thought again about being forced to leave the Admiral behind. The rational part of him knew there was nothing they could do for the man. Meriwether was probably already gone.

Kaylin seemed to read his thoughts. She squeezed his arm and then pulled him forward. "Come on. Let's get out of here." They hurried across the hall and into the tunnel that led back toward the well and, hopefully, safety.

This tunnel differed from the one they just left. There were none of the glowing stones on the wall, and they had to use their flashlights to find their way. Also, this passage gradually curved back to the right.

"Smell that?" Bones asked, raising his head and inhaling deeply. A smile spread across his dark face.

"What?" Maddock asked.

"Water. We're almost there." Bones claimed to have heightened senses due to his ancestry, but Maddock suspected that his friend was usually blowing smoke. This time, he hoped Bones was right.

Behind them, shots rang out again. They were muted, sounding far away. First one barrage, then another reverberated down the hall. The sound was unexpectedly drowned by a deep rumbling that seemed to come from within the bowels of the earth.

"Tremor!" Maddock shouted, dropping to the ground. The hallway shook as if some giant hand had grasped it and given it a jiggle. Chunks of rock fell around him. The vibrating lasted several seconds. As the force dissipated, he heard a loud crashing from down the tunnel ahead of them, and a cloud of dust filled the air.

"No way," Bones said flatly, his voice filled with resignation.

Maddock did not say anything. He stood and trotted down the hall. Just around the next bend, the ceiling had collapsed, blocking their exit. He and Bones climbed onto the pile of rubble, and attempted to dislodge some of the top stones, but to no avail.

"The tremors are getting worse," Kaylin said, a worried look on her face.

"Maybe they feel bigger because we're underground," Bones said. "What do you think, Maddock?"

Maddock took a deep breath and exhaled slowly. "I think we need to find another way out, and soon."

Chapter 28

Coming back out of the tunnel, Maddock led the group to the left, moving back toward the main room. When they reached the end where the passage terminated at the spiral staircase, they looked down the hall to the right. Meriwether lay where they had left him, obviously dead. Nearby, another body lay on the ground.

"He got him one," Bones said. "Good for him."

They walked over to where their friend lay. Maddock knelt and checked Meriwether's pulse, confirming that their comrade was, indeed, deceased. A lump in his throat, he opened the top button of the Admiral's shirt and removed his dog tags.

"I'll take care of these," he whispered, tucking them into his pocket. Then, he reached down and picked up the SIG P-210, and handed it to Kaylin.

The blonde looked down sadly at their fallen friend. She brushed at her eyes with the back of a sleeve and turned away from Maddock and Bones. Regaining her composure, she cleared her throat and turned back to face them. "You were right, Bones," she said. "We've just looped around."

"That means the only way out of here is up." Bones looked at the ceiling as if he could see through. "Where the bad guys are."

"What about the bad guy over here?" Maddock leaned down to inspect the man whom Meriwether had shot. He was surprised to see that this man was not clad in black, like the others. Instead, he was garbed in bulky, loose-fitting brown pants, and a pullover, white cotton shirt. The shirt was of an odd cut, with no collar and blousy sleeves. The man's features were obviously middle-eastern, but Maddock could tell no more. "He's definitely not part of the crossed swords group."

"The guys who were shooting from upstairs, I presume," Bones said. "We've got to get up there and somehow get past them."

"But who the hell are they?"

"I don't know but I'd rather avoid them if we can. Can't we get across the channel that cuts through the main room?" Kaylin asked.

"Too wide to jump," Maddock said, shaking his head, "and the current's too strong for us to swim across. We'll have to chance it upstairs. Bones and I will plow the field, and you can follow along." He forced a smile, hoping he looked more confident than he felt.

He led them back up the hall to the stairwell. Silently, they crept up the stairs, listening for the sound of approaching footsteps. The turn was so tight that they would be right on top of anyone coming in their direction before seeing them. The narrow staircase, hewn out of the rock, curled up and to the left. The walls were smooth, like those of the lower halls, broken up only by the occasional glowing stone high on the outside wall. Maddock winced as he took each step. The climb made him feel every pain in his feet, knees, and back, in a way that level ground did not. He gritted his teeth and focused on his anger, allowing his bitterness at the loss of Meriwether to overcome his pain. Slowly, he continued the seemingly interminable upward trek.

When they reached the top of the stairs, Maddock peered out cautiously. They were at a corner of the upper hallway. He looked to his left. The hall ran the approximate length of the main chamber, turning left at the end. Halfway down the hall, an arched window was cut into the inside wall at chest level. This must have been one of the windows from which the snipers had fired down upon their pursuers. Directly across from the window was a high, arching door set in the outside wall. Maddock could not see into the darkness beyond. Looking around the other corner, he could see that this upper hall definitely formed a hollow, walled balcony that wrapped around the big chamber below. This hallway also had a window at the center of the inside wall and a doorway on the outside. He turned and motioned for Bones and Kaylin to follow him.

Stepping out of the stairwell, Bones surveyed the area, just as Maddock had. "Another square up here," he whispered. "Everything seems to loop back on itself. But where are the bad guys?"

Maddock shrugged and led them down the hallway to the left. Reaching the window at the hall's midpoint, he glanced through, surveying the courtyard below. The black-clad bodies of their pursuers still lay at the top of the steps on the far side of the room. Nothing moved, save the water flowing through the canal in the center. He turned to see Bones peering into the dimly-lit room on the opposite side of the hall. Bones nodded and tilted his head toward the doorway. Rifle at the ready, Maddock hurried inside, with Bones behind him.

The crystals in this room emitted only the faintest light, but it was enough to see that they were standing in what looked like a quarter of a sphere hewn into the rock with laser-like precision. Carved into the rounded ceiling above, he thought he could just make out familiar constellations.

A whisper of warning from Bones brought Maddock's head down in time to see that he was staring down into a well like the ones in front of and behind the Goliath carving outside. The thought of the world outside gave him pause. The place in which he and his friends now found themselves was so surreal as to make it strange to think that somewhere up above, the world was going about its business, oblivious to what lay beneath their feet.

Kaylin hurried up and shone her flashlight down into the well. Unlike the other wells they had seen, this one was only a few feet deep.

"What's back there?" Bones asked, pointing into the gloom. Kaylin redirected the light to reveal a stone coffin. It was every bit as large as those of Goliath and his brothers. They moved forward to examine it. Kaylin shone her light across the lid. Something was carved on the surface, the deep shadows cast by the flashlight's beam distorting the image. As the beam fell directly onto the image, Kaylin gasped.

The being carved into the coffin lid was like no other Maddock had seen. It was tall, much like Goliath, but impossibly slender. Its arms were disproportionately long for its body and ended in large hands with long, wormlike fingers. The odd appearance did not end there. Its head was too big by a third. Garbed in a simple robe, the odd being had large, round eyes and a serene face. Just looking at it gave Maddock a strange sense of inner calm, as if this were the gentlest of beings.

"I told you, dude. Little green men," Bones whispered. "Well, big green men in this case."

He placed a tanned hand on the lid and pushed. With a soft, scraping sound, it gave way, exposing a sliver of darkness where the lid shifted from the lip of the coffin. "It's not beveled," Bones whispered in surprise. He pulled his own small flashlight from his pocket and shone it down into the coffin. Maddock and Kaylin hurried over to look inside, but Bones turned the light out before they could reach his side. He looked up, the disappointment evident on his face even in the semi-darkness. "Empty," he said.

The crystals on the wall had now absorbed enough stray light to cast a dusk-like glow around the room. Aside from the well and coffin, the room was obviously empty. Nonetheless, they made a quick search, looking for any sort of hidden egress, but they found nothing.

Leaving the room, Maddock led them to the right. They moved counterclockwise around the second story hall, turning left at each corner. They found that each hallway was exactly like the one before: courtyard window at the center of the inside wall, doorway to an empty burial chamber on the outside wall. At each inside corner, a spiral staircase wound down to the first floor.

The differences between the crypts, as Kaylin called them, were few. Two of the rooms lay directly above the underground river. The wells here emptied down into the water. The biggest differences lay in the images carved on lids of each empty sarcophagus. In the second room, they found the image of a squat, simian-looking hominid with a prominent brow and short, thickly-muscled legs. Its face was angry and exuded violence. In the third room, they found a representation of a small creature, no more than four feet tall. In terms of proportion, the body was very much like that of a human child. The features of its narrow face were those of an adult though its eyes were vaguely impish.

They stood now in the room that lay upstream of the main chamber. The carving on this sarcophagus was that of an angel, but unlike any angel Maddock had ever seen. No trumpet-bearing herald or Valentine cherub, this creature was fully ten feet tall, with broad, powerful shoulders, a narrow waist, and muscular legs. It wide forehead shaded narrow, slightly upturned eyes. Wrapped around its shoulders and cloaking its body were huge wings, rendered in such fine detail that Kaylin reached out and stroked the feathers.

"It's beautiful, yet somehow fearsome," she whispered. "The artistry… it's amazing."

"Yeah, but the coffins, the rooms, they're all empty," Bones said. "I don't get this place. All of these halls are just alike. I guarantee you that downstairs on the other side of the river is nothing but a mirror image of the side we were on. Just an empty, square tunnel."

Something clicked in Maddock's mind. "It's a deathtrap," he said, suddenly quite certain of himself. Anyone who finds this place just runs around in circles while whoever is defending the place picks you off one-by-one."

"So why haven't they gotten us yet?" Bones asked. He paced to the open doorway as he spoke, looking into the hallway.

"Maybe they're so busy slugging it out with the other guys that they haven't really paid us much attention," Maddock said, shrugging. The answer was not satisfactory, but he had no other at the moment. "That, and we've been lucky." He inwardly winced. The three of them had been lucky, but not Meriwether.

"Why did they even build this place?" Bones said, turning back to face Maddock. "If it's a killing ground, then it's here for a purpose. It has to exist to protect something else." He paused as a faint tremor shook the room. "So what is it protecting?"

"Don't know, don't care anymore," Kaylin interrupted, putting a slender hand on the sarcophagus as if to balance herself. "I'm sure I'll wonder about it later, but all I want right now is to get out of here." As if to punctuate the point, a quick burst of gunfire, the first they had heard since reaching the second level, echoed down the corridor.

"But where do we go?" Bones asked. "The tunnel's blocked."

Something in what Bones had said earlier gnawed at Maddock's consciousness. The thought broke through with a sudden and surprising clarity. "I've got it!" he said. "If the two halves of the first level are mirror images of one another, then there should be…"

"A tunnel leading back to the well!" Kaylin said, completing his thought. "There was more than one tunnel leading off of the well. The guys who shot at us in the main room must have come in that way."

"But won't they be guarding the exit?" Bones asked.

"They weren't guarding the other one," Maddock said. "Besides, if that's the only way out, does it really matter? Maybe our luck will hold, and we can slip out of here undetected." If the battle between the two yet-unidentified groups continued, perhaps the three of them could slip through the net. "You take the lead. I'll bring up the rear. With my legs the way they are right now, I can't keep up with you anyway."

"No freaking way. We're not going to leave you," Bones said.

"I'll make it. Just promise me that, no matter what happens, you are to get Kaylin out of here. I'll take care of myself." He gave Bones what he hoped was his most commanding stare.

Bones stared back for a moment before shrugging. "Whatever, dude. Let's try for the exit," Bones led the way out of the room. Turning left, they ran to the end of the hall, where it turned to the right. Like the other three corners, a stone staircase spiraled down from the inside corner. They mounted the steps, moving with care and listening for any sounds of approaching enemies. As they wound their way down to the bottom, he thought he heard distant shouts coming up from below. He bit his lower lip and steeled himself for another firefight.

They hit the bottom of the stairs at a trot. Bones looked around quickly and shouted, "Run!" He sprinted out the door, spraying bullets down the hall to the right.

"I'll cover you!" Maddock called to Kaylin. Gripping his Walther in his left hand, he reached around the doorway and blindly fired three shots down the hall. Then, giving Kaylin a push, he leaped out in front of her, opening up with his weapon.

Bones had taken out one man. He lay limp on the ground, his rifle near him. Two others, wearing the same style white shirt and brown pants as the man Meriwether had killed, charged down the hall, firing erratically. Maddock fired another burst, then turned and ran around the corner. Ahead of him, Kaylin reached the end of the hall and disappeared to the left. He had been right. There was a tunnel there!

Behind him, another shot rang out, and a voice shouted in English for him to stop. *Is this guy kidding me?* Maddock thought. He dodged right, then left, thankful that the pursuers did not have automatic weapons.

He was within twenty feet of the tunnel when another tremor shook the ground. This one was the strongest yet. He fell hard, his Walther clattering from his grip. He still held on to the rifle, and turned and fired another burst at his pursuers, who had fallen to the ground. Both had lost their weapons, and Maddock, still oozing with cold anger over Meriwether's death, took them out without compunction. He hopped to his feet and turned around. What he saw made him curse. The mouth of the tunnel had collapsed.

Chapter 29

Before Maddock had time to contemplate being cut off from his friends, shouts and footsteps reverberated down the corridor to his right. Not waiting to see who was coming, he turned and sprinted back the way he had come. How was he going to get out of here?

He reached the corner and the stairs they had just descended. More voices came from his left. Cut off from either avenue on the first floor, he dashed back up to the second floor. As he climbed, he considered his options. They were few. He supposed he could try to work his way back up the river, but the current was so strong, he would likely be swept away. It might be worth a try. He could always try going down one of the sacrificial wells. He had not seen any handholds or tunnels coming off them when he had examined them before, but he could have easily missed them in his haste.

He reached the top of the stairs and heard even more voices and footsteps that seemed to come from all around. Whoever these men were, they were converging on his position. His luck had run out. Taking a chance, he dashed to the north room, the one with the angel on the sarcophagus. Just as he ducked through the doorway, he caught a glimpse of several brown and white clad men rounding the corner. Their attention was focused on a black-clad man whom they held at gunpoint.

Maddock hurried to the edge of the well. Knowing that he did not have much time, he scanned the interior for handholds. Seeing none, he took one long look at the faint glimmer of the water far below. It was much too far to jump.

The voices were closer now. He turned and looked at the giant stone coffin. He had no other choice. Giving the lid a hard shove, he slid the end to the side, creating just enough room to squeeze through. He clambered in headfirst. Flipping over onto his back, awkward with the sword still strapped over his shoulder, he reached up and scooted the lid back into place.

The voices drew near. Maddock realized, to his chagrin, that the men were coming into the room where he was hiding. He strained to hear what they were saying. Someone was speaking in Arabic.

"I don't speak your language, primitive," a deep voice, brimming with arrogance, replied.

"Very well," a strange, almost musical voice said. "Tell us, please, who you are and why you come armed into the temple."

"I won't answer any of your questions." A heavy grunt told Maddock that the man had been punched in the stomach.

"Answer my questions truthfully, and you will be released." The odd voice spoke again. "I caution you: God will tell me if you lie, and it will go badly with you."

"We are the agents of God," the deep voice snapped, "the Order of the Blades has been sent to stamp out the heresy of the sword. God's dominion is at hand, and we shall not permit anything that could erode the faith of His believers to come to light."

"The sword has been gone from this place for many years. In any case, there is no heresy in this place, only a celebration of God's creation."

The prisoner laughed a sharp, nasal sound. "Don't you know? Someone has brought the sword into this very place. That is why we are here: to stop them and take the sword."

"Are you certain?" The speaker did not try to hide his surprise. "How do you know this thing?"

"A man confessed to his priest that he had found the key to finding the sword."

Maxwell, Maddock thought. *He must have been worried about how the world would receive the discovery of the sword, so he bared his soul to Father Wright. And he paid for it with his life.*

"Knowing the damage it could do if the sword came to light, the church neutralized the man," the speaker continued, "but he had passed the clues along to his daughter. We tracked her to this place."

"You have done an evil thing."

"Protecting the faith from this alien relic is not evil," the man said. "Rienzi spouted his heresies about God being a spaceman, and about alien creatures populating the earth. Had he been able to support his claims, the church might have been destroyed."

The man with the lilting voice laughed long and hard. "The sword is not an alien relic. True, its origins are not of this earth, but neither are they detrimental to the truth of God."

"The church believes that they are," the man hissed.

"Where does your loyalty lie, to your God, or to your church? They are not necessarily one and the same, you know."

"Heretic!" the man shouted. Maddock heard sounds of a struggle. "What are you doing? You said you'd release me!" the man cried, his voice strident.

"The well will be your release, my son. You will be released from the bondage in which your church holds you. Make your peace with God, whatever the name by which you know him."

The prisoner's angry cries were suddenly squelched by a gurgling sound. Maddock had heard that sound before: a knife across the throat. They had killed the man and dropped him into the well. He had to get away before the same fate befell him.

He waited, listening, as the men conversed in Arabic. A few forceful words from the man with the strange voice, and then footsteps running from the room. He waited. What if they were not all gone? What if they came back? He started to count backward from three hundred, struggling to count slowly. A new thought came to him. How much air was in this coffin? He had noticed cracks around the edge of the lid and hoped that some of them were allowing air inside.

He completed his countdown, five minutes, as close as he could guess and took a deep breath. He had not heard a sound since the men left the room. He could not remain here forever. He had to take a chance. Pushing the lid aside as gently as possible, he squeezed out. As his feet hit the ground, he heard a voice behind him.

"Welcome."

Maddock whirled about, rifle at the ready. The man who stood before him was old--very old. He wore a loose-fitting brown robe, cinched around the waist with a thick length of rope, over beige homespun pants and shirt. Short, snowy hair peeked out from under a brown head cloth. He had a closely-cropped white beard and mustache. Shining in his leathery face, heavily lined with age, his alert, gray eyes looked past Maddock, his gaze settling on the hilt of the sword.

"You did return the sword," he said in amazement. Maddock recognized the musical voice instantly. This was the apparent leader of the group-- the one who had ordered a man sacrificed. "It seemed too much to hope that the barbaric man spoke the truth."

"Who are you?" Maddock barked. The man was not physically imposing, nor did he seem to offer a threat, but Maddock kept the rifle trained on him just the same, ready to fire should the man call for his minions.

"I am Atiq Yomin. In your language, the "Ancient of Days." He pressed his hands together and bowed his head.

"Are you trying to tell me you're God?" Maddock asked, trying to convey in his voice all of the scorn that he felt.

"No," the man laughed, "it is but a title given to one of my standing in the community. You may call me Atiq."

"All right, Atiq," Maddock said, "are you planning on calling your cronies back?"

Atiq made a clucking sound. "Your behavior is very rude. I have given you my name, but you have not yet identified yourself. In any case, as you are an intruder in my domain, you should permit me to ask the questions. But I shall indulge you none the less, as I see you are agitated. No, I do not expect my men to return to this place anytime soon. They are scouring the temple."

Maddock knew that he had few cards to play, and Atiq was likely his only way out of here. "The name's Dane Maddock."

"Do you plan to shoot me, Mr. Maddock?"

Maddock was caught off guard, not only by the directness of the question, but also by the calm way in which the question was asked.

"I guess that depends on how things go," he said. "If that's what it takes to get out of here alive, I'll do it."

"You are an honest man. I appreciate that." Atiq scratched his beard. "May I know why you are returning the sword to the temple, Mr. Maddock?"

Maddock wanted to lie to the man, but something about Atiq compelled him to tell the truth. The man had a hypnotic air about him, almost holy. "An old friend of mine learned that the sword had been found and then lost almost two hundred years ago by a man named Rienzi. My friend was killed for what he knew. We found the sword, which led us here." Even as he spoke, he could not believe that he was telling this man his story.

Atiq turned and paced back and forth. He looked up at the ceiling. Each time he passed the stone sarcophagus, he let his fingertips trail over the edge of the stone lid. "So many came to Petra and left again," he whispered, "that we did not know who had taken the sword. We were inattentive to our duties." He stopped pacing, shook his head, and then turned to face Maddock. "On behalf of the Protectors, I must thank you for returning the sword. It lessens our shame."

"Well," Maddock said, "we weren't trying to return the sword. We just wanted some answers."

"We?" Atiq appeared calm, but his eyes retained their intense stare. "You are not alone?"

"The daughter of the man who was killed came with us, along with two of my friends. They got away. At least, two of them did." Inside, Maddock still seethed when he thought of Meriwether.

"And have you found the answers you seek?" Atiq sounded as if he were toying with Maddock.

"Not all of them," Maddock admitted. "Obviously, it was this 'Order of the Blades' that was following us. They killed my friend. But…"

"But you have other questions yet to be answered." Atiq was not asking.

"Yeah, like who built this place? What is it? What does it have to do with Goliath?" All the confusion he had felt, further clouded by adrenalin and grief came spilling over. "This place isn't anything! It's like you made it just to trap people and kill them. But what are you protecting here?"

"To answer your first question, God built this place," Atiq said, giving a small bob of the head.

"God," Maddock replied flatly.

"Yahweh, Allah, Jehovah, whatever you wish to call the supreme deity," Atiq said. "But I can tell by your tone of voice that you will not accept that answer. Consequently, I cannot answer your other questions, as you will not believe those answers either."

"There is no God," Maddock muttered. He looked Atiq directly in the eye. "If there's a God, who loves us out there, why do people die?"

"We all die, Mr. Maddock," the old man said with casual indifference. "That is a reality of our mortal existence. I should think you, as a man to whom violence appears to be a close friend, would be intimately familiar with the concept of mortality."

"I'm not talking about ninety year-olds who die in their beds. I mean young people who have their whole lives ahead of them. A God who loves us wouldn't let that happen." He had no idea why he was unloading years of pent-up anger on this strange old man. Atiq, for his part, took it calmly.

"You are obviously a military man. Odd that a man who has been trained to kill has such high expectations for his God in terms of saving lives. When you shoot a man, do you expect your loving God to come down and heal him so that you may shoot him again and again?"

Maddock did not answer. The man was talking nonsense.

"Do your parents love you, Mr. Maddock?" Atiq asked, folding his arms across his chest and sitting down upon the stone coffin.

"My parents were killed in an auto accident. So was my wife," Maddock said bitterly. "God didn't bother to save any of them. But yes, my parents loved me."

"I am sorry for your loss," Atiq said simply. For some reason, Maddock actually believed that the old man meant it. There was an air of simple sincerity about him that suggested he did not say things he did not mean. "Did these loving parents approve of your choice to take up arms for your nation?"

Maddock nodded. "My Dad was career Navy. So, yeah, they were proud of me." What was the old man getting at?

"But surely, loving parents would not permit their child to do something dangerous. Does a loving parent permit his child to go to school, where the child could contract an illness, or possibly be harmed by another child or even by an adult?"

Maddock stared at the ground. He did not have an answer for the old man.

"Free will, Mr. Maddock. Your loved ones exercised their free will to operate a motor vehicle, statistically a dangerous undertaking. Just as you made a choice to enlist in the armed forces. Just as you have, no doubt, exercised your free will to take a life, or perhaps more than one in your time.

"Sometimes we use our free will in ways that harm others. That is regrettable. But without free will we are little more than robots."

"But what about babies who die? What about cancer? Natural disasters?" Maddock pressed. "Why is everything so arbitrary?"

Atiq chuckled. His eyes took on a faraway stare. "I once had a discussion with a friend of mine from China." The man caught the surprised look in Maddock's eye. "I do live in the world. Being a Protector is my calling, but I live and love just as you do. My home is not in this place beneath the ground." He paused to let this sank in. "At any rate, my friend and I were discussing the ending of a Chinese movie. The character did something that flew in the face of all reason. Even with my friend's attempts at explanation, I could find neither practical nor symbolic meaning in that character's choice. He finally grew frustrated, threw up his hands, and said, 'You simply do not understand the Eastern mind.'" He turned and looked at Maddock. "It occurs to me that if I cannot understand the mind of my fellow human being, how can I ever presume to know the mind of God?"

Maddock stood in silent contemplation of the old man's argument. In his bitterness over losing Melissa, he had been so confident in his belief that there was no God. What Atiq said was far from satisfying, but perhaps it could be true.

"God is real," Atiq said, standing and moving to stand face-to-face with Maddock. "This place is the proof. If you have the courage to return the sword to its resting place, you will see that for yourself." As the old man spoke, another tremor shook the room. Maddock staggered back before regaining his balance.

"There were three tunnels coming off of that well shaft. Two of them are blocked. Show me where the third one is before this place comes down on our heads."

Atiq stared at the gun, his face void of all emotion. "Do you think I am afraid to die?" he asked. "For I am not." He fixed Maddock with an appraising look. "Here are my conditions: put down your weapons and return the sword to its proper place. Only then will I show you the way out."

"I don't have time for this," Maddock said. "These tremors are getting stronger. Take me out of here." The last, he said slowly, pronouncing each syllable.

"This place has seen worse," the old man replied. "You have heard my conditions. Do you accept them?"

"Why do I have to leave my weapons?" Maddock asked, suddenly suspicious. "Your goons waiting outside for me?"

"As long as you are in my company, no harm will come to you. You need to understand faith, Mr. Maddock. Leaving your defenses behind will be the first step."

Maddock looked long and hard at the old man, and read the resolve in his face. He considered shooting the man down on the spot, but quickly dismissed the idea. Atiq had not threatened him. Furthermore, he was the key to getting out of this place. Slowly, he laid the automatic rifle on the floor at his feet. Next, he drew the Walther, popped the magazine out, removed the unspent bullets, and slid the empty magazine back into place. "I've had this for a long time," he explained, holding the pistol up. "It has sentimental value. I can't leave it behind."

Atiq nodded his acceptance and silently led the way out of the chamber.

Chapter 30

Maddock followed Atiq down the stairs and into the main chamber, which the old man called the "temple." Walking to the stream that bisected the room, they followed it down to where it emptied under the wall. The man turned to face him.

"There are metal rungs in the ceiling of this tunnel. You must climb hand-over-hand for about ten meters. Where the rungs end, let go." Before Maddock could ask what he would be dropping down onto, the old man reached into the tunnel, grabbed a handhold, and swung into the darkness. He moved surprisingly well for his apparent age.

Maddock swallowed a curse. He reached into the tunnel with his right hand and felt along the curved ceiling, cool and slightly damp. His hand found cold iron, and he grabbed hold and swung forward. The faint glow from the temple did little to illumine the blackness of the passageway. He brought his left hand forward and was surprised to find the next rung right where he needed it to be. Just like the monkey bars, he thought. He found his rhythm with an ease born of harsh SEAL training. He moved along so effortlessly that he forgot that the handholds ended, and when after a short distance, his left hand grasped only air, he nearly lost his grip on the last rung.

"Atiq?" he called, feeling rather foolish as he hung by one arm. There was no answer. Had the old man somehow tricked him? "Hey!" He paused, waiting for an answer, but none was forthcoming. He listened to the sound of water rushing beneath him. No other sound met his ears. "Must be one of those faith things," he growled. He took a deep breath and steeled himself for a drop into the cold water below. Eyes closed, he let go.

He scarcely had time to feel the sensation of falling before his feet struck solid ground. With a grunt, he dropped to all fours, feeling every jolt and bruise his body had received from his earlier fall down the well.

"You are correct." From the nearness of his voice, Atiq stood only a few feet away. "I told you that you needed to learn about faith. Follow me."

Maddock stood and followed the faint sounds of the old man's footsteps into the darkness. He moved at a tentative pace, uncertain what lay before him. The floor beneath him was solid. The rustling of water all around suggested that he might be on some sort of walkway in the middle of the channel.

The faintest glimmer of light appeared in the distance. He could just make out Atiq's form about twenty feet ahead. He picked up his pace, moving to catch up with the strange old man, who did not acknowledge him but stared resolutely ahead.

The passageway grew brighter as they walked on. Soon, there was enough light for Maddock to confirm that they were, indeed, on a pathway in the middle of the underground river. The tunnel made a sharp bend to the right. Maddock turned the corner and gasped.

Stefan peered out through the arched doorway that led into the large central room. He watched with interest as first the old man, then Maddock, disappeared into the tunnel where the river flowed out of the room. Apparently, there were handholds of some sort in the tunnel roof. He smiled. They were leading him directly to whatever it was that this empty stone warren protected.

He stepped into the room and was disappointed to see that someone had removed the bodies of Peter and Michael, along with their rifles. Stefan had long since emptied and discarded his own weapon. No matter, he still had his knife and the other weapon. He resisted the urge to pat his midriff, just to make certain it was still there.

He hurried toward the tunnel where his quarry had vanished, all the while feeling vulnerable to the snipers that had dogged them throughout this debacle of an operation. Reaching the archway, he paused for a moment to feel for a handhold of some kind. His hand closed around some sort of metal rung, and he smiled again.

This place was a threat to the faith— that was certain. The things hidden here were abominations, as was the sword. The Dominion had been wise to finally call upon him. Only he could see this through.

He would kill Maddock first and recover the sword. Next, he would wring the old man's secrets out of him before taking care of him. Finally, when he had learned all that he could, he would blow this pagan abomination back to the hell in which it was conceived.

Maddock stared in amazement at the wondrous sight that lay before him. About fifty yards ahead, the tunnel opened into a broad, circular cavern, at least two hundred feet across. The river spilled over the edge and into the depths, but the pathway upon which they trod extended out over the chasm. Where it ended, hanging out over the abyss, was a sight unlike any he had ever beheld.

It was a giant cage, spherical, and about thirty feet across. It appeared to be constructed of the same material as the glowing crystals that illumined the temple and hallways. The thick, finely wrought bars, spaced vertically about a foot apart all the way around, gave it the appearance of being both delicate and sturdy at the same time. A doorway set in the near side stood open, revealing a bright, white object of indeterminate shape inside. Maddock could see no sign of bolts or hinges. Rather, it appeared to be one single piece. The entire object shone with the incandescence of a full moon, casting a faint glow around the cavern. Pearlescent light swirled and danced on the water as it tumbled into the darkness below.

"Your answer, Mr. Maddock," Atiq said. "This is the secret the temple hides."

Maddock could not begin to comprehend what he was seeing. Memories crowded in one after another in the span of a heartbeat: the fight in the slave market, diving for the *Dourado*, digging up the sword, Sowell's betrayal, and the battle in these very halls. All had led him to this moment, and he had no idea what stood before him. He only knew that it was breathtakingly magnificent. He stared in silence.

"God created many wonderful creatures, nearly all of which are long gone," Atiq said as if beginning a lecture. "The greatest of these, though few, were those we call the angels. They were beautiful, powerful beings, and they were God's favorite. But they were vain creatures, and they lorded their superiority over human beings, taking their pleasure with human women, producing the races of giants, the Anakim."

"What about the other creatures we saw carved in the sarcophagi?" Maddock asked.

"Two of them died out long ago," Atiq said, "but their legacy lives on in our fables." He paused, waiting for Maddock to catch on. After a moment, he continued. "Little people? Ancient alien visitors?"

"Ah," Maddock said, not certain what to think of this revelation. "And the ape-man? What is he? The missing link?"

Atiq chuckled. "Not precisely. All of the beings depicted in the carvings symbolize many beings of a similar nature. But yes, the simian-looking creature generally represents hominids."

"If all of these creatures lived on the earth, why is there no fossil record?" Maddock asked.

"I don't have all the answers," Atiq said. "These beings were historical before history existed. There were few." He shrugged. "Perhaps God removed their remains from the earth for some reason known only to Him? But there is one who remained." He gazed at the sphere in reverence and went on.

"One angel grew in wisdom and power. Legend has it he even developed a limited power to create. He gained a following, and he taught his followers how to make the crystals that illumine the pathways. It is not a certainty, though. Some say the crystals came from beyond the stars." He paused.

"He created the sword. He forged it in this very place, the center of his power, and he etched its location into the blade. Perhaps it was vanity, perhaps it was, in some way, a boast. 'Here I am. Come to me if you dare.'" He stared over Maddock's shoulder at the hilt of Goliath's sword. "Already an arrogant creature, when he learned to create, he was convinced that he was a god in his own right. He tempted the vainest of his race with promises of might and glory, and he led a rebellion against God himself."

Maddock felt cold. He took a step back, his heart racing. The sword seemed to hang heavy on his shoulder. It could not be!

"God crushed their rebellion. The bodies of the traitorous angels were cast into the depths of the earth. Their leader was locked away in a prison wrought from the stone of his own making, locked away in this cavern, his center of power, to contemplate the error of his ways. Angels take a long time to die." Atiq turned and dramatically swept his arm out toward the glowing cage and yawning chasm.

"Welcome to the bottomless pit."

Stefan crouched in the shadows, seething at what he heard. This was an even greater heresy than he had been told! The old man was clearly unhinged. None but God Almighty possessed the power of creation. Why did he spout this nonsense? Clearly he sought to mesmerize Maddock, dull his senses with false revelations, but to what end?

He freed his knife from its sheath and absently tested the edge against his thumb. Anger roiled inside of him. He had intended to slip up behind Maddock and kill him quietly. Now he wanted more. He desired to hurt the man, to make him pay. Maddock had caused this abomination to surface, and his actions could not go unpunished. Stefan wanted the man to know who was killing him and why. He wanted the man to feel fear. To know the power of the Dominion.

And when he finished with Maddock, he would deal with the old man. First he would cut out his tongue and then his eyes. He would make the man weep tears of blood. He would beg for mercy, but the only mercy he would receive would be a slow death.

He raised his sword and tensed every muscle, savoring the anticipation that came as he stood on the edge of dispensing justice. With a cry of rage, he dashed forward.

Maddock whirled and pivoted to his right as the shape hurtled out of the darkness and directly at him. He saw a glint of steel, and he struck out with his open left palm, turning the blade past his body. Ignoring the pain as the knife sliced into his hand, he drove his right palm into the attacker's face.

The man was quick, though, and turned his head, catching the brunt of Maddock's blow on the side of his head, just behind the right eye. He swung the knife backhanded in a vicious arc, scarcely missing Maddock's throat.

Leaning back to avoid the deadly knife stroke, Maddock delivered a roundhouse kick to the man's stomach, but to little effect. The guy's abs were like iron! The man struck again with his knife, low and hard. Maddock turned the thrust again, this time receiving a deep cut across the back of his left forearm. He stepped in close to his assailant and drove his elbow into the man's left cheekbone. He grunted and stabbed at Maddock again, this time a sloppy, overhand stroke. Maddock caught the man's wrist in his left hand, but immediately felt the man's arm slipping free of his bloody palm. Fingers clawed at his eyes, and Maddock grabbed the man's left hand in his right.

They struggled, nose-to-nose, strength against strength. If only Maddock could get some distance between himself and the attacker, enough to give him time to draw the sword. He squeezed tighter with his left hand, and pain shot down his arm from the gashes his opponent's knife had opened. Still hurting from the fall down the well, he felt himself gradually being forced back. As they came into the light, he could see the man more clearly.

The attacker had short, dark hair, and eyes to match. His olive skin and dark clothing made him appear a shadow in the darkness of the tunnel. He was an inch or two taller than Maddock, and solidly muscled. In the dim light, only his white teeth stood out as he fixed Maddock with a toxic smile.

"My name is Stefan," he said in a voice trembling with exertion and rage. "I am of the Blood Order. I wanted you to know who is killing you."

"The Blood Order? Sounds like a cheesy vampire movie," Maddock grunted.

"We serve God. His dominion is at hand."

Maybe that was supposed to mean something to Maddock, but right now he had survival on his mind. He felt his right heel slip over the edge of the path. If he went into the water, the current would sweep him over the edge in a matter of seconds.

"Time to die," Stefan whispered.

"You've got bad breath, pal," Maddock muttered. He thrust his head forward, driving his forehead into Stefan's nose. Letting go with his right hand, he grabbed the man by the hair and drove his head forward, butting him in the face again. He felt blood on his face and knew that it was not his own. A fierce tremor rattled the ground beneath them, and Maddock felt Stefan's footing give. Another blow and now Stefan was pushing away from him. Maddock gave the man a shove, reaching back for the sword as his assailant stumbled backward.

Stefan recovered himself quickly. The man's face was a mask of blood, and he fixed Maddock with a crazed, broken-toothed grin as he came forward, knife at the ready.

Maddock brought the sword free, swinging it in a sharp, downward arc. He heard Stefan scream as the sword parted hand from wrist. The dark-clad man reeled, staggering blindly toward the edge of the pathway. Maddock sprung toward him, delivering a vicious kick to the small of Stefan's back, and sending him crashing into the water. Maddock watched as the current swept him away. He turned to find Atiq waiting for him, hands folded across his chest.

"Thanks for the help," Maddock muttered, letting the sword hang down by his side.

"You were doing fine on your own," Atiq said. He turned and walked toward the glowing object. "Come."

Maddock followed, his eyes fixed on the apparition before him. As the light touched him, his cares seemed to drain away. All thoughts of the fight with Stefan, his concerns about escaping the underground temple, all evaporated as he marveled at the sight before him.

The light that radiated from the white sphere touched him as if it had substance. His pace slowed. He felt as if he were swimming in a sparkling stream of mother-of-pearl light. Overcome with wonder, he shuffled along the path. He scarcely noticed that he was now trailing the tip of the sword along the stone walk.

"It is all right, Mr. Maddock," Atiq said calmly, "come inside." The old man stood at the door, beckoning to him. Maddock took another slow step forward.

Stefan clutched the huge stone with all of his remaining strength, straining against the force of the current that threatened to drag him to his death. The tremor had jarred loose a sizable portion of the tunnel roof, blocking his descent over the falls and into the pit below. He lay motionless as first the old man, then Maddock passed only meters away. The rock lay between them, and the half-light in this portion of the tunnel rendered him nigh invisible. When the two men moved out onto the walkway that extended above the yawning abyss, he knew that he was safe.

Holding on tight with his left hand, he kicked hard, struggling to pull himself up. He gained an inch, then another. Soon, he was able to hook his right arm over the rock. The cold water had slowed his heartbeat, but blood continued to flow from the stump where his right hand had been. He pulled with both arms now, and felt the jagged stone tear through the fabric of his clothing and cut into his exposed flesh. He struggled forward, inching closer to the path in the middle of the passageway.

He felt no pain, only rage. For the first time, he had failed. His team had been picked apart by the old man's henchmen. The sword was beyond his reach now. He could not hope to recover it unarmed and in his present condition. His all-consuming goal now was to live long enough to obliterate the unholy sphere, Maddock and the sword along with it. He would cleanse this pagan sanctuary with holy fire.

Chapter 31

Maddock walked slowly into the glowing sphere, scarcely noticing the bars that seemed to envelop him like a porcelain web. In the center lay a rectangular slab of the opalescent stone. But it was what lay atop the block that drew his attention.

A huge skeleton lay in full repose. Its form was vaguely human, but with a broader chest and a tiny waist. Sturdy arm and leg bones spoke of powerful muscles. Its skull was like that of a human, but with a higher forehead. The face was like an inverted triangle, ending in a narrow chin. Spread out on either side of the body, curving up above the head and sweeping down below knee level was a lacework of delicate bones.

"He has wings," Maddock whispered. Even in death, the creature was both beautiful and terrible. He felt strangely serene in its presence. He stood silently for a moment.

"So, the Devil is dead?" he finally asked.

Atiq laughed and placed a hand on Maddock's shoulder. "A common misconception. Lucifer was a sinner like the rest of us." The old man paused, scratching his bearded chin. "Well, not like the rest of us, but a sinful creature still. Over time, his story became intertwined with theology, resulting in the Satan story that many people believe in today."

"How did Goliath come by the sword?" Maddock asked. It was all so confusing. "Did Rienzi know about…this?" He could not tear his eyes from the amazing creature before him.

"Tradition holds that Goliath found this place. Claiming descent from the Nephilim, he believed that it was his destiny to wield the sword. He and his brothers built their tombs in the rock above, in imitation of the upper chambers. The false wall, with the carvings of the Philistine giants, was built to conceal their resting place, with the sword as the key. Sometime after the death of King David, the sword was recovered and buried with Goliath."

"Behold, I saw a star fall from heaven to earth, and he was given the key of the shaft of the bottomless pit," Maddock whispered. He did not know how he managed to recall that bit of scripture, but in this situation it seemed to fit.

Atiq nodded and continued. "Centuries later, the Nabataeans rediscovered the temple. The sword was returned to this place, Goliath's cavern walled up, and the Protectors formed to guard the wonders of the temple. Sadly, as Petra's importance diminished, so did the diligence of the Protectors. When word of Rienzi's claims reached the Protectors, they verified the loss of the sword. They reconstructed the exterior wall, which Rienzi had broken through and reaffirmed their commitment to protecting the temple. My grandfather's great-grandfather was one of those Protectors."

Maddock drew his gaze away from the dead angel and stepped to the edge of the sphere. He looked down into the blackness beneath. The walls of the cavern plunged straight down, vanishing into the depths. The river that poured over the edge fell silently in a sparkling curtain of droplets. He could certainly understand why they called this the bottomless pit. Wherever the bottom was, it was a long way down. "So that isn't hell, down there?" He turned back to see Atiq shaking his head. "Why did you want me to see this?"

"I sense in you a need to believe in something." The elderly man paused as if expecting Maddock to say something. When no answer was forthcoming, he continued. "I do not expect to change your life in one moment, Mr. Maddock. I do have a question, though. Do you now believe that God is real?"

Maddock gritted his teeth. He looked back at the skeletal remains of the angel, of Lucifer, and then back to Atiq. "I don't know what I believe," he admitted, speaking slowly in order to choose his words carefully. His mind was still struggling to come to grips with all that he had seen and experienced. "But I'm more inclined to believe now than I was an hour ago." He looked again at the mythical seraph, and then stepped over to where the body lay. Raising the sword, he took one long, last look and laid it gently, respectfully on the surface of the stone. It was home.

Atiq nodded sagely. His brown eyes narrowed, and he raised his chin and fixed Maddock with an appraising look. "I wonder, when you leave this place, will you tell of what you have seen?"

Maddock thought for a minute, and then shook his head. He could not put words to it, but the very thought of sharing this place with the world felt wrong. The experience was too... intimate was the only word that came to mind.

"I believe you," Atiq said softly. "I should have you killed for what you have seen, but I cannot do that to the man who returned the sword. Come, I will show you the way out."

Maddock saw the man turn, and then stiffen as if frozen.

Stefan stood in the doorway, his olive skin pallid from immersion in the icy water. His right arm hung limply at his side, blood oozing from the stump and pooling on the stone by his right foot. His shredded pants revealed scraped and bleeding flesh. His black shirt was rent. What Maddock saw beneath it made his eyes bulge. A wide, gray swath of neoprene was wrapped around Stefan's abdomen, holding in place a device that was obviously a bomb.

"I told you," Stefan whispered, his voice slurring from cold and loss of blood, "I wanted you to know who it was that was killing you. I have come to complete the task." His left hand moved sluggishly toward the bomb strapped to his body. "Behold," he said, his eyes glassy and his speech deliberate, "I open the scroll and break the seal."

"You will not!" Atiq screamed. Springing forward at a speed Maddock would not have thought the old man capable of, he was on Stefan before the injured assassin could react, forcing him out of the doorway and back onto the walk.

Maddock watched as the two men as if in slow motion, tumbled over the edge, and into the emptiness below. He opened his mouth to call out, but Atiq was gone.

Stefan's mind was playing tricks on him. He seemed to be floating in darkness. A gentle breeze blew his hair. Where was he? What had he been doing? He thought for a long moment, and then remembered. His numb fingers sought the number pad on the side of the bomb. The Bringer of Holy Fire, as he now thought of it. He found it difficult to concentrate. The floating sensation was growing uncomfortable, and he was feeling dizzy. Deliberately, he punched in the five-digit code, then pressed the hot button.

The walkway beneath Maddock trembled, and the sphere rocked sickeningly from one side to the other. Another tremor, he thought. Then he saw, far below him, a faint orange glow appear in the depths of the pit, glowing brighter. He turned and dashed back up the walkway toward the underground tunnel. He felt the bridge that connected Lucifer's prison to the path in the river begin to give. He stumbled and fell down on all fours. He scrambled to his feet, then felt his footing slip as the stone rampart slowly fell away from the rock wall. He leaped up, extending his arms as far as he could reach, and grunted as his fingers caught the edge of the stone path where the walkway had broken free. He felt the stone collapse beneath him. Clinging by his fingertips, he looked back to watch as the final resting place of the rebellious angel dropped noiselessly into the bottomless pit. Lucifer had finally joined his comrades in arms.

The entire pit shook harder, and a wave of hot, dry air swept up the shaft, engulfing him. A hollow rumble rolled up on its heels. The river rushed angrily by on both sides. He felt the froth on his face. The cool spray seemed to give him a renewed surge of energy. Maddock's feet scrabbled against the rocky surface of the cavern, seeking a toehold. He gained a footing and pushed up, getting first his arms over the edge, then his chest. Finally, he lay sprawled face down on the cold stone. He was spent but knew he had to run.

As he regained his feet, a wave of heat coursed through the tunnel, searing his back. An intense, golden glow illuminated the passageway. The tunnel shook. He dodged to the left as a large block of a stone dislodged from the ceiling and came crashing down alongside him. He staggered forward, feeling the rock beneath his feet shift. The pathway was breaking up!

The rumbling grew louder as the ground heaved, and the river flowed over the broken ground. Icy waves crashed over the undulating pathway, nearly sweeping his feet from under him. He reeled forward, the glow from the flames scarcely evident this far down the passage. He gasped for breath. The fire was sucking the oxygen out of the tunnel. Only a frantic, desperate desire to live kept him on his feet as the stone crumbled beneath him.

The ground gave way beneath his left foot, and he dropped to one knee, cold water lapping over his leg. He staggered to his feet again, only to feel the path below him fall away. As he fell, a strong hand grasped him by the back of his collar.

He dangled in midair, the front of the shirt cutting off his wind. Whoever had hold of him was not strong enough to pull him up; at least not with one hand. Maddock reached up and felt for a handhold. His fingertips found a rung like the ones he had used to climb into the tunnel. He grabbed hold and pulled up with all of his remaining strength. The added lift of his rescuer was enough to vault him up and into a dark passage.

"That's twice I've fished you out of the river," Bones voice' sounded in the darkness. "Come on."

Dazed and unable to believe how close he had come to death, and how fortunate he was to be alive, Maddock let himself be hauled to his feet by the back of his belt. Someone slid beneath his right shoulder and wrapped a slender arm around his waist. Kaylin! His two companions half-carried, half-dragged him down the passageway. The rumbling continued unabated, the tunnel shaking all the while. Apparently, Stefan's bomb had exacerbated the seismic activity in the area.

They rounded a bend, and the tunnel glowed faintly in the light of a single glowing stone set high in the wall. Through the dust raised by the tremors, Maddock could barely see Bones' face.

"We came back up the third tunnel," Bones explained, pausing often to gasp for breath. "It branches off in several places, and we had to try them all. Kaylin thinks that one of them leads to the blocked passage you two found yesterday. Anyway, it isn't too much farther to the well."

"It better not be," Maddock gasped. "I don't have much left." The earth trembled again, and Maddock staggered to his right. He heard Kaylin grunt as she slammed into the side wall.

"I'm fine," she said. "Keep moving."

They turned another corner, and Maddock could see that the tunnel ended up ahead. He felt the damp cool of the well shaft and smelled the moist air. Both were welcome to his senses.

Reaching the end of the tunnel, Bones pointed to the handholds in the wall of the well. "You first," he said. "Don't argue with me, Maddock!" he shouted as Maddock opened his mouth to protest.

Maddock saw there was no point in arguing. He found two handholds and a foothold and began his ascent. He did not bother to look up. The memory of his fall down the well was fresh in his mind, and he knew how deep it was. Tired as he felt, if he were to actually see how far he had to climb, he would be tempted to give up and let himself fall back into the cool, inviting arms of the river.

One handhold at a time, one foot at a time, he scaled the cold, slick stone wall. Twice, he nearly lost his grip as the well shaft undulated with the tremors. Both times, Kaylin's voice spoke from beneath him.

"If you fall, I fall too," she said in a matter-of-fact tone. "No pressure."

Maddock climbed higher. Pieces of the well shaft broke away as the underground complex continued its collapse. Chunks of rock struck him on the head and arms, but he no longer felt pain. He wanted to live.

He was surprised when he finally reached for a handhold and found only air. He was so taken aback, in fact, that he nearly lost his remaining hand grip. Clutching the edge of the well, he drew himself up and over the side, and fell heavily to the floor. With the last of his strength, he stood and offered a helping hand first to Kaylin, then to Bones. Arms linked, the three of them ran from Goliath's tomb.

The bright morning sun was a shock to Maddock's eyes as he stumbled out into the daylight. The dry, dusty air burned his nostrils. A number of diggers were gathered outside the tomb, and they stared in astonishment as the friends appeared from within the heaving bowels of the earth. The shock wore off quickly, and several of them rushed forward to lead Maddock and his friends away from the collapsing tomb.

A safe distance away, Maddock turned and fell heavily to the ground. He sat and watched as a cloud of dust poured forth from within the stone sepulchre. With a final heave, the entire plateau fell in upon itself.

He stared in numb disbelief. The sword was gone. Meriwether was gone as well, with naught to mark his passing but a pile of rock. There was no tomb, no temple. It was as if none of it had ever been there. As far as Maddock was concerned, that was the case.

EPILOGUE

The sun shone bright across the green expanse of Arlington cemetery. The white headstones, arrayed with military precision, gleamed like polished buttons on a uniform. Many considered it an honor to be buried here. Bones, of course, thought it was bland and lacked the individuality that he so valued. He had already planned his own memorial and intended his cremated remains to be sprinkled into ashtrays at his favorite Vegas casinos and adult entertainment establishments.

Maddock had warned Bones that he had better produce offspring because Maddock was not about to carry out those final wishes. The picture of himself at eighty years old, tottering through a strip club with a bag of ashes in one hand and a cane in the other nearly made him smile.

Returning his thoughts to the present, he watched in silence as the honor guard folded the flag and presented it to Melinda Wells, Meriwether's granddaughter and only living relative. She accepted it with a firm nod of thanks.

She's got her grandfather's spirit, Maddock thought. As the uniformed men and women marched away, his gaze fell on the small mound of earth where they had interred Meriwether's dog tags, along with an urn containing the ashes of Rienzi's Bible.

The minister, a short, stocky young fellow with a voice much too big for his body, said a few words, none of which came close to doing justice to so fine a man. He closed with the Lord's Prayer.

When the mourners were dismissed, Maddock turned to leave. Bones caught his eye long enough to indicate that he planned to stay with Melinda for a while longer. Maddock nodded and turned to find Kaylin waiting for him. She stood with her hands on her hips and a slight, upturned smile on her face, tempered only by the solemnity of the occasion.

"What?" Maddock asked.

"I saw you back there," she said, a mysterious look in her eyes. "You were praying, weren't you?"

"I thought you weren't supposed to open your eyes when you pray," he kidded. "Come on, I'll buy you lunch." He offered his hand, and she clasped it in both of hers. Together, they strolled through the manicured green grass.

"You know," Kaylin said, "you still haven't told me what happened after we got separated back in the temple."

Maddock looked up at the azure sky and took a deep breath. Somehow, what he had experienced was too personal to share, even with Kaylin. Exhaling, he turned to her and shrugged.

"It's all so… I don't know what to say about it. I'm still trying to figure it out. It could take a while."

He could tell that she was dissatisfied with the answer, but she did not push. "I've got time. How long do you think it might take?"

"I don't know," Maddock said. "Maybe a lifetime."

~The End~

CIBOLA

A Dane Maddock Adventure

Under the tenth step entering to the east
Under the black stone at the Western entrance
Above the pillar of the northern opening of the cave that has two entrances

Under the stairs in the pit
On the third terrace in the cave,
on the eastern side inside the waterfall

At the edge of the canal on its northern side
Six cubits toward the immersed pool
In the sepulchre, in the third course of stones
Under the tomb
In the chain platform

This is all of the votive offerings of the seventh treasure, the ten is impure

Prologue
April 11, 1539

Fray Marcos de Niza muffled a curse as he dragged his shirtsleeve across the still-wet ink. He pushed the offending piece of fabric up to his elbow and surveyed the damage. Only a smear in the upper left corner. Nothing too grave. That ought to teach him to blot with better care.

Sighing, he turned away from the log book and refilled his cup. He held the bottle up to the light and swirled it around, looking mournfully at the very last of his wine. Three fingers, no more. Hopefully, something of a decent vintage would soon arrive at this remote outpost civilization had forgotten. He reflected on his fall from grace and hoped that word of it had not reached his family back home. He wondered if his father still lived. If so, he hoped his father had not heard tell of what he had done. If only he could tell him the truth. If only he could tell the world the truth. If so, he would not have been sent to this place to do nothing of value. Oh, they promised him he would return to Mexico some day, when he was no longer "needed" here. It was probably true. Whenever Coronado forgave him, he would be permitted to come slinking back, tail between his legs.

Had it all been worth it? Of course, it had. There were too many reasons that what he had discovered could not come to light. The truth of it alone might do the church irreparable harm. It had even shaken his faith, strong as it was. There was a greater reason, though. Who could be trusted with such power? Certainly not Coronado. Not the king, not even the Pope. Perhaps no one.

But was it right and proper for him to hide this secret for eternity? He was confident that he and Estevanico alone knew the true story. He had removed the sole written record of it from the library in which he had found it, and the final key was in Estevanico's hands... at least for now.

No. He could not let it die with him. It was not his secret to keep. This was God's secret, to be revealed in His time to the man of His choosing. Marcos would continue with the plan that had been laid upon his heart. He would leave a single clue for the world. If God wanted it to be found, it would be found. If not... well, it was in His hands. Marcos returned to his journal.

...I know that what I do is wrong in the eyes of the king, but I believe that it is good and proper in the eyes of God. Some secrets are meant to remain just that. I have seen the horrors wrought by my countrymen upon this innocent land. I shudder to think of the consequences if such power should fall into their hands. I do not fear for myself. They accepted wholeheartedly the tale I have spun, and only two of us remain alive who know the truth though the second is believed by them to be dead. At least, I hope he is still alive, and he lives to complete his task. I know that it is foolish of me to record these thoughts, but I feel that I must write them down, reflect upon them. I know the secret is safe.

Yet I find that I cannot bear to hide this secret from humankind. It is too terrible to reveal, but too precious to bury. I have prayed and searched the scripture for guidance, and I have received an answer. God Almighty willing, the day shall come when this secret comes to light. Only the chosen servant shall decipher the clues I and my faithful companion leave behind. He must begin by searching the depths of the well of the soul...

Sun-on-Lizard ducked down behind the stone outcropping and peered out upon the moonlit landscape. Silver light illumined the rocky plain, casting all in a ghostly glow beneath the blanket of darkness. It was a night for spirits.

The sound came again, much closer now. One less experienced might have missed the faint brush of foot on rock. Someone was moving almost silently through the night. It was possible that whoever it was meant no harm, but he would not take any unnecessary risks. Finding a comfortable position, his weight balanced on the balls of his feet, he settled in to wait. Patience, his grandfather had said, was a good thing, and Sun-on-Lizard had plenty.

With great care he lay the two small rabbits on the ground; a poor fare for an overlong hunting trip. He had been foolish to stay out so late. He did not fear the coyotes, but they could be more than an annoyance in this land where even the meanest game was hard won. And if the stories could be believed, there was more to be feared in this particular place. Slipping his short bow from his belt, he strung it with a practiced ease. Three arrows remained in his quiver, but he let them stay there. Should the need arise, he could put an arrow in the air faster than anyone he had ever met.

He stared up at the velvet blanket of the night sky, sprinkled with stars and washed in the pale moon glow. He had grown up with stories of the star pictures and the stories of the ancient ones in the sky. His brother, Sits-at-Fire, had always been fascinated with the lore, but he had no interest in such things. He believed in the earth beneath his feet, the bow in his hand, and the challenge of the hunt. He respected his adversaries, even the small rabbit and appreciated a resourceful quarry. He always thanked the game that fell to his bow for providing him with food and clothing. Yes, there were enough things of this earth to contemplate that he need not concern himself with things of the sky.

Once again, the shuffling sound whispered across the rocky landscape, and a glint of silver caught his eye. A dark figure appeared from behind a distant rock formation, moonlight outlining his dark form. Another figure emerged, and then a third. Sun-on-Lizard sucked his breath in between his front teeth, and he narrowed his eyes. It could not be! As the figures drew closer, he saw that he had been right. They had the heads, arms and legs of men, but their bodies were covered in snake scales! His left hand tightened on his bow, and he grasped an arrow in his right. Could such creatures be killed? Suddenly wishing he had listened to more of the elder's fireside tales, he hunched as low as he could without obscuring his vision. He willed himself to be a shadow, a dark patch on the night landscape.

A vagrant breeze, cool and dry, wafted toward him. He inhaled deeply but caught no odd scent. Of course, the snake had no scent of which he was aware. At least he was downwind of the strange creatures. They moved closer, and with each approaching step his heart pounded faster. Blood coursed through him, the vein in his temple pulsating with every beat of his heart. They were coming right at him. He would fight them if he must. There were three of them, and he had three arrows. He made up his mind that he would aim for their heads. That part of them, at least, appeared human, and as vulnerable as his own. It was only the serpentine scales that made them look unassailable.

He nocked his first arrow and drew it halfway. He was about to spring up and fire when the three suddenly veered from their path, the one in the lead gesturing toward a particularly bright star. They headed off to his right, to the north. As they made their way, Sun-on-Lizard had a good view of the snake men, and what he saw made him grin.

They were not beasts, but men. Men wearing the hard, silver vests of which he had heard tell. The same clothing worn by the fabled outlanders with their cloud-white faces and thunder sticks. Another story he had never believed. Sun-on-Lizard had traveled farther than anyone in his village, down to the red rocks and up to the great salt water, and he had never seen a man with a white face and a stick that made fire. Of course, he had not seen their silver vests before today, either. It struck him as more than passing strange that the men he saw were not white-faced, but dark. It was difficult to tell in the darkness, but the first two looked to be of the Dineh, as they called themselves, or perhaps some other southern tribe. The third man, though, was a head taller than the others, and as dark as night. So dark, in fact that his head seemed to vanish when he passed through the darkest shadows. Sun-on-Lizard had never seen such a man. When they were almost out of sight, he made up his mind to follow them. He had to know more.

Sun-on-Lizard rolled the pebble around in his mouth, trying to stave off thirst with the cool, round stone. Two nights and two days had told him precious little about his quarry. He was quite proud of himself that he had avoided detection during that time. He kept his distance in the daytime, remaining just out of sight, and relying on his tracking skills to keep him on the proper path. Twice he feared he had lost them, but in each instance a small sign reassured him. He had sharp eyes and could find a scuff on a dusty stone, or a pebble pressed into the sand by the soft tread of one trying not to leave a trail. He had to admit, the Dineh moved well, as did the dark fellow. From one that size, he would have counted on more than the occasional marking to indicate his passage.

It was full dark now, and he lay secreted within a rock fall surmounted by scrub brush. The rabbits were long gone, roasted over a banked and shielded fire the night before. He had eaten a bit of dried meat before creeping up on the others' camp. A discontented stomach could make all his stealth for naught. Reclining on his left elbow, he peered out from his hiding place at the strange trio of men. Or at the strange duo, rather. The dark fellow was gone. Careful not to move too hastily, he scanned the area around his hiding place but saw nothing.

He focused all his senses on the two men seated at the tiny fire. They had stripped off their serpentine vests, and now looked much less sinister in their native garb. The one on the left, a squat, muscular fellow with a scarred face and shaggy black hair was roasting lizard tail skewered on a long, sharpened stick. The other, equally short, but with a leaner build and a raptor-like face, sat with his knees against his chest, and his hands clasped together. They were speaking softly, but he could not make out the words. Of course, he spoke very little of their tongue.

A sound behind him caught his ear, and he whipped his head around, his hand going to his knife. The dark man stood behind him, a long knife at the ready. His smile shone in the darkness, and his eyes caught the starlight like dark pools. Sun-on-Lizard saw no threat in the man's countenance, but he did not doubt that the fellow could and would kill him if he so chose. He had the high ground and the better weapon. If Sun-on-Lizard were in the clear, he might be able to throw his knife at the man and get away, but not lying here in a tangle of brush. He spat the pebble from his mouth.

"You track well," he said to the big man, not that the fellow would speak his tongue. "You leave little sign with your passing, and I did not hear you coming up behind me."

"I thank you for the compliment," the man said in a rich voice, deep like the bottom of a canyon. "You are not without skill yourself. My name is Estevanico. Put away the knife and come sit by my fire." He leaned down and proffered an ebony hand.

It took Sun-on-Lizard a moment to recover from the shock of the strange fellow speaking his language. "I suppose you would have already killed me if that was your intention," he said, sheathing his knife and grasping the man's hand in his.

Estevanico hoisted him to his feet as if he was a child. The big man regarded Sun-on-Lizard with big, brown eyes for a long, silent moment before answering. "That remains to be seen."

Chapter 1

Jade tapped on the dive light strapped to her forehead. The beam flickered again and then shone at full strength. Shoddy university equipment. Drifting back to the wall, careful not to disturb the fine layer of silt that coated the floor of the subterranean cavern, she again ran her fingers across the striations in the rock. They were definitely man-made. Much too regular to be natural, and this part of the wall appeared smooth and level underneath the coating of plant life and debris that had accumulated over half a millennium. She scrubbed her gloved fingertips harder against the rock, instinctively turning her head away from the cloud of matter that engulfed her.

Turning again to inspect the spot she had cleared, she waited with heart-pounding anticipation for the sluggish, almost non-existent current to clear her line of sight. With painstaking slowness, the haze cleared away, and her eyes widened. It was a joint, where precisely-hewn stones fitted neatly together. She could see the vertical lines where the blocks met end-to-end. She scrubbed away another patch, revealing more worked stone.

Raising her head, she let her eyes follow the beam of light as it climbed the wall. About six feet above her head, the regular pattern of the ancient stones gave way to a rough jumble of broken rock and tangled roots. It was a collapsed well, just as she had believed she would find. Remarkably, the web of thick roots created a ceiling of sorts, preserving this bottom section almost intact. She made a circuit around the base, inspecting the rocks. They appeared to be solid, with no apparent danger of further collapse. Nonetheless, she grew increasingly aware of the mass of stone directly above her. It had obviously been in place for hundreds of years, but the thought of loose stone filling the shaft of a well made her feel distinctly vulnerable.

She checked her dive watch and was disappointed to see that she had exhausted her allotted time. She had carefully planned her exploration so that she would have time to return, plus two minutes, giving her as much time as possible to seek out the well.

Reorienting herself toward the upstream channel, she kicked out and felt resistance, like something tugging at her from behind. Cautiously she again tried to swim forward, and again she felt something pull her back. She was an experienced diver and knew that she needed to move slowly and remain calm. A sudden movement could tangle her further, or worse, tear a hose loose. She turned her head back and forth, seeking out the obstruction, but to no avail. Whatever she had snagged was directly behind her. Reaching back, she felt for the obstruction but found nothing. A moment's irrational fear rose up inside of her, but she quelled it almost immediately. She had to approach this rationally.

Reaching behind her head she ran her hands along the surface of her breathing apparatus, and soon found the obstruction. A root was wedged between her twin tanks. What were the odds? She tried moving backward, then from side-to-side, but to no avail. She freed her dive knife and tried to saw at the obtrusion, but it proved ineffective against the gnarled root. Besides, it was nigh impossible to accomplish anything while working blindly behind her back. She would have to unstrap her tanks and free them from the obstruction. The thought frightened her a little, but she had practiced the maneuver as part of her training. She again looked at her watch and realized she was now well past time to be done.

Her heart thundered, and her pulse surged. Stay calm, Jade, she reminded herself. Panic led to unnecessarily heavy breathing, which led to faster oxygen consumption which led to… Stop it! None of it mattered right now. She would work the tank free, and then she would make up the lost time on the return swim. Yes, that would work.

Taking two calming breaths, she methodically unbuckled the straps holding her tanks, and slipped free. With a last breath of sweet air, she took her mouth from the mouthpiece. Holding her breath and keeping a firm grip on the tanks, she turned about in the tight space. A few deft tugs and it was free. Putting the gear back on was awkward in the dark, confined space, but she managed nicely and was soon breathing the blessed air again. No time to pat herself on the back, though.

She set out at a rapid clip up the dark, narrow channel, swimming against the current, and what had seemed like a lethargic flow of water now seemed to be putting up serious resistance. Particles of silt and bits of vegetation flew past her face as she shot recklessly up the channel. She passed through a twisting section a little too carelessly and scraped her shoulder against the edge. She felt her neoprene suit tear, but under the present circumstances that was no great concern.

She wondered if Saul knew something was amiss. Did he even know how long she had been gone, or when she should have returned? Probably not. He was not a diver. Great. No one to send in the posse. When I get out of here, I'm finding a dive partner.

The ceiling was low at this point, and her tank banged against a low-hanging rock. She kept going, certain that the distance had not been so great on the way in. What if I've missed the way out? What if I've gone too far? Panic again threatened to seize control, but she forced it down. She remembered this low spot: it was about the halfway mark. Halfway! Down to the dregs of her tank, and she was only halfway.

Her legs pumped like pistons, her cupped hands pulled at the water as if she were dragging herself through sand. She tried holding her breath for longer periods, but soon gave up on the idea. Her body needed the oxygen that was no longer there. Her muscles burned, and the rushing of blood in her veins was now an audible roar. She tasted copper in her mouth, and her lungs strained against invisible bonds. Shadows appeared around the perimeter of her vision and slowly crept inward. She was going to die.

Still biting down on her mouthpiece, she screamed in mute frustration. She tried to fight, but her desperate flailing and kicking quickly subsided as the darkness consumed her. She released her bite on her useless air supply and surrendered. As consciousness faded, she saw a light coming toward her.

What do you know? All the stories are true. She watched with detached awareness as the light grew brighter. She was drifting up to heaven… or wherever.

The glare grew intensely bright, and then she could have sworn she felt arms around her. *An angel has come to take me to heaven…* A sudden tightness encircled her middle, pinning her arms to her sides, and before she knew what was happening, something was forced into her mouth. She tried to protest, and cool, sweet air poured into her lungs. A coughing fit immediately ensued. She had taken more than a bit of water into her mouth, and now it felt like all of it was in her lungs. She tried to twist free, but whatever it was held her tight.

Instinct took over, and she gradually regained control of her lungs and spat the water free. With the fresh flow of oxygen came a renewed sense of calm and awareness. Someone had come to her rescue after all. He was holding her tight so that she would not, in her panic, drown both of them. She took few long, calming breaths from the pony tank her rescuer was holding in his right hand. At least, she hoped those thickly muscled forearms belonged to a guy. Making a point to keep her body as relaxed as possible, she slipped her right arm down and tapped him twice on the thigh. His grip relaxed a touch, and she raised her hand and she circled her thumb and forefinger to make the "OK" sign. He slid the mini-tank into her hand and let go of her.

Turning to face her rescuer, she saw that it was indeed a man, but other than his blond hair, she could not tell anything about him. Giving him a nod and a quick wave of thanks, she led the way back up the channel. She could not believe how close she had come to dying. What's more, she could not believe someone had rescued her.

Relief gave way to embarrassment and anger as she neared safety. She couldn't believe how her own bad judgment had almost killed her. *Stupid!* She was a professional, not some weekend scuba diver. This guy, whoever he was, probably thought she was one of the dozen grad school bimbos working the dig aboveground. She was going to beat herself up over this for a long time.

The glow of sunlight flickered in the distance, and soon she was up the shaft and breaking the surface. Strong hands grabbed her under the arms and lifted her free of the water. Her feet touched the ground, and then she dropped down hard on her backside.

"Why were you down for so long?" Saul rounded on her, his square face marred by concern. "What happened in there? Are you trying to kill yourself? Because you nearly killed me from worry. Do I need to take up diving so I can keep an eye on you?"

"I'm fine, Saul. Really I am." She shrugged off her tanks and grinned, reaching up to pat his short, neatly coiffed brown hair like she would a faithful pet. "Thank you for sending someone for me. I was wondering if you had even noticed." She didn't catch his reply because her attention was focused on her rescuer, who was clambering out of the water.

He wasn't the tallest fellow, not quite six feet, even with the spiky blond hair, which was already sticking up as it dried in the hot Argentinean sun. He pulled off his dive mask to reveal a lightly tanned face, a friendly smile, and intense blue-gray eyes. Jade smiled back, taking a moment to admire the thickly muscled legs. The guy wasn't the type she usually went for, but he was definitely cute. He took a step toward her, and she hauled herself to her feet to greet him, but Saul was quicker.

"Thank you again for helping us." Saul stepped between them, clasping the man's hand in both of his. "She had been down for so long, and I always tell her she takes too many unnecessary risks. Thinks she's immortal, she does." He suddenly seemed to realize that he was still shaking hands with the fellow, and let go.

"It's quite all right."

She liked his voice. It was cheerful yet firm, and had a rich timbre, like one of those guys who reads audio books. What was she thinking about? She hadn't even spoken to the guy and already she was mentally babbling.

"I'm just glad I was nearby. It was a close thing getting her out of there."

Saul was about to say more, but Jade pushed him to the side and offered her hand.

"Thank you so much for your help, Mister…"

"Maddock," he replied, looking her directly in the eye. "Dane Maddock. And you're welcome."

"I'm just so embarrassed that I let myself run out of air like that. I'm really an experienced diver. I just pushed it a little too far." She stopped, realizing she was on the verge of babbling for real. He was still looking her in the eye, though, which scored him a few points in her book. Most guys would have let their gaze drift a little lower by now.

"You know what they say," he replied, waggling his finger like a grade school teacher. "One-third of your air going in, one-third going back out…" He was grinning ear-to-ear.

"…and one-third in reserve in case of an emergency, one of which I did arise. I'm well aware of the rule of thirds, Mr. Maddock. I just…" she felt her face grow warm. "I just didn't follow them this time." She wanted to be annoyed at his condescension, but his grin told her he was only joking.

"Understood. You can just call me Maddock. Incidentally, I still don't know your name."

"Oh, I'm sorry. I'm Jade Ihara."

"A beautiful name. You don't have a Japanese accent."

"My father was Japanese," she said. "My mother is Hawaiian. I was raised on Oahu."

"Well, that explains it." He cupped his chin and looked thoughtfully into her eyes. "I was trying to figure it out, but I couldn't place it."

"Explains what, may I ask?" She resisted the urge to squirm like a schoolgirl under his cool gaze.

"You have the traditional Japanese beauty, with just a touch of the robust splendor of Polynesia."

"I don't know whether to be flattered or totally creeped out." He had her laughing—another point in his favor. "Where did you get that line about 'robust splendor of Polynesia' anyway?"

"From a coffee commercial," he said, grinning.

"So, what are you anyway? Some kind of professional 'damsel in distress' rescuer or something?"

"I'm a marine archaeologist," he said. "We were working nearby. The discovery of this outpost has been a great opportunity for us."

Saul cleared his throat loudly, reminding them of his presence. He stood with hands on hips, tapping his foot. His mouth was twisted into a sour frown.

"Saul, if you will please pack up my equipment, I'll be with you in a moment." She cut off his protest with a raised hand. "Thank you, Saul. I'll join you shortly." She met his stare with a level gaze until he turned away, muttering something under his breath. He snatched up her dive gear and stamped off through the tangled growth. "I'm sorry," she said, turning back to Maddock. "Saul is very protective of me. He means well."

"Not your boyfriend, I hope."

"No, he's definitely not my boyfriend. He's my assistant." That was technically true, she supposed.

"Well, I need to get going," Maddock said. "By the way, did your mother ever teach you about the old Hawaiian tradition? When someone saves your life, you have to have dinner on his boat that evening." He made a show of checking the time on his dive watch. "At exactly 18:00 hours. Give or take a few minutes, of course."

"Is that so?" She really didn't have time to socialize with this, or any guy. But he had saved her life. Besides, an idea was forming in the back of her mind. "Who am I to flout tradition? Six o'clock it is. I'll need directions to this boat of yours." What was she getting herself into? "And Maddock? Dinner had better be spectacular."

Chapter 2

Man, I cannot believe you're kicking us out," Matt Barnaby, Maddock's engineer and first mate for this expedition while his partner Bones was on vacation, complained as he swung his leg over the side of their boat, the Sea Foam. "And for a girl of all things." He shook his head, turned, and hopped into the waiting motorboat. "Unbelievable."

"Hey, it's not that unbelievable," Maddock protested. Actually, it was. Since the death of his wife and unborn son nearly five years ago, he had sworn off women. Recent experiences had changed his outlook, and he was beginning to come to grips with some of his inner demons. "I like girls."

"I thought you liked Kaylin." Corey Dean, the ship's tech-head, and sonar guru stumbled out of the cabin, trying to slather on sunscreen and spray himself with insect repellant at the same time. His fair skin was no match for the intense sun, but he loved the sea. "I didn't know you were playing the field all of a sudden."

"Kaylin's my friend." Kaylin Maxwell was the daughter of Maddock's former commander. The two of them had been through a harrowing adventure together and come out of it barely alive. The experience had forged a strong bond between them, but sometimes it felt more like brother and sister than anything romantic. Perhaps it was because she was the first woman since Melissa to get close to him. "And she isn't your problem in any case."

"So you won't mind if I ask her out," Matt said, "seeing how you're just friends and all." He smiled a gap-toothed smile and ran his fingers through his close-cropped receding brown hair, pretending to primp in front of a mirror.

"She's from a Navy family. She'd sooner date a pig than an army grunt," Maddock jibed.

"See there, Corey? You've got a shot after all!" Matt helped Corey over the side and into the small craft.

"You know what really blows?" Corey replied, ignoring Matt's dig. "Bones goes on vacation, and now Maddock turns into the player. I thought we were going to get a temporary break from the college dorm room shenanigans."

Uriah Bonebrake, nicknamed "Bones", was Maddock's partner and a longtime companion. They had been best friends since their days in the Navy SEALs. The big

Cherokee had a way with the ladies and was known to kick his crewmates off the boat for an occasional evening of entertaining.

"That's right," Maddock called back, warming to the banter. "I'm picking up the slack for Bones. Bet you I..."

"You what?" Jade sat astride a jet ski just off the starboard bow. Maddock had been so busy bantering with his friends that he had not heard her approach. Her brown eyes sparkled, and her straight white teeth shone against her almond complexion. She was wearing a loose-fitting white tank top over a turquoise bikini top. Her black shorts were rolled at the waistband, showing off her flat stomach and a few extra inches of her firm thighs. "Come on now, I'm dying to hear."

"Epic fail!" Corey laughed and fired up the motorboat. "Good luck climbing out of that hole, Maddock."

"Hey, girl. How you doing?" Willis Sanders, the final member of the crew, gave Jade his warmest smile.

"I'd be doing better if you didn't call me 'girl.' I'm a bit old for that." Jade winked to show there were no hard feelings.

"I hear you. Y'all have a good night now." Willis joined Matt and Corey in the motorboat, and they cruised away.

When they had gone, Maddock turned back to Jade. "I'll bet you absolutely love the dinner I've prepared for us." Leaning over the rail, he offered her a hand, which she clasped firmly. He hauled her over with one tug, and she landed nimbly on the deck, her bare feet making barely a sound when they hit. Martial arts training, he supposed, or perhaps dancing. "By the way, totally unfair shutting down the engine and drifting up on me like that."

"I'm full of surprises." She gave him a coy grin. "If dinner's good enough, I might let you take it for a spin around the harbor." She surveyed the Sea Foam with an appraising eye. "Nice," she said. "She's obviously been worked hard, but I can tell you take good care of her."

"Done much sailing?" he asked, intrigued by this beautiful young woman who seemed to have a great deal of depth. "I suppose if you've done enough diving, you have to have climbed your share of rigging."

"Is that some sort of innuendo?" she teased. He shook his head, and she laughed. "I grew up around the water in Hawaii. My uncle had a fishing boat, and I spent a lot of time out with him. My mother hated it, said it wasn't ladylike, but I didn't care. Even then, I loved the sun, the salt spray, the dips and the swells." Her eyes had a faraway glint as she remembered. "I don't get out on the water as much as I used to. Mostly when I go back to visit my mother and uncle."

"What about your father?" Maddock asked. He could tell by the way she flinched that he had touched on a sore subject. "Sorry. I don't mean to pry."

"That's all right," she said. "He left before I was born. Went back to Japan. He wasn't really part of my life." She stared down at the blue-green water, her face now downcast. "I did all right, I suppose. What about you? What's your story?"

"Navy brat," Maddock said. "Did my time in the service, met my friend Bones, and we went into business together when we left the SEALs." He shrugged. "It's a good life. Lots of sun. The occasional interesting diversion," he gave her a meaningful look and grinned.

"I think you skipped over quite a bit in that lovely ten-second autobiography." She narrowed her eyes and stepped close to him. "But that's okay. I have all night to pump information from you." Raising her head, she closed her eyes and inhaled deeply. "What's on the grill?"

Dinner was one of Maddock's specialties: broiled sea bass with lime and herbs, steamed vegetables, and fresh fruit. Jade was duly impressed, and dinner conversation was relaxed and enjoyable. An archaeologist by trade, she had graduated from the University of Utah with a specialty in Native American tribes of the southwest, and now served on the faculty of Central Utah University.

"So," Maddock said, squeezing a lime into his second Dos Equis, "what is someone with your background doing working an early Spanish dig in Argentina? Seems pretty far out of your area." He took a long drink, savoring the strong flavor, the cool drink perfect on such a muggy evening.

"It's not as far afield as you might think," she said. "The Spaniards who founded this settlement were some of the same men who explored the American southwest, even up into Utah." She put her bottle down and folded her hands in her lap, suddenly serious. "I have a business proposition for you."

"Bummer," Maddock said. "And here I hoped it would be a proposition of a more personal nature." He smiled, put his beer down, and leaned forward, mirroring her posture. It was a technique by which Bones swore. He said it created empathy and identification. Then again, when had Bones ever cared about either of those things? Maddock suppressed a laugh and leaned back, letting his arms hang over the sides of the chair.

"Very funny," she said, misunderstanding the reason for the grin on his face. "Personal comes after I've known someone a great deal longer than one evening. Or did you think I was, shall we say, promiscuous?"

"Didn't think, only hoped." That was a comeback worthy of Bones, but it didn't gain him any points. Jade just smirked. Bones had a natural way with women while Maddock had to work hard at it. It wasn't fair. "Seriously, what's your proposition?"

"I need to have another go at that underground stream." She raised her voice and hurried on when she saw Maddock grimace. "I think it will take only one more time. I need to go back to the place where you rescued me." She paused, her brown eyes boring into him. "And I need a dive partner."

"I hate fresh water dives," Maddock protested. "They're dangerous, as you found out today, and they're not something I'm comfortable doing." Jade kept staring at him in silence. He knew what she was up to, waiting for him to fill the gap in the conversation. She would try to keep him talking until he talked his way through all his objections and right smack into doing what she wanted. Not biting, he retrieved his beer and took another swig.

"I don't blame you. I know it's dangerous work, which is why I need an experienced diver with me." Her voice softened. "This is very important to me. I've been working on it for ten years. It's not..." She broke off, uttered a distinctly unladylike curse, then mumbled something that sounded a lot like "Why do I get so flustered around you?" before turning her attention to her beer.

He made her feel flustered? He swore he would never understand women. The look of disappointment on her face was heartbreaking. "Why don't you tell me what you're working on?" he said.

"If I tell you, will you dive with me?" She cocked an eye at him.

"No," he lied, knowing full well that he was going to let her have her way because... well, just because that's what was going to happen. "But I'll think about it.

Tell me what you're doing here."

Jade leaned across the small table, close enough that he could smell her perfume. Jasmine or something like it. "Are you familiar with the story of the Seven Cities of Cibola?"

"I've heard the name," he replied cautiously. "That's about it." A creepy déjà vu feeling blanketed his mind, enveloping him in a muzzy semi-conscious state. He couldn't possibly be getting into another weird mystery.

"Part of the impetus behind the Spanish exploration of New Spain, what we could term Colonial Mexico, was the myriad of myths about treasure and magical places." As she spoke, she sat up straighter and her voice gained strength and confidence. She would make a great lecturer. "One of the greatest was the legend of Las Siete Ciudades Doradas De Cíbola, the Seven Golden Cities of Cibola. The myth was an outgrowth of the Moorish conquest of Portugal in the early eighth century. Allegedly, in the year 714, seven Catholic bishops and their followers fled across the Atlantic to a land called Antilia."

"The Antilles," he chimed in, to show that he was paying attention.

"Correct. The story goes that they fled to the New World and established the seven cities, where they hid gold, gems, and religious articles to keep them safe from the Moors."

At the mention of religious articles, Maddock bolted upright. "Oh no. No friggin' way!" He struck the table with his fist so hard that both their beers tipped over. Jade managed to catch hers, but his hit the table, spewing its foamy contents everywhere.

"Nice," Jade deadpanned. "Are you always this erratic? What did I say, anyway?" Her smooth features were tense with concern.

"Nothing," he muttered. "I just had a bad experience recently and..." What could he tell her that she would actually believe? "It's not important." Before she could reply, he hurried to the galley to retrieve some paper towels. Returning, he sopped up the mess as Jade looked on with an expression somewhere between amused and offended.

When the spill was cleaned up, she nodded like an officer at inspection time and inclined her head toward the bow. "How about we move back there and watch the sun set?" Maddock liked that idea just fine but was disappointed when, once they were seated, she resumed her story.

"The Antillean islands failed to produce the great quantities of gold and silver the Spaniards were expecting, so they set their sights on the continent and its purported riches. As soon as Cortes and his men finished conquering the Aztec Empire in the early 1520s, they set out to find these legendary Seven Cities of Gold. The expedition took them as far as the Texas panhandle, but, needless to say, they found no sign of Cibola.

"And then, in 1528 a Spaniard named Cabeza de Vaca was shipwrecked on the Texas Gulf Coast. He wandered through Texas and into northern Mexico before his rescue in 1536. He told of fantastic treasures he had seen in villages to the north, "with many people and very big houses." And thus, what is now New Mexico became targeted as the mythical Cibola.

"Viceroy Antonio de Mendoza soon became intrigued by the fantastic riches rumored to exist in the Seven Golden Cities of Cibola beyond New Spain's northern frontier. In 1539, he sent an expedition led by Estevanico, a black slave who had been shipwrecked with Cabeza de Vaca, and Fray Marcos de Niza to verify de Vaca's reports. Estevanico did not return. It is reported that he died in western New Mexico at Háwikuh, one of the Zuñi pueblos."

"I notice you emphasize 'reported' that he died," Maddock observed. "You don't think so?"

"Be patient, I'm getting to that," she reproved, smiling. She was warming to her tale and obviously thought he was as well. And he was, despite his better judgment. "Get yourself another Dos Equis and shut up. Get me one too."

He produced the drinks in short order and settled back in to hear the rest of the story.

"Fray Marcos returned to New Spain, declaring he had seen golden cities, the smallest of which was bigger than Mexico City. These strange people were said to possess in great quantities domestic utensils and ornaments made of gold and silver, and to be proficient in many of the arts of the Europeans."

"I think I know how this story ends," Maddock said, recalling a bit of history. "Coronado took a stab at it and failed miserably. Seems like these seven golden cities were just mud villages and such. Nothing but a pipe dream."

"Right. He spent almost two years searching for the seven cities, but finally concluded that they were a myth. His expedition was branded a failure." She bit her lip and stared out at the water.

"This Fray Marcos guy, why do you think he lied? Didn't want to admit to having failed? Maybe he didn't want his friend to have died in vain?"

Jade turned and met his gaze with wide-eyed seriousness. "The kindest historians think that, from a distance, he saw the sunset on adobe walls containing bits of silica and believed he was looking at glimmers of a city of gold."

"That doesn't make sense," Maddock protested. "Why would he see a city of gold from a distance, and never go close enough to get a good look? And what about all the details he provided? How would he know those things if he observed from afar?"

"You're right," she said. She took a sip of her beer, then rubbed the bottle across her forehead. Maddock watched the cool beads of condensation trickle down her tanned skin. Illumined in the setting sun, they put him in the mind of gold. "Marcos did find Cibola, and he concocted his story to protect the truth." She took another drink, waiting for his reply.

"Come on, now. Don't leave me hanging," he said. "You've got to fill in the blanks."

She reached into her small black bag and withdrew a plastic folder, opened the catch, and produced a small stack of paper-clipped sheets. "I'll hit the high points, so I don't bore you," she said, smiling mischievously. "Fray Marcos's journal turned up in a collection in Spain. I've scanned the pertinent pages. Translations are on the back." She held them out to him.

Maddock felt strangely detached as he took them. His fingers were numb, and his mind was muddled, and not because of the beer. "Another journal," he muttered. Jade cocked her head and frowned, but said nothing. "Unbelievable." He didn't feel like elaborating.

"Uh huh," Jade said. "He provides precious few details, but he makes it plain that he found something fantastic. He is also very clear that the story he told Mendoza was not only a fabrication, but a tale carefully crafted to lead them astray." She took a deep breath and held it, regarding him as if taking his measure. "I don't know why, but I feel I can trust you." Maddock nodded and waited for her to continue.

"The journal indicates that Marcos wanted to hide Cibola from Mendoza, Coronado, and the rest, but he didn't want to hide it from the world forever. I believe he left a clue in the bottom of a well." She paused, either for effect or to see if he had any response. "I found that well just before you rescued me. The top caved in long ago. No one even knew it was there. The bottom portion is intact." She leaned back, picked up her drink, and peered at him with an intense stare as she sipped her beer.

Maddock made a show of examining the papers, all the while turning things over in his mind. He could tell himself that he didn't want to get involved in another caper like he had before, but the truth was his heart was racing from sheer excitement. He had chosen his particular field not only because he loved the sea, but because he loved the mystery, the search, and discovery. This was right up his alley. And then, of course, there was Jade. He glanced up, his eyes meeting hers long enough to register the crinkled brow and tiny smile. She knew she had him.

"So, what exactly do you want me to do?"

Chapter 3

The water was colder than he remembered, and the tunnel darker. He supposed adrenaline had drawn his thoughts away from such things when he was coming after Jade. Now he had time to examine his surroundings, all of which reminded him how much he hated cave diving. Too many skilled divers had met their ends in caves just like this one. Dark, twisting, precarious arteries of peril, all of them. He couldn't wait to get out of here and make up for the sleep he missed the night before.

The two of them had stayed up late, planning the dive. By the time they were finished, Matt and Corey had long returned to the ship and called it a night. He had suggested that Jade stay the night, but she laughed and gave him a chaste hug before heading back to shore. Thoughts of her blended with images of gold and treasure until he couldn't say which was the most responsible for keeping him awake.

He snapped out of his reverie when the narrow channel opened into a wide chamber. They were in the well. He looked up, allowing the beam of his headlamp to play across the ceiling. A thick snarl of ancient roots held up massive chunks of stone, bound together by mud and clay that had seeped down into the collapsed well shaft. The whole thing had a precarious feel to it. He couldn't wait to finish up and get out of there. Jade drifted up alongside him and motioned toward the floor as if to say "get on with it." He needed no convincing.

Reaching into the small dive bag strapped to his waist, he fished out his metal detector. About three times the size of a cell phone, the rectangular instrument with its fat red buttons and large digital display reminded him of the hand-held football game he had gotten for his fourteenth birthday. The 'players' were little red dashes, and it emitted an annoying tweet whenever you scored. His parents had regretted buying it for him by the end of the first day. He grinned at the memory as he punched the buttons and waited for the instrument to boot up. It was still hard to think about Mom and Dad, but it didn't hurt the way it once had.

The screen was black, with green indicator bars up each side. He drifted to the downstream side of the well, chose what passed for a corner, and began his search. The little detector could penetrate about three feet in ideal conditions, and he was banking on the bottom of the well being silt and mud. He hoped that whatever they were looking for was made of metal. If it wasn't…. well, it wouldn't be the end of the world if they had to excavate the entire floor, but it was worth giving the unit a shot. Besides, it was an expensive toy, and he wanted to play with it. Better than a power tool any day.

Jade shone a high-powered dive light on the floor in front of him, leading the way as he crisscrossed the well bottom. Thankfully there were few obstructions, the gentle current having kept the floor swept clean over the centuries. He held the detector a half-meter off the bottom, sweeping it slowly back-and-forth, feeling like a hotel maid cleaning the floor.

The first hit came almost immediately, small and faint. He stopped and swept the area again. He felt certain that it wouldn't amount to anything, but he indicated the location to Jade, who swam over to meet him. She produced a long, thin digging tool and probed the area, careful not to stir up more dirt than necessary. The steady flow of the underground stream should keep the silt down, but it did not hurt to take care. In short order, she dug free a small, dark object about the breadth of his thumbnail. Perhaps a button or a coin, but they wouldn't know until they took it up top and cleaned it. Jade shrugged and deposited the item in her own dive bag.

The search continued with few results. They turned up a couple more unremarkable chunks of some metal or other, but nothing more. Maddock found himself growing impatient when suddenly his screen went supernova. The indicators on either side shot up, the bars hovering near the top. The display was a solid green square. He moved it back and forth over the spot, which was almost in the very center, trying to get a feel for the size of the object. He quickly determined that it was no larger than a meter square and no smaller than half that size. He switched the detector off and put it away. He would finish his sweep after they had exhumed whatever this was, but he had a good feeling that this was what they were looking for.

He withdrew his digging tool, a ten-inch titanium rod with a blunted, triangular tip and a six-inch rubber grip on the other end, and drew an imaginary circle around the target area. Jade nodded and began working on one side while he took the other. Firmly, but with great care, he probed the perimeter of the target area. Given the intensity of the signal, he hoped it was not buried too deep. The well bottom, mostly silt and clay, gave way easily as he pushed the rod in up to the handle again and again until finally he met with resistance. A glance told him that it was about seven inches down. He withdrew the tool and tried a spot six inches closer to the area where Jade was working. Again he struck something solid at a depth of seven inches. He tapped Jade on the shoulder, and indicated the area, giving her a thumbs-up, which she returned with enthusiasm. Together, they began removing a half-millennium of dirt, clay, and rock. A cloud of fine particles enveloped them, but the lazy current carried it away though not quite fast enough to keep pace with their digging.

When they had cleared a hand 's width channel about two feet in length, he was finally able to see what they were excavating. It was smooth and dark with a gently-angled edge. The exposed surface was slightly convex. Encouraged, Maddock produced a larger digging tool, a small shovel with a wide blade that Bones liked to call his "beach toy", and began scooping away the soil in large chunks. Jade tapped her wrist, and he consulted his dive watch. They had been down longer than he had thought. They had five minutes to get this thing out of the ground and start their return with a reasonable amount of time to spare. After Jade's near-disaster, he wasn't willing to take chances. They each carried a pony tank, but he would prefer to avoid using them altogether.

They worked fast, and soon had all but a thin layer of dirt and clay cleared from what he no longer thought of as an object, but an artifact. He swept the dirt away until his gloved fingertips touched the surface. It was hard and smooth with regular rows of raised bumps and lines. His fingers searched for the edge and found it, squared off and a half-inch thick. Increasingly confident in the solidity and durability of the artifact, he worked the edge of his shovel around the sides, clearing away the debris while Jade brushed the surface clean.

When the object was fully exposed, they paused, letting the silt drift away. As the water cleared, the object seemed to rise up toward them. It was a breastplate though its thickness and apparent weight made it obvious to Maddock that no man had ever worn it. Time and the elements had turned it almost black, but in the glow of the dive lamps he could discern raised markings. His heart pounded with eager anticipation as the two of them grasped it by opposite edges and pulled.

Nothing.

They tried again, but it would not budge. He checked his dive watch and found that they had less than two minutes. Retrieving his small digging tool, he worked it under one edge, and tried to pry it up, but to no effect. Jade did the same on her side. He reminded himself that, if need be, they could come back with better tools and fresh tanks. After five hundred years, the thing wasn't going anywhere soon, but he was stubborn enough to not want to leave it for even a short while. He managed to get the titanium blade underneath the breastplate, and levered it back and forth, working it along the edge. Soon he had enough leverage to try and pry it up from the bottom. Hoping that it was as sturdy as he reckoned, he braced his feet on the floor and lifted. The breastplate budged a millimeter, then two, and then it broke free with a massive upsurge of dirt and clay.

Knowing they were on borrowed time, Maddock motioned for Jade to help him with the breastplate, which was sitting on its edge on the well floor. She took hold of it, while he opened his mesh bag, pulled out two sturdy straps, and secured them around the breastplate. Where they crossed in the middle, he hooked a quick-connect, then snapped that onto a thick, folded object. Jade tilted her head questioningly. He unsnapped his pony tank from his belt and secured it to a valve. Jade nodded and gave him a "thumbs-up" as the object grew into a torpedo-shaped bladder with two handles on the top. He took hold of the bladder and lifted, the added buoyancy making it an easy burden. He was about to lead the way out when Jade pointed at his feet.

He looked down to where they had pulled up the breastplate. The silt had drifted away to reveal a dark circle embedded in the floor. A sigil, a cross inside a clover, was engraved on it. Jade dove down and began trying to work it free.

It looks like a seal, Maddock thought. A cold certainty swept over him, and he shook his head. He wanted to shout, for all the good it would do. He watched as if in slow motion as Jade gave a twist, and the edge of the seal crumbled. Cracks appeared on the surface, and then it imploded. Knowing she had screwed up big-time, Jade turned and headed for a tunnel leading out, with Maddock right behind her. Giant bubbles burst forth, and then a muffled sucking sound filled the watery cavern. The gentle current was now a daunting foe, and he struggled to make headway, the breastplate dragging him down.

A chunk of rock bounced off his mask, knocking it askew and letting in a small trickle of water. The ceiling was coming down! Invisible hands pulled at him, seeking to draw him back into the well. He was in the shaft, but he was making little progress. His legs burned, and his aching lungs reminded him that air would soon be in short supply. Letting go of the breastplate with his right hand, he grabbed for the side of the tunnel, searching for a handhold. His legs still doing double-time, his fingertips found a crack in the rock, and he pulled himself forward. He hoped Jade had made it out.

He suddenly felt himself being hauled forward, and he was dimly aware of a gloved hand clutching his shoulder. He kicked and paddled as Jade pulled him into a recessed area on the side of the tunnel. Thick vertical cracks ran down the wall. Still fighting the current, he shoved his free hand into one the cracks, made a fist and twisted until it was wedged tightly. Jade had done the same, and she wrapped her free arm around both him and the breastplate, helping him hold on.

The current raged, and Maddock's legs were slowly pulled out from under him. He kicked furiously as he felt himself drawn inexorably toward the well and certain death. Jade still clutched him tightly, and he was glad to know she was still holding on as well. His shoulder screamed in agony, and he feared it would pop out of its socket, but he tensed his muscles and held on. Dirt and debris battered them as it was sucked down the tunnel and into the well.

And then his hand slipped.

It happened suddenly. One moment his fist was painfully wedged in the rock, the next instant he was pulled free, taking Jade with him.

A tremendous crash sounded in the darkness behind them, loud in the watery tunnel, and then they were hurled back up the channel, away from the well. He careened into one wall, then another. He tumbled forward, the breastplate banging painfully against his shin. He was flipped upside down, and he crashed into a wall of stone, his breath leaving him along with his mouthpiece, and he slid to the bottom amidst a shower of dirt and rock.

Woozy, he tried to get a handle on his wits. He found his mouthpiece, forced it between his teeth, and tried to breathe, but his lungs were constricted from the blow. Schooling himself to calmness, he relaxed. It was no easy task to will himself to be at ease underwater in the dark, but soon he was able to take a sip of air. A few more tentative gasps and he was breathing again. He did not need to look at his dive watch to know he would soon need his reserve tank. He felt for it at his hip and was not completely surprised to find it gone.

Righting himself, he tried to get his bearings. The well must have finally collapsed, re-sealing the hole Jade had opened, and sending the wave of water that had sent them shooting back up the tunnel. That was good. It meant that he was closer to the way out. But how to find their way in the dark?

He ran his hand along the wall and discovered that he had struck a sharp curve in the channel. Trailing a hand along the edge, he swam forward, hoping he was headed in the right direction. Several times he collided with obstacles or banged into the opposite wall in particularly narrow stretches of the tunnel, but he kept moving forward. The darkness was absolute. *If I hit the collapsed well, I'm dead. I'll never make it back from there.* The thought did not strike him with fear so much as it disappointed him. He wasn't ready to go. *Where is Bones when I need him?*

A faint glimmer appeared far ahead of him and then a bar of yellow light sliced through the dirty water. Jade was somewhere up ahead with a flashlight. He swam furiously, the light shining brighter as the intervening space grew smaller. Before he knew it, Jade was with him. She took hold of the breastplate and together they swam out of the murky tunnel.

Maddock spat out his mouthpiece as he broke the surface, and sucked in a lungful of hot, humid air. Matt and Corey were waiting for them, along with Saul. The three of them lifted the breastplate from the water, and then hauled the two divers out.

Dropping to one knee, he removed his mask and turned to look at Jade, who lay on her side, breathing hard.

"I don't know about you," she panted, "but I'm thinking we shouldn't go back down there anymore."

"Do you think?" Maddock said, grinning despite the dozen or so pains he felt throughout his body. "Do me a favor. If we ever dive together again, check with me before you pry anything out of the floor." Still panting, he took a few deep, calming breaths. "I just hope that whatever we found was worth it."

"It will be," she said. "Did you see the symbol on the seal?" Maddock nodded, remembering the clover around the cross. "That was the mark of Fray Marcos de Niza."

Chapter 4

"Dude, this place is seriously dry. Somebody turn on the humidifier." Bones unscrewed the top of his bottled water, chugged half of it, and dumped the rest on top of his head. He let loose with a massive belch and tossed the empty bottle into the back of Isaiah's pickup. "You didn't tell me it would be like this, Cuz."

Isaiah frowned. "You realize this is a desert. What did you expect?" He hitched the backpack over his shoulder and leaned in through the driver's side window to grab his clipboard and notebook. Straightening, he fixed Bones with a level gaze. "Bones, this is a serious dig, and the first one I've ever directed. Promise me you won't be…" He paused, searching for the words.

"Be myself?" Bones asked. He had to laugh when his cousin nodded in affirmation. "All right Cuz, I'll behave. Honest injun!" He raised his hand like a plains warrior.

Isaiah rolled his eyes. "Bones, you know I hate it when you talk like that. It degrades our people." He shook his head. He knew Bones well enough to know his sense of humor would never change. "Forget it. Grab that other bag." He nodded to a black duffel bag in the bed near the wheel well on Bones' side of the truck.

"Are you sure we're related?" Bones kidded, hefting the bag. "Sometimes it's hard to believe we're swimming in the same gene pool, know what I mean?"

"Our mothers were related. I don't claim you at all, Cuz." Isaiah grinned and winked. "Let's get going. I don't want to be late on my first day." He led the way down a dusty gravel drive past a line of dirty trucks and SUVs that Bones assumed belonged to the workers on the dig. Falling a few steps behind his cousin, Bones licked his finger and wrote "YOUR MOM IS THIS DIRTY" on the back of a Range Rover before picking up the pace to catch up.

"You know you love having me around," he said, clapping a hand on the smaller man's shoulder. "By the way. Think you could explain to me how my Tonto act disgraces our ancestors, but it's all right for you to dig up their bones?"

"We're not exhuming any graves," Isaiah said. His long, thin face visibly pained.

"We're examining pictographs, and excavating artifacts from the site

"Oh," Bones said, shrugging. "I thought it was because these guys are Fremont, and we're Cherokee."

Isaiah snapped his head around and raised a finger, looking every bit the junior college professor that he was. His lecture was thankfully cut off by an attractive young woman in a business suit.

"Excuse me. Are you Dr. Horsely?" she asked though her tone indicated that the question was a mere formality. She knew exactly who Isaiah was.

Bones chuckled, drawing annoyed glances from her and Isaiah. His cousin's family name was Horse Fly, but Isaiah had legally changed it when he went to college.

"Yes, I'm Isaiah Horsely. How may I help you?" Isaiah took the woman's proffered hand, looking distinctly uncomfortable. He had always been shy around women.

"I'm Amanda Shores of the Deseret Bugle. I'd like to ask you a few questions about the dig." Not waiting for Isaiah's reply, she thrust a digital recorder in his face and pushed the record button. "What do you expect to find in this site?"

"I can't say yet," Isaiah said, taking a step back. "This site's very existence is a new revelation, and we've made only a preliminary survey. There are quite a few fascinating pictographs…"

Amanda cut him off. "Why do you think Mr. Orley has kept this site a secret for so long?" She took a step toward him, keeping the recorder in his face. "What do you think he has to hide?"

"He kept the site a secret in order to protect it." Isaiah looked decidedly uncomfortable. "I have no reason to believe he is hiding anything."

"We really have to go Miss Shores," Bones said, taking Isaiah by the arm and guiding him around the reporter.

Amanda was not deterred. She stepped in front of Bones, blocking his path. "And who might you be?" Challenge shone in her hazel eyes as she faced him.

"Uriah Bonebrake, but you can call me Bones. I'm just a grunt on this expedition, helping Dr. Horsely with his project. But if you're going to do a write-up on me, would you mention my band? We're called 'Custer's Next-to-Last Stand'. I've got a demo tape…"

"I'm sorry, that's not my department," Amanda said, cutting off the recorder and tucking it into her purse. She pointedly turned her back on Bones as she turned back to Isaiah, proffering a business card. "Here's my card, Dr. Horsely. If you find anything of interest, I would appreciate a call." She said it as if it was an order rather than a request.

Isaiah nodded and tucked the card into his pocket. Together he and Bones made their way toward the dig site.

"What is Deseret, anyway?" Bones asked.

"That was the proposed name of a state that Mormon settlers tried to establish back in the 1800's."

"So, you gonna' call her? The reporter chick, I mean." Bones stole a glance over his shoulder as Amanda climbed into her car. "She's cute in a brunette gymnast sort of way."

"You're crazy, Bones. I don't know how you lived this long." Isaiah chuckled and clapped a hand on his shoulder. "And yes, I just might call her."

They walked in silence for a short while. Bones took in the high skies and rugged terrain. It was beautiful, but a bit confined for someone accustomed to the sea. He tried to imagine being a native tribesman a thousand years ago, fighting to survive in this desolate land. Isaiah had assured him that despite appearances, Utah was far from barren. In fact, the land was teeming with life if you only knew where to look for it. Bones supposed that made it like the ocean in a way: bleak on the surface, but abundant life concealed within its depths.

They had not walked far when a short, square man in a weathered John Deere hat hailed them. He wore a flannel shirt in spite of the heat, and sweat rolled down his florid face. He drew a pack of Beech-Nut from the back pocket of his jeans and packed a wad into his cheek before speaking.

"You gonna' keep them diggers over at the site where they belong?" He looked at Isaiah as if daring him to say 'no.' "I don't want 'em nowhere else. This is a working ranch, and I ain't got time to be chasin' college kids all over the place."

"We're fully aware of the parameters of the dig site," Isaiah said. "Mr. Orley, I'd like you to meet my cousin, Uriah Bonebrake. People call him Bones."

Bones reached out to shake the rancher's hand, but the fellow just stared up at him for a long moment. He spat a small stream of tobacco juice onto the dusty gravel. "You're one big damned Indian. I think you're the biggest 'un I've ever seen."

"I used to model for the cigar store Indians," Bones said, "but chewing tobacco put us out of business. Now I just go around making white people hurt their necks."

Orley frowned and pursed his lips, glaring at Bones. He looked like he might spew out a stream of curses, but suddenly he laughed and clasped Bones' hand. "By God, you're a funny fellow too. This 'un here," he nodded at Isaiah, "you'd sooner get a tater out of a goat's behind than get a smile out of him."

Bones shuddered at the bizarre mental image. "He's a college fellow," he said in a conspiratorial tone, eyeing Isaiah out of the corner of his eye. "You know the type. Serious all the time."

"I do know it," Orley said. "You mean you ain't a college fellow yourself?"

"Me? Not a chance. Retired from the Navy." He left out the fact that he had earned a two-year degree while in the service. "You ever in the service, Mr. Orley?"

"Hell yes! Did my tour in 'Nam and got the hell out of there." He nodded at Bones, as if satisfied, and turned back to Isaiah. "Anyways, keep them diggers over there," he pointed to the dig site just visible in the distance. "And stay out of the small barn," he indicated a large shed built against a sheer rock wall about a hundred yards to the east of where they stood. "I got a sick bull in there. I don't know that you'd catch anything, but I don't need you upsettin' him. We clear?"

"Absolutely," Isaiah said, smiling. "And let me thank you again for opening up your ranch for this dig. I admire the way you've preserved the site for so many years, and I appreciate the opportunity to be the first to excavate it."

"Ah, forget it!" Orley waved a calloused hand at him, and spat another brown puddle on the ground. "Ever since that feller at Range Creek opened up his place, I knew it was just going to be a matter of time before you college 'uns started poking around. Might as well get it done." He turned away and strode off toward his small house just visible to the southeast.

Bones looked at Isaiah, who grinned and shrugged. "He's not a bad fellow," Isaiah said. "I can imagine that after the undisturbed Fremont sites were opened up on Range Creek, he probably did feel like he needed to share his site on his own terms."

"Whatever," Bones said. "Let's head on to the site. I'm anxious to do some digging. Should be fun."

This is the most boring thing I have ever done." Bones scuffed the ground with the toe of his boot. "I had this crazy idea that a 'dig' might involve some actual digging." He snapped another picture of the pictographs adorning the rock face and let out a dramatic sigh. They had spent what felt like hours photographing and cataloging the various pictures etched into the rock. The others members of the dig were mapping the lay of the land and making records of the artifacts that lay strewn across the ground. He had been surprised to see how plentiful they were, and that Orley had apparently left them untouched where they lay.

"Are you sure you've been on a dig before, Bones?" Isaiah did not turn to look at him, but instead kept his eyes on the pictographs. "You told me you loved archaeology."

"Yeah, but the last dig I was on, there was climbing and people shooting at me and stuff." He knew he sounded like a sullen schoolboy, but he didn't care, because at least it annoyed his cousin. "It was fun!"

"You're a piece of work, you know that?" Isaiah shook his head. "I swear, sometimes you even have me believing your wild tales." He paused to lean in close and scrutinize a picture that looked to Bones like a lumpy cow. "Anyway," Isaiah continued, "if you don't want to help me with this, grab a notebook and start counting the potsherds."

"Counting the potsherds. Thrilling. Forget it dude, I'll just stay here." He moved along the wall, looking with disinterest at the pictographs. Isaiah had called them "fascinating," said they were the best he'd ever seen. To Bones, all of them looked the same. The same people, the same four-legged beasts, the same weird shapes. Except for one that drew his attention. On the far right end of the rock face, where the overhanging ledge arched down, the wall receded back into the hill. The recessed area looked like it had been bricked over with inch-thick flat rocks and mud. To the left of the bricked in area was a rendering of a person. Unlike the pictographs, this one was a painting, and the fellow in the picture looked like he was bowing down to something or someone.

"Hey, check this out," he called out to Isaiah. "This one is different." He ran his fingers along the stone around the edge of the image, wanting to touch it, but fearing he might damage it in some way. His eyes drifted to the stacked rocks closing off the alcove. Perhaps it was his imagination, but they looked like they had been put there intentionally. He touched it with a tentative finger and found it solid. He pushed a bit harder to no effect. Stealing a glance at Isaiah, who was still scrutinizing the pictographs, Bones balled up his fist and rapped on the rocks. The sound rang hollow in his ears. There was a space behind there, he was sure of it! He knocked again, harder this time. With a loud clatter, the rock wall collapsed, falling back into the empty space behind in a puff of dust. Bones gasped when he saw what lay behind.

"Bones!" Isaiah shouted. "What did you do?" He rushed over to Bones' side. "I can't believe you…" Words failed him when he saw what Bones was staring at. His dark face blanched. "It can't be," he finally whispered.

A detailed cave painting, so unlike the simple pictographs that covered the rest of the rocky face, stared back at them. A man stood in the center of a group. Light shone all around him, creating a glowing aura about his beatific face. Although the artwork was primitive, it was clear that he was not an Indian. He had shoulder-length hair, a mustache, and a beard. He stood with his hands upraised and all around him the primitive-looking men bowed down to him.

Bones took a step back and shook his head. It was several moments before he found his voice.

"Who in God's name is that?"

Chapter 5

Maddock scrubbed the last bit of corrosion off of the breastplate, admiring its dull glow under the artificial light. It was iron with a copper coating unless he missed his guess. The artifact was not in bad shape considering its age. The clay and silt of the well had protected it all these centuries.

"What do you make of these markings?" Jade asked, her fingers resting lightly on his shoulders. "Some of them almost look like lines on a map." She leaned down for a closer look, her cheek brushing against his. He was painfully aware of her jasmine scent and the softness of her skin. "The cross is obviously the most significant marking, but what does it tell us?"

Running diagonally across the breastplate from top left to bottom right, a cross lay in raised relief. At each of the four tips, halfway up the longest segment, and at the point where the two lines crossed were seven-pointed sunbursts. Maddock looked at the etchings that surrounded it. It did look like a map. Lines that might have represented mountain ranges filled the top left and center. A low, oddly shaped range lay beneath the center sunburst, and a single jagged peak abutted the bottom left star.

There were pictures as well. There was a tall, squat tower at one point, and what might have been statues at another. And on the bottom, a semi-circle, its center filled with a variety of patterns.

"Is that the moon?" Saul spoke for the first time since Maddock had started cleaning the breastplate. Maddock didn't care one bit for Jade's assistant. There was something about the man's demeanor that rubbed him the wrong way. "These could be craters," he said, pointing at the circles that pockmarked the half-circle.

"I don't know," Jade said. "That wouldn't explain the squares. It looks familiar, though." She stepped to the side and folded her arms across her chest, scrutinizing the artifact. "Let me get some pictures of it, and then we'll see what we can figure out. All right," she said, raising her voice and clapping her hands twice like a schoolteacher calming an unruly class, "everybody clear the room. I like lots of peace and quiet when I work."

"Wait a minute," Maddock said in mock-protest. "I could have sworn this was my boat." The look Jade gave him, disapproval mixed with mild threat, told him not to push it farther. He followed Matt and Corey, who had been hanging out quietly by the door, out onto the deck, with Saul trailing behind.

Jade emerged twenty minutes later, a satisfied look on her face.

"We're finished for today," she said. She turned to face Saul, who stared at her with an air of impatience. "You can go back," she told him, ignoring his twisted scowl. "I'll be along in a little while. You and I can look at the pictures tonight if you like."

Saul's eyes flitted to Maddock and then back to Jade. He pursed his lips and worked his jaw. "Do you want me to help you with the breastplate? It's not really a one-man job."

Maddock expected a sharp retort from Jade at the word "man", but none was forthcoming.

"I've decided I'm going to leave it here," she said, "at least for the night."

"The university wouldn't like that," Saul protested. "I really think you should..."

"What the university would not like is my concern." Jade spoke over him in a firm tone. "Not yours."

Saul tensed, the veins in his neck standing out, and his face twisting into a scowl, then relaxed and gave a curt nod.

"Do you want me to come back for you later?" When Jade shook her head, Saul gave Maddock an accusatory look. "Of course," he said, his voice sour. Without further comment, he turned and walked away. Shortly thereafter, the sound of a boat motor heralded his departure.

"That guy is a real treat," Maddock said, shaking his head. "Wish I had ten just like him." Saul reminded him Marc Paccone, an upperclassman he'd encountered at the Naval Academy. Like most bullies, Marc was a sadist and used his station to abuse his underlings, but deep down he was a coward.

Years later, Maddock had encountered him in a bar. A few too many drinks and Marc invited him to step outside. Happy to oblige, Maddock had made quick work of the big fellow and been gone before anyone had even thought of calling the cops. Saul struck him the same way though what power the man wielded over Jade was not immediately apparent.

"You seem like a no-nonsense girl," he said. "Why do you keep him around?"

"I'm afraid he's a necessary evil," Jade said, smiling. "His father is my biggest backer." Maddock thought that explained a great deal. "But enough about Saul," Jade said, slipping her hand into his, "how about grabbing me a beer?"

Maddock tried to sleep, but slumber eluded him. He had spent a pleasant evening with Jade, but now the mystery was foremost in his mind. He would have gone back for another look at the breastplate, but at the last minute, Jade had decided to take it back with her. He bundled it up and gave her a lift back to shore.

One particular picture on the breastplate now gnawed at his mind. He was sure he had seen the moonlike image somewhere before, but he could not place it. It was driving him crazy. He rolled out of his bed, pulled on shorts and a t-shirt, slipped out of his small cabin and made his way up to the deck.

The night air was damp, but could only be considered cool in contrast to the day's heat. The full moon danced on the water, glistening on the gently rolling sea. It seemed to taunt Maddock, a tantalizing clue to the memory that lurked just beyond recollection. He rested his elbows on the stern rail and stared at the silver circle.

Something caught his ear. A sound that was out of place. He cocked his head and concentrated. He heard the scrape of a shoe on the deck on the port side. Moving quickly and silently, he hurried toward the sound, painfully aware that he was unarmed. Perhaps either Matt or Corey was also having trouble sleeping, but something told him that was not the case.

His instinct was correct. A small boat drifted just off the port bow. He heard its engine fire up as a dark form vaulted the Sea Foam's rail and landed in the smaller craft.

"Hey!" he shouted as the boat tore off, leaving a frothy wake. He didn't know why he had yelled, but it had seemed like the thing to do. He could make out few details of the rapidly receding boat. A hunched shadow was at the helm, but he could see no more.

He heard a commotion below, and soon the remainder of the crew joined him. He quickly explained what had happened, and they set about inspecting the Sea Foam. She was clean. The only sign of intrusion was the cabin door, which had been pushed to, but not quite closed. Inside, everything was in order; nothing was missing or out of place.

"Weird," Matt observed, shaking his head. "But you gotta' appreciate a burglar who cleans up after himself."

Maddock gave a half-smile, but he didn't have to say what he was thinking. There was only one thing anyone would have been looking for in the cabin. But how many people even knew that the breastplate had been here? The discovery was not a secret. News of the find had spread around the town and among the various researchers. He immediately suspected Saul, but that didn't make sense. Surely he would know that Jade had brought it back with her. And why would he want to take it anyway? As Jade's assistant, he had plenty of access to it. It was too much for his brain.

"I'm wide awake now," Corey said. "Anybody else want a beer? I'm dry as the desert."

The desert! Maddock glanced up at the moon, a broad smile spreading across his face. He remembered where he had seen the image on the shield!

Chapter 6

"Come on Cuz, your public is waiting." Bones clapped Isaiah on the back as they left the dig site. Up ahead, a throng of people stood outside the gate to Orley's ranch. He counted at least two vans from local television stations. A few others were too far away to identify. He spotted a bored-looking young man with an expensive camera slung around his neck, and two other men armed with notepads and tape recorders. At the front of the pack, looking quite pleased with herself, stood Amanda Shores. They were walking smack into a press conference.

Orley waited just inside the gate, his face even redder than usual. "You answer their questions and you get 'em out of here, or I'm shuttin' the whole thing down, you hear me?"

"Yes, I understand, Mr. Orley," Isaiah said, his voice tired. Public relations was definitely not his strong suit. "But you must understand, the discovery we've made might be of great significance. It's understandable that the public is interested."

"To hell with that." Orley cleared his throat and spat a wad of phlegm in the dust at Isaiah's feet. "Like I done told you, this is a working ranch, and I want 'em out of here." He shoved past Isaiah without giving him a chance to reply. Bones wondered at the man's comment. He hadn't noticed much work of any kind going on at the ranch, save the dig.

"Dr. Horsely," Amanda called out above the din of voices. "Amanda Shores from the Deseret Bugle. We spoke yesterday."

"Yes, I remember," Isaiah said. Warily he approached the crowd of reporters. Bones trailed behind, feeling wickedly amused. This ought to be good.

The photographer started clicking away while two men with television cameras appeared from the throng and started rolling. Amanda asked the first question.

"Dr. Horsely, is it true that your dig has found an image of Jesus Christ among some undisturbed pictographs?"

"Wait a second," Isaiah said, holding up his hands. "We don't know what the picture is, save that it appears to be a bearded man who is not Native American. Beyond that, we cannot say who the picture represents."

"Is it true that the image shows natives worshipping Jesus?" asked one of the news reporters, his hooked nose and piercing eyes giving his stare the intensity of a hawk on the hunt. He held his pen poised above the paper like something out of 'The Pit and the Pendulum".

"Um, the figures in the picture do appear to be bowing," Isaiah said, looking stunned. He obviously was not expecting the details to have gotten out so quickly. Someone on the dig needed to keep his or her mouth shut, Bones thought or have it shut for them.

"Was it common for the native peoples of this region to bow down to bearded men on a regular basis?" Amanda chimed in. People in the crowd laughed. Even Isaiah cracked a smile.

"You have to understand that there are any number of things that are uncommon about this find," Isaiah protested. "Aside from the fact we're talking about a painting rather than a pictograph, the representation is done with a level of detail unheard of for the time period, and in a style that is inconsistent with the other images found at this site. We aren't ruling out anything just yet."

"But do you have any reason to believe that the painting, or whatever it is, is not legitimate?" This reporter, a willowy blonde in a navy suit, looked and sounded unhappy to be out on this hot, dry, dirty piece of earth. "Aren't forgeries easy to spot?"

"As I said," Isaiah said, "we aren't ruling anything out. The image in question was concealed behind a false wall of sorts, and was not really a part of the other images, which are simply pictographs. I wish I could tell you more, but we just don't know very much."

"You are aware that the L.D.S. church has a belief that Jesus visited the New World?" Amanda asked. "Wouldn't that be the simplest explanation? These natives encountered Jesus and worshiped him?"

"There is no simple explanation for what we've found," Isaiah said. "At any rate, I'm not interested in the simplest explanation, only the truth."

One of the newspaper men, thick around the middle and thin and gray on top, raised a manicured hand, letting the sun glint off of his fake Rolex. "What sort of proof will you need before you can conclude that this is, in fact, the image of Christ?"

"I'm not gathering evidence to support any particular hypothesis. There are local legends that could tie in with this find. There are stories of men with scales that some believe represent Spanish armor. This could very well be evidence of contact with Spanish explorers."

Not liking the answer, Amanda turned to Bones. "What about you Mr. Bonebrake? What do you think about what you've uncovered? I understand it was you who discovered the painting?"

"No, it wasn't like that," Bones said, wishing she'd left him out of it entirely. "I accidentally busted up some rocks, and there it was. I stepped out of the way and let Dr. Horsely do his thing."

"We'd still like to hear your thoughts," the blonde interjected, sounding as if the only thing she'd like would be to get out of there pronto.

"I really wouldn't be of any help," Bones said, putting on his biggest dumb smile. "Like I told Miss Shores yesterday, I'm not an archaeologist, just a…"

"You're just a hard rocking Indian," Amanda said, her voice cynical. There was a triumphant look in her eyes that made Bones distinctly uncomfortable. "I did some checking on you. Fortunately, Uriah Bonebrake is not exactly an everyday household name."

"That's just my nickname," Bones said, his tension rising at what he suspected was coming. "My real name is Fred Smith. I'm a landscaper from Topeka."

The blonde actually giggled, but Amanda swooped in for the kill. "What would you like to tell us about first, Mr. Bonebrake? Your service in the SEALS? Your career as a treasure hunter and marine archaeologist?" The other reporters were now looking very interested. "I know," Amanda said as if she had just thought of it. "Why don't you tell us about the last archaeological dig you were on? I believe it was at Petra?"

"It was nothing," Bones said. "I was just a tourist on one of those volunteer digs. I didn't do much."

"That's true," Amanda said. "You only found a carving of Goliath that had been hidden since Petra's re-discovery." This statement elicited a loud murmur from the gathered crowd. The blonde reporter even appeared interested. Amanda continued to press him. "You seem to have a knack for uncovering ancient pictures of biblical figures, don't you?"

"I didn't actually find the Goliath carving," Bones said. Isaiah grinned at him, enjoying the turnabout.

"I'm sorry, was it your partner Dane Maddock who discovered it?" Amanda asked sweetly. "I have a call in to him."

"Don't hold your breath," Bones said. "He's not a people person like I am." He was filled with a growing certainty that he wasn't going to be able to talk his way out of this one.

"Tell us about the part where you and Mr. Maddock crawled out of an underground chamber behind the carving, having managed to bring down a whole mountain and effectively destroying the dig."

Bones thought fast. He had always been a risk-taker. Time to take a chance. "You're absolutely right, Miss Shores. I do have a fascinating story to tell." He strode to the gate and vaulted it, landing nimbly on the balls of his feet. Not bad for a sea dog. "I have decided to grant an exclusive interview to this young lady right here." Two steps took him to where the blonde stood, looking surprised and pleased with the turn of events. He hooked an arm around her waist. "Where is your vehicle Miss..?"

"Dixon," she stammered, blushing furiously. "Emily Dixon, from Channel.."

"We can discuss all of that later, Miss Dixon. Right now, what I need is a tall, cold cervesa. That's Cherokee for Budweiser. Care to join me?" Emily laughed and nodded her assent.

Bones turned back toward the tangle of reporters, all protesting vehemently. "I'll be leaving you now, but Dr. Horsely will be happy to continue this discussion with you." He ignored the frustrated look in Isaiah's eyes and turned back to his new friend. "Shall we go?" She nodded, and he led her toward his truck.

"Mr. Bonebrake!" Amanda shouted. "Will you at least tell us if you think it's possible that the image is that of Christ?"

"Who knows if Jesus came to America?" Bones shouted back. "I mean, he's the son of God. I guess he could… I don't know… fly."

Bones didn't know if it was the rattle of his cell phone vibrating on the nightstand, or the "Detroit Rock City" ringtone, but one of the two awakened him in a most unpleasant way. He rolled over, groaning at the pain in his head, and grabbed the phone. The number on the display was unfamiliar, but it was from the local area code. It was probably Isaiah.

He flipped it open and held it to the ear that was ringing the softest. "Bones," he croaked.

"Uh, I'm sorry," said a soft, feminine voice. *"What did you say?"*

"This is Bones," he growled. He really wasn't in the mood for a wrong number, especially after Emily had played him like a violin. He had been completely sucked in by her ditzy reporter act, and when he finally spilled the Petra story, she'd suddenly remembered that she needed to be home early. He'd always been a sucker for the sorority girl types, but they'd never been any good for him. In fairness, she had said goodbye with a kiss that had some potential, and a phone number that might even have been hers. He hadn't bothered to check it out. "How can I help you?"

"Did you say Bones? I'm looking for someone who knows Isaiah Horsely."

Bones sat up straight, his head clearing fast. Something was wrong. "This is Uriah Bonebrake. I'm his cousin. What's up?"

"Bonebrake, Bones, sorry about that. I'm just upset." A nervous laugh. *"And I'm babbling. I'm really sorry."*

"It's all right ma'am. What can I do for you?" He struggled to keep the impatience out of his voice.

"My name is Allison Hartwell. I'm Doctor Horsely's neighbor. I found your name and number on a notepad on his kitchen table. I need to let someone know that there's been…" The pause seemed interminable. He was about to tell her to speed it up when she finished the sentence. *"There's been an accident."*

Forty minutes later he was wandering through empty corridors of the local hospital looking for the pre-op room. There weren't many people to guide him this time of night, but thankfully it was a small place. He soon found the door and walked in without knocking.

"Excuse me, but what are you doing?" A gaunt young doctor with stringy ginger hair and a clipboard stepped in front of him. He had guts. The fellow was almost Bones' height but couldn't weigh more than a buck and-a-half. "You can't be back here."

"I'm here to see Isaiah Horsely. I'm his next of kin."

The doctor's eyes narrowed, and a look of skepticism crossed his face. "Mister Horsely is about to go into surgery."

"I understand the concept of pre-op," Bones said. He leaned in, the two of them now nose-to-nose. "I'm asking nicely. Please."

The fellow could take a hint. "Come with me." He turned and led Bones to a curtained room where a uniformed police officer stood.

"Who is this?" the cop asked. He wasn't foolish enough to stand in Bones' way.

"He is the next of kin," the doctor said. "He'll only be a moment."

"I'll want to talk to you when you're done in there," the officer said. Bones nodded and stepped into the pre-op room.

Isaiah lay under a pristine white sheet. His face was swollen, and his head heavily bandaged. His swollen lips were an ugly purple under the too-bright lights. He had taken a hell of a beating. The neighbor girl, Allison, had warned Bones, but it was still terrible to see. Isaiah's arms were badly bruised. Defensive injuries, Bones supposed. His eyes followed the I.V. drip from Isaiah's hand up to the bag. He looked at the vital sign monitors, but the numbers meant little to him. He couldn't believe someone would do this to Isaiah, who had always been so bookish and gentle of spirit, and was a good man. Bones grimaced. The culprits had better pray the cops got to them before he did.

A nurse stepped into the room and cleared her throat. "We're taking him back now. You can say your goodbyes."

Bones knelt down next to Isaiah's right shoulder and laid his hand on his upper arm. "I'm here. You awake?"

Isaiah opened one eye as much as his swollen lids would allow. The corners of his mouth twitched. He was trying to smile.

"They're going to get you all fixed up, man." Bones said, hoping this was true. "And when you're all better, we'll get this mess cleaned up. All of it." He gave Isaiah's shoulder a gentle squeeze and stood to leave.

"Bones," Isaiah said in a soft voice that was almost a wheeze.

"Yeah?" Bones leaned down so that his ear was close to his cousin's face. "I'm listening."

"Orley… doesn't have a bull." Isaiah closed his eyes and said no more.

"What was that?" Bones asked, but Isaiah's steady breathing indicated that he had lapsed into sleep.

"I'm sorry sir, but we have to take him now," the nurse said. "The waiting area is down the hall to your right. The doctor will find you when the surgery is over."

Bones thanked her and headed to the waiting area. He wanted to sleep, but something told him he would be up all night trying to figure out why in the world it mattered that Orley did not have a bull.

Chapter 7

Chaco Canyon was the root of Anasazi Culture. This desert country, with its long winters, short growing seasons and minimal rainfall seemed to Maddock an unlikely place for civilization to take root, yet it was once the center of Anasazi life. From the end of the first millennia to the middle of the second, people had farmed this canyon and constructed fantastic greathouses and kivas. In terms of architecture, life and social organization, the Anasazi of Chaco Canyon had reached heights unsurpassed by their kindred of the Four Corners region.

The Chacoans constructed their magnificent center of trade and worship on a nine-mile stretch of canyon floor, with an eye to longitude and the cycles of the sun and moon. Working with only primitive tools and without a system of mathematics, they raised massive buildings that still inspire awe.

Maddock was too focused on the sheer desolation of the land to take notice of the architecture. Most of the ruins were just far enough off the road to make it nearly impossible to see much of anything. He was road weary from the seemingly never-ending trek from the highway to the park, which lay in the midst of sparse, dry land.

Saul had insisted on driving the car even before their plane touched down in Durango, Colorado. Maddock sat in the back of the rented Range Rover, poring over a park map with Jade.

"Are you sure there's anything out here?" Saul asked, not for the first time. "This is the emptiest place I've ever seen. There aren't even any tourists around."

"Yes, I'm sure," Jade said, not looking up from the map. "Just keep going." She sighed loudly, but Saul was focused on his own thoughts.

"And people really lived out here? Hard to believe, it's so dry."

"Chaco Canyon was actually the center of Puebloan culture for a long time," Jade said. Saul snorted but said no more.

"So, go over the plan with me again," Maddock said. He remembered the plan well enough, but he preferred Jade's voice to Saul's any day. He was still weary from the whirlwind of the last three days. Since he had recognized the picture on the breastplate as being that of Pueblo Bonito in Chaco Canyon, they had scrambled to make arrangements. Willis, Matt, and Corey had stayed behind in Argentina to finish the job on which they had been working. Meanwhile, Jade worked furiously to research Chaco Canyon and any possible connection to Fray Marcos.

"The cross on the breastplate," Jade said, pulling a folder out from underneath the map, "is, I think, more than a cross." She laid the folder on top of the map and opened it to reveal the photos she had taken of the artifact. "A line with a sunburst at each end is a symbol commonly associated with a solstice or an equinox." Her finger traced the vertical bar of the cross, coming to rest on the top sunburst. "It can't just be a cross, or else why bother putting sunbursts there?" She closed the folder and slipped it back beneath the map.

"Here," she indicated a spot far from the park entrance they had passed not long before, "is Fajada Butte. Atop it sits the most famous astronomical marker in Chaco Canyon, perhaps the most famous in Anasazi Culture: the Sun Dagger. At midday, three large, vertical slabs cast a dagger-shaped shaft of light onto a spiral petroglyph carved into the rock face behind the slabs. The carving is used to demarcate solstices, equinoxes and phases of the moon. We'll climb to the top and check it out."

"And you're hoping we'll find what?" Maddock asked.

"We'll know when we get there," Jade said. "The pictures I found on the internet didn't tell me much, but there could be something there. I think there's a clue carved into the rock, or possibly buried." She sounded determined, if not confident.

"I still think we're going to have to blast through that petroglyph to get to whatever is behind it," Saul interjected. "That spiral looks just like a bullseye to me."

"We aren't going to blow up the Sun Dagger," Jade said. "We don't even have permission to climb the butte. Besides, the petroglyph was carved long before Fray Marcos came to the New World. In fact, the Chaco Canyon settlement was nearing its end during his time."

Saul shrugged. "Suit yourself. I'm still bringing my toys." Apparently Jade's assistant fancied himself a demolitions expert. "By the way, did I tell you what I learned this morning?"

"How to tie your shoe?" Jade quipped.

"No, really," Saul said, ignoring the jibe. "I was reading an article about Chaco Canyon. The people who lived here were famous for their Cibola-style pottery. Cibola! Pretty cool, huh?"

"Uh huh," Jade said, returning her gaze to the map. "I feel like we can get in and out of there pretty quickly. The park doesn't get many visitors, so they likewise have very few rangers. I'm figuring they spend most of their time inside the air-conditioned welcome center. The butte is off the beaten path, so we should be all right."

Saul stopped the car in a small turnoff amidst sand-colored hills. "We're hoofing it from here, ladies and gentlemen. Grab your jocks and your socks."

"Lovely, Saul," Jade mumbled as she stepped out of the car.

Saul opened the trunk, and they each donned a heavy backpack. They had outfitted themselves with climbing gear, analytical instruments, and water. Lots of water.

A twisting, sloped trail wound its way up into the bare hills. Maddock was soon reaching for a water bottle. They called a halt upon gaining the top of one of the rocky promontories. Years on the water had helped him grow accustomed to the sun beating down on him, but in this place the air seemed to suck the last drops of moisture from his body. He took a long, cool drink and scanned the horizon. It was beautiful if such a desolate place could be called so. The sky was high and slightly hazy with the heat. He tried to mop his brow, but the sweat evaporated almost instantaneously. How had people ever lived in this oven?

"Down the hill and to the east," Jade said, leading the way. The trail was gravelly but not particularly precarious. Saul lost his footing more than once, each time falling heavily onto Maddock's back, cursing all the while. The man was a buffoon, but there was nothing Maddock could do to get rid of him, so he gritted his teeth and continued bearing Saul up, hoping all the while that it wouldn't be much longer.

Twenty minutes later they stood at the base of Fajada Butte, staring up at the massive red rock. As Jade had predicted, there was no sign of a park ranger, or any other human being for that matter. Maddock circled the base, looking for the most promising climb. He finally settled on the southwest side, stripped off his pack, and began pulling out climbing gear.

"I don't know," Saul said, walking up beside Maddock. "This thing looks pretty tall to me."

"One hundred thirty-five meters, to be exact," Maddock said. "Not the easiest free climb I've ever made, but far from the most difficult." He and Bones had done their share of rock climbing together, and they had never agreed on who was the more skilled. Maddock was more agile, but longer legs and arms allowed Bones to reach crevasses and holds that Maddock could not. Until a few years ago, they had placed bets on all of their free climbs. Maddock chuckled and shook his head at the thought of his friend. Bones had promised to join them as soon as Isaiah was out of the woods. Maddock hoped it would be soon. It just wasn't right doing this without his partner.

"Are you all right?" Jade asked in her satin-over-sandpaper voice that reminded him of a young Demi Moore. "You look worried."

"No, I'm fine," Maddock said. "Just got distracted thinking about Bones' cousin. Wondering if he's going to be okay."

"I'm sure he will," Jade said. "He has to, so I can meet this Bones character you've been telling me about. In any case, if you're serious about free climbing this thing, you'd better keep your focus."

"Yes ma'am," he replied in his best military voice. He sprang nimbly to his feet. "When I get to the top, I'll set a rope for you. Send Saul up first, so you can belay for him." That, and if the rope breaks, we'll have one less problem to deal with. "You bring up the rear." No one had told him he was in charge of the climb, but sometimes a given set of circumstances seemed to dictate it. Since neither Jade nor Saul objected, it must have been the right thing to do.

He set to climbing and was pleasantly surprised at the ease with which he scaled the rock. The cracked, pitted surface provided ample handholds, and none of the angles were too treacherous. Soon, the three of them stood atop Fajada Butte, admiring the surrounding landscape. He found it truly amazing that a people had not only lived but flourished amidst this hard land.

"The Sun Dagger," Jade said, her voice filled with reverence and wonder. She indicated a spot against a high rock wall where three slabs of rock stood against the rock wall beneath an outcropping. The tallest was just over nine feet tall, and they all were tilted slightly to the left, like slices of bread.

"It's not much to look at," Saul said. And he was right. Despite having seen snapshots, Maddock had created an image in his mind of something larger than life, something magical and mysterious. This was something quite ordinary.

Jade's enthusiasm was not dampened in the least. She hurried over to the stone slabs and ducked down, vanishing behind them. Maddock followed her. Slipping into the shade beneath the stone pillars, his eyes were immediately drawn to the pictograph—a large spiral, twisting into a point in the center of the sandstone slab. He had read that the spirals carried different meanings depending on whether they spun out clockwise or counterclockwise, but he could not remember anything more.

"It's beautiful," Jade whispered, her fingertips mere centimeters above the rocks surface, tracing the spiral line without touching it. She was right. There was something in its simplicity, its balance, its perfection that moved Maddock's spirit. "Maddock," she said, "a thousand years ago people sat in this very place and followed the earth's journey around the sun."

"Sort of makes Mount Vernon seem trite, doesn't it?" Maddock was partial to the colonial period of American history, but this was truly American history.

They sat for a while in silence, neither replying when Saul stuck his head in and asked what the holdup was.

Jade finally let out a long sigh. "I guess we'd better get to work."

After making a thorough visual inspection and taking pictures with a high-resolution digital camera, they began work with a hand-held ground penetrating radar unit. Jade looked like a cop laying for speeders, her tanned face and almond eyes solid and serious as she held the radar unit in a two-handed grip. She first took readings below the slab, then around it, and finally of the slab itself.

"Nothing," she said after taking her third reading of the slab. "It's solid rock all around. Time to re-think the plan, I suppose." Her shoulders sagged, and her face fell.

"That means it's my turn," Saul said, picking up his backpack. "Stand back, ladies and gentlemen."

"Saul, you are not blowing up the slab." The downtrodden Jade of a moment before had vanished, and the stubborn ball of fire had returned. "If there was anything to be found underneath the rock, the radar would have picked it up. I'll not have you destroy a piece of history for your own amusement."

Saul turned around and was about to protest when something caught Maddock's attention.

"That's enough," he said. Jade rounded on him, but he did not give her a chance to speak, taking her by the shoulders and turning her toward the west where a black spot on the horizon was growing larger by the second. "You see that? That's a Sikorsky S-70, a military helicopter though it doesn't have any markings to indicate it's anything other than a civilian craft now. It probably has nothing to do with us, but just the same I think we should get out of here."

Chapter 8

Maddock was relieved that Jade did not argue with him. She squinted and looked at the approaching helicopter for a moment before nodding her assent. They collected their gear, and Jade and Saul made a rapid descent. Not wanting to leave any evidence behind, Maddock took the ropes loose and dropped them down to Jade. He looked back at the Sikorsky and found that it still seemed headed directly toward them, and it was coming fast. There was no way he could make the free climb to the bottom before it was upon them. He knew he was being overcautious, but his instinct told him that the black bird on the horizon was bad news.

"Go on! I'll catch up!" he shouted down to Jade and Saul. She put a hand to her ear and tilted her head. "I can't get down in time!" He pointed toward the path along which they had hiked. They understood then. Jade shook her head, but Saul took her by the upper arm and trotted away. Jade had to follow or be dragged. He's happy enough to get rid of me, Maddock thought.

He stole a last glance at the approaching helicopter before beginning his descent. It was slow going, feeling for the cracks and ledges he had climbed earlier. He wanted to look back and see if Jade and Saul had gotten away, but it was critical that he maintain his concentration.

A low hum filled his ears, quickly growing into a sound like a thousand angry hornets. The bird was almost there. Down and to his right was a crack in the stone face that looked almost wide enough to squeeze into. He made for it, his fingertips clutching at the most miniscule lumps of stone as he scooted across the rocky face. He slid his right foot out onto an egg-shaped protrusion and shifted his weight to his right hand and right leg. Almost there.

With a soft crunch, the rock broke away, and he was dangling by scraped, raw fingertips. He held on tight, not panicking. A less experienced climber might scrabble his feet against the stone searching for a foothold and actually force his body away from the rock. Maddock took a deep breath, ignoring the scorching hot pain that coursed through his wrists and forearms. Sliding his right foot upward, he found an angled crack in the rock into which he could push his toe. Soon he had found purchase for his left foot, and he was on steady footing four feet away from the fissure.

The helicopter was virtually on top of him now. Bits of sand and rock blown by the wash of the rotors rained down on his head. He searched for a way to get to the fissure, but the intervening space was worn smooth by sand and wind. He looked up to see the craft hovering over the butte. Had they seen him?

His senses sharpened by adrenaline, he spotted a crack running horizontally along the far inside wall of the fissure, level with his waist. Ignoring his better judgment, he flexed his knees, ankles, and wrists as much as possible, gathered his strength, and flung himself eaped sideways across the face of the rock.

For a panicked instant, he thought he was going to fall. As he had intended, he overshot the fissure, reached in and hooked the crack with his left hand. A violent yank nearly tore his shoulder from its socket, but he held on. His feet swung out, and he felt as if he were going to be upended, but then he swung back and caught hold with his right hand. Sucking in his breath he squeezed back into the shadowed opening.

He waited there, listening to the beat of the rotors. His arms burned with the effort of holding his weight, and he squeezed deeper into the crack, forcing the rock to bear some of the load. After about thirty seconds, though it seemed a half hour to his weary mind and body, the bird flew away to the east. As the sound faded away, he heard voices.

"See anything?" The voice was a man's, youthful with a Midwestern accent.

"Nothing. I wondered if we'd find anyone out here. This place is pretty remote." The second speaker pronounced "out" so that it rhymed with "remote". Canadian, perhaps. "I'm just glad we got here first."

"How can you tell? The rotors would have washed away any footprints. Never mind. What's the radar say?"

"It says..." The man Maddock now thought of as Canuck paused. "Rock. Lots and lots of rock." He paused again. "All over the damn place. Rock."

Midwest man uttered a vile oath and must have kicked a fist-sized stone because one nearly cracked Maddock's skull as it tumbled down. "You're absolutely positive?"

"Yup," replied Canuck. "The big man won't like it so much, but that's how it is."

"Fine." The tone of Midwest's voice said that it was anything but. "I'll call the bird back."

"Suit yourself."

The chopper returned less than a minute later, hovering over Fajada Butte long enough to pick up the two men, before heading west, back in the direction from which it came.

Relieved, Maddock scrambled down the rock faster than was safe, but he'd had all the rock climbing he could take for one day. At the bottom, he scanned the horizon but saw no sign of the helicopter. No reason it should return anyway. Not stopping to regain his breath, he set off at a jog toward the hiking trail.

Jade met him halfway back to where they had left their Range Rover. He wondered where Saul was, but did not care enough to ask. After assuring her that he was all right, he recounted what had happened on the Butte.

"Who could they be?" Jade frowned, her intense eyes boring into him. "And what are they looking for?"

"Probably the same thing we're after," he said, taking her by the hand and setting off down the trail. He had thought about it, and nothing else made sense. Surely Jade wasn't the only person in the world who had heard of Fray Marcos de Niza and his connection to the legend of Cibola.

"But how would they know?" she protested. "Do you think it's the same person who broke into your boat?"

"I suppose there's a connection," he said. "Right now, that's our only suspect in any event." With nothing left to them but idle speculation, they lapsed into silence.

Ten minutes later they stood in the empty spot where they had parked the Range Rover. Jade exhaled noisily and punched Saul's number into her cell phone. She made a face and snapped it closed. "No signal. The jerk! We had an argument. He read somewhere that Casa Rinconda, which is the largest kiva in Chaco Canyon, and not too far from here, has a solstice window. Every year at the summer solstice, the sun shines through into an alcove. He wanted to check it out, but I told him the kiva had been excavated before. Whatever sat in that alcove, if anything, is long gone."

"Let me guess," Maddock said, "He wanted to blow it up." The look on Jade's face was answer enough. "If he's fool enough to try it, let's at least hope he leaves the keys in the Range Rover before they cart him off to jail." That got a grin out of her. "Are you up for a hike?" he asked cheerily.

They took their time walking back to the park's main loop. Maddock went through two of his water bottles and still felt parched. They passed the time looking at park brochures Maddock had stuffed into his pack. As he was flipping through a pamphlet on Pueblo Bonito, something caught his attention. "Listen to this," he said, "it might be nothing, but in Pueblo Bonito there are seven corner doorways."

"The doorway is on the corner of the structure?" Jade echoed. "That's unusual."

"Very rare. And one of them is an astronomical marker. It's a second floor doorway, and at the time of the winter solstice, light passes through and shines on the base of the opposite corner of the room." Jade looked skeptical. "Think about it," Maddock said. "The picture on the breastplate was of Pueblo Bonito. It's a solstice marker, and it's cast by a highly unusual doorway. It's one in seven, as in…"

"Yes, I know," Jade said. "As in the 'Seven Cities.' All right, Maddock, I'll grant you it's worth a shot. But if we're wrong, don't say anything to Saul. He takes great pleasure in my mistakes."

"Few though they are," Maddock added.

"Of course."

Pueblo Bonito, the largest and most complex of the Chaco Canyon ruins, was an amazing sight. Set against the backdrop of sand colored hills, it was built in a half-circle, the outer rim a complex of multi-storied stone rooms that reminded Maddock of college dorm rooms, except of course for the odd, keyhole-shaped doors that led into each section. Another, narrow line of rooms ran across the straight edge, and another bisected the half-circle. There were many kivas here of varying sizes. He marveled at the scale and workmanship of the structures. Unlike the more famous Anasazi cliff dwellings that were constructed of large block, Pueblo Bonito was entirely constructed of small, flat stones that fit together with precision, giving the impression of a brick structure.

"The walls were built in the 'core and veneer' style," Jade explained. "The inner core is made of mud and sandstone. The shaped stones are the veneer. When people lived here, the veneer was plastered over and painted bright colors."

"So it wouldn't be out of the question for something to be hidden within the core of a wall?" Maddock said. Jade shrugged. "It's more likely than something being hidden under the slab atop Fajada Butte."

"I suppose so," she admitted. "The place is deserted. Let's find this room, and you do whatever it is you're going to do before someone shows up. By Chaco Canyon standards, this is the most popular attraction."

They quickly located the solstice room. A small, keyhole-shaped second story window was cut into the corner of one of the larger structures. It was about eight feet off the ground, no problem to reach, but it would be a tight squeeze to get inside.

"Make it quick, Maddock," Jade said, watching for any unwelcome approach.

"My, aren't we testy?" he teased. "I didn't take you for the nervous type." He took off his backpack and dropped it at her feet. He'd never fit through the window with it on his back. "Toss that to me when I'm inside." Not waiting for a response, he sprang up, catching the wider parts of the keyhole with his tender fingertips. He ignored the stinging- at least there were no helicopters around this time- and pulled himself up. It was not easy to find toeholds in the well-fitted stone wall, but he managed and was soon squeezing through the small window. He wasn't the biggest guy though broader of shoulder than average, but he was forced to go in on his side, which made for an awkward spill down to the bottom. The walls mercifully hid his fall from view.

"Everything all right in there?" Jade called.

"Sure thing. Toss me my backpack." She did not reply, but the black canvas pack came flying through the opening a moment later. He caught it and turned to inspect the opposite corner wall.

Protected to a greater degree from the elements, the inner walls of this particular room were in better condition than the outer walls. The plaster was still intact in several places, including the bottom corner opposite the window.

Using a small metal detector, he scanned the target area and was pleased with the resulting squeal that indicated something substantial lay behind the wall on the bottom left, a foot above the floor. Had he not gotten a hit, he would have tried Jade's radar unit, but he was satisfied. From his climbing gear, he pulled out a spike and small hammer, and began chipping away at the plaster over the area where the detector had found something.

He felt guilty at damaging a historic site, but he told himself that the damage would be minor, and the result might be of greater historical value. The plaster came away in half-dollar sized chips, and soon he had uncovered a stone two hand widths square. His heart raced as he noted how different this stone was from the others around it. All the rest were thin, rectangular slabs like those he had seen everywhere else. This one was out of place.

He scoured the surface of the stone, rubbing away the last of the plaster. His fingertips found something strange. Something was carved into the rock! Using the spike, he scratched at the surface. When he was finished, his breath caught in his throat as he stared at it. It was a clover with a cross in its center.

With renewed vigor, he worked the space around the stone. It was not fitted as tightly as the other stones. The space around it was filled with plaster. He had cleared the area around it and was about to pry it free when he heard Jade called a quiet warning. He stopped and listened.

He soon heard two elderly voices, one male, and one female, engaged in friendly conversation with Jade. He could not understand the words, but by their tone, it was doubtless small talk that was trying her patience as much as it was his. The conversation finally came to an end, and he waited for Jade to give him the go-ahead, but she did not speak. Should he call to her, and risk discovery? After a count of twenty, he called her name softly, but no answer. He dared not climb up to the window, not without knowing who might be outside. He made up his mind to finish the job as quickly and quietly as possible.

The stone came free with surprising ease. He placed it on the floor with care and scratched the hard, dry surface of the core. The mixture of mud and rock crumbled at the first touch. An inch below the surface, he struck something solid. Hastily he cleared the dried mud from around it and pulled it forth into the light.

It was a metal box, seven inches square and four inches deep. The clover and cross of Fray Marcos were engraved in the surface. It was neither hinged nor lidded, but a careful inspection of the bottom surface showed that it had been soldered closed. They would have to take it somewhere else to open it.

With a pang of regret, he wrapped it in a poncho and stuffed it into the bottom of his backpack. He flipped the stone over to hide Fray Marcos' cross, and slid it back into the wall. Quietly he gathered the loose sand and plaster and sprinkled it around the far corners. At a casual glance, he doubted anyone would notice what he had done, and how often was someone likely to enter this room?

Just as he was wondering what to do about Jade, he heard her call to him.

"Are we clear?" he asked. At her confirmation, he climbed up to the window and held the backpack out through the window. "Careful. It's heavy," he cautioned. Her delighted smile was almost as great a reward as finding the box. His good mood was dampened only slightly when he saw that Saul stood nearby, keeping watch. He managed to climb out of the window more gracefully than he had entered, and in a matter of seconds they were headed back through the ancient site.

"Sorry I ditched you," Jade said. "Those old people invited me to walk with them, and I couldn't very well stand in one place all that time without raising their suspicion. Saul showed up a few minutes later, and I told them he was my husband." Saul smirked and Jade grimaced.

"So," Saul said, sounding annoyed that Maddock had succeeded where he had failed, "what exactly did you find?"

"I don't know yet," he said, "but I've got a feeling it's something good."

Chapter 9

Bones had no particular desire to finish the dig. Isaiah had made it through the surgery successfully, but remained in what the doctors described as a "shallow coma". They assured him this was normal, and, in fact, a healthy way for a person with a brain injury to recuperate. This was not the sort of vegetative state from which patients did not come back; it was simply the body's way of healing.

Not completely reassured, but encouraged, he decided to go back to the dig. It was Isaiah's project, and he felt an obligation to see it through to the end. And perhaps he could pick up some clues to his cousin's attackers.

The dig site had changed much in the four days since Isaiah's attack. The ground around the rock overhang was roped off in squares and digging was well underway. But the dig lacked the pleasant air of people doing what they loved. Everyone worked in sullen silence. Only two of them even looked up from their work to greet him with curt nods. He headed to the rock face where a man in khakis and a starched pink oxford cloth shirt stood with a clipboard in hand, scowling at whatever he was reading.

"May I help you?" he said in a sour voice, not looking up from his clipboard.

"No, but I can help you. Your bald spot is getting sunburned," Bones said.

The fellow jerked his head up to scowl at Bones. One of the diggers snickered.

"Thank you. I shall attend to that right away. What can I do for you?"

"I'm Dr. Horsely's cousin, Uriah Bonebrake. I was helping him with the dig."

"I see. Well, I am sorry to tell you that we have all the help we need. I appreciate your visit and will thank you to leave without further disturbing our work." He turned his back on Bones and walked away.

"Wait a minute. This is Isaiah's dig," Bones protested.

"Not anymore." The fellow sounded disgustingly pleased with himself. "Dr. Horsely's financial backers have placed me in charge. I will thank you to leave my dig immediately."

"Who are these backers, mister…?"

"Doctor. Doctor William McLaughlin. And my backers are none of your concern. Now, if you will please excuse us, we have work to do. The Jesus picture is only the beginning."

"The Jesus picture? Have you established that's what it really is?"

McLaughlin was offended by the question. "Of course that's what it is." He turned and walked away before Bones could question him any further.

"Pompous ass," one of the diggers said in a hushed voice. Bones sidled up next to him. "All he cares about is fame." The man was tall and angular, with an expression of permanent disdain on his sunburned face.

"How about his backers?" Bones asked casually. "They after the fame as well?"

"Hardly. I don't know who exactly they are. No one on the dig knows. But I know they're Mormons. They want it to be true."

"What's that?" Bones asked.

"The Jesus thing. Mormons believe Jesus came to America and appeared to the people here. They would love to have the archaeological record support that." He spat in the dust. "They're going to spin this their way. No consideration of anything else. Oh, he has us going through the motions of excavating the site, but he's not at all interested in the artifacts. He wants more Jesus pictures." He spat another gob in the dust and kicked it with the toe of his boot. "Anyway, how's Dr. Horsely?"

"He's stable," Bones said. "Still not come out of the coma, but the doctors aren't too concerned yet. They say he'll wake up when he's ready. He's going to freak when he finds out what McLaughlin is doing to his dig."

"No kidding. Well, I'd better get back at it before McLaughlin jumps my case again. He and Orley got into it yesterday. You should have seen it. That old farmer was warning him away from that barn of his with the sick bull. McLaughlin couldn't care less about the barn or the bull, but he can't stand to be told what to do."

Bones didn't hear the rest of the story. He suddenly remembered the last thing Isaiah said before going into surgery. Orley doesn't have a bull. Grinning politely as the fellow finished his story, Bones shook the man's hand and walked away. Feeling dazed, he wandered back toward the farm until he came to the barn.

It looked no more remarkable than it did the first time he had seen it: a small, sturdy wooden structure built against the side of a hill, though he had to admit that it was unusual to construct a building directly against a rock wall. He paused two steps from the door and looked around. No one was in sight.

"Mr. Orley!" he called. "Hello?" He didn't truly think the old man was around, but no need taking chances. "Anyone here?" He noticed that the door was padlocked. He pressed his ear to the wood and listened. Silence. If there was a bull in there, it was dead. He walked around the left side of the barn. Near the back, the ground had washed away, leaving a hole a yard wide and eight inches deep under the wall. Bones looked around again, then cleared away the rocks and loose. When he could make the hole no deeper without a pick and shovel, he dropped to the ground.

He lay down on his back and squeezed into the opening. He had to exhale and relax his muscles in order to get his chest and shoulders through, but he made it with only a few scrapes. He climbed to his feet in the dim barn, brushed himself off and looked around.

It could not properly be called a barn. It was more of a storage shed; a simple wooden building with various tools and implements strewn about. Old bales of straw were stacked to the ceiling against the back wall. Bones pulled one down, covering his face with his sleeve against the thick cloud of dust that kicked up from the old, dry bale. There was no back wall- the shed was three-sided and abutted the rock face. That was interesting. He moved a few more bales out of the way, then, half out of intuition and half out of impatience, he took hold of the two bottom center bales and yanked.

The middle of the straw wall tumbled down, one of them bouncing hard off his shoulder. Dust burned his eyes and nose. He leaned down, plugged one nostril and blew the other out, then repeated with the other side. Maddock hated what Bones called "the farmer's handkerchief", and Bones took pleasure in disgusting his friend from time-to-time. As he was wiping his eyes, he was surprised to feel cool air on his face.

A four-foot-high fissure, three wide at the base, split the center of the stone wall. This was getting more interesting all the time. He fished the mini Maglite out of his pocket and ducked down to explore the opening.

The narrow beam of light shone on a long, narrow tunnel only a few feet high leading back into blackness. Never the one to ignore his curiosity, he made up his mind to explore. He had to crawl, holding his light between his teeth. The floor was smooth stone and cold on his hands. He had gone about thirty feet when the passage opened up into a room with a ceiling high enough for him to stand. He played his light over the walls. What he saw made him whistle in surprise.

The room was roughly rectangular with a fire pit in the center. The walls on either side of him were adorned with pictographs much more impressive than what they had found outside, the likes of which he had seen only in pictures of southwest Indian ruins. There were spirals, handprints, and images of animals. They were beautiful and remarkably well-preserved. But it was the opposite wall that took his breath.

A large circle, about a foot in diameter, was carved into the wall near the top. Seven straight lines descended from it, each ending in what looked like a hand.

On the left side of the wall, below the row of symbols, was a scene reminiscent of the "Jesus" picture he had discovered a few days before. It was clear, however, that this was not Jesus. The bearded man led a line of men in Spanish military uniforms, and others dressed in robes. These particular cave paintings clearly were not done by the natives who had carved the pictographs. Though not surprised, he felt a bit of disappointment at the knowledge that this was not Christ. The feeling, though, was quickly replaced by the excitement of knowing that there was definitely a mystery here.

The men were pictured moving through various scenes with landmarks behind them that probably would have borne significance to someone familiar with the region. On the right side, near the bottom, was a scene depicting the same men bearing heavy sacks, climbing what looked like a giant staircase. The final image was that of a distinctive-looking peak though one that was unfamiliar to Bones.

Near the base of the wall, a square niche was cut into the stone, similar to those in a kiva. Something glittered in the light.

A closer look revealed a golden disc about seven inches in diameter, with an image much like the one on the wall carved on the front. Intrigued, he turned it over. Fine writing spiraled in from the outer edge in an ever-tightening circle.

"Hebrew?" he whispered. "This is crazy." He took out his cell phone and used the camera feature to snap some pictures. Although his was one of the better phone cameras on the market, it still took several tries to get a few decent shots. He took care to replace the disc just like he had found it. He then took a picture of the front of the golden circle as it lay in the niche.

He backed up to the fire pit in the room's center and took pictures of the walls. Suddenly aware that he had spent a long time in this place, he shone his light around the room one last time. Satisfied that he had seen everything, he turned to leave. Dropping to his hands and knees, he crawled only two feet before the beam of his Maglite shone on twin shotgun barrels leveled at his face.

"Back it up," Orley growled from the darkness. "Move slow and stay where I can see you."

Bones did as he was told, crawling backward into the room, his options racing through his mind. He was fast and would stand a good chance of disarming Orley, but he'd have to injure the rancher in order to do so. He didn't want to do that if he could help it. For the same reason, he dismissed the .22 in his ankle holster. Besides, his instinct told him that the man was not a threat.

A flame blossomed in the darkness. Orley held a zippo in his left hand. He kept the shotgun trained on Bones with his right. "I didn't figure on it being you. By the way, you can take that pissant little flashlight out of your mouth."

Bones chuckled and tucked the light into his jeans pocket.

"This place is something."

Orley did not answer. He scrutinized the cave, his usual sour expression in place. "Well hell. You weren't gonna' take the disc?"

"Not me," Bones said. "My people aren't like that. I think you know that as well as I do." He stared at Orley, hoping he was right. If not, Bones would have to make a quick move for the shotgun. "I didn't take anything but pictures."

The silence hung between them in the semi-darkness for what felt like a minute before the rancher spat on the floor and lowered his gun.

"I reckon I do believe you at that. You ain't so bad for an Injun."

"And you're not too bad for a fat white man," Bones said, chuckling. Orley returned the jibe with a curse and a grin. "What is this place, anyway?" Bones asked.

"I don't rightly know. I found it near twenty years ago. A storm came through, one of them gully washers. Washed away enough of the rock to uncover this place. I've tried to figure some of it out, but I ain't too good at that kind of thing. I tried to keep it a secret, but once the government started pushing me to open up the other ruins, I knew this place would get found. If it has to be found, I reckon I'm glad it was you."

"Why do you say that?" Bones was flattered, but confused.

Orley was about to reply when a loud clatter came from the entrance.

"Mr. Orley?" a voice called. The speaker's tone of voice sounded taunting as if the man, whoever he was, knew precisely where the rancher was.

Orley whirled around, peering back in the direction from which he had come. "It's them! Take the disc and..."

"Who is 'them'?" Bones asked.

"The Dominion. Now shut up and do what I tell you. Take the disc with you. There's a way out up there," he gestured over Bones' right shoulder to the dark corner. "It's narrow, but you can do it. Go!"

Bones wasn't foolish enough to argue. He grabbed the heavy gold disc and shoved it into his shirt. Three long strides brought him to the corner. He ran his hands up the wall, his fingertips finding purchase on a small ledge. He pulled himself up, digging his steel-toed boots against the rocky face, reached out with his right hand and found the narrow passage. Clambering up, he twisted onto his left side and scooted into the crevice.

"Don't come back no matter what you hear," Orley said.

Feeling more guilt than he had thought himself capable of, Bones slithered forward, now understanding how sausage was made. He had never had much fear of tight places, for which he was now thankful. The cold rock sucked the heat from his body. He continued forward in the darkness, wondering how long this passage was and whether it would narrow to the point that he could not get through. His shoulders were almost touching the sides. One thing was sure; Orley had never crawled through this tunnel, or at least not in many a decade.

He heard muffled voices, then a shotgun blast. He froze as the staccato report of small-caliber handguns echoed down the narrow tunnel. One more defiant shotgun blast, a pause, a single shot, and it was over. Bones remained motionless for the span of a three heartbeats, entertaining the irrational notion that he should somehow wriggle backward, take the bad guys by surprise, and save the day. Common sense won out over guilt almost immediately, and he continued his trek, cursing Orley for his stubbornness and himself for not being a hero. He was certain the rancher was dead. Now he needed to save himself.

He crawled for what seemed like an hour, all the while wondering when bullets would ricochet down the passage. Had they killed Orley immediately? Did he tell them about Bones escape route? Would they find it themselves? None of it mattered. All he could do was keep going.

The tunnel curved, and for a brief moment panic threatened to overwhelm him as the walls closed in on him, but he was soon able to wriggle free and move on. Still grappling with guilt over leaving Orley behind, he was distracted by a pale sliver of light in the distance. Energized, he scurried ahead on hands and knees.

A gentle slope climbed toward the light, and the tunnel gradually widened. Suddenly aware that he had no idea where he would be emerging, or who might be waiting on the other side, he slipped his .22 from its ankle holster and quietly moved ahead. Dry air tinged with the aroma of sage and dust assaulted his nostrils. The tunnel ended in a narrow crack about seven feet high and a foot wide at its broadest point. Sage and scrub covered the entrance. Bones could see little through the cover of foliage, but the way appeared clear. His pistol at the ready, he moved forward.

Emerging on the slope of a dry, narrow gulch and carefully making his way down into the parched defile, the sun scorching his face after the relative cool of the cavern, he thought about the layout of the passage through which he had come, relative to the ranch, and guessed that he was due northeast of the dig, on the other side of the hills that backed Orley's barn and lined the eastern edge of his property. He couldn't be far away as the crow flies, but with gun-toting archaeologists, or whoever the hell they were, so close by, things felt decidedly unsafe. And what was the "Dominion" of which Orley spoke? He needed an answer.

Absently he ran his hand across his stomach and felt the disc underneath his shirt. He had actually forgotten about it. He withdrew the weighty gold circle and examined it in the sunlight. Its gold surface flashed in the brilliant light, displaying the spiraled writing in sharp relief. It was one of the most beautiful artifacts he had ever seen, and a complete enigma. What was a Hebrew artifact doing in Utah? "I hate puzzles," he muttered.

Flipping open his cell phone, he checked for coverage and was relieved to see that he had one bar. No way was he going back for his rental. He'd call the agency and report it broken down. He didn't have any personal items in the car anyway. Who to call? He thought of Emily Dixon, the television reporter. She had been loads of fun for about five hours, and then the obvious fluff between her ears had significantly detracted from her appeal. He needed someone sharp, someone who might know about the Dominion, someone with the guts to dive into what might be a dangerous situation.

A broad grin spread across his face as he called information and requested the number for the Deseret Bugle.

Chapter 10

Shouldn't we open this thing in a lab?" Saul asked, leaning over the makeshift worktable Maddock had created in his hotel room. A white sheet draped over the study table, plus all the lights they could garner, comprised his work area. The three of them wore gloves and dust masks they had picked up from the local home improvement store. All in all it was a poor excuse for a scientific environment, but Maddock had his reasons for doing this privately.

"What lab, Saul? And even if we managed to find one around here, who's to say it would remain a secret? I don't know who those guys in the helicopter were, but I'll assume they're no friends of ours until I have reason to believe different."

"I agree," Jade said in a distracted voice. Her attention was focused on the box Maddock had recovered from the wall at Chaco Canyon. Working with a set of tiny chisels and hammers, she gradually chipped away at the solder that had held the box closed for, they hoped, five hundred years. "Help me out here, Maddock."

Maddock took hold of one side of the box and, following Jade's instructions, they worked the lid free. It came loose reluctantly, but in short order the box lay open on the table. Ancient fabric enshrouded whatever was inside. Jade lifted it free, muttering soft curses as the dry linen crumbled at her touch. Saul laid out a square of clear plastic to catch the debris. Jade turned the bundle over, laid it on the plastic that covered the table and unwrapped it.

A shiny black object about half the size of Maddock's fist lay inside. It was black rock, carved into an eighth of a sphere.

"It looks like someone cut a grapefruit in half, then quartered the half," he observed. "Weird."

Jade held it up to the light. "Onyx," she whispered. "I'm almost certain." Maddock and Saul both leaned forward for a closer look. The rounded top was perfectly smooth, with an odd lip running along the curved bottom edge. Jade turned the artifact over and took a long, deep breath. Faint lines were etched into the bottom surface. They were worn and difficult to discern, but they were definitely letters of some sort. They gazed at the artifact for a long while before Jade laid it gently on the plastic.

"What do you think?" Maddock asked, puzzled by the odd piece. He had never seen such a thing though his background in marine archaeology was not the best preparation for this project.

"I think the artifact has been cut. Possibly into quarters based on the shape of this piece. Look at the straight edges. You can see markings as if someone sawed it. It's mostly smooth but lacks the perfection of the other sides. So..." she paused.

"So Fray Marcos has gone to the time and effort of setting us on a scavenger hunt through the American Southwest. Is that what you're thinking?"

"It's the only thing that makes sense, considering what we know so far. Marcos chopped up the artifact and hid the pieces, or had someone hide the pieces, in various locations. The shield provides us with a map of sorts."

"Find the pieces, put them together, and it leads us to Cibola," Maddock said. The prospect was exciting. "So what we need to do now is figure out where the next piece is hidden."

"Got it covered," Saul said, his perpetually sour face even more puckered if that was possible. He returned shortly with the briefcase in which they kept the pictures of the shield along with their maps and notes. "I have to tell you," he said, spreading the photographs on the bed, "I've given this a great deal of thought, and most of these images are a mystery to me. I also wonder if we need to visit them in any certain order."

"If we're collecting pieces of this artifact in order to reconstruct it, I don't imagine it would make any difference what order we found them in." Maddock rubbed his chin, feeling the stubble that announced evening was fast approaching. One of these days, he would grow a beard. "There has to be some key to understanding the instructions. Chaco Canyon was a lucky guess. The place had a distinct shape. I don't relish the idea of roaming the desert southwest looking at every landform and ruin that resembles these icons.

"These two," he indicated the images that lay at the center of the cross, and on the left, "could be two of I don't know how many different peaks. And the images on the right, at the cross point, and at the top look like ruins, but which ones and where?"

"How did we find this artifact?" Jade asked. "The solstice was important, and so was the number seven. Can we use either of those to help us?"

Maddock's mind was turning over an idea at a rapid pace. The number seven was tumbling around in his thoughts. There was something he had come across in their research. Something to do with travel and direction.

"Are you planning on telling us what you're thinking?" Saul snapped. He stood with his hands folded across his chest, leaning toward Maddock to emphasize the two inches by which he was taller than Maddock.

"The roads," Maddock said, ignoring Saul for what felt like the thousandth time since Jade, and her assistant had crossed his path. "Remember? The Chacoans built a series of roads leading out of the canyon. They were special because they were so straight and well-engineered."

"That's right. There were seven of them," Jade said, her voice indicating cautious interest. "What are you thinking?"

"Six of them scatter out in various directions and don't go very far," Maddock said. "But the one in the center shoots straight up, and it's much longer than the others. It stands out to me. I'm suddenly wondering if it points to anything in particular."

Saul hurried to the charts, obviously not wanting to feel left out. He sorted through them until he found the one with the ancient roads. "Is this the one?" he asked, pointing to the center avenue. Maddock nodded. Saul took his time, checking orientation and marking the roads on a larger map. Finally satisfied, he laid a ruler along the edge of the road and drew a faint line in pencil. The line ran out of New Mexico and into Utah. With his finger, Saul traced the implied path of the ancient road. "All of this is barren land. It doesn't seem to intersect any of the known sites. In fact, it pretty much covers empty land all the way to..." he stopped.

"Sleeping Ute Mountain," Maddock and Jade said at almost the same time. They looked at each other, and Jade grinned.

"Look at the image in the middle of the cross. It's not the entire mountain, but compare it to," she paused as she sifted through her papers until she found a silhouette of the famed mountain, "this picture. What do you see?"

"It's the foot of the mountain," Saul said. "That's why we didn't recognize it. The outline of the entire mountain, we'd have recognized, but not such a small section." He stared at the pictures Jade held up, then looked down at the spot where his finger touched the dot marked Sleeping Ute Mountain. "Does this mean the artifact is hidden on his foot?"

"I don't know," Jade said. "I don't know that something could be hidden there. I feel like there should be something more specific. We're onto something, but we're missing a critical piece."

Saul picked up his laptop that he had left running on the bedside table, and clicked on the icon for internet access.

"We have the number seven connection. I guess now we need the solstice connection." His frown quickly turned to a smile. "Aha! There's a flat area on the mountain where the Utes hold sacred dances, get this, in conjunction with the solstice! That's got to be it!"

Something did not ring true for Maddock, but he didn't have a better idea. "Can we get up there?"

"It says you have to have permission from the tribe, and be escorted to the top," Saul replied. "We can get around that, can't we?"

"I've never been there," Maddock said. "I don't know what's around there or if we can even get close to it."

"Let's try and do it the honest way," Jade said. "I'll make some calls tomorrow and see what I can arrange. If we can't work it out, we'll decide what to do next."

"What? You're going to ask some Ute bigwig if you can take a shovel and metal detector and maybe dig up their sacred dance floor? Yeah, that's really gonna' work," Saul sneered.

Jade pressed her palms to her temples. "Saul..."

"I know. The decision is yours. But I'm registering my objections, okay?" He shut down his laptop and snapped it closed. "I'm gonna' grab something to eat, and then hit the sack. I assume we're heading out early tomorrow?" He didn't wait for Jade's answer, stalking out of the room and closing the door just hard enough to make it obvious that it was intentional.

"I feel like I'm teaching Junior High," Jade groaned, falling down on the bed. "Maybe if this all works out, if we can solve the mystery, I won't need the backing anymore."

Taking a chance, Maddock sat down on the bed next to her. He pulled her hands away from her head and began massaging her temples with his fingertips. Her satisfied groans sounded like purring and set his nerves on an excited edge. Forcing himself to go slowly, he massaged her scalp, her neck, then her shoulders. Gradually the tension drained from Jade's face and was replaced by a satisfied smile. His fingertips trailed down her sides, stroked her stomach, and slowly made the climb up her taut belly. She breathed deeply. He ran his hands up her sides and across her chest. Propping on one elbow, he stroked her cheek and leaned in close, his lips close enough to feel her breath…

…His ears close enough to hear her snoring.

Chuckling, he carefully rolled off the bed and let himself quietly out of the room. Would his luck with women never change?

Chapter 11

Maddock rose early and enjoyed a long, quiet jog in the dim light of dawn. He did his best thinking when he was on the move, keeping his body and mind in sync. Something about Sleeping Ute Mountain did not seem right to him. He couldn't put a finger on it, but he had always been one to listen to his instincts, and right now they were telling him that something was just a little bit off. Returning to his room, he unwound with a hot shower, then sat down to do a little research. By the time, Jade appeared at his door he was on to something, but she was in no mood to hear about it.

"Saul is gone," she said, handing him a slip of notepaper. "He left this at the front desk for me. I'm going to kill him."

Jade, the note read, *I rented a car. Had some things to take care of. Don't worry about me. I'll call you this afternoon and we'll reconnect. Saul'*

"He isn't answering his phone. All of his things are gone."

"Did he take the artifact?" Maddock asked before he could stop himself. Though constantly annoyed with Saul, Jade was often touchy about criticism directed toward her assistant.

"Of course not," Jade snapped. "It was in my room." She dropped heavily into one of the leather padded chairs, picked up the remote and turned on the television. "Do you mind?"

Maddock wasn't much for TV at any time of the day but given the mood she was in, this was not the hill he wanted to die on.

"I guess we should go on as planned," he said. "Saul did say that he would catch up with us later. We can find rooms near Cortez and…"

"Hush!" Jade said, holding up a hand. She had stopped on a local news program. Behind the reporter was an image of Sleeping Ute Mountain.

"*…morning Ute Tribal Police arrested a man for trespassing on restricted tribal land. The suspect was reportedly trying to gain access to a sacred dance floor on Sleeping Ute Mountain. No motive for the trespas has been….*"

"Bloody hell!" Jade articulated the words as only an incensed woman can. She turned off the television and dropped the remote onto the table. "One guess who they arrested. What an idiot."

"I guess there's no point in me suggesting that maybe it wasn't him?" Maddock asked with an utter absence of sincerity. He had disliked Saul almost on sight, and nothing the man had done since then had convinced him otherwise. This stunt was exactly what Maddock would expect of the man.

"Not if you want me to continue respecting your intelligence," Jade said. "In one fell swoop the moron has killed any chance of us checking out the dance floor."

"I'm not sure we'll need to," Maddock said. Jade's expression was unreadable, so he hurried on with his explanation before it became a book he didn't want to open. "I didn't feel right about the dance floor. There's nothing to indicate that particular area was used for solstice dances at the time of Fray Marcos. Also, it's not just solstices and equinoxes that are significant. I think the sun itself is important. Remember the sunbursts on the shield, and the fact that the first piece was hidden in a place where the sun's rays actually strike on the solstice?"

"I'm listening," Jade said in a flat tone that hopefully indicated abating anger and rising interest. She sat with her arms folded beneath her breasts, her legs crossed, tapping her foot in fierce rhythm.

"I did some searches on the terms 'Sleeping Ute Mountain,' 'solstice,' and 'equinox.' I had to do some digging, but I found a likely spot. It's called Yucca House."

"Never heard of it."

"Neither had I. It's a site that's fallen into ruin. The National Park Service maintains control of it, but it's out in the middle of nowhere with no facilities or anything, just an occasional ranger making a drive-by. Anyway, it lies between Mesa Verde and Sleeping Ute Mountain. From there, you have a perfect view of the foot of Sleeping Ute Mountain." He thought Jade sat up a little straighter. "Supposedly, if you stand in the right place on the date of the equinox, the sun sets right on the tip of the Sleeping Ute's toe."

"It sounds... promising," Jade said. Her toe had stopped tapping, and she was now gripping the arms of her chair and leaning slightly forward. "It's not like we have anywhere else to go at the moment."

"Remote location," Maddock added, his convictions strengthened by her interest, "few visitors, and best of all; it's never been excavated."

"All right," Jade said, sounding unconvinced. "Let's give it a try."

Saul parked the car in a dense thicket of cottonwood and snakeweed, killed the engine, and double-checked the topographical chart he had printed out at the library. This appeared to be the right place. He took a long look around before exiting the car. He was crazy to try this, but it was necessary. If the Ute police caught him twice in one day, no way would they let him go again.

The rustle of cottonwood leaves in the sparse breeze put him to mind of a rattlesnake lying in wait. How could such an open, empty space seem so sinister? He had no time for such thoughts. He needed to hurry.

He hadn't believed it when he found it on the map: three hills, almost perfectly round, like the lobes of a clover, and a butte where the stem would be. And the place was perfectly positioned! This had to be it.

He crested the closest hill and gazed down into the valley. It was beautiful, as so much of this land was, but didn't look like much. Lots of scrub, yucca, juniper, and oxeye sunflowers. A flash of movement caught his eye, and he dropped to a knee though there was nowhere to hide up here. He relaxed as he realized it was a lone pronghorn wandering past.

He trotted down the hill and began picking his way through the tangle of flora. As he walked, he saw the remains of low walls, piles of stone, and a few overgrown holes that likely had been kivas. That was encouraging.

At the center of the valley, the ground dropped off in a circle forty feet across. His heart leaped. This once had been a massive ceremonial kiva. The roof had long since collapsed, but hopefully luck would be on his side.

Choosing a spot where the remains of the roof had piled at the edge, forming a ladder of sorts, he clambered down into the ancient center of worship and moved to the center, careful not to turn an ankle on the loose rock. He squatted down and started clearing away the debris when the ground suddenly seemed to churn, and something brown and black burst forth from the hole he had created. Scorpions!

He snatched his hand away and stumbled backward, landing hard on his backside. Seven or eight of the angry creatures scurried out across the rocks and vanished into the cracks and crevasses among the loose piles of stone. They were huge! Each one was at least five inches in length. He was no expert, but he thought they were called desert hairy scorpions. They ought to be called desert harrowing scorpions after that surprise.

He got to his feet, breathing a deep sigh, brushed himself off, and even more cautiously returned to the hole he had created. He really didn't want to get stung, but he had to do this. He would regret it if he didn't.

Slowly, one rock at a time, he cleared a hole about a yard in width. He bit his lip when he saw only hard, dry earth underneath. But he couldn't be wrong. It had to be here. If it wasn't in the center, he'd have to go back for the metal detector and inspect the whole place, and who knew how long that would take? He pulled out his pocketknife and scraped at the hard-packed earth. The blade caught on something. He continued to scratch the surface, revealing something round. This was it! Ten minutes of digging and clearing rewarded him with precisely what he had been looking for. A clay seal bearing the sigil of Fray Marcos de Niza!

Not wanting to waste time working the seal loose, he picked up a heavy stone, raised it above his head, and brought it crashing down onto the seal. The ancient clay shattered, falling into the dark hole that had been the sipapu—the ceremonial hole in the center of the kiva. He reached into the sipapu and his hands closed on a metal box. He had found it!

The pitted, dirt road bounced their rental, jostling them as they drove.

"Ow! My coffee," Jade sputtered, dabbing at her pants with a napkin. "Cheap gas station lids. When we get back to civilization, the first thing I'm going to do is find a Starbucks."

"Sorry," Maddock said. "I don't know how you can drink that stuff in this heat." The arid southwest climate was not as oppressive as the humidity of the Caribbean, but the feeling of perpetual dehydration was wearying. They came to a fence line with a gate blocking the way. "Are we in the right place?" he asked, bringing the vehicle to a stop. "This looks like a ranch or something."

"It says here that the road crosses private property," Jade said, consulting the directions she had printed from the web. "You don't need permission. Just close the gate behind you. I got it." She slipped out the door and strode into the hot midday sun.

Maddock watched as she walked to the gate and swung it open. He loved the way the sun played on her glossy black hair and lithe, athletic figure. Best of all, she was smart. Bones might like them dumb, but not him.

"Sometime today would be nice," Jade called, waving him on. Grinning, he stepped on the gas and pulled through the open gate. Jade secured it behind them and hopped into the cab. "It is seriously hot out there." She picked up his water bottle and uncapped it.

"Hey, what about your coffee?"

"Are you crazy? It's too hot for coffee. Besides, caffeine dehydrates you." She rolled her eyes at him as she took a drink.

Maddock shook his head and grinned. There was no point in trying to win.

They arrived at the site a short while later. There was no parking lot. The dirt road simply faded into flat, open ground, ringed by post and wire fences. A ranch lay off to the right, and a brown sign with white lettering directed them through an empty horse corral to the main gate on the other side.

Mesa Verde lay in the distance, clearly visible in the clean, clear air. Maddock looked out at the fabled Anasazi settlement and wondered what it was about that place that seemed to tug at him.

"Jade, have you checked any of the shield symbols against Mesa Verde structures? I mean, why wouldn't it be one the Seven Cities? Seems like an obvious choice to me." They arrived at a small gate flanked by a brochure box, and a dented, green garbage can on the left and a faded brown National Park Sign. He gave the sign a cursory glance, and helped himself to a brochure before opening the door and motioning her through.

"I have done some checking," Jade said. "The problem is that it's such a large settlement, and the images on Fray Marcos' shield are so small. It could be any little corner or section of a cliff dwelling. As to why it wouldn't be Mesa Verde, I suppose because it's too obvious. I'm still working on it, hoping to find a likely location."

Maddock followed her through the gate. He felt a little strange securing the gate behind them in this desolate place, but he supposed it was there for a reason.

"Have you checked out the solstice angle?"

Jade looked back over her shoulder at him, crossed her eyes and stuck out her tongue. "Yes, I've checked. There aren't any structures that are specifically designated as solstice markers. In such a big place, there might be some structures that fit the bill, but who knows?" She shrugged.

"Needle in a haystack," Maddock said. The thought didn't discourage him. In fact, the challenge made him even more determined to solve the riddle. Men who were easily discouraged didn't make good marine archaeologists. The countless hours going back-and-forth on sonar sweeps saw to that. "So, where is this place?"

"Right here." Jade pointed to a series of overgrown mounds ahead of them. "Not what you expected, I take it?"

"Hardly," Maddock said. The site was surprisingly large, but there seemed to be nothing still standing, except a single wall running along one side. "All of these mounds... is this it?"

"This is it," Jade said. "Really, Maddock, don't you read your own research? The largest one is Upper House." She indicated a mound in the center of the complex, then handed him a computer printout. "Here's a sketch drawn by William Holmes, the man who initially discovered the site. Of course, much of it is speculation. The site was already in ruins when he found it."

"Oh," Maddock said, scratching his head. "I stopped reading at the solstice part. Okay Boss, where do you want to start?"

"Honestly, I think it's going to be kind of arbitrary. I thought we'd scout it out, and then get the metal detectors and see if we can come up with anything that way. I still can't believe Saul took off with the ground penetrating radar."

"It was almost worth it to see the look on your face when you found it missing," Maddock said. He had not believed so lovely a face to be capable of such contortions. "You looked like something between Plastic Man and the Hulk."

"Do you always say the wrong thing, or is it only with me?" Jade lowered her sunglasses to peer at him like a schoolmarm. "No wonder you're not married." She must have noticed something in his face because she immediately forsook the mock disapproval and laid a gentle hand on his arm. "I just stepped in it really deep, didn't I?"

"My wife died a few years ago," he said. "Look, it's okay," he continued as Jade smacked herself on the forehead so hard he feared it would leave a mark. "You didn't have any way of knowing. I don't really talk about her."

"Oh, my..." she blushed furiously. "Maddock I am so sorry. Here I was accusing you of saying the wrong thing, and I make the blunder to end all blunders."

"Like I said, you couldn't have known. I really don't talk about it much."

"Tell me you accept my apology and I'll feel a little bit better. Not much, but a little."

"Apology accepted. Now how about we get to work?"

They spent the next thirty minutes clambering over and around the heaps of rock that had once been a thriving Anasazi settlement of some size. Try as he might, though, Maddock could not see how to even begin their search. It looked like an old quarry.

The midday sun was sweltering. They sought refuge in the thin shade of some scrub growing atop the remnants of what had been the largest structure in the settlement. They shared the tepid water from Maddock's canteen and stared out at the distant hills, hazy in the hot air.

"Do you miss her?" Jade asked, staring out at the ruined site.

It took Maddock a moment to realize of whom she was speaking. "Every day," he said.

"Does the hurt ever go away?" Something in her eyes told him she had a very personal reason for asking.

"Not exactly." He let the word hang between them, thoughts of Melissa seeming to choke off further words. Finally, the tightness in his throat subsided, and he was surprised at how normal he sounded. "But it dulls with time. At first you can't stand to think about it, but you can't think of anything else. Little by little, you distance yourself from it. After a while, it's only the little things that get to you; a certain song, a favorite place, a little gift you gave her that you thought she'd thrown away. Then it all comes back if only for a little while."

"I know what you mean," Jade said. She exhaled loudly and sprang to her feet. "Well then," she said, a forced cheerfulness in her voice. "I think the most likely place to start is down by Lower House. I saw an overhang that looked promising." She picked her way through the rubble toward High House without waiting for him.

When Maddock caught up with her, Jade was on her hands and knees crawling into a shady opening at the base of the rock pile that, according to the brochure, had once been an L-shaped Puebloan dwelling with a large central kiva, the round, sunken building that was the center of Anasazi worship. He dropped down alongside her, peering into the darkness. The air was cooler though not by much, but still it was a stark contrast to the sun blistering his back.

"It looks to me," Jade said, "like this part of the structure has actually held together. If we can scoop out some dirt, we might be able to get inside. I think I see an open space back there." She flicked on a tiny flashlight and directed the beam to the back of the overhang where the blackness was complete. She lay down on her stomach and scooted forward.

A flicker of movement caught Maddock's eye. Lightning fast, his hand shot out just as an angry buzz filled the small space. He grabbed hold of the rattlesnake's tail and with a flick of the wrist, slung it out into the sun. The fat, gray-brown viper beat a hasty retreat into the rocks and scrub, rattling furiously all the while.

"Oh, my…" Jade backed out of the overhang and rolled over onto her back, where she lay spread-eagled, her eyes closed and her breath coming in gasps.

"Are you all right?" Maddock asked. "He didn't get you, did he?"

"I'm fine," she said, still breathing rapidly. "Not my first rattler, but my closest call." She took a few deep breaths, gaining control of her breathing, before sitting up. "Western Diamondback?" she asked.

"I think so," Maddock said. "We don't get too many of those in the Caribbean, but I watched Wild Kingdom when I was a kid."

"How did you manage to grab that thing?"

"Fast hands and poor impulse control," he joked. "I caught sight of him when you turned on your flashlight. He was coiled to strike, but he was turned so that I had a clear shot at his tail. Probably wasn't the safest way of handling a snake, but at least I went for the less-dangerous end."

"I can't believe I was so careless," she said. "I'm just so mad that we wasted our time coming out here. It seemed so promising." She pulled the folded printout of Holmes' map out of her front pocket. She opened it and scrutinized it for a moment before balling it up and throwing it on the ground. "I give up," she said. "Let's get back to semi-civilization. Maybe Saul is back, and I'll have someone to take out my frustrations on."

"Wait a minute," Maddock said, picking up the crumpled map. Something had taken shape in his mind when she had opened it up moments before. He smoothed it out and laid it on his lap. "Got a pen?" Wordlessly she handed him a cheap ballpoint with a chewed cap and sat back with her arms folded across her chest and a look of skepticism painting her face.

"Look at how the site was originally laid out." He drew a faint outline around the layout as he spoke. "Notice how the general layout makes a three-lobed shape. And if you tie in this square ruin at the bottom…"

"A clover," Jade said, her eyes wide in amazement. "But wait a minute. This place would have been here before Fray Marcos's time. It would have to be a coincidence."

"Yes," Maddock said. "But imagine you're Fray Marcos or Estevanico, looking for places to hide pieces of this… puzzle or whatever it is. You don't want it to be too easy, but you also want to make sure someone will eventually find the clues. What better place to hide one of the pieces than in a village that is shaped like Marcos' personal symbol?"

"Which would explain why such a small place as this would be a likely spot," Jade said. "I like it. But where do we look?"

"If I draw a line right down the center," Maddock said as he drew, "see what it looks like when I cut a horizontal line right across this well in the middle?"

"It's a perfect cross!" Jade said. "But couldn't it be another coincidence?"

"It could," he agreed. "But there's only one way to find out for sure."

They made their way to a low spot that was, to the best of their estimation, the site of the small kiva. With great care, they began moving aside the jumbled rocks. After twenty minutes of tiring work, he was surprised to feel a cool draft on his face. He dropped to his belly and scooted down into the hole they had made.

"There's a tangle of interlocking roots holding up all of this rock," he said, dragging a heavy stone away to reveal open space underneath. "I think the kiva is intact down below us!"

"No way," Jade said, sliding up alongside him. "Just like the well where we found the breastplate." She took out her flashlight and shone it into the hole. Its slender beam sliced through the darkness, illuminating stones that had not seen sunlight in centuries. "Hard to believe it wasn't filled up with debris. I just assumed it wouldn't be worth inspecting when I saw the pile of rubble."

"If we can clear a large enough hole for me to fit through without bringing the whole thing down, I'll drop in there and see what I can find," Maddock said, sliding back from the hole and climbing to his feet.

"I'm going too," Jade said, standing and brushing the dirt and bits of rock from the front of her clothing. "I'm not letting you have all of the fun. This is much too cool to miss."

"One of us has got to stay up here with the rope in case something goes wrong," Maddock said. "If we're both down there and the roof comes down…" He did not need to finish the sentence.

"In that case," Jade said, "I should be the one to go down there. I'm lighter, so there's less chance of me bringing something crashing down. And if there is a problem, you'll have a much easier time pulling me up than the other way around."

Maddock wanted to argue, but her logic was impeccable. Besides, he had seen her in action, and she was far from helpless. Still he did not like it.

"I see your point," he said. "I just think I should be the one to go down there. We don't know what we're going to find."

"And why should you be the one to take the risk?" she asked. Her voice held a note of challenge. She folded her hands across her chest. "And you had better not say it's because I'm a woman."

Actually, that was exactly what Maddock had been thinking. He knew it was irrational, but it was the way he had been raised. He also knew Jade would not find it an acceptable reason.

"Suit yourself," he said. "Just promise me you'll be careful."

"Thanks, Galahad," she said, smiling. She put a hand on his cheek in a gesture that was somehow both condescending and affectionate at the same time. "I promise I'll be careful."

They began clearing way the rubble until there was enough space for her to wriggle through. They secured a rope to a nearby boulder and doubled it around the base of one of the larger scrub brush for added strength. Maddock took hold of it and held tight while Jade squirmed back through the hole and slid down into the darkness.

The oppressive darkness seemed to press down on Jade. She shone her light on the ceiling above her. The mass of earth and stone seemed to strain against the roots that bound it, seeking to pour down upon her. It seemed more threatening than the well in which she had dove. Somehow, the water had felt like a safeguard. Here, it was painfully obvious that nothing would protect her should gravity finally win this centuries-long battle.

"You're wasting time, Jade," she chided herself. She let the light play across the floor and then around the walls, searching for a clue. Maddock had better not have brought her on a wild goose chase. She continued to search, occasionally brushing the dirt off of a likely-looking stone, hoping to find something, but to no avail.

She paused, dropping to a knee and looking around. What might she be forgetting? Solstices were important. What was the connection between solstices and kivas? The axes of kivas were usually built on solstice lines, which meant the solstice sun would shine on...

She turned her light toward the heel stone that hid the tunnel through which the shaman would enter the kiva. Could it be?

She first inspected the heel stone but found nothing. Now for the tunnel. The Anasazi had been a small people compared to modern-day humans. The tunnel was going to be a squeeze. Holding her flashlight in one hand and her knife in the other, she squeezed into the opening and scooted forward. Inch by inch, she wormed her way back into the darkness. If I get stuck, there's no way Maddock will hear me call for him.

She finally reached the end of the tunnel. Above her, where the shaman had once climbed down into the tunnel, was another hole filled with a precariously loose clump of stone and debris. The wall in front of her would have been in direct alignment with the sun if not actually illuminated by it, so she started there. She started scraping away at the rocks in front of her. Nothing on the first one. Nor the second. Maybe...

A dull, dragging sound like a burlap sack being dragged across a rough floor filled the hole, and she looked up in time to see the ceiling cave in on her.

Maddock checked his watch. It had only been three minutes though it seemed longer. No word yet from Jade. He strained to listen, but could hear nothing. After a couple more minutes, he called down.

"Everything okay down there?" He hated not being down there with her. "Jade?"

No reply.

"Jade, what's going on down there?" What had happened to her? It wasn't so far to the bottom that she would not be able to hear him. "I'm coming in after you if you don't answer me." He suddenly had a vision of the rope giving way during his descent, leaving them both trapped at the bottom. But what choice did he have?

"Hold your horses, Buddy!" Jade called back. "I had to... I'll explain when I get up there." Another long silence, then "Go ahead and pull the rope up."

"You want me to pull you up?" he asked. "Are you hurt?"

"No, Maddock. Just pull up the rope." Her voice had the quality of a wife wearied of her obtuse husband. He remembered Melissa speaking to him in that tone many times, usually involving bright-colored laundry and the wrong temperature water. Duly chastised, he started hauling.

Whatever was on the end of the rope was light and came up easily. He hauled it out of the hole: a metal box like the one they had found at Chaco Canyon.

"You did it!" he called. Quickly untying the knots that held the box in place, he dropped the rope back into the hole so she could climb out.

Jade was covered in dirt, her face grimy, but her eyes were positively aglow. She immediately set to untying the rope.

"The interior of the kiva was still intact, just as we thought," she explained. "There was a tunnel. Shamans would use it to make a dramatic entrance while the room was smoky and the worshipers frenzied. It made them look like they appeared out of nowhere." She finished coiling the rope and headed back toward their vehicle, still lecturing. "I followed it to the end. The box was sealed up in a recess behind a rock like the one you described from Chaco. I had to scrub away the dirt to find the right stone and managed to bring a chunk of the ceiling down on me. It scared me more than anything, but I finally found a rock that had the symbol carved in it."

"Glad you're okay," Maddock said, looking her over just to make certain. "I wonder how many researchers have been in that room, never dreaming that if they just did a little scrubbing they'd find something amazing," Maddock said, holding the plain, metal box as if it were a priceless treasure.

"Lucky for us, this site doesn't seem to have gotten much attention," she said. "Let's get out of here before someone shows up. I can't wait to see what's inside this box."

Chapter 12

And you're sure he said "Dominion?" Amanda Shores turned back to the desktop computer in her office at the Deseret Bugle. The desk was cluttered with notes, a framed picture of what looked like Amanda and some friends in college, and a coffee-stained paperback fantasy novel. A framed graduation certificate from Colorado State University hung above the desk next to a small white board.

No boyfriend picture is a good thing, Bones thought.

"Yep," he said, picking up the picture to get a closer look. She had been cute in college but was definitely better-looking now. "The Dominion. Orley said it like some movie voice-over like I should know what he was talking about. Ever heard of it?"

"I think so," she replied, her attention fixed on the screen. She tapped a few keys and sat back. "Take a look."

Bones scooted the rolling chair closer. The website to which Amanda had surfed was royal blue with a beehive logo in the top, left corner. The heading read The Deseret Dominion.

"The Deseret Dominion, also known as simply, 'The Dominion,' is a para-political organization that supports independence for the former state of Deseret," Amanda explained. Seeing his blank stare, she continued. "In 1849, settlers in Utah proposed the formation of the state of Deseret. The proposal was basically for most of the land acquired in the Mexican Cession of 1848 to be included in the new state: all of present-day Utah and Nevada, and parts of Colorado, New Mexico, Wyoming, Idaho, and Oregon, and large chunks of California and Arizona. The United States didn't act on the proposal right away, and the provisional government actually existed unofficially for two years before the Utah territory was created."

"So this... Dominion," Bones said, "thinks it can start a new country inside the US?"

"It's complicated," Amanda replied. "Officially it's a small political organization that lobbies for Mormon interests. Take a peek beneath the surface, and you'll find all sorts of interesting things: rumors of training facilities for paramilitary troops, chemical weapons facilities, religious nuts. Who knows how much of it is true?"

"So you think these are the guys Orley was talking about?" Bones asked. "Why would they care about a farmer and an archaeological dig?"

"That picture you found. They're calling it the 'Jesus Image.' Anything in the historical record that could help support the Book of Mormon would be of interest to the Dominion."

"So they went after Isaiah to shut him up," Bones said, realization dawning on him, "because he wouldn't say that the image was of Jesus. But why would they go after Orley?"

"I don't imagine they were after Orley," she said. "But instead, they were after whatever was in the cave. Or maybe to keep what was in the cave from coming to the attention of the public. Those pictures you took suggest we're talking about a Spaniard rather than Jesus."

"I've got to do something to make sure Isaiah is safe from these guys," he said.

"I'll wager he is safe," Amanda said. "First of all, they haven't come back to finish the job. Also, they've gotten him off the project. The new foreman is probably their man, and if Isaiah comes out against him publicly, he'll just look like the envious professor who is angry because he didn't get to finish the dig he started."

"I hear you," Bones said, "but I still think I'll talk to Isaiah about getting out of town. How about Orley? Have you found anything out about him?"

"Whoever followed you two into that cave didn't try to hurt him. They subdued him and took him to a hospital. They claimed he had a fit. I also found out he's been transferred to a psychiatric hospital for evaluation. They can't hold him for long unless they can find something wrong with him. Problem is…"

"If the Dominion has connections in the hospital, his evaluation might not be the most honest or accurate," Bones finished.

"And," Amanda added, "they would have the drugs and know-how to question him in great depth. Anything Orley knows about that cave, the Dominion will learn sooner or later."

"My to-do list keeps getting longer," Bones said.

"Would you like to share it with me?" Amanda asked. "Maybe I can help."

"My list mostly consists of people I'm gonna' kick the crap out of," Bones said. "What you can do is help me find out exactly who to punch first."

"I can do that," Amanda said, her eyes glistening with excitement. "No one's ever really investigated the Dominion. Most of their critics are raving conspiracy theorists, but if Orley is correct, this is something worth pursuing."

"It could be dangerous," Bones said. "If we're right about this, they've already come after two people."

"I know," Amanda said. "But I want to do it anyway."

"All right," Bones said. "See if you can find out who it was that brought Orley to the hospital. They could be our link to the Dominion. Also, see what you can dig up on the guy who's taken over Isaiah's dig. Even if he's not one of them, we might be able to find out who's pulling his strings."

He removed the golden disc, now wrapped in cloth and hidden inside a plain, brown paper bag, from his jacket pocket. "So what do you think we do about this?"

"It's a tough call," she said. "The Dominion has members everywhere: in government, in business, even in universities. It's hard to know who to trust. We need someone we can complete rely on who has a background in local Native American history."

A sudden thought struck Bones. The girl who was working with Maddock might fit the bill.

"I think I know of someone who can help us out on that end," he said. "I'll also send the cave pictures and pictures of the disc to a friend of mine. He's sort of an über computer geek. If anyone can make something of the writing, it's him."

"Sounds good to me," Amanda said. "What do you want to do first?"

"First, we break Orley out of that hospital."

Chapter 13

Do you really think this is going to work?" Amanda whispered, peering across the dark parking lot at the glass-paneled entrance of the Central Utah University Neuropsychiatric Institute.

"No, I just thought it would be cool to get you arrested," Bones said. "Relax. It's going to be fine. I've got a feeling this won't be the first time you've bluffed your way into somewhere you weren't supposed to be."

"True, but I look like a tramp in this," she said, looking down at her tight, black leather miniskirt and fishnet hose.

"You say that like it's a bad thing," Bones said, leaning back to avoid her playful slap. "Seriously, you look great and you'll definitely get the interest of the guy at the front desk."

"What if it's a girl at the front desk?"

"You know, that never actually occurred to me," he said. "I guess you'd better hope she likes chicks. Either that or you're going to have to put on the coveralls, and I'll wear the skirt and hose."

"Let's just get this over with," Amanda said. She slid gracefully out of the car and set off across the parking lot in a purposeful, yet delicate, walk. Bones watched as she disappeared into the lobby, kicking himself all the while for not making sure the person on duty was a guy. Amanda would just have to wing it.

He wondered if he was being unnecessarily cautious. This was a university mental health center, not a prison or a military installation. But if the Dominion was holding Orley, they might have extra security. Then again, what reason would they have to think someone would be coming after Orley? He was banking on lax security to get them through.

He gave Amanda one minute, then retrieved the toolbox from the back seat and hurried to the door. Careful not to be seen, he peered into the lobby. Score! The kid at the front desk couldn't have been more than twenty-five and from the look on his face, he'd never seen a girl dressed this sexy outside his favorite websites.

Amanda and the rent-a-cop spoke briefly, with her doing most of the talking and the kid doing most of the mouth-agape, dumbstruck nodding. Finally, he gave a halfhearted shake of his head, at which point Amanda bent way over his desk and said something that must have done the trick. He removed his headset, stood and looked around before slipping out from behind the desk and leading Amanda down the hallway to the left.

Bones slipped in the front door and headed in the direction Amanda and the guard had gone. He moved silently- he told everyone it was an Indian thing, but actually it was just lots of practice- and soon he could hear Amanda somewhere up ahead. Good girl! She was sticking to the plan, acting the brainless babe coming to visit her sick uncle. The guard should be leading them to Orley's room.

He paused at a cross-hall, not sure which direction to go. He heard an elevator down the hall to his right, and he stole a quick glance around. Amanda stepped inside and the guard turned and headed back in Bones' direction. Crap! This wasn't the plan! He needed to get to the elevator in time to see at which floor it stopped, or he'd have a hell of a time finding Orley's room.

The footsteps came closer.

He looked around for somewhere to hide. He could deal with the kid if he had to, but he hated to involve someone who was just doing his job and had no idea what was going on. The only nearby door was the ladies' room. The light was on, but at this time of night there was probably no one in there. He took a deep breath and ducked inside.

The first stall was occupied.

Hoping whoever was inside would not see his boots, he moved to the far wall and made his way to the last stall. Shutting himself in, he sat down on the toilet tank, toolbox on his lap and his feet on the seat. *Hurry up, Lady!* He checked his watch. Amanda was definitely off the elevator by now. He pulled out his phone to text her. No signal.

Just then, a cell phone rang in the other stall, sounding like a fire alarm in the quiet room, and nearly eliciting a curse from Bones.

"Hello? Oh, hi! I've been meaning..." She dove into a lengthy conversation that left Bones fuming. He tried his own cell phone again. Nothing. *I need to find out who her carrier is,* he thought. Perhaps he could slip out while she was talking. He didn't know where he would go from there, but he could at least start looking.

"I've got to go," the woman said. "We've got this problem patient up on the fourth floor. A grumpy old rancher who keeps telling us he's been kidnaped. Totally paranoid. He's due for another sedative in about five minutes."

"Fourth floor," Bones whispered too low to be heard. "At least I caught one break."

Bones had no trouble finding Orley's room. He just followed the sound of profanity.

"...putting no needle in me!" The rancher's familiar voice lifted Bones' spirits. He liked the tough old fellow and was glad he had not been hurt. The fact that Orley believed he was being held against his will only served to confirm his and Amanda's suspicions.

"Mr. Orley, you need something to help you calm down," the woman from downstairs was saying. "Your niece..."

"I done told you I don't know this girl!" Obviously Amanda was in the room with them. Bones took a peek around the corner just as Orley turned toward him. The rancher scowled, but then his eyes widened as he realized who Bones was.

"It's okay," Bones mouthed, hoping Orley would understand that he and Amanda were there to help. Thankfully, Orley relaxed and quieted down.

"This will only take a moment, and then you'll feel much better," the nurse said. In short order, she had given him the injection.

Orley looked at Bones as if to say, You'd better know what you're doing. Bones gave him the "thumbs-up" and ducked into the bathroom just inside Orley's doorway. He hid in the shower until Amanda came to tell him the nurse was gone.

"Let's get you out of here," Bones said to Orley as he hurried into the room. He helped the wobbly man to his feet.

"Damn stuff's already gettin' to me," Orley mumbled. Amanda found his clothes and helped him get dressed.

"What's going on here?" A muscular man with a square chin and a shaved head stepped through the door. He wore a white hospital coat and held a clipboard, but Bones could tell this was no doctor. "I haven't discharged this patient."

"My uncle wants to walk a little," Amanda said. "He doesn't feel comfortable wearing the gown, you know."

"He can barely stand," the man said. Orley's knees were weak from the sedative. "Put him back in the bed now." He took two steps before Bones' presence finally registered. He glanced at the coveralls and toolbox, turned away, and then jerked back. Their eyes met and recognition shone in his face.

Bones swung his toolbox up at a tight angle, catching the fellow on the side of the head. The man had good reflexes and was able to turn away from the blow, catching most of the force on the back of his head. He spun away but recovered his balance quickly.

The man drew a pistol from the pocket of his coat, but Bones was ready. He swept a vicious crescent kick at the man, sending the gun flying across the room, and hurled his toolbox at the surprised man, who managed to dodge it. Bones sprang forward, landing a quick jab, and following with a right cross that just missed. Lab Coat Man bounced a punch off Bones' solid abs, and struck with a knife-hand that whistled past Bones' throat.

A meaty fist appeared seemingly out of nowhere, catching the man clean on the chin, and he crumpled noiselessly to the floor. Bones turned to see Orley slumped against Amanda.

"That's all I got left," the rancher said. "Get me the hell out of here. There's always at least two of 'em around."

They helped the stumbling rancher into the hall and back toward the elevator. Orley was heavy—years of ranching had turned him into a veritable chunk of muscle. Those muscles were not of much help, though, as the sedated rancher struggled to keep his feet beneath him.

"Hold him," Amanda whispered, shifting the weight to Bones' side and ducking out from under Orley's arm. She disappeared around the corner and returned with a wheelchair.

"Nice," Bones whispered. "I think I'm going to keep you around."

"Like it's up to you," Amanda replied with a wink. "Give him to me and let's get him out of here. Head for the elevator."

Bones took a moment to get everything situated, took the wheelchair and headed down the corridor. Reaching the cross-hall he made the left that would take him to the bank of elevators. He heard footfalls behind him.

"Hey! Where are you going with that patient?"

He glanced over his shoulder to see a man in a security uniform round the corner at the far end of the hall. This was not the rent-a-cop from down the hall. This guy had every bit of the military bearing that Lab Coat Man had.

"What did you say?" Bones shouted. He quickened his pace and was careful to keep his body between the wheelchair and his pursuer. "I didn't hear you!"

"Stop!" the man yelled and began trotting toward Bones. Good. The fellow wasn't overly concerned yet. "What the hell are you doing taking a patient out of here anyway?"

"He's being checked out. The nurse asked me to help her with him." He looked back over his shoulder. The man was closing the distance quickly. Bones kept the dialog going as he passed an empty nurse's station. "She was blowing chunks. You should have seen it. I think she had pizza for dinner."

"I'll take care of the patient," the man yelled. "Just leave him there for me."

Bones stole one last glance at the elevators, only ten feet away, and saw that all of them were on the first floor. The man was no more than fifty feet away.

"Suit yourself," Bones said. He turned and shoved the wheelchair through the nearest open door, a patient's room, and ducked into a nearby stairwell. As the door swung shut behind him, he heard a crash as the wheelchair spilled its contents: the toolbox he had hidden under a blanket. By now, Amanda and Orley were hopefully making their way out through the basement service exit they had discovered in the hospital floor plan they'd reviewed before attempting to retrieve the rancher. Angry voices told him he'd at least created a small diversion. He hoped he hadn't hurt any patients in the process, but what could he do? If anyone was injured, at least they were already in a hospital.

He jumped ten or so stairs and landed with a resounding thud on the landing. Ignoring the pain that surged up his legs and spine, he turned and hurtled down the next flight. A sign read Second Floor. They would expect him to go all the way down to the ground floor. He slipped through the door and hurried down another glistening white hallway, similar to the one above.

A middle-aged nurse with graying brown hair and a smudge of chocolate frosting on her cheek stood up and peered with alarm over the nurse's station desk as he ran by.

"Big mess upstairs," he huffed. "No nurse on duty, either. You might want to get up there."

"But I'm not..."

He was gone before she could finish her sentence.

Bones tightened his grip on the .22 he held hidden under his sleeve. He really didn't want to shoot anybody. Under any circumstance, it would be difficult to explain why he was kidnapping a patient. Considering the political clout the Domain apparently wielded, it would be doubly hard to justify putting a bullet in anyone.

He made a right turn and dashed down the empty hallway to the back of the building where he came to a break room with a huge plate glass window overlooking the back parking lot. Amanda sat parked directly under the window in the old van she had borrowed from her uncle. The magnetic "Patton Plumbing" sign Bones had stolen off a parked vehicle they passed along the way completed the ruse nicely. They'd mail the sign back to the rightful owners, and have the rental company pick up the car in which they had arrived. They'd rented it under a false name so it wouldn't trace back to either of them.

He was about to head to the back exit when he heard footsteps in the hallway. He had not bought himself as much time as he'd hoped. He took a long look at the window.

"Oh, what the heck?" he whispered. "Let's just hope it's not heavy-duty safety glass."

He picked up one of the break tables, a heavy, round job with a Formica top and black metal trestle, and heaved it into the window. The table rebounded with a crack and a thud, crashing to the tile floor, but the damage was done. A hole gaped in the middle of the window and a web of cracks spreading three feet all around. Hoping he'd judged the distance correctly, he got a running start and jumped, shielding his face as he smashed through the glass.

There was a moment of groin-tingling free-fall, and then he crashed with a metallic thud onto the roof of the van. Amanda yelped and stuck her head out the driver's window.

"Where did you..."

"Just drive!" he yelled. He grabbed the front edge of the van roof as Amanda hit the gas. The van surged forward, then sputtered and lurched to a halt. Bones tried to dig the toes of his boots into the pitted, dented surface, but to no avail. He slid forward and tumbled down the windshield and over the hood. He slowed enough to get his feet under him as he dropped to the asphalt.

"Sorry!" Amanda said. "I forgot the transmission on this thing sometimes..." The staccato crackling of gunfire rang out, and bullets whizzed past the front end of the van.

Bones returned fire, sending two well-aimed shots through the remains of the second-floor window. The van had rolled forward far enough to make for a difficult angle, and he had no idea if he'd hit his target, but it bought sufficient time for him to take the wheel from Amanda and hit the road.

"You have to baby the gas a little or else it stalls," Amanda said.

"Yeah, I sort of figured that out." He checked the rear-view and side mirrors and saw no pursuit. He doubted it would last.

He was right.

Headlights appeared behind them, growing fast as the vehicle sped toward them. Bones had no doubt it was their pursuers. He cut off the van's headlights and hung a right down the nearest street, careful not to tap on the brakes, lest the brake lights give them away. He stood on the gas, praying no one would pull or walk out in front of him. The odds were slim this time of night. He took another right, this time the van felt like it was going up on two wheels. Orley, lying on the back floorboard, groaned as he rolled over.

As they zoomed down another deserted street, Bones spotted an old white van nearly the twin of the one they drove. He slammed on the brakes, bringing the van to a halt.

"Why are we stopping? Are you nuts?" Amanda shouted.

"Here," Bones said, reaching out the window and yanking the magnetic sign off the door. "Slap this baby on that van. With any luck, it'll slow them down." When she was finished, he whipped the van around the next corner just in time to see headlights from the direction they had come. He sped up, hoping they had not been spotted. They flew down the darkened street with no sign of pursuit. The false trail had apparently bought them some time.

Bones made three more turns before he was satisfied they had left their pursuers behind. He slowed the van and turned the headlights back on.

"Can I breathe now?" Amanda asked, releasing her vise grip on the armrest. "I've never been shot at before."

"I think we're good," Bones said, still keeping a wary eye out for pursuit. "How's Orley?"

"Still doped. It isn't safe to take him home. Where should we go?"

"Considering we're both probably on hospital security video," Bones said, "I vote we get out of town."

Chapter 14

So your friend Bones is on his way here and he's bringing what?" Jade's attention was fixed on the e-mail they had received from Maddock's friend, computer geek Jimmy Letson, and she was only halfway paying attention to what he'd told her.

"He says he's found a gold disc with some kind of weird writing. He also has a bunch of pictures he took of cave paintings. He thinks you might be able to help him out."

"Did you tell him we're kind of busy here?" she asked, turning over another page. "Jimmy says the writing is something like Hebrew, but not quite. As if it's an older form that grew out of something else. He's identified a few phrases and thinks given enough time he'll be able to make some sense of it."

"What do you make of the two artifacts we've found so far?" Maddock turned the new piece over. It was almost the twin of the first one they'd found. Put together they made a quarter of a sphere. He wasn't certain, but the writing seemed to flow across from one to the other – they seemed to be a match. "Do you think maybe there are eight of them, so it makes a sphere?"

"I don't know," Jade said, still focusing her attention on the papers. "There are only six symbols on the shield, which makes me think there are six pieces."

"Six pieces, but seven cities," Maddock mused. He stroked his chin, feeling the stubble of a day's growth. "Yucca House was quite ordinary, and not even a city. Chaco Canyon qualifies as a city, but not golden."

"What are you getting at?"

"Just wondering what's at the end of the rainbow."

"Meaning?"

"I mean that obviously all seven 'cities' are not cities of gold or treasure. If your theory is correct, and all six locations point to a seventh, then is that where we find whatever it is Fray Marcos was hiding? And if so, what is it?"

"I wonder that myself," Jade said. "The only legend I've uncovered is that of the Moorish treasure and the religious artifacts, although the idea of an eighth-century crossing of the Atlantic, followed by going halfway across America to hide something seems a bit far-fetched."

"I've seen crazier. Trust me," Maddock said. "What do you…"

"Hey! It's another e-mail from Jimmy," Jade said. She took a moment to read the contents, printed it off, and handed it to Maddock. "He's managed to get what he thinks is a translation of the writing on the first piece." She handed him the paper from his computer guru friend and stood back with her arms folded across her chest and watched him read.

Maddock,
This is weird stuff- an unusual variation of Hebrew. Here's my best stab at the translation with

the help of a professor friend.

'In the sepulchre, in the third course of stones. Under the tomb. In the chain platform. This is all of the votive offerings of the seventh treasure, the tenth is impure.'

Doesn't look like too much. Sorry I couldn't help more.

Jimmy

"He's right," Maddock said. "It doesn't look like much. What do you make of it?"

"Nothing yet."

A knock at the door interrupted her. Maddock answered it and was surprised to see Saul standing in the doorway. He was covered in dirt, but otherwise looked no worse for the wear.

"What the hell, Saul?" Jade's soft voice was razor sharp, and her eyes were ablaze. "You take off with my equipment, you don't let me know where you are..." She stopped there, her hands in the air, looking as if she couldn't decide whether to scream at him or strangle him. Finally, with an exasperated sigh, she waved him into the room and stalked out past him.

Saul watched her go before turning to Maddock with a sheepish expression on his face.

"Guess I'm not on the invite list for her next soiree," he said.

"Not likely," Maddock replied. He had no idea how to take Saul, but the guy at least seemed contrite. "She's pretty stressed out, though. We have a translation from the artifacts we've found, but it doesn't seem to mean anything."

"You found another one?" Saul sat heavily on the corner of Jade's bed. "And you have a translation?"

"Yeah," Maddock said. He felt a little strange telling Saul this, but he supposed there would be no harm. The translation was close to nonsense; at least, it was of no use to them being incomplete and out of context.

He handed the sheet to Saul, who read it over silently, shook his head, and read it aloud.

"In the sepulchre, in the third course of stones. Under the tomb. In the chain platform. This is all of the votive offerings of the seventh treasure, the tenth is impure." He looked at Maddock, his expression unreadable. "It sounds like a treasure hunt. What could it be?"

"No idea," Maddock said though his mind conjured possibilities, each more far-fetched than the other, that set his heart pounding. He supposed he was just a kid at heart. He loved the thought of unraveling a mystery.

"Who did the translation?" Saul was staring at the paper again as if some secret were buried between the lines.

"A friend of mine," Maddock said. "Computer guy. He had some help."

"And he's certain of the translation?"

"As certain as he can be," Maddock said, feeling a touch of defensiveness rising. "He's reliable and very thorough."

"No doubt." Saul gave Maddock a measured look and opened his mouth to speak when a knock drew their attention. Maddock knew who it was immediately.

"Bones!" he said, swinging the door open. His friend grabbed him in a rough embrace and slapped him on the back.

"Maddock! Good to see you. How's the latest adventure?" Before Maddock could answer, a short, attractive brunette with the high cheekbones that spoke of native blood stepped up behind Bones. "This is Amanda," he said. "I think I mentioned her to you."

"Absolutely," he said, shaking hands with Amanda. "Dane Maddock. Good to meet you."

"Bones told me plenty about you on the drive here," she said, smiling.

"Half of it's not true and the other half's a lie," he replied. Remembering Saul, he turned and introduced him to Bones and Amanda. Maddock had told Bones of his discomfort with Jade's assistant, but Bones greeted Saul politely as they shook hands. Maddock was about to ask about the find Bones had made in Utah when Jade re-entered the room.

"Oh, hi," she said. Obviously her anger at Saul had distracted her. "Sorry. I'm Jade Ihara." She offered her hand to Bones, who surprised Maddock by neither hitting on her nor saying anything remotely inappropriate. He simply shook her hand and introduced himself and Amanda.

The two women shook hands politely but eyed one another as if they were sizing each other up. After an uncomfortable pause, Jade invited them to sit.

"What's the latest with Isaiah?" Maddock asked. "How's he doing?"

"Better. He's in Denver staying with friends while he recoups. He wanted to go back to the dig, but it's not his anymore, so..." Bones shrugged.

"So, where is the rancher guy you had with you?"

"Dropped him off with some relatives in Grand Junction," Bones said, settling into a chair opposite Maddock. "I think he's going to be fine. He's a tough old fellow."

"That's good," Maddock said. "So tell me about what you found in the cave."

Bones reached into his jacket pocket and extracted something wrapped in cloth. He removed the cloth with great care and laid the golden disc on the table. Bones had already described the disc to Maddock, but seeing it was amazing.

He turned it over in his hand, narrowing his eyes the writing that spiraled around the golden circle. It was like nothing he'd ever seen before. Or was it?

Jade slid her chair against his and leaned in close. Her soft hair brushed his arm and her soft intake of breath seemed to tingle in his ear.

"Maddock, she said. "The writing! Do you think it's the same?"

She didn't need explain what she meant by the same. It definitely looked to him to be the same writing they had found on the artifacts: a version of Hebrew. He couldn't say for sure, but Jimmy could find out for them.

"I think they are the same," he said. "It's one hell of a coincidence, though. Bones finding this disc and us finding the artifacts..."

"It can't be a coincidence," she said. "They have to be connected somehow. We've got to get this translated."

"I've already sent it to Jimmy," Bones said.

"Did he tell you anything?" Jade asked, her eyes sparkling with enthusiasm.

"Yes. He told me he already had a real job, and if we keep dumping all this crap on him he was going to start charging us for it."

Jade groaned and sank back into her chair. "I hate being stuck waiting around like this. I want something to do."

"Bones told me you were trying to identify some symbols on an artifact," Amanda said. 'Perhaps a fresh set of eyes would be of some help."

"Why not?" Jade said without much conviction. Maddock wondered what had gotten her so down all of a sudden. The possibility that Bones and Amanda's find could help them in their search had him feeling good about their prospects.

Jade brought out a high-resolution picture of the breastplate along with a set of papers. Each paper had an image from the breastplate at the top and a list of notes, thoughts and possibilities were jotted below.

"We've solved these two," she explained, indicating the moon-like icon that represented Chaco Canyon and the jagged promontory that was the foot of Sleeping Ute Mountain. "We believe that each has some association with solstices or equinoxes. We've also found Fray Marcos's personal symbol, a cross inside a clover, at each location. Maddock noticed that the layout of the second site, Yucca House, was clover-shaped as well."

Saul grunted in surprise and everyone turned to stare at him.

"What?" Jade asked her voice still cold with anger at her assistant.

"Well," Saul said, hanging his head, "I guess now is as good a time as any to tell you. I figured out another of the clues."

"Which one? Where?" Jade asked.

"This icon here," Saul said, pointing to the image that reminded Maddock of the palace of an evil sorcerer. "It's Ship Rock. It's not shown from the angle that most people see in photographs, but it's definitely Ship Rock."

"Heck, I could have told you that," Bones said, rocking back in his chair and grinning. "It looks like Dracula's castle. It's wicked cool."

"Bones, I e-mailed you a picture of the breastplate several days ago," Maddock said. "Why didn't you say something?"

"I didn't know then!" he said, still smiling. "But I saw that thing in the distance as we were driving down here, and that's the first thing I thought of just now when Jade showed us the picture."

Jade buried her face in her hands. For the first time, Maddock noticed that her knuckles were scarred—probably from field work.

"We drove down that long stretch of highway with Ship Rock in our sights and never once did I even think about it. All I had my mind on was Yucca House and wondering where Saul had gone, and I didn't even notice it."

"It doesn't matter now," Maddock said. "What's important is we know where to find another piece of the puzzle."

"It's not that simple," Saul mumbled. "When I got caught trying to get onto Sleeping Ute Mountain they took me in for questioning, but let me go after I convinced them I was just a flaky New-Ager trying to have a spiritual moment. While I was there, a photograph on the wall caught my eye. It was Ship Rock from the perspective you see on the breastplate.

"I thought about trying to climb it, but then I considered the solstice connection. I remembered that white settlers used to call it "The Needle" and wondered where the shadow of the most prominent point would fall at the various solstices. I found a library with internet access and started poking around with satellite images until I found a promising location: a formation of three hills and a butte that made a clover shape. I didn't have any way to perform the calculations necessary to test my theory, so I figured I'd check it out."

Everyone was silent. Even Jade now listened attentively, her anger abated.

"When I got there, I found a kiva right smack in the center, hidden by scrub and yucca. The roof was gone, of course, but when I cleared away the rubble, I found that the sipapu, you know, the ceremonial hole in the center, had been sealed. Or rather, it once had been sealed. The seal with Fray Marcos's symbol was lying broken off to the side. Anyway, there was a box like the one Maddock found at Chaco. Empty." He shrugged as his tale came to an end. "Somebody else found it. Probably the same guys we saw before."

Jade swore and covered her face with her hands.

"Well, at least we have two of the pieces," Maddock said.

"May I see the ones you already have?" Amanda asked.

Jade brought Amanda the pieces, and Amanda laid them on the table, pushing them together to form a quarter of a sphere."

"You know what this looks like to me? One of those Egyptian beetles."

Maddock stared at the piece which now was looking oddly familiar to him, but he could not name the shape.

"A scarab," Jade breathed. "Most are ornate, but this one is plain. That's why it was not readily obvious to us what it was."

"I see it now," Maddock said, feeling both excited and confused. "The ridges around the bottom are the legs." He thought for a moment. "There are six symbols on the breastplate, which means that the scarab was cut into six pieces. When we find them all, we'll have the entire message. Or at least, we'll have five out of six pieces. If Jimmy translates it all, I'll bet we can still make something of it." He paused, mulling over this odd discovery. "But why would someone take a scarab—an Egyptian artifact, write some lines in Hebrew on it, cut it up, and hide it in America?"

"The legend does say that they hid treasures of religious significance," Jade said. "And there was frequent interaction between the Hebrew kingdom and that of the Egyptians. Perhaps this scarab was a part of that treasure."

"Weird," Bones said. "It's not how I imagined the cities of gold." His face tautened. "Wait a minute…"

"What?" Maddock asked.

"Dude, does this mean we're going after another Bible treasure?"

"Whatever it is," Jade interjected, "we need to keep up the search. We've already lost one of the clues. I don't want to slow down and risk missing any of the others."

"Do you have any ideas on the other locations?" Amanda asked, mulling over the icons.

"Nothing definitive," Jade said. "This one," she indicated a tower-shaped structure, "is not distinctive-looking, but it could be one of a number of structures at Mesa Verde."

Bones whistled. "Talk about a needle in a haystack. That place is huge. How many ruins are there?"

"Oh, about six-hundred cliff dwellings and four thousand or so archaeological sites," Jade replied. "But I've scoured the maps, and it's the only likely location. Plus, I've used the solstice connection to narrow the search, and I have a few ideas." She smiled. "Shall we pack?"

Chapter 15

"And you want me to climb down there?" Maddock gazed down into the sheer-sided canyon. Set beneath a deep overhang, Square Tower House looked remote and inaccessible. "Isn't there a service road? How do the rangers get down there?"

"I told you," Jade said, sighing. "There isn't one. They use ropes and ladders to get down there. Unless, of course, you want to try the Anasazi handholds."

Maddock shook his head. "That's something Bones would go for. I'll take the rope." He paused and looked her up and down, admiring the snug-fitting faux ranger uniform she had cobbled together. The boots, khaki shorts, NPS t-shirt, and Mesa Verde cap looked good on her. Of course, she made everything look good.

"You know that getup would be more believable if you had not shaved your legs," he kidded. "You know-- go natural like the ranger women."

"Shut up and get going," she said, giving him a shove toward the edge.

"You did put up the sign, didn't you?" Maddock asked, knotting a rope in a bowline around his waist.

"Of course," she said. "This Trail Closed For Maintenance. It should fool tourists, maybe even a really lazy ranger. Now hurry." She took hold of the safety rope he had secured around his waist, wrapped it once around the base of a nearby tree, and secured it to a larger one. She would play the line out as he descended. He probably wouldn't need it on the way down. He would be sliding down the other rope they had hooked to the same tree. Where Jade would really come in handy would be on the way back up, when her added strength would help him with his free climb up the rope. It was the most unsafe, ridiculous-looking rock climbing setup he'd seen since he was a stupid teenager, but they didn't have the time or equipment for real rappelling.

Donning his climbing gloves, he got a good grip on the rope, hooked it around his ankle, and slowly backed over the rock face. Jade kept tension on the rope as he worked his way down. He was an experienced climber, and the first several feet made for an easy descent. The rock soon curved back beneath the hill, forming the overhang. His boots began to slip, telling him it was time to change tactics. The drop was just over one hundred feet, but it looked farther from this vantage point. Much farther.

"Okay! I'm going down!" he called.

"Go for it!" Jade shouted back.

He kicked free of the wall and immediately the hands of gravity yanked him downward. The rope burned his thighs and palms through his clothing and gloves as he shot downward. He squeezed tighter and his descent slowed a little. He felt the jolt from the balls of his feet to the base of his skull when he hit the ground. His foot tangled in the rope and he sat down hard, rolling a little on his hip to minimize the impact.

"Some action movie star I'd make," he muttered, looking around for spectators he knew were not there. He untied the safety rope and hurried over to Square Tower House.

Overlooking the ancient Anasazi ruins, Square Tower House loomed four stories high, set against the back wall like a lone skyscraper. He navigated through the remains of foundations and walls, worn smooth by wind and time. He soon found himself at the base of the tower. His destination was the top room, where, according to Jade's research, was a window through which the sun struck a peculiar outcropping on the day of the summer solstice. It wasn't the most definitive clue, but it was worth checking out. He hoped the climb would not be for nothing.

He entered the ground floor room of the tower. It was less than five feet high and cramped. The walls were blackened with soot from ancient fires, but here and there he could make out traces of the stucco-like substance the Anasazi used to cover their walls. Where it had chipped away, he could still see evidence of the fine stonework. There was a small hole in the ceiling through which he could gain access to the upper levels. He wasn't tall, but his shoulders were broad, and they made for a tight squeeze. With difficulty, he worked his way up to the top level.

Reaching the fourth floor, he stood, forgetting the low ceiling and banging his head. How small had these people been? Of course, Bones claimed the Anasazi were actually aliens who built fancy cliff dwellings then flew away, inadvertently leaving their pet chupacabras behind. He was pretty sure his friend was joking but was not one-hundred percent certain.

Where to begin? He looked out the front window and got his bearings, and then scanned the small room. Square Tower House sat on a south-facing cliff. Sunken as it was in a valley, sunrise and sunset would not be visible to the structure. Most likely, the solstice marker would have been based on the mid-day sun, meaning the center of the far wall. He used his knife to scrape away the ancient plaster. Once again, he felt guilty at damaging an ancient structure, but hoped the end result would reveal a prize of such historical importance that it would atone for his acts of minor destruction.

The plaster came away in sheets, and soon he was looking at the bare, ancient stone. The building blocks were much larger than those of Chaco Canyon, but they were pieced together with the same precision. For a brief moment, he wondered if Bones was right about aliens building this place. It was almost unthinkable that primitive people could create such an architectural marvel. He ran his fingers across the surface, feeling the joints where the stones fit together so neatly. He could find no indication of a compartment that would hide the next piece of the puzzle. Scratch this site off the list. No point in making the climb without giving it a good effort, though. He moved closer and scraped away at the stone. Something caught his eye.

In one spot, the consistency of the stone was somehow different. It dipped in ever so slightly and the stone felt grittier. His fingers traced the indentation like a blind man reading Braille, and they looped around in an oval pattern. He scraped away at the stone with greater intensity and soon uncovered a clover-shaped engraving that had filled with the ancient plaster, thus making him miss it at first glance. Given that Mesa Verde was abandoned a good three-hundred years before Fray Marcos and Estevanico made their journeys, whoever had secreted something here must have plastered over the stone himself. He obviously didn't want the clues lost forever, but neither did he want to make it too easy. But to what were these clues leading?

He worked the stone loose and was rewarded with a box exactly like the others they had found. He slipped it into a drawstring backpack and replaced the masonry as best he could. Peering out the window, he scanned the buildings and ledge for signs of rangers, but he could see no one. He felt a momentary pang of regret that he could not stay and admire the spectacular scenery for a while longer, but time was of the essence.

Climbing down was much easier than climbing up, though squeezing through the small holes was just as uncomfortable. He made his way quickly back to the ropes which still hung where he had left them. He gave the climbing rope two tugs-- his signal to Jade that he was ready to make his way back up-- but there was no answering tug. He tried again, but still no answer. She might have walked away, or encountered some tourists and had to perform her improv ranger act. He didn't want to entertain the possibility of anything more serious. He let two minutes tick away on his watch and tried again. Still nothing. He checked his cell phone though he knew he would have no reception at this remote location. Sure enough, there were no bars showing. He tried the call anyway-- a remnant of his upbringing by a father who believed in leaving no stone unturned and no detail unattended. No, dice. He debated calling her name, but a gnawing feeling of unease had crept up his spine, and he now felt that something was wrong. If so, circumstances might dictate that announcing his presence would be a bad idea.

Dreading the climb he was about to make, he took both ropes and scrambled up onto a nearby boulder. He pulled the safety rope taut and cinched it around his waist. Without Jade to take the slack out, it wouldn't keep him from falling should he lose hold of his climbing rope, but by starting higher than ground level, it would break his fall before he hit the ground. Of course, it could break his spine as well, but he was confident that if he lost one rope, he could grab the other before he went tumbling. With no more preparations to make, he donned his gloves, grabbed the climbing rope, and swung out.

He had scarcely begun his climb before something went wrong. A vibration like the plunking of a guitar string ran down the climbing rope and he dropped about a half-inch. He knew what that meant.

"Oh no!" He hastily grabbed the safety rope in his left hand, transferring as much weight as he could. The climbing rope shuddered again and he grabbed onto the safety rope with his other hand. He hung there catching his breath. Something had caused the climbing rope to fray. A few more seconds and it would have snapped completely. It was a brand new 11mm rope and should not have frayed under any natural conditions. That left the possibility that someone had tampered with it. And if they had tampered with the climbing rope...

The realization struck him just as the safety rope to which he now clung gave an inch. Cursing roundly he slid quickly down the rope. He reached the limit, forgetting he had shorted it to keep from falling, and found himself spinning like a wind vane ten feet above the rocky ledge. He had only a moment to consider the absurdity of the situation when the rope parted, dropping him like a sack of potatoes onto the ground. His breath left him in a sudden rush. He rolled over onto his back, his mind ticking off the curses his body lacked the breath to articulate.

His mind raced with possibilities as he recovered his breath. The likelihood that even one of the ropes would have broken was remote. But for both of them to not only break but to just happen to break at the same time? Not a chance. Which meant foul play and that something likely had happened to Jade. He scanned the rocky face above, seeing nothing amiss. Self-preservation dictated that he either find a place to hide until he felt certain that whoever did this was gone or that he climb all the way down into the canyon and search for a new way out. Neither one would work, though, because of Jade. He had to find out if she was all right.

It would take an experienced climber to make his way back up to the top. They wouldn't expect him to climb out on his own, but he was a skilled climber. He didn't relish the idea of a free climb, but he had no other acceptable choice. Then he remembered what Jade had said earlier. The Anasazi always carved hand and footholds in the cliffs in order to access their homes. All he had to do was find them.

His search seemed to take forever, scanning the weathered cliffs, inspecting each crack and shadow, but when he finally found the first shadowy concave space in the rock, his watch showed that only six minutes had passed. Perhaps he'd be doubly lucky and his hidden enemy had given him up for dead. Without further consideration, he set to climbing.

The ancient holds were eroded in places, some of them no more than shallow pits. He moved as quickly as he could, taking more time where the holds were almost gone. He did not look down, but instead kept his eyes on the top of the cliff. What would he do if someone appeared above him? Hope it was someone on his side, he supposed.

He made steady progress until he was about halfway up when the next handhold simply wasn't there. He paused, squinting against the sun's intense glare, and searched for it. His hands burned from scrabbling up the rock, and his muscles were knotted from the awkward contortions the climb had forced upon him. Where was the next hold? It was not long before a memory crashed down on him. The Anasazi coded their hand-holds. If you didn't start with the correct hand and foot, you could get just far enough along to get…stuck.

Keeping his body pressed as close to the rock as possible, he turned and looked back, seeking a way down. He could see the way he had come, but his feet and hands were all wrong and the intervening space too broad to permit him to move backward. He was in trouble. He certainly hoped Bones was faring better.

Chapter 16

Bones scanned the ruins of Sun Temple. Even now, centuries after the site had been abandoned, it remained an impressive sight. The remains of two towers, its stones fitted precisely together, stood within a D-shaped double wall. A few tourists milled about, snapping pictures.

"It doesn't look like a clover to me," Saul said, his constant scowl fully in evidence.

"No, but we need to check it out anyway," Bones said, wondering how he had gotten stuck with Saul as a partner. "The marker is supposed to be at the southwest corner." He indicated the direction they should go and led the way.

The walls were short and thick, the craftsmanship amazing. Sun Temple had never been completed, so Bones was skeptical about what they might find, but Jade had insisted they leave no stone unturned, so to speak.

Arriving at the southwest corner, they found a heavily eroded stone with three circles carved against a blurry-edged, diamond-shaped background. Bones knelt and ran his fingers across the surface of the marker up to the point where it curved into the wall. He didn't see anything here that would indicate Fray Marcos had chosen it as one if his hiding places.

"This is it, huh?" Saul said, putting his hands on his knees and leaning forward to gaze intently at the stone. "It looks a little bit like two planets crashing into a sun."

"It does a just a bit, doesn't it?" Bones looked all around the stone to see if he was missing anything. He didn't see anything that indicated a hidden compartment or Marcos' symbol. "I don't suppose the three circles could be the leaves of a clover?" he asked, somehow knowing it was not so.

"Doesn't look like what we've found so far," Saul replied, doubt clear in his voice.

A movement caught Bones' eye. Someone was moving beyond the farthest tower. That in itself was not strange, but it was the way they were moving—as if they were trying not to be noticed.

"Keep looking down at the rock like you're interested," he whispered to Saul. "Don't do anything else unless I tell you,"

"I hear you," Saul said. He didn't offer any argument or ask questions. Maybe the guy wasn't as stupid as Bones had believed.

He kept an eye on the far tower. There were two men moving slowly around the back of the chest-high structure. They were facing the back of the tower as if admiring the architecture, but it was obvious to Bones that they were watching him just as much as he was watching them. Their appearance was wrong as well. They wore casual clothes like any tourist would wear, but they were neatly pressed and their shirts were tucked in. Their haircuts were perfect. Everything about the way they looked made it seem they had checked in at the office before dropping by the ruins. Their bearing was not that of civilians. Their backs were too straight and they moved with too much purpose to be sightseeing.

Bones turned the lay of the land over in his mind. The men stood between them and the parking lot. The surrounding area offered little cover.

"Are you packing?" he asked Saul.

"Am I what?"

"Carrying a gun."

"Oh, no," Saul replied. "Why?"

Just then, the two men rounded the tower and moved toward Bones and Saul at a fast walk. They separated, each drawing a weapon and ducking low as they approached.

"Because I think we're going to need a little firepower."

Fatigue gave way to a bout of dizziness as Maddock baked in the sun on the face of the cliff above Square Tower House. Sweat ran into his eyes, but he scarcely noticed. He had considered and dismissed a dozen or more ideas, each more reckless than the next. He had just about settled on trying to slide down the cliff and hoped he survived the fall, when he began to hallucinate. At least that's what he thought was happening when a rope suddenly appeared six inches from his nose.

He blinked twice but could not dispel the image. He thought of thirsty men in the desert seeing mirages, their minds willing them to believe that which they most desperately sought was before their eyes. But he wasn't that far gone. Tired, aching, and frustrated to be certain, but not on the verge of death.

"Maddock, are you going to grab on to the stupid rope or not?" Jade's voice sounded tired and a bit hoarse, but it was her. Looking up, he could see the outline of her form against the bright, blue sky. Hoping this really wasn't a hallucination, and that he was about to grab a handful of empty air, he reached out and grasped the rope.

"It's the rest of what wasn't cut," she said. "I've got it secured to the base of a tree, but I think I'm strong enough to help you up. But you've got to hurry."

Shaking off thoughts of ache and fatigue, Maddock transferred his weight to the rope and started working his way up. Up above, Jade hauled on the rope. At first she seemed just to be dragging him across the rocky face, adding to his cuts and bruises, but then he saw a handhold. She had pulled him back over to the ancient egress. Keeping the rope twisted around his arm for safety, he scrambled up the ancient notches and quickly found himself face-to-face with Jade. What he saw made him grind his teeth in anger.

Her face was bruised, her lower lip split, and her clothing was ripped and dirty. She looked away as if ashamed to meet his eye.

"I don't know who they were," she said before he could ask. "They know we're after an artifact, but they didn't seem to know what it is. I didn't tell them." She kept her back to him, hastily gathering the rope and looping it around her hand and elbow.

"Why didn't they come down after me? Or wait 'til I got to the top and take it from me?" Maddock asked. "If they wanted the artifact, cutting my ropes wouldn't help them."

"I convinced them you had just called up to me to tell me that it wasn't there and that you'd be coming back after you put things right. They slapped me around a bit to make sure I was telling the truth. They finally knocked me unconscious. I assume they cut your rope to slow you down and then took off for Sun Temple."

"You sent them after Bones?" he said, unable to believe what he was hearing. "How could you..."

"No! They asked me about Sun Temple. I didn't say anything, but they seemed to already know about it, and that Bones would be there." She looped the last of the rope around her arm and finally turned to face him. The sight of her injured face brought a surge of guilt.

"I'm sorry," he said, taking her by the hand and heading off at a trot down the path. "I'm worried about both of you. Now, let's go find somebody for me to take out my anger on."

"You really think this is going to work?" Saul whispered. They had dived into a nearby kiva and were now squirming their way through the passage that connected it to another kiva on the far side of the ruin-- closer to their car, and hopefully behind the guys with guns, whoever they were.

"It might if you'll shut up," Bones muttered. It galled him to possibly be leaving the artifact behind, but he felt that he had little choice. He might have done something bolder had Maddock been with him, but all he had was Saul, and the research assistant didn't seem like someone to be counted on in a throw-down. Besides, this was the second narrow tunnel he'd had to squeeze himself through in the past week, and it was getting on his nerves.

His shoulders pressed against the edges. Bones was much too big for Anasazi architecture. Saul was a good-sized fellow in his own right though his bulk was spread around a little more evenly.

"Maybe they're more concerned about the artifact and won't notice us leave," Saul whispered.

"Maybe. Maybe not," Bones whispered though he doubted the men would give up so easily. "Either way, I told you to shut up."

Saul lapsed into sullen silence, broken only by the occasional grunt as he squeezed through a particularly narrow section of tunnel. They finally reached the end of the tunnel. Bones hoped Saul had enough sense to remain quiet while he checked things out. He peered out into the kiva, and along the rim as far as he could see. No one was there. He closed his eyes and let his ears take precedence as his grandfather had taught him when he was a boy. He heard a whisper of dry wind through stunted trees, but nothing else. This sparse southwestern wilderness was so different from the forests of North Carolina where he was raised. He heard no birds singing, no scrabbling of squirrels in the trees. No gentle rustle of a nearby stream. But most important, no voices or footfalls. Of course, they could be waiting out of sight for him to appear. He drew his Glock and sighed. He would have to take his chances.

"I hate these roads," Maddock muttered as he whipped around another tight curve. There was no direct path to anywhere in Mesa Verde. All the roads twisted, turned, rose, and fell along with the land. And there were just enough tourists to make things maddeningly slow. He whipped around an RV and stepped on it, barely making it around before a mini-van, horn blaring, appeared from around the curve ahead of them.

"Maddock," Jade groaned. "If you're going to drive like this, I probably should have just let those guys kill me. Traffic accidents are so... messy."

"Tell me about it once Bones is okay," he said. He fished into his pocket and pulled out his cell phone. He flipped it open and glanced to see if he had a signal. He did!

"Maddock!" Jade shouted and grabbed at the wheel. "Keep your eyes on the road!" He had let the car veer precariously close to the edge of a steep-walled canyon.

"Sorry," he said, this time keeping his vision focused in front of him as he punched up Bones' number on speed dial.

Bones peered over the edge of the kiva. As he had hoped, the two men had made their way to the far side of the ruin, and now seemed more interested in the sun marker than they were in finding Bones and Saul. The gray-haired man knelt in front of the stone, while the redhead stood with his back to them, looking out across the canyon as if he believed his quarry had gone over the edge.

Bones leaned close to Saul, who had exited the tunnel and was hunched down beside him.

"They're not looking," Bones whispered. "We'll crawl over to the other side of the kiva, and I'll check again. If they still aren't looking, we'll slip over the wall and back to the cars as quickly as we can without making any sound. Got it?

Saul nodded, and together they crawled across the floor of the ancient kiva. When they reached the other side, Bones dared another look and was relieved to see that neither of the men was looking their way. He nodded to Saul, who quietly climbed out of the kiva and began crawling toward their car. Breathing a sigh of relief, Bones hoisted himself up and over the ledge.

Just as his cell phone rang.

He cursed under his breath and took off, bending at the waist to present a smaller target. Saul followed behind, moving faster than Bones would have believed him able.

Something buzzed past his cheek and smacked into a nearby stone, spraying his leg with shards of rock as the sound of a gunshot reached him. He zigzagged, then hurtled the wall that surrounded the site. Bullets continued to fly as they dashed through the stand of trees and burst into the small parking lot. Saul rushed up to their rented Aztek, but he had not seen what Bones had seen.

"Keep going! They've flattened our tires!" He drew his Glock and fired off two rounds in the general direction of their pursuers.

Rather than following the road, where their pursuers could easily overtake them in their own car, Bones cut through the forested area of pine and blue spruce that separated the circular parking area of Sun Temple from the Mesa Top Loop Road.

There was no way that on foot they could beat these guys to Square Tower House and meet up with Maddock and Jade, but maybe he could raise them on the phone and meet them halfway, or at least get some much needed backup. His phone rang again, and he saw that it was Maddock on the other line.

"Maddock! Where are you?"

"Headed up the drive to Sun Temple. Are you all right? I tried to call you just a minute ago…"

"Yeah, and you almost got me killed. Thanks for that!" Maddock started to reply, but Bones cut him off. "Listen to me. The bad guys are at the Sun Temple. They're either in their car coming your way or they'll be chasing us through the woods on your right as you come to the loop." A bullet trimmed a branch from a nearby tree. "Okay. That would be the latter."

"Can you outrun these guys for a little longer? I'll turn around and meet you on the loop road."

"Can do," Bones huffed. "I don't know if Saul is going to make it, though. Gotta' do what we gotta' do. See you there. And don't call me back." He snapped the phone closed, pocketed it, and grabbed Saul by the arm to hurry him along. "Saul, I need you to keep running pretty much straight ahead as fast as you can. Can you do that?" He kept talking as Saul nodded. "Weave around trees when you can, but don't deviate too far from the direction we're going. Maddock and Jade are going to meet us. I'll catch up with you."

The news that help was on the way seemed to give Saul renewed energy. He took off at a faster clip. Bones ducked behind the first thick tree he could find, dropped to the ground, and waited.

The guys were making no effort to be quiet. Their footfalls pounded on the hard, dry earth, and soon they came into sight. He waited for them to sprint past before coming out from behind the tree. Two of them, one of me. Gotta' make it count.

He took careful aim and fired.

The redhead went down, clutching at his hip. He wasn't nearly dead, but he was out of the running, as it were. Bones immediately snapped off two more shots at the second guy, but the fellow was quick. At the sound of the first shot, he had veered to the left and dove behind a tree. Bones quickly ducked out of sight before the man could return fire.

Bullets struck the ground where Bones had just been standing. He fired a few rounds at the tree where the guy had ducked, and caught a glimpse of him scrambling away. He fired another shot and the man took off running in the opposite direction. Mission accomplished. Now for the next part of the plan.

Maddock whipped the car around the curve, keeping his eyes open for Bones and Saul. He caught a glimpse of something moving in the woods to his left, and then Saul staggered out onto the road. Maddock hit the brakes, the screech of rubber on pavement filling the air. He opened the door out, jumped out, and ran to help Saul, who leaned heavily on his shoulder as they headed back to the car.

"Where's Bones?"

"Don't…. know," Saul gasped, opening the back door and half-falling inside. "Sent me ahead… Heard shots and somebody yell."

"I've got to go back after him!" Maddock yelled, drawing his gun. "Jade, take the wheel and get out of here if anyone shows up."

"Maddock, you can't…"

Just then, a figure appeared at the edge of the woods. His casual clothes did not look nearly as sinister as the Taurus semi-automatic in his hand. He caught sight of Maddock and hesitated for a moment before raising his weapon. The brief pause gave Maddock the time he needed. He brought his Walther P-99 to bear and squeezed off two quick shots. The man reeled backward, firing blindly as he stumbled into the safety of the woods. Maddock dropped to a knee and kept his pistol trained on the spot where the man had vanished, but he did not reappear. He was debating whether or not to pursue him into the woods when the screech of tires caught his attention.

A black Pathfinder skidded to a halt next to their car, and a familiar face appeared in the window.

"Need a ride, pardner?" Bones shouted over the cacophony of heavy metal music he was cranking.

"Bones, what did you do?"

"Stole their car. Crazy Charlie taught me how to hot-wire a car when I was in seventh grade. Sweet ride, huh?"

Maddock couldn't keep himself from laughing at his friend's shenanigans. "Let's just get out of here."

Chapter 17

Amanda closed her laptop and took a deep, calming breath. She definitely had something here. She could feel it. The next step was to convince the others that she wasn't crazy. She fished her cell phone from her purse and punched up Bones' number.

"Yo, ho! What up?"

"That is, without a doubt, the rudest greeting I have ever received," she said, her voice not matching the smile on her face. "Try again."

"Sorry, let me try again. You have reached the voice mail of Uriah Bonebrake. I'm sorry I cannot..."

"I forgot your real name is Uriah!" she said with a laugh.

"What? You think my mom named me Bones? Ah, forget it. What's up?"

"I think I've come up with some promising leads," she said. "Where are you guys?"

"We just ditched a car I stole," he said. She couldn't believe the calm in his voice. "Now we're cruising out of the park and headed to Durango to meet up with you."

"Great! Meet me outside the library. And try not to steal any more cars while you're at it."

"It really wasn't my fault. They shot at me."

"Sure," she said. "What happened to your rental car, anyway?"

"That's another reason I had to steal their car. They were bad guys. You wouldn't have liked them."

"I don't know," she teased. "Were any of them cute? I might want an introduction."

"I wasn't attracted to them," he said. "I shot one in the butt. He probably won't be able to keep up with you for a while."

"I guess I could nurse him back to health." She couldn't believe she was engaged in such banter with a man who had just casually admitted to shooting someone and stealing his car. Of course, after what she'd experienced in the short time she'd known Bones, the extraordinary was becoming ordinary. "Then again, that's too much trouble. I guess I'll hang on to you as long as your butt is intact."

"More or less," he said. "Mine's always been a little flat. Maddock's the one with the booty."

She heard a raised voice and laughter in the background.

"I don't think he liked that," she said. "Forget the anatomy. Did you find it?"

"Maddock and Jade did. It was in Square Tower House. They had a bit of trouble themselves, but we came out of it all right. You said you've come up with some leads. Entertain me."

"Some of it I can't really explain until you've seen what I found. I can tell you that I'm almost certain one of the next places we need to go is called Hovenweep."

"Hovenweep? Never heard of it."

"It's actually pretty close to Mesa Verde. It's not very well known, but it's one of the finest known examples of Anasazi architecture."

"Keep titillating me with examples of Anasazi architecture, you naughty girl. So you were able to match it up to that little image on the breastplate? The image was kind of generic, wasn't it?"

"I matched the image to ruin at Hovenweep, yes. But I have another reason for believing I'm on the right track. That's the part I'll have to show you."

"Sounds good. We'll meet you at the library as soon as we can get there." He paused. "Amanda?"

"Yes?"

"Be careful."

The Elder reached for the phone on the first ring, then froze. It would not do to appear too eager… or apprehensive. He gave it two more rings before casually picking up the receiver.

"Yes?" he said, feigning disinterest.

"There is a Mister Jarren on the line for you," Margaret said, her nasal voice made even more annoying by the note of suspicion that rang clear. *"He declined to give his last name."*

"I'll take the call," he said, adding a sigh as if not interested in speaking to this semi-anonymous caller. The truth was, this was the call he'd been waiting for. *"What do you have to report?"* The Elder found his anticipation cooling as he listened until it finally froze in an icy block of frustration. "You are telling me that not only did you fail to retrieve the artifact, but Mikkel was shot and your car was stolen?"

"That is correct. The Indian used a secret passage. They got out of the ruin before we could get to them. We chased them into the woods and he somehow got behind us. That's when he shot Mikkel. As for the artifact, it did not seem to be at the site. That woman Jade must have lied to us."

"If they have it, we will find out soon enough," the Elder said.

"Can you get us out of here? The park rangers were easy enough to evade, even with Mikkel's injury, but he can't go much farther."

"It would be easier to deal with were you still in Utah. I can send the helicopter to follow your GPS signal." Another failure. Another headache.

"Perhaps I made a mistake coming after them," Jarren said. *"I could go back to letting them do our work for us. It has worked well for us so far."*

"Maddock has been useful," the Elder replied with restrained patience. "He is clever and resourceful, and would also be the one to go to jail if he were caught. But we are getting close to solving the puzzle, and with this friend of his involved now… well, I don't need to tell you what might happen. Maddock needs to be eliminated before the final clues fall into place, and his friend might as well be dealt with while we are at it."

"Could we not simply let him find it, and then take it away from him?"

The Elder had to tread carefully here. Only he and a very few others knew what they were truly searching for, and if Maddock found it first… well, he simply could not think about that possibility.

"Maddock has become a threat. What were the odds that he and this Bonebrake would turn out to know one another and, in fact, join forces? If they manage to put their knowledge together…" He shook his head. "We must take great care in eliminating both of them. And then we will complete the search on our own." It was important to avoid drawing attention just yet, but once they had it in their hands, no one would be able to stop them.

"I understand," Jarren said. *"I will, of course, make it look like an accident."* He paused. *"Elder, with all due respect, do you still believe our source is reliable?"*

The Elder's cell phone vibrated and he glanced down to see that he had received a text message. What he read made his frustration melt away. "Yes," he said. "In fact, I have just received further proof of the reliability of our source."

"How so?" Jarren asked, his increased interest clearly evident the tone of his voice.

"When you and Mikkel are picked up, I am going to have them take you directly to a place called Hovenweep."

Chapter 18

Their surroundings grew more and more barren the closer they came to Hovenweep. The land was beautiful in its own way, with occasional sprinklings of rich greenery or bright desert flowers, but it was a parched, unforgiving landscape with little in the way of trees and even less water.

"Man!" Bones said from the front passenger seat. "I thought Kansas was empty, but this… Hey! Check it out!" He held the travel brochure up in front of his face and scrutinized it with an intensity and seriousness that said to Maddock that his friend was being anything but genuine. "It says here that the devil's outhouse is just a mile or two away. We should check it out."

"What's the Devil's Outhouse?" Saul asked. "Some sort of rock formation?"

"No, dude. I mean this hot, dry, empty bunch of nothing must be where the devil comes to take a dump. We might even bump into him if we're lucky. I wonder how regular he is…"

Everyone chuckled but Saul, who pursed his lips and folded his arms across his chest. His severe, dour expression now filled Maddock's rear-view mirror in a most unpleasant way.

"I kind of like it out here," Maddock said. "The sea is pretty desolate sometimes, and there's a heck of a lot more sameness on the water."

"Not at spring break," Bones said, still reading the brochure.

A sign directed them to Hovenweep National Monument. The small visitor's center was visible from far across the desert terrain. Several police cars, lights flashing, took up a large portion of the parking lot.

"I wonder what's up," Amanda said, leaning forward to peek between Maddock and Bones. "Whatever it is must have just happened."

"Maybe it'll be newsworthy," Bones said. "Give your editor a scoop?"

"I can't imagine something down here would newsworthy at home, but you never know," she said. She had told her editor just enough about what Bones had found at Orley's ranch, plus a few hints about the Dominion, to convince him to let her accompany Bones to follow up on the mystery.

"I guess we'll find out," Maddock said, pulling into an empty space and shutting off the engine.

The heat blasted him like a furnace as soon as he stepped out of the vehicle. It was even hotter than Chaco Canyon had been, and not a breeze stirred the air. "Now I know how pottery feels," he said.

"You get used to it," Jade replied. "It's humidity that I hate. Makes you feel like you're drowning in the air. Around here it's the proverbial 'dry heat'."

No one was on duty in the visitor's center. They looked around for a while before finally concluding that everyone must be at the scene of whatever incident had brought out the police. Maddock left a twenty under a paperweight on the counter and they made their way into the park.

The brick path gave way to a primitive trail that wound down into a narrow, twisting canyon, thick with sun-baked rock and desert flora. Amanda clambered up onto a nearby boulder and scanned the canyon.

"Where to, hot chick?" Bones asked.

"I'm not seeing…" Amanda's voice trailed off as she spoke.

"I thought you said you knew this was the place," Jade snapped. "You said you were certain of it. But you won't show us whatever 'proof' you claim to have." The two had argued in the car on the way to Hovenweep. Jade had already researched and subsequently eliminated this site from consideration, the architecture of the ruin with the only known solstice room in the park did not match any of the images on the breastplate.

Amanda slowly turned and stared down at Jade, waiting for a moment to make sure the other woman had finished. "It is very rude to interrupt people, Jade. Didn't your mother teach you that?"

A slender young woman in an NPS uniform appeared on the trail behind them, cutting off Jade's retort.

"May I help you?" she asked, shading her eyes against the sun as she looked up at Amanda, who remained atop the boulder, hands folded across her chest. "Are you looking for a specific ruin?"

"Yes, actually," Amanda said, hopping down. "I'm Amanda Shores from the Deseret Bugle. I'm sort of combining business with pleasure on our trip. The article I'm writing is on Anasazi solstice markers. Do you have any structures in the park of that sort?"

"Well," the woman said, taking off her brown, mesh ball cap and running her fingers through her coppery hair which she wore in a loose ponytail. "Tracking the solstice and equinox was fairly common among the Anasazi. A room would often have a small window, and the family would follow the course of the sun by marking where it struck the wall on the opposite side. Some buildings were constructed in such a way that the sun would strike a specific place on the solstice, like a corner.

"In this park, Hovenweep Castle is about the only one that fits the bill. But you can't go there." The woman's hazel eyes flitted from person-to-person in Maddock's party. Her mouth was drawn in a tight, nervous frown.

"I didn't realize it was closed to the public," Amanda said.

"It isn't. I mean… it is today. I…" The woman closed her eyes and shook her head. "I apologize. I'm a little out of sorts." She took a deep breath, looked up at them and started again. "Someone vandalized it just a short while ago. In fact, they broke open the wall in what is called the Sun Room. It's where the solstice is marked. I guess your question just threw me off."

Bones muttered something inaudible and Jade made a sound that could have been sympathy but sounded more like annoyance. Maddock took a deep breath and released it slowly, taking control of his rising anger. Had there been any doubt before, it was now certain that someone else was on the same trail. And whoever they were, they had somehow gotten here first.

"Did they take anything?" Saul asked.

"There isn't really anything to take," the ranger replied, frowning. "The ruins have been empty for a long time. Strange, though. They booby-trapped it." She didn't wait for them to ask what she meant. Their quizzical expressions must have been enough. "Whoever it was placed some very large rocks above the doorway, held up with some posts, then tied a trip wire between the posts. The ranger who first investigated the damage didn't see the trip wire in the dim light."

"Is he all right?" Amanda asked.

"We think so. He'll need a few stitches in the back of his head, and he might have a concussion. Anyway, back to your question. You might be interested in the solstice marker at what we call the Holly Group. There is a sandstone wall with a number of carvings: a snake figure, two spiral circles, and some others. Nearby rock formations cause daggers of light to appear on the wall. It actually marks the summer solstice and the spring and fall equinoxes."

"Are you familiar with a ruin that looks like either of these" Amanda showed the woman a paper with the remaining undiscovered symbols from the breastplate.

The ranger scrutinized the paper, holding it close and staring intently. She broke into a sudden smile and tapped a picture of what looked like a cylinder floating on a rough sea.

"Yes! This ruin is in the Cajon group. It's a fascinating example of Anasazi architecture. They constructed a circular tower atop three very uneven boulders, yet the masonry is perfect. It's a very impressive structure, but the Cajon Group is more than eight miles from here, and not readily accessible, so it doesn't receive nearly the attention it deserves."

"Does it have a solstice room?" Maddock asked, suddenly excited.

"Not a solstice room," she said, "but there is a solstice connection. There is a set of three buildings. On every solstice and equinox, the shadows of two of the buildings meet at the corner of the third building as if the shadows are pointing to something. Few people know about it because it isn't a true solstice marker or sun room. It might be something interesting for you to write about." She turned a hopeful smile to Amanda.

"Thank you so much," Amanda said. "I think it will be perfect."

The road leading to the Cajon group took them along a winding, heavily rutted dirt road. It seemed much farther than the eight miles the ranger had told them it would be. They traveled in silence, knowing that whoever was after Fray Marcos' secret had somehow gotten ahead of them and might even be waiting for them at their destination.

Maddock wondered if they were even on the right track. He hoped so. It felt right, but this whole thing had been nuts. One close shave after another. How long could their luck hold?

They came upon a simple wooden sign that read, Cajon Group. Please do not leave the trail or climb on the ruins. He chuckled. Fat chance they'd be following those guidelines. He scanned the ruins for signs of their adversaries and found them blessedly empty.

It was a small settlement. The remains of a few lodges ringed a small reservoir. While the ruins might not have been as impressive to a tourist as, say, Mesa Verde, Maddock found them appealing because they had not been reconstructed by modern archaeologists, like Cliff Palace at Mesa Verde had been. What remained was in its original state, and clearly illustrated the fine craftsmanship that had been involved in its construction.

"I see the tower," Jade called, pointing across the ruin. "I'm going to go ahead and check it out." Without waiting for a reply, she strode away at a fast walk. Saul hurried after her.

Maddock started to follow, but Bones touched him on the shoulder.

"Let's talk for a minute while we walk," he said in an uncharacteristically soft voice. "Try to act nonchalant, though." He nodded toward Jade and Saul as they picked their way across the rocks toward the tower.

Maddock slowed his pace and fell in beside Bones and Amanda, but kept his gaze ahead of him. "What's up?" he asked.

"I'll make it quick," Bones said. "It's too big a coincidence that these people found out about Hovenweep at the same time we did, and actually managed to get here before us."

"What are you saying?" Maddock asked.

"If I have the story correct," Amanda joined in, "they were at Chaco Canyon, Mesa Verde, and Hovenweep. But they weren't at Yucca House."

"True," Maddock said, knowing where she was going with this and wishing he could disagree.

"And Yucca House was the only place Saul didn't know about because you figured it out while he wasn't there," Bones said.

"So you think Saul is a mole," Maddock said. "I hear what you're saying, but Jade trusts him. Doesn't like him all that much, but trusts him."

"You've got to admit it makes sense," Bones said. "It would explain how they know where we're going. What I don't get, though, is what these guys need with us if they have all these resources at their disposal?"

"They need Jade," Maddock said. "She's spent years researching the history and legends surrounding Cibola, and she's gotten farther than anyone before toward solving the mystery. She found the breastplate, which is more than anyone else can claim. Saul is a necessary evil- he comes with the financing."

Amanda made a "huh" sound that said she considered this merely to be further confirmation of what she already believed.

"I'm not completely sure why she needs me," Maddock said. "I guess I was in the right place at the right time. I know why she wanted me to help with the well. It was a dangerous dive."

"Maybe she thinks you're a stud," Bones jibed. "My sister always said you were a cutie, Maddock."

"Your sister scares me," Maddock said. Though undeniably beautiful, Angelica

"Angel" Bonebrake was nothing like her name. Hot-tempered, she'd been in more barroom brawls than Maddock and Bones combined. She was now fighting in a mixed martial arts organization under the name "Demonica" Bonebrake.

"I'd have to say that you've probably been very helpful to her," Amanda said. "You have some background in treasure hunting, and you helped her in Argentina. Why wouldn't she want you around?"

"I suppose," Maddock said. He sort of hoped Jade wanted him around for more reasons than that, but he felt like a high school kid even thinking that. "So what do you want to do about it?"

"Don't tell them where the next site is until we get there," Bones said.

"That's not going to be easy," Maddock said. "I don't care what we tell Saul, but Jade is technically in charge of the search. She's not going to like it."

"If Amanda is correct, we're going to need some special gear for this next leg. We'll just play it all mysterious and maybe we'll think of something better while we're on our way to pick up what we need. Worst case scenario, we just out-and-out lie to both of them."

A triumphant cry interrupted their conversation. Maddock turned to see Jade emerge from one of the ruins, a box tucked under her arm. When their eyes met, she smiled and raised the box above her head. "Got it!" she called.

Maddock gave her the thumbs-up. He couldn't help but notice that Saul wore an expression that was anything but joyful. He glanced at Bones and Amanda, who, by their expressions, had obviously noticed the same thing.

"Looks like he couldn't get his cronies here in time," Bones muttered. "Of course, I've been keeping an eye on him ever since we found out someone had gotten here before us."

"You missed all the fun!" Jade said as she and Saul joined them.

"Well, you know," Maddock said, "I've gotten two of them already to your one. I figured it was your turn."

"Thanks. You are such a gentleman," she said with a sly grin.

"What can I say?" Maddock grinned, his eyes locking with hers for a split-second.

"I don't know about you," Bones interrupted, "but I say we bolt before the bad guys stumble upon us again." He turned and headed away without explanation.

Maddock looked from Jade to Saul and back to Jade again, shrugged, and followed his friend.

Back in the car, the focus was on the newly-discovered clue. Jade opened the box with great care to reveal another part of what they were now certain was a scarab.

"I can't wait until we've pieced this puzzle together," she whispered, more to herself than the others in the car. "I want to know. I have to know."

Maddock expected Saul to ask about the next site, but he was strangely subdued. He gazed thoughtfully at the piece in Jade's hands, saying nothing.

Maddock looked toward the front of the vehicle. His eyes met Bones' in the rear-view mirror, and they both shrugged. It felt so strange, acting as if things were fine, all the while waiting for Saul to betray them. They settled into an odd silence as the barren land flew by.

Chapter 19

The silence did not last. As soon as they stopped for the equipment they would need for their next excursion, Jade and Saul had both raised questions, particularly when they saw what Maddock and Bones were renting.

"All right," Jade said. "You've kept us in suspense long enough. Where are you going and why do you need diving gear?"

Amanda glanced at Bones, then to Maddock. Seeing him nod, she began her explanation.

"I know that at one time you considered the possibility of the shape on the breastplate being more than just a symbol—that it could be overlaid on a map and give you the locations you sought."

"We tried that," Jade protested. "It didn't work. Some places were nowhere near any ruins."

"I know," Amanda said, her voice calm and patient. There was no sign of her usual annoyance at Jade's interruption. In fact, the longer the conversation stretched out, the longer it would be until she was forced to reveal their next destination. "When you lay it out over a modern map, it doesn't work. But…"

"But Fray Marcos didn't have a modern, scale map." Jade's voice was little more than a whisper, and her eyes faded into a distant gaze as she sunk into thought. "So if it were an overlay, it would be for a map from his day. What an idiot I am!" She snapped out of her reverie as quickly as she had faded into it. "You found a map from Fray Marcos's time?"

"A reproduction," Amanda said. "I wasn't even looking for one. I spent the morning in the library searching for hints of old legends that might give us a clue, but no luck. I gave up and was on my way out the door when I looked up, and hanging right there on the wall was a reprint of a very old Spanish map of the region. There was a brass plate on the frame indicating it was a reproduction of a map that had been drawn by… wait for it… Fray Marcos de Niza. Best of all, there were symbols sketched all over it, including those from the breastplate."

"And they let you examine it?" Saul asked. From the tone of his voice, he seemed genuinely interested, and not the least bit annoyed that he had neither made the discovery himself nor been let in on it earlier.

"Yep," Amanda said. "I showed the librarian my press credential and a few bits and pieces of the research I had with me. I told him I was looking into Spanish contact in the region, and he was happy to take it down for me and let me examine it. Of course, he kept looking down my shirt the whole time I was examining it, so he definitely had an ulterior motive."

"You should have punched him," Jade said.

"Hey, it got me the chance to look at the map." She dug into her bag and withdrew a rolled paper. "He even made a copy for me. It's not to scale, but it's a pretty decent size." She unrolled the paper to reveal the map she had described.

Maddock leaned forward as if drawn by some magnetic force toward what could be the key to the mystery. He reached out a hand toward the moonlike sketch of Pueblo Bonito that he had first recognized. He hesitated before his finger touched the paper, remembering that it was only a copy. Amanda had traced the outline of the shape on the breastplate, and he followed it from place-to-place until it reached their next stop.

"Rainbow Bridge," Amanda said. "Fray Marcos had all the right places on his map, but his distances and relative locations were way off. That's why the overlay wouldn't work on an accurate map."

"That's very, very good work," Jade said, her tone indicating a newfound respect. "But I still have two questions. Is there a solstice marker at or near Rainbow Bridge, and why do we need dive equipment?"

"There's no solstice marker," Amanda replied. "But once I knew we were looking at Rainbow Bridge, I found that, years ago, the shadow of the arch pointed directly into the window of a nearby ruin on the day of the summer solstice."

"But there aren't any ruins in that direction," Saul said. "I checked into that a long time ago. There's only…" his voice trailed away as the color drained from his face.

"Lake Powell!" Jade shouted. "That's brilliant! When the lake was created, the water covered countless ruins. No one really knows how much history lies beneath the water." She turned to Saul. "I'm feeling dumber today. How about you?"

"I couldn't believe they were able to find diving gear out here. I never even thought of Lake Powell."

"But why all the cloak and dagger?" Jade asked. "Why not just tell us?"

"I wanted the chance to explain it to you," Amanda said. "You know-- tell you the story, show you the map. If I had just announced we were headed to Lake Powell to find a submerged ruin, what would you have thought?"

"That you were wrong," Saul said. "It makes sense, though, the way you explained it." He turned to Jade, who nodded.

Maddock glanced at his cell phone, ostensibly to check the time. He was pleased to see he had no coverage, as was the case in most of the places they visited. He'd have to keep an eye on Saul as they drove, but hopefully there wouldn't be many opportunities to contact the outside world.

Rainbow Bridge stood in stark relief against the cornflower sky. More than three-hundred feet high, and nearly as wide, it was the largest natural bridge in the world. Maddock had never heard of this marvel of nature, but now he wondered how it was he had never learned of it. It was somehow magnificent in its simplicity. He continued to be amazed that someone who loved the water as much as he did could be charmed by this parched land.

"Sort of makes you homesick for St. Louis," Bones said, sidling up next to him and admiring the giant stone arch.

"How can you be homesick for somewhere you've never lived?" Maddock asked, not taking his eyes off the bridge.

"Same way you can call a girl a 'friend' who was obviously much more."

"What?" Maddock turned and looked at Bones in genuine puzzlement. "I don't get it."

"I've just realized how big a mistake you made with Kaylin," Bones said. "Don't get me wrong. Jade's hot and smart and feisty, but that's what you've got me for. Kaylin's the girl for you. You should call her."

"Besides the fact that this is a weird time to be talking to me about this," Maddock said, "do you really think you're qualified to give me relationship advice when you've never stayed with the same woman for more than four months?"

"Exactly," Bones said. "I know more about women than you do because I've had relationships with about a hundred times more women than you. And my record is seven months."

"So tell me; exactly how long was your second-longest relationship?"

"Nine and-a-half weeks," Bones said. "But we packed a lot of living into that time, so it really counts as about four months."

Maddock shook his head. He wouldn't even have this conversation with anyone else, but Bones had long ago earned the right to say whatever was on his mind. Of course, Bones said what was on his mind whether he had the right or not.

"Look, Maddock. You and I both know that the only reason it didn't work with Kaylin was because she was the first one after Melissa."

Maddock was proud of himself for not wincing at the mention of his deceased wife's name.

"But why the hell are we having this conversation here and now?"

"Because it needs to be said and I might forget to say it later. You know how distracted I get sometimes. Seriously, I see there's something between you and Jade. Might just be potential, but it's there, and that's cool. But she's not the port where you want to drop anchor."

"You're not you when you're with her. Well, you're you, but not all of you. I don't know if it's because she's so smart, or exotic, or whatever, but I can already see that you take a step back when you're around her. You're like eighty percent of you when she's around. You're too badass for that. Besides, my girlfriend thinks she's a bitch, and I don't want you bringing her to the wedding." He turned on his heel and strode away. "Time to dive!" he called back to Maddock.

"Whoa! What…? Did you say wedding?" He followed Bones away from the arch toward the lake where the rest of their party waited.

"Not so loud," Bones said. "I haven't let anyone in on this little secret of mine."

"Have you at least let Amanda know?" Maddock kidded.

"She doesn't yet know that she's in love with me," Bones said. "But she'll figure it out. They all do eventually." Bones gave him an evil grin. "Just kidding. I do like her, though, and I'll probably keep her around for a while. It would make things a lot less tense if those two would get along. Maybe I could tell Jade we're engaged, and then she'd lay off."

Maddock threw his head back and laughed, clapping his friend on the shoulder. There was no one quite like Bones, and having him here made everything better, even if he did occasionally cause Maddock to ponder things he'd rather not think about.

The water was pleasantly cool, and Maddock knifed through it like a dolphin at play. It felt so good to be back in fins and a mask, even if it was only for a brief lake dive. In no time, he and Bones had crossed the lake and were now treading water below the exact spot Amanda had indicated. They double-checked their tanks and valves, waved to the three who waited ashore, and dove.

The sun filtered through the greenish water in wavy beams of gold, putting him in mind of a jungle far away and a long time ago. He suppressed that unbidden memory before it was fully formed, and locked it back where his other demons were imprisoned. He supposed he'd have to exorcise them someday, but not today.

They worked their way along the face of the submerged canyon, their lights playing across the rugged surface. It was surprisingly free of silt and debris. The sunlight played out quickly, leaving them in a frustrating half-light that played tricks on their eyes and turned shadows into phantom doors and windows that vanished under closer scrutiny.

They reached the bottom and turned to ascend, spreading out to cover a new swath of rock. Bones hated this kind of methodical search, but Maddock enjoyed it. There was something about the precise, leave-no-stone-unturned method that appealed to him. It amused him that he and Bones could both be former military, but so different in their approaches. Maddock could have been a career officer had he wanted. Bones was fortunate to have avoided being kicked out of the Navy entirely. He'd been good at what he did, but lived on the edge of serious trouble.

Three passes later, Maddock was growing concerned that they might not have sufficient air for what was becoming a lengthy search when his light struck something that was definitely not a natural formation. Swimming closer, he saw the keyhole-shaped doorway of an Anasazi dwelling. He blinked his dive light at Bones until he received a return signal, and waited as his friend joined him. They shone their lights in and played them through the small room. It wouldn't be much to search, but there were other problems. One concern would be the inevitable silt that would be stirred up as they entered. The other was the size of the doorway. Maddock would be able to squeeze through, but not with his tank strapped to his back.

Getting Bones' attention, he traced the shape of the doorway, pointed to his tank, and drew his finger across his throat. Bone nodded and immediately helped Maddock remove his tank. Once free, Maddock took a breath of air, exhaled, and squeezed through the opening. They had not worn dive suits for what was to be such a brief dive in relatively warm water. The coarse rock tore his t-shirt and scraped his shoulders as he forced his way through. He managed to bark his shin for good measure as he swam inside. Once in, he turned back to the doorway, where Bones held his tank for him to take another breath.

The decades of silt that had blanketed the inside of the ruin now churned throughout every square inch of open space, limiting visibility to less than a foot. He began with the corners, feeling blindly until he collided with the far wall, working his way along the bottom edge. The right corner revealed nothing. The back wall seemed to be hewn into the rock of the canyon wall. There were no stones to break loose, and no sign of Fray Marcos's symbol.

He swam back to the doorway, startling Bones who jerked as Maddock appeared from the storm of silt. As he took a few breaths, waiting for his heart to stop racing, he shook his head to indicate he had found nothing.

A search of the other corner was no more fruitful. Based on their relative locations, he knew the shadow of Rainbow Bridge would strike the lower part of the back wall, so he took time to swim slowly across the back of the room, scouring the wall with his fingertips, hoping to feel if not see the cross and clover he sought.

By the time he had crossed the room, his lungs were screaming for air and his head felt like it would explode. He had always been able to hold his breath longer than anyone he knew, even the other SEALs with whom he had served, but this time he had pushed himself to his limit. He turned and pushed off from the wall, shooting toward the doorway.

Red light exploded in his head as he crashed into the opposite wall. He involuntarily sucked in and had to suppress a cough as the water burned his sinuses. He had miscalculated. The doorway could not be far, but where was it? He could see almost nothing in the cloud of particles that roiled around him. Had he overshot his target, or fallen short? His ears now rang from the combined effects of oxygen deprivation and the blow to his head.

Calming himself, he placed his hands on the walls and felt his way along. His body screamed for air, and it was all he could do to maintain control. It was a small space, he reasoned, and he would find the doorway soon.

His field of vision narrowed and the world was tinted red. He felt his lungs cramp, and he began to fade.

And then a beam of light sliced through the water directly above him. Bones must have known it had been too long and shone his flashlight through the hole to serve as a homing beacon for Maddock. Swimming up to the doorway, he felt a surge of relief as he bit down on the valve and felt blessed air fill his lungs again. It didn't take him long to feel revitalized and ready to renew the search. Where to look next?

He tried to visualize the position of the sun and the arch. Where would the shadow fall? The angle would be steep. Perhaps not the corner...

He remembered the dive he and Jade had made together in the well. Fray Marcos' symbol had been in the center of the floor. Of course, that had been a trap, breaking the seal to a drain. That wouldn't be the case this time. There was no way anyone could have had the foresight to know that these dwellings would someday be flooded by a man-made lake. In any case, it wouldn't hurt to check, and he was out of ideas.

A few more breaths and he was back to searching. With patient care, his fingers probed the floor, searching every crack and indentation until he felt a circle. Hastily he scrubbed the area around the shape until he had uncovered a clover. This was it!

He needed two more trips back for air before he could finish the job, but soon he and Bones were headed back across the lake, another box secure in his dive bag.

Chapter 20

Maddock and Bones sat in reclining pool chairs, soaking up the moonlight and the aroma of sage drifting on the dry breeze, barely suppressing the chlorine smell of the hotel pool. He trailed his finger absently across the condensation on his bottle of Dos Equis and pondered their next move.

"I suppose if I was a chick I'd say something like 'what are you thinking' or something equally annoying," Bones said. "Spill it, bro."

"We've hit a wall," Maddock said. "We've found all the pieces of the puzzle we're going to find, but the clues don't lead us anywhere."

"Au contraire," Bones said, "they will eventually lead us somewhere just as soon as we figure out where the starting point might be."

"And therein lies the problem," Maddock said. "And I can't shake the feeling that the other side might already know, and the only thing holding them back is waiting for Saul to get them the translation of the final pieces of the scarab."

"If that's the situation, the only thing we can do is get there first. At least we have a head start on them. We need to figure out the next step, and make certain that no more of Jimmy's translations fall into Saul's hands. This is going to be a race." Bones took a gulp of his Cherry Coke and belched the letters A through F. "I never make it to 'G'," he muttered. "So, have you thought any more about what I said this afternoon?"

"You mean about you getting married?" Maddock said.

"No, about you and..."

"I know what you mean," Maddock said, cutting him off in mid-sentence. He realized he had made a decision. "I've thought about it. Maybe it's not that Jade is wrong for me. Maybe I just need to quit being such a wuss around women. Melissa wouldn't want me to spend the rest of my life moping around. If the situation was reversed, I'd want her to have a good life, and to keep being herself."

"I knew you'd get there eventually," Bones said. "And thank you for not making me say it."

"Thank you for making me figure it out. Matter of fact, I'm going to go talk to Jade." He rose from his chair, chugged the last of his beer, and made it all the way to H.

"Show off," Bones said.

"Anyway, I'll catch you later."

Maddock knocked on Jade's door. He didn't know if it was the beer, his epiphany, or both, but he felt… different. Like whatever decision he made right now would be the right one.

You're not you when you're with her… you take a step back.

Bones was right. Jade was smart and sexy and a pain in the neck, but she wasn't too good for him.

Jade smiled and wrapped her lithe, brown arms around his neck, pulling him close.

"I was just about to come and get you," she breathed. "Your friend Jimmy just e-mailed me. He's been looking at the pictures Bones took and he thinks there's a connection to our mystery. He says he'll have something for us maybe by tomorrow. He's being a bit mysterious, but I get the impression he knows something already."

"Jimmy's like that," Maddock said. He had taken the look in her eyes and the hug as happiness at seeing him, and he was disappointed to realize that she was happy to see him, but only because of the new development in the mystery. "He likes to drop the bomb on you, then step back and take his bows. This piecemeal translation has probably been driving him crazy."

"Well, I hope he's…" Her gaze locked with his and her expression turned serious. "What's wrong?

"Nothing," Maddock said. His heart pounded out a relentless beat and his stomach felt like frozen cement. If he didn't do it now, he'd never do it. "I just wanted to give you something." Before he could change his mind, he cupped her chin in one hand, wrapped the other arm around her waist, drew her close, and kissed her.

He felt her stiffen and for a moment he thought he'd made a mistake of epic proportions, but then she relaxed. Her lips responded to his with a gentle insistence. Her fingers tangled in his hair and she drew away, kissing his cheek, his neck, his chest. He groaned and pulled her closer, pressing his body against hers.

She drew back long enough to help him out of his shirt before leaping fully into his arms, wrapping around him like a hungry parasite. For a brief moment, he was once again struck by her scent. It was like sage and cinnamon, and for some odd reason he found that quite remarkable. That was his last rational thought for some time, as he lifted her off her feet and carried her to the bed, where they collapsed into a writhing tangle of arms, legs, bed sheets, and discarded clothing.

He awoke in the semi-darkness with Jade leaning over him, speaking softly. He grinned and stretched luxuriously.

"Aren't you tired?" he asked.

"Get up," she whispered. "I've gotten a message from your friend Jimmy."

There was something in her voice that brought him instantly awake. There was a sense of urgency, and an underlying strain that puzzled him. It must be because of Saul. If Jimmy had made a breakthrough, she'd want to follow up on it before Saul could find out.

"What is it?" he asked, rolling out of bed and searching around for his clothes.

"He's found a connection between our mystery and the discovery Bones made. I'll tell you about it in the car. Come on!"

He barely had time to get dressed before she ushered him out of the room and hurried him to the car. Ten minutes later they were winging down the road, the aroma of cheap, gas station coffee assaulting his senses.

"So, are you going to finally tell me about this breakthrough?"

Jade paused before explaining.

"The writing on the disc Bones found was not exactly in Hebrew. Or, it was, but it was a cipher. Jimmy suspected as much when he first tried to translate it, so he set some computer programs to trying to crack it, and went back to our puzzle. The computer managed to crack the code late last night. The disc tells a very interesting story." She bit her lip, her eyes fixed on the road ahead.

"So, are you going to tell me or not?"

"Sorry," she said. "I'm just preoccupied." She paused again as if deciding how to proceed. "Have you ever heard of Akhenaten?"

"Wasn't he some sort of Egyptian sun god or some-thing?"

"Not quite. Akhenaten was pharaoh from about 1350 to 1336 B.C. You might have heard of his wife, Nefertiti."

"Okay, but I thought she was a fertility goddess or sex symbol or something."

"Maddock," she sighed, "it's one thing to not know, but you don't have to advertise it. Anyway, Akhenaten is known as the heretic pharaoh, or the enemy, because he tried to convert Egyptians to monotheism. He declared that the sun disc Aten, from whom he derived his name, was the one true god. This didn't set well with the polytheistic Egyptian people, and when Akhenaten died, there was a backlash against everything associated with his rule. Buildings were demolished and all ties to his religion were severed. Even his remains and those of his family disappeared. Egypt returned to what they considered normal."

"Wait a minute," Maddock said, remembering something Bones had once told him. "Wasn't he the guy with the weird body? He had feminine and masculine features, and some people think he might have had a disease?"

"Very good," Jade said. "You're smarter than I thought." Her laugh sounded forced. "There's a picture of him." She indicated a printout lying on the seat in between them.

The image was a familiar one, now that he saw it. The pharaoh was rendered with an elongated face and pear-shaped body.

"I remember him now. Bones thinks he's an alien."

"Oh, good Lord," Jade groaned. "Does Bones always connect everything to aliens?"

"Not everything," Maddock replied, trying to lighten Jade's mood. "He's pretty sure the Loch Ness Monster, Bigfoot, and Elvis are earthlings."

"Lovely. At any rate, the symbol of Aten was a disc with rays beaming down, each with a hand at the end. Sound familiar?"

"Sure," he said, immediately remembering the image on the gold disc Bones had recovered. "So, Bones' disc has an Egyptian symbol on the back. Our puzzle is carved into a dismembered scarab, which is also Egyptian. Is that it?"

"Nope, there's more. The translation of the writing on the disc tells the story of the downfall of Akhenaten. He and his most faithful follower recovered the treasures of the temple at Amarna and fled into the desert, where they lived in exile in the Sinai for forty years. He continued to teach his monotheistic faith and taught them ten laws for living, based on Spell 125 of the Egyptian Book of the Dead. They continued to revere him as the "mose" or "heir" to the throne."

"Whoa. Ten rules for living... the Sinai... mose... You mean Moses..."

"Moses and Akhenaten are one and the same, at least according to the writing on the disc. They eventually settled in what we know as the Holy Land. Aten became Yahweh, or "I Am," and the Jewish faith grew from the seeds planted by Akhenaten."

"Unbelievable." Maddock was stunned by what Jade was telling him. Of course, the story on the disc could be completely wrong, but he had seen enough on his last foray into the Middle East to make him realize that anything could be possible. "So, you're saying that God isn't God? That he's just this Aten in new robes?"

"I'm not saying that at all. In fact, I'm not much for religion one way or the other. You could look at is as Aten being the beginning of understanding the true nature of God. A polytheistic, pagan people were discovering the underlying truth. Maybe Yahweh, or God, is the culmination of that spiritual journey."

"I hear you. Anyway, is there a connection to our scarab other than the fact that they're both Egyptian artifacts with Hebrew writing engraved on them?"

"You left out the fact that both are in the middle of the American Southwest, and based on some of the cave artwork, both are associated with Spaniards. But yes, there's more.

"Akhenaten, now known as Moses, wanted to develop a cultural identity apart from that of Egypt. He ordered the treasures hidden away and appointed a sect of followers to be the keepers of the secret. This group, called the Essenes, recorded the secrets of the treasure on a scroll made of copper."

"The Copper Scroll," Maddock breathed.

"It's been generally assumed that the Copper Scroll leads, or led, to the treasure of the temple at Jerusalem, but the Egyptian connection makes sense. Another Essene scroll, the Temple Scroll, gives dimensions of a temple that coincide nicely with records of the size of the temple at Amarna."

"And the connection to our mystery?" Maddock still wasn't seeing the link, though he was fascinated by the story Jade was spinning.

"Jimmy also discovered that the writing on our scarab consists entirely of quotes lifted directly from the Copper Scroll."

"What? But..." His mind buzzed with conflicting thoughts. Why would Fray Marcos come to America to hide pieces of a larger treasure map that led to an Egyptian treasure hidden in Israel? What would be the point?

"This is where the cave art comes in. Legend has it that the Knights Templar found the temple treasure and carried it back to Europe. Another legend, one given less credence over the years, holds that the treasure was brought to the New World and hidden away. The idea seemed absurd. Why would anyone do that? But if you believe the story on the disc, well..."

"There's no way they could have revealed to the world that Moses was an Egyptian pharaoh who worshiped the sun," Maddock finished, the pieces now fitting firmly in place. "They couldn't bring themselves to destroy it, so they hid it in America. And that's why Fray Marcos left the clues. He understood how dangerous the secret was, but he wasn't willing to let it be lost forever."

"I think so too," Jade said. "The cave art depicts a group of Spaniards, transporting sacks of something a great distance. Obviously, someone thought this was worth recording. Fortunately for us, landforms in the pictures are very distinctive. Whoever made those images knew the place quite well. Jimmy was able to pinpoint it to a place in southern Utah."

"And our clue?"

"Snatches of phrases from the copper scroll, carefully selected to guide the seeker once they've found the site where the treasure is hidden. And you'll never believe the name of the place."

"Umm... Jerusalem National Park."

"Close," she said, turning to look at him for the first time. "It's called Zion."

Chapter 21

Bones re-read the printout of the e-mail from Jimmy. It was unbelievable. Could it possibly be true? Moses a pharaoh? The legendary Seven Cities of gold merely steps on a journey to a single, fabulous treasure? He checked his watch. It was early, but not too early to wake Maddock.

He rapped on the door that connected their rooms. Amanda groaned and turned toward him.

"What are you doing?" she moaned. "It's five o'clock."

"Solving a mystery," he said. "Get out of bed and I'll tell you all about it." He knocked again on Maddock's door, but no reply. "I'm going to get Maddock, and I'll tell you both."

"Maybe he's in Jade's room," Amanda said, rubbing her eyes with her fists.

"Yeah, I'll check." Bones replied. He hurried out the door but encountered Saul almost at once.

"Have you seen Jade?" Saul asked.

"Nope. You seen Maddock?"

"He's gone too?" Saul looked around as if Maddock or Jade might be hiding in the parking lot. "Oh, crap."

"What's up?" His distrust of Saul notwithstanding, there was something in the man's voice that worried Bones. Saul met his gaze with a long, level look.

"Can I come in? There are some things I need to tell you. I wish I had done it before, but..." He shrugged and set his jaw, still looking Bones in the eye.

"Sure," Bones said. "Just let me make sure Amanda is decent." Amanda had dressed and was brushing her teeth, so Bones let Saul in. She joined them around the small table and waited for Saul to explain himself.

"I don't exactly know where to start," he said. "Have either of you heard of the Deseret Dominion?"

Bones shifted uncomfortably in his seat and looked at Amanda, who nodded.

"Okay," Saul said. "The thing is... Jade works for them."

"What the..." Bones said, sitting up straight. "But we thought you..." *I stopped myself about three words too late*, he thought as Saul's eyes darted from Bones to Amanda and back.

"Me? Hell no. I'm working against them." He saw the skeptical expressions on their faces and hurried on with his explanation. "I didn't know at first. She seemed okay, but I got suspicious when I started noticing some of the calls and e-mail she got."

"What about it?" Bones asked, still not sure whether or not to believe Saul. "What caused you to be suspicious?"

"I recognized some names." Saul hung his head. "My dad was in the Dominion. I thought he was out of it, but it's too big a coincidence that he put so much money into Jade's expedition and set me up to work with her. I guess he's still involved." He took a deep breath but kept looking down. "Anyway, when those guys showed up at Chaco Canyon, I knew. I didn't say anything to Maddock since I didn't really know him, but it was kind of obvious what was going on."

"And what exactly were you going to do about it?" Amanda asked.

"I had hoped to stop her from getting some of the clues. Maybe I could beat her to them. I thought that if I could keep her from passing complete information to the Dominion, I could keep them from doing whatever it was they are trying to do. I even tried to steal the breastplate from Maddock's boat back when this all started, not knowing Jade had taken it with her after all. Of course, I didn't have a plan for what I would have done with it. If nothing else, I was hoping that, when the time came, I could take the information and get there first. But since the first few pieces turned up, I haven't had a chance to do anything. It's like you've been keeping me…" He looked from one to the other, understanding dawning in his eyes. "Oh."

"We've suspected you. No lie. But I don't know," Bones said. "How do we know you're not the one in the Dominion, and you're just trying to get information from us?"

"Oh, my…" Amanda's voice was cold with realization. "Bones, I'm so stupid. It never occurred to me before. Jade teaches at Central Utah University."

"And your point is?"

"When Orley was taken from his ranch, where did they have him?"

"Holy crap," Bones muttered. Orley had been at the Central Utah University Neuropsychiatric Institute. Even had he been aware of Jade's affiliation with the university, it was unlikely he would have made the connection, but it did seem to fit with what Saul was telling them.

"That's one reason to believe me," Saul said, "but I have another." He dug into his pocket and produced something wrapped in a handkerchief. "The Dominion didn't get the Ship Rock piece. I did." He unfolded the cloth to reveal the missing piece of the scarab. "There you go. My cards are on the table. Maybe I'm nuts for telling you this, but now that we're at the end, and Jade's disappeared, I don't know what to think. I've got this crazy idea that she and the Dominion know where Cibola is."

"They do," Bones said. With numb fingers, he slid Jimmy's e-mail over to Saul. The other man's eyes widened as he read. Bones was cold all over. How could they have been so wrong? And what about Maddock?

"He blind-copied this to you," Saul said. "So Jade doesn't know anyone else has the information. And we have the missing piece to the puzzle. If Jimmy can take care of the translation, we might have a small advantage."

"Saul," Amanda said, "what is it that the Dominion wants? What are they trying to achieve with all of this?"

"I don't know everything, and I can't be one hundred percent sure. It's a long, unbelievable story that I can tell you while we drive" Saul said. He sprang to his feet, almost toppling his chair. "I've made a scan of the artifact. We'll send it to Jimmy, find a car, and get the hell out of here. Maybe there's time to save Maddock."

"What do you mean, 'save'?" The disbelief that numbed Bones' senses was melting into anger.

"It's the endgame," Saul said. "Maddock was helpful, but Jade doesn't need him anymore. The Dominion won't let him live once they have the prize… if he lasts that long."

They didn't waste any time gathering their things. Bones grabbed Maddock's belongings as well. We'll catch up with them, he thought. Amanda was right. The woman is bad news.

Saul was back in their room in five minutes with his laptop in hand and his backpack slung over his shoulder.

"I e-mailed the scan to Jimmy," he said. "They don't have cabs out here in the middle of nowhere, but I checked and there's a rental agency a couple of miles from here. We'll be their first customers of the morning." His smile was grim.

Bones looked up at the dark sky and imagined the time slipping away as Jade drove Maddock right into the hands of the Dominion while the three of them hoofed it down the highway in search of a rental car. A single pair of headlights sliced through the darkness. As the vehicle drew closer, it slowed, then cut a sharp right into the hotel parking lot. Tires squealed and kicked up a cloud of the fine dust that coated the asphalt. His instincts told him that something was wrong. He grabbed Amanda and yanked her down as he ducked behind the nearest car. He opened his mouth to warn Saul, but he was too late.

A wet, slapping sound that Bones knew all too well preceded the muffled pop of silenced pistol. Saul grunted and staggered back. As if that first shot were a starter's pistol, a torrent of bullets sizzled through the air. Glass shattered, bullets ricocheted off of the brick wall, and Saul slid to the ground, his blood pooling around him, looking black in the dim light. The Dominion had arrived.

Trying to keep low and remain out of sight, Bones led Amanda along the row of parked cars. There were only four. The car that had zipped into the parking lot, a dark sedan, screeched to a halt. All four doors burst open and men poured out.

The last car in the row was an old mini-van. "When I start shooting, you run," he whispered to Amanda. She nodded. He held his Glock in his right hand and with his left he reached into his ankle holster and withdrew the snub-nosed .22 magnum mini-revolver that he carried for special occasions. He placed his left foot on the front bumper and launched himself onto the hood. A second leap and he was on the roof. He opened fire, dropping the two closest Dominion men, who were still scanning the parking lot and didn't expect an attack from above. The other two returned fire, their reckless shots well off-target. Lights were coming on inside many of the hotel rooms, but no one came outside.

Bones dropped down into the bed of an adjacent pickup truck and squeezed off two more shots, causing the men to hit the ground and roll. He was taking a risk exposing himself to gunfire like this, but he had seen how few shots had hit Saul, and concluded that these were not soldiers. Hired killers they might be, but these sorts of toughs never found themselves in real combat situations. He'd take the battle to them. Lying flat on his stomach, he slid to the end of the truck bed, raised up, and peered over the edge. The remaining two men had vanished into the shadows. Where were they?

A spare tire lay loose in the bed next to him. Cautiously, he tipped it up on its side and gave it a shove. It bounced once and rolled across the darkened lot. Dull pops sounded and bullets sprayed the blacktop all around the rolling tire. Bones spotted muzzle flash from a dark corner near the ice maker and squeezed off three quick shots. He heard a shout of pain and surprise. He had hit one of them. He ducked and rolled out of the truck just as bullets tore through the side of the truck near the spot he had just vacated.

Staying low and keeping to the darkest shadows, Bones crept forward, keeping a sharp eye out for any movement. Which way to go? A loud crash behind him made him whirl about, dropping to one knee, both guns at the ready. Instead of someone about to shoot him, he saw a man sprawled face-down on the ground, a hotel maid's cart lying on top of him. Amanda came charging down a nearby stairwell.

"Their car is still running!" she shouted. "Let's go!" Sprinting past the stunned man, she took Bones by the elbow and tugged him toward the waiting vehicle.

Bullets zinged past Bones' heel. One of the guys was still alive. He fired toward the hollow sound of the silenced pistol, which bought them enough time to leap into the Dominion car, slam it into reverse, and hurtle backward through the parking lot, zigzagging as bullets whizzed past. One pinged off the roof and another shattered the passenger side mirror, but nothing hit the windshield. Every moment took him farther from danger. He kept half an eye out for his assailant to come after him. Bones wished he would try it, but the guy was at least bright enough to remain hidden.

He didn't bother to slow down or turn around when they hit the highway, but kept it in reverse and floored it, hurtling backward down the narrow, two-lane highway before taking it into a controlled skid and bringing the front end about.

"Do you like my fancy driving?" he asked as they barreled down the road.

"That," she breathed, "was closer than the hospital. I didn't know what I was going to do. I couldn't just run away and leave you there, so I went up to the second floor and tried to keep a lookout, but I lost sight of you. And then that guy came out of the shadows, and the maid cart was there, so I…" She broke off, burying her face in her hands.

Bones reached over and laid a hand on her shoulder. He hated it when women cried, and hated it even more when it was his fault, which was frequently the case.

"It's okay," he said. "I'm all right."

"You're an ass is what you are," Amanda said, slapping his hand away and sitting up straight. Anger had replaced the fear in her eyes, and Bones was stunned to see that she was not crying. This woman was something else. "You could have given me one of those guns and I could have shot him instead."

Bones was momentarily speechless. She wanted to do what?

"Forget it," Amanda said. "I know you're trained and you can probably shoot better on the run with your left hand than I can when taking aim with both hands. I just wanted to help you. It sucks being scared for someone, and it's worse when you can't do anything for them."

"You were great," Bones said, trying to deal with the torrent of emotions that surged through him. "Tell you what. When this is all over, I'll take you sidearm shopping. I'll even train you."

"Promise?" Amanda's tone made it clear that she would hold him to it. "And you'll let me use it to shoot people?"

"Do you have certain people in mind, or just random people?"

"You know what I mean. If something like that," she tilted her head back in the direction from which they had come, "ever happens again, are you going to let me fight, or are you going to make me run away?"

"I…" His first instinct had been to tell her what she wanted to hear. He knew, though, that Amanda would detect his lie. She was the sharpest woman he'd ever known. Plus, for the first time in his life, the idea of lying to a woman really bothered him. "I promise that if it makes sense for you to… shoot people, I'll let you fight. But you're going to have to promise me that you won't argue if I tell you otherwise." He could tell she was going to protest, but he raised his voice. "I'm not old-fashioned about much, but your safety comes before mine. Always."

"Why? Because I'm a woman?"

"Because I like having you around. It would kind of suck if something happened to you."

Amanda unbuckled her seat belt, scooted up next to him, and wrapped her arms around his neck.

"You really are an ass," she whispered, and laid her head on his shoulder. They stayed that way, silent and content as they hurtled through the darkness toward the unknown.

Chapter 22

The bouncing vehicle jolted Maddock to full alertness. He scanned the barren landscape. Red rocks and sparse hills surrounded them, morning light casting their surroundings in a faint, golden hue. There was no road in sight.

"Sorry. Didn't mean to doze off on you," he murmured, rubbing his eyes. It was not like him to fall asleep like that, especially after the startling revelations from earlier. "Where are we?"

"We're close to Zion," Jade said. She sounded oddly subdued, so unlike her excited, almost manic behavior of earlier. Of course, she had been driving since early morning and was operating on very little sleep. "I had to go off-road a bit. This will take us in through the back door. Assuming, of course, you're up for a bit of a hike."

"Always ready," he said, though his head still felt thick from his nap as if his brain was filled with molasses. "Just need to finish waking up."

"If you don't have any coffee left, you can have the rest of mine." Jade inclined her head toward the two Styrofoam cups in the console.

Maddock swirled the contents of his cup before drowning the three remaining lukewarm swallows. One glance at the clock told him he had been asleep for only about a half-hour.

Jade brought the vehicle to a halt and hopped out before reaching into the back seat and grabbing a paper bag she had brought from the convenience store. Maddock assumed it held bottles of water for their hike.

They started walking. There didn't seem to be any distinct landforms by which to pinpoint their location, but Maddock trusted that Jade knew where she was going.

"There's a cleft in the rock over there." She indicated a spot in the distance where a dark, vertical line cleft the sun-illuminated stone.

He had to turn sideways and exhale in order to squeeze through the narrow opening, but on the other side it widened enough for two people to walk abreast. The way was strewn with loose rock and choked with cactus, but the slope was gentle and the path straight.

He shook his head, trying to clear the cobwebs. The moment of alertness he had felt when he first awoke was long gone, replaced by a feeling of increased heaviness as if his head was slowly filling with cement. He stumbled and barely caught himself before his face hit the path.

"You all right?" Jade asked. His sluggishness and heavy feeling made her words sound cold and flat.

"Yeah," he replied. "I think... I think I need to sit for a minute."

"There's an outcropping up here where you can get out of the sun. Come on." She took him by the hand and guided him like a child up to the sheltered overhang where she settled him against the bare rock. "Close your eyes," she whispered.

He fought to stay awake, but his eyelids drooped, and Jade faded from sight.

It was hot... dry... he was in the depths of a canyon. A winged, skeletal figure hovered over him, spreading its arms to welcome him into its deadly embrace.

"Aaah!" Red light flashed across his vision as he bolted upright and cracked his head on the low-hanging rock. "Stupid!" He rubbed his head and looked around for Jade, but there was no sign of her. He searched the defile, calling her name. No luck. Had she gone on ahead? Surely not, but who could say? Perhaps she had left a note in the car.

Utterly confused, he made his way back the way he and Jade had come earlier. Heat ripped up from the parched earth, the late morning sun hung angry in the sky. He rubbed a dry palm across his equally parched forehead. He was dehydrated. The single cup of coffee he had drunk hours ago was not remotely enough in this climate. On the positive side, he felt much more alert than he had upon arrival. His relief was short-lived, as he squeezed out of the rocky cleft to discover that their car was gone.

His mind raced. What had happened to her? She wouldn't have just left him. They must have found her, and she had hidden the fact that he was with her. That was the only possible explanation. So what was he going to do about it?

He considered his options, which were few. He didn't know how far it was back to the road, or exactly which direction they had come. For that matter, there was no telling how many back roads Jade had taken before leaving the road entirely. Were he to make it back to any sort of road, he wouldn't know where to go from there. The wide open spaces of the American southwest meant one could seemingly go forever without a glimpse of civilization. That had, for the most part, appealed to him until this moment.

The only thing that made sense to him was to keep on going. Jade had indicated that their destination was within walking distance. His limited examination of the map on the way here, and his estimation of the distance they had traveled provided a degree of confirmation. If Jade had been kidnaped, they would expect her to lead them to whatever waited in Zion. His only chance was to find her there. He checked his cell phone just in case, but he had no coverage, as usual.

His thoughts flew unbidden to a moment, years ago. He remembered the sound of Melissa's voice, the scream the crash... He had stood there staring numbly at his phone, knowing his wife was dead, and he could do nothing about it. It had been completely beyond his control, but this was not beyond his control. He would find

Jade and bring her back. Setting determined eyes on the horizon, he set off.

It was not long before the intense sun led him to tie his handkerchief over his head like a turban. The thin fabric was of little help in the heat, but it did serve to deflect the worst of the sun's rays. The wise course would be to find a bit of shade in which to wait out the hottest part of the day, and travel in the evening and at night, but he could not spare the time. He did not know exactly how far he was going, or where for that matter, but the fact that Jade had brought no water with them when they left the car indicated that she did not expect it to be far.

The shimmering waves of hot air seemed to resist his every step, as though he was swimming in molten lead. Sweat beaded on his forehead, and he wiped it off and licked it off his palm. I need to conserve every bit of moisture I can, he thought. He hoped it would not be far. He did not know what he would find when he caught up with Jade and whoever had taken her, but he was certain he would need every ounce of strength he could muster.

The path he walked was not truly a path at all, but a low area among the hills and mounds of rock, where water flowed through during the rare downpour that touched the desert with its brief, violent kiss. He came upon a bit of shade and rested for a moment, leaning against the rough, dry rock. His eyes searched the grounds for any bit of vegetation he could chew on for moisture, but he found nothing.

He continued to walk. The baked stone beneath his feet seemed to melt the soles of his shoes, and he imagined he was walking in mud, though it was only fatigue that made him feel like his feet were sticking to the earth. He came around a sharp bend, where the ground fell away to a narrow cleft where rocks and debris choked the bottom of the passage. His eyes fell on dark sand, and his heart pounded a hopeful beat. He half-climbed, half-fell to the bottom, and tumbled to his knees. He burrowed deep into the sand, working his way deeper until... yes! Moisture!

He continued to dig until his fingers struck rock. He twisted his arm back-and-forth, digging a tiny well for water to gather. He scooped up a bit of dirty, tepid water and carefully poured it into his mouth. He resisted the urge to gulp the water, instead letting it trickle back into his throat, keeping the grit and sand on his tongue. The hole yielded no more than another thimbleful, which he dribbled onto his swollen tongue. The moist sand he patted onto his sunburned arms and face. It did not come anywhere close to making him feel refreshed, but the worst of the heat seemed to dissipate. Renewed, he scooped up a couple of small, round, pebbles and popped them into his mouth before continuing his trek.

His pace grew torpid as he trudged across the unforgiving land. Concerns over lack of water and directions lay thin above the underlying fear that he might already be too late. What would they do with Jade once they found whatever it was they were looking for? He couldn't permit those thoughts. She had to be all right. She had to be.

By the angle of the sun, it was well past noon. He hadn't the energy to even consult his watch. For the first time, he felt hope wane. Had he missed a turn? Was there a sign of which Jade had been aware that he had not? His fatigue and thirst made it increasingly difficult to fight off despair. He needed something to drink. He remembered his survival training and groaned at the most immediate possibility. He could drink his own urine. It would be disgusting, and he had nothing in which to collect, but it would keep him going a bit longer. He really didn't want to do that. What would Bones say if he knew? The thought of his friend made him chuckle, and his spirits lifted, if only a shade.

What about food? He supposed he could poke around under some of the clefts and try to surprise a rattlesnake. If he could find one, and if he could manage to kill it without being bitten, he could eat the meat… raw. Of course, he would waste vital time and energy in what might be a fruitless quest. He would push on a bit further before making that decision.

He glanced up at the hazy, blue sky, the waves of heat rolling up like breakers on the sea. A lone wisp of cloud drifted lazily across the horizon, taunting him with the thought of the dark, heavy-laden storm clouds that visited his home in southern Florida every afternoon. Not a chance of that in this arid clime.

Something glimmered on the horizon. In his state, he could not tell if it was anything more than a mirage, but he continued to move toward it. His head swam, but he kept moving. Jade… Melissa… Jade… He stumbled but maintained his balance. He had to keep going.

And then something was moving toward him. A shadowy figure, little more than a dark outline against the sun-scorched sand. As it approached, the form took on a human shape. Hope welled inside of Maddock. He was too tired and dehydrated to wonder if the person might mean him ill. Maddock raised a hand in greeting, or tried to, but he could not lift his arm. His vision blurred, and an icy cool flowed down his back. Heatstroke. He stumbled to his knees as the figure drew forth. Maddock had only a brief glimpse of a hideous, beastly face before he slumped unconscious to the ground, the silent scream dying in his parched throat.

Chapter 23

The members of the small party picked their way across the narrow spine of rock that led to the top of Angel's Landing. Jarren kept his gaze fixed steadily ahead, refusing to look at the sheer drop-off on either side. Even the spectacular view of Zion National Park was not sufficient to overcome his touch of acrophobia and the myriad of thoughts that coursed through his mind. He had scoffed at the sign at the trailhead warning hikers of the potential danger this path posed, but now he saw the truth. The long, steep hike, particularly the switchbacks, had been challenging but not dangerous. This stretch was different. The ground seemed to flee from them as they crossed the narrow stone path. He could now see how several hikers a year managed to lose their lives on this perilous course. Why would anyone other than a skilled hiker be foolish enough to try and cross here? It was not that he had any sympathy for them; stupid people simply pissed him off.

A golden eagle circled far above, its lonely call drifting down from the heights. Jarren looked up for a moment too long and found himself struck by a moment of dizziness. He hastily dropped his gaze back to his destination, from which he was now only a few paces away. Angel's Landing. How fitting that the Lord's work would culminate in such an appropriately named place. He could scarcely believe it when the Elder told him. What were the odds that the Spaniards, more than a millennium ago, would have chosen a place that would later bear such a name? Zion indeed!

He knew little about what lay ahead. Excitement coursed through his veins. He suspected there still remained much the Elder had not told him. His instructions were clear: allow Ihara to guide them to the treasure, secure it until it could be removed, and then eliminate her at his leisure. It was the other part of the instructions he found most puzzling. If anything blasphemous is found, neither it nor word of it is to leave until I arrive. If that means eliminating your partners, so be it.

He grimaced at the memory of that last conversation. What might they find amongst the temple treasure that could blaspheme the Lord? Was he truly to kill the two men who accompanied him? Since those were his instructions, he was grateful for the small group. Initially, he had thought the concern over a large party drawing unwanted attention to be unfounded. This park did not have so many visitors compared to Mesa Verde or Grand Canyon. But, he supposed, a touch of prudence was not a bad thing though it went against his nature.

He turned his attention to his companions. Thaddeus was solid. He had done a few tours of duty in the army before joining the organization. He was very good with his sidearm and fair with his knife. He was dangerous, but his skill did not rival that of Jarren, nor would he be expecting an attack. If needed, Jarren would eliminate him first.

Jacob, the other member of their party, was a small-town police officer. He was steady, but was best suited for roughing up drunken Utes and the smart-alecky college kids who biked the scenic trails of southern Utah. His most redeeming quality was his zealous dedication to the Elder and to their cause.

As they neared the safe haven of the top peak of Angel's Landing, he relaxed and let his gaze drift to Ihara's trim figure. She was a fine-looking woman. A shame she had to die. He forced down the thoughts rising in his mind. Their sacred mission deserved his full attention, untainted by these stray thoughts.

"Almost there," Ihara called out.

"How is it," he asked, "that the entrance has been in this place all these years, yet no one has found it?" The question had gnawed at the back of his mind ever since he learned their destination.

"We don't know for certain that it has not been found," she said, not looking back at him. "It's entirely possible that others have found the entrance, but without the instructions we found, I assume you can't find your way to the treasure. I suspect the Spaniards made it very difficult to find."

"Maybe the monster ate them," Thaddeus said.

Ihara laughed and shook her head. They had arrived at the summit of Angel's Landing. She stood looking around, a half-smile belying her oddly sad eyes.

"Something funny?" Jarren asked. He hated being left out of jokes, always assuming them to somehow be at his expense.

"A local legend," Ihara said. "Some sort of chupacabra creature supposedly lurks around these canyons, killing the occasional goat or tourist. There have been a few disappearances, probably hiking accidents, but locals like to blame it on the monster."

"They found a body," Thaddeus said. "Mauled."

"Coyotes, most likely," Jarren scoffed. "Superstition is the tool of Lucifer, spreading fear in the hearts of those lacking sufficient faith." Thaddeus scowled, but Jarren ignored him.

"If you say so," Ihara replied. She fished into her pack and drew out a notebook. "I want to make sure we get this right. The first clue reads, 'Pass under the tenth step leading to the east.'"

"Step?" Jacob asked, shielding his eyes from the sun and looking around. "But there are no buildings here."

"Must be a natural formation resembling steps," Ihara said, "or steps hewn into the rock in a place that's not readily visible. In any case, the cave paintings discovered at Orley's ranch definitely indicate the presence of steps coming down from the peak. Let's look around." They made a cursory inspection of the top of Angel's Landing, and then made their way around the edge, carefully inspecting the steep cliffs below for any sign of the mysterious stairs.

"Tell me," Ihara said, "why didn't we come in your helicopter? We could have gotten a better look at the cliffs, then been dropped off up here without the big climb."

"Not worth the risk of notice," he replied.

"That didn't stop you before," she said.

"It was not so great a concern then. As long as we found the missing pieces, it did not matter if others grew curious about why we were there. Once we found what we needed, it did not matter if the authorities poked around. They would find nothing. But this..." his sweeping gesture took in the entire panorama "...this is where the treasure is. We positively do not want undue attention drawn to this place."

"There's something else I don't understand," Ihara said as they walked along. Her foot slipped and he grabbed her upper arm, steadying her. "Thanks. Anyway, I was reporting in regularly. I was doing the job. Why did your goons keep trying to get ahead of me?"

"That was my decision," Jarren said. He wondered if Ihara knew that he was one of the "goons." Likely, she would not care if she gave offense or not. "Initially, I did not know if you could be trusted, so we moved on Chaco Canyon as soon as I learned of your plans. You proved yourself at Chaco when you found what we did not, and you reported in as expected. At that point, I was content to let you continue on your own. Closely monitored, of course. That is until Bonebrake showed up. He had already given us trouble, and we could not take a chance with a wild card like him."

"You weren't worried about Maddock?" Ihara asked, shielding her eyes against the intense sunlight and looking down over the edge of the precipice.

"He had shown himself to be loyal to you, so we were content to let things move along as they were. Too bad cutting his rope at Mesa Verde didn't kill him."

"Right," she said, her voice tight. "Wait a minute!" She whirled around to face him. "You recovered the Ship Rock piece, and that was before Bones showed up."

"What do you mean?" Jarren asked. He suddenly felt cold all over. What piece was she talking about?

"The piece you recovered from Ship Rock."

"You said you had all the pieces," he replied.

"I said we had all the pieces. I have five. You have the sixth. Please tell me you brought the translation with you. I was so distracted by... everything I had to do today that I just assumed..."

"Ihara, I don't know what you are talking about. We did not recover any of the artifacts, and you certainly never reported anything about Ship Rock."

"There wasn't time," she said. "Saul actually figured it out, and by the time he told us about it, you had already..." Her eyes widened in shock. "Oh... my..."

"What?" Jarren was not certain he wanted to hear the answer. He was completely sure, however, that the Elder would not like to hear whatever it was that Ihara was about to tell him."

"Saul figured out the Ship Rock clue and took off without telling us. He came back and said that you had beaten him to it. He must have kept the piece himself. I'll kill him!"

"I imagine that has already been taken care of," Jarren said, relaxing a little. By now, Saul, Bonebrake, and the woman would be long-dead.

"We need to find out whether or not the missing piece was among Saul's things."

Jarren grabbed his walkie-talkie and called down to Ian who was waiting near the trailhead.

"I need you to contact the team. Have them search Saul's and Bonebrake's possessions. There should be a small stone artifact…"

"Sir," Ryan's voice came back fuzzy but discernible, "the team has not yet reported in."

"What?" Jarren checked his watch. Too much time had passed. Something was wrong. He quickly turned over the possibilities in his mind. Notify the Elder? No, that was the last thing he wanted to do. He needed to be certain before he told the Elder anything. There had been too many failures already. He couldn't hike back down and investigate it himself, and he certainly didn't want to sit atop this rock while he waited.

"You're going to have to go there," he told Ryan.

"Sir? My instructions were to remain here and…"

"Your instructions have changed. Get there and back as quickly as you can. You won't be able to communicate with us once we've found the entrance. Leave Jedediah to man the post, find out what happened to the team, and get back here as quickly as you can."

"What should I tell the Elder?" Ryan's voice quavered.

"Should the Elder contact you, which he will not, tell him that the last update you received from me was that everything was proceeding as planned. Otherwise, play dumb." Shouldn't be a problem for him, Jarren thought.

"Something wrong?" Ihara asked.

"Nothing you need to worry about. Let me ask you; do you believe we can find our way to the treasure without the missing clue?"

"I don't know." Ihara shrugged. "I assume every clue is important, but I don't see that we have any choice. Even if it was among Saul's things, we'd have to get it translated, and I don't relish waiting that long, do you?"

"Definitely not. We'll begin our search, and in the meantime, the others can work on searching for the piece. Worst case, we are unsuccessful and have to start again with the additional information."

"Suits me," Ihara said. She led them on a circuit around the top, before coming to a sudden halt, her eyes gleaming with triumph. "The solstice!" she exclaimed. "I'll bet they would have chosen a location that caught the sun most of the day. Somewhere where a rock formation could have cast a shadow…" She did not complete her thought but hurried toward the edge and lay down flat, her head hanging over the edge. She looked for a minute, and then cried, "I see it!"

Jarren joined her on the cliff edge and lay flat on his stomach, his head hanging over the edge. He could see why no one had discovered it before. Down below them, the rock receded into a deep overhang. A deep cleft wound through the rock and vanished into the shadows of the rocky ledge. No one would be able to see this from anywhere other than where he lay. The floor of the cleft resembled large stairs. This was definitely the spot. They wasted no time in working their way down. Ihara did not wait for them but counted down ten steps as her translation instructed, dropped to her knees, and began brushing away dirt and loose rock. She drew a long-bladed knife from the sheath on her belt and began probing the area.

"See anything?" Jarren asked, moving in behind her.

"Not.... wait a minute!" Her knife had caught in something. She carefully worked it to and fro, and then drew it back toward her in a straight line. "I think I've found an edge. Get your knife and help me." Soon they had uncovered a slab roughly three feet square. With Thaddeus's help, they pried the stone loose, and upended it to reveal a tunnel descending at a sharp angle and curving out of sight.

"What's this carved on the bottom of the stone?" Thaddeus asked. A shamrock with a cross in the center had been scratched into the underside of the rock.

"It's Fray Marcos' sigil!" Ihara gasped. "If we needed further confirmation, this is it. We are in the right place. Follow me!" Without another word, she thrust her legs into the hole, scooted forward, and slid out of sight.

"Ihara!" Jarren called, but she did not answer. "Hell," he mumbled. "We'll have to follow her. Jacob, you come down last and be certain to replace that stone before you follow." Gripping his flashlight in his left hand and his pistol in his right, Jarren took a deep breath and plunged into the darkness and out of sight.

Chapter 24

"**Angel's Landing. Strenuous** climb. Narrow route with cliff exposures. Hazardous during..."

"Bones, I know how to read," Amanda snapped. "I'll be fine. Besides, I've got you with me."

"If you say so," Bones said. "Of course, it's not so much the climb, but who might be waiting for us at the top that worries me."

"Then you'll just have to look after me that much more carefully." She smiled, took his hand, and led him up the trail.

The trek thus far had been strenuous, though nothing either of them could not handle. Truthfully, Bones was more worried about Maddock than Amanda. The few times he had gotten cell phone coverage, he had tried to call his friend but failed to reach him. He had spoken to Jimmy, who had not heard from Maddock but had managed to translate the final clues from Saul's piece of the scarab.

"One other thing I wanted to tell you," Jimmy said, *"is that I made a mistake translating a piece of the artifact. Instead of 'the tenth is impure,' I'm fairly certain it should read 'the ten is impure.' Doesn't make much sense, but there you go."*

Bones didn't have time to think about the subtle nuances of language. He wanted to find out what had happened to Maddock. Tough as he was if Jade had surprised him by delivering him directly into the hands of the Dominion..."

"It might be all right," Amanda said, reading his thoughts. "You've told me before he's the toughest, most resourceful guy you've ever known. Besides, it might not be what you think. She seems to care about him. Maybe she's double-crossing the Dominion and he's helping her."

"I don't know," he said. He didn't know what to think. He just wanted to find his friend.

A young park ranger appeared from around a bend farther up the trail. He approached them, an easy smile on his face.

"Afternoon," the ranger said. He was short and stocky with light brown hair and a faint splash of freckles across his sunburned nose. He removed his ranger's cap and fanned his face. "Enjoying your hike?" he asked, a twinkle in his bright blue eyes.

"It's beautiful," Amanda said, "but tiring."

"Walter's Wiggles," the ranger said knowingly, nodding in the direction of the steep switchbacks they had climbed a short while ago. "It'll do that to you."

"We're trying to catch up with some friends," Bones said in what he hoped was a friendly tone. "Did you pass anyone on your way down? We're pretty sure they went on ahead of us." He gave a quick description of Maddock and Jade.

"Sure!" the ranger said. "I definitely saw the girl. She's hard to miss! She was with, like, three guys, though."

"Was one of them my friend?" Bones asked, every muscle tense.

"Probably," the ranger said, shrugging. "I just noticed the girl." He arched an eyebrow at the sound of Amanda's muttered curse but did not comment. "They're probably up at the top by now. Even if they don't wait around for you, you'll definitely pass them on their way back down. There's no other way off this rock."

"That's great," Bones said. He stood, ready to resume their hike, when a glint of gold on the ranger's chest caught his eye. "What's that you're wearing?"

"Oh, this?" Hanging from a leather necklace was a heavy gold cross with a wide loop at the top. "It's an ankh," he said. "Pretty realistic-looking isn't it?"

"It looks very old," Amanda said, leaning in for a closer look.

"Yeah, but I'm sure it's not," the ranger said. "I found it in a stream here in the park. A visitor must have dropped it. Kept it in the office for a year and no one ever called about it, so they let me keep it."

"It's pretty cool," Bones said. "Well, we'd better be going. Nice talking to you."

"You too," the ranger said. "By the way, I wouldn't stay too long. I think there's a storm coming. I can smell something on the wind. It's going to be a big one."

"We won't dawdle," Bones said. He and Amanda shook hands with the ranger and continued up the path. When they were out of earshot, Bones turned to Amanda and said, "Well, what do you know about that?"

The top of Angel's Landing was void of human life. They stood in the eerie silence, catching their breath from the last stretch of trail, which had required hanging on to heavy chains bolted into the stone in order to make the climb. There was no sign of Maddock, Jade, or the other men with whom the ranger had reported seeing her.

"If Jade put these clues in the proper order, we're looking for something that resembles steps," Amanda said, consulting her notepad. "I don't see anything that looks like steps around here."

"They must have found them." Bones took in every detail of the top of Angel's landing. "I'll find them."

"And how do you plan to do that?"

"I'm an Indian. I'm going to track them." He had been a skilled tracker in his youth, and the knowledge had served him well during his military service.

"Right." Amanda sounded skeptical. "You're going to track on rock."

"It's not all rock," he said. "Look over there." He pointed to a small patch of dirt that had gathered in a low spot on the rock. "See that curved imprint on the left side? That's the edge of a shoe. Whoever left it went that way." He led her across the rock, pointing out an occasional scuff, a bent patch of dried grass, and even an occasional footprint, finally coming to a halt on the southeast edge of the cliff.

"End of the line," Amanda patted him on the shoulder. "Sorry. You did a good job on the tracking."

"Oh, it's not a dead end," he said, grinning broadly. Had they more time, he would have let the suspense build before explaining, but that was a luxury they did not have. "See this smooth patch here? Someone hung a rope over the edge and climbed down. Their weight, plus the rubbing of the rope smoothed out this patch. I'll bet if we get a good look down below…" He lay down on his belly and hung as far over the edge as he dared. He immediately spotted what he was looking for. "There they are!"

"Seriously?" Amanda hauled him to his feet and threw herself into his arms, crushing him in a hug and almost sending them both tumbling over the edge. "You are amazing," she whispered in his ear before giving it a playful bite. "Okay, Mr. Indian, this time you get to be the cavalry."

They used a nylon rope he carried in his pack to reach the steps. Once they were down in the rocky cleft that hid the rough staircase from sight, they immediately spotted the tenth step where someone, obviously Jade and her companions, had uncovered what looked like a large, square stepping stone. Bones pried it up, revealing a tunnel down below.

"It looks like one of those playground slides," he said, peering into the round, curving tunnel. "Should be fun. Got your gun ready?"

"Got it," Amanda said. Bones had lent her his snub-nosed .22.

"Good. We'll go down as quietly as we can. Keep your flashlight turned off for the time being. Whoever is ahead of us will have lights of their own. We want to see them before they see us." He turned on his own flashlight and cupped his hand over the end, spreading his fingers just enough to allow a sliver of light to illumine their path.

He had been correct when he compared the tunnel to a playground slide. It was smooth and round, corkscrewing in a sharp, downward spiral. Gravity pulled him inexorably downward, and he had to use his heels as brakes. I hope my pants still have a seat when I get to the bottom, he thought as he skidded downward. Their dizzying spin through the darkness seemed to go on forever, but finally, without warning, the tunnel dumped them out into an open space. He grunted as Amanda tumbled onto him.

"Where…" Amanda began, but Bones clapped his hand over her mouth and whispered for her to remain quiet.

They lay there in the deathly black silence, ears straining to hear any sound that might indicate danger. The roaring of his own blood filled his ears, and the rapid tattoo of his heartbeat seemed so loud that he was certain it would bring the mountain down on top of them. After a minute, he relaxed and let go of Amanda. He stood and helped her climb to her feet. Playing his light around the room, he found that they were in a cavern about fifty paces across. Vaulted passageways stood to their right and directly across from them. The wall to their left was unnaturally smooth and regular. Amanda turned on her light and went over for a closer look.

"It's some sort of plaster," she whispered. "This must be how they brought the treasure in. Nothing of any size could have come in the way we did." She turned away from the wall and consulted her notebook. "Okay, the next clue reads, "under the black stone at the western entrance."

Bones consulted his Pathfinder watch, which included an altimeter, barometer, thermometer, and a digital compass. "We're almost a thousand feet down. Still four-hundred feet above the canyon floor." He switched the watch from altimeter to compass. "And the western passageway is over there." He pointed to his right.

Directly in front of the passageway lay three paving stones similar in shape and size to the one through which they had accessed the tunnel: one gray, one reddish, and the third black. They raised the black stone to reveal a vertical shaft with handholds carved into the wall.

They descended another twenty-five feet and found themselves in a narrow tunnel with a squared-off roof. The ceiling was scarcely high enough to permit Bones to stand upright, and he had to resist the urge to duck as he walked. The pathway sloped down in a gentle incline. He kept moving his light back and forth, up and down, looking for any potential hazard.

"What are you doing?" Amanda asked in a soft voice. "That's driving me crazy."

"Looking for booby traps or falling rocks or whatever. I don't know. I guess I read too many pulp novels as a kid."

"What do you think would have happened if we had not known about the black stone and just gone down the tunnel?" she whispered.

"Hard to say. Might loop back around on itself, or maybe come to a dead end, or even something worse. The last time I was in a place like this..." He paused, forcing down the memories of what had happened then. "Never mind. Looks like we're coming up on another chamber."

This chamber was smaller than the previous one. Two massive caves, each flanked by ornate pillars hewn directly into the rock, gaped dark and forbidding directly in front of them.

"Okay," Bones said. "These are the clues Jade doesn't have. What's the first one?"

"Above the pillar of the northern opening of the cave that has two entrances. Okaaay."

"Both caves are set in the west wall of the chamber, so the northern opening would be the one to the left." They shone their lights on the cave wall above the pillars that stood on either side of the northernmost cavern. "I see something," Bones said. He had picked out a spot of deep blackness above the pillar to the left of the cave. Had he not been looking for it, his eyes would have passed right over it, dismissing it as nothing more than an irregularity in the rough stone. As he moved closer, he could make out a small shaft a few feet above the pillar. He began to search the wall for the best way to climb up when Amanda gasped and clutched his arm.

"Bones, look!" She pointed to the mouth of the cave. Thirty feet back, the passage was blocked by a pile of rubble. At the bottom of the pile of stone, her light shone on a human leg sticking out from beneath the mass of stone. "You don't think..."

They moved cautiously forward, their lights sweeping across the ceiling, but it appeared solid. Reaching the scene of the cave-in, Bones knelt and touched what was obviously a man's leg. It was cold. He hastily stripped off the man's hiking boot and wool socks, and placed his fingers on the dorsalis pedis artery atop the foot for a pulse, but there was none.

"He's dead," he said, rising to his feet and inspecting the pile of rock. "It's not Maddock. This dude's foot is way too big."

"Do you think they're all buried under there?" Amanda whispered.

"No way of telling," he said. "I don't think it would be a good idea to try to move this rock. That is unless..." He left the rest unspoken. *Unless we find the treasure, but don't find Maddock and the others.* "Let's just assume that one of the Dominion guys bit the big one. Score one for our side."

Something stirred in the darkness. The creature did not see it. Generations of its kind living in complete darkness had rendered it and those like it blind. It did not smell it... yet. It did not hear it though its sense of hearing was easily its most acute. Rather, it felt something moving. The creature and its pack were one with these caverns, perfectly attuned to their environment. Not a stirring of dank air escaped their notice. And nothing moved in these halls of stones without alerting the pack with both the sounds and the vibrations that rang through the walls of stone. Yes, something was stirring.

The creature rose and moved down the tunnel toward the source of the vibration. Its stunted, muscular legs and low-slung, broad body slunk easily through crevasses that would deny passage to larger creatures. Its heavily padded feet made no sound on the cold stone, and it kept its razor claws retracted until it needed to climb... or to kill.

The source of the disturbance was closer now. The creature could discern sounds alien to its experience. Harsher than the tumbling of water through the underground river that snaked through its domain. Steadier than the staccato clacking of a rock fall. This sound was new and enticing. It followed the sound with a single-minded purpose until a cloying scent assaulted its nostrils. Yes!

The creature knew this smell. It had ventured outside the caverns only one time in its life. It had run down and devoured a small, soft thing that had squealed as the creature's powerful jaws snapped its back. The warm blood, so unlike the cold, slick things of the river that were the staple of the pack's diet. Yes, this was a warm blood smell.

The creature sent out a call to the pack. There were no words, nor were there sounds. There was simply a shared understanding among the creatures of the pack. The message was simple.

We hunt.

Chapter 25

A lukewarm dampness pressed down on Maddock's face. He grabbed at it as he sat up, and his hand came away clutching a sodden, green dish towel. Where was he? He quickly took in his surroundings. Faded curtains permitted a hazy glow to fill the small room, revealing twisted covers and a moldy pillow on the small bed upon which he sat. Above him, a water-stained ceiling drooped like a low-hanging storm cloud, and below him threadbare carpet of burnt orange failed to entirely cover the cheap subfloor. The walls were covered in murky gray-brown paneling and were plastered with sketches. He was no art expert, but dating Kaylin Maxwell, a professional painter, he had enough familiarity that he could tell that this artist, whoever he or she was, was a talented amateur. Maddock recognized the peak of Angel's Landing from a picture Jade had printed out. There were other landscapes done in pencil or crayon, and all were pleasing to the eye. Others, however, were more sinister. Dark caverns filled with grotesque figures were rendered in broad, heavy lines of crayon. Something was chained over a river. And most disturbing of all were the shadowy renderings of a fanged creature with dead, black eyes, and glistening claws. The beast was always drawn in a night scene, and never in complete detail, which made it seem all the more malevolent.

A sliver of light appeared in the wall as a door opened. He tensed as a figure appeared in the doorway, the brighter light outside the door bathing its features in shadow.

"Wake?" A slurred voice asked. "Wake?" There was no malice in the odd voice. The figure stepped into the room, and the dim light from the window fell upon the most hideously deformed person Maddock had ever met. He was a young man, perhaps about twenty years old though it was difficult to tell. His right leg was six inches shorter than the left, emaciated, and was twisted so that his left foot was pointed to the side. His right arm was also noticeably shorter than his left though both were heavily muscled. It was his face that was the most disfigured. His right eye was tiny and beady, and the left bulged so far out of its socket that it looked like it would pop out if someone were to clap the young man on the back. His nose was not fully grown, giving it a pig-like appearance. His lips curled back in a permanent smile, revealing a few twisted teeth. His patchy, brown hair was long and fine, and seemed to float behind him whenever he moved his head. Despite his horrific appearance, though, there was somehow an air of gentle kindness about him.

"Yes, I'm awake," Maddock said.

"Dink!" The young man thrust a glass of water into Maddock's hands, sloshing half of it onto his lap. "Dink mo."

Maddock was parched, and he gulped it down. It was lukewarm and had a coppery taste, but he did not care. He finished it and was brought another, which he forced himself to drink more slowly.

"I guess you saved me out in the desert," he finally said to his Good Samaritan, who had sat down on the floor and was staring happily at him.

"Eah!" He nodded vigorously. "Eah!"

Maddock was torn between the urge to get back to looking for Jade, and the sympathy and gratitude he felt for the youth. In any event, he needed to figure out exactly where he was, and how to get to Angel's Landing from here. That was it!

"Did you draw these pictures?" he asked.

"Eah! Daw." The young man climbed unsteadily to his feet and pointing to various pictures and talking rapidly. Maddock could understand very little of what he was saying. When he indicated the pictures of the creature, he said something like "Choo. Choo." It didn't look like any choo-choo Maddock had ever seen.

"Is that place close by?" Maddock pointed to the picture of Angel's Landing.

"Eah." A noncommittal shrug.

"Have you been there?"

"Eah!" This time the young man seemed very excited. "Eh dah, eh dah, eh dah." He pointed to the cavern sketches. "You see." He dropped to the floor, reached underneath the bed, and pulled out a shoebox, which he opened with great care. He took out a handful of smooth pebbles and handed them to Maddock. "Got dah." He indicated a sketch of what looked like a twisting river running through a dark cavern.

"You found these in that cave?" His question was answered by a vigorous nod. He needed to connect with this young man if only to learn the way to Angel's Landing. He made a show of admiring the smooth stones, turning them over in his hand and rubbing them between his fingertips. But he did not have to feign interest in the next object that came out of the box.

The young man dropped a golden ingot into Maddock's palm. Maddock was no Egyptologist, but as a marine archaeologist, he had enough knowledge of Egyptian artifacts that he easily identified its origin and could tell that it was very, very old.

"Where did you get this?" he whispered.

"Dah." Again, the same picture.

"Is this a cavern and an underground river?" He stood and walked over to the picture.

"Eah!"

"And you've been inside it, and it's where you found this?" He held up the ingot.

"Eah. Eh dah, eh dah, eh dah." The boy stood and this time poked each cave drawing with his index finger. He held the open box right in front of Maddock's face. "Fi dese too!"

Maddock gasped. Among the collection of native rocks lay a golden ankh, several scarabs of various sizes, a few amulets, and some beads.

"Can you show me where you found these?" Maddock whispered.

"Eah!" He dropped the box, its contents scattering across the floor and bolted out the door. Concerned that he might be left behind, Maddock hurried out behind him.

The young man was standing in a small, dark living room babbling to an elderly woman who sat in a wheelchair with a blanket draped across her lap. She turned to Maddock and greeted him with a toothless smile. Beneath the blanket, her twisted legs came well short of the floor. Other than this deformity, she seemed to have escaped the young man's misfortune.

"I see you're awake," she wheezed. "Justin brought you back from the desert. Put you in his bed and kept damp cloths on you. He's a good boy."

"He is," Maddock said. "I thank you both for your help. What can I do to repay you?"

"Nothing," the woman said in her coarse, faint voice. "I taught him to do right by others, but we don't see many others out here. We mostly like it that way. Our family's lived here for generations, but there's nobody left but me and my grandson. We sure don't see many people out walking in the desert without any water. What were you thinking?"

"It's a long story and it wouldn't make much sense if I told you," he said. "Ma'am, would you happen to have a phone I could use?"

"Afraid not," she said. "And them fancy cell phones don't do no good out here either."

"Can you tell me if we're anywhere near Angel's Landing?"

"The Land of Zion?" she croaked. "You're heaven-bound, are you? We're not too awful far, but I think Justin wants to take you somewhere."

"Eah!" Justin said, taking Maddock by the hand and leading him to the front door of the house.

"You boys be careful," she said as they stepped out into the blistering sun.

Justin led him through a twisting dry wash, up a rocky hill, and through snarls of cactus and gnarled pine, and down into a tiny box canyon surrounded by steep walls of red rock. At the far end of the canyon abutting a sheer cliff a small pool lay hidden behind a screen of juniper and sagebrush

"Eah," Justin said, pointing down into the water. "Go dah." He made a diving motion with his right hand, dipping it down and bringing it back up. "Sim."

Swim under there. Maddock was growing accustomed to Justin's manner of speaking. He thought it over. Could this possibly be a way to the treasure? If they were close to Angel's Landing, who was to say Justin had not happened upon the treasure, or at least a small portion of it that had been carried away by the underground stream. In any case, there was no harm in checking it out.

"And the cavern where you found the treasure is in there?" He pointed to the cliff face.

"Eah." Justin nodded vigorously and again made the down-and-up motion with his hand.

"All right," Maddock said. "Guess I've got nothing to lose. Thank you for everything, Justin. You're a good man." He gave Justin's shoulder a squeeze and turned away, but the youth grabbed his arm and pulled him back.

"Choo choo," he whispered. His eyes no longer danced with infectious good nature but were serious. He looked Maddock straight in the eye as if trying to convey a message beyond his capacity to verbalize. "Choo choo." His voice took on a pleading tone. "Choo choo."

"Right. Choo choo." Maddock said. "Thanks again." He pulled off his boots, tied the laces together, and draped them around his neck. Taking a deep breath, he plunged feet-first into the water. The icy jolt as he broke the surface felt like an invigorating boost of energy. With powerful kicks and easy strokes, he swam down into the waiting shadows. A circle of absolute darkness tugged at him like a black hole. As he swam toward it, he could see that there was indeed an opening in the rock. He swam through, an eager sense of hopefulness surging inside him. The waning light from outside faded away, and he fished into the thigh pocket of his hiking shorts and took out the mini dive light he always carried with him. He hadn't actually expected to do any diving, but he preferred a waterproof light in any case. He clicked it on, and the intense beam knifed through the dark, clear water. The water above him churned in a torrent of milky bubbles.

He broke the surface in a large cavern. A roaring filled his ears, and he saw that the pool in which he swam was fed by a dozen narrow cascades of water pouring in from all sides. At the far end of the pool, the cavern wall sloped gently upward to the yawing mouth of a tunnel, above which was carved the shamrock and cross of Fray Marcos de Niza. He had found it!

Chapter 26

Jade muttered a curse as the tunnel ended in a blank wall. She had realized this tunnel was a mistake as soon as the booby-trapped ceiling caved in on Jacob. Obviously the missing clue contained something more vital than she had assumed. They gave up the idea of digging out almost immediately. There was no way to make it through the mass of rubble. They continued on, their nerves stretched like piano wire as they watched for further traps, but all they found was a long stretch of tunnel coming to this dead end.

"Any ideas?" Jarren asked, letting his light play up the wall and across the ceiling.

"Put your light back up there in the corner of the ceiling." She thought she had seen something. She added her light to his and the twin beams revealed a gap in the ceiling where the rock had crumbled away. There was a passage above theirs! "Boost me up."

Jarren hunched down and Jade clambered up onto his shoulders. He was very strong, and had no problem lifting her up to the gap in the ceiling. She peeked through, shining her light back and forth. It appeared that this passageway ran directly above the one in which they had been traveling, but unlike the lower passage, it continued on. She hoisted herself through, and then turned back to the others.

"Who's next? I can help one of you through if you need it, then we'll drop a rope and haul the last person up."

"I'll give Jarren a boost up," Thaddeus said. "I'm lighter, so it'll be easier to bring me up the rope."

A few seconds later, Jarren's head and broad shoulders appeared in the hole, and he clambered through. Jade had already fished the rope out of her pack and was looking for a place to secure it. Finding none, she instead secured it around Jarren's waist and tossed the other end through the hole.

"Ready when you are."

"Just a minute." Thaddeus's voice was soft and urgent. "I hear something in the tunnel. I'll be right back." He drew his pistol, turned off his flashlight, and headed off down the passageway.

"There can't be anyone in the tunnel," Jade said. "Both ends are blocked off, and we didn't see any side passages.

"He's an idiot," Jarren muttered. "I ought to go down there, but in the dark, he'd probably mistake me for a gentile. I should just go shoot him myself and be done with him."

Jade wanted to laugh, but the sounds that suddenly burst out through the hole in the floor chilled her marrow. A shout. A single gunshot. A shriek of agony that died into a wet, choking squelch.

"What the…" Jarren sprang to his feet. "Wait here. I'll be right back." He untied the belt from around his waist, slipped feet-first through the hole, and dropped with a thud to the floor below.

Jade sat in the darkness, her heart racing. What had happened to Thaddeus, and what would she do if Jarren did not come back? She entertained the frightened thoughts for only a moment before steeling her resolve. She would find the treasure by herself. How many years had she dedicated to finding the truth behind the story of Cibola? She had joined forces with an organization she despised, and betrayed a man about whom she cared deeply in order to fulfill her personal quest. She had heard of treasure hunters catching "the fever" and she knew it was true about her. Cibola was her passion, her purpose, her very life. She could not go on until she had seen it through. Perhaps, when it was over, she could find Maddock and make him understand that what she had done, she had done to protect him. Drugging him was the hardest thing she'd ever done, but if it kept him from walking into the hands of the Dominion, it would be worth it. Whether he would even believe her, much less forgive her, was another question altogether.

The thoughts fled as Jarren returned. It was all she could do to help him get back up to the second level, but they managed.

"I take it you didn't find him," she said.

"I found this." Jarren held up a Taurus PT92 that she assumed belonged to Thaddeus. "And lots of blood." Only now did she notice the reddish tinge on the Taurus's grips.

"Nothing else?" she whispered, unable to believe he could have just vanished like that.

"There were smears of blood along the passageway as if he'd been dragged away, but after about forty feet the trail just vanished at the base of the wall. I swear, I searched that wall from tip to toe and didn't find any sort of passageway, trapdoor, not even a seam." His voice was dull and he sounded understandably shaken. "I don't know who is in here with us, but I don't believe Bonebrake did that."

"All we can do is go on," Jade whispered. She did not wait for an answer, but turned and headed down the passageway. They continued for another five minutes until the tunnel gave way to a narrow staircase that wound around the inside of a deep pit. Grotesque gargoyles ringed the upper edge of the pit, each contorted into a different, agonized pose, all holding out their hands in supplication.

"Ugly," Jarren observed, shining his light upon one particularly gruesome figure. "What now?"

"Obviously, we don't know for sure that we're in the right place, and we're missing the fourth clue, but the fifth clue reads, 'On the third terrace in the cave.' And that," Jade shone her light across the pit, "looks like the mouth of a cave to me." As they crossed the pit, Jade noticed that the clover and cross insignia of Fray Marcos was embedded in the very center of the floor in polished marble. "This is encouraging," she said. "We found this symbol everywhere one of the clues was hidden." She shone her light around the room and saw that the insignia was also carved on the wall where the stairs began. "I have a good feeling about this. Let's go."

Chapter 27

"Get as close as you can!" the Elder shouted over the whir of the rotors. He looked down at the surface of Angel's Landing, taking in every detail. There was no sign of his people or Bonebrake. They must have found the way in. Where was it?

"The wind has picked up." The pilot looked nervously at the roiling black clouds sweeping toward them. "And I think it's only going to get worse. Are you sure you want me to leave you here?"

"You have your instructions." The Elder grimaced as fat raindrops spattered the windscreen. "I will contact you when you are needed. In any event, I want you out of here before the local authorities are notified of our presence. Hopefully this storm is keeping people inside and you won't be seen at all."

"Yes, Elder." The pilot grimaced and took them down. Strong winds buffeted the craft.

"Hold it steady," the Elder said. The rocky peak seemed to grow larger as they hovered lower and lower, until they were almost touching.

"Now!" the pilot shouted.

The Elder leaped out, followed by twelve handpicked men, all armed with Kalashnikov RPK 74M light machine guns. It was perhaps overkill, but he was finished allowing Maddock and Bonebrake to make a fool of him. First it had been the call from Bradley, gravely injured, telling him that Bonebrake had killed three of Bradley's men and escaped in their car. That made the second time the Indian had managed to steal a vehicle out from under the nose of the Dominion. Unable to contact Jarren, the Elder had then called that fool Ryan, who pretended everything was all right before finally admitting he had been instructed to find an artifact among Saul's possessions. Apparently he had held something back from Ihara, and now she, Jarren, and their party were apparently lacking critical clues to the treasure. It had taken a simple hacking of Saul's e-mail to confirm it, and to obtain the translation of the missing clue. The icing on the cake had been when Jedediah reported seeing a man and woman matching the descriptions of Bonebrake and Barnes climbing the trail to Angel's Landing. Of course, he had made no effort to stop them. The Elder had given Ryan the task of killing Jedediah. A fitting punishment for them both, as Jedediah and Ryan were brothers. Then the Elder had killed Ryan. Ihara had supposedly taken care of Maddock, but he no longer believed it. Too much had gone wrong to trust in any of his underlings anymore.

A jagged fork of lightning sizzled through the air much too close for comfort, and a deafening thunderclap seem to shake the very stone upon which they stood. He turned and waved his arm at the pilot, who gave him the thumbs-up and maneuvered the craft up and away. The helicopter had almost cleared the peak when the world was ripped apart. A blinding flash, and an explosion as lightning shattered a dying pine at the cliff's edge. The helicopter, already heeling over from the heavy wind, was directly in the path of the explosion. Chunks of tree tore through the spinning rotors, shattering the blades and sending shrapnel hurtling out in all directions. One of the deadly missiles cleanly decapitated Reuben, who was standing next to the Elder, but he did not notice; he was watching his helicopter tumble over the edge of the cliff and out of sight.

Rage boiled inside him, but he was its master. He stared for a moment at the empty space where the craft had been, listening for the explosion as it hit bottom. The fiery fate of the craft seared his determination. He would succeed where the others had failed.

Maddock clambered up out of the tunnel into a warm, dark chamber. A strong animal odor immediately assaulted him. It was a heavy, oppressive smell, like that of a great cat. He shone his light around the cavern. It was oval in shape, with many ledges, crevasses, and overhangs cratering the walls. A steady stream of water poured down from a crack in the ceiling above, pooling in a circular indentation in the stone floor, likely created by centuries of falling water. All around him was the smell of wild animal.

He inspected the chamber, finding small bones, mostly those of fish or snakes, and lots of scat. The droppings were long and cylindrical, and tapered at the ends like that of a wolf or mountain lion, but free of the bits of fur you would expect to see from an animal that ate deer and small rodents. He didn't know what these creatures were, but he had found their lair.

An angry snarl filled the cavern, and he whirled around to see three beasts out of a nightmare come hurtling out of one of the crevasses. He opened fire with his Walther, bringing down the creature in the lead. The other two beasts kept coming.

He leapt up onto a nearby ledge, turned, and pumped three more rounds into the second creature. Another shot went wild, and the third beast was scrambling up onto the ledge. Maddock kicked him twice in the snout, sending him tumbling back to the ground. As it crouched, ready to spring, he put a bullet between its eyes.

He leapt down from the ledge and dashed toward the only tunnel that looked large enough for him to pass through. He hadn't gone ten steps when another of the beasts came hurtling down the tunnel right at him. He stopped and squeezed off three shots before bringing it down. Five bullets left in the clip. Jade had hurried him out of the hotel so quickly that morning that he hadn't even thought to grab any reloads.

The tunnel opened up into a yawing cavern. A stone bridge no more than three paces wide spanned the depths. Maddock didn't spare a glance at the darkness below, but dashed across, keeping his light on the ground in front of him.

He was halfway across when he again heard the snarling sound that told him the beasts were coming again. One burst out of the darkness ahead, and he fired once, twice, but the creature kept coming. A third shot and it fell mere yards from him. He had no time to breathe a sigh of relief because now the sound was behind him. He whirled about, bringing his Walther to bear.

The creature was hurtling through the air, its gleaming white fangs shining in the darkness. He fell backward, firing as he went down. The beast hurtled past him, regained its feet, and leapt again.

Maddock regained his feet, and as the monster flew toward him, he let his Walther fall to the ground and struck out with his open hand, catching it below its snapping jaws, striking in the throat with all his might. Sharp claws raked his shoulder and he caught a whiff of fetid breath as he knocked it back. Before it could spring again, he kicked it hard in the side with both feet, sending it tumbling over the edge and into the darkness.

He allowed himself only a moment to recover and holster his empty Walther before regaining his feet and continuing along the path. Whatever lay ahead, he would have to meet it with his bare hands.

"What's our next clue?" Bones stood in the center of the pit, directly atop Fray Marcos's symbol, letting his light play across the faces of the gargoyles. He couldn't help but be amused at the way the moving shadows seemed to make them come to life.

"If you'll stop playing for a minute, I'll tell you," Amanda said. "Under the stairs in the pit." She turned and shone her light back toward the stairs they had just descended. "Under the stairs…"

"This is the other clue Jade doesn't have," Bones said. "If she made it this far, she probably went down that passageway over there, which means we're ahead of her." He inclined his head toward the tunnel on the other side of the pit. There was no way of knowing whether or not any of Jade's party had survived the cave-in, but he held out hope that Maddock was alive and well, and somewhere in this warren of dark tunnels.

"I just don't see anything 'under' the stairs," Amanda said. "They hug the edge of the pit. It's just solid stone. Maybe one of the steps comes up, or something."

"Could be," Bones said. He decided they should take the systematic approach. "Tell you what. We'll start at the bottom. You check each step, I'll work my way along the wall."

The steps had been carved into the natural rock, and everything about them seemed solid. He ran his hand across the smooth surface, seeking an imperfection, a recessed area, anything that would indicate a doorway. He was just beginning to think they were in for a long day when his light fell on a sight they had somehow missed.

"Amanda, get down here!" Her hurried footsteps padded down the heavy stone, and she was at his side in seconds. "I was so busy checking out the gargoyles that I didn't notice it."

"Fray Marcos's symbol," she breathed. "Do you think…?"

"It's got to be." He said. "The entrance to this place was under the tenth step. The symbol here is…"

"Under the tenth step!" She squeezed his arm with delight. "I wonder why ten and not seven?"

"Who cares? Let's go."

The clover outline was carved in shallow relief, but the cross in the center was cut deep. A closer look revealed a thin circle two feet in diameter encompassing the symbol. Bones slipped his fingers into the grooves of the cross and twisted. Nothing. He tried again. Still nothing.

"Maybe counterclockwise?" Amanda suggested.

"What am I thinking?" he muttered. "Righty tighty; lefty loosey." He changed his grip and heaved with all his might. The stone moved an inch, then another, and slowly began to turn until it had rotated ninety degrees and then stopped. Bones kept pushing, but to no avail. He stepped away from the wall, about to try out some of Crazy Charlie's favorite Cherokee curse words, when a hissing sound filled the pit and the stone shot back into the wall with a pop like a champagne cork.

"They hermetically sealed it!" Amanda whispered. "You must have broken the seal and the suction pulled the stone through."

"Glad I wasn't still holding on," Bones said, imagining tumbling down a dark tunnel with his fingers stuck in the disc like a drunken bowler on ten cent beer night. He shone his light through the hole and saw another set of stairs leading down into more blackness. He went headfirst through the opening, with Amanda close behind. From somewhere down below, a sound came like a whisper but, as they drew closer, grew to a roaring crescendo. Water. As they continued their descent, a hazy, green glow emerged in the distance, first as a fuzzy pinpoint of light, growing to an arched doorway ten feet tall.

They stepped out onto a walkway running above an underground river cutting through an oval-shaped cavern. Shining bands of green twisted in irregular paths through the natural rock all around them, giving the entire chamber an ethereal glow.

"What's making it glow like that?" Bones asked. "It's nothing biological; it's in the rock." He knelt to get a closer look at one of the glowing streaks. "Radiation?"

"Radioactive material doesn't typically glow," Amanda said. "But sometimes radiation can cause other minerals to glow. I wrote an article on it once." She stood and took his hand as they paused, admiring the sight.

On the far end, water poured out of a clover-shaped opening forty feet up the wall, and tumbled over a series of seven terraces before emptying into the channel that flowed beneath them. The walkway on which they stood ran directly down the middle of the channel, ending at the seven-terraced waterfall.

"Where is all this water coming from?" Amanda asked.

"We're pretty far below ground level," Bones said, consulting his Pathfinder. "I suppose some sort of underground stream runs through here."

"Well, this fits, at least. I think the next two clues go together," Amanda said, taking out her notes. "'On the third terrace in the cave on the eastern side inside the waterfall.' Looks like we're going to get wet."

"And to think I didn't even bring my umbrella," Bones said. "Who'd have thought we'd need one down here?"

From the stairwell behind them a cold voice spoke.

"I wouldn't worry about that. You won't be needing it."

Chapter 28

Issachar knew something was wrong the moment he entered the chamber. A foul stench filled the air, the faint sound of something... many somethings... running, and then...

A vicious snarl, and then a bloodcurdling scream. Confused shouts. Gunfire. Muzzle flashes. Confused interplays of light as the squad members searched for their attackers. And then he saw one.

A flash of gleaming white fangs, a slick, black snout, and burning eyes hurtled toward him from out of the darkness. He brought his Kalashnikov up and blew its head apart. So they could die. That was all he needed to know.

A flare blossomed in the darkness, setting the cavern aglow. Some of the creatures shied away from it, but others continued to attack. The surviving members of the squad fell in together, keeping up a steady fire and moving as one across the cavern.

Issachar picked off another leaping beast. In the glow of the flare he could see a little more of them. Their low-slung bodies were lithe, like greyhounds, and covered in dark hide. What were they?

"This way!" The Elder shouted. "Keep moving!"

Another squad member fell to one of the creatures. Issachar fired at it and missed. The beast began dragging the body away. He fired again and brought it down.

Reaching the far side of the cavern, Issachar and Benjamin laid down a steady rate of fire, trying to keep the creatures at bay as the men climbed into the passageway, but the creatures had fallen back into the darkness. Issachar caught a glimpse of booted feet as the beasts dragged the corpse of one of their men away into the darkness.

That's everyone, Elder," Benjamin said as Issachar scrambled into the tunnel. "The rest are dead. The creatures are..." he paused, his face twisted in disgust. "The creatures are dragging their bodies away. They're even dragging away the carcasses of their own dead." Sweat shone on his florid face, and he voice quavered.

"What are they?" Levi asked in scarcely more than a whisper.

"I don't know," Benjamin said. "Their heads are like wolves, but their teeth..." He shuddered and swallowed hard. "I wish I had could have gotten a better look at them. I've never seen anything like them."

The Elder had gotten a good enough look at them, however. In the first chamber, they had found Jacob's remains buried under a rock fall, and had just seen the passageway above the pillar, when surprised shouts and agonized screams shattered the silence. As the rattle of gunfire filled the air, he turned back to a horrific sight. Like a macabre slide show, each muzzle flash revealed demonic creatures, somehow doglike, reptilian, and catlike at the same time. He could make no more sense of them in the strobe-like flashes of gunfire and wavering beams of their high-intensity flashlights. They stood little chance against these lightning-quick creatures that could apparently see in the dark. He had dropped a flare and guided his men to the escape, but already his elite twelve had been reduced to seven.

"It doesn't matter what they are or what they look like." Issachar's voice was a low rumble like a rockslide. "They can be killed. That's all that matters." He stood, his hulking form seeming to fill the tunnel in shadow.

The Elder nodded. He stood and shone his light down the passage ahead of them, seeing nothing threatening.

"We are seven now," he said. "A fitting number for uncovering the secret of the legend of the Seven Cities. God has seen fit to cull our flock. We will not be taken unawares again. Naphtali, you will be the rear guard. Keep an eye out behind us." The hulking blond man nodded. "Benjamin, watch for any passages or trapdoors on our right, Asher you mind the left. Levi will be on the lookout for anything coming from above. I will take the lead." His words seemed to renew his men's confidence, and they set forth at a slow jog.

The Elder set his jaw, channeling his frustration into a sense of righteous rage. It was his destiny to bring the Dominion to power. No longer would they be a clandestine organization, little more than a well-funded paramilitary group. The treasure would bring them greater wealth, no doubt, and the notoriety associated with the discovery would certainly cause many true believers to finally abandon the Mormon church and join the Dominion. But the true prize was something none other than him even suspected. Not even Ihara knew what the Elder believed lay beneath these stones. He suppressed a shiver of excitement as he thought of the moment he would finally lay hands upon it and the Dominion would truly live up to its name.

"Put your hands up very slowly." A man stepped out from the shadowy passageway, his pistol trained on Bones. He was just a shade over six feet tall, solid and muscular. His flat-topped hair was prematurely gray and looked like it had been cut with a laser level. He fixed his intense gaze on Bones. "Ihara, will you please relieve them of their weapons?"

Jade stepped out from behind the man. She did not meet Bones' eye as she relieved him of his Glock and Amanda of the .22. She didn't check his boot sheath, which struck Bones as odd. He was certain she knew about the knife he always carried.

"I remember you now," Bones said. "You're the idiot whose car I stole at Mesa Verde." Bones said. "Where's Maddock?"

Jade did not answer. She stepped back to stand beside the man with the gun and went about storing the confiscated pistols in her pack before drawing her own weapon, a snub-nose .38 revolver, and trained it on Amanda.

"Maddock is dead," the man said. "You can thank Ihara for that."

"Shut up, Jarren," Jade muttered.

"I'll kill you," Bones whispered. "Slowly and painfully." He wasn't sure which of them he was talking to. Right now, he wanted them both dead. He might have taken his chances going after Jarren, but not at the risk of Jade killing Amanda. "You're both going to die."

"You'd better do it quickly," the man said. "As I'm about to kill you. I just wanted to give you some time to think about it before you died. You deserve to suffer a little. As a matter of fact," he lowered his gun from Bones' chest to his abdomen, "I think I'll make it slow and painful, as you suggested."

"You might want to think again." He was trying to think of anything to keep them talking. Anything to buy time in hopes that Jarren would make a mistake and give him an opening. "We've heard from Jimmy again. Seems he made some mistranslations in the final steps." It was almost true. "We saw what happened to your little friend in the first chamber, so you know what a bad idea it is to proceed without complete information."

"We'll take it off your dead body," Jarren said.

"I didn't write it down, you half-wit. It's in my noggin."

"We should keep them alive anyway," Jade said. "In case the treasure is booby-trapped. Let them lead the way and they can spring whatever traps are waiting for us."

"Not a bad idea," Jarren said. "But we don't need both of them to do that. And since Bonebrake here is the one with the knowledge, that makes his girlfriend expendable. Kill her."

It was like Bones had been dunked in freezing water. His eyes locked with Jade's and he saw her look from him to Amanda and then at Jarren. Her face was a mask of uncertainty. She looked at Amanda and frowned as if trying to communicate something. Her eyes fell, as did her hand in which she held her gun.

"Ihara?" Jarren turned his head to look at Jade. That was all Bones needed.

He sprang forward, striking Jarren's wrist with a vicious downward chop that numbed his fingers. He ripped the gun out of Jarren's grasp, but before he could get control of the weapon, Jarren knocked it out of his hands. Green light glinted off the barrel as it spun through the air and splashed into the water. At the mouth of the passage, Amanda had pounced on Jade and was grappling with her, trying to wrest the revolver from her. Bones landed a solid right to Jarren's jaw, sending him tumbling backward. He leaped past Jarren, stumbling as he dove for the weapon.

He, Jade, and Amanda landed in a heap at the mouth of the passageway. Bones grabbed the short barrel of the revolver and pointed it up toward the ceiling, aware that Jade's finger was still on the trigger.

"No!" Jade grunted. "You... don't ... understand."

Bones twisted onto his side, and with his right hand, pushed the hammer back and forced the webbing of his hand inside the hammer, preventing it from firing. With a snarl of pure rage, he ripped the pistol away from Jade. Before he could turn the weapon on Jarren, though, burning agony exploded inside him as Jarren landed a solid kick to Bones' groin. Dizzy with pain and grunting with the effort, he rolled onto his back, raising the revolver. Jarren kicked it out of his hands and dove onto Bones, his hands clutched at Bones' throat.

Bones had plenty of experience in ground fighting, but the direct blow to the groin had weakened him. He struggled to get the clutching hands away from his throat. He worked Jarren's right hand loose, and struggled in vain to wrap it up. He pushed with both feet and twisted, trying to turn the man over, knowing he did not have the leverage or remaining strength to do so. His air almost completely cut out, his vision swam and Jarren's eyes glowed in triumph. Bones twisted again, trying to free himself. Amanda could not help him; she was still struggling with Jade. He knew the fight had lasted only a minute if that, but the moments stretched into eternity as they struggled for their lives.

Jarren ripped his hand loose from Bones' weakening grasp and clenched his fist, ready to rain down blows, when something caught his eye. Bones' pants leg had slid up and Jarren had seen the knife. Before Bones could react, Jarren wrested it free and raised it above his head.

"Time to die."

Chapter 29

Maddock burst into the glowing cavern, his eyes taking in the scene in a split-second. Jade and Amanda wrestling on the floor, rolling precariously closer to the edge of the walkway and the dark water that waited below. A man with an upraised knife. Bones clutching desperately at the man's arm.

His Walther useless, having expended all his bullets fighting off the dark creatures that whose lair he had penetrated, he sprinted forward, leaping into the air and catching the man full in the chest with a flying side kick. The man fell onto his back, still clutching the knife. Maddock tumbled to the walkway, catching most of the impact of his fall on his shoulder, rolled over, and sprang to his feet.

"Jarren! No!" Jade shouted. She and Amanda lay on the ground, their fight forgotten, both staring open-mouthed at Maddock. Bones rolled over onto his stomach, choking and gasping for breath.

Jarren crept forward, his knife held low, a vicious look in his eyes, still panting from the fatigue of his fight with Bones. He chanced a glance behind him, apparently to gauge how long he had to dispatch Maddock before Bones was able to join the fray. He sprang forward, slashing at Maddock's inner thigh, trying to sever the femoral artery.

Maddock slipped out of the way just in time, the blade slicing a shallow cut across the outside of his thigh. He sprang forward, driving his elbow into Jarren's throat. Jarren reeled backward, gasping, but immediately resumed the attack, stabbing at Maddock's midsection. Maddock pivoted and with an open palm, knocked Jarren's knife hand to the side. As the blade thrust met empty space, Maddock trapped Jarren's elbow with his right arm and struck him twice in the side of the neck with vicious palm heel strikes. Jarren's knees buckled and the knife clattered to the ground. Maddock released his grip.

As Jarren staggered away, Bones stepped in front of him.

"I owe you this," he said, and drove a devastating right cross into the man's temple. Jarren's eyes went glassy. He took two steps to his right, and then went limp. He tumbled like a rag doll over the edge of the walkway and into the water below. They watched the current carry him out of sight.

Bones grasped Maddock by the shoulders and held him at arm's length, looking at him like he had not seen him in ages.

"Bro, I thought I'd never see you again," he said. His eyes grew suddenly hard and he whirled about, picked his knife up off the ground where Jarren had dropped it, and stalked down the walkway toward the women, who were standing and looking at him in trepidation. "All right, Jade. What do you want me to cut off first: your fingers or your toes? I would cut your eyes out, but I want you to watch yourself bleed to death."

"Bones! What the hell are you talking about?" Maddock shouted. He couldn't believe his friend was saying this.

"She's one of them," Bones snarled. "She's part of the Dominion. All along, it was her feeding information to them. As soon as Jimmy sent us the final translation, they sent men to kill us. They killed Saul and almost got us. She," he pointed at Jade, "was supposed to kill you. She told them she had."

Maddock felt like a detached spirit floating in blessed unfeeling. He had not felt this numb since Melissa died. Everything fell into place. She had used him, used them, to help her find the clues she sought. When she didn't need them anymore, she drugged him and left him to die in the desert, and left the others to be taken unaware by the Dominion men."

"Don't kill her," he said in a voice like ice. He couldn't bring himself to do that. "Find something to tie her up. We'll figure out what to do with her after we find the treasure."

"Maddock, no!" Jade cried, her voice cracking. "You read my note, didn't you? I explained everything!" Tears welled in her eyes, and she took a tentative step toward him.

"What note?"

"They wanted me to kill you, but there was no way I would ever do that. I gave you something to put you to sleep and left you somewhere safe I knew of, somewhere close by until I could come back for you. I explained it all in the note."

"You left me in the desert to die." He said.

"I left you in a sheltered place with six bottles of water, a bag of trail mix, and a note telling you to stay out of sight until I came back for you because the Dominion wanted you dead. Don't you remember when we stopped for coffee? The paper bag I carried out of the convenience store?" She was pleading now. "I tucked it between you and the wall of the overhang."

Maddock vaguely remembered her taking a paper bag out of the back of the car. He certainly could have missed a brown paper bag stuck in a shadowy overhang of red rock. Could it be true? He wanted it to be, but he didn't know if he could trust her.

"Maddock, if I wanted you dead, don't you think I could have killed you while you were asleep? Why do you think I left you so close to Zion instead of out in the middle of nowhere? How could you think I could do that to you after we... after..." Her voice faded away. Tears now flowed freely down her cheeks, but she did not look away from him. "Please," she whispered. "I really do care about you."

He couldn't take it. He had tried so hard not to let himself have feelings for anyone since Melissa had died. There had been Kaylin for a short while, and then after last night, he had thought... He turned his back on her and stared into the water tumbling from the center of Fray Marcos' symbol and down onto the glowing terraces.

"Explain a few things to me, then." Bones said, taking up the slack in the conversation. "You admit, then, that you're in the Dominion."

"No," Jade replied. "Maddock, please look at me. I'll tell you everything. I promise."

"Telling me everything from the start would have been a good idea," he said, turning around to face her. "Now I don't know if you're going to tell me the truth or a carefully crafted story."

"I know. When I first met you, I didn't want to scare you away by telling you. I actually knew your name, and yours," she said to Bones, "from reading about what happened in Jordan. Then things got dangerous, and I was afraid you'd bail on me, and I was scared and I needed you. When I realized I was falling for you, it had been so long that I didn't see how I could tell you after waiting all that time."

"Fine, just tell me whatever truth it is you want to tell me." He folded his arms across his chest and stared at her.

"My passion has always been solving the mystery of the Seven Cities. Saul was one of my students, and one day he approached me with something I had only dreamed of ever finding: the missing final page from the journal of Fray Marcos de Niza."

"Great. Another journal," Bones muttered, fingering his knife.

"Fray Marcos uncovered evidence of a "great and terrible" secret. That secret was somehow associated with an order that acted under the sign of the cross-and-clover, the one we now know as Fray Marcos's sign. He journeyed through the New World and managed to confirm the truth of that secret. Seeing the depredations they committed upon the native people, and not wanting the Conquistadores to discover his secret, he concocted the story of the Seven Cities of Cibola, both to explain his wanderings and to throw the Spanish off. He did not, however, think it was his place to hide this secret from the world forever, so he and Estevanico concocted a plan. He remained in the southwest, planting clues in places he and Fray Marcos had chosen. Fray Marcos returned to Mexico, telling everyone that Estevanico had been killed and spreading his tale of seven cities containing more gold than the Incas ever dreamed of.

"Unfortunately for Fray Marcos, Coronado couldn't wait to get his hands on the gold. He took Marcos as his guide and set out to conquer the Seven Cities. When the Spaniards never found the cities of gold, Fray Marcos was branded a liar, and eventually died in disgrace. According the journal page Saul gave me, he hid a single clue that would unlock the secret. He hid it in a well in a remote outpost in Argentina."

"The breastplate," Bones said, still holding his knife.

"Right," Jade said. "When Saul showed me this, I dove into the research and learned of a recently discovered Spanish outpost in Argentina. I wanted to get down there and investigate right away before someone beat me to it. Saul introduced me to his father, who offered to fund my expedition through the organization of which he was a member. I would get all the credit for the find. The catch was, when I found the final location, his organization wanted to cherry pick a few of the artifacts before I documented the find. I thought it was a simple matter of black market artifact trading, which I loathe, but I didn't see any other way I could fund the expedition on such short notice. By the time I learned I was being funded by the Dominion, it was too late to back out. In part, I was afraid of what they might do if I broke our deal, but I have to admit that I had the fever. I probably would have taken their money had I known from the start, as long as it meant realizing my life's ambition."

"I don't get why they needed you," Amanda said. "If they had the journal page, why not go after the clue themselves?"

"I can't be one hundred percent certain." Jade's eyes took on a faraway glint. "The only things they had were the journal page, which makes no sense if you don't know the rest of the story, and some local legends about a hidden treasure. They needed my knowledge and expertise. If you have a choice, why send a team of grunts when you can send an archaeologist who's studied the Seven Cities for her entire life? Besides, even if they had managed to find the well and uncover the breastplate, which I doubt they could have done without the benefit of my research, they would have had needed an academic to help them get the clues deciphered. They also had Saul to keep tabs on me, and I was required to report back to Saul's father on a regular basis. I guess the answer to your question is, 'Why not me?'"

"Then why did they show up at Chaco Canyon, Mesa Verde, and Hovenweep?" Maddock asked. "Why did they snatch the clue at Shiprock before we did?"

"Actually," Amanda said, "Saul found that clue. He didn't tell us because he knew Jade was working with the Dominion."

"He did?" Jade looked flabbergasted. "I didn't think he knew. He didn't seem to know his own father was in the Dominion." She shook her head. "He must have wanted to find the treasure before them. Why didn't he tell me?"

"You still haven't answered my question," Maddock snapped. He wanted desperately to believe her, to feel about her the way he had before learning of her connection with the Dominion. Anything that did not make sense, anything that did not strengthen her story, eroded the trust he was trying to rebuild.

"That was Jarren's doing." She gestured toward the spot where Jarren had been swept away by the current. "He works for someone who is known only as The Elder. He's the head of the organization. Jarren wasn't sure I could be trusted, so he took it upon himself to try to find the first piece without us. When I reported in, as instructed, he backed off. That is until Bones showed up."

"Why did that matter?" Bones had sheathed his knife, and now squatted on the walkway, listening with keen interest.

"You were a new variable. You had already made trouble for them by taking the sun disc, and by rescuing Orley. At Mesa Verde, Jarren and another thug showed up at Square Tower House. They wouldn't answer my questions, but they wanted the clue and they wanted you dead though I think they were acting on their own in that respect. I told them you had just reported back to me that Square Tower House was a dead end, and I convinced them that I was going to ditch you anyway because I didn't need you. One of them cut your rope and knocked me out 'just to be safe.'"

"So you didn't set them on Saul and me at Sun Temple?" Bones asked. Amanda had sat down next to him. Both seemed to believe what Jade had told them so far.

"No. I had reported that we were looking at both locations. I kept giving them only the minimum information: what we found, and where we thought the next location might be, so they never knew about the solstice connections or any of our speculation. We were a little off regarding the site at Hovenweep, so we unintentionally threw them a curve there. And you guys held back the information about Rainbow Bridge until we were already there."

"We thought Saul was the mole," Amanda said, "but we weren't sure."

Jade nodded.

"When Jimmy made the connection that led to Zion," Jade continued, "I reported in that all the pieces were in place. I believed Saul that the Dominion already had the Ship Rock piece. They, in turn, assumed that when I said 'all pieces' that I meant I had all of them. I thought I could ditch you guys at the hotel, complete the mission, and then when the Dominion picked whatever artifacts it was they wanted, I could let you in on everything. But they told me to kill Maddock."

"Why only me?" Maddock asked. Now they were at the heart of it.

"I think they suspected there was something between us." She was looking him right in the eye. "It was a test of my loyalties. What I did to you was the only thing I could think of on short notice. I almost told you the truth that night, but I didn't know what you'd do. I was half afraid you'd hate me and half afraid you'd insist on going with me and manage to get yourself killed. I never planned to hurt you, and I did not know they would send men after the rest of you." She now knelt and spoke to Bones. "When I came into this chamber and saw you and Amanda here, I was in shock. It was like my brain was frozen. Jarren had his gun on you, and I didn't know what to do that wouldn't get you killed. You had to have noticed that I didn't take your knife, not that it did you any good." She took a deep breath. "I've never killed anyone. Never even dreamed of it. But I swear to you, I had just made up my mind to shoot Jarren when you jumped him. I swear."

Bones did not say anything. Apparently he was having as much trouble making up his mind as Maddock was.

"I really don't like you," Amanda said. Both women stood and faced one another, Amanda's eyes ablaze and Jade's dull with remorse or regret. "But I believe you." She held out her hand, and after a moment, Jade took it in hers.

"Okay," Bones said, rising to his feet. "I don't know if I forgive you, but I believe you."

"Thank you," Jade whispered. She let go of Amanda's hand and turned to face Maddock, the questioning look in her eyes making words unnecessary.

Maddock did not know what to say. Though every fiber of his being ached to believe her, to forgive her, to take her in her arms and make things be the way they had been, he just could not. It just wasn't that easy.

"Let's find this treasure," he said, his voice hoarse with emotion. He could not help but see tears flood Jade's eyes as he turned his back on her.

Chapter 30

The icy water drenched Maddock as he ducked through the waterfall, chilling him to his core. It brought him to his senses after feeling dazed by Jade's revelations. Behind the waterfall, a door in the face of the rock led to a spiral staircase. As Maddock led the way up, Bones filled him in on the events that had brought him and Amanda to this point, including the attack at the motel, Jimmy's updated translation, and their trek through the chambers beneath Angel's Landing. Finally, the stairway ended at an ornate stone door. The door was carved with an elaborate scene of a storm at sea, complete with angry clouds, crashing waves, and a sea monster writhing in the depths. Where a knob would be found on an ordinary door, the cross and clover was carved, hovering just above the horizon. Hebrew words were carved above the doorway.

"I've seen these words before," Jade said. "When I was studying the first temple. 'Shaar HaMayin. The Water Gate. I wonder what's behind there."

"Only one way to find out," Maddock muttered. His anger had lent him a sense of reckless disregard. He pressed the symbol and the door slid back, revealing another glowing cavern. Here, the glow was more intense, the light brighter, and the chamber was noticeably warmer, almost humid. A cross-shaped channel ran down the center of the room, the water disappearing into a hole at their feet. On the far end of the chamber near the point of the cross, and on either side, lay circular pools, their dark waters speaking of great depth. "The cross and clover," Maddock said, noticing the layout of the pools. "This must be the source of Fray Marcos' symbol."

"Either that or Estevanico spent a lot of time with a hammer and chisel," Bones said with a smile. "So, what's the next clue?"

"At the edge of the canal on its northern side, six cubits toward the immersed pool," Amanda recited. "Which way is north?"

"To the left," Bones said, consulting his Pathfinder.

They skirted the edge of the cross-shaped canal. Reasoning that the northernmost point of the cross would be the logical place to begin, Maddock led the others to the far left point of the cross.

"A cubit is the distance between a man's fingertip and elbow." The hurt was still evident in her voice. "So, probably about eight feet toward the pool."

Maddock paced off the distance, dropped to his knees, and shone his flashlight across the floor. He saw nothing but smooth stone.

Bones dropped to the floor next to him and ran his fingertips across the smooth stone. He frowned.

"Shine your light here, Maddock. I think I feel something." Maddock turned his light on the spot Bones indicated, and saw the cross and clover traced into the rock in such fine lines it would have been almost impossible to see if they had not been searching so intently for it. "But what do we do?" Bones asked. "It's just a picture." He pressed it, but nothing happened.

"Boys, how about that big chain hanging up above you?" Amanda asked, her voice playful

Maddock looked up. A massive chain hanging down from the ceiling, ending about eight feet above them.

"How long have you known that was there?" Bones asked.

"Since we walked in," she said. "There's another one on the opposite side." She pointed to the far side of the channel where Jade stood looking up at the twin of the chain under which they stood. "I imagine there's an unpleasant surprise waiting for the first person who doesn't know his north from his south."

As she said those last words, Jade reached up to take hold of the chain.

"Jade! No!" Maddock took off at a sprint, leaping across the center channel and dashing over to her. She looked into his eyes in complete astonishment as he clutched her tight against him.

"I wasn't going to pull on it," she whispered. "What's gotten into you?"

"You have," he said, so soft that only she could hear him. For in that moment he thought she might die, he knew his true feelings for her. All uncertainties and hurt aside, he had cared only that she lived. He cared. "We have a lot to work out between us, but I do care about you."

She did not reply but twined her arms around his neck and kissed him very seriously. After what seemed like an hour, Bones interrupted them by loudly clearing his throat.

"Excuse me, but don't we have a treasure to find here?"

"I found my treasure," Maddock said, holding Jade tight to his side. "Let's get out of here."

"Are you serious, Maddock?" Bones' eyes were wide and his mouth agape.

"Hell no," Maddock said after a suitable pause for effect. "I was yanking your chain. How about you yank that one and see what happens?"

"I suppose you think that's funny too," Bones said to Amanda, who was covering her face.

"Of course not," she said, her smile belying her words. "I would never make you the butt of a joke."

"Forget it," Bones said. He took hold of the chain and pulled. A sound like thunder filled the room and the floor shook.

"Bones! Are you sure this is the north side?" Maddock shouted over the roar.

"Trust me!" Bones called back. "Look there!" He pointed to a spot on the ceiling directly above the pool, where a circle of stone about twelve feet in diameter had begun to turn. As the stone rotated, it gradually descended, revealing another spiraling stone staircase. It settled to the floor with a thud, fitting perfectly over the top of the pool. "Told you," Bones said. "Trust me."

Maddock again took the lead. As they ascended, he finally told them how Justin had rescued him in the desert and showed him the pool that gave him access to a back entrance through a long, spiraling tunnel, much like the one at the top of the peak through which the others had entered. Finally, weary from the climb, he had emerged in the center of the gargoyle-lined pit. He had immediately been set upon by the dark creatures from Justin's drawings. He had retreated back into the tunnel, where he could pick them off one at a time. Finally, he made his way back out, praying he would not meet any more of the beasts, as he had exhausted his ammunition.

Upon learning that his friend was unarmed, Bones gave Maddock the .22 Jade had returned to him. She had given Bones his Glock back as well, but her revolver was lost. When they reached the top of the stairs, they were again faced with a stone door. This one was engraved with a large circle at the top, with seven lines descending from it, each ending in a hand.

"That's the same symbol that was painted in Orley's cave," Bones said. "And on the sun disc." He took the disc out of his pack and held it up for comparison. They were identical. "Do you think whoever painted it was here?"

"Whoever the artist was," Amanda said, "he certainly knew the way to Angel's Landing. His paintings led the way. And that giant spiral slope Maddock climbed sounds a great deal like the spiral staircase that was painted in the cave. I'll wager," she said, reaching out to touch the disc, "that even if the artist was never here, the disc was once here."

"It's also the symbol of Aten," Jade said. "I think this just about seals the connection if there was any doubt."

"Can you translate what's inscribed above this door?" Maddock asked.

"Shaar HaKorban. The Gate of the Offering."

"Sounds promising," Bones said, putting the gold disc back in his pack. "Maddock, do you want to do the honors?"

This door pivoted as the others had done, and as he stepped through Maddock was greeted by a sight that took his breath. Like the chamber below, a cross-shaped channel flowed through the middle, but this was a massive, vaulted chamber with ornate columns, all shot through with the same intensely glowing streaks, that climbed to a ceiling far above them, supported by shining arches. Here, the light burned with such intensity that it had lost most of its greenish hue and was almost white. A similarly vaulted chamber was carved into either side. It was like a giant cathedral! It was not, however, the magnificence of the room that amazed him, but the treasure.

The floor was carved into seven terraces rising up from the channels in the chamber's center. Every inch was packed with more wealth than Maddock had ever imagined. Huge chests had dry rotted and burst, spilling their contents upon the floor. Coins and ingots of gold, gold, silver and bronze coins lay scattered on the floor. Bars of gold and silver were stacked like firewood. Casks that probably contained oils or perfumes stood on the upper levels, interspersed with sculptures and pottery. Much of it was obviously Egyptian, but not all of it. As they made their way through the room, they saw other treasures. Some barrels held precious jewels, while others held ivory, or moldering bolts of what must have once been the finest cloth.

"Man, something's messing up my phone," Bones said, holding up his cell phone. "I wanted to take a picture. Bummer." He looked down at a pile of Egyptian artifacts that had spilled down from somewhere up above and lay strewn haphazardly across the bottom level. "This must be how that ranger found his ankh, and Justin found his treasures. They washed down the channels and eventually made their way out."

"Let's see what's in the transepts," Jade whispered, using the name of the side chambers that gave cathedrals their cruciform shape. She took Maddock's hand and led him forward. The left transept was shallow, perhaps forty feet deep, and held no treasure, but at the far end, perched atop the seventh tier, stood a golden lampstand larger than any Maddock had ever seen. Three golden arms curved up on either side of its central column, and its solid base was inlaid with rubies. Jade squeezed his hand in a crushing grip. "Maddock! It's the menorah! The menorah!"

"I can't get my camera to work either," Amanda said as she and Bones walked up behind them. "It's almost as if…" She stopped in mid-sentence as her eyes fell on the menorah. "I can't believe it. I thought the Romans took it."

"That was the one that was made after the Babylonian Exile," Jade said, her voice soft with reverence. "This must be the original. Many believe that the shape of the menorah is influenced by the Aten symbol."

"So what's in the other transept?" Maddock found that he could not bring himself to speak above a whisper in the face of such a holy sight. Moving as one, they all turned slowly about, and again were stunned by what they saw.

This transept, too, held no treasure save what stood at the end.

"I have to get a closer look at this," Maddock whispered. He hurtled the center channel, the others following behind, all in rapt silence. The steps of this chamber were lined with white marble, and the walls were lined with cedar. On the bottom level of the left side of the transept, spaced at three-foot intervals, stood a line of twelve golden lions. On the right, facing their counterparts, were twelve golden eagles. Each step at the far end of the transept was also flanked by a golden creature: A lion facing an ox, a wolf and a sheep, a tiger and a camel, an eagle and a peacock, a cat and a cock, and a sparrow opposite a dove.

"Six steps lead up to…" Jade whispered.

On the seventh step stood a throne of such magnificence that it almost hurt to look upon it. The seat was made of ivory, its frame of gold. Atop the seat stood a golden candelabra topped by a golden basin. Twenty-four golden vines entwined above the throne and topping it all was a dove clutching a tiny hawk in its claws.

"…Solomon's throne."

Maddock dropped to his knees, and the others did the same. He took Jade's hand in his left and Amanda's in his right, who in turn took Bones' hand. They remained there, in reverent silence, gazing upon what, until now, had only existed in memory and legend.

"I don't understand," he finally whispered.

"Understand what?" Jade asked, turning to stare at him.

"There are more clues," he said, unable to take his eyes off the throne of the greatest king in Hebrew history. "This isn't the end. But what else can there be?"

Bones stood and one-by-one hauled everyone to their feet. He looked at Maddock with an unreadable expression.

"As to that question, my friend, there's only one way to find out."

Chapter 31

At the far end of the chamber, the steps led to a simple doorway, so out of place amongst the splendor of the treasure that surrounded it.

"In the sepulchre, in the third course of stones," Amanda read. "Is that a sepulchre?"

"In ancient Hebrew practice, a sepulchre was usually carved into the side of a hill," Jade said. "Perhaps that's what the simplicity is supposed to symbolize."

Golden statues of Anubis guarded the door, each holding a spear. Bones paused for a closer look."

"Hey! They come out!" he exclaimed, removing one of the spears and hefting it. "It's heavy!"

"Put it back," Amanda said as if speaking to a child.

"You're no fun," Bones said, but he returned the spear to its proper place and followed her up the steps.

The chamber they entered was nothing more than a perfect square carved into the rock. Down the center of the room stood a line of seven piles of loose rock. Maddock and Bones immediately set to moving the third pile of stones, and soon they uncovered a manhole-sized cross and clover disc. Together, they lifted it from its place and moved it to the side. Maddock could hear the rush of water down below, and another sound he recognized immediately.

"Get out of here!" He shouted, pushing Jade toward the door and drawing the .22. A dark blur burst from the hole, snarling with unearthly rage. Maddock pumped three rounds into the beast, but when it hit the ground, it turned toward him and tensed to spring. Before it could leap, Bones blew a hole in the back of its head with his Glock. They weren't out of the woods yet, as two more of the beasts clambered out of the hole. Maddock emptied the .22 into the first, then drew his knife, and backed up to the door, ready to protect Amanda and Jade. Bones put four rounds into the second beast, then moved cautiously to the hole and peered down inside.

"Here, kitty, kitty," he called. No sound came from the hole save the steady flow of the underground stream. "Hopefully that's it," he said. "What are these things?"

In the light, Maddock could clearly see the beasts for the first time. He squatted down next to the nearest of the fallen creatures. Amanda and Jade returned to the room, Jade clutching her knife and Amanda holding one of the Anubis's spears. Amanda shrank back from the dead creatures, but Jade dropped down on the balls of her feet next to Maddock.

The creature's body was long and sleek, with a broad chest and a sturdy rib cage. It was hairless, its flesh a mottled, dark green and as tough as old leather, with a pronounced spinal ridge that jutted up like the plates of a stegosaurus. Its haunches were so thickly muscled that they reminded Maddock of a kangaroo. The front legs were also short and powerful. Jade lifted one of the padded front paws and squeezed it, causing its wicked, black claws to extend, and retract when she let go. The head was vaguely catlike, save for the long snout, with oversized ears and large, black eyes. Its mouth was filled with razor sharp teeth, two of which extended below the lower jaw line like fangs.

"Chupacabra," Bones whispered. "It's got to be!"

"Choo choo. Justin was trying to warn me of the chupacabra. He must have seen one at some point in the past, and it scared him enough to draw those pictures. Unbelievable."

"So, do we go on?" Bones asked. "There could be more, and I don't have many bullets left."

"There could be more behind us as well," Jade said. "I didn't come this far to stop now. I vote we go on."

It did not escape Maddock's notice that Jade was no longer taking the lead, but treating everyone as an equal member of the group. This was no longer her expedition, but a shared experience.

"Me too," Amanda said. "Let's finish this."

Maddock went feet-first through the hole, landing on a stepping stone inscribed with the symbol that had become so familiar. He was in the middle of a fast-moving underground river. Stepping stones like the one on which he stood were set at three-foot intervals in five rows running the length of the passage all the way to the end, where another arched doorway waited. He was about to hop onto the next stone when something caught his eye. He stopped himself at the last second, almost losing his balance and flailing his arms as he fought to keep himself from tumbling into the fast-flowing current.

"Are you doing some kind of bird imitation down there?" Bones called to him. "What's the holdup?"

"There are stepping stones down here," he called back. "But they're not all the same. Some of them have the symbol on them, but some only have the clover. Pass the spear down here." Bones handed him the spear, and he reached out and tapped the stone upon which he had almost jumped— one with only a clover. It sank beneath the surface, floating back to the top when he pulled the spear away. He tested his theory on another stone that had both the cross and clover on the surface. It held. But would it support his weight? Here goes nothing! Bracing himself for a swim, he hopped onto the stone. It held.

"All right!" He called up to the others. "Come down one at a time, and only jump on the stones that have the cross and the clover. Make very sure where you're stepping. Got me?" He led the others on a zigzagging path through the river, testing each stone with the spear before moving on. Soon, he hopped out of the river to stand at the doorway.

"Beit Adonai," Jade again read the inscription. "The house of God."

Maddock stepped through the doorway, and the spear clattered to the ground from his limp fingers.

The chamber was carved into the shape of the interior of a pyramid, and all its walls were gold plated, save the cap of the pyramid, which was natural stone. The light that shone down from that small section at the top, and up from the floor, was so intense that it set the entire space aglow with a flickering golden light as it reflected off the water and the shining walls. High above him, a golden chain hung from the capstone, supporting a platform though he could not see what it held. Water poured down through the seams of the capstone as well, soaking the hanging platform and falling in a curtain that enshrouded an island in the very center of the pyramid floor. Through the haze of falling water, Maddock could just make out a stone sarcophagus on either side of the island. The island seemed to beckon to him, and he continued, as if in a trance, along the walkway that led to the island.

Jade moved to the first sarcophagus and ran her fingers across it. The lid was carved in the image of a woman of unsurpassed beauty. Her striking face and swanlike neck were reminiscent of the famed bust of Nefertiti. She was not rendered in the Egyptian style, with royal headdress and accoutrements, but as she might have truly looked, with long, flowing hair and simple garments.

"Nefertiti," Jade whispered.

"And the other one?" Maddock asked.

"Let's see."

The man on the lid of the other sarcophagus had the long face, prominent nose, broad cheeks, and hooded eyes of Akhenaten. His shoulders were narrow and his hips wide for a man, but nothing like the exaggerated images portrayed in art. Like Nefertiti, he was not rendered in his kingly Egyptian garb, but as a regular man. His hair was long and flowing, as was his beard. His slender arms lay folded across his chest, and in his right hand he gripped a staff engraved with Hebrew writing.

"The staff of Moses was reputed to bear the names of the ten Plagues of Egypt," Jade said.

"So this is..." Bones said, his voice quavering.

"The mose," she said. "Moses."

"I have to see this for myself," Maddock said. He didn't know why, but the compulsion was so strong that he could not help himself. He needed to see. "Bones, will you help me with this."

"Maddock, maybe you shouldn't," Amanda began. "I mean, it's..."

"Babe," Bones said, "this is the only man on earth who's seen the dead body of Lucifer himself and lived to tell the tale. Amanda smirked, obviously assuming he spoke in jest, but Jade paled visibly.

They carefully drew back the lid. Maddock peered into the stone coffin. There was no second, ornate sarcophagus, as was the Egyptian tradition. There were no mummified remains.

Moses lay in the bottom of the sarcophagus, his body somehow perfectly preserved despite the thousands of years.

"He looks like he could stand up and walk out of here," Jade said, peering over the side along with Maddock and Bones.

"Wrong testament," Bones said.

Maddock reached down and touched Moses' staff. Unlike many of the legends, it was not made of sapphire, but of solid wood, polished to a high sheen. The Hebrew words were there, worked in gold along the length of the staff. The ends were capped in bronze, with the symbol of Aten etched in the top.

Amanda screamed and turned to see two dark-clad men burst into the room. They dashed across the walkway, the first clutching a military-style knife, the second holding the spear Maddock had dropped. Bones brought down the first man, a powerfully-built blond man, with two well-placed shots. His final shot went wild as the man with the spear, a veritable brute of a man with dark hair cut G.I. style and arms and legs like tree trunks, bore down on them.

Without thinking, Maddock grabbed the closest weapon, Moses' staff and dashed out to meet him. The man thrust the spear at Maddock's chest, but Maddock parried the blow and cracked his opponent's elbow. It wasn't much of a blow; enough to sting, perhaps, but the man hissed as if he had been burned. Maddock pressed his momentary advantage, driving the larger man back. Staff met spear with crisp, sharp clacks. His opponent was not tiring, he was obviously in peak condition, but his inability to penetrate Maddock's defenses was clearly frustrating him because he began taunting Maddock, trying to distract him.

"You think you can win, little man?" He bared his teeth in a predatory grin.

"Issachar has killed better men than you."

"Does Issachar always speak of himself in the third person?" Maddock shot back. The surreal nature of this entire experience gave things a dreamlike quality, and with it, a subtle feeling of unreality, as if nothing could harm him, no matter how reckless he might be.

"Funny man!" Issachar growled. "You'll die whimpering like those pathetic beasts I killed in the tunnels. I ran out of bullets and had to strangle the last one with my bare hands." His blows rained down harder, but Maddock turned them with ease. A quick side thrust to the chest and Issachar gasped in pain. Now, clearly frustrated, he barreled forward, seeking to knock Maddock down by main force, but Maddock was too quick. He dodged to his right, swept Issachar's feet from under him, and gave him a smart rap on the back of the head. The blow would have rendered a weaker man unconscious, but Issachar bellowed with rage and kicked out, catching Maddock's heel and bringing him down hard on his backside.

They both sprang to their feet, but once again Maddock was quicker. As Issachar tensed to make an impaling thrust, Maddock whipped the staff around with all his might, cracking Issachar on the right temple. Issachar screamed in agony, covered his face with his hands, and staggered backward. Maddock pursued him, the staff whirling like a windmill. Issachar shrieked as each blow struck him. To Maddock's great surprise, everywhere the staff struck his opponent, angry boils rose on his flesh and slowly began to spread. Issachar drew his hands away. The festering sores now covered all of his exposed flesh. He cried out again, this time in sheer horror, and dove into the water. His cries trailed away as he vanished from sight.

"Most impressive." Maddock recognized the cool pressure of a gun barrel pressed against the base of his skull. "Very slowly, hand me the staff."

Maddock's first reaction was to fight, but even the feeling of invincibility that still flowed through him was not sufficient to conquer common sense. The man, whoever he was, need only to pull the trigger to end Maddock's life. Careful not to make any sudden moves, Maddock handed the staff back to his captor.

"Very good. Now, get down on the ground and put your hands behind your head." Despite the circumstances, the man sounded completely at ease as if he was accustomed to his orders being obeyed. Maddock complied with the man's instructions, lying face-down on the cold stone. With Maddock no longer standing between them, the others finally got a look at the intruder.

"Mr. Zollinger!" Jade gasped.

"As in Jude Zollinger, the bank president?" Amanda blurted.

"He's also Saul's father," Jade said.

"I am all of those things," the man replied as if making introductions at a formal party, "but you may call me Elder."

Chapter 32

"You're the Elder?" Jade's ashen face reflected her stunned disbelief. "But... you had your own son killed."

"Saul was no longer a true believer," the man said. His voice was cool and uncaring as if he was discussing something stuck on the bottom of his shoe. "He was no longer of use to me. Besides, the Lord has shown us that it is noble to sacrifice your son. You, however, might have earned your reprieve. I was going to kill you all, and I still might, but I think perhaps I shall let you live."

"Why?" Bones eyes burned with fury as he stared at the Elder.

"As Ms. Ihara is well aware, there are a few items of particular interest to me. I cannot remove them alone. I shall carry the staff, keeping my gun hand free, while the four of you carry the other."

"And what item is that?" Maddock asked.

"Oh, forgive me, Mr. Maddock. I have left you lying on the cold floor for too long. Please stand, keeping your hands behind your head of course, and proceed out to the island. If the rest of you would please move to the side and kneel, also with your hands behind your head?" The congenial manner in which he made his requests was chilling. "Please understand that I have no qualms about shooting any of you, and I have the skill to do so."

Maddock complied, moving cautiously toward the island. The others also cooperated with the Elder, moving off to the side and dropping to the ground. Maddock joined them, and they knelt there looking up at the Elder who leaned casually against Moses' sarcophagus. This was Maddock's first good look at the man. He had a distinguished-looking man with intense blue eyes, graying black hair, but his athletic build and confident bearing removed any doubt as to whether or not he could handle himself.

"All of you seem to have forgotten that we have not exhausted the remaining clues. There is one discovery yet to be made, and it hangs above us."

Their eyes went to the platform suspended from the top of the pyramid. The intense glow that emanated from the walls of the pyramid made the water seem to sparkle and dance as it cascaded down. For the first time, Maddock noticed a haze of steam around the platform. He thought about what he had seen when he had first entered the pyramid.

"You know, I don't think I would mess with that platform," Maddock said. "That water isn't supposed to be coming down from there. It's leaking through the seams of the capstone. You try to bring that platform down, you might just bring the whole place down with you."

"I'm disappointed," the Elder said. "I thought yours was a more adventurous spirit than that." He turned to Jade. "Miss Ihara, as you are the last remaining member of my organization who has any knowledge of this quest, I shall permit you to do the honors. If you will please?" He pointed his gun at her. "I am not really asking."

"I'm not part of your organization," Jade muttered as she slowly rose to her feet and looked uncertainly from the Elder to Moses' tomb, and back to the Elder again.

"Details. The next clues read, 'Under the tomb, in the chain platform.' I assume there must be a hidden mechanism to lower whatever that is up above us." She cast uncertain eyes to the platform hanging above them. She moved to Moses' tomb and circled it, inspecting the floor all around it.

Maddock kept his gaze fixed on the Elder, who moved away so that he could keep an eye equally on Jade and the others who remained on the floor. Obviously, they could charge him, but at least one of them would die in the process. He couldn't risk it... yet.

"It's not here," Jade said, her voice uncertain. "It's either inside or it's somewhere there." She nodded to Nefertiti's resting place. She looked inside the sarcophagus where Moses lay, inspecting every inch. Her eyes narrowed. "Could that be it?" she whispered. "Bones, give me the Aten disc." Once again focused on solving the puzzle, her air of command had returned.

Bones removed his backpack and tossed it to Jade, who retrieved the disc and leaned down into the sarcophagus.

"There's a space just above his head," she explained, "that looks to be the mirror image of the Aten symbol side of the disc. It might be nothing, but I wonder…"

Jade's hands were not visible from where he sat, but Maddock could see the look of concentration on her face. He watched her lean back down into the sarcophagus, biting her lip. There was an audible click, and then a roar like the grinding of great, invisible gears. He looked up to see the platform descending toward them. He, Bones, and Amanda sprang to their feet almost as one.

"Careful, now," the Elder cautioned, training his gun on Maddock. "I won't have you crushed underneath the platform. Move slowly toward me."

Maddock took a hesitant step toward the Elder, his heart pounding. He needed an opening and he needed it soon because he had just understood the final clue, and now he knew what lay on the platform. All the pieces fell into place: the glowing veins in the stone, the increased intensity of light and heat as they moved closer to this place, the decaying capstone, even the deformed creatures. It was all connected.

"Elder, you have the wrong translation of the final clue." He held out little hope that the man would listen to reason, but he had to try. "It should read '…the ten is impure.' Not the tenth. The ten."

"Meaningless." The Elder gave him a dismissive glance. His eyes flitted back to the platform and a beatific smile spread across his face. "The wealth of the treasure is a mere pittance compared to the power the Dominion will now wield."

"You can't even touch it!" Maddock shouted. "It kills anyone who puts his hands on it! Don't you remember the stories?"

"You've seen too many movies, Mr. Maddock. Besides, I shan't touch it. The four of you shall."

The platform was no more than thirty feet above them now. Maddock was sure he could feel the heat emanating from it. His eyes locked on Jade's and a look of horrified realization dawned on her face. She understood. Her expression became stern, and she tilted her head ever so slightly toward the Elder. Maddock couldn't say for certain how he knew, but the message was clear— Let's get him.

"Bones," he whispered. His friend gave an imperceptible nod and tapped Amanda, who paled visibly and also nodded her assent.

A golden light fell upon the Elder's face and he looked up toward its source, letting his grip on his gun slacken.

In a flash, Jade snatched the sun disc out of the sarcophagus and sent it hurtling, Frisbee-style, at the Elder. It cracked across the bridge of his nose in a spray of blood, and he cried out in surprise and pain. Maddock and Bones were on him before he could recover. Bones ripped the gun out of his hands and Maddock wrested the staff away.

"No!" The Elder grabbed futilely for the staff, his eyes filled with tears from the pain of his broken nose. Maddock cracked him across the forehead with the staff. Instead of boils, a dark stream of flies erupted from the Elder's forehead and engulfed him in a dark, buzzing cloak. The Elder shouted and staggered back, flailing his arms at the swarm that now completely enshrouded him.

"Come on!" Maddock cried, taking Jade by the hand and sprinting down the pathway toward the exit. He heard an anguished scream behind him, and he stole a glance over his shoulder. The platform had completed its descent, settling neatly between the tombs of Moses and Nefertiti, and the Elder had not made it out from underneath. His head, arms, and shoulders jutted out from beneath the massive stone block. The swarm of flies was gone. Maddock heard Bones gasp, and he realized they had all stopped in the doorway, staring back at what the platform held.

The Ark of the Covenant.

Jade took two steps back toward the island, entranced by the sight. Maddock took her by the arm and yanked her back, not bothering to be gentle.

"You can't," he said. "Don't you feel it?" His body tingled as if he was badly sunburned. "We have got to get out of here!" As if to punctuate his statement, the water that had been pouring from the leaking capstone chose that very moment to become a deluge. The movement of whatever mechanism it was that operated the chain had put undue stress on the surrounding rock. Cracks appeared at the pyramid's peak, creeping down the walls like the claws of a hungry predator. "The ceiling's going to come down! Let's go!"

Chapter 33

Maddock led the way back across the stepping stones. The water level was rising, and by the time he reached the final stepping stone, it was underwater. He clambered out of the hole and helped the others out. They dashed through the cathedral-like treasure vault, where the canals there were also roiling with the increased flow of water. He spared a glance at Solomon's throne as they sprinted by, a pang of regret pinching the back of his throat as he realized it might be the last time human eyes gazed upon its beauty.

"Maddock!" Bones shouted. "Behind us!"

Maddock looked over his shoulder to see a pack of the chupacabra creatures pour out of the doorway from which they had just fled and hurtle toward them with relentless rage, gaining ground with every leap. Where were these things coming from? "Keep running!" he shouted to Jade and Amanda, and turned to face the beasts.

Bones dropped to one knee and opened fire with the Elder's gun. He brought down the one in the lead, but the others jumped over him and kept coming. When he brought down two more, the rest slowed down. Apparently they had some degree of intelligence, because they spread out, encircling Bones and Maddock.

"Any ideas?" Bones muttered, letting the Elder's gun fall uselessly to the floor and drawing his knife.

Maddock's mind raced. Could they survive an attack from seven of these beasts? Then he realized he was still holding the staff. In his desperation to think of a way to get everyone safely away, he had not spared it a thought. It obviously had power. The creatures slunk closer.

"Maddock?" Bones' voice was strained.

What could the staff do? Assuming what happened with Issachar and the Elder held true, he could kill one of the creatures by striking it, but one at a time was not going to be good enough against these lightning-fast predators.

"Get back!" he shouted, striking the end of the staff to the floor. He immediately felt foolish. Were these beasts truly going to obey him like a well-trained pet? But then...

"What the hell?" Bones stepped back as a hole appeared in the floor where the staff had struck it, and out poured... frogs!

Hundreds of the small amphibians poured forth, hopping in all directions. The chupacabras began to turn in all directions, sniffing the air and snarling.

"They're confused! They must rely on their sense of smell!" How long would it be, though before they singled out the scent of humans? He and Bones took off toward the exit, leaving the confused beasts behind, but not for long. They had not gone forty yards when the monsters again took up the pursuit. "Leave me. Find the girls and get them out of here."

"No way. We stay together."

They turned to face the charge of the remaining beasts.

Figuring he had nothing to lose, Maddock struck the floor again, and this time a writhing, contorting ball of bronze grew out of the floor. The ball split into seven pieces that each twisted into a bronze serpent that slithered out to meet the chupacabras. The beasts never smelled the snakes, which must have been actually made of bronze. The snakes went for the creature's throats, and with each bite came instant death. Maddock and Bones slowly backed away from the scene as, one by one, the bronze serpents swallowed the beasts. Then, as the final creature was devoured, the serpents flowed together, melted into a ball, and dissolved into the floor.

"Time to go," Maddock whispered.

They sped out of the cathedral and down into the water gate chamber. Here, the canals had overflowed, and the water was an inch deep. The spiral staircase that descended to the room of waterfalls was now a waterfall itself, and they took care to keep from falling. Jade and Amanda waited at the bottom.

"Thank God!" Jade cried as she wrapped her arms around Maddock.

"You don't know how true that statement is," Maddock replied. "Let's go."

"There's a problem. Amanda and I already tried going through the waterfall. The bottom level is completely submerged. You can't even see the tunnel we came down. We could try to swim for it, but the current..." She shrugged and stared at the curtain of water that blocked their view of the next room.

"Should be no problem," Bones said. "You've got Moses' staff. Did he ever let a little water get in his way? You know, '...and Moses stretched out his hand over the sea...'"

"'The waters were divided,'" Amanda whispered.

"You two left out a little bit in the middle," Maddock said, "but I get your point." Maddock's first thought was that Bones was crazy. There was no way he could do what his friend suggested.

"You already made boils, flies, and frogs, Mister Plague-Bearer. Then you made serpents that devoured the chupacabras. Does somebody need to whack you over the head to make you see the obvious? Now hurry up! This water is cold."

Bones was right. Even more water poured out of the stairway behind them, and the level had risen almost to his calves. His feet were going numb from the cold. He extended the staff.

Nothing happened.

And then, as if a strong breeze were blowing into it, the waterfall in front of them wavered, and then the curtain of water parted. Down below, a channel opened along the pathway that led to the way out.

They walked between walls of roiling water. It surged and pulsed, and with every step he took, Maddock was more and more certain that it was all going to collapse in on them at any moment.

"It's like Sea World!" Bones said. "But without all the cool fish."

They reached the other side safely and ascended the exit tunnel that was now a vertical tube of water.

"Anybody else feel like a hamster?" Maddock asked, watching as the water raged around the circular passage. The path opened for them as they made the climb and closed behind them when they passed. The glowing cavern was soon left behind, and they had to rely on their flashlights to light their way.

They emerged in the gargoyle pit, which was now an angry vortex. Water gushed from the gargoyle's mouths, swirling about the circular pit and spiraling into a violent maelstrom that was swallowed up by the tunnel through which Maddock had originally entered the pit. He had hoped that would be the avenue of their escape, but now they would have to retrace the path by which Bones and Amanda had come.

Maddock extended the staff again, and a pathway opened that led them to the stairs that wrapped around the pit wall. He took the steps two at a time, the narrow beam of his flashlight bobbing as he climbed.

When he reached the top, a flash of movement caught his eye, and before he could react, something struck him hard above his right ear. He crashed to the ground, landing hard on his back, the staff slipping from his grasp. He reached out in desperation but only succeeded in brushing it with his fingertips before it rolled out of his reach and disappeared over the edge of the pit.

He didn't have time to even think about what had happened because something was hurtling directly at him. Bones and the others had not reached the top, but the faint light cast by their flashlights shone on Issachar, his face now little more than a mass of bleeding boils. With a bellow of inhuman rage, he hurled himself at Maddock. Maddock drew his knees to his chest and caught Issachar's stomach on the balls of his feet, and grabbed his shoulders. Using his attacker's momentum to his advantage, he kicked up, somersaulting Issachar into the pit.

He rolled over, snatched up his flashlight, and shone it down into the depths of the pit below. He saw nothing but dark, angry water.

"It's gone," he said in disbelief as the others arrived at his side. "I just lost the staff of Moses."

"Brother, at the rate we're going, there won't be any biblical treasures left in a few years." Bones clapped Maddock on the shoulder. "Next week let's blow up Noah's Ark."

Faint lines of pink brushed the velvet sky on the edge of the horizon when the weary party found their way back to the top of Angel's Landing. They replaced the cover stone and heaped mounds of loose rock over it. No one before them had found it, and likely no one would again, at least not for a long time. There had been no more sign of the Dominion or the chupacabras though they did find a Kalashnikov lying in a sticky pool in one of the chambers and had taken it with them just to be safe.

Now they stood together letting the first rays of the morning sun wash away the memories of their hellish night underground. Jade leaned against Maddock's shoulder and he slipped his arm around her waist.

"None of it seems real now," she whispered. "My life's ambition realized and lost again in one night. And what do I have to show for it?"

"You're alive," Maddock said. "And hey, you've got me."

"So it's kind of a wash," Bones said. "Life with Maddock can be an absolute pain."

"So the Ark of the Covenant was radioactive?" Amanda asked after a long silence. They had all been too focused on getting out alive to discuss what had happened.

"I think the plates on which the Ten Commandments were carved were highly radioactive. Unbelievably so considering the half-life it must have for it to still be radioactive today."

"How did you guess?" Now that they were back in the real world, Amanda was regaining some of her reporter's instincts.

"I kept wondering what could be a greater treasure than what we saw in the cathedral chamber. What is associated with Moses besides the staff? Then I remembered what Bones said about Jimmy's corrected translation: The ten is impure. The Ten Commandments! I thought of the Ark of the Covenant, and how the Bible said that if someone touched it, they died. And then it all fell into place: the glowing veins of minerals in the stone, the fact that every cavern seemed to get warmer and brighter as we moved closer to the final chamber, the chupacabras, which are probably descendants of population of native animal, maybe a mountain lion that has mutated for generation after generation. Their lair smelled of wild cat. Justin's grandmother told me that her family has lived in that spot for generations. They've probably been drinking contaminated groundwater."

"Why wouldn't it affect the park?" Jade asked.

"I don't know. It would probably take years of drinking it to have any effect. Besides, think about how far we traveled down there. The chambers are miles from here."

"I get it!" Bones said. "The Ark of the Covenant is gold-plated, which acted as an imperfect shield. You could get close, but not too close."

"How could Moses have carried the Ten Commandments down from Sinai if they were so highly radioactive?" Jade asked.

"The same way he parted the sea, caused the plagues, all that good stuff," Bones said. "No matter how much science you throw into the mix, you can never quite factor God out of the equation, can you Maddock?"

"I guess not," Maddock said. He and God had not been on good terms since Melissa's death. The experiences of the past year, though, had made the universe a much bigger and more complicated place than he had ever imagined. It was certainly beyond his small capacity to comprehend. He looked at Jade, thinking of how he had every reason not to trust her, yet he trusted her. More than that, despite the hurt she had caused him, he wanted to give it a go with her. Maybe that was a small taste of what faith was like.

"Does it bother any of you," Amanda remained in reporter mode, "knowing that Moses was, in actuality Akhenaten?"

"I don't know." Bones looked out across the beauty of the landscape. "Does it bother you to know that Akhenaten was really Moses? It doesn't change what Moses did, or why he was so important. Heck, I think it's cool. Things like that sort of bring us all a little closer together. Shared history and all that. I don't know. It's not as bad as if we found out Elvis was really Tiny Tim."

"You can ask Elvis next time we see him," Maddock said. He noticed that

Amanda had turned away from the rest of the group and was staring up at the sky. "Are you all right?"

"I was just thinking that I helped uncover the story to end all stories, and I can't tell anyone. It's got Pulitzer written all over it, but even if there is anything left down there, would it be a good idea for the world to know? Look at what the staff could do. What other powers might some of those treasures have? Imagine them in the hands of the crazies of this world."

"The Elder indicated that no one is left in the Dominion who knows anything about any of this," Maddock said. "That leaves Jimmy and the four of us. Personally, I think Fray Marcos was right. It's too terrible a secret to share with the world. Someday, if it's meant to be, the right person at the right time will find it."

"So we weren't meant to find it?" Amanda asked, returning to Bones' side.

"I'm not a philosopher," Maddock said. "But I think maybe we were meant to stop the Elder from finding it. I know that's not much, but at least you know you were part of something important."

"Man! I thought I was being cheesy," Bones said. "But I think you're right."

"It's all right," Amanda said. "I think that with a little digging I can craft a major story about a bank president and community leader who was secretly the head of an underground paramilitary organization. I might even be able to blow the lid off of Central Utah University as well." She looked at Jade, concern in her eyes. "But what are you going to do? I mean, you can't go back, can you? Not with the university's connections to the Dominion. And finding out the truth of the Seven Cities was your life's ambition, and now you can't even take any credit. Oh Jade, I'm sorry."

"Thank you," Jade said. "But I did find out the truth, and that's what matters. I guess I need a new life's ambition. As for where I'll be working," she turned to look into Maddock's eyes, "I'm a pretty fair diver. Know anyone who's hiring?"

"I just might at that," Maddock said. "Bones and I have been talking about expanding our operation."

Now Bones turned to Amanda. "That leaves you," he said. "What are your plans?"

"My plan is for you to buy me a meal and give me the back rub of my life. Long term? When my story comes out, I'll be a girl in demand. Maybe I'll find my way down to Florida and blow the lid off some scandal or other. Think you'll be free?"

"You never know," Bones said. "I'm already a man in demand."

"I think it's light enough to safely make our way down now," Maddock said, taking Jade's hand. "Are we ready?"

"We need to take it slow," Amanda said. "By the time we get to the bottom we should probably have a good explanation for the shootings at the hotel. Some of our names are bound to be on the hotel registry, after all."

"No, they aren't," Jade said. "Saul always registered us in his father's name and paid with one of his father's credit cards. I never thought anything about it. Now, all signs point back to the Elder."

"The snake bites its own tail," Bones said. "Maddock, you ever notice how things just seem to go our way?"

"You know," Maddock said as they stepped around a large outcropping and into the light of a new day, "I'm starting to think you just might be right."

Epilogue

Justin sat at the edge of the pond, rocking back and forth, letting his bare feet soak in the cool water. The sun sparkled on its surface, lending a sense of joy to the early morning. He held up his hand, letting the dancing reflections of sunlight play across his palm. It was a favorite game of his and could occupy him for hours at a time. But not today. Today he was worried about his new friend.

Justin had waited by the pond until almost dark, hoping his friend would come back, but he did not. What if the choo choo's had gotten him? He hoped not. His friend was nice. He liked Justin's pictures, and he didn't seem scared by Justin's funny eye. He talked to Justin like a regular person.

There still was no sign of him. No footprints around the pond. Nothing. The pond was bigger this morning, which was strange. The water went all the way past his favorite sitting rock and around the pine tree where he liked to get his shade. Probably his friend had found a different way out. He wouldn't have wanted to walk across the desert again. Yes, that was it.

Feeling much better, he decided it would be okay to leave now. As he stood, something in the water caught his eye. Down at the bottom of the pond, the sun glinted off of something shiny and gold. He had found shiny treasures in the pond before! His friend had liked those too. He waded into the water as far as he could, took a deep breath, and dove. He was a good swimmer—he could swim better than he could walk, anyway.

He reached the bottom and his hand closed around the shiny thing. It was much bigger than he had thought. It wasn't too heavy though. He swam back to shore, excited at his new find.

Back on dry ground, he held his treasure up so he could see it better. It was long, dark, and shiny, with golden letters that glowed in the sun. There were shiny things on either end, too. He liked it!

"Stick!" he said. There was a note of pride in his voice. This was the nicest stick he had ever found. He wouldn't show grandma. She always let him keep his sticks for a while, but in the winter she burned them in the wood stove. This stick would be his secret.

Happier than he had felt in a long time, and no longer worried about his new friend, he decided this would be a perfect morning for a long walk-- just him and his new treasure.

~The End~

QUEST

A Dane Maddock Adventure

But of the tree of the knowledge of good and evil you shall not eat, for in the day that you eat of it you shall surely die."
Genesis 2.17

Prologue

149 B.C.E.

"Why have you summoned me? I should be at my place on the walls." Hasdrubal's eyes were afire and his hand trembled as he gripped the hilt of his sword. His anger was understandable, considering who he was and to whom he was related. But, he had come right away when summoned, and that was to his credit.

"You are needed for something greater than waiting to die." Aderba'al laid a hand on the man's shoulder, but he shrugged it off. It was an affront which, under different circumstances, would merit severe chastisement, but this was not the time for such things. Time was of the essence. "Hear my words before you so impetuously assume that you know what is best."

"Very well, but do not delay me unnecessarily." He looked around as if, at any moment, enemies would be storming the temple.

"It is you who is delaying me," Aderba'al snapped. "What I do is the last hope for the survival of our people. You have been chosen for a sacred task."

Now Hasdrubal was curious. "Tell me." Suspicion hung heavy in his words, but at least Aderba'al had his attention.

"That is what I have been trying to do. Follow me, listen, and do not interrupt."

They passed through the temple, now dark because they could no longer spare the oil required to light the lamps. Everything, it seemed, was needed in defense of the city. Behind the altar, he knelt, running his fingers across the carved surface, the smooth stone cool to the touch. He stopped on an image of a flooded field. "Aretsaya," he whispered as he pressed down.

With a click, a door swung open, revealing a dark passage in the base of the altar.

"What…" Hasdrubal must have remembered Aderba'al's warning against interruption because he clamped his mouth shut and followed without protest as Aderba'al led them down into the tunnel.

He required no light, so familiar was he with this passage. They walked along in silence as complete as the absence of light. Their footsteps echoed in the empty corridor and it was almost possible to forget the enemy at the gates. Not once, in all the time he followed Aderba'al into the unknowable blackness, did Hasdrubal speak though he surely was wondering where they were going and why.

When he tasted the salty tang of sea air, Aderba'al knew they had almost arrived at their destination. They emerged in a grotto overlooking a sheltered cove. This place was a temple secret, but it was far from the most important one he would reveal today. Down below, sailing ships were being loaded and made ready to sail.

Hasdrubal looked scandalized at the sight and he rounded angrily on Aderba'al, his face red and his eyes flashing. "You want me to flee like a coward? I shall not do it. You know my bloodline and the obligation it carries with it. How can you ask me to run?"

"What I ask you to do requires more courage than anything you have ever done before." This gained Hasdrubal's attention and he lapsed into an uneasy silence.

Aderba'al drew from his robes an oilcloth pouch and handed it to him. "As you are well aware, our ancestors were the greatest sailors in history. They passed down to us knowledge of a land, wild and unconquered by civilized man. It lies far across the great water beyond the white stones. These maps will show you the way."

"Beyond the white stones? *Across* the water?"

Aderba'al nodded gravely. "There is no other choice. You must go beyond the reach of our enemy."

Hasdrubal held the bundle in his hands, looking sadly at it. "Surely there are other sailors who can take this command. Other men…"

"But there is only one man with your blood. One man who can sail, fight, and command their unwavering allegiance. It must be you."

"So I am to find this faraway land and found a new colony?" Regret filled his voice and it was obvious the man would rather fight to the death on the walls than abandon his home.

"That is a part of it, but there is something much more important that you must do. It is a sacred duty that reaches back beyond the history of our people. Few know of it and should our city fall, as I fear it will, you will perhaps be the only living man with that knowledge."

Aderba'al remembered the day the secret had been passed down to him. He had not believed it at first, but when he had seen the proof with his own eyes, it had been a wondrous revelation. He wondered how Hasdrubal would react to what he was about to be told. Taking a deep breath, he began his tale.

"The ship on which you will travel carries…"

148 B.C.E.

Hasdrubal stepped off the ship onto sand as white as snow and as hot as a forge. The deep green of the forest was a pleasant change from the months of unrelenting blue sea under blue sky. They had sighted land a few times in recent days, and the others had pleaded with him to take the ships ashore, but he had refused. The maps indicated that these were small islands and wholly unsuitable for their purpose. They needed to disappear in this strange new world. He would lead them into its dark depths until the gods told him they had found their new home. When they reached that place, they would plant the seeds of their new civilization… literally.

A man stepped out from the darkness of the forest. Short of stature, with dark skin and glossy, black hair, the man looked at him, not with enmity, but curiosity. He carried a primitive spear, but no other weapon. Hasdrubal's hand itched to reach for his sword, but he remained calm. Step by hesitant step, the man came closer, until he stood only a few feet from Hasdrubal, certainly close enough to use that spear if he chose to do so.

A tense silence hung in the air as everyone waited to see what would happen next. The roar of waves crashing on the shore filled Hasdrubal's ears and the cool breeze ruffled his hair. This would not be the worst place to die, but he somehow sensed this was not his day. His mission was not yet complete.

The dark man looked up at him in wide-eyed wonder. The moment stretched into an excruciating span of three heartbeats. Then, without preamble, he let his spear drop and fell face-down alongside it.

Hasdrubal thought, for a moment, that the man had died, but then, more figures melted out of the jungle. Like the first man, they too laid down their weapons and fell prostrate in the sand.

"It is as if they think we are gods," Shafat whispered. A fine sailor, his was one of only four ships that had survived the journey.

"It is well that they do," Hasdrubal replied. "Perhaps they shall be of some use as we search for our new home."

"And where will that be?" There was no disrespect in Shafat's voice, only curiosity.

"I will know it when I find it."

1922

"Colonel! You must come quickly!" Adam poked his head into the tent, his excited eyes shining, in contrast to his dirty face. "Someone has come to the camp!"

Percy Fawcett looked up from his book and frowned. "Tell me, would you open the door to someone's house and shout to them, Adam? Or would you knock first?" Adam hung his head. "And wash your face. You embarrass me." Apologizing profusely, the man backed out of the tent.

Fuming, Fawcett pulled on his boots. Weak men who could scarcely maintain their humanity in the jungle were an affront to his sensibilities. Why was it so difficult to find men with pride, dignity, and a bit of backbone? Disappointments, every one of them.

He pushed aside the flap of his tent, wondering what absurdity had prompted them to bring him out so late. Despite the lateness of the hour, it was still hot and muggy out. The others had kept their cookfire burning and were huddled around it, seeming to find comfort. Weaklings! Doubtless they had called him out here for something preposterous. Perhaps a large insect or something of the sort. When he saw the young man lying beneath a blanket by the fire, however, he revised his opinion at once.

Fawcett knelt down beside the young man and pushed back his hair to get a better look. He did not resemble the natives of this region. In fact, he had a distinctly Mediterranean look about him.

"Who is he? Where did he come from?"

"We don't know," Adam replied. "He came staggering into camp and collapsed. He hasn't stopped babbling. Alberto understands some of what he says, but he can't make out the half of it."

Fawcett listened closely. The language was an odd one. Some of the words were recognizable as a dialect similar to that of the natives of this region. The rest was...

Fawcett gaped, the pipe falling from his mouth. He found that he could understand much of what this young man was saying, but the language was...

It couldn't be!

"Adam, be a good fellow and fetch my book and my pen." Heart pounding, he stared down in excitement and disbelief at the strange young man who had so fortuitously stumbled into his encampment. And if Fawcett understood his words correctly, this youth just might be the key to what Fawcett had been searching for all these years.

Chapter 1

Thomas had never felt so hot in his entire life. The heat was sweltering, unrelenting, and scarcely a breeze stirred beneath the canopy of green. Creeping, clutching foliage dogged his every step. And the insects! They were an unrelenting cloud, biting and stinging him, and invading his every orifice. Civilization's finest insect repellent had waged a losing battle against the onslaught.

"It's getting late." Denesh, his neck twitching in that annoying nervous tic of his, glanced up at the tattered bits of sky visible through the tangle of trees. "You know how quickly night can come on in this jungle. I don't want to be stuck out here when it does."

"I know." Thomas took another look at his notebook. He had found all the landmarks up to this point, but this next one continued to elude him. Perhaps just a bit farther. Of course, he'd been telling himself that for the better part of the last hour, with no success. With a sigh, he tucked the notebook back into his pocket. They were close. He just knew it. His research had proved to be accurate up to this point, with all the landmarks exactly as they should be, so there was no reason to assume it would not continue to be so. They were on the verge of a discovery that would rock the world.

"Did you hear that?" Denesh shifted his weight from one foot to the other, looking all around. He looked like a nervous bird, his head jerking to and fro as his eyes probed the jungle.

"I didn't hear anything." The truth was, Thomas was so focused on his thoughts that a truck could have driven over him and he probably would not have noticed until it was too late. "Let's head back. Tomorrow we'll get an earlier start and see how far we can get. We might even break camp and haul the gear along with us. That way we can range even farther."

Denesh's coffee complexion paled at the suggestion, but he nodded. A brilliant graduate student, he was finding the expedition difficult, to say the least, but he had braved it all without complaint. The young man had potential, assuming Thomas could ever get him back out into the field after this experience. He now stood stock-still, his knuckles white as he clutched the hilt of his machete. "I'm not crazy, Professor Thornton, I swear I heard something. It was the strangest sound. Like a giant sheet of sandpaper being dragged across the ground."

"That's probably what it was, then. Congratulations. You've solved the mystery." He elbowed Denesh in the ribs, coaxing a weak smile. "All right, it's time to test your woods craft. Do you think you can guide us back to camp without getting us hopelessly lost?"

Denesh took up the challenge and only managed to lead them off course twice, but both times he found the trail again without any help from Thomas. By the time camp was in sight, he had a bit of bounce in his step. The promise of food, no matter how poor, and a camp bed beneath a screen of mosquito netting, seemed like high living in this part of the world.

Thomas sensed something was wrong the moment he entered the camp. A quick inspection revealed nothing obvious that might be amiss, but still, things were not right. There was a tension in the air as if the world were strung as taut as piano wire.

Derek and Emily appeared from the shadows on the far side of the encampment and hurried to meet him. They both appeared agitated.

"Doctor Thornton, I did not sign up for this trip only to be stranded in the middle of nowhere." Emily's freckled face was bright red, but whether from sunburn or anger he could not tell.

"Wait, what are you talking about? We're not stranded." The psychological toll this place took on travelers sometimes caused a person to crack. He hoped this was not the case with Emily, who, despite having a face and body that screamed 'delicate flower,' had been a trooper up to this point.

"Victor is gone." Her voice trembled as she spoke and she looked like she was on the verge of tears. "He said he was going to hike back to the lagoon, take one of the boats, and go home."

The news struck Thomas like a punch to the gut. If their guide was gone, that left him alone to get three students back to civilization. He supposed he could do it, but this meant the expedition was over. Damn. Another day or two might have done it. With serious effort, he regained his composure. Under the circumstances, it would not do to appear rattled in front of the others.

"But we still have the other boat, so we aren't stranded." He stared through the trees in the direction of the lagoon, as if his eyes could penetrate the miles of tangled greenery and see their remaining boat, their only path back to civilization, waiting there beside its dark waters. "But why did Victor just up and leave? Did he say anything?"

Emily gave Derek a look that said, *"I told you so,"* and Derek nodded.

"I think it's been coming on for a few days, Professor," Denesh said. "He didn't like it here and kept telling us it was a bad place and that we should not stay. He knew it would do no good to say anything to you, though. You were so focused on whatever it is you're still doing out here." He held his hands out to his sides in a gesture of confusion. "I do think Victor was on to something, though. There's a wrongness about this place, and it's got us all spooked."

"Superstitious nonsense." Thomas was embarrassed that he had been so focused on his search that he had failed to notice that one of his team was on the verge of abandoning the group. "He got into your heads, that's all. He fed you tales about spooky stuff, and it took root in your psyche. Don't let it control you."

"It's not just that, Professor," Derek said. "I had to kill an opossum today."

"Chestnut-striped," Emily chimed in, proving she had been paying attention to her field guide.

"An opossum," Thomas repeated, unable to keep the disbelief from his voice. He could not begin to fathom where Derek was headed with this.

"I know how it sounds," Derek protested. "You had to be there, I suppose, but it's not just that I killed it. I *had* to kill it. It came marching into camp in the middle of the day, which is strange enough in itself, and it went straight for our food. It ignored me when I tried to shoo it away. Then I kicked it and it..." He swallowed hard. "It attacked me. Turned on me, made this crazy noise and sprang up like a mountain lion or something. It tore up my pants leg, but I got hold of it by the tail before it could bite me. Even then, it kept snarling at me."

"An opossum snarled at you." Thomas didn't get it. Perhaps this was all just an elaborate ruse to get him to pack up and leave. Or maybe it was a joke.

"It was a snarl," Emily added. "It sounded like a ferocious predator."

"I flung it across the camp and it smashed into that tree over there." Derek nodded at a kapok tree with a trunk nearly ten feet in diameter. "It should have crawled away, but it got up and came right at me again. I kicked it away and it still kept on coming at me. Finally, I had to stomp it to death." Derek's eyes fell, clearly upset by the memory.

"So you had an encounter with a rabid opossum and now you believe Victor's stories about the bogeyman. I'm disappointed in you."

"It was not rabid." Frustration was now clear in Derek's every word. "You don't understand. It didn't appear crazed at all. Its actions were purposeful, and, I don't know, it was almost as if it thought it was a giant predator and I was the small animal in its way. It never seemed the least bit frightened, or even wary, just determined. It was like there was no question of it doing what it wanted to do, and I could pose no threat to it in any way."

"I work at a vet's office every summer," Emily added. "Even in the early stages of rabies, if an animal goes into the aggressive state, it's accompanied by other symptoms, like disorientation, trembling, loss of muscle coordination. I saw none of that. That animal was different. We kept the body if you would like to look at it."

They led him to the spot where the opossum lay. Thomas took his time examining the disfigured remains of the small mammal though, in truth, he doubted he would recognize even the late-stage signs of rabies. He kept his features calm, letting the silence and his own serenity settle the nerves of his upset students. Finally, he gave a diagnosis of "perhaps" and rose to his feet.

"Our notebooks are complete, Doctor Thornton. They have been for two days. Victor took half the remaining supplies. Let's just go home." Emily sounded as if she were on the verge of tears.

The pleading tone grated on his nerves. They had to leave, he understood that, but that did not mean he had to be happy about it. To have come so close and yet failed. It would be another year, at the soonest, before he could return, and that was assuming his sponsors would fund another trip. He had promised results, and they were not going to be happy when he returned empty-handed. "Fine," he said, rising to his feet. "Pack up as much as you can. We'll leave in the morning."

Derek's and Emily's faces relaxed, and each thanked him profusely, assuring him that this had been the best field ecology trip ever and that they couldn't wait to get home and tell their families all about it.

Denesh did not appear to share in their joy. He frowned, his eyes fixed on a spot deep in the jungle.

"What's wrong with you?" Emily nudged him. "Lighten up a little."

"Quiet." The tone of his voice silenced everyone in the group. "Something's coming."

Thomas turned to look in the direction Denesh indicated in time to see three figures stride out of the jungle. They were short and stocky, with glossy black hair cut short in the Yanomami style. Their bodies were painted orange-brown with black smudges all over that put him in mind of a jaguar. Each was armed with a stone-tipped short spear and a stone axe. They moved directly toward the camp, their faces blank, and their strides resolute.

"Who are they?" Derek whispered. "There aren't supposed to be any natives in this area."

Actually, very little was known about this region. The area was so remote that it had remained unexplored in modern times. The satellite photos Thomas had inspected revealed nothing but a blanket of unrelenting green.

"I have no idea. They must be from an undiscovered tribe." Thomas shook his head. These men had the general look and build of the natives of this region, but he noticed subtle differences. Their faces were narrow, and their noses longer. He could not discern eye color from this distance, but they were definitely not the brown one usually found here. Curious, he took a step forward, but Denesh stopped him with a firm grip on his forearm.

"Let me do it. I know a smattering of languages from this area. Perhaps I can get them to understand me. If this actually is a tribe that has avoided outside contact, and we can communicate with them, I could write quite the paper on it."

He walked toward them, his open hands at his sides, and spoke to them in a language Thomas did not recognize. The natives neither acknowledged his words nor broke their stride. Denesh tried again in three other languages unfamiliar to Thomas and then in Portuguese. Nothing.

The men continued their silent approach, their faces still devoid of emotion. Their movements were not exactly robotic but were steady and measured, almost military in their regularity.

"They're like zombies," Emily whispered.

Thomas grew more nervous with each step they took. Maybe he too had been spooked by Victor's suspicions, but something was very wrong. His hand itched to take hold of the machete that hung from his belt, but he dared not make any movement that insinuated violence. The results could be deadly.

Denesh gave up his attempts at verbal communication. He dropped to one knee, slipped off his wristwatch, and held it out as a supplicant would a tribute.

The men stopped in front of him. The one in the center gazed down at the wristwatch and then, as casually as a businessman would brush lint off of his suit, he raised his hatchet and brought it crashing down on Denesh's head. The young man crumpled to the ground, blood pouring from his split scalp.

Emily screamed at the sight of her friend lying dead on the ground, and she turned and fled. Derek drew his .38 revolver and emptied it in a wild spurt of gunfire. At least two bullets hit one of the warriors, punching through his chest and spraying gore on the man who strode directly behind him—yet the wounded man did not stumble, nor did he so much as blink. He kept coming.

Derek stood like a statue for a moment that seemed frozen in eternity. With a sudden gasp, he shot a glance at Thomas, and then back to the bloody warriors who bore down upon him, their implacable gazes locked on the frightened young man. Derek shrieked, threw his pistol at the first warrior, watched it bounce harmlessly off his chest, and then fled after Emily.

Thomas felt for his own pistol and realized he had not bothered to carry it today. He didn't own a gun in his "real life," and still was not in the habit of keeping one at his hip. Now he was quickly altering his opinion on the necessity of firearms.

As the silent warriors turned their attention to him, he slid the machete from his belt and raised it in what he hoped was a threatening pose, but they stalked after him, undeterred. His courage draining faster than his bladder, he turned on his heel and fled blindly into the jungle.

Chapter 2

Kaylin looked up and down Meeting Street for what must have been the tenth time. Traffic was light in the historic section of Charleston. More importantly, there was no carriage to be seen. Also for the tenth time, she re-read the text message she'd received the night before.

be in front of circ church at 10 get in carriage drop you at powder mag leave your car there its about thomas – andy

Andy was Thomas's closest friend, and in the time she and Thomas had been dating, she and Andy had gotten to know one another fairly well. That was why she knew there were several things wrong about this message. Foremost was the fact that he had texted her rather than calling, which was unusual for him. Second, was the lack of capitalization and punctuation, to which the English Literature professor always paid fastidious attention, even in text messages. Finally, the text had not come from Andy's phone, but from an unfamiliar number.

Thomas was more than two months overdue from the field ecology trip he had taken with his graduate assistant and two other students. He had assured her something like this might happen, and told her not to worry. The Amazon, he said, was not like other places. Plans frequently got fouled up, connections were missed, or wires crossed, resulting in a giant mess. She wanted to believe him, but could not help wondering if Thomas was penning a cover story which would allow him to spend more time with Emily, the cute redhead who called, texted, and emailed Thomas far more often than Kaylin thought appropriate for a professor-student relationship. Now she regretted having entertained such ideas. Andy's message had filled her with a dark sense of foreboding.

Right on time, a carriage appeared in the distance. It belonged to one of the small, private companies that catered primarily to couples looking for a romantic ride around the old parts of the city. As it drew closer, she recognized Andy's shock of short, dark hair, high brow, and fair complexion. The carriage came to a halt and Andy offered his hand to help her inside. His palms were sweaty and his eyes were alive with a manic energy.

"Take this but don't look at it until you're somewhere safe," he whispered, handing her a small manila envelope as the carriage rolled forward. He leaned up and whispered instructions to the driver, who nodded and began loudly describing the historical significance of the Circular Congregational Church.

"Andy, what's going on? You said it's about Thomas. Have you heard from him?"

"We don't have much time." Andy looked around as if expecting someone to leap into the carriage with them at any moment. "Before he left, Thomas gave me that." He indicated the envelope. "He said that he might be delayed on his trip, but if I had not heard from him for sixty days after his expected return date, to get help from someone I trust, and come for him. He said I should do it without drawing unnecessary attention." Andy paused, his expression tense. "He also told me to watch my back."

"But I've already contacted the authorities. They say they've checked the entire stretch of river where his party was to have traveled and found nothing. Their best guess is that Thomas and the others probably went into the rainforest and their boat was stolen while they were gone. They tell me they'll keep an eye out, but they figure Thomas will show up at one of the settlements along the river and send for help. What else are we supposed to do?"

"Thomas didn't follow his planned path. This field ecology trip was just a front to get the university to approve an expedition into the Amazon. He's gone after something bigger. Much bigger."

An icy sensation of disbelief crept up Kaylin's spine. Something much bigger? What was Andy talking about?

"For several years now, Thomas has been working on a research project that he's kept top-secret, except to say it was a very old mystery. He said he couldn't share it, even with the people he trusts. He seems to think knowing nothing might keep us safe though he didn't say from whom. In fact, he said he didn't have all the pieces, but he thought he had enough to succeed."

"This is nuts! Are you sure he didn't just concoct this crazy story as a cover so he could spend more time with Emily?" She regretted the words the moment they left her mouth.

Andy gave her a soft smile of understanding, took her hand, and gave it a squeeze. "There is nothing between him and Emily. He's in love with you. You can take the word of his closest friend on that."

"I'm sorry." She buried her face in her hands. "That was so selfish of me. It's just something that's been bothering me for a long time. God, I feel like such an idiot. Thomas is lost, maybe in danger, and I'm acting like a jealous teenager."

"Don't beat yourself up over it. Thomas needs your help, not your regrets. Now listen carefully. I can't be the one to do this. I'm an English Lit professor, not an explorer, and I don't have any friends who are. Thomas specifically wanted me to tell you if it came to this. He seemed to think you might be able to mount a rescue mission." Andy looked puzzled. "No offense, but you're a Fine Arts teacher, so it seems odd to me. Maybe because of your father's military background?"

Kaylin shrugged, too lost in thought to form a reply.

"So, *do* you know someone, anyone, who could go into the Amazon, find him and the students, and bring them back out alive?" He didn't add *if they're still alive.*

Actually, Kaylin did know one person who fit that bill. She knew him quite well, in fact, but the mere thought of asking him to risk his life to save her boyfriend made her stomach churn. "I think so." She bit her lip and stared out at the street. "But I don't know if he'd do it."

"Thomas swore that solving this mystery, whatever it is, would rock the world—his words, not mine. He seemed to think he was going to be rich and famous."

"But that doesn't make sense. He's an academic. Even if he solved some sort of mystery in the Amazon, there's no money in that. What would he get out of it? Mostly fame among scholars, maybe a few mentions in the media." Closing her eyes, she took two deep, calming breaths and rubbed her temples. Before getting Andy's message, she had convinced herself that Thomas was not truly in danger. He'd been overdue before and always returned safely. Now, her whole world had been turned upside down. She almost wished for a return to a few hours ago, when her greatest concern had been an irrational fear that her boyfriend was cheating on her. She needed to think about this calmly and logically. "Okay, so we don't know what mystery he was working on. What do we know?"

"Nothing. I've looked at what's in the envelope, and I'm baffled, though he insisted it would be sufficient to set us on his trail without giving anything away were it to fall into the wrong hands. I think you might have more luck with it than me. When you see it, you'll understand why."

"There's so much about this that doesn't make sense. Why didn't he tell me anything? If he thought he might not come back, why didn't he leave us a map or something? He could have written a note saying, *"Look for me here,"* and put it in a safe deposit box. And why did he confide in only you?" She wanted to add *"and not me,"* but she'd already embarrassed herself once today with her jealousy.

"In respect to the first two questions, I can only tell you that he believed someone might be after not only him, but anyone else who might know something about what he was doing. I think he was right. I've been on holiday for the last week, and yesterday I received a call from a colleague who told me that a man has been asking after me around the university. I called a neighbor, who said someone had come to her door asking about me as well. Now I'm afraid to go home." He sighed. "As to the latter question, he knows I keep his secrets."

Before Kaylin could follow up on that last cryptic comment, his head snapped up and he once again looked up and down the street before turning to face her.

"There's no more time for talk. The Powder Magazine is coming up on the right. The carriage is not going to slow down, but he will pull as close to the curb as he can. I want you to slip out right in the middle of the tour group that's waiting at the gate, and then get to your car as quickly as possible. I don't know if you should go home, but you definitely need to get help. In fact, you should probably get out of town, just to be safe. I've gotten you involved now, and I regret it."

"Andy I…"

Ever the professor, he hushed her with a raised index finger as if she were his student. "I'm sorry to bring you into this, and I hope the situation is not as grave as I fear, but who really knows?" He gave her a small, sad smile. "Here's your stop."

He gave her a gentle shove and she sprang from the carriage. Her last thought, before she hit the ground, was, *Why did I wear heels?* And then she was stumbling into the midst of a dozen or more tourists waiting to see the colonial-era gunpowder magazine and its museum.

She landed in the arms of a dark-skinned young man in sagging jeans and an Under Armour shirt. He helped regain her balance and looked her over though his expression was one of concern rather than lewdness. Satisfied she was all right, he looked toward the carriage, which was now rounding the corner onto Church Street. "Did that dude try to push you out?"

"Oh, no." She forced a laugh. "He didn't want me jumping out of the carriage in heels, and he tried to grab me, but I was too quick. I guess I should have waited for the carriage to stop."

"Why didn't you?" He was still staring at the carriage as if he didn't want to let it out of his sight until he was satisfied with her story.

"That's my divorce attorney. My estranged husband's kind of crazy, and while we were talking, I saw his car come around the corner. I guess I freaked." Someday she would have to write a note to Mr. Harper, her high school drama teacher, thanking him for all those improv lessons. She looked around, not needing to feign nervousness. "I just want to get to my car and get out of here before he finds me."

"I'll walk you there." The young man offered his hand. "Tariq."

"Kaylin." He had a strong grip, but his hand was surprisingly soft. "I appreciate it, but I wouldn't want you to get into trouble because of me."

"It's all good. Which way's your ride?" He stayed right beside her, shielding her from the view of passing vehicles. As they walked, he told her a little bit about himself. He was a high school senior and hoped to attend Citadel next year. She told him that she was a Navy brat, which elicited a nod of approval.

As they neared the spot where she'd left her car, she looked down the street and gasped. The carriage was stopped on the side of the road, and someone was pushing Andy into a waiting vehicle. Another man, tall, barrel-chested, with short, ash-blond hair was talking to the carriage driver, who turned and looked back down the street, spotted her, and pointed. The man turned, his blue eyes locked on her, and he started in her direction.

They want to take me too! Her heart pounded and she nearly stumbled.

"That's him, isn't it?" Tariq pushed her behind him and made a beeline for the man. "Get in your car and go."

"I don't want you to get hurt because of me. Just run." She couldn't believe this was happening, and she hated that she'd gotten an innocent young man caught up in it.

"Just get in your car, alright? I got this."

Kaylin fished her keys from her purse with trembling fingers and struggled to unlock the driver's side door.

"Hey, lady! I need to talk to you!" The unfamiliar voice must have belonged to the man who was coming after her.

"Yo man, what's up?" Tariq stepped in front of the larger man as Kaylin pulled the door open and slid inside.

"Get out of my way."

"I said, what's up?" Tariq gave the man a hard shove, but he barely budged. Kaylin slammed and locked the door, and promptly dropped the keys. Spewing curses, she retrieved them and started the car. Outside, Tariq was grappling with her would-be abductor. Horns blared as she gunned the engine and backed blindly out into the street. The man broke loose from Tariq, shoved him away, and ran toward her car.

She spun the wheel, did a donut in the middle of the street, and floored it, heading the wrong way back up Church Street. Glancing in the rear-view mirror, she saw the man quickly give up the chase, and run back to the vehicle in which they'd put Andy. She wondered why the driver had not given pursuit, but then she saw bodies twisting and jerking inside the car. Andy was trying to fight them so she could get away.

Her inattention almost cost her. She returned her attention to the road in time to see a van blowing through the yellow light, coming right at her. She yanked the wheel hard to the right, going up on the sidewalk as the van shot past her, the stunned driver staring at her as he whizzed past.

Back on the road, she took another look behind her and saw the man who had come after her reach the car, draw a gun, and point it through the window.

She lost sight of the vehicle as she turned back onto Market Street. She gunned the accelerator, flew past the Powder Magazine, and blew the red light as she turned onto Meeting Street, skidding through the intersection, and barely missing a taxi cab, which swerved and took out a garbage can on the corner. She hoped no one got her tag number, but an appearance in traffic court was small potatoes compared to kidnapping.

By the time she turned onto Broad Street, she finally dared to hope she was not being followed. She prayed Andy was alive, and that the man had drawn the gun only to get him to stop fighting. Her eyes clouded with tears as she thought of the gentle professor fighting for his life.

She finally breathed a sigh of relief when she pulled into the parking lot of the Charleston Police Department Administrative Building. She knew someone there she could trust, and hopefully he could help her, Andy, and Thomas.

Chapter 3

"Let me see if I've got this straight." Captain Ray Gerard tapped his square chin with the envelope Andy had given to Kaylin. A friend of her father, Hartford Maxwell, during their Navy days, he had remained close to Kaylin after her father's passing. "Your boyfriend is overdue returning from the Amazon and you think he's in trouble." Kaylin nodded. "But the only evidence you have is this." He held up the manila envelope.

"I know it sounds crazy, but putting that aside for the moment, Andy was definitely kidnapped. I watched it happen." She winced at the fresh memory and thought of the gun the man had drawn. "He might even be dead."

"Yes, about that." Gerard looked down at his desk, perhaps not wanting to meet her eye. "We can't file a missing person report just yet. Andy hasn't been gone long enough. What I did do was put out an alert, giving the description of the vehicle and the passengers. Hopefully something will turn up."

Kaylin knew the odds were slim. She had been so surprised by the entire incident that she had not gotten a good look at the car. The best she had been able to tell the police was that it was a silver sedan as if there weren't thousands of those out on the road. She had been able to give a fair description of one of the men, the one whom Tariq had confronted, but not the driver.

"I don't know what to do now. I don't feel safe going home, but I also wonder if I'm being foolish. This all really has nothing to do with me, except for the fact that I'm dating Thomas. But I don't know anything about his expedition."

"Well, if this thing," Gerard taped the envelope, "is of any significance, and I don't see how it could be, the people who've kidnapped your friend might come after you if they find out if you've got it."

"But I no longer have it. That was the whole point of turning it over to you."

"Even if they find out you've given it to me, they'll figure you at least looked at it. They might want to make you describe it to them, or to stop you from telling anyone else about it. Either way, you could be in danger. Do you have anywhere you can go? Is there anyone you can stay with for a couple of days?"

Kaylin sighed. "I'll get a hotel for tonight, and then maybe I can stay with friends. But what about Thomas? Isn't there anything you can do?"

"If your friend Andy is right, and Thomas didn't follow his planned path, I don't see that there's much anyone can do, short of going down to South America and asking around. But even that would probably be a waste of time, especially since we don't even know for certain where he started his expedition."

"But there's got to be some way you can help!" Kaylin realized she was grasping at straws, but the thought of Thomas being in trouble and her doing nothing to help was more than she could bear.

"Kaylin, I want to help you, I really do, but we're just a local police department. We don't have any international connections, and even if we did, what would I tell them? A professor is missing in the Amazon? That happens all the time. What if they were to ask me for his itinerary, and I tell them we don't think he followed it, but we have this here clue..." Once again, he held up the envelope and gave Kaylin a meaningful look.

"I understand." She wished she could keep the disappointment from her voice. Gerard was a good man, and she knew he would do what he could. Unfortunately, in this situation, what he could do was not much. "I suppose I'll try the dean of his college, and maybe my congressman's office. I have to do something." She rose from her chair, shook Gerard's hand, and thanked him for his help.

"I really wish I could do more for you, but my hands are tied. I will keep up the search for your friend Andy, though."

She assured him that she understood, and gratefully accepted his offer of a police escort to a nearby hotel. He walked her out to the lobby and they made small talk for a few minutes, and she promised to drop by for dinner with him and his wife sometime soon. A young officer walked her out to her car and followed behind in his squad car. Her mind was abuzz with a swarm of confused thoughts and jumbled questions. What should she do next? Was Andy okay? Where was Thomas? And, perhaps most important, what should be her next move?

Jay Newman watched Gerard leave his office with the blonde and escort her down the hall. The moment they turned the corner, he looked around to make certain no one was watching. Certain he was in the clear, he hurried to Gerard's office and tried the door. He was pleased to find it was unlocked, and he slipped inside and closed the door behind him.

A manila envelope lay on the desk. He had seen the girl carrying it when she entered the captain's office. It must be the one to which the message had referred. Jay opened it and removed the single item it contained. He frowned. What was this and how could it be important? Not his problem. He laid it on his desk, snapped a couple of pictures with his iPhone, and slipped it back into the envelope.

Knowing time could be short, depending on how long Gerard took walking the girl out, he hurried back to the door. Easing it open, he peeked out and was relieved to find that the hallway remained empty. Closing the door behind him, it occurred to him that he should have just stepped out of the office acting normally, as if he'd simply been looking for the captain and had not found him in his office. All of this cloak and dagger was not for him. If he hadn't needed the money, he would never have agreed to help these guys.

"Detective!" Gerard's voice boomed down the hall. "Are you looking for me?"

Newman was proud of how calmly he turned around to face Gerard, who, despite nearing mandatory retirement, still could intimidate him with a mere glance. "Yes, Captain, I was just wondering if there was anything I could do to help you with that young woman's situation."

Gerard fixed him with an appraising look, but then his stony features cracked into a smile. "Don't bother with that one. She's all broken up over her missing boyfriend."

"You mean the guy that was kidnaped?" Newman's heart raced. Perhaps he could glean some useful information from this conversation, which could mean more cash, and hopefully being shut of these guys sooner.

"No, a different fellow. Went on a university field trip and got himself lost." Gerard smirked. "College man. We'd all be better off if everyone had a mandatory tour of duty in the service after high school. It made a world of difference for me."

Newman had heard Gerard's pontifications on mandatory service more times than he cared to remember. He thanked the captain, reiterated his offer of help, which elicited another smirk from Gerard, and returned to his cubicle.

He wasted no time in sending the photos to his contact number, and wasn't surprised when he received a response less than a minute later.

CALL ME

This was not a conversation he could risk having overheard. He hurried to a small, single-head restroom near the break room and locked the door. Inside, he turned on the water and retreated to the stall before making his call.

"You sent the wrong attachment." Not so much as a hello. *"What the hell is this picture you sent me, anyway?"* The voice belonged to the man who had first contacted him with the business proposition.

"No, really, that's it. That was the only thing in the envelope."

"The next two words out of your mouth had better be 'April Fool' or else my employers are going to be very unhappy with both of us."

"I'm serious." Newman forced himself to remain calm though his heart was racing. What kind of people had he gotten himself hooked up with? "That is what the girl turned over to my captain."

"And you're certain it was the right envelope?" Suspicion lay beneath every word. *"If you're messing with me, you won't see one penny of the money. And that's only if they take the news well. If they don't…"*

If I don't get that money, certain other people are going to be after me, too. Either way, I'm toast, Newman thought. "I'm one hundred percent sure. I saw the girl take the envelope into the captain's office."

"Fine." The caller gave an exasperated sigh. *"What about the back? You didn't send me a picture of the flip side."*

Newman froze. Had he even looked at the back? Surely he had taken a quick glance to see if anything was there. He must have looked at it, seen nothing, and just taken pictures of the front. In any case, he wasn't going to tell this guy that he might have overlooked something that simple. No way was he going to make this fellow any angrier than he already was.

"The back was blank. What you've got right there is everything." He held his breath, wondering what the reply would be, and what it might bode for his future well-being.

"All right, whatever. I don't get why this thing is such a big deal, but that's not for you and me to decide. We do need to make sure this is the real thing, and the girl didn't pull some sort of switch on us. I'll check her place. You find out if she might have decided to stay somewhere else."

It was a good thing Newman was in the head because he felt like he was going to throw up. He'd agreed to provide information, not help track down and interrogate innocent women. He hoped the man had nothing in mind more serious than an interrogation. He swallowed hard. "I understand. Do you have her name?"

"Yeah, it's Kaylin Maxwell."

Thirty minutes and the walls were already closing in on Kaylin. She sipped a cup of hot tea, which was not bad for a complimentary hotel brand and tried to relax. It was lunchtime, but she had little appetite.

Her conversation with Thomas's dean had been a waste of time. The man claimed to have no connections in South America but promised her he would "ask around." The call to her congressman's office was equally fruitless. She'd left a message with a skeptical-sounding aide, who asked that she email him with the details so he could look into it, whatever that meant.

Now that she was calm enough to reflect, she felt like a fool for panicking when the man had come after her, and letting a teenager fight her battle for her. What happened to the tough, self-reliant girl her father raised? She'd been in worse situations before. Since she and Thomas had become serious, she had allowed herself to get soft. Why, she didn't even carry her .380 in her purse anymore. It was still in her glove compartment where it had lain for a couple of years now. What would her father think if he could see her right now, cowering in a hotel room, hoping other people would solve her problems for her?

No more of this. It was time to take action. She took out her phone and scrolled down to the D's. There was the name, still there though the two of them hadn't talked in... she didn't know how long. What if he had changed his number? No, that wouldn't be like him. Never mind. She'd call him later. Telling herself she was putting first things first, and not being chicken, she called her neighbor, Amber. Perhaps she could safely go home and get her laptop, clothes, and personal items.

Amber picked up on the first ring.

"Hi Amber, it's Kay. Would you mind taking a peek over at my apartment and seeing if things are... all right?"

"Sure. Your key's hanging right here. I'll go check it out. Is everything all right?"

"No! I mean, I think things are okay, but no, you don't have to go inside. Just take a look and see if things look... normal." She was feeling a little foolish. What exactly did she want Amber to look for? Masked men hiding on the balcony? The door kicked in? "You know what? Don't even worry about it."

"It's no problem. I'm already here. Besides, what are next-door neighbors for?"

"No, really. Forget about..."

Amber's scream cut her off in mid-sentence. She heard the clatter of a phone falling to the ground.

"Amber!"

The call ended. She punched up the number again, but no answer. She tried again and, this time, it went straight to voicemail. That sealed it for her. She snatched up her purse, the only item she had with her, and headed for the door, calling 911 as she went. She gave the operator an abridged description of the phone call and the scream, making it sound like she and Amber had been on the phone when Amber screamed and the line went dead. She worried that the incident she described would not seem serious enough to merit police attention, but the operator assured her they would check it out.

The elevator reached the first floor, the doors opened, and she hurried toward the side entrance nearest the spot where she had parked her car. As she passed the front desk, she heard someone say, "Kaylin Maxwell's room, please." She jerked her head around in surprise and caught a glimpse of a tall, lean man in a navy suit. Distracted, she bumped into an elderly man who was engrossed in a large print novel.

"I'm so sorry," she said, hurrying away.

"Not at all," he called to her. "I wasn't watching where I was going."

She glanced back to discover she had caught the attention of the man at the counter, who was now following after her.

"Ms. Maxwell!" he called. "Hold on a minute! Please!"

She banged through the door and hurried out to the parking lot, once again cursing her high heels and vowing to wear flats for the rest of her life. She was just slamming the car door when she heard the man call out to her.

"Wait! I'm with the police!"

She locked the door and turned to see him approaching, holding up his shield and identification. She let her shoulders sag and lowered the window an inch.

"I didn't mean to freak you out." He tucked his badge into his coat pocket. "I'm a detective. Can we talk?"

"First, you can send someone to my apartment. I think my neighbor is in trouble."

"I know. I mean, I came to tell you not to go home." He leaned down, putting his face inches from the window, and lowered his voice. "You're in danger."

Kaylin tensed. "How did you already know about my neighbor? I just called it in maybe two minutes ago."

"I didn't." She was certain he was lying. The way his eyes shifted to the left as he spoke, his demeanor, even the sound of his voice set off alarms. "I just wanted to warn you about going home. If something has happened, then I guess I was right."

"Thank you for your concern. If you'll please follow up on it and make sure help is on its way, I need to go." She put the key in the ignition and started the car.

"Wait! The envelope you brought into the station. Are you sure you gave us everything? Was there anything else inside?"

"What? No. Captain Gerard has everything. Why would I go to him for help and then withhold the only piece of evidence I have?" Why was he asking about the envelope? This situation was all wrong.

"That's fine. Just one more question before I go. Was there anything on the back?"

"I don't know. Flip it over and look for yourself." Not waiting for a reply, she put the car in drive and hit the gas, leaving him standing alone, looking dumbfounded as she sped away. She looked back, praying he wouldn't follow her. If the man was truly working on Andy's case, why did he need to ask her a question he could easily answer for himself simply by taking a look at the evidence? It just didn't add up.

Just then, her phone vibrated. The number was local but unfamiliar. She hesitated for an instant, then remembered her vow to start taking action.

"Hello."

"Kay, it's Amber." Kaylin breathed a deep sigh of relief at the sound of her friend's voice. *"I'm sorry about that, but there was somebody in your apartment. He ran for it when I opened the door. He knocked me down and I dropped my phone. I'm talking it went flying. Two stories to the parking lot. Toast."*

"I'm so glad you're okay. I'll buy you a new phone."

"Crazy!" Amber laughed. *"I've got a replacement plan."* Her tone now turned serious. *"Kaylin, I'm not stupid. Something's wrong with you. What's going on?"*

Kaylin would have liked nothing more right now than to unburden herself to her friend, but she couldn't do it. She needed to stay strong, and crying on Amber's shoulder wasn't the way to do that. "It's one of those proverbial long stories. I'll tell you about it when I get a chance, but not now."

"The police are here. They want you to take a look and let them know what's missing."

"Oh, okay, I can be there shortly." She was about to hang up, but a thought crossed her mind. "By the way, did you get a look at the guy?"

"I got a look at the huge hand he thrust in my face when he shoved me out of the way. Other than that, I don't know. The apartment was dark. He was a big white guy with short hair. Sorry."

"No problem. I'm just happy you're safe. I'll be there soon."

She ended the call and stared blankly ahead as she drove along Murray Boulevard. A few boats, gleaming in the midday sun, plied the waters of Charleston Harbor. Looking at the boats, she sighed. They probably did not constitute a sign from above, or anything like that, but regardless, it was time to make the call.

Chapter 4

Daylight was fading, and the murky waters of Altamaha Sound grew dark. This would have to be the final dive of the day. That was all right. It had been a productive one, and the beer and ribs would go down nice and easy while they sat around a pile of Spanish gold. Dane Maddock tapped his wrist and motioned toward the surface. His partner, "Bones" Bonebrake, nodded, and they returned their attention the spot they had almost finished excavating. Bones held the dredge over the spot, sucking away the sand and silt while Maddock scooped up coins and deposited them in a mesh net. A few more minutes' work, with limited success, and he was finally satisfied that this area had been thoroughly culled. He gave Bones the thumbs up and, together, they began their ascent.

He broke the surface on the port side of their boat, the *Sea Foam.* To the northeast, the shadowy form of Wolf Island was already growing dark as the sun settled down for the evening. To the west, the Altamaha River shone blood red in the fading light.

Matt Barnaby, a stocky, dark-haired crewmate, offered a hand and hauled him up and over the rail.

"We did it!" Matt clapped him on the back, relieved him of the coins he had collected on this last dive, and held them up for a closer look. "These babies will clean up nicely! Good work, guys. How about we find ourselves a place to anchor and fire up the barbeque?"

"Sound like a plan." Maddock grinned and turned to give Bones a hand. They stripped off their dive gear and settled into deck chairs, letting the fatigue from the day's work melt away in the cool air.

"It's Miller time!" a loud voice proclaimed. Willis Sanders, an old comrade and longtime friend, came up from below deck carrying a cooler, followed by Corey Dean, the last member of the crew. They two made an odd pair—Willis was tall and muscular with mahogany skin and a shaved head, while Corey was a short, fair-skinned ginger. As Matt guided the boat toward shore, Willis passed out the drinks.

"You'd better have something better than a Miller in there." Bones said, languidly stretching and yawning. "I am beat and I deserve a Dos Equis at the least."

"At your service." Willis produced a dark bottle with a black label, popped the top, and handed it to Bones, who rubbed the cool condensation across his forehead before taking a long pull. "It needs lime." His eyes suddenly narrowed, focusing on something in the distance. "Hey, Maddock." Bones sat up straight. "You see that blonde on the shore over there? Looks like she's trying to get our attention." He pointed to the south shore of Wolf Island, where a young woman stood waving.

Maddock smiled. "I forgot to tell you guys. We're expecting company."

"No way, man. Why didn't you tell me this was a coed trip?" Willis jibed. "I'd have brought me some company."

"I don't think your mom would fit in with this crew." Corey blushed as soon as the words passed his lips.

"Ooh! The computer geek is trying you!" Bones clinked bottles with Corey. "Whatever you and that chick are going to get up to, make it quick, Maddock. It's your night to cook, and I'm hungry."

"Okay, but she won't appreciate you referring to her as 'that chick.'"

Matt slowed the boat down and Maddock headed to the stern, where they had secured their Sea Doo jet ski craft. He hopped on, fired it up, and headed out across the smooth waters of the sound.

Kaylin Maxwell waited on the shore. A wave of nostalgia passed through him when he saw her smile. The daughter of his former Navy commanding officer, he and Bones had once helped her solve a mystery her late father had been working on and murdered over, and she had joined them on one of the improbable adventures that seemed to have become the norm for Maddock and Bones in the past few years. Maddock and Kaylin had dated for a short while afterward, but it had fizzled, mostly due to distance and disparate lifestyles. Maddock was now seeing someone off-and-on, but long distance was an even greater impediment to that relationship. In any case, he had been surprised to get Kaylin's call earlier in the day, and was curious why she wanted to see him on such short notice.

He was thirty yards from shore when a shrill scream split the air. He looked to his left to see a young girl on a canvas raft paddling furiously toward shore. Behind her, the long, dark form of an alligator swam toward her, its broad snout cutting a v-shaped wake in the water. Gators preferred fresh water, but it was not unusual to see them in brackish water, especially when they were hunting.

Maddock veered the Sea Doo toward the intervening space between the girl and the predator that pursued her. For a brief instant, he considered trying to scoop her up onto his jet ski, but that would require perfect timing and impeccable balance, his craft being too wide for him to simply reach out and grab her. Meanwhile, Kaylin had spotted the girl and was splashing into the water toward her and the gator. Great! Maddock would have to go for the alligator.

The primordial reptile, which looked to be a twelve footer, closed the gap on the girl, who was still paddling furiously. In the distance, a man and woman were running along the shore in their direction, shouting and frantically waving. Maddock was barely aware of them, so focused was he on his target. The alligator opened its jaws wide and Maddock sprang off the Sea Doo.

He came down on the gator's back, his momentum pulling it to the side, and causing its jaws to clamp down on empty air. Maddock got an arm around its snout, wrapped his legs around its torso, and held on as the beast rolled in the water. Maddock went under, had time for a quick breath as he came up, and then was taken under again.

Okay, I've got ahold of it. Now, what am I going to do with it? he thought. He broke the surface again and took another breath of sweet air. He felt like he was riding the world's wildest bucking bronco as the gator thrashed and twisted in the water. His body shifted forward and, for a moment, he feared he might lose his grip on the deadly jaws. He locked his legs tighter around and punched it in the head once, twice, three times. If the blows had any effect on the beast, they served only to further annoy it. It rolled again, and Maddock banged into the seabed, almost losing his hold. He had not realized they had reached the shallows. If he could wrestle the gator to shore, he could get safely away, but, in the water, the gator had the advantage, and he did not dare take the chance of letting go of it.

With one arm around the gator's snout and another around its head, he unlocked his legs and scrambled for purchase on the sandy bottom. The beast thrashed its tail wildly, sending up a furious salt spray, and Maddock felt the snout slipping from his grasp. He gritted his teeth and roared with the effort of holding on, but inch by inch he was losing his grip.

Dark forms burst from the water. Bones and Willis had come to his aid. Willis took hold of the gator's tail and fought to keep it under control. Meanwhile, Bones hastily looped a rope around the snout and wrapped it around several times. Holding the rope in his right hand, he took control of the head, wrapping his left arm around its head, covering its eyes. Maddock moved to take hold of it around the middle, and the three of them hauled the gator, its struggles now subsiding, to shore.

"On the count of three," Dan instructed. "One, two, three!" Everyone let go of the gator at the same time and moved well away as it twisted and shook until Bones' rope, which he had not tied off, came free. Giving an angry hiss, it turned and took to the water, and soon had disappeared back into the sound.

The little girl, frightened but unharmed, had been returned to her parents, who thanked Maddock and his friends profusely before departing.

"Not bad, Maddock." Bones grinned. "But gator wrestling's a sport for Indians, not white guys. You should know that."

"Bones, you're a Cherokee, not a Seminole. How many gators did you wrestle up there in North Carolina, anyway?"

"All I know," Willis interjected, "is I don't want the tail next time. Reminded me too much of a snake." He shuddered and exhaled sharply.

"Dude, how many hard, knobby snakes have you handled?" Bones looked at him with a mix of amusement and scorn.

"That's what I asked your mama last night." Willis grinned wickedly. "Seriously, though. I ain't handled no snakes, and I ain't ever going to. You feel me?"

"Did you guys plan this show just for me, or is this all in a day's work?" Kaylin walked up and stood between Maddock and Bones, who gaped when his eyes fell on her.

"Maxwell! Maddock didn't tell us it was you he was hooking up with! We'd have cleaned up the cabin before you got here." He pulled her into a crushing bear hug, which she didn't seem to mind, despite his salt water-soaked body. Willis greeted and hugged her as well.

And then she turned to look at Maddock. "You told him we were hooking up?" Her flinty stare took him aback, and he found himself at a loss for words. She folded her arms and moved closer until they were almost touching.

"No, I didn't say that. Really."

Her eyes softened and she broke into laughter. "Come on, Maddock." She wrapped her arms around his neck and pulled him close. "Like I'd really take Bones seriously. I know him better than that."

He looked down into her emerald eyes and remembered all too well their time as a couple. Funny how time could erase the bad memories and leave him wondering how he had ever let this picture of perfection get away. "It's good to see you." He wondered if his words sounded as lame to her as they did to him.

"You know, I always liked you two as a couple," Bones said, drawing their attention away from on another. "You're both short and blonde. Of course, Maddock's got the baby blues while you're rocking the green, so I don't know which color your kids would have."

"I'm six feet tall, Bones," Maddock said. "That's not short."

"It is when you're standing next to me."

That was true. At nearly six and a half feet tall, the powerfully-built Native American dwarfed most of the people he met.

"Six feet?" Kaylin patted the top of Maddock's head, where his short hair was already drying. "Maybe if you use enough hair gel."

"So Kaylin, what brings you here, girl?" Willis rescuing Maddock from further abuse.

Kaylin grinned. "Actually, I feel kind of bad coming to you guys like this after not having stayed in touch, but there's no one else who can help me." She shot Maddock a pleading glance and continued. "I'm pretty sure I'm in danger, and…" she bit her lip "…I sort of have a mystery I need help solving. I think it might be your kind of thing."

"You're freakin' kidding me." Bones took a step back and raised his hands. "If you tell me we've got to fish the Holy Grail out of a volcano or some crap like that, I'm retiring." He smiled to assure her he was joking.

Kaylin grinned. "No, it's nothing like that, but I do need your help." She looked at Maddock again, and he knew that, no matter what it was she needed him for, there was no way he could refuse.

"Well," he began, "why don't you come aboard and tell us all about it?"

Chapter 5

They sat on the deck of *Sea Foam*, watching the sun set and enjoying cold drinks after a long day. After a few minutes of awkward starts and stops to the conversation, they settled into an easy give-and-take. He and Bones filled Kaylin in on their exploits since the last time they had seen one another, and she, in turn, told them about her current faculty position at Charleston University, where she taught Fine Arts, and about her boyfriend Thomas, who was also a faculty member at the university.

Not wanting to seem like he was engaging in one-upsmanship, Maddock did not mention his girlfriend, archaeologist Jade Ihara, but Bones being Bones, her name came up almost immediately.

"So, Maddock, have you told Jade that you're hanging out with your ex?" Mischief glinted in his dark eyes as he grinned at Maddock.

"Jade? Is that your girlfriend?" Kaylin's expression was one of polite interest though her voice sounded hollow. "Tell me about her."

"She's also a college professor and an archaeologist. I met her on our last little 'adventure.'"

"You do seem to have a knack for that, don't you?" Kaylin's coquettish smile brought back good memories.

"It sure seems that way, doesn't it?" Maddock laughed. "I guess I can't really call her my girlfriend. We don't have any sort of commitment, what with her working about six thousand miles away."

"You never change, Maddock. You know that? There's always a reason not to get too close." Seeming to realize she'd revealed something a bit too personal, Kaylin blushed and took a long drink while an uneasy silence fell over the group.

"That's me," Maddock added lamely, trying to ease the sudden tension. "So, are you going to tell us about this thing you need help with?"

Kaylin's face fell. "My boyfriend, Thomas, is missing in the Amazon." She dug into the small backpack she had brought with her, took out a picture, and handed it to Maddock. "He left this picture with a friend of ours. It's supposed to be a clue, the only thing we need in order to find him."

Maddock held the picture up in order to best catch what remained of the fading daylight. Bones pulled his chair closer in order to get a better look.

"This isn't the original," Kaylin said. "I left that with the police. I took my own picture of it before handing it over to the authorities, and I had a print made on the way down here."

It was a painting of a lean, angular man with a beard and a handlebar mustache seated in a Victorian-style armchair. His close-set eyes seemed to burn into Maddock. It was a busy image by the standards of the time. The man held a book in his left hand, and a painting of a steamship hung prominently in the background over his right shoulder. A seascape, a dark island looming in the midst of a stormy sea, hung on the wall just over his left shouldeer. Exotic plants in amphorae framed the image.

"That dude looks familiar." Bones took the picture and gave it a closer look before handing it back to Maddock. "Not sure where I've seen him before, but I know he's somebody famous."

"It's Percy Fawcett," Maddock said, passing the picture around so everyone could have a look. "He was probably the most famous explorer of the early twentieth century. He disappeared in the Amazon looking for the lost city of Z." His stomach was doing somersaults. As a young man, he had been fascinated by stories of the famed explorer, and the man had always been something of a hero to him. He had a bad feeling about the direction this conversation was about to take.

"I'm sorry, Kay. If the only clue your boyfriend left you is a picture of Percy Fawcett, that isn't going to be enough to go on. Not even close. People have been trying to find him ever since he disappeared. That trail has been cold for almost a century."

"There's a message in this picture," Kaylin insisted. "And there was a code written on the back. Here!" She handed him another picture.

"Numbers and letters. It's not longitude and latitude. We can't punch it into a GPS." Maddock truly did want to help her, but he didn't see how they had anything at all to help them even know where to start.

"But, the friend I mentioned, the one to whom Thomas entrusted this, was kidnaped, maybe even killed."

"I'm sorry to hear that, but how do you know that picture is the reason this happened?" Maddock asked.

"He warned me and then they took him! They wanted me too, but I got away. They searched my apartment. Maddock, you know I'm not a drama queen, and I wouldn't come to you unless I really needed your help."

The need in her eyes took him back to another time and place, and he shook his head to return himself to the present.

"Okay, I understand. So you want us to go to the Amazon to find your boyfriend? I don't know that we're the best men for that job. It's not our specialty."

"I want you to help me solve this mystery, wherever it might lead. That *is* your specialty. Don't deny it." Her eyes bored into him. "I also need someone who can keep me safe." Her voice fell with the admission. "Whoever these people are, they probably don't know I've given the picture to the police. Even if they do, they might want to make sure I can't tell anyone else what I've seen."

Maddock rubbed his chin, feeling the stubble that had cropped up over the course of the day. He felt for her, truly he did, but was he really the right man for the job? And frankly, if it was Kaylin lost in the Amazon, he'd go after her in a heartbeat, but to risk life and limb for her boyfriend? It was… weird.

"You could stay with us," Corey suggested, "and have the authorities search for your boyfriend. You'd be safe here, and there must be people who are better trained for an Amazon rescue."

"It's not that simple. When Thomas first turned up missing, everyone's attitude, the police, the university, was he'd probably just been delayed because that's fairly normal down there. Now that it's been a while and still no word from him, I'm getting subtle hints that he's probably not coming back. No one really wants to help. If he's going to come out alive, I've got to make it happen."

Bones took the picture from Kaylin, took a long look at it, and dropped it into Maddock's lap. "You know we're going to do it, Maddock. You might as well save us all some time and go ahead and say yes."

"Please, Maddock," Kaylin's eyes glistened on the verge of tears. "There's no one else in the world I can trust. I need you."

"All right." His voice was hoarse. "I'll do it, and it sounds like Bones wants in."

"Hell yes, I do." Bones pumped his fist. "Gonna' lasso me a kangaroo and ride it clear across the jungle."

"They don't have kangaroos in South America." Willis looked at Bones as if he wasn't quite certain if Bones was kidding or not.

"Seriously?" Bones face fell. "Well, I'm not going. I was only in it for the kangaroo rides." He gave Kaylin an evil grin and she laughed.

"That's another reason I need you guys to help me. You can always make me smile no matter how bad the situation gets."

"Maddock's the best at making a woman laugh." Bones spoke behind his hand in a mock stage whisper. "Just not on purpose."

"Hey, I'm not the one whose nickname was 'Mister Shrinkage,'" Maddock retorted. The others guffawed as Bones sputtered an explanation about gossiping women and the temperature of a particular hotel pool.

When the laughter subsided, Corey spoke up. "I take it that, once again, the three of us will be left to finish up the job here while you guys do your thing."

"That's pretty much the size of it," Maddock said. "Look on the bright side. You have a boss who trusts you with every aspect of the business."

"Right." Matt downed the rest of his beer in two gulps, belched, and tossed the bottle back into the cooler before fishing around in the ice for another. "You know, such trusted employees just might deserve a raise."

"Seriously," Maddock said, his voice sober, "if Kaylin needs help, it's probably going to take all of us. We'll have to do some research on the front end, but if I'm going to venture into the Amazon, I'd like to have all you with me if you're willing. There's no better crew in the world and no one I trust more."

"I'm there." Willis raised his bottle and nodded.

"Me too," Matt said.

All eyes turned to Corey, who sat staring down at the deck. Unlike the other members of the crew, he was not a veteran of the armed forces, and didn't get the adrenaline rush from dangerous situations that his friends often did. He sighed and shook his head. "I guess it would get lonely around here if the rest of you jerks were off saving the world and left me to swab the deck. I'll do whatever you need me to do."

"That's settled then." Maddock stood and knuckled the small of his back. "Bones, Kaylin, and I will follow up on this... clue." The simple picture scarcely merited the title, but it was all they had. "You guys shouldn't need more than a few days to finish up here. If we aren't back by then, we'll meet you at home."

Home was the Florida Keys, where Maddock had been planning to spend a couple of weeks after this job, fishing and being generally useless. That would have to wait. If he was honest with himself, though, the prospect of trying to solve another mystery from the past had his heart racing.

"Well," he said to Bones, trying to keep the excitement from his voice. "I guess we need to pack."

Chapter 6

"That's the last one." Bones tossed another book onto the table. "There's not much relating to Fawcett in this library. I did find a freakin' awesome book about cryptids of the Amazon, though. I wonder if they'd let me have a library card."

"Bones, what kind of luddite are you that you're actually looking at books?" Kaylin grinned and returned to the library computer. "I wish I had my laptop, but I didn't want to go back home. Not after, well, you know." Lapsing into silence, she looked around as if danger might lurk behind any shelf.

"I'm going to pretend I know what that word means," Bones replied, "and we'll skip to the part where I tell you to kiss my big red butt."

"A little quieter, you two," Maddock said, making an apologetic wave to the two scandalized-looking old ladies who sat at the next table. He was reading an article online about The Lost City of Z, the subject of Fawcett's alleged obsession. It made for interesting reading, but mostly consisted of speculation founded on rumor, with very little substance to it. "And Kaylin, you don't need to look so nervous. The real danger begins when we head to the Amazon. I think we're safe in the library."

"So, what did Jimmy say when you asked him to help us out on this?" Bones asked. Jimmy Letson was an old friend and a high-level computer hacker. His system, NAILS, could access secure databases all around the world, and he had assisted them with key research on their previous adventures.

"Well, he used a few phrases that curled the hair on my toes, and then he told me he didn't do fairy tales or dime store novels, and to call him when we had something real for him to investigate." Maddock chuckled. "When he finally took a breath, he explained that, while he could probably turn up plenty of information on Fawcett, it wouldn't be anything we can't find ourselves, and a lot of it would be junk. He's a subject of historical interest, and an important explorer, but it's not like there are secret government documents about the guy."

Kaylin sighed as she clicked on another link. A website opened, filling the screen with old photographs of Fawcett. "I can't find anything relating to this Fawcett painting. What few portraits he posed for are pretty ordinary—nothing as busy as the image Thomas left for us." Her shoulders sagged, and she took her hand off the mouse. "I'm already getting discouraged here, guys. Tell me something that will lift my spirits."

"You know," Maddock said, "I think what you've found is actually helpful, in a way. If all the other portraits for which Fawcett sat are plain and ordinary, that actually reinforces the idea that our painting is special. I'll bet you that every detail in that picture is critical to understanding Thomas's message, whatever it might be." Maddock turned away from his computer and looked at Kaylin and Bones. "What do you say we take each element of the picture separately, and see where each leads us?"

"What do you mean?" Bones had abandoned his book on cryptids and was now hunched over an old book, trying to erase Fawcett's huge mustache from a black-and-white print. Kaylin snatched it away from him, shooting him a reproving glance.

"We take each item in the picture one at a time, and try and figure out how it relates to Fawcett. Take the ship, for example. Did Fawcett make a voyage on that particular ship or one like it?"

"We'd have to know her name," Kaylin said. "But I think you might be on to something." She took the picture out of its envelope and slid it onto the table where they all could see it.

"Amphorae," Bones mumbled. "Could be Greek, or, really, any of several Mediterranean cultures."

"I always forget you're not as dumb as you act." Kaylin shook her head.

"Thanks, I guess. Anyway, I don't think I've ever heard of Fawcett doing any explorations connected to the Mediterranean, but it won't hurt to check."

"Let's see what we can find." Kaylin typed a few words into a search engine. "We have a couple of hits." She frowned as she read. "There's speculation that Fawcett's lost city of Z might have actually been an ancient Greek city."

"Wait a minute. A Greek city somewhere in the middle of South America?" Bones frowned. "How does that make sense?"

"It doesn't." Kaylin turned a knowing smile upon him. "But you and Maddock, of all people, should know something doesn't have to make sense in order to be true." She turned back to the computer. "Kephises is a legendary lost city of Amazonia, settled in ancient times by the Greeks. Nothing else of substance, though."

"Do you think that might be what Thomas was searching for?" Maddock asked.

"It doesn't sound like him. He's a scientist, so I can't envision him searching for lost cities. I could see him searching for Bigfoot before he went after a lost city." She shook her head. "Then again, I wouldn't have expected him to have any interest in someone like Percy Fawcett, either. I guess I didn't know him as well as I thought."

"Okay, so we have the possibility that Thomas was looking for the lost city of Z. That's not much to go on." Maddock cracked his knuckles and picked up the picture. "If he truly believed this picture was enough for someone to come after him, there's got to be much more here than meets the eye." He gazed intently at the picture as if the famed explorer could speak to him. "How about the book? Is there a connection between Fawcett and…" He took a close look at the picture, turning it so he could make out the title on the cover. "*The Lost World* by Arthur Conan Doyle?"

"I loved that book when I was a kid." Bones smiled and, for a moment, his eyes took on a faraway cast. "Seems like the connection would be obvious, though. That book was written around the time Fawcett was exploring. What other book would you put in his portrait?" Then his eyes lit up. "Dinosaurs! Kaylin, you said Thomas might go after Bigfoot. What if he believed dinosaurs still live somewhere in the Amazon? Would that be something he'd go off in search of?"

"I… suppose." Kaylin frowned. "It doesn't feel right, though."

"I agree," Maddock said. They were thinking about this all wrong. They were looking at the picture from the perspective of a Fawcett scholar, deepening the mystery of his quest for Z. What they should be doing, however, was put aside what they thought they knew about Fawcett and Z, and instead, treat this image as a set of bread crumbs that would lead them to Thomas. "Look up Fawcett and *The Lost World*."

Kaylin typed the terms into the search engine, and the screen filled with hits.

"Wow!" she whispered. "Look at all of these." Maddock and Bones scooted closer to the monitor. "It appears that Fawcett and Conan Doyle were friends. Some of Fawcett's explorations inspired the story, and the main character in *The Lost World* was even modeled after Fawcett." She continued reading. "Conan Doyle presented Fawcett with a signed copy of the book, and…" An excited smile spread across her face as she went on. "Percy Fawcett took it with him on his next-to-last expedition in the Amazon. Members of his party said he used it as sort of a personal journal, making notes in the margins."

"That's got to be it!" Bones pounded his fist into his palm. "Thomas must have found something written inside that book that told him where Fawcett was headed on his final expedition. Find the book, find Thomas."

"But why wouldn't someone have discovered it before now?" Kaylin looked as if she was afraid to believe it could be true.

"Maybe it's in code or something, like what was on the back of the picture," Bones said. "We don't have any better ideas, do we?"

"Does it say where this book is kept?" Maddock's heart was racing. This felt right. "Is it in a museum somewhere?"

"It's kept in the headquarters of the Royal Geographical Society in London."

"Did Thomas make a trip to England at any time in the last few years?"

Kaylin frowned, her brow furrowed. "He actually did, shortly after we started dating. I remember thinking it was odd because he was gone much longer than he had planned, but I didn't want to be nosy. We weren't serious at the time. You know, he seemed excited when he got back, and he stayed that way. I assumed it was because he and I were getting along so well, but maybe it was something else." Her face flushed, and she hastily called their attention to a thumbnail-sized image of the book inside a glass display case.

"Here's the book." She clicked on the image and the snapshot filled the screen.

There was nothing remarkable about the book itself, but something else had caught Maddock's eye.

"Go back to the previous screen for a minute." Kaylin clicked the back arrow. "Click on this picture here." He pointed to a thumbnail image farther down on the page. Kaylin clicked it, opening an image of one of the rooms in the Royal Geographical Society.

"Look at the picture hanging on the wall in the background." The resolution was low, and the image blurred, but there was no mistaking the portrait.

"It's the same picture," Kaylin whispered. "Thomas's picture. Our picture!"

"You know what this means." Maddock smiled. "Time to pack our bags for England."

"Well, I have mixed feelings about this." Bones frowned, looking disheartened.

"What's wrong?" Kaylin asked.

"I've been to England," he said. "The beer's okay, but the food sucks."

Chapter 7

You are telling me that this is the sole piece of evidence you have collected?" It was only with the greatest of effort that Salvatore Scano kept his voice calm. He found cold serenity to be much more intimidating than anger or annoyance. Let them wonder what was going on behind that calm façade, and they would always fear that you were about to do something rash. "With all the resources you have at your disposal, the best you can offer me is nothing more than a poor quality photograph of an early twentieth-century painting?"

Silence reigned in the conference room as everyone exchanged sideways glances. No one wanted to be the first to speak. Finally, Alex, his son, cleared his throat. "That is the only piece of evidence there is, Father. Thornton left no other clues regarding his plans." He fell silent, wilting under his father's cold gaze.

Shane Kennedy took up the explanation from there. "We searched everything, Sir. Thornton's office, his apartment, even his girlfriend's apartment. Nothing that would tell us where he's going. We were thorough." Few men could meet Salvatore's stare for very long, but, when it came to Kennedy, nothing seemed to intimidate the gritty former Marine, a quality that Salvtore both appreciated and found annoying.

"Details." He reached for his cup of espresso, his eyes never leaving Kennedy's.

"Breaking the encryption on his office computer was child's play, but all the files dealing with the Amazon expedition pertained to the trip he was *supposed* to take with his students—not the one he actually took. He had no computer at home. It's either hidden, been destroyed, or he's taken it with him. No paper trail, either. He cleaned up after himself nicely."

"What about his phone records, credit card charges and such?" Salvatore took a small sip of the hot, dark liquid, its bitter taste a perfect match for the information Kennedy relayed.

"Nothing helpful in the phone records. We believe he used a disposable cell phone for whatever calls he needed to make. We're still working on obtaining the rest of his credit card information, though what do we have doesn't reveal much." He drew a sheet of paper from a manila envelope and slid it along the table to Salvatore, who eyed it dispassionately. It was a copy of a credit card statement with a charge for a round-trip ticket to London highlighted. "Thornton went to London several months before his expedition. While this doesn't tell us anything specific, it suggests that the painting is of significance. Percy Fawcett was from the U.K. after all."

"Anything else?"

"Not yet, Sir, but we are still working."

"I expect nothing less." Salvatore nodded and returned his attention to his son, Alex, who sat chewing his lip and staring daggers at Kennedy. "And what of the man we have in custody? Thornton's colleague?"

"A waste of our time." Alex's voice was scarcely audible across the long conference table. "He knows nothing."

"What *did* he tell you?" Salvatore took another sip and waited.

"Thornton gave him the picture with instructions to use it to find him should Thornton not return from the Amazon. The man's a Literature professor, a school teacher, he didn't know what to do with it, so he passed it off first chance he got."

"And he confirms that this picture is the only piece of evidence Thornton left behind?"

"Yes." Alex feigned a yawn. He thought his reticence made him look strong and aloof, but it served only to make him appear childish. More and more, Salvatore had considered the likelihood that Alex would not be a suitable choice to take the reins of ScanoGen. Alex was not half the man his brother had been. If only…

"You're sure of this?" Noticing Salvatore's distraction, Kennedy had taken over the questioning. "He's not hiding anything?"

"He is a worm." Alex's twisted frown suggested a hint of something foul in the air. "He broke under questioning in less than ten minutes. I worked on him several other times just to be certain. He knows nothing else." Alex actually smiled, something he seemed to do only when he was inflicting pain on someone, or thinking about doing so. How was it possible he was Salvatore's progeny?

"Very well." Salvatore resumed control of the conversation. "What about the girlfriend?"

"We are still working on that as well, sir." Kennedy consulted his notes. "Our contact with the Charleston Police Department tells us she left the hotel they put her up in, and now she's disappeared."

"She is completely off the grid?" David Romani was ScanoGen's Chief Operations Officer, and Salvatore's best friend since college. "You can find no trace of her anywhere?"

"Our contact confirms that she hasn't used her credit card at all in the past two days, and hasn't drawn out any cash since shortly after she disappeared." Kennedy consulted his notes once again. "She made two calls to a cell phone number in southern Florida. That's all."

"Our guest insists that the girl knows nothing. She was shocked to learn her *boyfriend*," Alex sneered as he spoke the word, "had hidden so much from her. She was quite heartbroken over it. Such a tragedy." He breathed on his fingernails and polished them on his shirt. "I don't think she is of much concern to us. As soon as Thornton's friend gave her the picture, she headed straight to the police station and handed it over to them."

Salvatore turned his attention to Mitchell Vincent, an agent who was reasonably bright, but severely lacking in the backbone department. "Returning to the topic of Doctor Thornton. I assume your inquiries in the Amazon region have not uncovered any helpful information?"

Vincent shook his head.

"I am sorry Mister Vincent, I did not hear you."

"No, sir." Mitchell's face reddened. "We located the town where he and his students began their expedition, but we don't know where they went from there. No one admits to having seen them."

Salvatore rose to his feet and looked down the table. "We invested a great deal of time and money on the Pan project. Doctor Thornton has clearly betrayed us. If we cannot locate him and force him to deliver on his promises, the project is dead in the water, and ScanoGen is in serious trouble." He paused to let that sink in.

"Mister Vincent, you will continue the search for Thornton." He next turned to his Chief Research Officer, Julius, who had remained silent thus far. "Mister Julius, I want you to take all the information we have on Thornton's work and have our people conduct their own research. Perhaps we can discover his secrets independently." Julius nodded, but the look on his face mirrored Salvatore's thoughts. It was unlikely they could replicate Thornton's work—they knew too little of what he had discovered, and much of his information was comprised of nuggets sifted from heaps of myth and legend. "David, Kennedy, you two stay with me. The rest of you are dismissed."

Everyone except Alex hurried out of the conference room.

Salvatore fixed him with a blank expression. "Do you require something of me, Alex?"

"No, sir." Alex scowled and flashed resentful looks at Kennedy and David. He was ever envious of their place in his inner circle, but he did not understand that their places had been earned. Alex, however, was content to rely on his family name, indulging his sadistic urges as needed while he waited for the day he would take over ScanoGen. A day that likely would never come. "I mean, what do you want me to do with Thornton's friend?"

"I shall think on it and let you know. You may go now."

Salvatore turned his back on his son and moved to the window overlooking President's Park. Reston, Virginia wasn't the most picturesque place in the world, but the view from Salvatore's office always calmed his nerves.

He waited for the sound of the closing door before he turned back to face the two who waited at the table, still in their seats. He first addressed himself to Kennedy.

"Tell me how you intend to proceed, considering what we have to work with."

"Obviously, we are researching Percy Fawcett and any connection he might have to the items in the painting. We think the book is important. I've got men on their way to England as we speak, with orders to search any places connected with Fawcett, and try to find and obtain anything pictured in this painting. Until we can figure out what exactly this painting is telling us, the least we can do is make sure that if any of the items pictured in it are important, no one else can get their hands on them."

"That is a good start. Anything else?"

"Not at this time, Sir."

Salvatore dismissed Kennedy with a flick of one finger, sank into his chair, and closed his eyes. Only in front of David did he ever let his guard down. "Can you believe that dirtbag Thornton screwed us over like this, David?"

"Relax, Sal, we'll get him." Now that Salvatore's wife had passed, David was the only person in the world who dared call him by his nickname. "Odds are, the guy's dead anyway. What was he thinking, going into the Amazon with nothing but some college kids?"

"That doesn't make me feel any better, David. If we don't find Thornton, we might not be able to complete Pan, and then what?"

"The company will get through it like we always do. So we piss off some defense contractors, and we lose a little money…"

"It's *my* money!" Salvatore slammed his fist down on the conference table, rattling his empty espresso cup and the phone that sat to his left. *And there's more money at stake than anyone knows*, he thought. "Never mind that. We have another problem. I received a call today from a Reverend Felts."

David sat up ramrod straight and frowned. "That idiot with the cable show? The one who blames everything from hurricanes to hangnails on our *'sinful, humanist government?'*"

"One and the same. He wants to meet with me this afternoon."

"Pardon the expression, but what the hell for? Is he on another of his anti-cloning crusades, and accusing us of…" David froze in the midst of running his fingers through his thinning, gray hair. The color drained from his face as he slowly turned to look at Salvatore, his hand falling to his side. "Does he know?"

"He knows something. He wouldn't lay all his cards on the table, but he said enough to convince me it's no bluff."

"You want me to take care of it?" David's features hardened.

"Please do. I'm thinking, though, if he knows, it's because someone let something slip. What I need you to do is find out if there is a leak. And if there is, plug it…

permanently."

"I'll do it. Anything else you need from me?"

Salvatore shook his head. As David left the room, he closed his eyes, rubbed his temples, and groaned. "My head is killing me," he said to no one in particular. Opening his eyes, he tapped the call button on his phone.

"Yes, sir?" Tam's rich voice filled the room.

"I need you."

"I'll be right there, Mister Scano." In ten second's time, Tam Broderick, his personal assistant, was coming through the door carrying a glass of Wild Turkey with two ice cubes, just the way he liked it. "I could tell by the sound of your voice that you needed a little something for your headache. She smiled, her teeth pearly white against her rich, chocolate complexion. Her big, brown eyes radiated motherly concern as she moved behind his chair and began massaging his scalp with her strong fingers.

Kennedy had found her in training for the Washington D.C. police force, and persuaded her, with a little help from Salvatore's bank account, to come to work at ScanoGen. She had a well-organized mind and a gift for details. She was also cute enough to be believable as a secretary, but that petite body packed a wallop. She'd done a bit of kickboxing and Brazilian jiu-jitsu, and could handle a gun as well as anyone in the organization outside of Kennedy. It was little wonder she had risen so rapidly up the company ranks. At times, he had been tempted to expand their working relationship, but pragmatism always won out in the end. Tam was too valuable an asset for him to risk affecting her job performance for the sake of a little entertainment.

"You are aware that I have a late lunch scheduled this afternoon with Reverend Felts."

"Yes, Sir. Two o'clock at the Bastille. I have a private table reserved for the two of you, your car is ready. In fact, you leave in ten minutes. You'll have the usual security, plus two of our people in plain clothes dining a few tables away." Her fingers traced circles across his scalp, her thumbs pressing firmly in the indentation at the base of his skull. The dull pain seemed to flow into her hands, draining him of all tension.

"Very good." He was referring to her thorough planning, but his words could have applied to the scalp massage as well. Was there anything this woman could not do? "I need you to take care of one more detail." Her hands worked their way down his neck, her thumbs working deep into the muscles. "Reverend Felts will not be able to make it to our lunch meeting today. I don't want my time to go to waste, so schedule someone of consequence to dine with me. I trust you can line up someone suitable on short notice."

"I'll see to it right away." Tam gave his shoulders a firm squeeze before departing. "Don't forget your drink," she called back over her shoulder.

Salvatore smiled as he raised his glass in a silent, mocking toast to Reverend Felts's health. He brought the amber liquid to his lips and closed his eyes as it warmed his insides. If only all of his problems could be solved so easily.

Chapter 8

Traffic was sparse on Kensington Gore as Maddock, Bones, and Kaylin approached the red brick mansion that was the headquarters of the Royal Geographical Society. Maddock could not tear his eyes away from the massive chimneys, the many gables, and the steep, multi-leveled roof.

"Freakin' cool!" Bones took out his digital camera and snapped a few pictures. "Why don't we have office buildings like this in America?"

"Lowther Lodge." Kaylin sounded mesmerized. "It was a private mansion before the Society bought it in 1912. That section over there," she indicated a nondescript wing of plain red brick adorned with a pair of statues set back in alcoves high in the wall, "was once the stables, but was converted to a lecture hall."

"Who are the stone dudes?" Bones squinted and aimed his camera at the statues.

"Ernest Shackleton, Antarctic explorer," Kaylin said, "and David Livingstone."

"Doctor Livingstone, I presume?" Bones mimicked a British accent.

"Bones, I'll give you five bucks if you can tell me anything about Livingston besides that quote." Maddock didn't bother to reach for his wallet.

Maddock's phone vibrated and he was surprised to see Jade's name on the screen. The last time they spoke had been four days ago and she expected to be away from any kind of service for a week or more. Feeling more than a little bit weird about talking to Jade with Kaylin standing right next to him, he walked off to the side as he answered.

"Jade! Didn't expect to hear from you for a few more days. How are you?"

"Ugh. It was a disaster, Maddock. We got all the way out to the dig site only to find out Charles hadn't filed all the proper paperwork. Two days hike in, another two out for nothing."

"I'm sorry about that. You should treat yourself to a massage." *"Already on the docket. You know me too well. I wish you were here, you're actually pretty good at back rubs, but you really suck at rubbing feet."*

"That's because I don't like to rub feet. If I was any good at it, you'd want me to do it all the time." The banter felt good and he realized how much he missed her.

"So, what are you up to? Still down in South Carolina finding sunken Spanish gold?"

"Actually, Bones and I are in London." He gave her a quick run-down of the mystery and what they knew.

"Oh, Maddock, you suck! I want in on this!" Her voice was a mock-wail. *"You're going to find a lost city while I'm sitting here waiting for Charles to get his pen out of his orifice and get us some permits."*

Maddock laughed. "It probably won't come to that. We just want to find my friend's missing boyfriend and come home."

"Oh, so it's a female friend you're helping out?" she teased. *"Who is she? She'd better not be prettier than me."*

"Um," Maddock felt like he was a kid again, about to confess to his mother that he'd broken a prized family heirloom. "Kaylin Maxwell." Her silence was so complete that he thought, hoped actually, that he'd dropped the call. "Jade, you still there?"

"Yes. I'm just waiting for you to say 'psyche' or for Bones to get on the phone and tell me I just got punked."

"Jade, there's nothing going on. It's her *boyfriend*."

"Even so, it's inappropriate, Maddock. You know that. She's your ex-girlfriend."

"She doesn't have anyone else, Jade."

"Fine. I just don't get why you always have to be the knight in shining armor, always rescuing people. Can't you just be a little selfish every once in a while?"

"You didn't mind so much when I rescued you."

Jade gave an exasperated sigh. *"I know, and you're right. It's one of those things I hate and love about you. I just... Look, I gotta go. I'll text you when I know when we're heading back out into the field."*

"Okay. Be safe."

"You too." She ended the call without a goodbye.

Maddock closed his phone with a sick feeling in the pit of his stomach. Jade was so confusing. Was she mad at him or not? Did he really care?

"Yo, Maddock! If you're done with girl talk, how about we go inside?" Tucking his camera into his pocket, Bones sauntered past the black wrought iron gates framed by tall brick columns, and up to the front door. To the right of the arched doorway, a black, marble bust of a man of late middle years sat on a white stone pedestal.

"Churchill!" Bones exclaimed. "I love this dude! Let's rub his head for good luck." He turned toward the bust, but Kaylin took him by the elbow and pulled him back.

"That's not Winston Churchill; it's one of the former presidents of the society. Let's just go inside."

"President? Shouldn't he have been Prime Minister?"

"You keep proving you're smarter than you look, Bones." Kaylin gave him a playful elbow to the ribs.

"Don't tell him that," Maddock said. "He prefers to lower people's expectations so he can catch them by surprise with his occasional flashes of brilliance."

He opened the door, held it for the others, and stepped through. The interior of the Royal Geographical Society smelled of books, lemons, and age. The years seemed to emanate from the walls, ghostly echoes of the many great men who had walked these halls.

"Welcome to the Royal Geographical Society. How may I help you?" The speaker was an attractive woman of early middle years dressed in a business suit. Her white shirt was unbuttoned a bit farther down than was strictly professional and, as she leaned toward Maddock, elbows propped on the counter, she pushed her breasts up for full effect. Bones stifled a cough and turned away, but not before Maddock saw him grinning.

"Yes," Maddock said, glancing at her name tag, which read *Sarah Richards*, and quickly redirecting his gaze to the woman's eyes, which were actually a very pretty bluish-green, "we're hoping to do some research on Percy Fawcett. Do you..." he broke off as Kaylin ran her fingers along his forearm. What was she playing at? And after he'd just assured Jade there was nothing to be jealous about. Struggling to suppress the heat that was rising up the back of his neck, he recovered his train of thought and started again.

"Do you have a Fawcett section, or anything like that?" He hoped that if he played the polite, but uninformed, American, he might gain a little extra helpfulness from the woman at the counter.

"We have many documents pertaining to Fawcett." Her eyes flitted toward Kaylin for only a fraction of a second, but Maddock did not miss the disapproval, if not outright anger, that burned there. "Might you be looking for something in particular?"

"Yes, we particularly want information on his last expedition." She pursed her lips and her eyes narrowed, doubtless wondering if he was one of the many whack jobs seeking Fawcett's legendary lost city, so he hurried on. "Also, we're looking for a particular painting. It's a portrait of him seated, holding a book..."

"Of course." The smile was back. "That portrait hangs in the room just up the staircase and to the left. For your research, you should go to the Foyle room. Ask for Benjamin and he will be happy to assist you. He is our resident Fawcett expert." After checking their identification, and entering their names into a computer, she pointed them to a grand staircase, its ornately carved banisters polished to a high sheen.

Maddock thanked her for her help, and as they turned to walk away, Kaylin hooked her arm in his and laid her head on his shoulder.

"What are you up to?" He kept his voice low.

"Ditch me," she whispered. "And make it obvious."

"Say what?"

"I want to know if Thomas was here. That lady's got the hots for you. Make an excuse, go back and flirt with her a little bit, and then ask her to check and see if Thomas was here."

"You are one wicked woman." Now her flirtatious behavior made sense. As they reached the stairwell, he pulled away from her. "I'll meet you up in the reading room," he said to Kaylin, his voice loud enough to be heard in the quiet lobby, but not so much as to make it obvious that he wanted to be overheard. "I have a few more questions I forgot to ask. I'll be there in a little while."

Kaylin pouted and shot an angry glance toward the front counter before flouncing away up the stairs. Maddock had to hand it to her. She was quite the actress when she needed to be.

"Your girlfriend seems upset," Sarah observed as Maddock headed back in her direction. The smile on her face said that she, by contrast, was anything but unhappy at this turn of events.

"Not my girlfriend." Maddock leaned easily against the counter and grinned. "My ex. It's complicated though. We still have to work together, which isn't exactly easy. You saw how she is."

"Some women just don't know when it's time to let go." Sarah ran the tip of her tongue across the bottom of her upper lip. So ostentatious was her attempt at flirtation that Maddock nearly choked. "So," she continued, "what *else* can I do for you?"

Why couldn't Bones have been the one to hit on her? He was a natural with this stuff. Nothing to be done for it now, so Maddock plunged in. "I need a recommendation of a nice, intimate place for dinner tonight, and a phone number for someone to join me."

He flashed his most winning smile, feeling all the while like a buffoon. Surprisingly, it worked. Sarah hastily jotted her name and number on a slip of paper and tucked in into his pants pocket. He forced himself not to react when her fingers roved a bit too far afield. *This girl would be perfect for Bones, but then again...* Realizing his thoughts were drifting, he refocused his attention on the task at hand.

"I do have one other, much less important, request. Can you tell me if a friend of mine visited here sometime in the last year or so?"

"I'm not supposed to do that." Sarah looked at him uncertainly. "Those records are private."

"And I'm not supposed to make dinner dates with beautiful women when I'm supposed to be conducting research." He gave her a wicked grin. "I don't want any private information; just tell me whether or not he was here."

"All right, but if you get me sacked, you owe me two dinners. What's the name?"

"Thomas Thornton." He watched as she typed in the name. She was actually kind of cute in a lush, full-figured sort of way. Perhaps he *should* make time for dinner tonight. What was he thinking? He already had one girl mad at him. He didn't need any more complications in that area.

"Ah! Here he is. Thomas Thornton. I can't tell you exactly when he visited, but I can confirm he was here."

"That's perfect. You've been a big help. I'll just head up and meet my friends." He turned and headed back toward the staircase.

"Maddock?" He glanced back at her. "I get off at five o'clock. No pun intended."

"Gotcha." He hurried up the stairs, already wondering if he should make an excuse, or just not call her at all.

He found Bones and Kaylin checking out the original painting of which Thomas had left them the picture, which hung between two more traditional portraits of the famed explorer.

"He looks like he's made of old leather," Maddock observed. "Hard to believe he never came back from his last expedition. He always seemed like the kind of guy nothing could stop."

"Not much to see here, I'm afraid." Bones said. "No small, semi-hidden images that we couldn't see in our picture. No secret codes." He glanced at the other two portraits. "Both of these have little plates at the bottom. Let's see, *Donated by Andrew Wainwright, grand nephew of Percy Fawcett.* No brass plate on our painting, though."

They looked at the portrait a little while longer. Finally, agreeing there was nothing else to be found here, they headed for the Foyle Room.

The Foyle Reading Room was a pleasant surprise—a contemporary oasis inside this classic Victorian structure. Sunlight shone through wide plate glass windows that angled inward, illuminating the counter that ran the length of the wall, wrapping around the bends in the oddly-shaped exterior wall. Workstations were set up along its length, with permanent computer setups in the center and laptop connections on either side. Bookcases lined the wall to his right, and various cabinets, counters, and worktables were arranged throughout the room. It had the feel of a university library.

A short, stocky man, with blue eyes and short brown hair looked up as they entered the room. "What can I do for you?"

"We're looking for Benjamin," Maddock said, giving the room a quick scan. "Can you tell us where we might find him?"

"You just did." He smiled and shook hands with Maddock. "Expected an old fart, did you?" He didn't wait for an answer, but motioned for them to take seats around a nearby table.

"If you're looking for me," he said with a sigh of resignation as he settled into a chair, "you must be interested in Fawcett. We've had quite a bit of that lately. People looking for the lost city, trying to track his last expedition. Those are the normal ones. Then there are the weirdoes…" He dismissed the thought with a wave, propped his feet on the table, and folded his hands on his chest. "So, into which category do you three fall?"

"Technically, we're searching for someone who falls into the first category," Maddock said. "We are looking for information on Fawcett's last expedition, but only in order to find a friend who went off in search of him."

Benjamin's face remained impassive.

"We're not making this up." Kaylin showed him a copy of the missing person's report she had filed with the Charleston Police. He scanned it with bored eyes, made to hand it back to her, then snatched it back.

"This chap looks familiar." He held the paper close, scrutinizing the photo of Thomas which Kaylin had paper-clipped to the report. "I remember him. He didn't want to look at any of the usual Fawcett documents. He only wanted to see Fawcett's copy of *The Lost World.*"

Maddock sat up a little straighter. "Did he find anything in it?"

"Couldn't say." Benjamin shrugged. "Truth be told, he seemed a bit disappointed. Looked at it for over an hour. He wasn't reading it, mind."

"How could you tell?" Maddock didn't understand. What else would Thomas have been doing?

"He was flipping through too fast, looking at the margins and the spine through a magnifying glass. Even turned it upside-down a few times. I don't know what he was hoping to find, but whatever it was, I don't believe he found it. Left here quite down."

Maddock felt hope draining away, but as long as they had come this far, they might as well take a look at the book. "Could we see it? Is it still on display?"

Benjamin frowned, the lines in his forehead deepening. "Sorry, but it's gone missing. It was gone from its display when I arrived yesterday morning."

"Someone stole it?" Kaylin's voice was soft with dismay.

"I assume so. Odd, though. No alarms, nothing on the security cameras."

Maddock's heart sank. "Can you tell us; was there anything... unusual about the book? Was there anything written inside of it?"

"It is one of a kind. It was inscribed to Fawcett by Sir Arthur Conan Doyle himself. Beyond that, I couldn't say. It's not like I handled it on a regular basis." Benjamin frowned. "As long as you're here, is there anything else you want to take a look at?"

A cool sense of conviction flowed through Maddock's mind. This was no coincidence. It couldn't be. Someone had gotten here first and taken the book.

"Did Thomas say anything about where he might be going, or what he had planned?" Bones had reversed his chair and sat with his chin resting on his arms. "Maybe the dude had something more in his head than just following Fawcett's last expedition."

"Not that I recall. As I said, I only remember him because I thought it odd that an American would come all the way to London simply to look at a copy of one of Fawcett's personal possessions." He flashed them a knowing grin. "But I see now that it's not as unusual as I had thought."

"Is there anything..." Kaylin bit her lip. "Sorry, I don't exactly know how to ask this. We think this might be more than just a simple matter of someone getting lost in the Amazon. Are there any stories that connect Fawcett to something that might interest people today? I mean, interest them enough to..." She swallowed hard.

"I understand what it is you're asking. There are more legends surrounding Fawcett than I care to know. To call them far-fetched would be an understatement. Fawcett found Z and lives there as a white king like Prester John. Fawcett found a lost white race that has preserved the secret knowledge of the ancient civilization of your choice. Even if one of them were true, it would be of great academic interest, but nothing more." He raised his head and pondered the ceiling for the span of three heartbeats. "If your friend has gone chasing after Fawcett, and has not returned, the most likely explanation is that the same thing happened to him that has happened to too many Amazon explorers in the past. I am sorry."

Maddock ground his teeth in frustration. The stolen book couldn't be the end of the line. The book was significant—he was certain of it. But Benjamin had said that Thomas had examined the book, yet seemed disappointed, as if he had not found what he was looking for.

"Do you know of any museum or library that has Fawcett's personal items on display?" Maddock asked.

"There is no Fawcett museum. Most of the items of interest relating to Fawcett are here. Is there anything aside from the book that I can show you?"

"I don't suppose so," Maddock said. For some reason, he did not feel comfortable asking about the Fawcett painting, and, in any case, it was the book they wanted, and the book was not here.

"You might look up Andrew Wainwright and give him a ring."

"The guy who donated the portraits downstairs?"

"Yes. He's a descendant, and has probably forgotten more about Fawcett than I've ever known. At any rate, good luck with it."

They shook hands with Benjamin, thanked him for his time, and made their way back to the entrance.

"Bummer," Bones said as they descended the stairs and passed through the lobby. "I thought we'd get a little farther than that."

"Me, too," Maddock agreed.

Sarah hailed them as they approached the exit. "That was a short visit. Did you find what you were looking for?"

"Benjamin was a great help," Maddock said.

"You'll call me about dinner, then?" She eyed him like a tigress contemplating exactly how she wanted to play with her food before eating it.

Before Maddock could answer, Bones sidled up to the counter.

"*You* didn't steal the Fawcett book, did you Sarah?" He grinned lasciviously. "We really wanted to see it. Maddock might have to frisk you…"

"Thanks, Bones!" Maddock grabbed his friend by the arm and steered him toward the door. "I'll talk to you later, Sarah. Thanks again."

As soon as they were out the door, Sarah left the front desk and hurried to the nearby break room. Terry looked up as she entered, and gave her a hopeful smile. Sooner or later she would have to break down and go on a date with the poor tosser, but for now, the occasional flirtatious smile or touch on the arm was enough to make him as helpful as she needed him to be.

"Terry, would you be a dear and mind the front for me? I need to phone someone, and it's rather private."

"Not a boyfriend, I hope." He tried to play it off as a joke, but failed.

"No, it's nothing like that." She forced a laugh. "I just need a chat with my doctor—female stuff, you know."

Red-faced, Terry assured her that he understood completely. She doubted he knew much of anything about female anatomy or the issues relating to it. In fact, she harbored a suspicion that he still lived with his mum, but he could be counted on to do what she asked of him, and that was what mattered.

She hurried back to her office, took a card from her purse, and punched up the number on her cell.

"Yeah?"

"Hi, this is Sarah from the R.G.S."

"Yeah."

Not a great talker, this one. "You asked me to call you if anyone came around asking after Fawcett's copy of *The Lost World*."

Silence.

"Are you there?"

"*I am.*"

Five hundred pounds, she reminded herself. She could put up with rudeness for that. And it wasn't as if she was doing anything wrong—just passing along a bit of information. She quickly gave the man on the other end the names of the three visitors, and a brief description. She felt a pang of guilt when she mentioned Maddock's name. She rather liked him and he was quite handsome.

"*Okay, good. Are they still there?*"

"No, they just left." She looked out the break room window, and was surprised to see that the three were standing on the pavement, engaged in a serious discussion. "They're just outside the building, though."

"*Good. Keep an eye on them until I get there. There's another five hundred in it for you.*"

The call ended. Sarah took a deep breath and peered outside again, hoping Maddock and his friends had departed, but no, they were still there. She had a sinking feeling that she had just made a terrible mistake.

Chapter 9

They had almost reached the street when Maddock hesitated. Something was bothering him—a feeling that he was right on the verge of making a connection. But what? He was sure it was important, if only he could put a finger on just what it was.

Turnin back to look at Lowther Lodge, his eyes fell on the entrance and the bust next to the door.

And it struck him.

"Kaylin, what was it that Thomas wrote on the back of the picture?"

"Let me see." She fished in her purse, looking confused. She pulled out a sheet and handed it to him.

There were five letters at the top, and then a series of number pairs.

MRKHM
2-5 1-17 1-1 2-13 4-10 3-3 1-10 1-22 1-12 3-3 1-19
1-23 1-6 1-8 4-6 4-11 6-9 7-1 7-10 8-16

Could it be that simple?

"Did either of you catch the name on the bust by the front door?"

"Markham!" Kaylin's eyes widened as realization dawned on her face. "Do you think it could refer to the bust?"

"I think it's worth a look. Let's go."

They hurried back to the front door and Maddock read the inscription aloud.

"This monument to the memory of Sir Clements Markham, KCB, FRS, and for 12 years President of the Royal Geographical Society, was erected in the year 1921 by the Peruvian Nation in gratitude for his services as historian of their country."

"And this means… what, exactly?" Bones rubbed his chin and peered doubtfully at the sculpture of Markham.

"I wonder," Maddock said, looking again at the numbers Kaylin had written down, "if these pairs of numbers correspond to lines and letters in the inscription." He knelt to take a closer look. "If I'm correct, the first letter would be…" He consulted the paper, and then counted over to the letter *L*. The next number pair gave him the letter

E. As he continued, his certainty that he was on the right track grew. His heart beat faster as he called out each letter. When he was finished, he looked at the paper on which Kaylin had recorded the letters, though he already knew what the message said.

"Let Albert be your guide."

"Great," Bones said. "Now we just need to find this Albert dude and ask him where to go next. Any idea where to start looking?"

"Across the street."

At first, Maddock thought Kaylin was joking, but her expression was deadly serious. She arched her eyebrows in an *'Are you doubting me?'* look, and put her hands on her hips.

"Okay," Maddock said. "I'll bite. Who or what is Albert?"

"Just across the street, in Kensington Gardens, is a well-known memorial to Prince Albert."

"Seriously?" Bones crowed. "Is he in a can? Do we need to let him out?"

"I'll wager that's what the message is referring to," Kaylin said, rolling her eyes at Bones's weak attempt at a joke.

"Sounds good to me. Let's check it out."

The Albert Memorial consisted of an ornate canopy, nearly two hundred feet high, set above a gilded statue of a seated Prince Albert. Mosaics decorated portions of the exterior, and sculptures devoted to the arts and sciences sat atop the pillars and in corner niches. Around the base was a marble frieze, and at each corner a sculpture representing one of the Victorian era industries: Agriculture, Commerce, Engineering, and Manufacturing. Steps on each side led up to the memorial, and ringing the base were decorative railings, with even more elaborate sculptures at each corner. It was this set of sculptures that caught Maddock's eye. Each displayed a group of figures on and around a beast of burden, and was named for a region of the world: Africa, Europe, Asia, and America.

The America sculpture featured a bison, with three figures, one male and two female, all rendered in the classic style—European facial features, flowing robes and, as Bones put it, "topless." Each wore a headdress that reflected Native American stylings, and two of the figures held stylized spears.

"It's got to be the America sculpture, right?" Bones asked, walking over to lay his hand on the bison's head. "I mean, we're looking for connections to the Amazon, so what else could it be?"

They scrutinized the sculpture with care, examining every last detail, but none of them could infer even the most tenuous connection to Fawcett or his expedition. Finally, they were forced to conclude they were on the wrong track. They circled the base of the memorial, first examining the other sculptures, then stepping back and taking in the memorial as a whole, hoping something would leap out at them. It did not.

"I don't understand." Kaylin, usually so positive, hung her head. "It says to let Albert be our guide. How could it not be this memorial? It's right across the road from the R.G.S., and there's Albert just sitting there. This has got to be it."

Maddock agreed with her. He was convinced a clue of some sort was right there for them all to see, but, for the life of him, he could not see what it might be. He looked up at the gilded figure of Prince Albert, as if the answer lay in his lifeless gaze.

And it struck him like a slap in the face!

"Bones, I need a big diversion." To his friend's credit, he did not so much as bat an eye.

"How long?" He was frowning thoughtfully, the mental gears obviously turning at a rapid pace.

Maddock took another look at the memorial— the rail, the steps, and the sculpture itself—and did a quick calculation. "Two minutes ought to do it. Can you handle that?"

"Are you kidding, bro? I thought you were going to give me a challenge. I got this."

As Bones turned away, Maddock slipped off toward the opposite side of the memorial. Thankful for the sparse assemblage of tourists, he quickened his pace, reaching the far side just as Bones began to shout.

"Ladies and gentlemen, may I have your attention please? I need everyone over here for just a moment!"

Maddock stole a glance in his friend's direction. Bones was holding Kaylin's hand and calling out for everyone to join them, beckoning to the recalcitrant ones. Judging by the look on her face, he had not clued her in on whatever it was he was about to do. A few curious people were making their way toward the couple, but several more hung back, uncertainty painting their faces.

"That's it! Just gather around right here!" Bones called. He spotted the few who were hanging back near Maddock. "You folks as well, please! I want to make this a moment that my lovely lady will never forget." At these words, the confusion in the crowd melted away, and everyone hurried toward Bones and Kaylin. Wishing he could spare time to watch the spectacle, Maddock took a last look around, took a deep breath, and vaulted the rail that surrounded the memorial.

"That's right! Video it for us. You can even put it on the internet. I want the world to know how I feel."

Maddock grinned and kept moving.

"When I first met this beautiful young woman, I knew then and there that someday she would be my wife!" Everyone had gone silent, listening raptly to Bones as he proclaimed his love for Kaylin.

Maddock sprinted toward the monument, closing the distance in a flash.

"Of course, when I asked her out, she told me she wouldn't go out with me if the world was covered in 'my dung,' to put it delicately, and I had the last roll of toilet paper." The crowd laughed and jeered as Kaylin, playing along, protested that she had said no such thing.

Maddock took the steps two at a time, and soon found himself beneath the canopy where Prince Albert sat gazing off into the distance.

"As you can see, she didn't hold to her vow, and I'm the luckiest man in the world for it. And so…"

A sigh escaped the spectators gathered around Bones and Kaylin, and Maddock was certain the Bones had gotten down on one knee. An unexpected feeling of envy crept up inside of him. There had been a time he had envisioned the day when he would propose to Kaylin. Of course, that was a long time ago, and they had both moved on. He shoved the thought out of his mind and clambered up onto the statue of Prince Albert. He hoped no one was watching, but if so, it was too late now.

Bringing his head level with Albert's, he stared out across the lawn, trying to follow the prince's line of sight. In the distance, he could clearly see an old brick building. It was as if someone had cut a passage through the sparse trees so that the structure was framed by wooded patches on either side.

"Kaylin, you have made my life worth living. And I have never minded that you're transgendered."

Maddock choked down a guffaw and almost fell off of the statue. Internally cursing and laughing at Bones, he moved his head directly above Albert's, just to be certain his line of sight was correct. It was.

"You know I never wanted kids anyway. So…"

His heart pounding with excitement, he sprang down, and dashed down the steps.

"Will you marry me?"

As Maddock sprang over the rail, he heard polite applause ring out, and knew that Kaylin must have said 'yes.'

"Thank you!" Bones shouted. "And I was kidding about the tranny thing. I took one home once, but that was beer-related." More laughter, and a deeper round of applause.

Maddock felt a tug at his elbow. He looked around to see a freckle-faced young boy looking up at him.

"What were you doing up there?"

"Oh, I was checking for… rust."

The boy considered this for a moment before nodding sagely and walking away. Breathing a sigh of relief, Maddock made his way through the dispersing crowd, and back to his friends.

"Congratulations," he said. "When's the big day?"

"Oh, we haven't set a date yet." Kaylin was looking at Bones with an expression Maddock knew all too well. It was her 'I'm pretending to be happy because we're in public, but you will pay later' look. In the time the two of them had dated, she had only given him that look twice, and he had forgotten neither incident. Both had been caused by Maddock giving his honest opinion on her friends' artwork: one a so-called sculpture titled "Patriotism" that consisted of strips of the American flag wrapped around toilet paper rolls; the other a performance art piece that he still could not wrap his mind around, though he did remember a country song played backward, and lots of grunting.

"I think I'm onto something," he said. "Follow me." He headed off in the direction of the building he had spotted. Bones and Kaylin strolled along in his wake, holding hands and doing a reasonably good job of acting as if they'd just gotten engaged. When they were back on the main street, Kaylin yanked her hand away and rounded on Bones.

"Tranny? How'd you like to be a eunuch? I dare you to go to sleep…"

"Not now!" Maddock hadn't intended to bark an order like that, but he'd been a military man, and some old habits die hard. "We don't need you calling attention to us," he said in a calmer voice. "Yell at him later, if you need to."

Kaylin directed a contemptuous glare at Bones, but said nothing.

"The statue of Albert looks directly at that building right there." He pointed across the street to their destination.

"What is that place?" Bones asked, stepping out into the street and almost being run down by a passing car. He ignored the blaring horn and kept walking.

As they drew closer, Maddock could read the sign by the front door. "Royal Institute of Navigation. No way! My dad talked about this place. He visited here when he and Mom were still dating. She spent the day seeing the sights, and finally had to drag him out at closing time." After all these years, the memory of his parents, and of their tragic deaths, was still bittersweet.

"My father came here as well, looking for information on the *Dourado*," Kaylin said, her voice thick with emotion. Her father, a former officer and friend of Maddock and Bones, had been murdered a few years before, and the three of them had completed his quest for the lost ship and its unbelievable cargo.

"So what do you figure we'll find here?" Bones asked. "Doesn't seem like a Fawcett kind of place."

Maddock and Kaylin suddenly exchanged excited glances, each arriving at the same conclusion. "The ship in the picture," they said in unison.

Maddock drew the picture from his pocket and looked at the portrait of the ship hanging in the background. The two-master, with its single smokestack, was the only possible link between their single clue and the Institute of Navigation. Hope rising anew, he led them inside. As he stepped through the front door, Maddock was actually relieved to see an elderly man working the front desk. He didn't think he could handle two cougars in one day. The man greeted them warmly, and when Maddock asked if anyone on staff was versed in early twentieth century British ships, he directed them to the Cundall Library of Navigation, where shelves strained under the weight of aging tomes. The smell of old paper pervaded the room.

"Good afternoon. How can I help?" The speaker was a woman of middle years, with silver-streaked brown hair and a sharp nose that contrasted with her dull eyes. She pushed a pair of black-rimmed reading glasses up onto her head, where they joined the two matching pairs already resting there. She did not quite meet Maddock's eye when she looked at him. All told, she gave off an air of casual disinterest.

"Yes," Maddock said. "We're doing some research and I was hoping we could find something out about this ship." He handed her the picture and held his breath. Unless this vessel was famous, he was searching for a single grain of sand on a seriously large beach.

The woman squinted at the photograph, held it out at arm's length, and began patting her pockets.

"Bugger it all! Where did I leave my glasses? That's the third pair I've lost today."

Suppressing a smile, Maddock pointed to the top of her head. Neither thanking him nor noticing the two other pairs of glasses atop her head, she pulled them back down over her eyes, and held the picture up again. "Ah! *Quest!*" she proclaimed.

"Not exactly a quest," Bones said. "We just want to find out about the ship."

"That's the name of the ship. *Quest.* It belonged to Ernest Shackleton."

"The polar explorer?" Maddock asked sharply.

"One and the same." She narrowed her eyes as she looked down at the picture. "Odd that it would be Fawcett in the painting. You would think it would be Ernest."

"Do you know of any connection between Fawcett and *Quest*, or Fawcett and Shackleton, for that matter?" Excitement was rising in Kaylin's voice, and with it rose Maddock's spirits. "I'm sorry; we didn't ask your name."

"No matter." She waved away Kaylin's apology as if shooing a fly. Still gazing at the picture, she took a second pair of glasses off of her head and began tapping her lips with them. "Fawcett and Shackleton," she mumbled. "The only connection I can recall is Fawcett went on an expedition with…"

"James Murray!" Maddock exclaimed.

If she was annoyed with Maddock for finishing her sentence, it did not show.

"Yes. Murray was part of the Nimrod expedition." Bones snickered, but he need not have bothered. The woman, who still had not given them her name, seemed blissfully unaware of most of what transpired around her. "Shackleton, of course, led that one. Two years later, Murray joined Fawcett on an Amazon expedition. It went badly and Murray hated Fawcett after that. I don't think they ever settled that grudge."

"Interesting," Kaylin said, though her tone said otherwise. This connection was tenuous at best.

"Do you have any information on *Quest* that we could take a look at?" Maddock asked.

"Of course." She walked between Maddock and Bones, both of whom had to step aside to avoid her bumping into them. Maddock watched her disappear between two heavily laden shelves. She had not instructed them to come with her, but who knew if that was intentional? With a shrug, he followed after her. After a moment's pause, Bones and Kaylin came along. They wound through the shelves, coming out at a small wooden table next to a tall window giving them a view of Hyde Park and the Albert Memorial.

"Wait here," their guide instructed. Feeling like schoolchildren, they took their seats around the table and waited. She returned in short order, bearing an armful of books. "These," she laid two books on the table, "are specifically about *Quest*. These three," she laid more books on the table, "contain chapters or sections referencing her, and this," she dropped an oversized tome down in front of Maddock, "is a collection of entries and clippings about Shackleton. Leave them here when you are finished."

Maddock thanked her, but found himself talking to the back of her head, as she had already turned and was walking away. Shaking his head, he pulled the large book toward him and opened it up. He soon found himself absorbed in the details of Shackleton's exploits.

Bones and Kaylin also took books and began reading. It was not long before Bones spoke up.

"Dude, it sank."

"What?" Maddock looked up from a clipping of an interview with Shackleton. "Where? When?"

"Back in 1922, near a place called Ascension Island. Cool name, huh?"

"Seriously?" Kaylin asked. "Or do you have some kind of pulp adventure book hidden in there?"

Bones laid the open book flat on the table so all three of them could see it.

"I'm serious. It was Shackleton's final expedition. He died of a heart attack and, on the way back, *Quest* sank."

Maddock pondered this new bit of information. Could the shipwreck be of significance? "Does it mention any connection to Fawcett?"

"Let me see... Fawcett..." Bones turned the page and he suddenly did a double-take. "Yes! Right here!" He read on for a moment, and then spun the book around so Maddock could see. "It says Shackleton and his friend Rowett were on their way to the Antarctic, and they stopped in Rio. Shackleton had what they thought was a heart attack, but he refused treatment. There, they met up with Fawcett, who was returning from a trek in South America, and he joined them on their expedition."

Kaylin snatched the book away, found the spot where Bones had left off reading, and took over the explanation.

"Shackleton suffered another heart attack, died, and was buried in South Georgia.

They tried to continue the expedition, but failed. *Quest's* engines were not powerful enough to battle the tough Antarctic waters, and she had a serious leak. They finally turned back, but the ship foundered and sank off the coast of Ascension Island. Fawcett is credited with keeping them alive until help arrived. He spent long hours exploring the small island, brooding, keeping mostly to himself, and cursing the "infernal birds," but he did make sure they had adequate food and water." She continued turning pages until she finally declared that there was nothing more to be gleaned from that particular book.

With a renewed sense of purpose, they focused in on Shackleton's final expedition, searching for more references to Fawcett. Maddock found the next clue.

"Listen to this," he began, his pulse throbbing in his temples and his skin electric with excitement. "Fawcett said he lost something valuable in the shipwreck. He never said what it was, but he tried to recreate it, whatever that means, but feared his effort was incomplete." He continued reading, and suddenly came upon a passage that gave him such a start that he almost dropped the book.

"Sorry," he said, finding his place again, "but you have to listen to this." He lowered his voice, though no one seemed to be about. "Fawcett was quoted as saying he was thankful he managed to save his copy of *The Lost World*, which he treasured."

"But we already knew that," Kaylin objected.

"Just wait." Maddock's voice trembled with excitement. "He said that it was the most treasured of all of his books, and he'd sooner lose the first edition Arthur had given him than lose his personal copy."

It took Bones and Kaylin a moment to comprehend the full implications of the statement, but then Bones whooped and pumped his fist.

"The stolen book is the first edition given to him by Conan Doyle!"

"So the real book is still out there somewhere." Maddock thought about it for a while. "Let's take Benjamin's advice and look up this Wainwright fellow."

They had scarcely passed through the exit doors when Kaylin glanced up and her face went pale. "That's one of the guys who kidnapped Thomas. I'm sure of it."

Maddock looked up to see a tall, thick man with ash blond hair striding toward them. "Bones, get Kay out of here right now. Go!"

Bones didn't have to be told twice. He took Kaylin by the arm and ducked back into the building.

The man was almost on top of Maddock, and as he reached inside his jacket, Maddock sprang into action. He leapt in close and drove an uppercut into the man's chin just as he was drawing a pistol from underneath his jacket. The man grunted and stumbled back, but Maddock stayed on him. Grabbing the man's wrist in both hands, Maddock drove his forehead hard into the taller man's mouth, and heard the satisfying crack of breaking teeth. Still controlling his wrist, Maddock swept his legs out from under him, and rode him to the ground. He punched him once, twice in the temple, and banged his head on the pavement for good measure. The gun slipped from the stunned man's limp fingers. Maddock picked it up, tucked it his belt, then relieved the man of his wallet before getting to his feet and giving him a solid kick in the temple to keep him down. Keeping an eye open for more potential attackers, he untucked his shirt in order to hide the gun.

"Say! Did that bloke just pull a gun on you?" A paunchy man in a suit stood at the corner, looking at Maddock as if he was radioactive. He held a cell phone, but appeared uncertain if he should use it.

"Yes, he did. Call the police." Not waiting for the man to grow bolder, Maddock turned and dashed back inside the building after Bones and Kaylin.

"Did you happen to see which way my friends went?" he asked the frightened desk clerk. "The blonde girl and the tall Indian."

"Through that door." The man pointed a shaky finger down the hall. "And another man came in after them while you were… fighting outside."

As he dashed through the door the clerk had indicated, he heard a loud crash, and turned a corner just in time to see Bones punch a man in the throat, grab him by the back of the head, and drive a knee into his face. Kaylin, her face pale, but her expression resolute, hurried out and took Maddock's hand.

"What was the crash?" Maddock asked as they turned away from the front desk and headed down a narrow hallway, following the sign that read 'Emergency Exit.'

"Bones knocked down some books," Kaylin said. "I don't know why."

"I was trying to push the freakin' bookshelf over on the dude." Bones sounded defensive, almost hurt by her criticism.

"Those are huge shelves, and they're anchored to the floor. You can't just push one over." Maddock couldn't help but grin, despite their perilous situation.

"In the movies, one shove and the whole library goes down like a bunch of dominoes."

"Yes, Bones," Kaylin said in a patient voice, as if speaking to a child, "but real life isn't always like the movies."

"Sure, you tell me that now," he said in a sullen voice, "after I almost got us killed. We could see the guy through the shelf. He had a gun, and looked like he was up to something, so I tried to knock the shelf over on him. All I managed to do was hit him in the side with a few books."

"Some of them were big books," Kaylin said, "with lots of pages. Who knows? Maybe he got a paper cut."

Bones muttered something Maddock was certain was obscene, but Kaylin owed Bones for the tranny comment.

Outside, they hurried across the street and tried to blend in among the tourists in Hyde Park. After five minutes' walking, they felt safe enough to stop and talk. Maddock took out the wallet and looked at the driver's license. It belonged to a Cyrus Wallace of Manassas, Virginia. The credit cards bore his name as well.

"Why did you take his wallet?" Kaylin frowned and looked at him in confusion.

"One, I wanted to know who he is. Two, having no cash, credit cards, or identification might make it harder for him to come after us." Spotting a garbage can nearby, he hurried over to it and stuffed the wallet down to the bottom. "Screen me," he instructed. While Bones and Kaylin moved in close to block him from view, he took out the pistol, removed the clip, and hastily wiped it down.

"You can't have a handgun, here!" Kaylin gasped. "It's against the law."

"Yes, but bad guys don't always follow the rules," he said, stuffing the pistol down into the garbage and pocketing the clip. He would ditch it elsewhere.

"I know," she mumbled, her cheeks pink. "And our next step is?"

"Now," Maddock said, "we pay this descendant of Fawcett a visit."

Chapter 10

The first thing Cy was aware of was a faint, quavering voice in his ear.

"Just lie still there. Help is on the way."

He didn't know the voice. In fact, he wasn't sure where he was. All he knew was he hurt. A lot. Groaning, he rolled over and spat blood on the ground. Running his tongue across his teeth, he counted two chipped, and one that was broken. Muttering a curse, he climbed to his feet. Damn! Now he remembered.

It was that Maddock guy he'd been warned to look out for. The chick from the R.G.S. had called to let him know that Maddock and his friends were asking about Fawcett. She'd lost sight of them as they headed toward Hyde Park, but once he showed a picture around, people remembered the big Indian, and had pointed him toward the naval library. He groaned as the memories returned. They'd warned Cy not to underestimate Maddock and Bonebrake, but neither had looked like much to Cy, and he'd had the element of surprise on his side, or so he'd thought.

The world swam into view and resolved into an image of a portly man peering down at him. Cy snarled and climbed to his feet. He grabbed the man by the tie and pulled him close.

"Which way did they go?"

"Uh, the fellow who... who kicked your arse? He went back inside the building there."

Cy shoved him away and barged through the front door, hoping, praying someone would try to stop him. Inside, a frightened old man warned him that the authorities were on the way.

"You listen to me, you old fart." Cy reached across the counter and took hold of the man's lapel. "If they get here before I'm gone, you tell them I ran into the park. You do anything else, I use my gun on everyone I see. Got it?"

The man nodded.

"Now, what were those three looking for?"

"I don't know. They went to the Cundall Library. That way."

Cy hurried up the stairs. The average police response time in London was seventeen minutes, and a call about a fight that was already over probably wouldn't be considered urgent. A glance at his watch told him he'd been out for three or four minutes, and had wasted another minute with the fat guy and the old man. If he made this quick, he should be okay.

Inside the Cundall Library, he met a chunky woman with two pairs of reading glasses on top of her gray hair, and another pair perched on the end of her nose. She blinked at him like an owl.

"May I help you?"

"Yeah, you can help. The people who were in here earlier: the guy, the girl, and the big Indian. What were they looking for?"

"Looking for?" She looked around, a dazed expression on her face, and stared at a nearby table as if she had never seen one before. He had a mind to shake an answer out of her, but then she seemed to wake from her trance. "Oh, the Fawcett people."

"Yes, that would be them. Why did they come here looking for information on Fawcett? This is a naval library."

"Why, yes, I know that." She smiled faintly, as if pleased by the thought.

Where did they find this crackpot? Cy tried again. "Do you know if they found anything? Did they write down anything? Make any copies?"

"No copies. No notes."

"All right, lady, listen to me." He reached for his gun... it wasn't there. Where was it? He patted himself all over. It wasn't in his front pockets, nor his back... Wait a minute! Where was his wallet? Hell! He had lost it in the fight. Who was this Maddock, anyway? Kennedy had probably given him a bio in his email, but Cy had skimmed it. He wasn't much of a reader.

The old lady was looking at him like he was the one who was nuts. The expression on her face infuriated him.

"All right, you crazy old cow. Listen to me very carefully. I want to know what they learned and I think you can tell me. Now start talking."

"All I heard was something about an item that Fawcett treasured." Her voice was serene, as if she was unaware of the danger she was in. Her eyes seemed to be focused on a point somewhere just above Cy's head and, for an instant, he thought about looking behind him, but he could not act nervous. He needed to intimidate this loony toon if he could.

"What else did you hear?"

"They also mentioned Shackleton," she said, "and I heard the phrase 'buried in South Georgia.' I did not hear anything else."

"Who is Shackleton, and what part of Georgia?"

"Shackleton is the famed polar explorer, a contemporary of Fawcett. And South Georgia is an island. I believe Shackleton is buried there."

"Nothing else? They didn't say what this thing is that Fawcett treasured?"

"No. I do not eavesdrop." She folded her arms and tapped her toe. "I only happened to overhear a few snatches of conversation as I went about my work."

"Did they seem... excited? Like they found what they were looking for?" She just stared at him. "Fine." Cy let go of her and gave her a shove. "You just sit tight and don't tell anyone about any of this. You don't want me to come back, do you?"

"No. You are much too loud for a library."

A thought occurred to him. "Did they look at any books?"

"Yes. They seemed particularly interested in that one right there." She pointed to a battered old tome with a gray cover.

Cy picked it up, tucked it inside his jacket, and turned to leave.

"I am sorry, but we do not permit patrons to check books out. I will have to ask you to remain here if you wish to read it."

Unbelievable. Ignoring the old cow, Cy barreled toward the exit, keeping his eyes open for Maddock and his friends. Of course, if they had his gun, he had to be extra careful. He wondered if Jay had gone after them.

Jay! Cy had forgotten he hadn't come here alone. His bell must have been rung hard for him to lose track like that. He made his way down the stairs and through a side exit just as a siren wailed in the distance. Good response time, but not good enough.

He still had his phone on him, so he dialed up Jay's number.

"Yeah?" Jay sounded as groggy as Cy felt. "Where are you?"

"On Kensington. Where are you?"

"I'm in the car. I'll pick you up." Jay broke the connection, and Cy kept walking, trying to look interested in the sights. A police cruiser flashed past him, skidding to a halt in front of the institute.

Moments later, a metallic green Ford Fiesta pulled up to the curb. Habit led him to take two steps around the front of the car before Jay waved him back. Cursing any country that would put the driver on the right side of the car, the car on the left side of the road, and him in a Ford Fiesta, he threw open the door and folded his frame into the compact vehicle.

"You forget again?" Jay grinned as he pressed the accelerator.

"Screw you. What happened to Maddock and the other two?"

"Don't know," Jay said. "That Indian sucker-punched me. He knocked me clean out. I haven't been hit like that since I…"

"Yeah, I know. You boxed in the service. You're a regular Brown Bomber."

"Is that supposed to be a racist comment?" Jay regarded him out of the corner of his eye.

"No, I just can't think of any other boxing nicknames at the moment."

"C'mon, man. There's Sugar Ray, Iron Mike, Smokin' Joe, Gentleman Jim. Lots of great nicknames."

"So, what should I have called you?" Cy had no interest in boxing, but he wasn't in any hurry to admit what had happened to him.

"The Motor City Cobra." Jay savored the words, saying them almost like a prayer.

"But you're not from Detroit."

"Forget you, man. You don't know boxing." Jay glanced in the rear-view mirror. "Don't seem to be any cops following us. So, what happened to you back there?"

"I gotta call in." Cy took his phone out again and scrolled down to Kennedy's name. He took a deep breath, steeling himself, and hit the call button.

Much to Cy's chagrin, Kennedy answered on the first ring. *"Cy, what's the status?"*

"I think I've got something." He filled Kennedy in on the enticing clues regarding Fawcett, Shackleton, and South Georgia, as well as his having procured a book that was of interest to Maddock. He was careful to make it sound like he and Jay had arrived after Maddock and party had departed, and had gleaned these kernels of information through solid detective work. He omitted the part where the two of them got their asses kicked, and Cy got his gun and wallet lifted.

Kennedy was silent for a long time—longer than Cy could stand it.

"It's good, isn't it Kennedy? I mean, we are after Fawcett, and if…"

"We'll follow up on it," Kennedy said in a clipped voice. *"Anything else?"*

"I've already shipped Fawcett's copy of *The Lost World* to you like you asked. Fastest available post."

"Fine. Send the book you found today along to us, and then lie low until you hear from me."

The call ended. Kennedy wasn't much of a people person.

"Thanks for not telling him about… you know." Jay stared straight ahead, his expression blank.

"No problem." Now it was Cy's turn to feel like an idiot. "Say, I'm going to need you to spot me some cash for a few days."

"What? How come?"

"Maddock sort of stole my wallet." Cy would have given anything to be somewhere else at that moment, as Jay threw back his head and laughed. "And when I see him again," Cy muttered, "I'll kill him."

Chapter 11

Maddock parked the car in front of a modest, two-story, detached brick house in Blackheath, a suburb southeast of London. Despite the pleasant surroundings, he couldn't help looking up and down the street, searching for potential danger, wondering if the guys who attacked them at the naval library would track them down again. He'd given the name and address of the man with whom he'd fought to his friend Jimmy, in hopes he could shed some light on exactly who these people were of whom they'd run afoul.

A tiny man with a shock of unkempt white hair answered the door. He eyed them through thick glasses that gave him the appearance of a snowy owl.

"Mister Maddock and party, I presume?" If his body was small, his voice was huge. He could have done voice-overs for NFL films.

"Yes. Thank you for seeing us, Mister Wainwright." They shook hands, and Maddock introduced Bones and Kaylin.

"Bloody hell," Wainwright said, craning his neck to look up at Bones, "are all American Natives your size?"

"They wish. My mother just fed me good."

"Fifteen stone, I'll wager." Wainwright cupped his chin, looking Bones up and down with a critical eye.

"Dude, I haven't been stoned since I was a teenager."

Wainwright did a double-take, laughed and ushered them into a living room overflowing with books. Every wall was lined with floor-to-ceiling shelves, with volumes stacked two deep and tucked into every open space: aging hardcovers, old pulp novels, and textbooks of varying age and subject. Four overstuffed chairs circled a round table, also stacked with books. Books were even piled haphazardly in the corners, and a basket stuffed full of newspapers, magazines, and mystery novels sat next to one of the chairs. He urged them to make themselves comfortable, and returned a few minutes later with hot tea, sandwiches cut in small triangles, apple slices, and sugar cookies.

"Hold this, young man." He handed Maddock the tray, then bent down and cleared the coffee table of books with one sweep of his arm. "Ordinarily I would not treat books so," he said, placing the tray on the table and pouring a cup of tea for each of them, "but they are romance novels my late wife's sister thought I would enjoy reading. Perish the thought! If I want pornography, I shall search for it on the internet."

Bones choked on his tea, and Kaylin's eyes were suddenly wide as saucers at the comment. Maddock merely grinned and nodded.

"You have quite an impressive library," Maddock said, looking around the room.

"Thank you. I fear this is, as they say, only the tip of the iceberg. All of my rooms, save the kitchen and bath, are in a similar state. I have always had a fascination, and perhaps an obsession, with books."

"You know, I'll bet you could put all of these on one e-reader." Bones cocked his head, as if performing the calculations in his head. Kaylin frowned and nudged Bones's leg with her toe, but Wainwright laughed.

"I have one of those as well. Most of my books, however, are too old and obscure to be available electronically. If you would like to scan them for me, I'm certain it would not take you more than a few decades."

"You don't want Bones touching your electronics." Maddock took a bite of a sandwich and forced down a grimace. It tasted like cream cheese and cucumber, or something like that.

"I scanned my butt once and emailed it to *Playgirl*. They didn't write back, though." Bones stuffed two of the small sandwiches into his mouth at once.

"I'm sorry, Mister Wainwright." Kaylin laid a hand on the man's arm. "We are not as crazy as we must seem. Well, Maddock and I aren't."

"Nonsense. It is a delight to have young people in the house. I was a university professor for many years, and I miss the absurd humor of youth."

Maddock couldn't remember the last time he'd been categorized as young, much less youthful, but he'd take it. "The reason we are here is actually in regard to a book. One that belonged to Percy Fawcett."

Wainwright gave him a shrewd look. "What book might that be?"

"A copy of *The Lost World*. A personal copy in which he took notes. It was supposedly one of his most treasured personal possessions."

"I see." The temperature in the room seemed to drop ten degrees. Wainwright sat up straighter, his posture stiff. "May I ask why you are interested in this book?"

Maddock sensed he would have to tread carefully. His instinct also told him that anything short of the truth would not suffice. Wainwright impressed him as a sensible, perceptive man.

"We are searching for a friend who disappeared in the Amazon. From what we have learned so far, we believe he was on the trail of Fawcett's final expedition, and we think he found information in this book that guided him on his search."

"He has been missing for some time now." Kaylin sat her cup on the table and folded her hands together in a supplicating gesture. "He is not some crackpot—he is a college professor, like you were. We need to find him."

"What is his name?" Wainwright still eyed them with suspicion.

"Thomas Thornton." Kaylin took a photograph from her purse and handed it to Wainwright, who looked at it for a long moment, and then seemed to sag.

"I warned the lad. He was here, I don't recall for certain, perhaps a year ago, if that. I let him look at the book, and told him what I know, and what I suspect about my granduncle's final expedition. I'm sorry. I tried to dissuade him. Truly I did."

"Thomas was here!" Kaylin's face and voice were filled with hope. "Did he show you this picture, or a picture like it?" She handed him the image of the Fawcett painting.

"Ah! The portrait that hangs in the Institute. No, he did not show this to me, though I am familiar with it. It is, in fact, the final portrait Fawcett commissioned of himself."

"Thomas left this for us as a clue to his whereabouts," Maddock said.

"Did he? Well, it certainly ties several things together. Fawcett, *The Lost World*, the island, *Quest*, and, of course, the amphorae." Three seconds' tantalizing silence followed the statement. Maddock's heart raced, and he found himself inching forward in his seat, as if the old man's words would reach him sooner. Finally, Wainwright shook his head and continued.

"I fear Fawcett was losing his mind prior to his final expedition. The story has been passed down through the generations of my family. It is said that he paced the floor, muttering to himself about something he lost on the shipwreck. He spent long hours poring over his copy of *The Lost World*, works of ancient history, and the Bible."

"The Bible?" Maddock was puzzled. "What was the connection there?"

"No one knows. At any rate, something happened on his next-to-last expedition into the Amazon that made Fawcett more certain than ever that the lost city of Z was real, and that its inhabitants were descended from the ancient Greeks. Hence the portrait he had commissioned and donated to the Institute just before his departure. He knew he could not make public what he believed about Z. He was already a subject of some skepticism because of his beliefs. To share the conclusion he had come to would have held him up to public ridicule."

"But if this portrait represents what he thought he was going to find," Bones began, a look of deep concentration on his face, "he could come back later and tell the world, *'See, I knew it all along. In your face!'"*

"That is one way of saying it." Wainwright smiled. "Fawcett was a proud man, and it would have been important to him to prove that he had not simply stumbled upon the lost city by happenstance, but had set out to reach it, already knowing it was there."

"What exactly happened on the previous expedition that affected him so?" The familiar feeling of anticipation that always came when he was on the verge of a breakthrough, surged through Maddock. Bones and Kaylin also sat in rapt silence, waiting for the answer.

Wainwright, clearly enjoying his captive audience, took a sip of tea, and carefully placed his cup and saucer atop a stack of books before beginning his tale.

"Understand, what I am about to tell you is conjecture, partly supported by cryptic phrases jotted in the margins of Fawcett's copy of *The Lost World,* and partly based on family legend of the things he supposedly said during his final months at home."

Maddock nodded, and Wainwright continued. "Fawcett was just completing an extended trek through the Amazon. Supplies and morale were low, and he and his party were making their way out of the jungle, when a young man stumbled into their camp one evening. He was in bad shape: weak from hunger and dehydration, eaten up by insects, and nursing old wounds. He looked, according to Fawcett, decidedly Mediterranean, and he spoke an odd language, containing enough words familiar to Fawcett and his native guides that they could piece together bits of his story. Some of his words, however, sounded Semitic to Fawcett. He recorded a few of the words, spelling them phonetically, and eventually concluded they were Punic."

"You lost me there," Bones said.

"Punic was the language of Carthage," Maddock said.

"Oh yeah! Hannibal and the war elephants. Cool!"

"They were descended from the Phoenicians," Maddock said, "the first great sailors in the ancient world. Some say the Phoenicians reached the New World centuries before Christ." Maddock wondered if this could possibly be true, or had Fawcett fallen prey to hope and wishful thinking?

"Precisely." Wainwright took another sip of tea. "From what they could gather from the young man's ravings, he and a young woman had fled their home, a place he called 'Keff Sess.' You have, I presume, heard the legend of Kephises?"

Maddock nodded and motioned for him to continue.

"The young woman was lost along the way, the victim of what the young man called 'the Dead Warriors.' He offered, as proof, fragments of pottery Fawcett believed were Mediterranean in origin, as well as some sort of plant material that the young man said had strange, mind-altering properties. He also gave Fawcett a map carved in stone. It was very old, and showed the path his ancestors had taken to Keff Sess. His home, he said, was 'in the air,' and could only be reached by taking a secret path—the Path of Five Steps. These steps, Fawcett wrote in his copy of *The Lost World.*"

"What about the map?" All thoughts of rescuing Thomas were forgotten. In his mind, Maddock was already trekking through the Amazon, following Fawcett's last journey.

"Lost when *Quest* sank, along with the only copy Fawcett made of it. The pottery and the strange plant material were lost as well. Only *The Lost World* was saved."

"So, when he went on his final expedition, what did he do? Just go by memory?" Bones asked.

"It is odd, that. After the shipwreck and the loss of his maps, he grew paranoid. He claimed to have made a map from memory shortly after the wreck, and he said he put it where no one could get to it. When he set off on his final expedition, he left his book behind, presumably after copying the five steps, and whatever other information he needed. And, as the story goes, he was never heard from again." Wainwright folded his hands in his lap and gave them a small, sad smile.

"Why has none of this ever been made public?" Kaylin asked. "It could have shed light on Fawcett's final expedition."

"My dear, you can't possibly believe the story to be true. Fawcett had clearly let his dream of finding Z overcome his good sense. To his mind, the raving young man's Kephises was his fabled city of Z. He was already believed to be… eccentric. The family could not reveal the story of his last months to the rest of the world. It would have sullied his memory and cast a shadow over all the good work he did in his life. He was perhaps the most important explorer of the twentieth century." Wainwright sat up a little straighter as he spoke the last. "He did not deserve to be remembered as a fool who believed in myth and superstition."

"But, couldn't the family have used the information to search for Fawcett?" Kaylin persisted.

"If the map had been available, perhaps, but all the family had were the five steps. As it stands, many have searched for him and failed."

"Mister Wainwright," Maddock began, "could we please see the book?"

"Young man, you seem a sensible sort. Don't tell me you would actually set off on this fool's errand."

Maddock had seen enough strange things in his life that he had little trouble believing Fawcett's tale, though he sensed this was not what Wainwright wanted to hear.

"We aren't looking for the lost city; we're looking for Thomas. If he believed in the lost city, maybe there's something in the book that will help us find him."

Wainwright stared at him, and finally, hung his head. His voice was rough with regret. "How can I possibly show it to you after what happened to your friend? I fear I encouraged him by letting him read it, and now he is gone."

"Bones and I are highly capable. We have spent more than our share of time in hostile environments and dangerous situations. I assure you, we are also going into this with eyes wide open. You have made it clear to us that this is, in your opinion, a wild goose chase, and a potentially deadly one. To us, this is a rescue mission, not an adventure, and we need your help."

The old man took his time considering Maddock's request. He sipped his tea and stared into the distance. Finally, he nodded. "Very well. As long as we are clear that I am actively discouraging you from this quest. Make no mistake, that's what it will be. I can see it in your eyes. You have the same spirit that my ancestor had. You might begin by searching for your friend, but sooner or later, the longing will overcome you, and you will not be able to rest until you have solved the mystery, or at least tried. Don't try to deny it." He held up a liver-spotted hand. "I would have no lies between us." He eased himself out of the chair and shuffled off into the adjoining room, returning a few minutes later with a tiny flash drive, which he handed to Maddock.

"After your friend visited me, I worried that the story might get out, and what it would do to Fawcett's legacy if it did. I have not decided what should become of it after my passing, but it is in a safe deposit box for the time being. I have scanned all the pages with his notes on them. I trust that you will do me the courtesy of not sharing these with the world."

"You can count on us." Maddock tucked the flash drive in his pocket and shook hands with Wainwright. "I should warn you. Someone else is on the trail of Fawcett's last expedition, and they could be dangerous."

"I will take all necessary precautions," he said. "I have considered taking a holiday outside the country. Perhaps now would be a good time."

They all thanked him profusely and bade him goodbye. As they piled into the car and drove away, a sense of excitement filled the air.

"So, what next?" Bones asked.

"First of all, we give Jimmy some more homework. We need him to see what he can do to help us pinpoint *Quest's* location." He grinned. "We are going to find a lost shipwreck."

Chapter 12

Tam rapped twice on Salvatore's door. She was the only person whom he permitted to do so, because he knew she would only interrupt him if it was important.

"Come!" he called.

"Boss, we have a problem. Two men fitting the description of the bumbling idiots Kennedy sent to London are wanted for questioning." She laid a folder in front of him and went on. "It seems they confronted Maddock and Bonebrake at the Royal Institute of Navigation. Cy was caught on a security camera getting his ass handed to him by Maddock. Jay apparently didn't make out any better with Bonebrake. Jay, at least, had the good sense to get out of there, but Cy stormed inside, threatened the staff, and told them he had a gun and would kill everyone if he had to."

"I would love to ask if this is a joke, but I know better." Salvatore closed his eyes and took a few deep breaths. "Tell me, what do we know about Maddock and Bonebrake?"

"Ex Navy SEALS. Now they find shipwrecks, search for sunken treasure, that sort of thing."

"Why did Maxwell reach out to them in particular?"

"There's a history there. Her father was their commanding officer at one time. She and Maddock also had a relationship a few years back."

"Interesting. She asks her old boyfriend to help her find her new boyfriend. What else can you tell me?"

"About Maddock and Bonebrake? Not a great deal, except for rumors. Sketchy stuff related to archaeological finds. Nothing firm." She wasn't sure what to make of what she had heard about them.

"Anything else?"

"I think Cy lost his wallet. It appears Kennedy had to scramble to secure new identification and a passport for him, as well as a credit card. Now I.T. tells me someone hacked into the personnel files looking for information on…"

"Cyrus Wallace." Salvatore slammed his fist down on the table. "Get Kennedy on the phone. I want Cy on the next plane back here. I'll flay that idiot." He stood and walked to the window. "The hacker, how far did he penetrate?"

"Not very deep, as far as we can tell. Just the basic personnel files."

"How did he get past the firewall?"

"The techies are working on that as we speak. They understand it means their jobs if they don't find that breach and seal it. I took the liberty of suggesting it might mean their balls, too."

Salvatore didn't smile, but Tam thought she saw a hint of a twinkle in his eyes. "Did they back trace him?"

"Couldn't. Whoever it is, he or she is good. We'll keep trying, of course."

"I know you will. Now, get Kennedy in here."

Kennedy frowned when he saw Tam seated at the conference table. He took a seat across from her and waited for Salvatore to speak.

"I want a full report on Cy and Jay." Salvatore's voice was ice.

"Of course." As always, Kennedy was unflappable. "They acquired Fawcett's copy of *The Lost World*, but there was nothing in it, except for an inscription from the author to Fawcett. I'm having it checked for invisible ink, and the inscription reviewed for any irregularities that might suggest a code of some sort, but nothing so far. They almost got themselves into trouble with the authorities, but we got them out of England, and they're now following up on a possible lead." He glanced at Salvatore's face and didn't wait for a follow-up question. "I've sent them to South Georgia Island to check out Shackletons' burial site. Cy thinks there might be a connection there."

Salvatore grunted a subdued, mirthless laugh. "Good. That will get them out of the way for a while, at least. So, you are telling me that England was a complete failure?"

"Perhaps not." Kennedy grinned and opened his briefcase.

Tam kept the surprise from her face. What had Kennedy found that he had kept so well hidden?

"Dane Maddock was reading this book." Kennedy made a funny face as he said Maddock's name. He placed an aged volume on the table. "It makes reference to a voyage on which Fawcett embarked prior to planning his final expedition. The ship he was traveling on sank and Fawcett lost something important. We don't know what it was, but it's not inconceivable that it's connected to our situation. I think we should find the site of this sunken ship and see what, if anything, is there."

Sal looked at Tam. "What do you think?"

"It's thin," she said, "but it's a possibility, which is all we have right now. I haven't yet read the passage, since Kennedy has kept this to himself." She paused, hoping Kennedy was at least squirming on the inside, since he never showed anything on the surface. "I don't, however, see any harm in following up on it. We have the resources to get the help we need." She thought for a moment. "If Kennedy isn't mistaken, which is possible, since his information comes from Cy, Dane Maddock will probably be coming for whatever is inside this wreck. Do we want to go for it ourselves, or simply wait for him to get it, and take it away from him?"

"I don't like waiting around for anything," Salvatore said. "Kennedy, I want you moving on this immediately. We have to assume that we're in a race with Maddock; a race you will win, or we shall have a conversation." He dismissed Kennedy with a flick of his finger.

Kennedy rose, nodded to Sal, and spared a steely glance at Tam before striding out, his phone already to his ear. He would not soon forget that Tam had questioned him in front of Sal. That did not matter now. The two of them would have it out one day, and he had no idea what he was up against. Some people resented being underestimated, but Tam found it a useful tool in her arsenal.

"I'm going to roll the dice here," Sal said, his eyes boring into hers. "We need to go after Thornton, and quick. Assemble a team and be ready to move on my command. You have your choice of the agents. If Kennedy finds something, that is well and good. If not, use what information we have about Thornton and about Fawcett, and begin the search. We can't put this off any longer."

"Sir, are you saying…" She didn't dare let herself believe it could be true.

"I'm putting you in charge. You might not have Kennedy's experience, but you're a hell of a lot smarter than him, and you haven't screwed up… yet. Choose your agents, outfit your team, get down to Brazil, and await my instructions."

Heart pounding, and dizzy with triumph, Tam stood and gravely nodded her head. "I won't let you down, Salvatore."

He rose to his full height, and looked down at her with a ghost of a smile on his lips. "I know you won't, *figlia mia.*"

Chapter 13

Sea Foam **sliced** through the gently rolling sea, its rising and falling barely noticeable. Maddock sat on the bed in his below-deck cabin, scrolling through the latest report from his hacker friend, Jimmy Letson.

"The guy who attacked me works for a company named ScanoGen. Sound familiar?"

Kaylin shook her head. "No, why should it?"

"Because, according to Jimmy, they made a substantial transfer into Thomas's bank account a few months before he left on his expedition."

Kaylin's entire posture changed. She sat ramrod-straight in her chair, her lips pursed. "He never said anything to me. Not about ScanoGen, and certainly not about any money." Her shoulders sagged. "Of course, all of this came as a surprise. It's hurtful to know that he had a whole part of his life that he wouldn't let me into." She suddenly looked right at Maddock, and then something passed across her face, and she turned away.

When the two of them had been a couple, she had accused him of locking her out of various parts of his life—mostly memories of his time in the service, and of his deceased wife. That was probably what was on her mind now, but he was not about to go there with her. Not now, at least.

"I'm sure he had his reasons." He tried to make his voice soothing, but his throat was dry, and his words lacked conviction. Trying to make an ex-girlfriend feel better about her current boyfriend was not his thing. The sadness in her eyes, however, convinced him to try again. "Look, he obviously knew these were dangerous people, and he wouldn't have wanted you mixed up with them."

"Well, I *am* mixed up in it, in case you didn't notice."

"Yeah, I think I noticed. I'm in the middle of it, too." He held up a hand, forestalling her retort. "The guy tried to keep you safe. That's what guys do for the women they care about. He probably figured he could do for ScanoGen whatever it was they wanted done without involving you, and then the two of you could enjoy the money he made off the venture."

"He just... the lying..." She stood and began pacing the room, which only required a few steps, but she moved to-and-fro, fists clenched, until he couldn't look at her without feeling dizzy.

"If you're that upset with him, we can call this thing off if you like. You can lie low with us until ScanoGen gets off your case, and then you can go back to your life."

Kaylin froze. Slowly, she turned to face him. The anger on her face melted, replaced by an amused smile.

"Right, Maddock. You've waded knee-deep into a mystery, and you'd just turn back and walk right out again without seeing it through to the end?"

He had to laugh. "Fine, you know me too well. Now shut up and let's finish going over this."

The ice broken, she plopped down beside him on the bed and leaned against him. The closeness should have been uncomfortable, but its familiarity was welcome and natural.

"ScanoGen is a bioengineering firm. Most of their money comes from military applications. That's not a big surprise, considering the Amazon is believed to hold countless species of plant life that could have properties previously unknown. People have searched the rainforests for everything from recreational drugs to a cure for cancer." For a moment, he was sadly reminded of their mutual friend, Franklin Meriwether, who had joined them on one of their adventures. Another place to which he didn't want to let his thoughts drift.

Kaylin seemed to know what was on his mind, and she slid her arm around his waist and laid her head on his shoulder. "So Thomas found something, or believed he would find something, that ScanoGen wanted. It's the whole Fawcett connection that doesn't make sense to me. In all the research we've done, there hasn't been any mention of Fawcett going after some super plant, or whatever it is they want."

"You remember the story Wainwright told us. The young man had with him a plant that had some sort of great power." Maddock tried to ignore her closeness, the softness of her hair against his cheek. "That's the only way I can see how a company like ScanoGen fits in."

Kaylin looked up at him, her green eyes sparkling.

"What is it?" Maddock dropped his papers on the bed and met her gaze.

"You know, you never would let me all the way in, Maddock, but when we were together, you were never dishonest with me."

Before Maddock could reply, her arms were around his neck and her lips pressed firmly against his. His surprise dissolved in the familiarity of the moment. It was as if the two of them had never broken apart. He returned her kiss, pulling her tightly against him.

"Ahem."

They jerked away from each other like two teenagers caught parking. Kaylin smoothed her clothing and Maddock sat up straight.

Bones leaned in the doorway, grinning. "Sorry to interrupt, but I thought you'd like to know, we've found *Quest*."

Unable to contain his excitement, Maddock bounded to his feet, offered Kaylin a hand, and followed Bones out of the cabin. Bones arched an eyebrow at him and grinned, but Maddock ignored him.

Above deck, Willis was already suiting up. "It's about time we got into the water. Man, I hate this searching stuff."

Inside the cabin, Matt and Corey were looking at a small monitor.

"Uma's down there right now," Matt said, his eyes not leaving the screen. Uma was an unmanned submersible camera, so nicknamed by Bones, who was a big fan of Uma Thurman's character in the movie *Pulp Fiction*. On the screen, the outline of *Quest*, blue-gray in the deep water, suddenly filled the screen. She had settled on her port side, the bow resting on a rocky formation on the seabed, and the ship's distinctive profile made her easy to recognize.

"She's in great condition," Matt observed. "Smokestack's still intact and everything."

"According to Jimmy's information, Fawcett's cabin was most likely in the aft section on the starboard side," Corey said, scrolling down through a document. "Take her in that direction and let's see what we can see."

"Are you going to send Uma inside the ship?" Kaylin asked, leaning forward to get a better look. She touched Maddock's arm, a detail not missed by Bones, who smirked.

"Not a good idea," Maddock said. "She could get tangled, or the ship's hull might cause us to lose our signal. There's higher-tech equipment out there, but Uma's usually all we need for our work."

"Maddock, take a look at this." Matt sounded surprised, and not in a good way. He pointed at a dark spot on *Quest's* hull. Growing larger as Uma came closer, the image resolved into a square hole cut in the ship's side."

"Sorry to state the obvious, but that's not natural." Bones said.

"Look at the edges. They're sharp and clean. The cut is fresh, too." Mat shook his head. "Somebody got here before us, and not too long ago."

Maddock stood up straight, clenching and unclenching his fists. "It has to be ScanoGen. As far as we know, they're the only other player in this game, and I'm sure they have the resources to pull it off fast."

"So what do we do?" Bones enunciated each word. When he spoke like that, he was right on the verge of breaking something or someone.

"We go through with the dive. Maybe they missed something. It would be crazy to come all the way here and not even take a look."

"Then what?" Matt already sounded defeated.

"I've got something up my sleeve," Maddock said. "We'll talk about it after the dive." Really, all he had was a nugget of an idea buried deep in his mind. He didn't know if it would pan out, but they'd find out soon enough.

Maddock plunged into the water, letting the cool depths envelop him. Down here he could put thoughts of Kaylin and Jade out of his mind, and focus on the dive. This was the one place in the world that always felt right. Bones swam on his right, Willis his left. They glided through the water like three phantoms, slipping down into the semi-darkness. If only he had gills, he thought, he'd never leave the water. He'd felt that way since the first time his parents had taken him to the beach. Maddock, just a toddler, had slipped his hand from his father's grip and wobbled toward the surf as fast as his legs would carry him. He had two memories of that day: the salt spray on his face, and his parents' laughter as they trotted alongside him. Smiling, he kicked harder, plunging toward the sunken *Quest*.

The hole in the ship's hull was exactly as Matt described it. It had clearly been made very recently, and the clean, straight cut indicated the use of the modern tools. It was large enough for two men to swim abreast through it, but they took it one at a time, just to be safe.

Maddock took the lead and found himself in a small room that fit the description of the cabin in which Fawcett had resided during his voyage on board *Quest*. He gritted his teeth. ScanoGen had done their homework, all right, and the likelihood of Maddock and his crew finding the missing artifact, whatever it was, was now even smaller.

Bones and Willis followed him in, moving with caution, so as not to stir up too much silt. As planned, the two of them exited the room to explore other cabins in case Jimmy's information had been incorrect.

Maddock scanned the cabin. Though *Quest* lay on her side, one of the advantages to being underwater was that he could easily orient himself, creating the illusion that the ship still sat upright. Everything in the cabin had gradually slid to one corner, so he began his investigation there. A few items were scattered about, probably by ScanoGen's divers. Maddock sifted through the crumbling remains of what had once been personal items belonging to the legendary Fawcett. Aside from crumbling bits of furniture, most of what remained had been reduced to silt and muck, and was no longer recognizable, though he did find a broken mug, a few buttons, which he stashed in his dive bag, and a corroded spoon, which he also kept. He searched every inch of the cabin, but found nothing else of interest.

Discouraged, he checked his watch. Two minutes until time to head back to the surface. Bones and Willis would be returning any moment. With no time to check out any other section of the ship, he returned to the pile of accumulated detritus in the corner and slid his hand down below the pile of muck. He ran his fingers along the seam where the cabin floor met the wall and was rewarded when he felt something hard that had wedged into a crack.

Exercising care, he slowly worked the thing back-and-forth until it came free. Holding it close, he grinned as his dive light shone on a fragment of pottery. He'd seen enough of these to know what it was. Feeling a little bit more positive about things, he secured it in his bag as a glimmer of light appeared in the darkness beyond the cabin door, telling him that his friends were on their way back. Maddock gave each of them the "thumbs up" sign as they passed through the cabin, indicating they should head back up top.

Back aboard *Sea Foam*, Maddock wasted no time in showing the others what he had found.

"It's a fragment of pottery, and it's definitely Mediterranean in origin. This at least confirms part of Fawcett's story."

"So," Bones began, "that probably means that Fawcett really did have a map carved in stone that showed the way to Kephises."

"And now, ScanoGen has that map," Matt finished. "So, where does that leave us?"

Maddock thought about all they had learned of *Quest's* sinking, and the aftermath. He gazed out at the ocean, his eyes drifting to one of the small islands near Ascension. He wondered…

"I have an idea." Maddock pointed to the small, rocky island in the distance. "Matt, take us there, as close as you can get."

"What are we looking for?" Bones gave him a speculative look, the amused twinkle in his eye showed that he could tell Maddock was up to something.

"I'll know it when I see it."

Kaylin frowned. "But Maddock, what is the point..."

"Don't bother," Willis interrupted. "When he's like this, there ain't no point. *That's* the point. He'll tell us when he's ready. Me, I'm gonna get a beer and wait for the big reveal." He headed below to retrieve the beer cooler from the galley.

"What is that place?" Kaylin asked as Matt took *Sea Foam* in the direction Maddock had indicated. Out here on the water, with her blonde hair flying in the breeze, she was as beautiful as Maddock had ever seen her. He looked into her green eyes, so open and honest, and thought how different she was from the dark, exotic Jade. One was his seemingly perfect match, the other his perfect counterpoint.

"Did you hear me?" Kaylin grinned. "Typical man. I'd ask you what you're thinking about, but I know how much you hate that."

"Sorry. It's called Botswain Bird Island."

"Interesting name."

"The name comes from all the birds that nest there. We've been assuming that Fawcett and the others took refuge on Ascension Island after *Quest* sank, but I noticed before we made the dive that Botswain is closer to the spot where she went down. Also, remember what we read in the naval library, about Fawcett complaining of 'the infernal birds' that annoyed them while they waited for rescue."

"Okay, so how does that help us?"

"You'll see." He met her annoyed look with a roguish grin, and headed into cabin where Matt was piloting the ship in while Corey kept one eye on the depth readings and the other on a navigational chart.

"Are you looking for anything in particular?" Matt asked, keeping his eyes trained on the water.

"Yep. Just get in as close as you can and circle the island. I'll tell you when to stop."

"It shouldn't take long," Corey observed. "The island's small enough."

His words proved to be correct. Within five minutes, they were circling the shore of Botswain Bird Island. The tall, gray rocks gave it the appearance of a giant molar rising up from the sea. Maddock kept his eyes on the shore as they circled, *Sea Foam* plowing through the chop. Time crept by, and he was about to admit that he had been wrong, when they found what he had been looking for. A natural stone arch rose up from the water, joining the steep, rocky cliff at the water's edge.

"Does that look familiar?"

"It's the island in the painting!" Kaylin had joined them in the cabin. "You think it means something?"

"Matter of fact, I do."

Chapter 14

Tam sat in the shade of an umbrella in an outdoor café in Cuiabá, the capital city of the state of Mato Grosso, Brazil. Under different circumstances, she would have found it a delightful place to visit. The city was tourist-friendly, and boasted a rich local culture of music, dance, and cuisine all reflecting African, native American, and Portuguese influences. At the moment, though, she was focused on the job at hand, and anxious to get started.

Her sat phone rang and she answered immediately. It was Salvatore.

"How are things?"

"We're ready. I've got three guides lined up. Just say the word and we're off."

"I am pleased to hear it. I knew I made the proper decision in sending you. You shall begin very soon. It also seems that Kennedy was successful in his efforts to find the sunken ship." Salvatore did not try to keep the satisfaction from his voice.

"That's wonderful." She wasn't sure how wonderful it actually was. On the one hand, she didn't like Kennedy and never cared to see him succeed. On the other hand, if he found something that helped her complete her part of the mission, good on him. "What did he find?"

"A map carved in stone. After all this time in sea water, the images were faint. Our people were, of course, able to make laser scans of the carvings and create enhanced digital images. We are now cross-referencing it with existing maps of the Amazon region. It appears, however, that the map has no particular scale, and little is known about the region into which you shall be traveling. They tell me that, assuming Fawcett followed this map, it appears that what the world knows about his final expedition is wrong."

"Interesting, but not surprising. That certainly would make it difficult for anyone to have followed his trail, much less find him."

"Indeed. I shall send whatever they come up with along to you as soon as it is ready."

Tam's heart beat faster. It was really happening. *Don't blow it,* she told herself. This was her first assignment and she could not afford to fall out of Scano's good graces by blowing it. She had worked too hard to get where she was in the organization, and it would be a serious blow indeed if she slipped up. "Very good. When can I expect it?"

"Soon. But you be patient. I'm sending a few…disposable items your way."

"Sir?" She did not like the sound of this one bit.

"Thomas Thornton's colleague, the one whom we questioned about Thornton's only clue, has proved useless. The Charleston Police Department has been investigating his disappearance. We could go to the trouble of doing away with him and making it look like a crime, but it would be much cleaner if you would simply lose him in the Amazon. Besides, there is still a possibility he knows something useful, though I doubt it. Assess him, and eliminate him when you deem he is of no use. It should not be a problem."

"No sir, it will not." Tam felt a weight in her stomach. Damn! Another loose end to tie up. "You said 'items,' as in more than one." *Not Alex,* she prayed. *Don't send me your snotty, psychopath son.* That was one distraction she could live without.

"Yes. Cyrus and Jason have outlived their usefulness as well." Tam had to remind herself that he was referring to Cy and Jay. *"They seemed to think it a good idea to exhume Shackleton's remains. Getting them off South Georgia Island and covering their tracks was a close thing. I cannot afford to have men with so little sense in my employ. Kennedy will arrive tomorrow with all three expendables. He knows your orders, but I fear he might grow sentimental about Jason, in particular. See to it that the job is done."*

"Kennedy's coming here?" Her stomach was in a twist. Kennedy posed a problem of an entirely different sort.

"You need not worry. He understands that the command is yours. He's a good soldier and he'll follow orders." She doubted that. *"Kennedy is one of our best."*

She didn't know what to say to that, so she kept her silence. A quiet ensued, enduring for so long that she wondered if the connection had been lost. Finally, Salvatore continued. *"Our investors have grown anxious for Project Pan to get underway. They are growing impatient. We do not need them to take a direct hand."*

Tam's heart raced. "You've never told me who our investors are, Mr. Scano."

"Nor will I." His voice was sharp with implied rebuke.

"Forgive me. I only wonder what I might come up against should they decide to get involved."

"*You need not worry about it.*" Salvatore's voice had regained the fatherly, reassuring tone he often took when talking to her about a difficult situation. *You and Kennedy have a head start, and you are well-equipped. Finish the job, and finish it soon, and we won't have to concern ourselves with anyone else.*"

"Yes sir."

"Good luck, *figlia mia.*"

The call ended and Tam sat staring at the wall. The last thing she needed was Kennedy and two of his lackeys, no matter how moronic, interfering. She was close, she could feel it. But if they interfered…

She ordered up another Baden Baden Stout, the signature beer of the Brazilian microbrewery of the same name. Beer was seldom her drink of choice, but this particular beverage complemented the spicy food nicely. She took a sip, enjoying the rich, smoky flavor with a suggestion of dark chocolate and burnt coffee. She let the cool drink and calm atmosphere sooth her jangled nerves. She was a professional, and she would face whatever came her way.

She took another drink and smiled.

A complicated job had just turned into a Gordian knot. Oh well, a knotty problem required a bold stroke, and she had plenty of those up her sleeve. She wondered for a moment if Salvatore would still think of her as "daughter" when this was all over.

Chapter 15

As they drew closer to the arch, Maddock's certainty grew. This was the same place shown in the painting. It had to be significant.

"So, now will you tell me all about your brilliant idea?" Bones asked, leaning on the rail and gazing intently at the stone formation.

"It was Fawcett's complaints about all the 'infernal birds' that got me thinking. I believe they took refuge on Botswain Bird Island, not on Ascension."

"The book did say it was a small island," Bones agreed. "I get it. You think the arch in the painting was more than just a signpost to Botswain Bird Island. You think the arch itself is important."

"Yep. And we're told that Fawcett tried to recreate the map to Kephises. I think, while he was off keeping to himself and brooding over their situation, he carved a new map from memory, or least tried to."

Bones thought for a while. "You know, Maddock, you could be right. Didn't the book say that Fawcett screwed it up, though?"

"He said it was an incomplete map. Fawcett was a perfectionist. If he felt he'd left out even the smallest detail, he would have been unhappy with the finished product. I'm wagering he did a reasonably good job of replicating what the native had given him. It's the best hope we have, in any case."

They anchored *Sea Foam* a safe distance from the shore and began their search. Willis and Matt headed for a spot that looked like a likely place for the crew of *Quest* to have taken refuge. They would head out from there, scouting out any possible pathways Fawcett might have taken. Maddock and Bones went to take a closer look at the arch itself.

It wasn't spectacular, by any stretch, but it was impressive in its own way. It was a thick column of stone rising up from the churning surf, curving in to meet the imposing cliffs of Botswain Bird Island.

They inspected the base of the arch, then used binoculars to scan its surface on either side, but they saw nothing that looked like a map, or even a hiding place where one might be secreted. A search of the island in the immediate vicinity of the arch proved fruitless as well. They checked in with Willis and Matt, but the two had not had any luck either. Discouraged, they sat down on a stone slab in the shade of the arch, letting the salt spray cool them.

"I'm thinking we're going to have to expand our search area." Bones didn't sound disheartened, but neither did he seem pleased at the prospect. "Of course, covering every square inch of this island might suck, but it's better than the alternative."

"Which is?" Maddock was only half-listening. He gazed up at the underside of the arch, turning the problem over in his mind.

"Scouring the entire Amazon basin looking for Thomas. I don't know about you, but I want to be done with this and back home in time for football season."

Maddock had to laugh. "You know there's nothing in the world you'd rather be doing than what we're doing right now."

Bones look affronted. "What? Sitting on a rock in the middle of nowhere getting our butts wet?"

Maddock grinned and stretched, working the kinks out of his head and neck. "Maybe we should get back to the search," he said, tilting his head back and popping his neck. And then he spotted something. It was only a shadow, a pool of black below the spot where the arch met the cliff face, but as his eyes fell on it, a bird took flight from somewhere inside its dark depths. He stood transfixed, keeping his eyes on the spot as if he feared it might disappear if he looked away even for a moment.

"What is it?" Bones craned his neck to see. He spotted it almost immediately. "No freakin' way! Do you think it might be?"

"Only one way to find out." Maddock turned a conspiratorial glance his way. "Race you to the top."

The first fifteen feet of the climb were a challenge. Here the edges of any cracks, protrusions, or irregularities in the stone had been rounded off by the surf, but the way grew easier as they ascended. Maddock reached their destination first and hauled himself up into a cave just wide enough for two men to squeeze inside. He turned and gave Bones a hand, hauling his friend in behind him.

"You cheated, dude," Bones grumbled. He prided himself in his climbing ability and hated not being the first one somewhere.

"Your arms and legs are just too long," Maddock replied, unhooking his mag lite from a clip at his waist and shining it around.

"Tell me how that makes any sense at all." Bones took out his own light and together, they inspected the cave. The passage cut straight back into the rock, with no end in sight. "Do you really think Fawcett could have found this place? I mean, we almost missed it."

"I think Fawcett could do just about anything." Maddock was confident in his assessment. "He was maybe the greatest explorer of the twentieth century, and he was stuck on this pile of rock with nothing else to do. I think he would have explored every nook and cranny. Let's just hope you don't get stuck in here."

"I'd better go first in case it gets narrow farther back," Bones said. "Anywhere I can fit, we'll know you can get through, too. If I'm behind you and get wedged in, it could get ugly."

"Oh, I'd just kick you in the head until I jarred you loose, but if you want to go first, be my guest." The two switched positions and Bones headed off into the darkness, Maddock right behind him. They had only gone about twenty feet when he stopped short. "Whoa, dude!" The passage came to an end at a deep crevasse. They shone their lights down to reveal a fifty foot drop onto jagged rocks. "Not fun."

"See that?" Maddock trained the beam of his light on a tangle of bone and decaying fabric amongst the rocks below. "We're not the first to come this way." He wondered who the person was and what had led them up to this place. Another adventurer on the track of Fawcett, or just an unfortunate soul who had gotten a bit too curious or too careless?

"You want to try to jump across?" Bones shone his light to the spot across the way where the tunnel continued on the other side of the chasm.

"I don't think this would have stopped Fawcett, do you?" Maddock gauged the distance. It wasn't too broad a leap. It was the consequences of failure that made it a bit more interesting.

"No, but I don't think your little legs will carry you that far, do you? It's a good ten feet. That's a long way for an old man like you"

"I'm a month older than you." Maddock arched an eyebrow at Bones. "You've already lost a climbing contest. Do I need to beat you in long jump, too?"

"Just don't beg me to climb down and get you if you fall. I hate it when a grown man whines."

They both made the leap with ease and continued their search. The way grew wider as they progressed and soon they could walk side-by-side. It was slow going, as they kept a careful eye on the stone walls all around in case Fawcett had hidden the map somewhere, or perhaps carved it directly onto the wall. They came upon two side passages, but neither led anywhere, each of them narrowing until they were impassable. Finally, the passageway came to an end. No twists and turns, only stone.

"Oh, no way." Bones cursed and kicked at the pile of loose rocks at the base of the wall. "To come all this way and find nothing. This is crap."

Maddock sidestepped as a rock bounced off the wall and rebounded his way. He felt like picking up one of the rocks and bashing something.

And then a thought struck him.

"Bones, help me move these loose stones." Holding his mag lite in his teeth, he leaned down and hefted the largest one, setting it off to the side. Bones didn't ask what Maddock had in mind, but lent a hand. They had only moved about five of the biggest stones when cool air flowed across their arms from somewhere behind the rock pile.

"Maddock, you are the man!" Bones clapped him on the back and attacked the rocks with vigor.

At the base of the wall was an opening just high enough for a man to worm his way through. Maddock lay down and shone his light into the opening, revealing a small chamber on the other side, and on the far wall…

"A map!" he breathed. "Bones, this is it!"

They squeezed inside and moved to take a closer look. A curved line, presumably a river, snaked across the wall. Tributaries crept down like menacing hands. At various points, distinctive shapes were carved, signifying landmarks. At one bend, a smaller line wended away, perhaps another tributary, ending at a giant question mark.

"This question mark must signify the thing Fawcett couldn't remember,"

Maddock said. "The final landmark."

"Who cares?" Bones began snapping pictures of the map. "If the map can get us that far, we'll figure out the last clue when we get there. After that, we have the five steps from Fawcett's book. Mystery as good as solved."

"Of course, we might not even have to figure out the last clue," Maddock said. "We could find Thomas along the way, or find out what happened to him, and then we could go home."

Bones lowered his camera. "Maddock, are you telling me that you would just give up like that?"

Maddock considered the question. Kaylin had asked them to help find Thomas, but now the adventure bug had bitten him again, and he knew he would have to see things through. He, like so many others, wanted to know the fate of Percy Fawcett, and to learn what, if anything, lay in the heart of the unexplored Amazon. Maddock was no longer on a rescue mission. He was on a quest.

Chapter 16

Maddock knocked on the door of the tiny house. A tired-looking little woman of late middle years opened the door. She frowned when she saw him, but her expression softened a bit when she noticed Kaylin.

"Hello," Kaylin said. "My name is Kaylin Maxell, and this is Dane Maddock. We're looking for Victor. We were told he lives here."

The frown deepened. "Victor don't talk."

"I see. We are looking for someone who we think might be lost in the jungle, and we were told that Victor might be able to help us."

The woman frowned and shook her head.

"Could you at least tell us if you have seen our friend?" Maddock asked. Kaylin took out a photograph of Thomas and handed it to the woman.

She stared at it for a long time, her sour expression curdling.

"I seen that man. Long time ago. Many weeks."

"Are you sure?" There was a note of excitement in Kaylin's voice.

"He came with a pretty girl and two young men. He was a teacher."

Maddock's heart leapt. This was the first solid lead they'd had on Thomas, and if he'd been seen here, in this tiny frontier town, the same one to which Fawcett's map coupled with Jimmy's research had led them, that confirmed that Thomas was on the same trail they were.

"Do you know where he is now?" Kaylin looked like a bubble that, at any moment, would either soar into the air or burst, depending on the woman's reply.

She nodded vigorously. "They go into the jungle. The river, then the jungle. They don't come back. Only Victor come back." She shook her head. "They hire him to…" Unable to find the word, she made a motion with her hand like a snake slithering through the grass. "… into the jungle."

"And Victor came back without them?" Deadly scenarios played out in Maddock's mind. What might this Victor person have done to Thomas and his students? Had he led them astray and abandoned them? Or had it been something worse?

"Yes. But he is… not right. He does not talk since he come back."

"Could we please see him? It's important." Kaylin bit her lip. "We're just trying to find out if he and the others are all right."

The woman shook her head. "I think they don't come back."

"Ma'am," Maddock said, "could we please see Victor? Maybe he could tell us where they went. If they are still in the jungle, we will need to go in after them. If Victor was their guide, perhaps he can tell us which way he took them."

"He don't talk," she said again, but she opened the door and motioned for them to come inside. The tiny home was sparsely furnished and smelled of coffee. Dim light filtered through a small window, giving the room a gloomy, oppressive feel.

A man a little younger than Maddock sat on the floor, staring at the wall. He did not acknowledge their presence. In fact, he did not seem to register they were there at all. The old woman nodded at him, indicating that this was Victor.

Kaylin sat down cross-legged beside him. "Victor," she began, in a gentle voice, "my name is Kaylin. I'm looking for someone who is lost. You guided him into the jungle a few months back, and I am hoping you can help me find him again."

Victor continued to stare straight ahead. It seemed like the man was in a catatonic state. Maddock glanced at the old woman, who looked at him with sad eyes.

"He hears. He don't talk."

Kaylin tried again. "Would you please take a look at this picture and tell me if you remember anything at all about this man or the people who were with him?" She held out the picture of Thomas.

Victor let out a screech and crab walked as fast as he could away from Kaylin. When he banged into the wall, he rolled over into the fetal position, covered his face, and wailed. Both Kaylin and Victor's mother tried to calm him down, but he continued to cry and shiver, and refused to remove his hands from his face.

Finally, they were forced to give up. They apologized to the woman, who, Maddock realized, had never given her name, and left.

Kaylin looked like a deflated balloon, so thoroughly defeated was her posture as they walked along the street. Maddock nudged her.

"Hang in there. At least we know we're on the right track. Thomas was here, and it looks like he was headed in the same direction we're going."

"I suppose that's true." Kaylin sighed. "It would be much worse if we didn't at least know we were headed in the right direction." She glanced at Maddock. "Now what?"

"Now," he said, "it's time to begin our jungle adventure."

The flat-bottomed aluminum boat slid through the dark waters of the Kuluene, the largest of the headwaters of the Xingu River in the Mato Grosso, or "Thick Woods," region of Brazil. The third-largest state in Brazil, the western state featured diverse ecosystems, including the Pantanal, the world's largest wetland, in the south, and the Amazonian rainforest in the north. Piloting the craft through the debris that choked the surface, Maddock could not help feeling a thrill at the thought that they were actually on the trail of Percy Fawcett's final expedition. He had fantasized about this as a youth, wandering the forests near his home, imagining deadly creatures, dangerous tribesmen, and lost cities, but now it was real.

Bones and Kaylin sat in the boat with him. He had not wanted to bring Kaylin into this dangerous place, but she had informed him that, should he leave her behind, she would mount her own expedition, and probably get herself killed doing it. He knew she was serious and had relented, though he had briefly contemplated marooning her on

Botswain Bird Island until this was over. If he was honest with himself, he wanted her with him. He felt guilty about that, but it was what it was. He'd sort out his women problems later… much later.

Up ahead, Simáo, their guide, piloted a craft identical to the one in which they rode. Willis and Matt rode with Simáo. Only Corey had remained behind in the city of Cuiabá. He had protested, but not too vehemently. Everyone agreed he would best serve them as their link to civilization via sat phone, and could also be a go-between to Jimmy, should they need his assistance.

It had not been easy to secure a guide. There were plenty of cons in the region who would get a party lost and then demand payment to lead them back out, or who would conspire with friends to rob or even kill a party of explorers. Maddock and his crew could take care of themselves, of course, and given the information Jimmy had assembled by cross-referencing Fawcett's map with satellite imagery, could probably find their way to their destination, but an experienced guide could get them there much faster. Since they had to assume ScanoGen had a good lead on them, they needed to move as quickly as possible.

It was a shame that Victor had not been in any condition to provide any helpful information which might have sped up their progress, though. After leaving his home, they had gone about hiring their guide. A priest in Mato Grosso's capital city of Cuibá had given them the names of three guides whom he knew to be reliable men, and directions to the frontier town where they could be found—the same one in which Victor and his mother resided. The first two had been interested at first, but had flatly refused when Maddock had shown them a map with their probable destination marked. Neither had given a reason for his refusal, but had simply walked away.

The final candidate, Simáo, had been hesitant at first, but finally agreed, saying his wife was pregnant and he needed the money.

"Are you watching where you're going?" Kaylin's voice cut through his thoughts. Her hair was pulled back in a ponytail, and a few loose strands whipped across her face in the gentle breeze. "You look like you're in a trance."

"Just thinking about things. How about you?"

"I was just wondering what's waiting for us out there. What do you think Simáo meant when he said the 'Dead Ones' live in the area where we're going?"

"It's probably just a nickname for one of the native tribes, but it might even be one that has avoided contact, and thus legend has grown up about it. That happens here. Mato Grosso is basically the size of France and Germany put together, and very little of it has been touched by modern man."

"That's fine by me," Kaylin said, looking out at the dense greenery that lined the river.

"Me, too. The fact that such a huge place has seen so little exploration means that there really could be undiscovered people or places hiding right under the noses of modern man."

"So you think there really could be a Kephises out there waiting to be discovered?"

"Crazy as it sounds, there just might be. More likely, there's a more mundane explanation for it. Perhaps a tribe with a higher than usual prevalence of albinism sparked the legend of a lost civilization of European origin."

"That would be boring." Kaylin winked to show him she was kidding. "Whatever is out there, I hope Thomas found it, and we find him. I can't explain it, but even though I'm no longer sure he and I have a future together, I need him to be okay. Does that make sense?"

It made a lot of sense to Maddock. He already felt guilty for playing both sides of the coin with Kaylin and Jade. If the situation was reversed, and something were to happen to Jade, his having feelings for Kaylin would make it feel a thousand times worse.

"You do realize you're doing way more than you're obligated to? Thomas can't possibly have expected a college art professor to go trekking into the Amazon after him."

"We've already had this discussion, Maddock. Yes, he probably imagined I would sort out the clues and then send someone in after him, but I don't care. I'm already on the expedition with you. There's no point in arguing about it now."

"That's not my point." Why did she always take his words and turn them in an entirely different direction than he intended? "What I'm saying is, no matter what happens, you've done all you can do, and then some. You have nothing to feel guilty about. Life is too short to live with guilt. Besides, there are no guarantees. It can be over in a flash. Thomas had a dream, something that drove him, and he went for it. If the news is bad, don't beat yourself up for the rest of your life. Don't let guilt stop you from being happy."

Kaylin looked surprised and a little upset, but then her expression softened. She was about to say something when Bones called back from the bow.

"Hey Maddock, are there piranha in this river?"

"Some. Why?"

"Because if I have to listen to one more minute of this relationship talk, I'm swimming for it." He pulled the brim of his Washington Nationals baseball cap down low over his eyes, folded his hands across his chest, and leaned back against a sack of provisions. "Besides, it annoys me that you obviously don't understand irony."

Kaylin flashed a wicked grin, gave Maddock a satisfied look, and turned to look downriver. "How far do you think we'll have to go?"

"I don't know. The Xingu runs north all the way to the Amazon. Could be a long way." He thought about it. "Thanks to modern transportation and roadways, no matter how badly in disrepair, we've already covered a distance that took Fawcett a month or more to trek. We'll just see how it goes."

The sun beat down on them as the day wore on and the heat of the Amazon shrouded them like a blanket. Maddock kept a close eye out for danger, especially the human sort. According to Simão, the natives in the area through which they would initially travel were usually easy to deal with, provided one treated them with courtesy and respected their lands. Maddock was more concerned about the threat posed by ScanoGen. He had no doubt they too were following Fawcett's trail, and he wondered what resources they might bring to bear.

By late afternoon, however, the only potential threat he had spotted was the occasional black caiman peeking up out of the water, dark eyes and black, scaly skin gleaming in the sunlight, but the deadly reptiles all kept their distance from the boats.

Up ahead, in the lead boat, Matt waved for him to pull up alongside of them. Maddock brought his craft around to their starboard side and slowed to match their speed.

"Simão says he thinks the first landmark should be up ahead. If we're reading the map correctly, we'll have to make a short portage."

"No problem," Maddock said. "I'm ready to stretch my legs anyway."

When they rounded the next bend, everyone sat up straighter. Bones raised the bill of his cap and took off his sunglasses to get a better look.

"Dude, is that the ruins of some lost city?" He turned to Simáo. "How long have you known about this place?"

Their guide laughed. "Many people are fooled. It is natural formation in the rock. I can no say how it happen."

As they passed alongside the rock formations, Maddock could see how someone could mistake this place for the site of ancient construction. The natural rock lay in regular, even layers, giving the impression of stone work. Vertical shears created the illusion of corners and right angles. One shape even resembled an arched doorway.

"Man, this is unbelievable." For the first time all day, Willis actually laid down the Mossberg 501A1 shotgun he carried, and looked on in fascination. "And you're sure this ain't the real thing?"

"Is real, yes. Made by man? No."

Following Jimmy's application of the Fawcett map to modern maps, they left the river just beyond the stone formation. Maddock thought they might have to search for the hidden branch of the Xingu to which they had to portage, but Bones solved that problem immediately.

"Someone's been through here. Several someones." He squatted down to inspect the ground about ten paces from the river's edge. "I see scuff marks and some bent grass."

"How long ago were they here?" Kaylin knelt down next to Bones and squinted in the direction he was looking, as if she too could see the signs.

"I'm not that good, but I appreciate your confidence in me, chick. There are a few plants back home that, if they're broken off, I can make a fair guess by the amount of wilting, but not here. I can tell you, though, that they went thataway." He pointed off into the distance, like a general commanding his troops.

Leaving the others behind, Maddock and Bones scouted ahead, making sure they had a clear path for the boats. The trail snaked through a dense patch of jungle growth, leading them back toward the rock formation, where they passed between two high walls of stone that Maddock, despite knowing their natural origin, still could have sworn were wrought by human hands.

They emerged on a bluff overlooking a waterfall that poured out from an underground channel below their feet, feeding a narrow river that churned its way into the jungle and out of sight.

"Somewhere back there, the Xingu runs underground and comes out here," Maddock said, looking down. "And with this branch of the river being so narrow, it's no wonder it escaped the notice of map-makers. It didn't even show up on Jimmy's satellite images, though, thanks to Fawcett, we knew it was here. I'll wager not many people outside local natives even know about it."

"Dark and dangerous. Sounds like my kind of place." Bones cracked his knuckles. "So, are we ready to haul all those freakin' supplies and the boats over here?"

Maddock would have groaned in mock-complaint, but just then, something caught his eye. Twenty feet away, almost completely hidden by undergrowth, a body lay face down on the ground. Maddock drew his Walther and dropped to one knee. Glock in hand, Bones was at his side in an instant, looking all around.

"What are we looking for?"

"Probably nothing," Maddock replied. "See that body over there?" Bones cursed at the sight. "Not a local, unless the tribes around here are African-American with a buzz cuts, t-shirts, and camo pants."

He looked around. Obviously, if anyone had a gun and meant them harm, they'd already be dead, or at least have been shot at. Besides, from the looks of things, the dead man's head had been bashed in, which meant he'd probably been attacked by a local. After they'd waited long enough to satisfy themselves that no one was about to attack them, they went for a closer look.

The back of the man's skull was crushed. Maddock didn't have enough experience with such things to know how many times he'd been hit, or with what type of object, but he definitely had not been shot. He rolled the man's body over onto his back and his eyes widened in surprise.

"That's one of the dudes that came after us in London," Bones said, kneeling to check the man's pockets for identification. He came up empty. "I guess a local killed him and took whatever he was carrying."

"If he's from ScanoGen," Maddock said, looking around, "where is the rest of his group?"

"I guess they left him behind. Those are some cold characters, bro."

"Another reason I'm going to keep my eyes open and my guard up," Maddock said. "Let's get those boats down to the river and see if we can't ruin their day.

Chapter 17

"There's the second landmark." Kennedy pointed straight ahead, where a large, gray object rose up out of the water. It was a dome-shaped rock at least ten feet high, and it looked to Tam like a giant tortoise cutting through the water as the river rushed past it on either side of it. Centuries, millennia of erosion had worn away a few inches of the base on either side, adding to the tortoise-shell illusion. Faint lines carved into its surface indicated that, at some point in the past, humans had also seen the resemblance and sought to augment it by carving a tortoise shell pattern into the stone. Had she been a tourist, she would have stopped to take pictures, but time was a luxury she did not have. In fact, it bothered her that these stray thoughts even entered her mind. What was wrong with her? She had a job to do.

"That's a relief," she said, though she hated speaking to Kennedy at all. "I was hoping the map-maker didn't intend for us to take a right at the first turtle that came swimming up to the boat."

The corner of Kennedy's mouth turned up in a false half-smile, but that was the only response. He was angry about Jay's death, but if he knew the truth, he'd kill Tam, or at least, try to. She had a feeling the two of them were headed for a reckoning sooner or later, but for now, she needed him.

"Go right at the fork," she told the guide who piloted their boat. Now that two of the landmarks had proved to be real, her confidence was bolstered, and she was eager to press on toward their destination.

"When can we stop and eat?" Even riding in a different boat, Cy managed to get on her last nerve. Despite his recent spate of screw-ups, and the death of his partner, he seemed to believe he was only a notch below Kennedy in the pecking order, and in his mind, Kennedy was at the top of the food chain on this expedition. He bullied their guides and condescended to the three ScanoGen security agents, all of whom were ex-military men Tam had brought along for extra muscle and firepower. Add in the fact that he made no bones about his belief that Tam was in charge in name only, and she was seriously considering going ahead with Salvatore's orders regarding Cy, no matter what her conscience might tell her.

"Later," she snapped. "Keep a lookout on both sides of the river for something that looks like an open mouth. Once we find it, there's a side channel somewhere around it that we'll need to take."

"Shut up and look," Kennedy snapped, not looking back at Cy. Perhaps Tam should have appreciated the support, but she knew it was simply Kennedy trying to assert some authority over the only man on this trip who was clearly loyal to him.

"If *you* say so." Cy made it clear that the "you" to whom he was referring was Kennedy, not Tam. He took off his cap and fanned at the cloud of mosquitoes that swirled around his head.

Biting and stinging insects were just a few of the minor perils of the Amazon. They all wore long pants and long-sleeved shirts, and frequently doused themselves with the finest insect repellent money could buy. Cy, however, still managed to draw a cloud of swarming pests. They hovered around him, seemingly waiting for his repellent to wear off so they could suck him dry. He complained about it incessantly, pointing out that no one else received similar treatment from the flying nuisances. She could not help but laugh at the man's petty annoyance, which was far less than he deserved.

Seated in front of her, Smithson, one of her hired guns, leaned back, let his arm hang over the edge, and trailed his fingers in the water.

"Don't do that!" Her tone was harsh. He jerked his hand back immediately and gave her a look that was a mix of annoyance and embarrassment. "You can lose a finger that way, or worse. There are piranha, caiman, snakes, even electric eels in these waters. Unless you want to lose your trigger finger, keep your hand inside the boat."

Smithson lost the annoyed look, nodded, and turned around to face forward. At least the security guys were willing to take orders from her. Rather, they had been willing up to this point. She worried that Kennedy would insinuate himself in-between her and the men. She would just have to deal with that as it came.

Shafts of late afternoon sun bathed the river in a burnished orange glow when they finally spotted it. The river twisted sharply to the left, and directly in front of them loomed the arched outline of a dark cave. Its façade resembled a macabre face. The cave was the mouth, a stone jutted out directly above the opening, forming the nose, and jungle growth hung like thick hair up above it.

"If that's our landmark," Kennedy said, "where's the side channel?"

"I think we're supposed to go inside the cave." A deep sense of foreboding filled Tam. She didn't like the look of this cave, but she knew she was right. She could tell by the flow of the water that the cave was not a dead end, but a passage leading... somewhere.

Kennedy turned to her. "Have the third boat take the lead."

She understood his thinking. The third boat held supplies, a security agent, a guide, and Andy, the professor of whom she was to dispose since he had no useful information to offer. To Kennedy's way of thinking, they were the most expendable.

To her mind, however, she was at least a little more certain of the loyalty of her handpicked members of the expedition than that of Cy or Kennedy, though the guides frequently gave her dark looks, and muttered under their breath when she gave them orders. Besides, it wasn't his place to give orders to her, even if he had almost made it seem like a suggestion. At least he hadn't given the order outright, a sign that he, too, thought the guides and security men might properly acknowledge her as leader.

She decided to split the difference. *She* wasn't expendable, but Cy was. She instructed the guide piloting his boat to take the lead. Cy probably should have been annoyed, but he quickly rummaged for a flashlight, drew his side arm, and crouched over the bow like an eager pirate ready for plunder.

Kennedy gave her a dirty look, which she met with a smirk. "You know what Salvatore's instructions are in regard to our friend Cyrus," she said softly. "Maybe something in there will do the job for us."

Kennedy looked, for a moment, like he was about to argue, but he held his tongue. He turned around and fixed his eyes on their destination.

The cool, moist air of the cave was a welcome relief from the oppressive heat on the river. Nonetheless, Tam did not relax. Weapon in hand, she played her light back and forth in the darkness, wondering what might lay in wait. Her mind conjured images of vampire bats, or the glowing eyes of a jaguar lying in wait.

Her pulse quickened as they penetrated deeper into the darkness. The low ceiling gave her the feeling that the world was pressing down upon her. As they passed through the tunnel, the water was filled with sharp rocks that had to be carefully skirted, lest they damage their boats. Several times the boats hung up on the shallow bottom, and they were forced to get out and drag them, all the time worrying about the dangers that might lurk in the dark water just out of sight.

She breathed a deep sigh of relief when they finally emerged unscathed into a mist-shrouded lagoon. It was nearly sundown; the waning light and the thick canopy of the jungle cast the place in sinister shadows.

She spotted a clearing on the far side of the lagoon and directed them to go ashore there to set up camp. The jungle was silent here, and when they cut the engines and let the boats glide the last few feet to shore, the discomfort she felt in the cave filled her again.

Her grandmother had taught her that some places were "just bad," and were to be avoided. She hadn't meant dangerous places, like bad neighborhoods, but wicked places, places where evil resided so strongly that one could literally feel it. Tam had never believed her, but now she did. This was a bad place.

It happened in the blink of an eye. There was a sudden blur of motion as something sprang up from underneath a low-hanging branch. The guide in the lead boat had only a moment to cry out in surprise and pain before something clamped down on the back of his neck. Tam's mind registered only a flash of olive and yellow before the man was snatched down into the water.

"Anaconda!" she cried, springing to her feet and almost capsizing their boat. Her Makarov was in her hand and her head was on a swivel, searching for a target.

Kennedy, cursing like a sailor, fired blindly into the water. The lagoon was filled with shouts as the two remaining guides called their friend's name, while Cy cried out in panic and dove for the unattended motor. All the boat engines suddenly roared to life as everyone tried to get to shore as fast as human possible.

Tam wobbled as their boat struck ground, but she kept her feet and sprang nimbly onto shore. Their guides scrambled out of their boats and fled blindly into the jungle. Everyone else stood watching and waiting.

"Over there!" Cy shouted as, on the far side of the lagoon, the water roiled and a mass of coils surfaced for an instant. Only the man's left arm was visible, desperately tugging at one of the coils. Cy and the two agents sent a flurry of bullets in the anaconda's direction, but if they hit it, there was no sign.

"Stop!" Tam shouted. "You're wasting ammunition. There's nothing we can do for him now, and we don't know what else we might run into." Deep in her bones, she knew her words to be prophetic. Something told her their troubles had only just begun.

Chapter 18

This place was wrong. Everything about it sent up warning flares in Maddock's subconscious mind. He scanned the shore of the lagoon, but saw no obvious threats. Of course, in the Amazon, the unseen threat was often more dangerous than the one you saw coming.

"I don't know, dude." Bones was searching the trees with the same intensity as Maddock. "There's some serious wrongness here. It's too quiet, and I don't know what else, but I feel it."

"Man, check out that snake." From the other boat, Willis pointed to a spot along the bank where the biggest anaconda Maddock had ever seen lay sunning itself.

Bones cursed and reached for his Glock, but Maddock grabbed him by the wrist. "Don't bother. Looks like it's already eaten."

Bones's eyes went wide when he saw what Maddock had already noticed. The middle of the snake's body was swollen and distended almost beyond recognition, but it was evident that its last meal had been a human being.

"He won't be going after anyone for a while. He'll be too slow, and won't have much of an appetite. What we need to do is make certain there are no brothers and sisters ready to make a meal out of us."

All eyes went to the surrounding trees, scanning the branches for the giant predators. Matt hefted his Heckler and Koch MP5 submachine gun and his expression made it clear he was ready to shred anything that moved. Willis kept his Mossberg trained on the sunning anaconda, his finger on the trigger. He despised snakes, and all manner of what he termed, "squiggly things."

"Come on Maddock! Let me take care of this thing." In the shadowed lagoon, Willis's eyes seemed to glow against his dark skin. "It ain't hungry now, but it just might be by the time we come back this way."

"No. The ScanoGen people might be somewhere close by, and they'd hear the gunshot. If it can be helped, I don't want to warn them that we're catching up to them." They had taken a risk and traveled through the night. One person in each boat took a turn piloting the craft while the other two slept in the bottom of the boat, using mosquito netting for a blanket.

They had not let Kaylin take a turn, a decision about which she vigorously protested. Maddock reminded her that she was on this expedition against his better judgment, and that her carping was liable to draw the attention of unfriendly natives or worse. Now she satisfied herself with the occasional resentful look, or an "I told you so" stare whenever Maddock or Bones yawned.

"Fawcett claimed to have killed an anaconda that was sixty-two feet long." Kaylin gazed at the snake in admiration. "He was generally ridiculed by scientists, but I think he might have been telling the truth. That thing has got to be close to that long." She raised her camera and snapped a few pictures. "Hey Bones, why don't you swim over there and stand next to it so I can get some scale perspective?" She winked at him.

"Will my middle finger be enough scale for you?" The anaconda chose that moment to slither away at a glacial pace, slowed no doubt by its heavy burden. "See that? It's camera shy."

The banter ceased as Maddock's boat slid gently onto the bank, followed moments later by the second craft. Willis and Matt sprang out of their boat like commandos storming the beach, alert for danger.

"You're not fooling anybody," Bones told them as he helped Kaylin to shore. "You two think if you stand there like you're on guard duty, you won't have to help unload the boats."

"True that," Willis said. "But I got out first, so guess I'm gonna be the guard." He looked at Matt, who was glowering at him. "What? What? You too slow, ranger boy. Get to work."

"How did I ever get lassoed into hanging out with a bunch of SEALs?" Matt slung his MP5 across his back and turned to help Simáo unload their boat, while Maddock and Kaylin unloaded the other. In a matter of minutes, they had divided their provisions and loaded up a backpack for each person. Matt and Willis hid their boats within a thick stand of trees, camouflaging them with foliage. Bones, meanwhile, scouted the jungle nearby. He returned just as the rest of the group was donning their packs and getting ready to move.

"We're definitely in the right place," he pronounced, "and so is ScanoGen. They left plenty of prints on their way out of town. I also found their boats hidden close by."

"Hopefully that means the guy inside the anaconda is one of theirs." Matt bared his teeth in something between a grimace and a grin.

"How many boats did they have?" Maddock wondered how many men they'd be facing.

"Three. I couldn't guess their numbers by the tracks they left behind." Bones was thinking along the same lines as Maddock. "But if you figure they needed room for supplies, there can't be more than a dozen in their group. Probably fewer."

"Minus the one inside the snake," Matt added.

"All right. Let's move on, then." Maddock consulted the map on which Jimmy had projected their path, then re-checked Fawcett's rough map. "It looks like we're headed that way." He pointed in the direction from which Bones had come. "Think we should just follow ScanoGen's trail?"

"As long as they're on the right track, why not?" Bones nodded. "If it looks like they're drifting off course, we'll change directions."

"We'll need to move as quietly as possible." Willis and Matt did not need to be told, and perhaps neither did Kaylin and Simáo, but Maddock did not wish to leave anything to chance. He and Bones took the lead, with Matt and Willis bringing up the rear.

The farther they trekked from the lagoon, the denser the jungle grew, with the shafts of sunlight sifting through the treetops fewer and farther between. The unnerving silence continued, with no sounds of any kind, save their soft treads and the occasional rustle of branches up above. He glanced back to check on the others. Kaylin appeared transfixed by the beauty and mystery of this dark place untouched by modern civilization, though her knuckles were white from the tight grip with which she held her M6 Scout, a multi-purpose weapon, an over-under weapon that fired both .410 shotgun shells and .22 bullets. It wasn't a high-powered combat weapon, but it was the right fit for her. Maddock had no concerns about her using the weapon. She was the daughter of his and Bones' former commander, and knew how to handle any number of firearms.

Simáo, on the other hand, was trembling and sweating profusely. He periodically stopped short, aiming his bolt-action hunting rifle in the direction of some unseen enemy. The third time he did this, Bones threatened to take the weapon away from him. The guide shook his head profusely and muttered something in his native tongue; but after the scolding, he ceased pointing his rifle at every sound.

They had hiked for hours, following the trail left by ScanoGen, when the path suddenly fell away in a deep trench that had been reclaimed by the native flora. Maddock halted at the edge and held his hand up for everyone to stop. It was difficult to discern the lay of the land beneath the dense foliage, but he could make out a series of circular terraces rising up behind the trench. This was not a natural formation, but something many centuries old, or perhaps older.

"It's like a moat," Kaylin whispered, looking down at the circular ditch that wrapped around the terraces. "They've found formations like this in Xingu National Park, though not as formidable as this."

"This must be the next landmark." Bones tapped the paper Maddock held in his hand. The image, carved so long ago, looked like a layer cake, and had baffled Maddock until this moment.

"Circular terraces, one on top of the other, ringed by a ditch. You're right. This is it." His heart pounded. Despite the perils inherent to the Amazon, he would have been thrilled with the tantalizing possibility of discovery, were they not facing the threat of armed men from ScanoGen somewhere up ahead. "Okay, the map makes it look like we're supposed to go right over the top of this thing. I wonder if we couldn't just go around?"

"Help me!" No sooner had the faint voice floated up from somewhere below than the crack of rifle fire shattered the silence. "Don't shoot! Please!"

Cursing, Bones snatched Simáo's rifle and gave the man a shove. He landed hard on his backside and sat glaring at Bones in bitter resentment.

"Don't you realize there are people out there who want to kill us?" Bones hissed. "If they're anywhere close by, they heard your shot, and they know we're right behind them. Idiot!"

"I thought it was the dead ones." The man trembled, the anger already gone from his eyes.

Maddock didn't have time for native superstition. He raised his M-16. "Whoever you are," he called down into the ditch, "come out slowly."

A small, bedraggled man crawled out of the foliage and wobbled to his feet. Maddock could not imagine anyone looking more out of place in the depths of the Amazon than this slender, fair-skinned man.

"Andy!" Kaylin gasped. "What are you doing here?"

"You know him?" Maddock frowned.

"This is Thomas's colleague. The man who gave me the Fawcett picture! The one who was kidnapped."

Maddock gave Andy a hand up the embankment, and the little man stood trembling as Kaylin hugged him. His quaking finally eased enough that he accepted a drink of water from Matt's canteen before sinking to the ground.

"Tell us how you got here." Maddock squatted down so he could look Andy in the eye. Depending on how long the man had been wandering in the jungle, his information might not be reliable. He seemed lucid, however, as he began his explanation.

"The people who kidnapped me brought me down here with them. I didn't understand at first. I mean, I didn't know anything at all about Thomas or what he was up to. They held me forever, it seemed like. They'd interrogate me, sometimes hurt me, but I didn't know anything. Finally, I started making up stuff just to get them to stop, but I think they knew I was lying." He swallowed hard. "I thought they were going to kill me, but one day they told me I was going on a trip, and they brought me out here."

"I don't get it," Maddock said. "Weren't they taking a risk bringing you along?"

Andy managed a rueful laugh. "What danger am I? They've got all these fancy weapons, and they all look like... them." He pointed at Matt and Willis. "And you guys." He nodded at Maddock and Bones. "They didn't even handcuff me or anything. Just shoved me into the plane, then the helicopter, and so forth. When we got to the edge of nowhere, the girl told me I was free to run away any time I wanted. Everybody laughed like it was some big joke, which it was. I'm useless."

"What girl are you talking about?"

"Her name's Tam, or at least, that's what they call her. She's in charge, but I don't think the guys in her group like that very much. She questioned me at different times along the way, stuff about Thomas. I tried to bluff her into believing I knew some final clue, thinking she'd keep me alive, but she didn't buy it. They kept making little comments about getting rid of me. We'd see a caiman and this one guy, Cy, would say it looked hungry for professor meat, stuff like that. I was starting to wish they'd just go ahead and get it over with. I hate this place." He glanced up at the trees and shuddered.

"So, how did you manage to get away?" Maddock could not conceive that this little academic had outfought or outwitted his captors.

"She let me go."

"She let you go. Just like that?" Bones interjected, suspicion heavy in every word.

Andy shook his head. "We got up to the top of that hill, or whatever you call it," He indicated the terraces, "and we found the tunnel."

Bones did a double-take. "What tunnel..."

"That can wait." Maddock said. "One thing at a time. Go ahead, Andy."

"So, the others started going down into the tunnel, and the girl told them to give her five minutes, because she had something she needed to do. She took me down into the ditch, fired her gun off into the woods, and then gave me a canteen and told me to stay hidden until she came back for me, and that's exactly what I did until you got here."

"That's odd." Maddock rubbed his chin. "Do you know anything about her? Anything at all?"

"She's a killer. She doesn't know I saw, but I watched her bash a guy's skull in with a rock because he put his hands on her. She told the others a native had done it. I don't know if they believed her, or if they just didn't care. Every one of them is cold-blooded."

Maddock remembered finding the body of the dead man. "How many of them are there?"

"Eight," Andy said after a moment's thought. "There were eleven, including me. Tam killed the one guy and an anaconda got another." He shivered. "Two of the remaining guys are guides, locals, but they seem as nasty as the rest of the group."

"So, five professionals at most. I'll take those odds." Bones patted his M-16. "Do they have any idea we're after them?"

Andy shook his head. "I don't think so. At least, they didn't let on that anyone was after them. I heard one of them, Kennedy, say they had the only map, so I'm guessing they think they're in this alone."

"Good." Maddock smiled. "Let them go on thinking that. How far ahead of us are they?"

"Less than a day. It was just this morning she let me go. I don't think I'd have lasted through the night, though. I already drank all the water she left me and lost the canteen while trying to get to you."

"It's all right. We're glad you found us." Kaylin gave him a reassuring pat on the shoulder.

Maddock disagreed, but there was no point in saying so. Andy wasn't cut out for this environment, and was liable to get himself killed. Maddock doubted the professor was even capable of walking quietly in the woods.

"I will not go!" Simão, like the others, had been listening in silence, but now he was on his feet. "That hole is the… the doorway to the land of the dead ones! You will all die if you go there."

Maddock contemplated this turn. They didn't need Simão. Frankly, they had really only needed his boats, but his services as guide had come with the rental. He had been of some use at the outset, but as soon as they left the beaten path, he had been of little help.

"Can you find your way back to the boats?" The man nodded. "Bones, the ScanoGen boats. Could you hotwire one if you had to?" Bones rolled his eyes, which, coming from Bones, was a strong affirmative. "All right. Give him back his rifle." Bones gave him a quizzical look, but handed the weapon back to Simão.

"I want you," Maddock said to the guide, "to take Andy here back to the boats. If you ration them, your provisions will hold the two of you long enough to get back to your village. Look out for him until we come back, and I'll double what we paid you."

Simão nodded vigorously. He likely would have agreed to anything that would get him out of this place and away from the "dead ones," whoever they were.

Maddock turned to Kaylin, but she waved him away.

"Don't even bother, Maddock. I'm staying with you all the way."

"But we know where the ScanoGen people are now, and we're headed right for them. You'll be safest if you keep as far away from them as possible."

"I'm safest with you." Her tone was hot, but her eyes were soft. "I always have been."

Maddock could tell it was pointless to press the argument any farther. They bade Andy and Simão goodbye and good luck, and headed down into the ditch.

The climb to the top terrace was a challenging one, and they were all scratched and dirty when they reached the top. Maddock took a breather and looked around. The mound on which they stood was below the level of the tallest trees. All he could see in every direction was dark green.

Chunks of sod and rotten wood lay strewn about, indicating the opening to the tunnel had been camouflaged prior to the arrival of ScanoGen. *Less work for us,* Maddock thought.

The way down was a dark, sloping passage with no obvious steps or handholds. Maddock leaned closer for a better look, and crinkled his nose at the dank, musty air.

"Too bad there's no rain," Bones said, kneeling down next to him. "This would make one hell of a waterslide."

Maddock chuckled. "Actually, I know we haven't had any luck since we left the main branch of the Xingu, but if we can get a signal, we should try to raise Corey on the sat phone before we go down there. Maybe Jimmy can pinpoint our location before we go in."

"What's the matter, Maddock?" Bones elbowed him. "Afraid we're going to get us a little Jules Verne action going on underground? Maybe slide to the center of the earth?"

"Afraid we'll get to the bottom and have no way back up is more like it. I'm surprised the ScanoGen people didn't secure a rope before they went down, in case they had to climb back out."

"Well, we can't all be as smart as you, Maddock."

Matt tried, but was unable to get any connection with the sat phone. Maddock wondered what Corey was thinking right now, sitting and waiting for them to check in, and hearing nothing. Everyone took a moment to secure their packs and get ready to move.

Maddock stood, looked down into the waiting darkness, and then back at his friends.

"All right, who wants to be the first one down into the creepy, dark tunnel?"

Chapter 19

Everything is going as planned, gentlemen. My team is in the process of completing the job as we speak. I estimate we shall be able to move on to the next stage of the project in less than two weeks time." Salvatore stared across the table at the two smartly-dressed men in power suits and forced a polite smile.

Senator Nathan Roman of Utah, member of the Senate Arms Committee, sat back, a condescending smile painting his face. "You understand, Mister Scano, that we can tolerate no more delays. There are deadlines to be met, and you are far behind the promised timetable. If we are forced to start over somewhere else, I fear our armed forces will choose to do business elsewhere. In fact, the government might be forced to dig deeper into some of ScanoGen's more questionable practices."

The man did not intimidate Salvatore in the least. A Senator, no matter how powerful, derived his power from the consent of the governed, a fickle lot at best. One scandal and the good senator just might find himself back in Utah selling real estate. In fact, the groundwork for such a scandal had already been laid in the form of a young lady who would soon be leaking cell phone pictures of the senator engaged in some very embarrassing costume play. And that was just the tip of the iceberg. He glanced at David, and saw a shadow of a smile cross the man's face. Senator Roman would play ball soon enough. It was the other man who worried them.

"Now, now, Nathan. There is no need to bandy threats. Mister Scano and ScanoGen have always been reliable business partners, and doubtless that will not change. I have every confidence in them." The man turned an icy smile toward Salvatore.

Frederick Hadel was an enigma. He was the leading figure in a large, independent religious organization known as The Kingdom Church. What bothered Salvatore was that was all they knew about him. Hadel had clout, there was no denying it, but how much he had, and whom he had under his thumb, had eluded Salvatore and his people.

That bothered him.

"Senator Roman simply wants you to understand how important this project is to us," Hadel continued. He paused to take a sip of tea. "It is no longer merely a matter of scientific speculation. The work your people have already done has set an excellent foundation, and major plans have been laid with that work at its core. We must, however, move forward."

"Your concern is duly noted, Mr. Hadel," David assured him.

"Bishop Hadel, if you please. Perhaps it is vanity, but I do prefer to be addressed by my title. I worked very hard to earn it."

"My apologies." David made a placating gesture. "It did take some time, but things have fallen into place. Our people are on the ground as we speak."

"I have people of my own at the ready if you require assistance." Hadel raised his eyebrows. "I can call on them at a moment's notice."

"That will not be necessary, but we appreciate the offer." Salvatore stood and David quickly followed suit. "Your concerns are duly noted."

Hadel and Roman exchanged looks, clearly not appreciating the curt dismissal. Finally, the two stood, and Roman shook hands with David and Salvatore.

"We will talk again in two weeks," Roman added, squeezing Salvatore's hand tighter than was necessary. The imbecile actually believed that, in the twenty-first century, musculature was a sign of power? He would not last long in Washington.

"I look forward to it." Salvatore tapped a button on his phone, indicating that Alex, who was temporarily and unhappily filling Tam's role as receptionist, should see his guests out.

Hadel stepped through the doorway, paused, and turned back to Salvatore and David. "Traffic in the Washington area is dangerous, is it not?"

"It is." Salvatore had no idea where Hadel was going with this, but he was certain the man would not bring it up without reason.

"Perhaps you heard about the death of a dear colleague, Reverend Felts. He was killed in a tragic accident very recently."

"Yes, I did hear something about that." Salvatore kept his tone conversational, but his mind was racing. How much did Hadel know?

"Truly a tragedy." Hadel grimaced. "How Reverend Felts, who was a competent driver without a blemish on his driving record, could have run off the road like that is beyond me." Now he looked Salvatore in the eye. "I wish I could say I was sorry to hear the news, but I fear my friend had lost his way. It is a shame, but accidents do happen." His smile was mirthless and his eyes cold.

"Yes they do," Salvatore agreed.

Hadel nodded and closed the door.

"He knows." David's fists were clenched tight. "He knows we are behind Felts's death, and he obviously approves. Why doesn't he just say so?"

"He's sending us a message." Salvatore pursed his lips. He wants us to think we can't do anything without him knowing about it." Perhaps it was the truth. So much they did not know about Hadel.

"So, do I proceed with our plans regarding the senator?" David eyed him in trepidation.

Salvatore took a deep breath. "Hold off until Tam has completed her mission. Perhaps it will not be necessary." He hated the feeling that someone else was controlling him, but he had not risen this far by putting ego before wisdom. *Tam,* he thought, *do not let me down.*

Chapter 20

Maddock was the first into the tunnel. The initial drop was so steep that he was forced to slide down, using his Recon 1 knife as a brake to control his descent. About fifty feet down, the way became less steep, and he was able to stand, though he kept a steadying hand on the ceiling, which was no more than six feet high.

"Come on down!" he called to the others. "Bones and Willis, the ceiling's low, so don't bump your heads when you stand up!"

Kaylin came down, springing gracefully to her feet at the end of her slide. Her eyes widened as she played her light down the tunnel. "Awesome!"

"You sound like Bones." Maddock had to grin. Though Kaylin looked like she belonged behind a news desk or reporting from the sideline of a college football game, she was a Navy brat through and through, and wouldn't let something like a dark tunnel bother her.

"Oh well. You're the one who keeps him around. If he rubs off on me, it's not my fault." The rest of the group joined them in short order and they proceeded down the passageway.

The floor was made of stone, but the walls and ceiling were lined with wood, much of it succumbing to various stages of decay. Roots peeked out in various places and Maddock wondered if they were strengthening or weakening the structure. He hoped it was the former.

"This whole place looks like it could come down at any moment," Kaylin observed, shining her light on the ceiling. So engrossed was she in the construction of the passageway that she almost didn't see the pit in front of them.

Maddock grabbed her by the arm and snatched her back just as her foot came down on... nothing. He shone his light down on a deep pit. Twenty feet below them, a body lay impaled on a wooden stake. Other stakes lay shattered on the floor, confirmation of Maddock's assessment of the weakened condition of the wood due to years of dry rot. One of the stakes, though, had held together, to the detriment of the man who had fallen. He was lying on his stomach, the stake jutting out of the small of his back. His face was turned to the side, and Maddock could make out his native features.

"One of the guides," Bones observed. They're down to seven. Sweet!"

"Hey! Anybody got a notepad or an index card?" Willis looked around at the others, grinning.

"What for?" Kaylin cocked her head to the side.

"I want to make a scorecard, like baseball. I know I'll kill more of them than y'all." He elbowed Matt.

"Want to put some money on that? A hundred bucks?" Matt offered his hand to shake on it.

"Hell, Army boy, you don't even *get* to be on the scorecard. You're gonna' carry my backpack and let the SEALs do the killing." Laughter drowned Matt's profane response.

Beyond the pit, the tunnel sloped down and they were again forced to descend in a controlled slide. Maddock kept a sharp eye out for more pits or other hazards, all the while thinking that the condition of the tunnel made the whole place a potential booby trap.

Faint light glimmered in the distance and they reached the bottom of the tunnel without incident. Weapons at the ready, they followed the winding passageway toward the glow that grew brighter the farther they progressed.

They emerged in a deep canyon, walled in by sheer cliffs that ran out of sight to the north and south as far as the eye could see.

"No wonder they had to build the tunnel." Maddock looked behind them at the wall of stone. "There's no way you could climb down that."

"Speak for yourself," Bones said. "I am Spider-Man on rock walls."

Maddock rolled his eyes. "And," he turned back around, "no telling how far this canyon runs. This might be the only way across for miles or more."

"This place has a weird vibe to it." Willis stepped forward, looking all around, his eyes narrowed and his jaw set. "It feels like we don't belong here."

He was right. The canyon was very different from the jungle through which they had trekked thus far. The trees here were smaller and grew farther apart than they had up above. It was as if the valley had once been cleared, but later left to lie fallow. On the opposite side of the valley, a waterfall poured over the canyon rim.

"It's like a lost world," Kaylin whispered.

"Let's hope it's not as dangerous as the one from the book." Maddock's eyes scanned the valley, all his senses alive, seeking out any potential threat, but the silence was complete.

"Looks safe to me," Bones said. "Should we keep following ScanoGen's tracks?" He didn't wait for Maddock to say yes, but moved ahead.

They had walked only five minutes or so when they came upon an abandoned campsite. Four tents had been slashed and trampled, and camping gear lay strewn everywhere. Maddock noticed a spatter of something dark on a tree trunk, and took a closer look.

"Looks like blood," he said to Kaylin, who was peering over his shoulder. "Can you tell anything from the tracks?" He called to Bones.

"Only that everyone scattered in a big hurry." He looked at Maddock. "There are about five paths we could follow, and I assume you want to stay together?" Maddock nodded. "Good call, I think. So, the question is, which path do you want to follow first?"

Maddock pondered the question. They had come to the end of Fawcett's imperfect map. They did not know the final landmark, which left following ScanoGen, or wandering until they found something as their only choices. The first option was out for the moment and the second was unappealing.

A shot rang out in the distance, breaking the silence, and then another.

"That way," he said, pointing toward the waterfall on the opposite side of the canyon. He wasn't sure why he chose it as their destination, except that it would be an easy landmark for everyone to find should they get split up. That, and it just felt like the right way to go. "Everyone stay concealed as much as you can, and be careful."

Chapter 21

Cy felt like a bumper car as he careened from tree-to-tree in his mad dash for safety. He had emptied his rifle and hadn't had time to reload before being forced to abandon it. His pistol was gone, dropped in the midst of hand-to-hand fighting with those freakish, silent natives that had swarmed their camp.

They won't die!

He had put bullets in a half-dozen of them at least, and stabbed one in the gut, but they kept coming! What were these things? Zombies? Couldn't be, but he had no explanation for how a man could take a bullet in the chest and keep coming. He had seen Kennedy blow the leg off of one and it kept on crawling forward like it hadn't felt a thing. That's when Cy panicked and ran.

He could hear the sound of the waterfall somewhere up ahead. His only hope was that Tam had been correct in her assertion that the final landmark would be found somewhere in its vicinity. If he could find it, maybe he could get away from these... things.

A limb smacked him across the face and he reflexively covered his eyes. He stumbled a few steps, and then the ground went out from under his feet. He had only a moment to cry out in surprise before he was enveloped in cold darkness.

Water filled his mouth and nose, and he choked. His feet hit the slimy bottom and he pushed up. He emerged gasping and coughing. He vomited a stream of water, and then blew out through each nostril, clearing them.

Eyes burning, he looked around to see he was in a dark waterway surrounded on all sides by thick vegetation. The channel was straight and narrow, obviously man-made, and he could see that it cut a straight path to the waterfall! His feeling of relief was cut short by a rustling in the foliage.

The jungle growth parted, revealing two of the natives armed with primitive stone axes. They were broad-shouldered with glossy black hair and weird orange body paint with black spots, like a giraffe. What made them frightening were the blank, inhuman eyes that gazed down on him as if he were no more than a fly to be swatted. He heard a sound behind him and whirled to see another of the zombie-like warriors emerge, pointing a spear at Cy's chest.

Cy slowly raised his hands above his head. There was no fighting, no running, only the hope of surrender.

"Please." He was so frightened that he didn't know if he had said the word aloud or not. The native pressed the tip of his spear against Cy's throat, and Cy felt his bladder release.

Excruciating pain, the like of which he had never imagined was possible, erupted not in his throat, but his groin. He screamed in pain and staggered back, clutching his burning genitals.

Perhaps taken by surprise, the native drew back his spear, leaned down for a closer look at him, and then looked at his companions. Was it possible that a ghost of a smile played across his stony face?

A fragment of a memory flashed through Cy's mind as his body crumpled down into the water in sheer agony. Something he had learned about the Amazon and its native fish.

Candiru. Enters the urethra. Locks its spines in place. Agonizing death.

He screamed again, staggered backward, and found himself facing the two club-bearing warriors. "Please," he wailed. This time he was not begging for his life, but for release from this agony.

Still staring at him with empty eyes, one of them raised his club and brought it down in a swift motion. The world fled, and with it, the pain.

Tam ducked down in the shadow of a thick shrub, her Makarov at the ready.

Kennedy crouched beside her, his eyes gleaming with the thrill of battle. How had she gotten stuck with him? This would be a good time to put a cap in him, but she probably needed all the allies she could get against this swarm of seemingly-unstoppable natives. Well, that wasn't entirely accurate. They'd killed several, but they were nigh-impossible to bring down, and didn't seem to feel pain the way a normal human being would.

"See if you can raise ScanoGen on the sat phone," Kennedy barked. "Maybe they can get a read on our position and send help." The tone of his voice said it was futile, but they were in a desperate situation.

"Already did," Tam lied. "They said they'd do what they could for us, but it would take some time."

"That's not very promising." Kennedy scowled, still searching the surroundings for the natives.

"It is what it is. We can't count on anyone but ourselves to get out of this." She bit her lip. How was she not only going to get out of this situation alive, but then get away from Kennedy?

"Have you figured out the final landmark yet?" he snapped. "That would help."

"Yes!" Sudden inspiration struck her and she forced down a smile. "It's that rock formation up there." She pointed to a nondescript outcropping.

"How can you tell?" Kennedy tilted his head to the side and squinted. "It doesn't look like a skull."

"You have to see it from the other side. I was trying to work my way to it when these... things blocked my way, and I had to double-back. That's it though, I'm sure of it. Think we should make a break for it?"

"Why not?" Kennedy sneered. "Even if you're wrong, I'd rather be doing something than hiding here like a scared woman."

Tam didn't know if that last comment was meant as an insult to her, or was simply a reflection of his misogyny. She was just happy to see Kennedy take off at a dead sprint in the direction she had indicated. *Scared woman? How about gullible man?* Hopefully, he'd get himself killed. If not, she had bought herself enough time to get to the waterfall and see whether or not her theory was correct. She raised her Makarov and took a deep breath.

Time to roll the dice.

Chapter 22

Maddock halted and dropped to one knee as dark figures appeared from the cover of the surrounding trees, stalking toward them. They were natives, armed with axes, spears, clubs, and wooden sword-like weapons with teeth, probably those of a caiman, set in either edge like the Aztec macuahitl. Oddly, they didn't charge Maddock and his party, nor did they halt, but stalked toward them, weapons at the ready.

"Stop! Don't come any closer!" Maddock shouted, hoping they would get the gist of his words, despite the language barrier. No luck.

He fired off a warning shot with his M-16 just over the head of the foremost warrior, held up his hand with his palm toward them, and again shouted for them to stop. It didn't do any good.

They charged.

Gunfire opened up on all sides, shredding the line of attacking natives. Some stumbled, some reeled or staggered backward.

But they did not go down.

Bloodied and torn, the warriors kept coming. Some stumbled forward, slowed by their wounds, but none of them stopped.

Willis, pumping and firing his Mossberg at a steady rate, blew the legs out from under an attacker. The man tumbled to the ground, shook his head, and began crawling forward. Willis fired another shot, taking the man in the top of the head, and he lay still.

"No body shots!" Maddock ordered. "Legs or head!"

"That's what I'm talking about!" Bones shouted, taking aim with his M-16 and hitting an attacker with a clean head shot. Matt opened up with his MP 5 submachine gun, spraying a thigh-high stream of lead across the line of attackers. The withering gunfire was taking its toll, sending the attackers to the ground, but more were appearing, drawn by the sounds of gunfire.

Maddock emptied his M-16, drew his Walther, and opened up on the attackers. "Everybody retreat back to the tunnel entrance!" Maddock ordered.

"No can do, boss man." Bones spoke as calmly as if he were discussing the weather. "They're behind us."

Maddock glanced back to see an even larger group of warriors stalking toward them. They wouldn't be getting through that way any time soon.

"Scatter and meet up at the waterfall!" he called. "Kaylin, follow me!"

He dashed to their left, where only a few warriors stood in their way. Two shots with his Walther put bullets through two skulls. He trained his weapon on the next warrior who impeded his path, and was about to pull the trigger when Kaylin screamed.

His shot caught the attacker in the shoulder, and he turned to see Kaylin use her shotgun to deflect a spear thrust by a warrior who had just emerged from behind a tree. He had time to fire off a hasty shot that caught Kaylin's attacker in the chest before the warrior whom he'd shot in the shoulder was on him.

Maddock ducked beneath the vicious stroke of the primitive sword, and fired off two rounds into the man's chest, emptying his clip. The warrior staggered backward, but before Maddock could finish the job, another attacker charged in, from behind. Still holding his M-16 in his left hand, Maddock deflected the downstroke of the man's club, but the rifle was battered from his hand. He lashed out with his right foot, sweeping the stumbling warrior's legs out from under him, and delivered a kick to the temple. The warrior groaned and slumped to the ground.

He heard someone coming at him from behind. Dropping his empty Walther, he snatched up the warrior's club, drew his Recon knife, and turned to face the second attacker, who was charging back in despite gouts of blood pouring from twin holes in his chest. They didn't seem to feel pain, but surely loss of blood would take its toll. The problem was, before that happened, the man just might live long enough to finish Maddock off.

The warrior, snarling through gritted teeth, swung his weapon in a deadly arc with much more speed and precision than Maddock would have expected from someone who had taken two bullets to the chest. Maddock dodged the stroke and lashed out with his knife, opening a cut on the man's arm. It might as well have been a mosquito bite for all the difference it made. The tooth-lined sword came around in a vicious backhand stroke. Maddock deflected it with the club and stabbed twice for the heart in rapid succession. The warrior staggered backward, clearly on his last legs. He raised his weapon, his arms quaking, but before he could bring it down, Maddock leapt in, opened his throat with the Recon knife, and shoved him backward, where he landed atop his stunned tribesman, who was just beginning to rise.

Maddock retrieved and reloaded his Walther, then finished each man with a head shot. His life no longer in immediate danger, he looked around for Kaylin. Her shotgun lay abandoned on the ground, but she was gone.

Kaylin fled from the natives with reckless abandon. She didn't know which way she was headed, and she didn't care. All that concerned her right now was getting away from the silent attackers who, despite their usual measured paces, could move quite fast when they wanted to.

She leapt across a fallen log and landed awkwardly. Her ankle rolled over and she went down in a heap, pain shooting up her leg. Something moved behind her, and she reached for her .380, but she was too slow. A sharp blow to the head sent flares of pain through her skull and stars swirled across her field of vision.

Strong hands hauled her to her feet, and she felt someone relieve her of her pistol and knife. She stamped down on the man's foot, eliciting a grunt of surprise, and spun, throwing out an elbow, but she struck only air. Her injured ankle twisted beneath her as she spun, throwing her off-balance, and a blow to her stomach sent the breath shooting out of her in a rush. Before she could recover, her assailant had her by the hair, raising her head. She felt the cold pressure of steel against her throat, and she froze.

"What have we here?" A tall, blocky man with a scarred cheek, outfitted in jungle camouflage stepped in front of her. He had the bearing of a military man, his every move suggesting scarcely-contained danger. "You would be Kaylin Maxwell, Thomas Thornton's special friend."

She finally regained her breath, gasping and coughing, still very much mindful of the blade pressed against her throat by unseen hands. "Who are you?" she croaked.

"I represent the company who paid Doctor Thornton a lot of money to do a job. He didn't live up to his end of the bargain, and I'm here to find out why."

"He's lost out here in the jungle is why, you idiot!" She didn't know where the words came from, because she was more frightened than she had ever been in her entire life. Perhaps she had just enough of her father in her to give her a measure of courage.

The man slapped her, just hard enough to sting. The coppery taste of blood filled her mouth. She spat at him but he sidestepped, and slapped her again, this time on her ear. A loud pop like a bursting balloon made her ears ring.

"No more playing around. I want answers." He drew his knife and moved in close.

"I won't tell you anything. You're just going to kill me anyway."

"Oh yes. But if you tell me what I need to know, we won't make it hurt." He touched the tip of his knife to the corner of her eye. She squeezed her eyes closed and tried to turn her head, but he pressed the blade harder against her flesh. "Open your eyes or I'll cut your eyelids off." He didn't sound the least bit annoyed with her, and that's what convinced her he would do what he threatened. She opened her eyes to meet his cold, impassionate gaze. "Good. Now, tell me how you found this place. Did you follow us?"

"Yes. We tracked you." It was technically true, though not the whole truth.

"How about the river? You can't track us on water."

Kaylin couldn't think of what to say next. Her lips moved, but no sound would come.

"Tell me, or I take out your right eye." The man brandished his knife.

"Fawcett's map," she gasped. "We followed it until we found your tracks."

"You're lying. We have Fawcett's map. You couldn't have followed it." He grasped her right eyelid and yanked it up. She couldn't pull her head away, no matter how she tried. The tip of his knife touched her eyeball and she broke. A swift death might have been one thing, but torture was something she wasn't prepared to endure."

"Okay! Okay! We also found the book."

"The book." The man sounded like something important was falling into place. He didn't take the blade away from her eye, though. "Tell me everything and tell me fast, and you keep your eye."

Tears poured down Kaylin's face as she hastily told the man about Fawcett's other map, and about the copy of *The Lost World* that one of his descendants had preserved. She was ashamed of her weakness, her moment of bravery evaporated in the face of mortal fear. She should have held on to that fighting spirit, but she couldn't. This wasn't like books or movies—the terror was real, the knife was real, and the possibility, no, the probability of her death was real, too. As much as she wanted to hold back information, she was too afraid.

"After you get past the last landmark," she gasped, "which we don't have…"

"We already have it," the man snapped. "Go on."

Tears trickled down her face. She tried to summon the courage to resist, but the razor sharp knife hovering inches from her eye made that impossible.

"You have to follow the path of five steps…"

Chapter 23

Maddock heard voices up ahead, and saw someone or something moving away from him. He crept forward, his Walther at the ready.

"Do whatever you want to her," a voice called, "but make it fast. Meet me beneath the stone outcropping."

Her? That had to mean Kaylin. His suspicions were confirmed moments later when he heard her cry out. Moving quickly and silently, he caught a glimpse of blonde hair, and heard her whimper.

"Easy. You don't want me to cut you, do you?" The heavily accented English had to belong to one of the guides with ScanoGen's group. Careful not to be spotted, Maddock ducked behind a tree and peered around it.

Kaylin was being held by a tall, dark-skinned man. In one hand, he had a knife pressed to her throat, and was pulling up her shirt with the other. Half of his head was obscured by Kaylin's. It was a small target, but it would be enough if he was fast.

He stepped out, Walther in a two-handed grip. The man spotted him and froze for a split-second. That was enough.

Maddock's first bullet took him in the eye, and Kaylin pushed the dead man's body away as he fell. Weeping, she ran to Maddock, who swept her up in his arms and held her tight.

"We've got to get behind cover," he whispered, moving backward. "We don't know who might be coming. There's the natives, and now these guys to contend with. Are they ScanoGen?"

Kaylin nodded. "Maddock, I'm sorry, but I told them about the Path of Five Steps. That guy, he was going to cut my eye out. I'm so sorry."

"It couldn't be helped." He pulled her close. Their one advantage over ScanoGen was now gone, but he couldn't expect Kaylin to hold up under threat of torture. It was stupid to have brought her here in the first place, no matter what she said.

"I did lie to him about one of the steps. The one about Rome. That might help. I just couldn't do more. I was so afraid he could tell I was lying. I'm so sorry." There was a longing in her eyes, and he knew she wanted him to tell her all was forgiven.

He managed a sympathetic nod. "What matters is you're all right. We need to find the others quickly. Did they take your gun?"

"I think the dead guy has it."

Hastily, they retrieved Kaylin's knife and pistol from the dead guide. As she tucked the knife back into its sheath, they heard the sound of many feet shuffling through the underbrush, coming right toward them.

"It's those zombie native freaks," she hissed. "They must have heard the sound of your gunshot."

"Let's go, and be sure to stay with me this time." Maddock took her by the hand and together they took off in the direction of the waterfall.

Bones trained his M16 on the figure hiding behind the bush. It wasn't one of the natives, but an attractive woman with short, black hair and skin the color of dark chocolate. She was dressed in fatigues and armed with a Makarov. This must be Tam, the ostensible leader of the ScanoGen group. She was good with a handgun. Bones had already watched her put a bullet through the skull of a charging native at fifty feet.

Of course, she was no SEAL. Bones was now twenty feet away from her and she had no idea he was there. He could take her out any time, but it suited him to let her waste her bullets taking out the natives while he waited here by the foot of the waterfall for Maddock and the others to arrive.

Also, something told him there was more to this girl than met the eye. He kept coming back to the fact that she'd set Andy free instead of killing him. Also, Andy implied that the ScanoGen crew didn't truly accept her as a leader. Something was stinky in Dodge, or however the saying went. Perhaps there was a rift in the ScanoGen group—one big enough for him to worm his way into. He decided to take a chance.

"Don't move a muscle." He kept his tone low, just loud enough for her to hear. She didn't flinch. She kept her body still and turned her eyes in the direction of his voice. "Don't even think about it, sweetheart," Bones added. "Doc freakin' Holliday isn't that fast."

"I can't see you, but I can tell where you are by the sound of your voice. I put enough bullets in the air, one of them will hit you."

"Look, chick," Bones said, knowing how much women hated being addressed that way. "First of all, we can sit and talk all day and my concentration won't lapse one bit. That's a promise. Second, you'll have a bullet in your skull at the first sudden movement you make. Now, open your hand and let the gun drop."

She grimaced, but did as she was told.

"Good, now put your hands on top of your head."

"I've never let anyone sneak up on me like that," she said as she slowly followed Bones's instructions. "I must be sleep-deprived."

"Don't let it bother you. It's all part of the training." He loved this girl's calm demeanor, but it also made her dangerous.

"I'm guessing you're either Maddock or Bonebrake."

"Why the hell does Maddock always get top billing? I'm the badass."

She smirked. "Look, I know you won't believe me, but I'm F.B.I. I'm on your side."

"Bull. If you're F.B.I., what are you doing in a foreign country?"

"I'm a plant inside ScanoGen. Have been for a long time. My primary assignment is domestic. My orders were to find out all I can about a shadow organization that's funding them and other groups, but I failed. I worked my way up through the organization and all I got was a name. The Dominion."

"What the hell are you talking about?" Bones's blood ran cold. It couldn't possibly be true, but then again, neither could it be a coincidence. "Do you mean the Deseret Dominion?"

"That's one small segment of a nationwide organization. I'm surprised you've heard of them. That cell has been quiet for a while."

"Maddock and I sort of had something to do with that." He probably shouldn't have made that admission, but he couldn't help himself.

"You're kidding me." Her eyes were wide with surprise. "Is this a joke to mess with me?" He had finally rattled her, though only a little bit.

"Nope. If you convince me not to kill you, I'll tell you all about it when we get out of here." He realized he had already decided to let her live, and he hoped he wasn't making a mistake.

"My cards are on the table." Her voice was calm and he detected no deception. "I've done my job the best I can, and tried not to do too much harm along the way. ScanoGen ordered me to kill a man, Thornton's colleague, but I let him go instead, although he doesn't stand much of a chance out there if I don't get back to him quick."

"We found him and he's all right. We sent him back with an armed guide." Something occurred to Bones. "You said your primary job was to investigate the Dominion. What else were you supposed to do?"

"To find out the truth behind Project Pan," she replied glumly, "and either steal the science behind it for the government, or put a permanent stop to it."

"What is Project Pan?"

"Something the Dominion hired ScanoGen to do. I don't know exactly what it is, but we believe it has a military application, and that it's somehow related to modifying the human brain."

"You mean like turning soldiers into semi-zombies that can't feel pain and keep on coming at you until you blow them apart or blow their heads off?"

"Maybe." She gave a sad smile "All I know for certain is Thomas Thornton claimed that he knew where to find the key, and I'm sure it lies somewhere beyond that waterfall. Look, I can't offer you any proof, but I'm telling you the truth. Take away all my weapons if you like. Do whatever you need to do to feel safe around a little girl like me, but let me come with you. While we're sitting here chatting, Kennedy and what's left of the ScanoGen guys are getting a head start."

"All right," Bones said. He moved to her side, pocketed her Makarov and relieved her of her knife and spare clips. His eyes fell on a strange-looking weapon lying nearby. "What is this?"

"Personal Halting and Stimulation Response rifle. PHaSR for short. Some call it a dazzle gun. It temporarily blinds your enemy. I tried it on the zombie things, but they just stopped and sniffed the air and came after me again like they were hunting dogs or something."

"Sweet!" Bones hefted the high-tech weapon. It was bulkier than a machine gun, and looked a bit like something you'd see in a science fiction movie. "I'll have to save this for Corey. He loves to get his Star Wars on!" He looked at down at his new pseudo-ally. "I am sorry about disarming you. You understand, don't you?"

"Don't worry about it." Tam looked up, turning her large brown eyes and bright smile on him. "I can take my weapons back from you any time I like."

"Bring it on any time." Although he was only ninety-seven percent sure she wasn't going to try to kill him, Bones couldn't help but like this girl. "My friends and I are to meet up here. If they agree to it, you can come along." He had to laugh. He could only imagine what Maddock was going to say.

Chapter 24

Maddock was not sure what to make of this new development, but he trusted Bones's judgment, and his own instincts told him that Tam was all right. He didn't know what to think about her claim that she was investigating the Dominion. What were the odds that name would crop up again? Until she proved herself, however, he was going to watch her closely.

He heard a rustling over the sound of the waterfall, and turned to see Matt and Willis come into view, the former supporting the latter's weight. Willis's right pants leg was soaked with blood.

"He caught a spear in the thigh," Matt grunted as he helped his friend ease down onto a nearby rock. "It looks worse than it is, I think."

"Says you." Willis winced as Bones ripped open the gash in the fabric in order to get a better look. "How come it's always the black man that has to die first? Tell me that, any of y'all."

"You're not dead. If you were, you wouldn't be so freakin' talkative." Bones chastised. They stood guard as Matt hastily cleaned, dressed, and bandaged the wound. "I'd stitch it up, but that would take a while, and there's no telling when those natives will be back."

"I think we just ran out of time!" Maddock had spotted movement in the distance. Shadowy forms were coming their way, and that meant danger, whether it was the natives or ScanoGen who were on their trail. "Let's get to the waterfall. Even if Tam's wrong about that being the last landmark, that will cut down on the approaches they can take to get to us."

They picked their way across the narrow, rocky path that ran between the base of the cliff and the dark pool fed by the waterfall. Cool mist coated their faces and made the way slick. Maddock put Tam in the front so he could see if she tried anything. Willis refused further help, and managed the trek reasonably well, though Maddock was worried about his comrade. Bones had confided in him that the wound was deep, and would require better attention than the quick treatment Matt had given it.

As they drew close to the waterfall, Maddock could see that the cliff face was hollowed out behind it. Hope rising, he urged Tam to quicken her pace before they were spotted. Skirting a head-high boulder, they stepped behind the curtain of water into a cave ten feet across running twenty feet back into the rock. Light filtering through the water cast the place in a flickering glow, and made it easy to see what awaited them inside the cave.

A giant skull was carved into the back wall. The mouth, nose, and eye sockets were all large enough for a person to crawl through. The irregular light sent shadows wavering across its surface, seeming to bring it to life.

"Wicked," Bones observed as he, bringing up the rear, entered the cavern.

"This is it." Tam put her hands on her hips and stared at the huge stone skull. She seemed to have already forgotten her position as a prisoner amongst a group of armed captors. "The problem is, I don't know where we go from here. Fawcett's map only takes us this far. It's entirely possible this is rigged so that someone who doesn't know the trick gets it." She dragged a finger across her throat and made a squelching noise.

"I think, for safety's sake, we should assume that's the case," Maddock said. "We can help you here. You see, we found Fawcett's *personal* copy of *The Lost World*." He grinned at Tam's look of surprise. "Now we need the Path of Five Steps. Kaylin, what's the first one?" He hoped that by asking her to contribute, even in a small way, he could assuage some of her guilt at surrendering their secret.

"All about me I see enemies. Rome, the scent your funeral pyres is the finest perfume."

"Weird." Matt frowned. "Couldn't they just say, *'Push this button and go here*?'"

"You have definitely been spending too much time with Bones." Kaylin shook her head. "Remember, this is a combined translation from Fawcett and a native. It's not going to be crystal clear, especially if it was some sort of secret code."

"So what does it mean?" Tam looked and sounded impatient.

"You like what you see, but not what you smell." Maddock said. "Sounds like we need to pick its nose." He looked at Tam. "Go for it."

She smirked. "Scared to try it for yourself?"

"Nope, but if I'm wrong, I don't want to lose one of my people."

"Fine by me." She strode over the skull and peered into the hole where the nose should be. "There's a handhold in here." She glanced up at the eye sockets and down at the gaping mouth. "Also one in each of the eyes, but not the mouth. That's just a blank wall." She looked back at Maddock. "Mister Maddock, you had better be right about this." Gingerly, she reached into the sinus cavity, set her jaw, and pulled.

Nothing happened.

Tam stepped back, hands on hips, looking at the skull like it was a man she'd just caught with another woman. And then a loud, creaking sound resonated above the sound of falling water, and with a scraping like the opening of a crypt, the wall at the back of the skull's mouth slid down into the floor, revealing deep, impenetrable darkness behind it.

A ragged cheer went up among the group. Maddock grinned and tossed Tam a flashlight. "In you go."

They had to proceed on hands and knees through the mouth of the skull. On the other side, they could stand, though Bones and Willis had to duck down in places to keep from hitting their heads. The tunnel ascended at a steep angle, and Willis, his leg bleeding again, was forced to accept help as they made their way up.

They reached a spot where the path leveled out and the way opened up into a large chamber. Standing before them were two statues: a horse and an elephant. Each stood about four feet tall at the shoulder. They could see no door, nor any other obvious means of egress.

"Now this is a puzzler." Maddock scratched his chin. "What's the second step, again?"

"The vile Numidians," Kaylin replied.

"What else?" Tam turned to Kaylin with a quizzical look. "That can't be all."

"That's it." Kaylin nodded insistently. "It was the easiest one to remember. Maddock has them written down if you want to double-check."

"No need," Maddock said. Something had clicked into place. "The Numidians were the finest cavalry in the ancient world. The horse would represent them."

"So who is the elephant?" Bones asked.

"Carthage." The more Maddock thought about it, the more certain he was that he was correct. "Carthage was known for its elephant cavalry. It used the Numidian cavalry against Rome early in the Punic wars, but the Numidians later turned on them, and things went downhill from there. When you consider that Rome was the bitterest of Carthage's enemies, the first clue also makes sense in that context."

"You think Kephises is a Punic city?" Kaylin suddenly gaped. "Remember what Wainwright said! Fawcett recognized some of the words the young man spoke as being Punic."

"It could be," Tam mused. "They were descended from the Phoenicians, the greatest sailors of the ancient world. There are legends of the Phoenician sailors reaching the Americas. Perhaps the knowledge was preserved and passed down, and someone from Carthage came here."

"That's how I see it," Maddock agreed.

"So if these are cavalry mounts," Tam said, "we hop on the back of Carthage's finest." She took two steps and sprang up onto the back of the elephant.

"You see, Maddock?" Bones said. "I did the right thing keeping her around. She's our very own canary in a coal mine."

His words were drowned out by a rumble as the elephant began to sink slowly into the floor. Tam's eyes bulged, but she kept her seat. The girl was brave, no doubt. She disappeared from sight, and the rumbling ceased, leaving them standing in awed silence.

"You can come down!" Tam called. "There's another passage heading back from here."

Matt went down first, and he and Bones helped Willis down. Willis grumbled and cursed the whole way, but did not refuse the assistance. When the last person had climbed down, they took a minute to bandage up his wound again. As they were working, the elephant suddenly rose back up and locked into place with a loud clack, closing them in the tunnel. They could see now that it was supported by a rectangular block of stone.

"How do we get back out?" Kaylin looked the column up and down with nervous eyes.

"We'll figure it out. Don't worry." Maddock gave her hand a quick squeeze. "Time to move on."

"This can't be right. Tam lied to me." Kennedy hated to admit he'd been duped, but there was no hiding it from the others. "When I find her, I'll kill her."

"Where do you think she is?" Smithson tapped the trigger of his F88 as if he, too, was eager to dispose of the woman. The three ScanoGen agents were still alive, and had managed to meet up with Kennedy. He'd had doubts about their loyalties, as Tam had hand-picked them for a the mission, but they were all ex-military, and not inclined to take orders from a civilian, even if that civilian was Salvatore Scano's favored son, or daughter, as it were.

"I don't know, but the mission remains our top priority. We won't seek her out, but should we come across her, your orders are to shoot on sight. Anyone have a problem with that?" No one spoke. "Good. Our first order of business is to find the last landmark, and then see if this Path of Five Steps is for real. I'll bet we find Broderick somewhere along the way."

"Sir, I saw her headed in the direction of the waterfall." Wesley was the youngest of the group, and a bit too eager, but he wasn't stupid. "Should we try there?"

"That's as good an idea as any. Remember to keep an eye out for Dane Maddock and whoever he brought along. Don't underestimate him or his companions. They know what they're doing."

"Same orders as with Broderick?" Brown, a big, red haired brute with a southern twang, grinned.

"Correct. Shoot on sight. But do it right, gentlemen. You are professionals. We want every man, and woman, in their party dead."

He bit the inside of his jaw, relishing the pain and the taste of blood. It always whetted his appetite for action. Despite all that had gone wrong on this mission, it felt good to be back in the field, ready to kill if necessary. And now, with Maddock and Bonebrake on the prowl, he had additional targets. Eliminating them would be a pleasure.

Chapter 25

They came to a fork where the passageway to the left was guarded by lions carved in the walls on either side, while wolves stood sentinel on either side of the passage on the right. Maddock grinned. He doubted he even needed the clue for this one.

"Time for the third step," Kaylin said. "Rome is forever cursed."

"There's got to be more," Matt objected. "You know, something about wolves and lions. This is crap! If we go down the wrong tunnel, we don't know what's going to happen."

"Don't worry. I got this one." Tam smiled, and Maddock could tell she was thinking the same thing he was thinking. "Romulus and Remus were the founders of Rome. They were abandoned as babies and…"

"…nursed by a mother wolf!" Kaylin exclaimed. "So it's a choice between the African lion and the Roman wolf."

"No choice at all, really." Tam smiled and took the passage on the left.

The way continued upward in a steep ascent. They must be nearing the top by now, Maddock thought. Just then, the tunnel leveled out, but after only a few paces, Tam stopped and put her hands out.

"Wait!" she snapped. "I think we've come to the next step." She shone her light across the floor. It was made up of square tiles, five wide and at least twenty deep. Each tile had a symbol engraved on it.

"Too far to jump across," Bones observed, walking right up to the edge and looking things over. "Bummer. That would simplify things."

"This step is an odd one." Kaylin knelt down in front of the tiles. "Walk safely across the moon."

"None of them look like the moon to me," Bones mused. "They aren't even round."

"I actually know something about this one from a religions course I took in college." Kaylin bit her lip, like she always did when she was deepest in thought. "At least, I think I do. I'd hate to be wrong."

"Your guess is better than anything else we have to go on," Maddock said. "What are you thinking?"

"The main deities of the Punics were the god Ba'al and the goddess Tanit. I remember her symbol because I thought it looked like an angel without wings." She pointed to one of the tiles.

"It also looks like an ankh," Tam added, "except for that strange thing at the top."

"Exactly." Kaylin's voice grew stronger as she warmed to her subject. "That's the moon clue, I think. Tanit is the moon goddess, and that symbol is a crescent moon!" She looked up at Maddock with a hopeful expression. "What do you think?"

"Makes sense to me. Anyone else have a better idea, or another suggestion?" He looked around, but the others shook their heads.

"Alrighty then." Tam rose to her feet with a sigh of resignation. "I hope you're right."

"Wait a minute. You've taken enough risks. It's my turn." Maddock took of his pack and handed it to Bones.

"No way, Maddock." Bones shoved the pack back into his arms. "We need you. I'll do it."

"We're all needed, Bones. I'm going."

"I'll go," Kaylin interrupted. "I'm sure if I just keep to the tiles, I'll be fine. Besides, I'm the most expendable one here."

"You are not," Maddock said.

"Excuse me." Tam moved between them. "How about I just go, while you and your girlfriend argue?"

"She's not my girlfriend," Maddock muttered.

"Really?" Tam raised her eyebrows. "She's cute. You should go for it."

"That's what I keep telling him," Bones chimed in. "But does he listen? Not a chance. He's all about figuring women out instead of just chilling and having a good time."

"You two both suck." Maddock looked at Bones. "Give Tam back her dazzle gun."

"Are you sure?" Bones and Tam said at the same time.

"No, but let's do it anyway." Bones unslung the gun from his shoulder and handed it to Tam. "You've done everything we've asked, and you could have easily stolen Kaylin's gun or her knife when she knelt down beside you just now."

"You would have shot me." Tam didn't look or sound accusatory, but spoke in a matter-of-fact manner.

"Yep, and I still will if you try anything, but I believe Bones is right about you. You didn't kill Andy, when it would have been easier to do so, and that says a lot. Besides, we're coming up on the final step, and we don't know what's waiting for us. You need a way to defend yourself."

"Thanks." They shook hands and she looked at him with a solemn expression. "I want to finish this as much as you do, and I give you my word. I'm not against you."

"We'll see," Maddock said. "Now, I don't care what anyone says. I'm taking the lead on this one."

He focused on each tile, choosing those carved with the Tanit symbol. He could not let go of the thought that these tiles were probably more than two thousand years old. It would be just his luck to be the one under whom they finally broke. One step, then the next. Each stride was uncomfortably long—just enough to make it difficult to maintain his balance. The third tile shifted as he put his weight down, and he froze.

"Hurry up, Maddock!" Willis shouted. "Even the army boy could go faster than that."

Maddock kept his eyes on the tiles and saluted his friend with an upraised middle finger. When he finally stepped off the last tile, everyone cheered him with sarcastic applause.

Willis had been resting up, and he went across next. He had been weak and wobbly on his feet, but you couldn't tell it from the confident manner with which he crossed the tiles, each foot firmly set in its proper place. Maddock breathed a sigh of relief when Willis was finally across. The others followed in short order, with Bones last.

"Glad you could join us," Maddock joked as Bones made a mocking bow.

"I just scouted ahead," Tam said from behind Maddock. "It looks like the fifth step is just around that corner."

Maddock couldn't help but smile. "We're there!"

Kennedy stood and stared at the two paths— the lions on one side, the wolves on the other. This clue had him stumped, though he hated to admit it.

"What did the girl say, again?" Smithson asked. "Something about Rome?"

"Rome is forever glorious."

"Well, that's easy, then. The lions, the arena, gladiators. We go that way." Smithson gestured to the tunnel guarded by the lions.

"Perhaps, but the wolf is associated with the founding of Rome. Also, the first clue was anti-Roman, saying their funeral pyres were perfume."

"Maybe they're burning the bodies of their enemies," Wesley suggested.

Kennedy thought about it. He couldn't wait too long. Maddock was out there somewhere, and so was Tam. The longer he stood here thinking, they were either gaining on him, or perhaps extending their lead if they had managed to get in ahead of him. Furthermore, indecisiveness instilled no confidence in those who followed you.

"Let's go with the wolves," he finally said. "But keep your eyes open and stay close to one another."

Wesley took the lead, his eagerness tempered only by Kennedy's order to remain close together. He stalked between the wolf carvings, their bared fangs seeming to portend doom. He had taken only six steps when the floor gave way beneath him. Wesley cried out in surprise as he plunged downward. Kennedy dove forward and grabbed his collar a split-second before Smithson and Brown grabbed Wesley by the arms. A good thing, too, else Wesley's weight would have dragged Kennedy down as well. They hauled the shaken man out of the pit.

"I guess it was the lion," Kennedy said, massaging his shoulder and staring down into the dark hole which had no visible bottom. Now he *really* wanted to kill Tamara Broderick and Dane Maddock.

Maddock rounded the corner to find that the passageway ended at a wall carved with a landscape. To the left was a lake, at the center a field, and a wooded ridgeline to the right. An iron ring set in a round plug hung below each image. On the floor in front of each, a seam outlined a six foot square, perhaps a pair of trap doors. A similar outline in the ceiling above each indicated something else potentially dangerous. He had visions of the floor dropping out from underneath him, or a giant block turning him into strawberry jam. He'd better interpret the last clue correctly.

"Here lies victory." He stared at the image until the edges blurred, and the water seemed to ripple. There wasn't any battle going on in the carving. What could it mean?

"If it was me, I'd take the high ground," Bones said. "Of course, they're probably looking for something a little more 'out there' than simple strategy."

"I think you've hit it on the head." Maddock smiled as the pieces came together. "Before the Romans destroyed them, Carthage's two greatest military victories were at Cannae and at Lake Trasimene. At Trasimene, they trapped the Roman forces between a ridge line and the lake, and slaughtered them. Some tried to escape by way of the lake and were also cut down. At Cannae, they pinned them against a river, and the slaughter was even worse. The Punic forces gradually gave way until the Romans were stretched out all along the river, and then the cavalry came down from the high ground, encircled, and slaughtered them. Rome's force was so large, and their defeat so complete, that they say many of the soldiers were just waiting to be killed when the forces of Carthage finally cut through the outer ranks to get to them. They even found Roman soldiers who had grown tired of waiting for the inevitable and had buried their heads in the dirt and suffocated themselves.

"That's crazy, dude." Bones shook his head. "So no safety on the low ground or in the water."

"Here goes nothing." Maddock stepped onto the square in front of the mountains and took hold of the cold, iron ring. He took a deep breath, turned and winked at Kaylin, and pulled.

The plug slowly gave way and, when it was extended about six inches, it stopped with a loud clunk. The floor began to vibrate and Maddock tensed, but nothing dropped out from beneath him, nor did anything come crashing down. Instead, the block on which he was standing sank slowly down into the floor. Sheer, dark stone slipped past, and a new passageway rose up before him. He smelled fresh air, saw a glimmer of light, and he knew they had made it.

When the remainder of the group had reached the bottom, they all stared in silence toward the end of the tunnel, which was partially obscured by hanging vines and low-growing flora. The question seemed to hang in the air. What would they find on the other side?

Chapter 26

Maddock stepped through the curtain of vines and into the late afternoon sun, then stopped in stunned amazement. Below him stretched a valley teeming with life. A stream ran down the center, wending its way between cultivated gardens on one side and orchards on the other. Giant kapok trees were scattered here and there among the fields. He could see people tending to the crops, but none of this was what shocked him. At the far end of the valley, beyond the orchards and cultivated fields, the jungle grew wild in a thick, dark, tangle, and rising up behind it stood a pyramid. Its dark, weathered stone speaking of age and mystery. Trees and plants had rooted in various places on its surface as the jungle struggled to claim it. What was a pyramid doing in this part of the world?

"Mayan?" Tam asked, staring at it in confusion. "But it couldn't be. This is the wrong place for it."

"Right." Maddock continued to stare at the pyramid. It bore some resemblance to Mayan architecture, but something wasn't quite right about it. Something about the angles gave it a different feel than the Mayan pyramids he had seen. "It almost looks like it has some Incan influence, or something, doesn't it?"

"The influence was Egyptian, actually."

Maddock was surprised to see a man staring up at them from down the path that descended into the valley. He had wavy brown hair, dark eyes, and a large, curved nose. His skin was deeply tanned, making his teeth seem even whiter when he smiled. He carried a small bow, but he did not have an arrow nocked.

Good thing for him, Maddock thought. He was not sufficiently armed to cause them any trouble.

"I am Mago and I welcome you to Kephises." He bowed. "Please put down your weapons. You have my word that we mean you no harm."

"I only see one of you," Matt scoffed.

"That, I think, is the point." Mago's smile widened.

"There's at least two guys hiding in the brush over that way," Bones said, inclining his head to the right. "They've got arrows trained on us. I'm guessing there are a few more I haven't spotted."

"You would be correct," Mago said. "Your weapons, I'm sure, are formidable, but you would be killed."

Maddock had to go with his gut. They were in an exposed position, and this man truly did not seem to want to hurt them. Could he blame these people for wanting to protect themselves from intruders in their realm? Besides, what choice did they have? Sure, they could fight, but at least some of their number would be killed, and probably for nothing. They had come this far to find out the truth behind Fawcett's final expedition, and hopefully to find Thomas, and that was what they were going to do.

"All right," he said, laying first his M-16, and then his Walther, on the ground. "But I have to warn you, there are dangerous men after us, who are better armed than we are. We mean you no harm either, and it would be a good idea to let us keep our weapons."

"We shall see," Mago said. When the remainder of Maddock's party had laid down their weapons, he made a quick gesture and several figures appeared, as if from nowhere, to collect their weapons. "Now, if you will please follow me."

He led them down the trail into the valley, with his comrades trailing behind, some carrying the confiscated weapons and backpacks, and others keeping arrows trained on their backs.

Maddock ignored them, hungry to take in the incredible scene. This was Kephises, the lost city so desperately sought after by Fawcett. Its very existence defied belief. He understood how this place had gone undiscovered. It was too far off the beaten path, and too well hidden, not to mention protected by the tribesmen below, for an explorer to stumble across it. Furthermore, with the heavy jungle growth all around, and the trees interspersed between the gardens, it would take the most detailed scrutiny of an aerial photo or satellite image to realize this was anything more than another patch of green in the midst of the vast Amazon region.

The people tending the crops stared at them as they passed. They lacked Mago's distinctive Mediterranean features, and instead bore some resemblance to the natives of the area, though their height, eye color, and complexion suggested a mixed ancestry.

"May I ask you a question?" Maddock actually had a hundred or more questions he wanted to ask, but he thought he'd start small.

Mago shook his head. "I am not the person to answer questions. When we reach the temple, there are others who will speak to you."

A jaguar emerged from the cover of the trees and slunk toward them. Maddock tensed, wishing he had a weapon, but their escort smiled at it as it padded up to him and nuzzled his hand. He scratched it behind its ears and spoke to it in gentle tones, as if it was a favorite pet. It left Mago and sidled up to Maddock. He froze, wondering if this beautiful but deadly beast was docile only for its master, but then the big cat rubbed against his thigh and purred.

"Isa likes to be scratched behind the ears and between the shoulder blades," Mago said. "Go on. She won't hurt you."

Maddock reached down and scratched the jaguar, whose purr sounded like a Harley revving up. Kaylin knelt down and stroked Isa's back.

"She's magnificent. And she is tame?"

"She will do violence only in defense of her life. All the animals in Kephises are that way." That raised another question Maddock wanted to ask, but Mago was already moving again. One of their armed escort motioned with his bow, indicating they should move on.

They entered the shade of the thick patch of jungle that barred the way to the temple. The path wound back and forth, almost like the coils of the Amazon River as it snaked its way across the continent. This was likely the only path through the jungle, and was cut this way in order to slow down invaders. Defenders could hide at each curve to repel invaders. The only alternative would be for the attackers to come through the jungle itself, which he imagined each citizen in Kephises knew like the back of his hand.

The jungle gave way to a sparsely wooded area. Stone houses, built in the style of the ancient Mediterranean world, stood in the center, with huts resembling those of native Amazon tribes scattered all about. The trees, all tall with broad limbs, cast this village area in mottled sunlight.

"This would be hard to spot, even from a satellite," Bones observed, looking up at the massive trees. "And the pyramid, as eroded and overgrown as it is, probably just looks like a hill."

"I wouldn't have believed it was possible for a place like this to exist undiscovered," Tam said. "But it makes sense to me now."

Mago ushered them into the largest stone building, a rectangular structure with small windows and an arched entryway. A fragrant scent, like incense, greeted Maddock as he stepped inside. Three men looked up as they entered, one of them springing to his feet.

"Kaylin! Oh my God, what are you doing here?" It was Thomas, and he hurried forward, arms outstretched.

Maddock stepped aside, and a spark of jealousy flared in his heart, but it was extinguished almost immediately as he saw the look of hesitation in Kaylin's eyes. It was only there for an instant, long enough for her to steal a glance at him before Thomas crushed her in a tight embrace.

"I didn't mean for you to come," he mumbled, his lips pressed against the top of her head. "You were supposed to send help."

"Things got complicated," she said. "I had to come along for my own safety."

Thomas drew back and frowned at her. "You went into the deepest, most unexplored region of the Amazon for your own *safety?*"

"ScanoGen was after us. Is after us," she added. "I don't know who you need to warn, but they might be right behind us."

"I have taken precautions, Father," Mago said, addressing a broad-shouldered man who remained seated, staring impassively at them. Finally, he nodded, and Mago bowed himself out of the room.

Kaylin introduced everyone to Thomas, who shook each person's hand and thanked them profusely for coming to his aid. She saved Maddock for last, and a shadow crossed Thomas's face when he heard the name. Clearly he knew Maddock and Kaylin had once had a relationship. He recovered immediately, and gave Maddock the same warm thanks he had given the others.

"I imagine you have many questions." A tall, lean man of lighter complexion than the others waved them to sit on a wooden bench that ran the length of one wall. Of middle years, he was lean and athletic-looking, and had about him an aura of abundant energy. "We will answer what we can. You have obviously taken a great deal of personal risk to come here."

Maddock frowned at the man. There was something familiar about him. Perhaps it was his eyes, which, though friendly, were lighter than those of the others Maddock had seen in Kephises, and burned with an intensity bordering on zeal. His accent was different, too. It almost seemed to have a touch of the U.K. in it.

"Would you care for food or water?" the man asked.

"Actually, my friend has a wounded leg that needs tending to." He nodded to Willis, who waved dismissively, but his smile was a tired one.

"We shall see to it at once." Now it was the big man who spoke. He rose to his feet and clapped his hands twice. A young man, another of those who looked to be of mixed race, hurried in and dropped to one knee. "Take the Nubian and see to his hurts."

Willis's jaw dropped in surprise, but he was too tired to reply. Tam covered her giggle with a forced cough, and Bones looked like it was taking all he had not to chime in.

"I'll go with him," Matt said, rising to his feet and helping Willis stand. "I have first aid supplies that might come in handy." They followed the young man out the door, Willis leaning heavily on Matt. Clearly, he was in worse shape than anyone had suspected, and the climb up the five steps had taken its toll. Maddock had to admire his friend. He was resilient.

"Is that word amusing to you?" The big man had not missed their reactions. "Or is it no longer used?"

"Forgive us." Tam spoke up quickly. "The word is still in use, but it is typically only used when complimenting a beautiful woman. You might call her a Nubian queen or princess."

"Ah." The man settled back into his seat. "Your amusement was not disrespect, then."

"No disrespect was intended," Maddock assured him. "I am curious, though. Your settlement has clearly been here for many years."

"Two thousand, one hundred, forty four, to be exact. My ancestors wandered in the wilderness for a long while before finding this place."

"Were your ancestors from Carthage?" Maddock had a feeling he knew the answer to that question, but did not want to make assumptions.

"Yes, they were." The man with the British accent spoke up. "You have the honor of addressing Hamilcar of Kephises, descendant of Hannibal Barca, the greatest of the Punic generals."

Hamilcar inclined his head, the expression on his face almost kingly. Under different circumstances, this would have been a stunning revelation, but considering they had just discovered Percy Fawcett's legendary lost city, Maddock found it merely surprising.

"So, Kephises was not a Greek city," Kaylin said, half to herself. "The legend was inaccurate."

"The name is of Greek origin, for reasons that have to do with the purpose of my people's journey here so long ago," Hamilcar said.

"May I ask what that purpose was?" Tam's voice was hopeful. Obviously, the answer to this question lay at the core of her, ScanoGen's, and the government's interest in Fawcett's last expedition. Assuming, of course, she had told the truth about her government connections.

Hamilcar shifted uncomfortably in his seat.

"I can show you later," Thomas said. "I owe you all an explanation after you came all this way to find me." He sat next to Kaylin, holding her hand, though she did not look pleased about it.

"If I may ask," Maddock began, turning his attention away from the discontented couple, "how is it that you speak English?"

"I'm afraid the fault lies with my grandfather and great-grandfather." The man whom Maddock had thought familiar-looking took over the explanation. "I am Brian Fawcett, great-grandson of Percy Fawcett and grandson of Jack Fawcett."

Maddock's heart raced. "So Fawcett did make it here!"

"Why, yes he did." Brian smiled, clearly proud of his ancestor. "Mister Thornton, here, tells me my great-grandfather is quite famous, though it is generally believed he died in pursuit of a folly."

"That's true. But now people will know the truth." Maddock imagined revealing the true story of the heroic explorer, and validating the man's life's work. But then he imagined what would happen next. The very best scenario he could envision was a swarm of researchers: archaeologists, anthropologists, historians, even geneticists wanting to learn more about this place and its people. They would destroy Kephises as it existed right now. "Sorry, I wasn't thinking."

Fawcett nodded. "I understand. It must be an even greater surprise to you than it was to my grandfathers." He leaned back in his chair and smiled, as if he was telling a story by a campfire. "Of their party, only Percy and Jack reached Kephises. The rest died along the way, or were killed by the 'dead ones' as Thornton tells me they are known to the outside world. The people of Kephises welcomed and honored them, though they were not permitted to leave."

Bones shifted uncomfortably and cast a dark glance at Maddock, but did not interrupt.

"I do not think they wanted to leave, frankly. They were treated well, and Jack was even permitted to marry into the Barcid family, which had been kept to a pure Punic bloodline. I have the rare honor to be descended both from the great Percy Fawcett and the legendary Hannibal."

"You would be a famous man in the outside world." Maddock smiled. "Have you ever been tempted to leave?"

"No." Fawcett's face darkened. "I have not."

Hamilcar suddenly rose. "You will be given food and drink and a place to stay."

"If I may be so bold." Maddock had no idea how to address this man. If there was an honorific due him, he didn't know what it was. "Please do not underestimate the men who are after us. They are well-armed and I seriously doubt they care who they kill as long as they get what they came for." He glanced at Tam, who remained silent. "My friends and I are trained soldiers. We can help you defend yourselves."

"I will consider your words." Hamilcar made a back-handed gesture, like brushing away an insect, and inclined his head toward the door.

"I'll show you around." Thomas stood, nervously brushed invisible dirt from his pants, and ushered them out the door.

The sun was an orange ball perched on the edge of the horizon as they stepped out into the light. Maddock looked around, unwilling to relax. He and the others had not put up a fight when they met the protectors of Kephises, but this would not be true of ScanoGen. They would be looking for a fight, and though they would most likely be on the lookout for Maddock's group, if they encountered anyone from Kephises, they would probably shoot first and ask questions later.

"I get the impression they think they're going to keep us here." Bones kept his voice low so that no one else could hear.

Maddock nodded. Yet another reason they needed to retrieve their weapons as soon as possible. But how to do it without coming into open conflict with people they would prefer to protect?

Kennedy stood in the shadows at the end of the tunnel, letting the darkness and the vegetation conceal his presence. He could not make out much from this vantage point, but he could see there was some sort of valley or canyon below them, and what looked like a pyramid in the distance.

"See anything?" Smithson whispered.

"Not much, but there's at least two men hiding out there, keeping watch. If I can see them, there have to be more of them I can't see."

"You think it's more of those zombies?" Wesley actually sounded eager for a return engagement with the mindless natives.

"I don't think so. They didn't seem like the type to hide out and guard an entrance. There's something else going on here. I think we've reached the end of the line."

"Well, let's go get 'em then!" Wesley bobbed up and down on the balls of his feet. His near-death experience in the booby-trapped tunnel had not dampened his enthusiasm one bit.

"Not yet." Kennedy despised inaction, but he wasn't stupid. They needed intel. What waited for them out there? How many men? How were they armed? What was the key to Project Pan, and where was it?

"Yes, sir." Wesley's disappointment-soaked words were respectful. The man might be a pit bull, but he was a well-trained one. Good thing, too. Kennedy didn't tolerate men who could not or would not follow orders.

"We'll wait for dark. Our night vision goggles will give us a major advantage. I'll take one of them alive if I can, and find out just what's waiting for us out there. Then we'll move in." A grim smile crept across his face. He did not know if Maddock or Broderick had reached this place ahead of him. It would probably be an easier fight if they had not, but somehow, he hoped they were here. He had a bloodlust that needed to be satisfied.

Chapter 27

"You should see the pyramid. It's really something." Thomas's speech was clipped and his expression grave. He was moving fast, as if he didn't care if they kept up with him or not. When they reached the pyramid, he began climbing. "Watch your step." He didn't look back as he spoke. "It's crumbling in places, but if you stay behind me, you'll be all right."

Maddock wanted to tell him that they really weren't interested in sightseeing right now, but he sensed Thomas had a purpose behind his actions, so he followed without complaint. When they had climbed about halfway, Thomas stopped, and indicated they should sit down.

"I'm sorry about the climb." The words were interspersed with gasps as he sucked in air. "It's steep, but necessary." Finally composing himself, he drew in a few slow, measured breaths. "Anyway, this is the one place we can talk without anyone listening. Not everyone here speaks fluent English, only the Punics, but the natives all speak at least a little bit, and understand a lot. This way, we can have a bit of privacy, and can also watch to see if ScanoGen shows up. The way in is that way." He pointed to the ridge on the far end of the valley.

"Tell us the story," Maddock said. "The whole story. We risked our lives to save you, and we deserve answers."

"That's why we're up here." Thomas would not meet his eye. "Where should I begin?"

"How much have you learned much about this place?" Bones asked.

"Quite a bit, actually. Fawcett is very talkative, and the others are fairly free with information since they know I'm no threat to escape. Kephises was founded by refugees from Carthage who escaped at the end of the third Punic War, just before the fall of Carthage itself. Those who survived the voyage made landfall far to the north, most likely near the southernmost regions of the Mayan empire. The first natives they encountered worshiped them as gods, and followed them into the jungle. Their leader was Hasdrubal, Hannibal Barca's grandson."

"That's one of the things that confused me," Maddock said. "I didn't think Hannibal had any children."

"History has been hazy on that topic," Thomas replied. "I suppose that's because his only living descendant headed off to the Americas." His thin smile only made him look more nervous. "Anyway, Hasdrubal was on a mission, given to him by the priesthood, to protect Carthage's greatest treasure. When they arrived in the New World, he told the others that the gods would let him know when and where it was time to stop. They journeyed deeper and deeper into the jungle, picking up some native followers as they went, but losing their fair share of people along the way. When they finally found this place, he deemed it safe and remote enough to settle.

The tunnel, the Path of Five Steps, and the pyramid all were built over the generations using combined labor of the Punics and natives. That's why the pyramid is a bit odd-looking. The Barcids wanted something like the pyramids of Egypt, but the pyramid has distinctly Mayan features, which is why I believe their first landfall was in or near Mayan territory."

"So, the people who live here are a mix of Punics and Mayans?" It bothered Maddock to feel like the ignorant half of a conversation with Kaylin's boyfriend, but he wanted to hear the story nonetheless.

"Mostly. Also local natives, some of whom they collected as they went in search of this place, others they collected over the years. There seems to be something of a hierarchy here, depending on how much Punic blood one has, with the Barcids being the most pure. That's actually how Fawcett came to find this place. I assume you found Wainwright?" They nodded. "The young man whom Percy Fawcett encountered was a Barcid who wanted to marry one of the low blood girls. That isn't acceptable in that family. In fact, the only reason Jack Fawcett was permitted to marry into their line was because the husband of one of the women of the line had died. She was of late middle age and thought to be past childbearing years. Anyway, the young man and his lover escaped, and he took with him the secret to the five steps, and he also carved a rough map in stone. I suppose he thought they'd come back some day once they'd had a few children and it was too late for his family to do anything about it. If it hadn't been for him, this place might still be a secret." He lapsed into silence, gazing out across the valley.

"You said you weren't a threat to escape," Bones said, "are they keeping you here?"

"I'm sure if they let you go, they'll let me go, too." Thomas sighed. "Once they understand their secret is out, there's not much reason for them to keep us here."

"I'd like to see them try." Bones grimaced, and his gaze turned flinty as he looked down on the settlement.

"The truth is, unless Salvatore Scano has told the world, which I can almost guarantee you he hasn't, the only people from the outside world who know about this place are sitting right here." Tam frowned. "And what's left of the ScanoGen men, if they survived those zombie people."

"The Mot'jabbur, they call them." Thomas looked up at the sky. "The Dead Warriors."

"Who are they? *What* are they?" Maddock asked.

"I suppose you could call them experiments that went wrong, but that wouldn't be entirely accurate."

"What *I* want to know is how you came to have any dealings with ScanoGen in the first place." Kaylin's voice was white hot rage. "You never told me a single thing. Then you disappear, with nothing but a picture as a clue, and leave killers after us. What happened?"

Thomas hung his head for a moment, as if gathering his thoughts, and then stood. "For you to understand that, you'll have to see the tree."

He led them around to the back side of the pyramid and pointed down to a clearing, in the center of which stood the strangest tree Maddock had ever seen. It resembled a baobab tree in miniature, with a thick trunk and a few root-like branches spreading out at the very top. But the similarities ended there. The bark was silver and gleamed in the orange sunset. The round leaves were concave and glossy like those of a magnolia, but they were dark on one side, nearly black in color, and a creamy white on the other. A single piece of fruit was visible through a gap in the bizarre foliage. It was the size of a cantaloupe, and it, like the leaves, was dark on one side and light on the other.

"Percy Fawcett was on to something even crazier than anyone ever suspected.

Much of what he professed to believe was a smokescreen designed to throw people off the trail of what he knew would be an earth-shattering discovery. It took half a lifetime, but I pieced together, and kept for myself, enough evidence to realize what he was truly after."

Down below, a woman was watering the tree. She glanced up at them, but paid them no particular mind, and went back to her work.

"This tree is the secret the Punics traveled her to protect. It has passed through many hands: Athenian Greeks, Spartans, Persians, all the way back to ancient Israel and beyond."

Maddock turned a quizzical glance at Thomas, but did not interrupt.

"The leaves, when divided, have powerful properties if made into a tea and drunk regularly."

"What sorts of properties?" Maddock asked.

Thomas gazed into the setting sun, as if uncertain how to explain. "The human propensity for violence exists on a spectrum. Some people have such a tremendous aversion to violence that they cannot abide the thought of it, and will only raise a hand to another human being in the final, most desperate defense of their life, or that of a loved one, if then. On the other end of the spectrum are those who will pull a trigger with no compunction whatsoever. Most of us lie somewhere in between."

"That's one of the things military training does." Maddock thought about his own experiences. "From the beginning, you are never told to kill the 'other man;' everything is referred to as a target, even human targets. There are a lot of other techniques they use as well to try to get you past thinking of the other side as human, because most of us have at least some aversion to killing others."

"When I was doing some research about an ancestor who fought in the Civil War," Bones said, "I read that a good many soldiers couldn't even bring themselves to fire their gun. As soon as the shooting started, they'd hunker down and wait it out."

"Very true." The professor in Thomas was emerging. "Those who can kill without thought make our deadliest soldiers, because they don't flinch in the face of danger, and they never hesitate when it's time to pull the trigger."

"They also make for serial killers," Maddock added, "because they have no empathy."

"Precisely. Imagine a fighting force in which every man is completely without fear, yet preserves his intellect, and is thus able to follow orders and make appropriate decisions without fear getting in the way. It would make a difference today on the battlefield, but think of the effect it had in the ancient world, where all the fighting was hand-to-hand, face-to-face, hacking apart another human being. It was vicious and very, very personal."

"But an army, even one that was outnumbered, that drank this tea would make for a better fighting force than a larger force filled with frightened men." The pieces were falling into place for Maddock. "Hannibal gave this tea to his troops during the Punic Wars, didn't he?" Thomas nodded. "And the Spartans must have drunk it before the battle of Thermopylae."

"Spies stole it right out from under the noses of Xerxes and his so-called Immortals. Took all the leaves and the sole remaining seed. Xerxes apparently intended to plant a new tree in the western half of his new empire. It didn't work out for him." Thomas grinned. "It passed from Sparta to Athens, which had the most success in cultivating it. They managed to build up a stockpile of seeds, which eventually fell into

Punic hands."

"So how did Carthage not win the war if they had the greatest general of his day, plus this tea?" Bones asked.

"The supply is always limited. The tree is slow-growing and produces a limited number of leaves every year. The priesthood that tended to the trees could not produce enough to keep up with the army's demands. Only certain, special units were given the tea in any case."

"So, when Carthage fell, they took what remained of the seeds and escaped?" Maddock tried to imagine the courage or desperation required to cross the Atlantic Ocean in an ancient sailing vessel.

"Their Phoenician ancestors had visited what is now the Americas and the priesthood held on to that knowledge. When it became clear that Carthage was going to fall, they sent a remnant to the New World. Hasdrubal and his followers found this place, settled down, and planted a new tree."

"What does the white side of the leaf do? Mellow people out?" Bones grinned.

"Yes. White tea will pacify the drinker for a short period of time. They will temporarily forsake all thoughts of violence. In a way, it's more deadly than the black tea. Slip your enemy some white tea and you can slaughter them. I imagine you could do just about anything you want to someone who drinks enough of it."

A cloud of suspicion passed through Maddock's mind. "Do you think that's how they pacified the natives? Maybe it wasn't that they thought the Punics were gods."

"If that's not how they initially gained their allegiance, they definitely have used it since then as a way of developing a servant class that won't be quick to fight back. They even give it to the animals to make them more docile."

"So ScanoGen hired you to bring them, what, seeds, fruit, leaves from this tree?" Maddock asked.

Thomas nodded. "They want to develop this into a weapon. Modify people at the genetic level to make them perfect soldiers."

"And turn enemies into pacifists," Bones finished.

"So, what about those zombie guys?" Maddock felt something was not adding up. "Did they get too much black tea or something?"

Thomas took a deep breath. "You aren't supposed to eat the fruit, or at least that's what legend said. But the people here didn't heed that warning. There were natives living in the next valley, and once the five steps were in place, the Punics saw in them a potential extra line of defense. Problem was, the effects of the tea were only short-term, and the supply of leaves limited. They took a chance and used the fruit. At first it seemed like it had worked, but slowly, the people changed. They not only became killers, a threat to anyone who was different than them, but they lost the ability to feel altogether. They don't feel physical pain, and they don't seem to have any emotions, either. They live in caves, hunt, eat, reproduce, and try to kill anyone who enters their realm. It's a miracle I made it through."

"What does the white half of the fruit do?" Maddock tried to imagine the polar opposite of the condition in which those natives now lived.

"It puts them in a state of utter contentment, to such an extreme that the person no longer feels the need to do anything. They forsake all human interaction, and just sit and smile. They don't want anything. They stop eating and drinking, and eventually they stop breathing."

"That's even more horrible than the Mot'jabbur." Bitterness singed Kaylin's every word.

"I can see why the Dominion wants this." Tam pursed her lips, deep in thought. "Shoot, I can see why anyone would want this. Governments, terrorist organizations, the potential is unthinkable." Her eyes grew wide.

"Wait a minute! Project Pan. The Greek pottery..." She gasped. "It can't be."

"Pandora's Box." Thomas nodded. "The Greek urn in which the seeds of the tree were kept."

"You're telling us that *the* Pandora's Box is here?" Why this was surprising to Maddock, after everything else they'd seen, he could not say.

"It goes deeper than that." A mysterious smile played across Thomas's lips. "Think for a moment. Have you ever heard of a tree that bore forbidden fruit?" Maddock's mouth went dry as Thomas went on. "A fruit that, when eaten, could cause you to be cursed. Could give you the ability to know evil and do evil things."

"No freakin' way." Bones was on his feet. "That is the tree from the Garden of Eden?"

"Hardly." Thomas chuckled. "But I suspect it is a descendant of the tree or trees that inspired the Garden of Eden story."

Maddock stared down at the silver tree with its black-and-white fruit, and wondered if his life could get any stranger. How was it that these things kept happening to him? The others were equally silent, gazing at the wondrous sight in awed, reverent silence. As he looked at the tree, though, something else occurred to him.

"You know what that tree reminds me of? Look at the leaves and the fruit. A circle, half black, half white."

"The Yin and the Yang," Tam whispered. "Maybe it's all tied together somewhere back in very ancient history."

"All I know," Maddock stood and looked at Thomas, "is you've uncovered a deadly secret, and because of you, we just might have led men here who would like nothing more than to unleash this on the world."

"Thomas, how could you do this?" Kaylin looked angrier than Maddock had ever seen her. "You're helping them do Lord knows what? I never dreamed you were this kind of person."

"You don't understand," Thomas pleaded, dropping to his knees in front of her. He reached out to take her hand, but she slapped it away. "For me, it was always about Fawcett. ScanoGen funded my expeditions, and, yes, they paid me well. The money was going to be for us, for our future together. I swear. Once I solved the Fawcett mystery for myself, I was going to tell them I had failed. That I didn't find anything."

"And you thought they'd just let it go like that? I can't believe you." Kaylin buried her face in her hands.

"Kaylin, I..."

"Just forget it. We'll talk about it later." She waved him away. "Talk to them."

Thomas stood, clearly exasperated. "You have to believe me. I didn't intend to give the information over to ScanoGen. I was just using them to finance my work on Fawcett. I've been fascinated with his story all my life. The mystery grabbed hold of me and wouldn't let go. You," he said to Maddock, "of all people, understand that, don't you?"

Maddock rose to his feet and looked Thomas in the eye. "Do I know that feeling? Yes. Do I think that makes it okay to do something rash and reckless out of utter selfishness? No way."

Thomas looked like he was about to argue, but words must have failed him. He lapsed into a sullen silence and turned away from Maddock.

"What do we do now, Maddock?" Bones asked. "I could throw this dude down the pyramid if you like."

Tam suppressed a chuckle as Thomas's face reddened.

"It wouldn't help us any. We need to get our weapons back and be ready in case ScanoGen shows up. I say we give them a couple of days, and if they don't show, that means they're either lost or the Mot'jabbur got them. If Willis is up to it by then, we'll make our way back home."

He turned to Tam. "Do you think there's any chance of keeping this," he pointed at the tree, "under wraps? You said only one person at ScanoGen knows about it."

"As far as I know, he's the only one. I suppose there's a chance he shared the information, but I doubt it. Other than the Fawcett map, Salvatore Scano only knew in a very general way what it was Professor Thornton here thought he would find—an Amazon plant that would allow them to manipulate human aggression. No one dreamed of this."

"If you're really F.B.I., what do you plan on telling your superiors when you get back to the States?" He searched her big brown eyes, seeking whatever truth might wait there.

"I don't know." She didn't look away as she answered him. "I have a duty to my country, and I take that to heart, but I'm almost as afraid of it falling into our government's hands as I am of ScanoGen and the Dominion, whoever they are, getting hold of it."

"I'd say we chop the thing down and get the hell out of Dodge." Bones stood and stretched. "But I suppose they'd plant another one.'

"There's only one seed left." Thomas said in a soft, almost inaudible voice. "Fawcett told me. Some of what they brought with them from Carthage never took root, nor have many of the seeds the trees here have produced. The trees also don't live as long in this place as they did in the old world. They don't say so, but the people here are worried."

"It would be a blessing for them if the tree had already died," Maddock said. Of course, it was too late now. "Let's head back down before it gets dark. I have a bad feeling about tonight."

Chapter 28

Brian Fawcett was waiting for them when they reached the bottom of the pyramid, a nervous look painting his face. Armed guards stood nearby, eyeing Maddock and the others. He had the feeling they were not there by coincidence.

"Quarters have been prepared for you." Brian cleared his throat. "I shall show you to them. We have food and drink waiting there for you as well. Also, your friends are already there."

"These quarters wouldn't happen to be guarded, would they?" Maddock was not certain how long he would tolerate being caged, and he knew Bones to be doubly impatient with such things.

"For your safety, only. Some people are suspicious of new arrivals, you know." The words sounded artificial, and Fawcett reinforced Maddock's instinct with a quick shake of the head. He mouthed the word "later," and led them away from the pyramid.

To Maddock's disappointment, they were given a room, not in one of the huts, which would have been easy to escape from, but in one of the ancient stone buildings. A contingent of guards escorted Kaylin and Tam away to separate quarters. "Don't drink any tea," Maddock warned them as they parted ways. Kaylin looked at him with fear-filled eyes, while Tam merely looked calculating, like she was already planning their escape.

At the room that was to be their quarters, Fawcett entered with Maddock and Bones, and a guard closed the door behind them. They heard the lock turn, followed by the sound of a bar sliding into place.

Willis, looking weary, sat on a mat of woven reeds, his bandaged leg stretched out in front of him, and his back against the wall. They all stared at Fawcett, who began pacing the room.

"I understand," he said, "how you must feel."

"I doubt that," Bones said. "And I doubt you have any idea who you're messing with."

"Please, give me time," Fawcett pleaded. "You only just arrived. We need to convince Hamilcar that you only came in search of Thornton. Then, he will believe you mean no harm."

"So Hamilcar is in charge?" Maddock asked.

"Technically, no, but everyone on the council defers to him and follows his lead."

"If ScanoGen shows up, he's going to regret locking us up and confiscating our weapons. I doubt there's a person here, besides us, who can use them." Maddock kept his voice calm. "We came to rescue Thomas. That's all. We're not here to steal anything from their tree."

"Thornton told you about it, did he?" Fawcett chuckled. "I should not have told him, but I fear holding my tongue is not a talent I possess. Besides, I felt that I owed it to him after he told me all about my grandparents and their homeland. The man is quite the expert on Percy Fawcett, you know."

"We know; believe me." Maddock grimaced. "If he'd been a little less interested, we wouldn't be here right now, and neither would ScanoGen."

"Maybe the ScanoGen guys were killed by the Mot'jabbur." Matt's flat voice was devoid of optimism. "Then we'll just have to worry about getting ourselves out of here."

"You are welcome to come with us," Maddock said to Fawcett. "I know this is your home, and I won't pretend it's not going to be a dangerous trip back, but if you wanted to see the outside world, you can come along. Like I said before, you'd be a famous man."

Fawcett shook his head. "No. I fear it is not so simple in my case. At any rate, I don't want to see anything happen to Kephises, which is why I am trying to convince you to remain patient. If you try to fight, you will be killed, but I don't doubt you are capable of doing your share of harm, even without your weapons. I don't want to see anyone hurt, especially my brothers and sisters here." He ceased his pacing. "This is a magical place. We live peacefully, work together, care for one another, all without the interference of the outside world."

"I hate to tell you, but that's probably over for you." Maddock truly did hate the fact that the secret of Kephises was out of the bag. Hopes of keeping it hidden from the world hinged on the silence of a few ScanoGen members, not to mention that of Thomas, once they got out of here. Maddock trusted the rest of his group to keep their silence, including Tam. For some reason, he had already developed confidence in her. He hoped she would be an asset, and not prove to be a mole, cleverly placed by ScanoGen. He had been there before. "Forget the Grecian urn you guys have hidden away somewhere," Maddock said. "Thomas opened a Pandora's Box when he got in bed with ScanoGen."

Fawcett flinched at the mention of Pandora's Box. "I really should not have been so free with what I told Thornton. But, I suppose it does not matter now. Promise me you won't try anything reckless."

"That's not a problem." Maddock ignored the frowns Bones, Willis, and Matt directed at him. "Just make sure Hamilcar understands that, if ScanoGen attacks, the four of us, with our weapons, will give your people their best chance at survival."

"I shall try." Fawcett made an awkward bow and backed to the door. At the sound of his voice, the door was unbarred and opened slowly, several gleaming spearheads filling the empty space. When the guards were satisfied that their prisoners were not making a rush for escape, they drew back and permitted Fawcett to exit.

No sooner had the door closed than Bones was on his case.

"Are you kidding me?" Bones stared at him like he was from Mars. "What do you mean, telling him we wouldn't try anything?"

"What I said was, we won't try anything *reckless*." Maddock grinned. "That word, my friends, is subject to interpretation. And what other people think of as reckless is just another day at the office for us."

"That's what I'm talking about." Willis nodded. "You just say the word and I'm ready to move. I can deal with the leg."

"Wouldn't expect anything less." Maddock took a careful look at the room in which they were imprisoned. It was a wonderful example of ancient architecture, made of solid stone, each block precisely fitted together. The floor consisted of smooth, square tiles, so precise they looked as if they were manufactured by modern machinery. Truly, they had stepped back in time.

Which was what he was counting on.

Moving to the far wall behind Willis, he put his hand against it, and found it was cool to the touch. He put his ear to the smooth stone, listened intently, and smiled at the soft sound of running water.

"Okay, everybody look around for a hole, or maybe something in the floor or at the base of the wall that looks like a vent."

"Care to let us in on your little secret?" Bones, to his credit, was already searching the floor even as he asked the question.

"This building has Roman-style air conditioning," he explained. "Well, not actual air conditioning, but water is piped through the walls, which cools the room. It might also have an ancient heating system, which consisted of vents that carried warm air from a fire in a central location throughout the building. Also, when archaeologists excavated the ruins of Carthage, they found that the houses had waste holes that ran down into a communal drain. If they went to the trouble of installing the cooling system, I'll bet you they put in waste disposal."

It required only a few minutes to give the room a thorough search, which turned up nothing. Maddock gritted his teeth, thinking hard. There had to be a way out.

"Any more ideas?" Matt asked.

"I've got one," Bones chimed in. "Maybe Willis could move his fat butt so we can see if there's anything underneath him."

"Oh, sorry." Willis winced as Maddock and Matt hauled him to his feet.

Maddock pushed aside the mat with his toe. Up against the wall, where Willis had sat, lay a square floor tile four times the size of all the others. Grinning, he dropped to his knees and ran his fingers along the edge of the tile. Centuries, or more, of dust and dirt had accumulated in the cracks. As he began scraping and brushing it loose, Matt and Bones lent a hand. Finally, the edges were clear. Maddock slipped his fingers down into the open space, and felt a groove running all the way around.

"All right," Maddock said. "Everybody grab hold and let's do it."

The ancient stone must not have been moved in a long, long while, for it held tight. Veins stood out on Bones's neck as he tugged. Sweat beaded on Matt's forehead, and his face was screwed up in intense concentration. Maddock shifted his weight, gave the tile a jiggle, and was rewarded by a bit of movement.

"Come on, you mother." Bones hauled on the stone with renewed vigor, and, a millimeter at a time, the stone tile came free. They laid the heavy tile to the side and Maddock looked down into the hole. Cool air drifted up into the room, carrying with at a faint scent of something unpleasant.

"Okay, Andy Dufresne. You going to crawl through the sewage to freedom?" Bones clapped him on the shoulder.

"Matt and I are the only ones who'll fit," Maddock said, looking down into the darkness. The drain was just wide enough that he could work his way through, provided it did not grow narrower at any point further up.

"At least it's a small population," Matt observed. "In a bigger settlement, this thing would be stanky." He sighed deeply. "All right. You first, or me?"

"I'll take the lead. You can pull me out if I get stuck." He turned to Bones. "We'll get back as quick as we can to let you out."

"No problem, bro. If they find you're gone, I'll just bash them in the head with this tile." He grinned at the thought.

"Don't get yourself killed, Bones. I'm serious. Worst case, they come looking for us. I doubt they'll hurt you, unless you give them reason."

"You take the fun out of everything." Bones frowned.

"You heard me. I need you to stay alive in case I have to sacrifice you to the Mot'jabbur on the way back." He ignored Bones's insult and, crinkling his nose, slid headfirst into the tunnel.

Four inches of cold water flowed along the bottom of the drain. He headed upstream, in the direction from which the drain would be fed. Matt was right—the smell was not as bad as it could have been, and soon his olfactory senses tuned it out entirely.

"I hope nobody decides to take a leak right now." Matt couldn't hide the disgust in his voice.

"At least we could see something," Maddock whispered. They were moving forward blindly, feeling their way through the dark, smelly drain. Maddock's shoulder's scraped the walls, and he felt that familiar warning flash of alarm that divers feel when they find themselves in a precariously tight position. He wasn't diving right now, of course, and if he were to feel like he was getting stuck, he and Matt could simply back up.

They continued on, time seeming to grind nearly to a standstill in the darkness. It was difficult to tell what kind of progress they were making, which made it feel even more frustratingly like they weren't moving at all.

"What do you think?" Matt finally whispered. "Did we make the wrong move?"

Just then, Maddock caught a glimpse of gray in the distance. "I see light. I think we're almost there." Now, with a visible goal in front of him, Maddock moved as fast as he dared, devouring the space between himself and what he could now see was the night sky shining into the drain.

When they reached the end of the drain, he took a breath of fresh air and peeked his head out. Here, a stream, probably the one that fed the waterfall back in the valley, wrapped around the edge of the village. The drain angled in from the side, so the current and gravity would naturally carry water through it. The calm rush of water was the only sound in the quiet night.

Staying low in the water, Maddock crawled out of the drain, and Matt followed. The faint moonlight cast the village in a silvery haze. Firelight flickered in a few nearby windows, but no one was out. He was about to lead the way out when a figure appeared from the darkness, strolling their way.

Fawcett!

Maddock froze. He didn't need to warn Matt to be quiet. The man knew his business. He waited until Fawcett passed them, then rose up quickly and quietly, grabbed Fawcett in a chokehold with one arm, and clamped a hand over the man's nose and mouth. Fawcett grabbed Maddock's forearm, but could not dislodge his powerful hold.

"Don't make a sound," he hissed into Fawcett's ear. "It's Maddock. He felt the man relax. I don't want to hurt you, but if you call out, I will. Blink twice if you understand."

Fawcett deliberately closed and opened his eyes two times.

"Do you know where our weapons are?" Fawcett blinked twice. "Good. I'm going to uncover your mouth, and you're going to tell me where they are. Try to give us away and I knock you out and hold you face-down in the water until you stop kicking. Understand?" Two more blinks.

Fawcett sucked in a rasping breath, and coughed. "For God's sake, man," he gasped, his eyes and nose running, "I'll not betray you. I'm trying to help you, remember?"

"Where are our weapons and supplies?"

"They are in Mago's quarters. Right there." He indicated the first door of the building from underneath which they had just crawled. "He is with his father right now, but his door it is locked up tight. You won't get in, at least not without bashing in the door and drawing attention."

Matt smiled at Maddock. "I got this" He took a long look at the space between the stream and the stone building, gauging the distance. "You just be ready when I open the door."

Fawcett frowned as Matt slipped back down into the water. "I'll assume he knows what he is doing." He rounded on Maddock like an angry schoolteacher. "You promised me you would not do anything reckless."

"I didn't. If I'd wanted to be reckless, I would have sent my friend Bones through the tunnel. He'd have scalped you and set half this place on fire. And that would just be for starters."

"I actually believe you." Fawcett grinned. "Let's move closer to Mago's door and wait for your friend."

They slipped into the shadows of a nearby palm tree and waited for Matt.

"Did you talk to Hamilcar about us?" Maddock whispered.

"Yes. He said to treat you well until he decided what to do about you." Fawcett's eyes narrowed and his lips pursed. "I am worried about these ScanoGen people. I fear he does not take the threat seriously enough. He believes our guards will suffice."

Just then, Maddock caught a glimpse of movement in the shadows of a nearby hut. He ducked down behind the pitiful screen of the tree trunk, pulling Fawcett down with him. The figure moved closer, the moonlight outlining its frame. Maddock could not believe his eyes.

"Tam," he whispered, just loud enough for her to hear. At the sound of her name, she jerked like a hooked fish. Her eyes searched the darkness and finally fell upon Maddock. Maddock held up a hand, signaling her to wait, and she nodded.

Less than a minute later, they heard a rattling sound, and the door to Mago's quarters opened. Maddock waved for Tam to come on, and they all hurried into the room and closed the door behind them.

"How did you get out?" Maddock asked Tam.

"They underestimated me, like always. They only put one guard on us. I acted all girly and helpless, and yelled to him that I was hurt. When he opened the door, I took him down and tied him up. You know the drill."

Fawcett looked dumbstruck, but Maddock just grinned as he and Matt gathered their weapons. He handed Tam her Makarov and her flash gun.

"How about you?" she asked. "I was trying to figure out how I was going to disarm four guards and spring you guys."

"Came through the drains," Matt proclaimed proudly proclaimed. "That's how I got in here, too."

"So that's what that smell is." Tam grimaced. "Okay, what's the plan?"

"We leave the tents and the camping gear. Just take ammunition and what food we can carry in a day pack. We'll get the others, and get out of here."

They grabbed packs for everyone, and Maddock remembered his sat phone, which he hastily pocketed, just in case. Now ready to move, he turned to Fawcett. "Do you know where Thomas is?"

"I saw him a short while ago. He was on his way to talk to your friend, Kaylin."

Tam frowned. "I guess we're going to have to fight our way back through the Mot'jabbur."

"Can you think of another way?"

Fawcett cleared his throat. "I should not tell you this, but there is another way out. An ancient escape route put in place early in Kephises's history. But I warn you, it might be even more dangerous than the way you came. There is a legend about a monster..."

"We'll take it. It can't be any worse than the Mot'jabbur. Where is it?"

"It is inside the pyramid," Fawcett said. "There is a sanctuary at its center, and a passageway behind the altar. You will not be permitted to just walk in, though. You have to get past the guards and the priests. Perhaps I can help you with that, and show you the way. Understand, I don't want anyone hurt."

Distant cries of alarm rang out in the night. For a brief instant, Maddock feared their escape had been discovered, but then he realized the voices were much farther away than their quarters. And then he heard gunshots, followed by an explosion.

"Too late for that." He turned and looked at Tam. "ScanoGen is here."

Chapter 29

The world glowed like an alien landscape through Kennedy's night vision goggles. He gripped his F88 AuSteyr combat rifle with M203 grenade launcher attachment, the same weapon with which the three agents had also been outfitted. He'd managed to get by without using it so far, slipping past the guards outside the tunnel while Wesley created a diversion, blowing up a few of the locals. He now crept forward, keeping to the jungle well away from the path that led toward the pyramid.

They all knew their roles. Kennedy and Smithson would take opposite sides and work their way silently through the jungle, moving toward the pyramid, where he was convinced the secret of this place lay. Wesley was to stick close to the path, keeping behind cover and making enough noise to draw defenders his way. If Kennedy had read Wesley correctly, it would not be long before he lost patience and barreled his way down the pathway like a bull in a china shop. For that reason, Brown was to back Wesley up and wait for orders.

"Wesley, don't overdo it," he whispered, his throat mic picking up his barely-audible voice.

"*Roger,*" came the disappointed voice in his earphone.

"Save your ammo. You're going to need it." The promise of carnage in the near future should satisfy the man.

"*I've got targets coming my way,*" Smithson whispered. "*I think they're moving toward the explosion.*"

"Let them pass. Your job is to get to the pyramid as quickly as possible."

Smithson acknowledged the order and went silent.

"*Here they come.*" It was Brown's voice. "*Wesley, you got a line on them?*"

Wesley's reply was a barrage of gunfire.

Kennedy grinned. If that didn't draw the defenders down the path, nothing would. He set off at a quick pace, careful not to make too much noise, and to keep his eyes peeled for movement. Something burst through the brush in front of him and he raised his rifle.

A deer.

He smirked and kept moving. It would take more than that to get him to lose his cool and fire off a shot that would warn the enemy of his approach. Another sound, this of measured footfalls headed his way, and he ducked behind a tree. Through his night vision goggles, he spotted a figure moving toward him. The man was armed with a spear, and his head was turned in the direction of the road. He moved closer, still looking away, and Kennedy attacked.

Dropping his rifle, he struck the man hard in the temple. He staggered backward, his legs tangling in the underbrush. Kennedy kicked the spear from the man's limp hand and leapt atop him, sliding his KA-BAR from its sheath and holding it to the fallen man's throat.

His eyes went wide at the feel of the cold metal against his throat.

"Do you speak English?" Kennedy whispered.

"A little." The accent was weird, but the words were easy to understand.

"What is the secret of this place? What's your special power?"

"Do not know." The man gasped as Kennedy pressed down, cutting into his flesh. "The tree, I think. The tree!"

"What tree? What's so special about it?" Was the fellow trying to toy with him?

"Priests guard it. Is good tree." His words were faint, punctuated by soft gasps. Kennedy hadn't cut his windpipe, so the breathlessness came from fright. Good.

"What makes it good? Come on!"

"Don't know words. Is good tree!" There was a pleading tone to the man's voice, as if he were begging Kennedy to believe him. He was telling the truth, or at least what he believed to be the truth.

"How many of you are there? How many fighting men?" He needed to make this quick, before someone heard him and he lost his advantage.

"Don't know." Tears flowed freely down the man's face. "Nine! Nine!"

"You've got a hell of a lot more men here than that," Kennedy growled. Nine was probably the largest number for which he knew the English word.

"Nine!" The man screamed.

Kennedy cut off his words with a slash of his knife. He hoped he'd silenced the man before his cries alerted the other defenders. His information hadn't been that helpful, but Kennedy would check out this tree, whatever it was.

The men no longer approached. After Wesley had picked off the first few who came his way, no more had charged in. He had seen movement in the alien green landscape painted by the night vision goggles, and taken a few shots, but he didn't know if he had hit anything. He figured they must be waiting out there, hiding and watching for him to make a move.

But what if he was wrong?

What if they had figured out the ruse and backtracked toward the pyramid. It was Wesley's job to keep them off Kennedy's and Smithson's backs. He picked out a spot where he'd seen movement earlier and fired off a grenade, turning his head away from the blinding flash of the explosion.

The sound was awesome. Better than the roar of the crowd at a metal concert. He heard a cry of pain, and knew he'd at least wounded one man. They had to realize he could keep on like this if they didn't flush him out.

"Come out and play," he whispered. Sure enough, something moved, coming his way. "Time for some target practice."

The door to the room in which Bones and Willis were being held was unguarded. Some of the guards had run into the jungle to meet the threat, while others ran about in confusion. Someone was hammering on the inside of the door, voices calling for someone to let them out.

"It's us!" Maddock shouted.

"About freakin' time!" Bones yelled back. "What's going on out there?"

Maddock unbarred the door, but didn't have the key for the ancient iron lock. "Stand back!" he ordered. He blasted the lock with his M-16 and kicked the door open. "ScanoGen is here," he said as the others hurried out. "Let's get going."

Bones and Willis, who was limping badly, reclaimed their weapons and each donned a backpack.

"Are we buggin' out, or do we fight?" Even injured, Willis sounded ready for either option.

"We can't leave these people unprotected," Maddock said. "All they have are bows and arrows."

"Works for me." Willis chambered a round in his Mossberg and grinned. "Who do I shoot first?"

"Maddock!" Kaylin's voice rang out. He turned and spotted her and Thomas leading a group of women and children toward them. "We're taking the children to the pyramid. They tell me there's a safe room there." She inclined her head toward two of the women, who nodded in agreement.

"That's good. Willis, you go with them. Don't argue!" Willis was about to protest, but Maddock's words stopped him short. "That leg is slowing you down. Besides, if ScanoGen breaks through, all they have to protect them is Kaylin and her .380."

"Oh, yeah!" Matt pulled Kaylin's pistol out of his pocket and handed it to her. "Reloads are in here," he said, handing her a backpack.

"All right." Willis scowled, clearly unhappy with his assignment, but he wasn't one to let ego get in the way of doing the right thing. He knew he wasn't anywhere near one hundred percent. "Let's get going."

"What do you want *me* to do?" Thomas's face was white as a sheet.

"Help Willis. Kaylin takes risks. Don't let her do anything stupid."

"Right, because she always listens to advice." Thomas managed a faint smile, clearly relieved that he hadn't been asked to take part in the fighting. "Good luck." He offered his hand, and Maddock shook it. "And thank you." With that, he was off.

Maddock found it odd that, in the midst of an attack, he was contemplating how he felt about shaking hands with Kaylin's boyfriend. Shrugging off the distracting thought, he turned back to the others.

"I think these explosions are a diversion. They've been far away, and always in the same place. Whoever is firing grenades, or whatever they are, isn't coming any closer. I believe they're trying to draw the defenders down the path, and maneuver around them." He turned to Tam. "I killed one of their men during the fighting down in the canyon. How many do you think they have left?"

"Five at the very most, and that's if that idiot Cy is still alive. Last I saw of him, though, he was running like a debutante toward a surgeon's convention." She saw Maddock's confused look. "You know, husbands on the half-shell."

Bones chuckled. "I like you."

"Everybody likes me." Tam gave a coquettish smile. "What's the plan?"

"They're going to have to come out of the jungle sometime. The four of us should spread out and take up defensive positions where we can get a good line of sight and maybe pick them off."

"They have night vision goggles," Tam said. "So stay out of sight. They'll see you before you see them."

"All right," Maddock said. "We'll rendezvous at the pyramid if they get behind us."

Tam looked at Bones. "Want to be killin' buddies?"

"Don't mind if I do. We'll take the left flank." The two of them disappeared into the darkness.

After a quick look around, Maddock positioned Matt on top of one of the nearby stone buildings, and then headed off to guard the edge of the settlement opposite where Bones and Tam had set up.

A group of defenders, led by Hamilcar, rounded a building and froze when they caught sight of Maddock. Hamilcar pointed at him and shouted something in his native tongue. His men looked at him in confusion.

"There's no time to argue!" Maddock shouted. "The men out there can see in the dark. They have special glasses." With one finger, he drew circles around his eyes, wondering if he was making any sense at all. "If you run into the jungle, they'll just shoot you."

Hamilcar, to his credit, didn't waste time on indecision. "What should my men do?"

"Bows and arrows are your best bet. We have to assume they are coming after the sacred tree. Hide your men all along the way, and shoot them if they come near. You have to stay hidden, though, because their rifles can shoot a lot farther than your bows."

As if the emphasize the point, one of the Carthaginian men crumpled to the ground, his head ruined, just as the report of a rifle reached them. Maddock hit the ground and rolled behind the relative safety of the closest hut. Another man fell and his companions scattered. Another report came from behind them as Matt returned fire.

"Get back to the tree!" Maddock shouted, peering around the edge of the hut for a muzzle flash that would give away the attacker's position.

Hamilcar barked an order and the men followed him back through the dwellings, toward the pyramid and their sacred tree.

The next shot buzzed high overhead, obviously aimed at Matt, and Maddock saw only the faintest flash of muzzle fire. They must be using flash suppressors. He didn't waste time, but immediately aimed a shot at the place where he'd seen the shot. Matt's answering shot came a split-second later, and from a different spot on the roof. Maddock rolled to his right before their attacker could return fire. No shot came, though. Obviously, the man was on the move. He would be a tough nut to crack.

"Next shot, you fire left, I'll fire right!" Maddock called out, hoping Matt was close enough to hear him.

"Gotcha!"

The night grew eerily silent as they waited for their unseen attacker to make his next move.

Smithson was running out of forest cover, and he had two shooters to dislodge. Maddock and his crew must have beaten them to Kephises. "Locals are retreating to the pyramid," he whispered into his throat mic. "I've got two shooters in the village."

"Can you slip around them?" Kennedy sounded unperturbed, as always.

"I'm going to try."

"I want you to stay put for a minute," Kennedy ordered. *"Brown, do you copy?"*

"Roger that." Brown sounded equally calm.

"Change of plans," Kennedy instructed. *"I want you to swing around the right and come in hard. Blow the bastards to hell if you have to."*

"Roger that. Over."

"Smithson," Kennedy continued, *"you wait for Brown's attack, and then make your move."*

"Roger." Smithson hoped Brown would be quick about it.

"What about me?" Wesley sounded like an eager kid on Christmas morning who was afraid he hadn't gotten any presents.

"Keep doing what you're doing."

Wesley didn't acknowledge. It was a good thing Kennedy didn't insist on strict military decorum, or he'd have the man's ass. Kennedy wasn't one you messed around with. Smithson grinned. Maddock and his crew didn't know what they were in for.

Chapter 30

Bones heard the shots exchanged, but stayed put, despite his inclination to help out. Maddock wouldn't want him to abandon his post. Besides, it had been a while since he'd heard the last shot. He wondered what was going on. Perhaps this meant the battle would soon be shifting in his direction.

No sooner had the thought passed through his mind than he heard the sounds of lots of feet running through the jungle. He raised his M-16 and waited.

A group of men broke through into the clearing, all of them natives of Kephises. From within the depths of the jungle, someone fired off three shots in rapid succession, and two men went down. This was it! His eyes probed the darkness, seeking out a target.

He saw a burst of muzzle flash, and the ground erupted beneath the running men. Bones squeezed off two quick shots and hit the dirt, rolling behind a giant fern. Bullets sizzled through the spot he'd just occupied. Nearby, men cried out in pain. A few struggled to regain their feet, but others did not move at all. Bones had seen too many of those glassy eyed stares in his lifetime.

He wondered if the attacker could see him hunkered down here. The fern wouldn't offer much protection, but it would hopefully hide him from the night vision-enhanced eyes of the ScanoGen men. Another muzzle flash and, before he could return fire, another explosion, this one too close. He squeezed his eyes shut and turned his head as rocks and debris scoured him. Over the ringing in his ears, he heard an explosion from somewhere in Maddock's direction, and then footsteps pounded close by—the guy was coming right at him. In fact, he was almost on top of him!

"Hey!" Tam shouted. Bones looked up to see the man turn his head in her direction just as she pulled the trigger of her dazzle gun.

The man's scream was one of sheer agony. Reeling, he dropped his rifle and ripped off his goggles. A dazzle gun temporarily blinded a man, but what would it do to someone wearing night vision goggles? Bones had no sympathy for this scumbag who had so callously cut down the men of Kephises, who were only defending their homes and families. As the man turned, Bones drew his Glock, took careful aim, and shot him in the groin.

If the man's screams had seemed agonized before, he now reached a whole new level. He collapsed, one hand pressed to his eyes, the other clutching his ruined groin. Blood seeped between his fingers. His screams quickly gave way to pitiful wails, echoing those of the hurt and dying Kephises men. Bones stood and approached him slowly, ready to finish him off, but Tam beat him to it.

She drew a knife and pressed the tip to the man's heart. "All right Brown, who else is with you?"

"Broderick, you traitor!" The man spat. "I'm not telling you anything."

"I'm not a traitor. I'm a Fed. Now tell me, and I'll make the pain go away. Don't tell me, and I'll leave you here to die. I'll even stab you in the gut to make *sure* you don't make it. Of course, you might enjoy being a blind man. Then again, you're not really a man any more, are you?"

"The hell with you!"

"Last chance." She pressed her knife to his abdomen. "Who is here?"

"Kennedy, Wesley, and Smithson. Everybody else is dead." He groaned again and shuddered as a spasm of pain racked his body.

"What's your plan?"

"They're going for the tree behind the pyramid. Smithson's swinging around the left, Kennedy's going to sneak through wherever he can, and Wesley's holding back until he's called." He convulsed. "That's all I've got. Now finish it like you promised."

Tam nodded and rose to her feet. She drew her Makarov, took aim, and fired a single shot to Brown's head.

"It sounds like Maddock has engaged with Smithson," Bones said. "If this guy, Wesley, is hanging back, that just leaves this Kennedy guy trying to get to the tree. I say we fall back there and wait for him."

"I agree." Slinging her dazzle gun over her shoulder, Tam took up the fallen man's rifle, checked to see if it was loaded, then took off toward the pyramid.

The defenders who had not been killed or seriously injured were dragging the wounded men to safety. "They're going after the tree!" Bones called to one of them. The man nodded, and then barked orders to his men. Two of them put down the injured men they were carrying, picked up their bows and arrows, and followed Bones.

Great! My army is me, a crazy chick, and some dudes with bows and arrows. Bones grinned in spite of himself. *I kind of like my chances.*

As soon as Smithson heard the explosion, he fired off a grenade of his own and took off running. A sharp, stinging pain sliced across his shoulder as bullets buzzed through the air like angry hornets. Whoever was shooting at him hadn't aimed for his muzzle flash, but to the side. A lucky shot, but he'd had worse. It would take more than that to stop him.

Forty yards and he was out from behind cover. Another bullet clipped the ground at his heel, and then he was behind the cover of an old stone building.

He paused and leaned against the wall, catching his breath, when a hissing sound filled his ears and something cracked against the wall just above his head. He ducked down just as another projectile whizzed past. Arrows! He fired off two shots in the direction from which he thought the arrows had come, and kept moving. This was, without a doubt, the craziest operation he'd ever taken part in.

At the first glimpse of muzzle flash, Maddock pulled the trigger on his M-16, aiming to the right, just as he and Matt had planned. He assumed Matt fired to the left, but the world was suddenly engulfed in flame as an explosion rocked the hut behind which he was hiding. Burning debris showered him, and he rolled away as quickly as he could. Up above, he heard Matt fire off a single shot.

"Missed him!" Matt called down. "Are you all right?"

"Yeah." Maddock climbed to his feet. "I'm going after him."

Kennedy could not believe his eyes. Brown's limp body lay splayed on the ground, blood pooling around his head and between his legs. Rage boiled up inside of him.

"Wesley, do you copy?" He didn't bother to keep his voice down. Nearby, one of the local men who knelt tending one of the wounded cocked his head, as if he'd heard something strange.

"I'm here," came the eager reply.

"Your objective is the tree behind the pyramid. Come at them will everything you've got. I want to kill every last one of them."

"Roger! Over."

Kennedy didn't bother to hide; he didn't bother to creep. He strode forward, cutting down the men one at a time. One actually charged toward him, brandishing a spear. Kennedy's shot took him in the throat. Another managed to fire off a single arrow, which went wide, before Kennedy shot him down, too.

He strode through the village, putting a bullet in every man who didn't look dead. He killed everyone he saw: those who fought, those who ran, those who tried to surrender. The pyramid rose up in front of him, and he smiled. His objective lay just on the other side, and anyone who tried to stand in his way would regret it.

Wesley barreled down the winding path, his rifle at the ready, but no one rose up to challenge him. Not a single arrow flew. He didn't even see anyone running away from him. Damn! Kennedy had held him back so long that all the defenders had retreated, probably to the pyramid. It wasn't fair. He had made the same trek everyone else had, and survived the zombie Indians down in the canyon. He deserved his chance to see this operation to the end. He quickened his pace, determined *not* to miss any more of the fighting.

He burst forth into a residential area. Dirt paths worn smooth over the ages ran between stone houses and wood and thatch huts. He saw the glow of fire to the left and to the right. Some of the huts must be burning. He kept an eye out for anyone who might take a shot at him, but still saw nothing. The sound of gunfire told him that fighting was going on up ahead where the pyramid lay.

He rounded the giant stone structure at full-tilt and came out on a well-tended greenspace. Up ahead, a ring of defenders knelt at the base of a tree. One of them spotted him, shouted a warning, and a cloud of arrows flew in his direction. He dropped and rolled, letting the projectiles pass over him. Shoot at him, would they? He'd show them. Springing to his feet, he unloaded with his grenade launcher.

Gunshots rang out up ahead as Maddock dashed forward, careful to remain behind cover as much as possible. He heard more shots, and cries of pain as men fell to ScanoGen's assault.

The pyramid loomed up in front of him, and he clambered up to the first level to get a better vantage point.

He reached the far side and stopped short as gouts of flame burst all around the sacred tree. Every man who stood in its defense was blown off his feet by the blast. The shooter kept coming, firing two more grenades, and then switching to rifle fire.

Maddock took aim, but before he could squeeze the trigger, something invisible thwacked the ScanoGen man in the gut, and he tumbled backward, rifle falling from lifeless hands. Maddock recognized Bones's whoop of delight. Good man.

That was when the shooter Maddock had been stalking made his presence known. He fired off a grenade that exploded somewhere near Bones's hiding place. Maddock didn't have time to look for his friend. He had finally spotted the attacker, who wasn't watching the pyramid, but was looking to see if he'd gotten Bones.

Cold determination fixed Maddock's resolve. He lined up his shot, took careful aim, and squeezed the trigger. He didn't need to look to know he'd hit his target, but he took a grim satisfaction in watching the man fall from a perfect shot to the head.

He dashed around the pyramid, the faint light of the burning tree flickering across its eroded surface. Reaching the far corner, he sprang down and called Bones's name, and was relieved to hear his friend answer, though his voice was weak.

His relief was short-lived, because just then, a dark figure smashed into him, and he tumbled to the ground, his M-16 clattering to the ground. As he grappled with his attacker, he struck out blindly and his fist met bone in a glancing blow that didn't do much damage. The man struck back, but Maddock ignored the punch, focusing on trapping the man's arm.

He was a big man with a buzz cut and a scar on his right cheek. This was Kennedy, whom Tam had described as the most dangerous of the ScanoGen force. Maddock barely had time to register the thought when Kennedy raised a knife and brought it plunging down.

Maddock put up an arm to block the strike, but before the knife could find its target, a snarling black shadow flew out of the night. Kennedy shouted in surprise as he was bowled over. He rolled to the side beneath the dark shape that continued to snarl.

Unburdened by Kennedy's weight atop him, Maddock clambered to his feet and saw the man fleeing from Hamilcar, who was brandishing an ancient sword, and three men armed with spears. Isa the jaguar stood protectively in front of Maddock, her teeth bared at the retreating figure. She had come to his aid at just the right time.

Maddock knelt and scratched her between the shoulder blades. She nuzzled his arm and purred contentedly. "I should take you home with me, girl. Do you think you'd like it on the beach?"

He heard Bones call his name, followed the sound of his friend's voice, and found him lying on the ground, shaking his head. Tam lay in a heap nearby, bleeding from a scalp wound.

"She's not dead," Bones grunted. "But she's out cold. How many did we get?"

"I got the guy who shot the grenade at you."

"Nice one, bro." Bones rubbed his temple. "He gave me one hell of a headache. Tam got one and I got that guy over there. That just leaves one more."

"Kennedy. He just bolted." Maddock hauled Bones to his feet.

"Looks like we failed." Bones shook his head sadly as he stared at the ruined tree. Despite his devil-may-care exterior, Bones retained some of his people's values, and his regard for nature was one of them. He would not relish the destruction of any ancient tree, but this one was particularly tragic.

Maddock looked at the charred remains of what, just minutes before, had been a one-of-a kind, miracle of nature. Its silver bark was now a scorched, black hull. The limbs had been blown apart, the leaves incinerated, and now the single fruit was a shriveled ruin in the midst of the burning remnants. No one would ever make use of its power again, but perhaps that was for the best.

"Do we go after Kennedy?" Bones asked.

"I don't think you're up to it. Besides, he's alone and unarmed. I think they can handle him. Let's get help for Tam."

"I'm all right." Tam was sitting with her head between her knees. "Just a little cut."

Maddock knelt and inspected the wound. It wasn't deep. Still, the girl was tough. "Let's get this patched up, and then we'll get out of here."

Chapter 31

Matt met them at the entrance to the pyramid. Willis stood guard just inside.

"Is it over?" Willis asked, a touch of disappointment in his tired voice.

"We think so." Maddock helped Tam inside, where Matt hastily cleaned and bandaged her wound. Thomas and Kaylin joined them, and Maddock and Bones recounted the details of the fight.

"At least it's finished," Kaylin sighed. "Please tell me we can go home now."

"Kaylin, can we talk?" Thomas shifted his weight from one foot to the other, his eyes flitting from side-to-side.

"What is it?" There was a wariness in her voice, as if she feared the subject he was about to broach.

"Let's go somewhere private, all right?" Thomas took her hand and turned to lead her away, but froze at the sound of someone running down the corridor.

Fawcett burst into the room. "You've got to get out of here right now!" he gasped, sweat pouring down his pallid face. "They're coming for you!"

Maddock couldn't believe what he was hearing. "Who is coming? More ScanoGen agents?"

"No. The locals. They blame you all for leading the ScanoGen men here, and they plan on punishing you for it. They're still arguing amongst themselves, but it won't take them long to work up the courage."

"We saved their butts." Bones looked like he was ready to take them all on. "And this is how they thank us? Bring 'em on!"

"Forget it, Bones," Maddock said. "We'll go. No point in fighting to save their lives only to kill them ourselves. Let's get the hell out of here."

Hand on his Walther, he pushed past Fawcett and headed down the corridor, headed toward the exit. He didn't want to fight these people, but he and his friends *would* walk free, whether they liked it or not. No going quietly; no being locked up again.

"Not that way!" Fawcett snapped. "You'll walk right into the middle of them. You'll have to take the other way out. The escape route I told you about." He indicated the dark, downward-sloping passageway that led deep in the heart of the pyramid.

"You heard him," Maddock said to his friends. "Let's go. Anyone need a hand?" He looked at Willis and Tam, both of whom shook their heads. They, along with Bones and Matt, followed Fawcett down into the darkness while Maddock hung back to cover the rear. Kaylin tried to follow the others, but Thomas pulled her back.

"Kaylin, wait a moment. I wish I could do this another way and," he glanced at Maddock, "in another place. I want you to stay here with me." Kaylin gaped. "Hear me out. It's wonderful here. The people have lived in peace for over two thousand years. Even the animals are tame. You didn't see the real Kephises. It's a paradise! We could have the perfect life here. There's a lifetime of study here. You can learn about their history, culture, language, architecture, even their art and music. There is a whole Kephises you haven't seen yet, and we can discover it together in a place of peace and beauty."

Maddock thought this was the most absurd thing he'd ever heard. These people would likely hold Thomas, and certainly Kaylin, just as responsible for the carnage ScanoGen had inflicted on their home as they did Maddock and the others. He expected Kaylin to laugh, or at least tell him he was insane, but instead she looked... uncertain. Her eyes flitted from Thomas to Maddock, and back to Thomas again.

"I don't know..." she began.

"Stay with me." Thomas dropped to his knees. "Be my wife. They accepted me here. They'll accept you, too. We can help them rebuild their city. Just think, we can be a part of an ancient race that has lasted for two millennia. No one gets that chance. Not ever!"

Kaylin appeared frozen in place. How could she even consider this? She looked at Maddock, and a question seemed to hang in the air. What did she want him to do? Talk her out of it? The hell with that! If she was crazy enough to stay here, let her.

And then it struck him. What was it that really bothered him? The fact that she might choose, in his estimation, the dangerous course of staying here and risking the wrath of the people of Kephises, or that she couldn't seem to decide whether she wanted him or Thomas? In any case, there was no time to ponder it further.

"I think you're both crazy if you stay here," he said. "Mobs aren't known to be judicious, and if they're half as angry as Fawcett seems to believe, it's not a risk you should take. Whatever you decide, though, you need to make up your mind now. They could be here any second, and we're bugging out."

Kaylin took Thomas's face in her hands. "Come with us," she whispered. "It's not safe for you here."

"I see." Thomas's tone was as flat as the expression on his face. He pulled her hands away and stepped back. "You made your choice." His eyes flitted in Maddock's direction for the briefest of moments. "Now go."

"Thomas, please."

"No!" Thomas turned his back on Kaylin, crossed his arms, and stared at the wall. "Hurry, before they catch up with you all. I'll tell them I think you went into the forest. That should buy you some time."

Tears running in rivulets down her cheeks, Kaylin bolted the room, and Maddock followed. He didn't know what to say to Kaylin, and frankly, he wasn't inclined to talk to her right now. Maybe, if they both got out of this mess in one piece, they would talk about it then.

The passageway led down into an antechamber, the walls of which were carved with scenes from Carthage's history, mostly great military victories. Maddock felt a pang of regret that he could not stop to examine them more closely. *I find Fawcett's lost city and I don't get to stay but for a few hours,* he thought.

The antechamber opened into a room about forty feet square, its walls angled inward, approximating the shape of the pyramid outside, meeting at a tiny shaft far overhead. Two flickering oil lamps flanked an ancient Grecian urn atop a stone altar, which was supported by a four foot-high block of stone, in the room's center. Maddock did a double-take, realizing this urn was very likely the legendary Pandora's Box.

"About time," Bones greeted them. "Thought you'd decided to stay here and play hero a little longer."

Maddock shook his head and inclined his head toward Kaylin. Bones took one look at her face, still wet from tears, and understanding filled his eyes. "Gotcha. Sorry, Kaylin."

"This is the temple," Fawcett explained unnecessarily. "The way out is back here." He waved for them to come around to the back side of the altar.

"I'm surprised no one is in here," Maddock observed. "No priests?"

"The guards have all left to fight. The priestess who was to have been here tending the flame is, um, a close friend of mine. She chose to tend to the wounded for a little while. Long enough for you to make your escape."

Maddock rounded the altar and watched Fawcett place his hand over a symbol carved in the stone block on which the altar rested, and press down. A trap door sprang open, revealing a low, dark tunnel.

"In here," Fawcett said, motioning toward the opening. Bones took the lead, and the others followed, until only Maddock remained. Fawcett grabbed his arm. "Listen carefully. You will come out at an underground river. Follow it down to where it ends in a box canyon. At the far end of the canyon, you will find the black water.'

"What is the black water?"

"You followed my great-grandfather's map, did you not?" Maddock nodded, and Fawcett continued. "All I know is that you should have left the river and passed into the black water."

"Okay. I know the place you're talking about." He meant the lagoon where they had left their boats. Perfect.

"Take this." Fawcett shoved a small pouch of woven grass into his hand. "It is the last seed from the tree. Take it somewhere safe. Its power is great, as is its potential for harm, and for that reason, we cannot risk those men coming back for it." He paused. "But something so wondrous should not pass from this world."

"But, this rightfully belongs to Kephises!" Maddock protested. "It's their secret to guard, not ours."

Fawcett laughed. "It is a secret that once belonged to Carthage. Before that, it was Athens's secret, Sparta's before that, and so on. The tree does not belong to any one people. Not forever, at any rate."

"What happens when they find it gone?"

"I rubbed ash on an avocado seed and switched them out. It looks quite similar. I don't doubt the priesthood will discover the switch when it comes time for planting. By that time, you will be long gone, and hopefully they will blame one of you. No offense."

"None taken." The bag had a long drawstring of vine, so Maddock hung it around his neck and tucked the pouch inside his shirt. "Thank you." He shook Fawcett's hand and turned to make his escape.

"One last thing," Fawcett said. "The legends say the box canyon is the domain of the mapinguari. Be careful."

Maddock was halfway into the passageway, but he stopped and looked back. "What is a mapinguari?"

"A monster, I suppose. That's all I know." Fawcett looked around. "I had better go. They can't know that I helped you. It is not my life I care about, but my friend's. Good luck!" He hastily pushed the trapdoor closed, leaving Maddock in darkness.

It had been far too easy to elude his pursuers, Kennedy thought. They certainly lacked the tracking skills of the natives of this region. If this place truly was a remnant from the ancient world, isolation had caused them to go soft. He had outdistanced them, doubled back, and slipped past their line. It might have appeared that he'd fled in panic, but it had been a strategic retreat. He was out of allies and weapons, save his KA-BAR.

How had he let himself lose it like that? When he saw Brown lying dead, something inside him had snapped, just like in Kandahar. He couldn't let it happen again. This mission was a hair's breadth from failure, and it would take all his skills and a bigger dose of luck to get him through.

The minutes crept by, and gradually the people retired to their quarters, leaving only a few out on patrol. He needed to catch one of them alone so he could get some answers.

As if on cue, a man came strolling down the path toward Kennedy's hiding place. Incredibly, he appeared to be unarmed and unconcerned about his own safety. When the man passed by, Kennedy raised up, grabbed him from behind, and dragged him into the undergrowth.

"You speak English?" Kennedy growled his hand pressing down on the man's nose and mouth. The man nodded, though his eyes were on Kennedy's KA-BAR, which hovered a few inches from his face. The man held Kennedy's wrist in a firm grip, keeping the knife at bay, but Kennedy was stronger; even as the man held on, the knife moved incrementally closer.

"I want to know what Thomas Thornton was after."

The man gave his head a little shake, as if he did not know what Kennedy was talking about, but there had been a momentary flash of understanding in his eyes that Kennedy did not miss. He knew something! Kennedy leaned a little harder, and the knife moved closer. The man was turning purple from lack of air, and the blade of the knife was dangerously close to his eye. Finally, the fight went out of his eyes and he nodded.

"Tell me everything, tell me quiet and fast, and you might live." He removed his hand and the man sucked in a breath. In short order he had spun an incredible tale of a tree with the power to make a man a killer or a pacifist—at least that was how Kennedy understood it. Apparently, it was also what had spawned those zombie men they had encountered previously. The warrior he had questioned earlier had also claimed the tree was special. A sudden, disturbing thought turned his insides cold.

"Tree? You mean the tree Wesley blew up?" He had seen it happen from a distance. The reckless soldier had gone barreling in to the fray, not even thinking, and started blowing up everything in sight.

"Yes." The fellow was either too smart or too frightened to look triumphant. "It's gone."

Kennedy thought hard. Had he lost all his men for nothing? There had to be an answer. "Can they plant a new one?" Once again, the truth was in the man's eyes, and he didn't try to deny it. "What do they have? Cuttings? A seed?"

"The seed is in the temple, in an urn on the altar."

"Show me." Kennedy yanked his knife hand free from the man's tiring grip, stood, and hauled him to his feet. "Don't make a sound. If we see someone, we hide. Don't you do anything, *anything* to rat me out. I can spill your guts and be gone in an instant, and you'll die slowly and painfully for nothing. Got me?"

The man nodded, turned, and guided them back down the path, Kennedy holding on to his shirt tail. They reached the pyramid without incident, and the man led him up a sloping tunnel, then down a steeper one. He wondered if he was being led into a trap, but how could one have been set?

He spotted the urn the moment they stepped into the gloomy temple.

A brown-haired woman with olive skin knelt before the altar. At the sound of their entry, she turned and her eyes went wide with shock. "Brian," she gasped. "What has happened?"

"Miri, I…"

"Don't say another word, or you both die!" Kennedy might just kill them anyway. He'd had more than his fill tonight. "Is this the urn?" The man, Brian, nodded, and Kennedy gave him a shove that sent him sprawling on the ground at the woman's feet. She knelt beside him, scowling at Kennedy and taking Brian in her encircling arms like a mother bear protecting her cub.

Kennedy mounted the steps to the altar, reversed his KA-BAR, and brought it down hard. Miri cried out as the urn shattered. Fishing through the shards, he pulled out a large, grayish seed. He held it up in the lamplight to get a closer look.

"That is not..." the woman began. Too late, Brian clapped a hand over her mouth.

"What do you mean?" Kennedy formed each word like a death sentence, because that's exactly what it was—Brian's death sentence.

The woman shoved Brian's hand away, and they both clambered to their feet and backed away. "That is not the seed," she whimpered. "That man must have taken it. The one from outside."

"Dane Maddock?" The name was a curse on Kennedy's lips. He leapt down and stalked the pair as they backed around the altar.

"I suppose so. He and his friends took the seed and left through the door. Look back here!"

"Miri! No!" Brian's words fell on deaf ears as Miri ran to the altar, pressed something, and a hidden door swung open.

"This is the way out," she said. "It will take you under the land of the Mot'jabbur. The dead warriors. You will not have to pass through their lands this way."

Kennedy's eyes narrowed. What if this was a trick? Maybe she had just opened the door to a pit like the one that had taken the life of one his guides just two days before. Then again, why would you build a death trap into the back of an altar?

Kennedy leaped forward, grabbed the woman by the wrist, and yanked her to him. "Tell you what, lady. You go first and show me the way." She screamed and clawed at his arm, trying to get loose.

"No!" Brian yelled. "Take me! I'll show you the way." He started babbling, explaining how he had stolen the seed, replaced it with a fake, and given the real one to Maddock. He even described the woven grass pouch in which he'd placed the seed.

Kennedy was seriously considering killing him just to shut him up when a roar filled the temple, and he whirled to see a burly man with brown hair and a short beard bearing down on him, holding an ancient sword aloft. This was Hamilcar, the one who had chased him earlier. Kennedy owed him. He turned and charged.

Hamilcar's sword sliced through empty air as Kennedy dodged to his left and delivered a swift kick to the man's foreleg. The man was sturdily built, though, and the kick didn't faze him. Hamilcar was also faster than Kennedy expected, and his backhanded swipe nearly opened Kennedy's throat, but the miss left him vulnerable. Seeing the opening, Kennedy struck, and his KA-BAR opened a gash in Hamilcar's side.

Hamilcar didn't even wince, but took a step back and resumed his attack. The Bronze Age sword was no more than two feet long, but that still gave Hamilcar a decided reach advantage over Kennedy with his knife. Kennedy parried a thrust and danced to the side, looking for an opening.

Something flew through the air, just missing his head. Brian was atop the altar, hurling pieces of the broken urn at Kennedy's head as fast as he could.

The distraction was almost the death of him. Hamilcar aimed a vicious thrust for his heart, but Kennedy spun at the last second. The sword whistled past him. Hamilcar had overextended his attack, and before he could draw back, Kennedy lashed out with his KA-BAR, going for the throat. Hamilcar ducked, and the blade caught him on the crown of his head, nearly taking his scalp. He roared in pain and swung his sword at Kennedy's legs. Kennedy sprang back and crouched, ready to finish it, when a half-dozen armed men burst out of the passageway and through the antechamber.

Out of options, Kennedy turned and ran for the trapdoor.

Chapter 32

The passage spiraled downward as if a giant had twisted a corkscrew into the ground. Maddock walked hunched over, one hand on the wall, the other on the cold stone above, until the ceiling was finally high enough that he could stand. Deeper into the darkness he went, with every step seeming to heap a greater weight upon him. Two thousand year-old passageways didn't inspire confidence, but he reminded himself this place had stood for this long. Why shouldn't it last a bit longer? He soon caught up with the others, and was pleased to see Matt had held on to his flashlight.

"You didn't think to snag a few of those for the rest of us?" Maddock joked.

"Nope. You were all guns and munchies, so that's what I got for the rest of you. Besides, we were sort of in a hurry." Matt let the light play around the sloping passage. The stonework was solid, with every block fitted together with precision.

Breathing easier now, Maddock checked on Willis and Tam, both of whom insisted they were fine, though Willis was keeping one hand on the wall and moving slowly.

"What's supposed to be down here?" Bones asked. "Jimmy Hoffa?"

"A subterranean river. We follow it, and it will take us to a canyon close to the lagoon where we left the boats. This way, we won't have to fight our way through the Mot'jabbur."

"Sweet!" Bones clapped him on the shoulder. "Looks like things are finally going our way. In fact," he cocked his head to the side, "I think I hear the river up ahead."

Maddock listened intently, and could just make out the whisper of water running over rocks. "Great. Now, let's take stock. What do we have in the way of weapons and provisions?"

"I have my flashlight!" Matt replied. "But you already knew that."

Willis still had his Mossberg, but was running low on ammunition, and everyone except Tam still carried a side arm. If they did manage to avoid the Mot'jabbur, they should be okay. Food was in short supply. Everyone carried a pack with a few freeze dried meals and a canteen. They would try to supplement along the way back, but there was no reason they couldn't make it back to what passed for civilization in these parts on what they had, though they'd all probably be a few pounds lighter when they arrived. The worst part would be listening to Bones complain, but it would hardly be the first time.

The passageway came to an abrupt end at a rock ledge that jutted out into the swift-moving water. Matt directed his light downstream. Stalactites dangled from the ceiling like sinister chandeliers, waiting to fall on unsuspecting travelers.

"So, do we swim it?" Tam pursed her lips, looking doubtfully at the dark water.

"We can take off our pants and make flotation devices out of them." Bones sounded eager. "Ladies first!"

"You couldn't handle it, sweetie," Tam said. "Not in a million years."

Something in the corner of his eye caught Maddock's attention. "Matt, turn your light this way." Leaning against the wall, just a few feet upstream from where they stood, was a raft.

"A two thousand year-old raft from Carthage? No thank you," Bones scoffed. "I say we put my 'no pants' idea to a vote. Who's with me?"

Maddock and Matt took a closer look and were surprised by what they found.

"This thing is new." Matt rapped on the logs and tested the vines which bound it together. "I wonder who put it here and why?"

Maddock knew in an instant. "It was Fawcett. He was the one who told me about this place."

"How do you think he got it down here without them noticing?" This was the first thing Kaylin had said since leaving the temple.

"I got the impression he has someone, maybe a girlfriend, in the temple priesthood. I suppose she could have let him slip a few things down here at a time. It wouldn't have taken much."

"Look here, Maddock!" Matt knelt and looked behind the raft. "There's a basket of food here: nuts, dried fruit and meat. There's even a gourd for water. You don't think…" He looked up at Maddock.

"He was planning on leaving." The full impact of what Fawcett had done for them hit him hard. Fawcett had been preparing for his escape, was possibly even planning on taking his priestess girlfriend with him, but he had given it up so they could get away.

"We'd better not let his sacrifice go for nothing, then." Kaylin's voice was husky with emotion, but her resolve was clear. "Let's get out of this place."

The raft could not bear everyone's weight, so Maddock and Bones handed their guns over to the others for safe-keeping, and swam behind, holding on to the back. The water was frigid and Maddock immediately missed his diving suit.

"Dude, I am never going to be able to have kids after this," Bones said. "Matt, we're trading places in a few!"

"Can't. Somebody has to hold this flashlight."

Maddock laughed. "Bones, you don't want to have kids anyway."

"I don't know. Heck, I might already have kids scattered all over the world. Who can say? Lots of little Bones running around."

"Stirrups," Tam said absently.

"Say what?" Bones looked at her like she was crazy.

"The stirrup is the smallest bone in the human body. You know, 'lots of little Bones…'"

Bones grimaced. "Science hurts my head. Of course, I'm not feeling any other pain thanks to this ice water. I might not feel anything ever again."

"Do us all a favor," Maddock said, "and stick your mouth in the water until it's numb."

Everyone, including Kaylin, laughed, and they relaxed as the current swept them along. They shared some of the food Matt had found, and as the distance between them and Kephises increased, their spirits rose in turn. Soon, they were laughing as they ducked low-hanging stalactites and the miles swept away behind them.

It was difficult to track the passage of time, but Maddock knew they were making much better time floating down this river than they had hiking through the jungle. He assumed they had to be getting close to their destination.

"Um, Maddock," Matt called. "Do you see what I see?"

Maddock peered up over the raft and saw a faint glow in the distance.

"We must be getting close to the end. Cool!" It would be a relief to get out of this cold water and onto dry ground."

"That's not what I'm talking about!" Matt's voice rose as he called out. "Look in front of us!"

At first, Maddock saw nothing but low-hanging stalactites shrouded in gray mist. Then he realized that the sound of the river had been growing progressively louder for some time now. He raised up a little higher to get a better look.

"Aw, hell!" Willis exclaimed. "Waterfall!"

Thirty feet ahead and closing fast, the river poured out over a rock shelf and tumbled into a void. There was no way they could all leap from the raft to the rock shelf—the water was moving too fast.

Maddock and Bones grabbed hold of the vines that knotted the raft together and began kicking furiously, trying in vain to swim against the current and arrest the raft's momentum. Tam and Willis both began paddling backward on the same side, almost upending the craft.

"It's not going to work!" Maddock looked all around, but the walls were worn smooth by the passage of water and time. There was nowhere to get a handhold. And then he looked up. "Grab a stalactite!"

Everyone looked at him as if he was crazy, but then understanding dawned on Willis's face. He reached up and grabbed hold of the closest one.

It broke off in his hand.

"Damn!" Willis tossed the stalactite aside and reached for another, but by this time, Matt had stood and wrapped his arms around the biggest stalactite he could reach. The raft pivoted under his feet and Maddock and Bones were spun about so that they were now downstream of the craft, their feet precariously close to the edge of the fall.

"It's going out from under me!" Matt shouted, still hanging on. By this time, Willis had gained his feet and found two handholds. He stood, arms spread apart, holding on for dear life.

"You look like Samson!" Bones shouted. How he could still make his wisecracks at a time like this was beyond Maddock.

"Let's hope for a better outcome than that story." Tam grunted, struggling to find a handhold of her own without tipping the raft.

"Bones, can you at least be serious when we're feet from going over a waterfall?" Maddock was working his way to the corner of the raft, which would put him close to the rock shelf, but still not close enough to reach. "Okay," he called to the others on the raft. "We need to start working the raft over to one side. Willis, can you reach a little to your left and grab that next one?" Willis nodded and shifted his grip. The raft wobbled as he reached out, but didn't tip. One at a time, each person on the raft took hold of a new stalactite and, on Maddock's command, pulled. The raft inched closer to the side.

"Again!" Maddock shouted. He was holding on, still kicking for all he was worth, but he could feel the water inching him closer to the edge. The moments seemed to melt into hours as they hauled the raft ever closer to the edge.

Finally, the raft struck the side and Maddock scrambled out onto the ledge. He hauled Bones up, and the two of them helped Kaylin and Tam to safety. Now only Matt and Willis remained.

"You first!" Matt shouted.

"Naw, man. I'm closest to the edge. You'd never make it over."

"But you've got the hurt leg."

"Just go, and make it fast. And when you get off this thing, get the hell out of my way." Willis took a deep breath and tightened his grip. Veins bulged in his neck and cords of muscle on his powerful arms rippled in the half-light under a sheen of sweat and mist as he held the raft in place against the powerful current.

Matt took two steps, leaped, and rolled as he landed, clearing the way for Willis, from under whom the raft was already moving.

Willis let go, bent his legs, getting his balance, and, as the raft came even with the rock shelf, jumped. The wobbly foundation of the moving raft, plus his injured leg, betrayed him, and his leap fell short. He hit the water inches short of the ledge and was swept downstream.

Maddock leaped and caught Willis's wrist. His wet skin was hard to hold on to, but Maddock maintained his grip as the heavier man pulled him down toward the edge of the waterfall. Maddock tried to dig in with his feet in order to arrest his slide, but he found no purchase on the smooth stone.

Then he felt strong hands grasp him by the legs, holding him fast. Matt stepped over him and hauled Willis up out of the water.

"You don't have to do everything by yourself, Maddock." Bones stood and helped Maddock up.

"Like I'd be anywhere without you guys." He took a moment to assess their situation. No one was hurt. They had lost his and Bones's backpacks, the basket of food, and Willis's Mossberg.

"There goes our raft." Kaylin pointed down to where the river flowed across the subterranean chamber in which they stood, dropping out of sight at the other end, continuing its descent to places unknown. Pieces of the shattered raft bobbed in the churning water, carried away by the current.

"That's okay. We don't need it anymore." Maddock pointed to a spot on the far side of the chamber, where a shaft of light shone through the mist. "We've found the way out."

The climb down was an easy one, save for Willis, but he managed. They picked their way across the stone, buoyed by the promise of daylight and warmth.

Bones crinkled his nose. "You smell that?" He sniffed and frowned. "It's like a pole cat or something."

He was right. There was an unpleasant odor in the air, faint, but definitely that of an animal. "Could be anything. All sorts of creatures in the Amazon."

"Can't be any worse than what we've already bumped into." Bones grinned. "It's not a zombie native smell, so I'm game for whatever we find."

The morning sun was a blessed relief to Maddock's waterlogged body, and he soaked in its warmth with a smile on his face. As Fawcett had described, they were in a high-walled box canyon. Kapok trees towered above a forest of palm, Brazil nut, and other trees he couldn't identify. All around, he heard the calls of bird as they welcomed the break of day.

"Now this is nice." Kaylin managed a weak grin. All they had been through was taking its toll on her, even more so than anyone except Willis, who, despite his brave exterior, looked like he was about to drop. A blue macaw landed in a nearby tree and turned its head to look at them in curiosity.

"How about we find a place to rest for a few hours?" Maddock suggested. No one looked at Willis, but they all knew why he made the suggestion.

"Naw, I'm good. We all got some sleep on the raft."

Maddock knew it was pointless to argue, so they set off. The going was excruciatingly slow as they hacked their way through the tangled undergrowth. If any non-flying creature lived here, it would have to be one that either slithered on the ground or swung through the trees.

"My kingdom for a machete," Matt grumbled as he hacked away with his knife. "Why didn't I grab them when I broke into Mago's quarters?"

"Hush!" Tam waved a hand at Matt. "What's that sound?"

A high pitched sound, somewhere between a squeak and a chirp, rang out above the sounds of the jungle. "It's over there. Take my pack." She slipped off her pack, shoved it into Willis's arms, dropped to the ground, and crawled into the underbrush.

"Seriously?" Bones shook his head. "Just crawl around down there with the creepy critters. We'll wait for you."

Tam returned a minute later clutching something small, white, and fluffy to her chest. "It's a baby harpy eagle. It was nuzzled up against its dead mother. Must have tried to fly to her and fell."

"I've never heard of it." Bones leaned down for a closer look.

"It's the largest eagle in the world, and they're nearly extinct in some parts of the world. Deforestation is wiping them out." A grim expression fell across her face. "Something else wiped out this one's mother. She was nearly torn in half."

"Wonder what did that to her?" Maddock was suddenly wondering if there was something to the mapinguari legend after all. "Say, have any of you ever heard of the mapinguari?"

"Hell yeah!" Bones fist pumped. "It's like Bigfoot meets the giant sloth."

"How do *you* know about it?" Tam asked as she took her pack from Willis and set about making a comfortable place for the baby eagle to rest. Apparently they now had a mascot. "You don't seem the scholarly type."

"Bones only studies things that are, umm…" Kaylin began.

"Controversial," Bones finished.

"Bullcrap is more like it," Willis said.

"Hey, somebody's got to know about Bigfoot and Nessie and all that good stuff. That somebody is me."

Tam finished making a nest for the bird inside her backpack, and put it on backward, like a baby carrier. Bones took the lead as they resumed their trek, happily carrying on about the mapinguari.

"There are all kinds of stories about it. The far-fetched ones say it has caiman skin, backward feet, and a mouth in its belly."

"The 'far-fetched' stories?" Kaylin smirked.

"We just discovered a two thousand year-old Punic city in the middle of the Amazon. Do you really want to take a tone with me?"

"Fair enough," Kaylin said. "Go on. We're all ears.'

"Anyway, it seems most likely that it's a descendant of Mylodon, an ancient, ground-dwelling sloth. It was ten feet tall." Bones slashed at a low-hanging limb and dodged as it sprang back at his face. "Supposedly, the mapinguari is a carnivore, and it can move in total silence through the thickest vegetation. Then again, some people think it's not a ground sloth, and can swing through the trees, as long as the limbs are strong enough to hold it."

"What else?" Maddock found himself searching the upper reaches of the kapok trees, keeping an eye out for the legendary beast.

"It's hard to kill because of its thick skull, and sturdy bones. And it's got a tough hide and this coarse, matted fur that arrows bounce off of if you don't hit it just right. It hates the scent of a human, and people get dizzy when they look at it, but that's probably because of its strong odor…" His words trailed away and he stopped and turned to face Maddock. "Just out of curiosity, why do you ask?"

"Oh, it's no big deal, really. According to Fawcett, this canyon is where it, or they, supposedly live, and it's supposed to be death to pass through here."

Five seconds of stunned silence hung in the air as everyone stopped and stared at him.

"Why are you just now telling us this?" Matt sounded uncannily like Maddock's father, back when Maddock was a child and had neglected to mention something important, usually a failing grade or a paper that needed signing.

"What would have been the point? We didn't have any other choices. Besides, it's probably just a legend, anyway."

"And if someone asked you if the chupacabra was real?" Bones arched an eyebrow.

"Fine! I get the point. Let's just get the hell out of this canyon." He brushed past Bones, who, unlike the others who were still staring at him in disbelief, was looking crestfallen.

"What's wrong with you?" Maddock frowned.

"We came all the way to the home of the mapinguari, and I don't have a camera."

Kennedy knelt in the shadow of a kapok tree, chewing on a Brazil nut and letting the humid air bathe his frozen body. It had been child's play to use his clothing as a flotation device as he rode the river, but the frigid water had nearly been the death of him. He'd scarcely been able to pull himself out of the water before what would have been a certain fall to his death over the waterfall. His body temperature had fallen, too, and he found himself feeling sluggish and confused as he made his way out of the underground cavern.

He would be all right, though. He'd been through worse in the service. Already, his senses were sharpening. He'd immediately spotted tracks left by Maddock and his party, and followed them to where they had cut a trail through the undergrowth.

He grinned. Nice of them to clear him a path. It would take him minutes to cover distances that had taken them hours to hack their way through. Best of all, he doubted they had any idea he was on their trail.

Chapter 33

"Did you hear that?" It was about the third time Matt had asked the question, but this time, Maddock did hear something. It was a rustling somewhere in the distance, and it was coming closer.

"Can't be the mapinguari. It's silent, but deadly." Maddock could tell Bones was trying to sound more positive than he felt.

"Smells like a silent but deadly." Willis grimaced.

He was right. Borne on a gentle breeze, the same foul odor that was evident in the underground cavern now assaulted Maddock's nostrils. He drew his Walther, regretting the lost backpack with his reloads. He had four bullets left in this clip.

"Bones, do you have any more wisdom to share about this thing?" The rustling grew closer and the stench was almost overpowering.

"They're afraid of water. Won't cross it." Bones said, tapping the handle of his Glock. Unlike the others, who were visibly nervous, Bones was as calm as ever. Then again, perhaps he was just crazy. "I'll bet there's a stream or something running across the end of this box canyon. That would explain why they haven't expanded their territory."

"All right, everyone. If we get separated, make for the end of the canyon as fast as you can. We'll meet up at the lagoon."

The rustling sound ceased. They all turned and looked in the direction from which the unseen thing had been approaching. What was it doing? From inside Tam's backpack, the little harpy eagle sounded a shrill cry, and then, all was bedlam.

The attack came from behind. With an unearthly roar, a monstrosity of tangled reddish-orange fur dropped down in the midst of their group. It swiped at Matt with a clawed hand, cutting him across the chest. Maddock whirled and fired, catching the moving beast in the head. It roared again and vanished in a flash, scrambling on all fours into the jungle.

It wasn't over.

Another of the creatures, probably the one they'd heard stalking them, burst from the tangled forest, knocking Bones to the ground. Maddock aimed for the gut this time, but the mapinguari was fast, and his bullet caught it in the thigh as it sprang toward him.

Maddock dropped and rolled as the beast flew past him. It rounded on him. It had a long snout, beady, black eyes, and a mouth full of razor sharp teeth. Its body was covered in red-orange fur, like that of an orangutan, except its belly, which was leathery, dark red flesh. Moving faster than Maddock would have thought possible, it attacked, but Matt, Bones, and Willis were ready. They all opened fire. There was no telling how much damage the bullets actually did to the strange beast, but it fled, leaving a trail of blood behind.

"Whew!" Bones said. "That was freakin' crazy."

Just then, the jungle behind them came alive with the cries of angry mapinguari.

Bones looked at Maddock. "What now?"

"Now we run!"

"What the hell?" Kennedy stopped short, looking all around. Up ahead he heard the cry of an animal like none he'd ever heard before, followed by gunshots, people shouting, and more roars. The outburst only lasted for a matter of seconds, and then silence...

...followed by bedlam.

They were in the trees and in the jungle all around him. Big, furry, orange things swinging toward the sound of the gunshots. He didn't know what they were and he didn't care. He just wanted to get out of there.

The jungle seemed to grab at him as he ran, as though nature itself was working in concert with the unseen creatures. Gunshots occasionally broke through the din of bestial roars. He didn't know whether to hope Maddock's men were killing these creatures, whatever they were, or if he should root for the beasts. Then again, he had to have the seed. He *had* to have it.

One of the monsters broke through the foliage to his left and came for him. He saw a flash of white teeth and long, razor-sharp claws. He hit the ground and rolled under it, stabbing up into its exposed gut as it flew past him. His KA-BAR dragged across the tough hide, but didn't pierce the flesh.

He came to his feet, knife at the ready. The creature turned, circling him warily. He didn't understand why. He certainly hadn't done it any damage. Snarling, the beast struck at him with its wicked claws.

Kennedy leapt back, breaking through a tangle of brush, and nearly falling into a twenty foot gorge. He teetered on the edge, staring down at the swift-moving stream that tumbled over and around jagged boulders. Righting himself, he turned to face the monster. Its head broke through the foliage and it froze. It sniffed the air, roared, and turned and ran.

What had just happened? Why had it not finished him?

There was no time to contemplate this turn of events, because just then, he looked around and spotted Maddock helping the blonde, Kaylin Maxwell, up onto a fallen tree that spanned the gorge. On the opposite side he saw figures vanishing into the forest. The others had already crossed. He was almost too late.

Maddock stood with his back to Kennedy, watching the girl. Perfect. Kennedy drew his KA-BAR and attacked.

Maddock heard the approach of his attacker only an instant before the man was upon him. He whirled around, barely dodging the knife thrust. It was Kennedy. How had he caught up with them? It didn't matter now.

Maddock drew his Recon knife just as Kennedy rolled to his feet and came at him again. Maddock wished he had even one bullet left in his Walther, but he had expended them all fighting off the mapinguari, which, just as Bones had said, did not seem to want to come anywhere near the water.

Kennedy feinted and Maddock stepped to the side, flicking his knife at Kennedy's eyes. The man moved his head just enough to avoid the blow, and slashed at Maddock's knee. Maddock shifted his feet and made the man pay with a quick slash that missed his throat, but opened a gash in his cheek. Now he'd have another scar to match his first one.

Kennedy, baring his teeth, crouched, looking for an opening. They circled one another in silence. Maddock could see Kaylin out of the corner of his eye. She was more than halfway across, and must not have heard the attack over the sound of the rushing water far below her. That was fine with him. She didn't have any bullets left either, and even if she did, he wouldn't want her involved. He wanted her to get to safety with the others.

"Just give me the seed and I won't kill you," Kennedy growled.

"What do you want it for?" Maddock kept his voice conversational, though his every nerve was charged.

"I don't want it, but those whom I serve want it very badly."

"Those you 'serve'? What kind of talk is that for a tough guy? ScanoGen must pay you pretty well if you'll grovel like that for them."

Kennedy barked a laugh. "You're as ignorant as I thought. ScanoGen pays me well, but I only work for them. I serve the Dominion. Perhaps you've heard of them?"

The words caught Maddock totally by surprise, and Kennedy used the moment of shock to make a quick thrust at Maddock's midsection, one which he barely avoided.

"I don't know what you did in Utah, Maddock, but rest assured, the Dominion knows your name, and they know Bonebrake. When I make my report, you're both dead men. If you give me the seed, though, I'll ask them to spare the lives of your friends Barnaby, Sanders, Dean, and Maxwell." His confidence was growing as he spoke. "I know your type, Maddock. You don't want their blood on your hands. Not that I think you're noble, I think you just don't like feeling guilty."

"Thanks for the therapy session. My copay's in the mail." Maddock made a feint of his own and Kennedy danced back out of reach. So he wasn't so caught up in his little speech that he could be taken unaware. "Sorry to disappoint you, but I don't have the seed."

"Liar! That guy, Brian, gave it to you. He told me himself. He even described the pouch he put it in!"

"True, but I gave it to Tam Broderick. You remember her," Maddock taunted. "By the way, she's F.B.I. Did you know that? She's got the seed, and she's already on the other side of the river." He hoped Kennedy could not see that the pouch still hung around Maddock's neck. "You can go after her, but you're going to have to get through me first, and then she's got all those friends of mine you mentioned to protect her. Good luck with that."

Kennedy's eyes flitted across the river for a split-second, and then he attacked. He thrust for Maddock's midsection, but changed his direction at the last second. Maddock felt the blade slice across his thigh. It would hurt later, but the adrenaline coursing through his veins dulled the pain.

Maddock lashed out, cracking Kennedy across the forehead with the butt of his knife, and slicing back down at an angle, opening a gash over his collarbone. Kennedy's return stroke was not quick enough to catch Maddock's throat, but it sliced open his shirt and left a shallow cut across the breastbone. Maddock had been ready for the strike, though, and as Kennedy's knife hand swept past him, he struck him with a vicious backhand swipe that nearly severed Kennedy's wrist.

Kennedy roared in pain and leapt at Maddock, his good hand clutching at Maddock's throat. Kennedy's shout had finally caught Kaylin's attention, and she screamed Maddock's name as he was borne backward by the heavier man. Maddock plunged his knife into Kennedy's exposed midsection, but it seemed the man was as far beyond feeling pain as Maddock was. They were now only inches from a fifty foot fall to the rocks below.

"Ready to die?" Kennedy growled, his eyes afire with madness as he pushed Maddock backward. Then his gaze fell on the grass pouch hanging from Maddock's neck, and understanding dawned on his face. "The seed!" He released Maddock's throat and ripped the pouch free.

The moment of distraction was all Maddock needed. Free from Kennedy's controlling grasp, he pivoted to the side and shoved Kennedy to the edge of the gorge. As Kennedy staggered and caught himself just at the edge, the small pouch holding the sacred seed slipped free from his grasp.

"No!" Kennedy cried as it fluttered down and was swept away by the fast-moving water. Roaring like an angry bear, he turned on Maddock, who was ready for him.

Maddock drove the heel of his palm up into Kennedy's chin with all of his might. Kennedy's eyes rolled back in his head and he wobbled, out on his feet.

"I think we're done here." Maddock placed his index finger on Kennedy's chest and pushed. Like a felled tree, Kennedy tumbled to the rocks below. Maddock watched as his lifeless body was swept away. With a deep sigh, he turned away.

Kaylin waited on the other side of the river, her face buried in her hands.

Maddock made his way across to her, and she fell into his arms. This time, it felt... different, like the comfort shared with an old friend. Whatever he had felt for her, or thought he had felt, was gone. He searched his heart, like a tongue probing the empty socket of a lost tooth, but he found nothing there.

"Are you all right?" he whispered.

"No," she sobbed. "I just can't take this anymore. I'm not like you, Maddock."

"I know. I think I finally get it. You're a tough girl, and you can handle yourself, but that doesn't mean it feeds your soul to go traipsing through the jungle risking life and limb. I saw the look on your face when Thomas asked you to stay. I don't even think you wanted to stay with *him* so much as you loved the idea of the life he was describing." He held her at arm's length and looked down into her teary eyes. "You're a beautiful woman, a talented artist, and you love beauty. It's not your fault your father also made you a badass."

She laughed a little. "Not badass, exactly, but I guess I can take care of myself."

Hand in hand, they headed off through the jungle in the direction in which their friends had gone.

"Exactly, but just because you can do something doesn't mean that's what you're meant for."

"Kind of like us? We're not bad together, but maybe we aren't meant for each other."

"Could be," Maddock agreed. "Of course, I wouldn't say no to being friends with benefits." He fixed her with a roguish grin and she smacked his chest. "Ow! Did you forget my lovely knife wound?"

"I'm sorry!" she gasped. "I'll tell you what." Now she was the one who looked like she had something up her sleeve. "Get me somewhere where I can get a hot meal and an even hotter shower, and I'll make it up to you."

"You've got a deal." He laughed inwardly as they came in sight of the dark lagoon, where the others were just dragging two boats into the water. Maybe Bones was right. Maddock needed to spend less time trying to figure life out, and more time enjoying it.

The return trek, though grueling, was blessedly uneventful. They encountered no more deadly natives, giant anacondas, or legendary beasts, not to mention ScanoGen agents. By the time they had returned to the main branch of the Xingu River, Maddock felt like he was waking up from a bad dream.

"You know something, Maddock?" Tam stroked her baby eagle, which she had clearly adopted. "You guys are wasting your talents finding sunken treasure."

"I don't know about that." Maddock closed his eyes and laid his head back, soaking in the warm sun. "We're pretty good at it."

"You know what I mean." She laughed as the little eagle snatched a grub from her hand. "Seriously, though." She fixed him with a grave expression. "The government could use guys like you and Bones. Men like you are rare."

"We've served our country. Now we're doing our own thing, and we're happy."

"It's not only that. Kennedy said the Dominion knows about you. What if they come after you? You and Bones might need us on your side."

"We can handle ourselves." Maddock's voice was as cold as his insides. She might be right. If the Dominion was truly the powerful organization Tam said they were, and he and Bones were on their radar, no telling what they might try.

"I know you can," Tam sighed. "That's why I need you. I've already talked with my superiors." She held up her sat phone. "It looks like the Dominion is going to be my white whale." She lowered her voice. "I'm forming a team whose sole job is to find out who and what they are, and put a stop to their schemes. I told them I want you and Bonebrake."

"You're taking me by surprise here." Maddock's head was spinning. "I'm flattered, but, I don't know. I like my life the way it is."

"I don't blame you, but if the Dominion comes after you, your life will never be the same." She smiled down at the eagle, which now lay asleep in her lap.

"How are you going to get that thing through customs?"

"Don't have to. I got our ride home all taken care of, and we ain't flying commercial." Tam grinned. "Sometimes it pays to work for Uncle Sam."

"Works for me." He looked out at the lush, green forest as it slid by, trying to imagine going back to work for the government. He couldn't fathom it.

"You don't have to give me an answer right now," Tam said. "But think about it. I can just about guarantee you'll be paid a visit by my employers sometime soon. Maybe you can decide on your answer by then."

"We'll see." Maddock closed his eyes again and lost himself in the gentle rolling of the boat as it cut through the water. He had thought trekking off into the Amazon was a challenge, but he had the feeling his life was about to get a whole lot more complicated.

Epilogue

The small grass pouch was no match for the rapid current and sharp stones that tore at it as it rode the water. It snagged on a limb and hung there, buffeted by the current, until it fell apart.

A gray seed, large enough to fill a man's palm, floated free. For days, weeks, the water carried it deeper into the depths of the jungle, into land which no human foot had trod, until it came to rest on a sandbar.

A parrot, its emerald feathers glistening in the sunlight, took the seed in its beak and carried it away. Choosing a suitable perch, it set about trying to crack the seed, but soon gave up trying to penetrate its hard exterior. In a rustle of wings, it took flight, letting the seed fall to the ground.

It came to rest in a sun-kissed clearing, where it lay undisturbed. It baked beneath the warm sun, and, in time, it settled beneath the soft earth, nestled in its nourishing arms.

The rainy season came and went, and, in the fullness of time, the seed sprouted, and brought forth life into its secluded domain.

A tree grew in the jungle.

~The End~

AZTLAN

A Dane and Bones Short Story

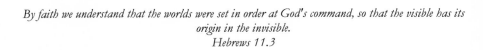

By faith we understand that the worlds were set in order at God's command, so that the visible has its origin in the invisible.
Hebrews 11.3

AZTLAN

"Holy crap, it's hot out here." Bones Bonebrake mopped his brow and cast a challenging look at the sun high in the cornflower blue sky. "And don't give me that 'It's a dry heat' stuff. Hot is hot."

"No argument here." Dane Maddock plucked at the neck of his sodden shirt. It wouldn't stay damp for long in this dry climate. He hunkered down on the tiny rock ledge where they'd stopped to take a breather, took a bottle of water from his pack, and took a long drink. He gazed out at the parched red landscape of southern Utah. Sharp peaks and low hills dotted the horizon, all shades of the same reddish-brown as the mountainside on which they perched. It had been a long time since he'd ventured into this part of the country, and he realized he'd missed the open skies and sweeping vistas.

"Are we close to the top?"

"Why? Are you ready to wuss out on me?" Bones' heavy breathing belied his bravado.

"Hardly. We both know I'll reach the summit before you do. Why don't you just give it up?"

"Not on your life." The tall, powerfully-built Cherokee squatted down beside Maddock, removed the tie from around his ponytail, and let his long hair blow in the breeze.

The two made an odd pair: Maddock was fair-skinned with blue eyes and short, blond hair. He stood just a shade under six feet tall, but alongside the six and a half foot tall Bones, he looked small.

Bones stood, knuckled his back, and turned to examine the rock face above them. "Only about fifty meters to go. Shouldn't be too bad."

"Remind me again why we decided to free climb here?" Maddock asked, tucking the water bottle back into his pack and rising to his feet.

"Because no one ever has. Because it's awesome." Bones bared his straight white teeth in a wolfish grin.

"How'd you find out about this place, anyway?"

"My cousin Isaiah." Bones' cousin, Isaiah Horsely, was a professor and archaeologist working the American Southwest. "He found out about it from a local storyteller who says few people even know this place exists."

"I don't wonder," Maddock said. "Considering how much trouble we had just getting here, much less climbing it."

Motec Mountain's height and steep sides made it look less like a mountain and more like a butte that had been stretched out until it touched the sky. Nestled in the heart of Utah's Red Rock region, it was one of the most remote locations Maddock had ever visited in this part of the country.

"He told me some other stuff about it. Legends mostly. Weird stuff but pretty cool."

"Tell me when we get to the top. The longer I stand here, the more I think about the cooler of beer waiting in the car."

"Dude, you can drink beer any time. How often do you get to boldly go where not very many men have gone before?"

Maddock frowned at Bones. "Seriously? We do it all the time."

"And that's why we rule. Now let's get back to climbing."

Upon reaching the summit, Maddock expected to be rewarded with a refreshing breeze and a spectacular view, but he found neither. A fine mist hung over the landscape, slowly swirling in a clockwise pattern and giving the air a tepid quality.

"This is weird." Bones waved his hand in front of his face, the mist curling around his arm. "It's like it wants to grab ahold of you."

"Nothing about this makes sense," Maddock said. "We're in an arid climate. Why doesn't the fog dissipate, or at least burn off? And where is the moisture coming from?"

"The storyteller said there's a lake up here. Want to check it out?"

Maddock gazed at the curtain of mist. It was odd, to be sure, but it didn't seem to be dangerous. Curiosity winning out over caution, he nodded. "Let's see what's up."

The way was smooth, with only a few scattered boulders here and there to impede their way. Though the mist shrouded the landscape in white, it was thin and visibility was more than adequate. Soon they came to the edge of a dark lake.

"Want to go for a swim?" Bones asked.

"I don't know." Maddock felt uneasy as he scanned the surface of the water. He realized in an instant what caused his discomfort. "The water doesn't move at all. Look at it. It's like a sheet of glass."

"Maybe it is." Bones knelt down and touched the surface. It scarcely made a ripple. "This is jacked-up. It's water, all right, but it's like there's a surface tension holding it in place. I don't know how to describe it."

"I think you describe it just fine," Maddock said, dipping his own finger into the water. "It's warm, too."

"Isn't there a lake in the Middle East where people float really easily?" Bones asked. "You know, like without an inner tube or those water wings you love?"

"The Dead Sea." Maddock ignored his friend's jibe. "But that's because of the high salt content. I don't think that's the deal here."

"If it's all the same to you, I'm not going to taste the water." Bones wiped his hand on his shirt.

"And I think we'll pass on the swimming, too."

They stood and began to walk along the shore. They quickly discovered that the lake was perfectly round, or something close to perfect. As they walked, Maddock's discomfort lessened. Maybe this place was more odd than sinister. None the less, he took a moment to dig into his pack for the dive knife he always carried, and hooked the sheath onto his belt. Bones did the same, and they continued their exploration of the mountaintop.

Maddock estimated they'd reached the side of the lake opposite where they'd begun their circuit when Bones halted in his tracks.

"Look at this."

Maddock followed his friend's line of sight to where a complete skeleton grinned up at them. A tarnished breastplate covered its chest and a tarnished helmet and the rusted remains of a sword lay nearby.

"Spanish," Maddock noted. "Probably an explorer."

"And he climbed all the way up here in his armor?" Bones said doubtfully. "I'm not buying it."

"It wouldn't be the strangest thing we've seen. Who knows? Maybe there is, or was, another way up."

"I have another idea." Bones folded his arms and turned to face Maddock. "Hear me out on this. This is an alien hot zone." He raised a big hand before Maddock could argue. "Just listen. That could explain the weird water and the mist. And like you said, we've seen enough strange crap that it's not the most far-fetched idea in the world."

"So the aliens abducted the Spaniard and then dumped him here?" Maddock couldn't believe he was indulging his friend's fixation with extraterrestrials, but Bones wasn't wrong. They'd seen and experienced enough strange things that nothing could be discounted.

"Now you're thinking like an honest-to-goodness conspiracy theorist. I knew I'd win you over sooner or later."

"Just trying to follow your train of thought, and believe me, it's a scary ride."

They continued on and made it only twenty or so paces before something on the lake caught Maddock's attention.

"Bones, look at that." Far from the shore, a dark shape loomed in the mist. At their feet, flat round stepping stones formed a bridge.

"Another of the storyteller's details I forgot to mention," Bones said. "There's supposed to be an island in the middle of the lake. And, of course, it's cursed."

"Do you believe in curses?" Maddock asked.

"Other than a woman scorned? Nope." Bones grinned. "Lead the way."

Maddock tested the first stepping stone and found it was solid. He tensed slightly as he put his full weight on it, and relaxed when it held. "I don't know if it'll support your fat butt," he said to Bones, "but I'm good to go."

"Screw you, Maddock."

Maddock almost felt like he was dreaming as he moved through the mist across the motionless lake.

"I bet this is what Heaven is like," Bones said in an uncharacteristically soft voice.

"You'll never find out."

"That's cool. Better parties in hell, anyway."

At the center of the lake, they stepped onto solid stone. It didn't take long to discover that what Bones had believed to be an island was, in fact, a giant stone disc.

"I told you, dude," Bones said. "Aliens."

"Aztecs, more like. See?"

Symbols and other imagery covered the rock beneath their feet. Though he didn't know the meanings of most of them, the patterns and motifs were familiar. "It looks like a giant Aztec Calendar Stone."

"You're right." Bones dropped to one knee to get a closer look. "Doesn't mean aliens didn't help them, though."

"True. Let's keep going."

They moved deeper into the mist and soon the dark form toward which they'd been moving began to take shape. They soon found themselves at the foot of a miniature pyramid. At the top stood a small temple, surmounted by a sculpture of the feathered serpent head of Quetzalcoatl. That sealed it. The site was definitely Aztec.

They climbed the dozen stairs to the top, where, just inside the temple door, a tight spiral staircase descended into the darkness. They clicked on their mini Maglites and headed down. Time seemed to slow down as they wound deeper into the heart of the mountain, Bones grumbling all the while about the low ceiling and tight quarters.

Finally, they emerged in a large chamber. Maddock halted at the entrance and ran the beam of his light across the floor, looking for potential booby traps, but saw nothing. He took a few cautious steps inside and waited for Bones to join him.

"Interesting," Bones observed, shining his light all around.

The room was round with a low ceiling. Spaced equally were the mouths of seven caves. At the center stood a waist-high pedestal.

"There's an Aztec legend," Bones began, "about a place called Chicomoztoc, or 'The Place of the Seven Caves.' From here, seven tribes, for lack of a better term, came together and settled at Aztlan, the ancestral home of the Aztecs."

"So if this is Chicomoztoc, then you think Aztlan is somewhere around here?" Maddock asked.

"The Aztecs called Aztlan 'The land to the North', and this is well north of Mexico. It was reputed to be an island within a lake." Bones scratched his chin. "And the word itself means 'the place of whiteness.' Think about it: the island within a lake, the white mist, the connection to the caves. I think the island up above us is Aztlan."

Maddock frowned. "But Aztlan is supposed to be the Aztecs' ancestral home. An entire nation couldn't live up there. It's just a single mountaintop."

"You know how legends work. They get passed down from generation-to-generation and it changes a little at a time until it's an entirely different story with only a few recognizable details remaining. Maybe Aztlan was the place the Aztecs emerged from, I don't know, under the earth."

Only a few years earlier Maddock would have scoffed at this, but such a story no longer seemed far-fetched. "Let's check out the caves."

They began by exploring the first cave to their left and quickly discovered that it plunged downward at a steep angle, going on and on with no end in sight. A cursory inspection of the other caves produced similar results.

"This isn't a two-man job," Maddock concluded. "It would take a team, maybe several teams, of researchers to explore this place, depending on how far down the caves go." He turned and shined his light on the pedestal at the center of the main chamber. "Let's check this out."

At first glance, the pedestal was merely a simple cylinder, but closer inspection revealed a detail that had gone unnoticed. At the top, set in the center of the cylinder, was a turquoise disc.

No more than a hand's length across, it was engraved with several symbols. Around the outside ran what looked like a seven-lobed clover. Inside that lay a ring of five suns. Finally, at the center, two figures faced one another. Only a few minor details kept them from being mirror images of one another. The images meant nothing to Maddock, but Bones gasped when his light fell on them.

"Holy crap, Maddock. I know what this is!"

Maddock was not surprised that Bones had some knowledge of Aztec lore. His friend had a keen interest in myths, legends, and ancient prophecies, and the Aztecs were strongly associated with the end of days, and also with aliens, another of Bones' favorite subjects.

"This," he said, hovering a finger over the cloverlike outline, "represent the seven caves. The sunbursts represent the five suns of creation. And they," he pointed at the figures in the center, are Ometecuhtli and his female partner, Omecíhuatl, the highest of the Aztec deities." He looked at Maddock. "This is the Duality Stone."

"What does that mean?"

"I can't say for sure. Only the craziest conspiracy theorist believes it exists." He broke out into a broad grin. "Tell me again what nutbags those guys are."

"You know what they say about a blind squirrel," Maddock said. "But in this case,

I tip my cap to you and your eccentric friends."

Bones stood for several moments in silent contemplation. "I think we should tell Isaiah about this place. After all, he's the one who tipped me off about it, and he's got the resources to study it properly.

"Agreed," Maddock said. "This is one heck of a discovery."

The sun was setting over the hills, painting the landscape in shades of orange, by the time they made it back to their vehicle. Both men were utterly spent, yet buoyed by their discovery, their spirits remained high. As they drove along the rutted dirt road back to civilization, Bones spied a small bar. It was a squat, adobe style building of faded brown, nearly the color of the surrounding earth. A faded sign, the paint peeling, proclaimed it the White Bear Pub.

"I don't remember seeing that place on the way here," Bones said. "It's not often that a watering hole escapes my notice."

"It was six in the morning. I hope you weren't keeping an eye out for bars," Maddock said.

Bones nodded thoughtfully. "That must be it. Let's stop for a while."

"We've got beer in the cooler."

"Yeah, but this place has different beer. No reason we can't drink both."

Bones slowed and turned off the main road. He parked alongside the only other vehicle in the dirt lot— an aging sedan of unfamiliar make. As they mounted the single, rickety step up to the building, he glanced back at their rented SUV and frowned.

"I could have sworn we rented a CRV," he said.

"I thought so too." Maddock walked around the back of the vehicle to check the model name. "What the hell is a GAZelle?"

Bones shrugged. "Who knows? Must be a Hyundai or some crap like that. It got us here. That's what matters."

Inside, they found themselves the lone customers inside the dusty bar. Narrow beams of sunlight filtered in through dirty windows, shining on the ceramic tile floor, which was pitted and cracked in places, and setting the dust motes aglow. Maddock and Bones took seats at the bar where the local news was showing on an aging television set.

"Couldn't spring for a flat screen?" Bones asked.

"Don't worry about it."

The bartender, a stout man of late middle years with lightly tanned skin, copious ear hair, and a bald head, greeted them enthusiastically.

"My first customers of the day. I am Alexei. What can I get you?"

Maddock noted a slight Russian accent to the man's speech. Unusual for this part of the country.

"Dos cervezas, por favor." Bones held up two fingers. "Dos Equis if you've got it."

Alexei frowned. "I don't know this beer."

"That's cool. Just give us two of the best beers you've got."

The man smiled and handed them two bottles labeled Tinkoff Golden. Bones tipped him generously and clinked bottles with Maddock. "To discovery."

"Discovery," Maddock agreed. He took a long drink, taking the time to savor the light, tangy flavor. He nodded approvingly and took another drink. "Not bad."

They finished their drinks quickly and Bones called out to the bartender. "Yo,

Axel. Another round."

"Alexei," the man corrected though he smiled to show no offense was taken.

"Who's your pick to win the Superbowl this year?" Bones asked, trying to make conversation.

Alexei tilted his head. "You mean the Soccerbowl?"

"What? No, dude. The Superbowl. Football."

"Football and soccer are the same." Alexei picked up a greasy rag and began wiping the counter. "Or do you mean gridiron?" Bones nodded and Alexei grimaced. "Nasty, violent sport. I didn't think they played it anymore."

Bones made a confused face but continued to make small talk with Alexei. Meanwhile, Maddock turned his attention to the television, where the reporter was saying, "Today the American Politburo sent a strongly-worded message to Moscow, warning the Premier that America will not be treated as a lesser member of the Soviet Union."

Maddock almost spilled his beer. Bones had heard too.

"Are we on a hidden camera show?" Bones looked all around.

"I don't understand your jokes," Alexei said, "but I like you all the same."

"You're pretty cool too," Bones said. "Say, who's the president nowadays?"

Alexei cocked his head. "How do you not know that?"

"I can't really talk about it. Let's just say I've been out of circulation for a while."

"No television in prison?" Alexei grinned. "The president is Vladimir Putin."

"I meant the President of the United States."

Alexei laughed. "Now I think I am the one on hidden camera. There has been no president since the war. The American Politburo governs but reports to Moscow, just like all countries in the Soviet Union."

Maddock's head swam and he felt as though his tether to reality was slipping. He took a closer look at their surroundings, truly taking in all the details. Everything was Russian—posters of soccer and hockey teams and framed photographs of Soviet premiers dominated the walls.

Alexei walked away, shaking his head, and Maddock looked at Bones.

"What the hell is going on here?"

Bones stared at him, and then he closed his eyes and let out a groan. "I did it." He buried his face in his hands. "I took the duality stone. It's in my pack. I don't know why I did it. It was like the stone wanted to be taken."

Maddock was surprised at what Bones had done, but that wasn't his primary concern at the moment. "Why should that matter?" he asked.

Bones sighed. "According to legend, the duality stone holds the worlds together." He shook his head. "No, that's not quite right. More like, it tethers the different versions of the world."

"Different versions?"

"You know, like alternate timelines. I know it sounds nuts, but I think it's taken us to a timeline where the Russians won the Cold War."

Maddock looked at the label on his beer and considered what Bones said. Unless they were both experiencing the same hallucination, nothing else made sense. "Maybe we're dreaming," he said lamely.

A sharp pain blossomed in his shoulder. Bones had punched him. "What the hell?"

"Does that feel like a dream?" Bones asked.

"I don't know. Does this?" He returned the favor and Bones winced.

"Okay. We can rule out dreaming."

Alexei, who was polishing the end of the counter, scowled at them. "You fight outside. Not here."

Maddock was about to apologize when his phone vibrated. He looked at it and his jaw dropped.

"You all right, bro? You're pale as a... well, as a you."

"I just got a text. From Melissa."

Bones looked poleaxed. "That can't be right."

Melissa was Maddock's wife who had died years before.

"If we're in an alternate timeline, maybe she's..." Maddock couldn't say it aloud. Holding his phone in a trembling hand, he read the message aloud.

Hope you can come home soon. We miss you.

"We," he whispered. "Melissa was pregnant when she died. Maybe..."

"Don't do this to yourself, Maddock." Bones said.

Maddock scarcely heard him. He was scrolling through his contact list. He saw familiar names: Bones, Willis Sanders, Pete "Professor" Chapman, and Jimmy Letson.

But he also saw names that hadn't been there before: Hartford Maxwell, their old commander who had been murdered by the Dominion. Franklin Meriwether, a beloved officer who'd died in the Holy Land, and then he gasped.

"Mom and Dad," he breathed. "Bones, look at this! My parents are still alive, and Maxie and Meriwether."

Bones snatched the phone away and scrolled through the list, his brow furrowing deeper as he read. "This is not good."

"What do you mean? Melissa, my parents! Bones, I need to go home."

"Just chill for a second. Listen, we don't belong here. Right now, some alternate Maddock is probably driving home from his job selling insurance, and I'm sure there's another version of Bones who's getting busy with a Russian tennis player. But they're not us and we aren't them."

"How do you know? Maybe the alternate version of us are on a climbing trip in Utah. Maybe we've taken their places."

"It doesn't matter. This isn't our world. Look at this." Bones turned Maddock's phone around so he could see the display. "Yeah, there are some new names here, but you know what? There are some missing too. Matt and Corey aren't here. That means we don't have a crew. There's no Kaylin Maxwell, no Jade, no Tam Broderick. All those mysteries we solved? All we did to fight the Dominion? Never happened. Not here. And there's another important name missing."

They exchanged a level look and Maddock felt his resistance crumbling. He knew precisely who Bones meant. Pain stabbed at his heart. How could he have wanted to stay here, but how could he want to leave?

"Besides, do you really want to live here, under Soviet rule?"

Maddock shook his head. "I suppose not."

Just then, the phone vibrated again. Bones glanced at it and his eyes went wide. "What is it?"

Bones shook his head. "You're better off not knowing. Trust me."

"Give it to me." Maddock spoke slowly, pronouncing each syllable in a tone that said he would brook no nonsense. Reluctantly, Bones handed it over.

Melissa had texted him again. This time she'd sent a photograph. There she was, her smile and her big brown eyes were just as he remembered. But it was the little boy, a blue-eyed blond who sat on her knee that captivated him. It was his son.

"He looks just like you," Bones said.

Maddock's throat was tight and he only managed a single nod. He felt as if his heart were being torn into a million pieces. It was more than he could take. He took a deep breath and cleared his throat. When he could finally speak, his voice was husky.

"Bones, let's put that stone back where we found it."

The moon hung low on the horizon when they once again emerged from the temple atop Motec Mountain. It shone dully through the mist that still hung over the mountaintop. Between the climbing and the strain of this afternoon's experience, Maddock had nothing left. He crossed the lake and made his way back to the spot where they'd made their ascent only scarcely aware of his surroundings, his mind as foggy as the air that surrounded them.

"I think we should stay here until morning," Bones said. "It's too dark and we're both too tired to climb down."

Maddock nodded and sank to the ground.

"It sucks that we won't know until tomorrow whether we made it home or if we're still stuck in our own version of Red Dawn."

Maddock took out his phone. He scrolled through the contact list and then checked the text messages. The photo and message from Melissa were gone. His list was back to normal, though, and the name at the top brought a smile to his face—Angel.

"It's all right," he said. "We're back."

~End~

Works by David Wood

The Dane Maddock Adventures
Dourado
Cibola
Quest
Icefall
Buccaneer
Atlantis
Ark (forthcoming)

Dane and Bones Origins
Freedom
Hell Ship
Splashdown
Dead Ice
Liberty
Electra
Amber (forthcoming)
Justice (forthcoming)

Stand-Alone Novels
Into the Woods
Arena of Souls
The Zombie-Driven Life
You Suck
Callsign: Queen (with Jeremy Robinson)
Oracle (with Sean Ellis)
Destiny (with Sean Ellis)
Dark Rite (with Alan Baxter)

David Wood writing as David Debord
The Silver Serpent
Keeper of the Mists
The Gates of Iron (forthcoming)
The Impostor Prince (with Ryan A. Span-forthcoming)

About the Author

David Wood is the author of the bestselling Dane Maddock Adventures and Dane Maddock Origins series and many other titles. Writing as David Debord, he writes the Absent Gods fantasy series. When not writing he co-hosts the Authorcast podcast. David and his family live in Santa Fe,New Mexico. Visit him online at www.davidwoodweb.com.

40758341R00243

Made in the USA
Middletown, DE
31 March 2019